Horace

Campbell Johnston

First published in 2023 by Blossom Spring Publishing
Horace Copyright © 2023 Campbell Johnston
ISBN 978-1-7394532-0-6
E: admin@blossomspringpublishing.com
W: www.blossomspringpublishing.com
All rights reserved under International Copyright Law.
Contents and/or cover may not be reproduced in whole
or in part without the express written consent
of the publisher.
Names, characters, places and incidents are either products of
the author's imagination or are used fictitiously.

For Wendy with gratitude and love

CHAPTER 1

The summer of '76 was a scorcher; everyone wanted to be on the beach. I was in Weymouth and could smell the surf and taste the salty air but I was never to see the sand, never to touch the water. Sergeant Major Busty Burton would see to that. Busty had us marching around a parade square and doing rifle drill from dawn to dusk so we would be the finest soldiers in the Army. Busty wore his crown on his sleeve to show his rank but it could have been on his head. He was the main man and, what is more, he knew it. He also had a chip on his shoulder because he was not a full-time soldier, but a welder. By day he joined lumps of metal but at weekends he was a warrior. The two-week camp in Weymouth every summer was Busty's war. But more of Busty later.

Me? I was a final year polytechnic student living in a house with four friends. At the end of term, we were obliged to give up our student house and occupy ourselves until starting gainful employment. I had feared having to return home to Essex and live with my mother, father and younger sister.

We, I use the term advisedly, as it was almost impossible to get all the housemates in the same room at the same time, but, somehow by default, we all agreed to keep the house for the summer. The landlord was content as he was being paid whether it was occupied or stood empty. I was anxious about paying the rent as I was already overdrawn. I hoped something would turn up. One flat mate, Colin Hipgrave, was the first southerner I had ever met. He was from Watford but we all called him a Londoner as that was near enough. He was on my Civil Engineering course and we had been on the same floor of the student flats during our first year and became flatmates in second and third year by continuity, as we were too lazy to sort out alternative accommodation or housemates. Colin worked Friday and Saturday nights in the White Rose as a barman. On both nights, when he finished, he would pick up a Chinese takeaway. He never ate them on the night of purchase but would eat them cold and congealed the next morning for breakfast. He was a difficult man to live with. When the five of us would go out together he insisted on drinking Stella Artois. This was more expensive than the normal draft Heineken the rest of us would drink. I got round this by always buying the second or third round. I would buy all Heinekens but ask for one to be in a dimpled glass with a handle. I would take the tray back to the table and say 'Colin, you're the Stella' and he would smile. He never noticed the difference. Colin let me down a couple of times and I should have been more wary of him but I had never met anyone in my life I could not trust, so it never occurred to me that Colin was not everything he seemed. Once I asked him to hand my soil mechanics coursework direct to the tutor. My tutor wanted it before the weekend and I promised I would deliver it to him. Colin told me he was walking over to the Civil Litigation Department and would drop it in. I thanked him and my last words were, 'Please hand it directly to Dr Jenkins' and Colin said, 'Yes, no problem.'

I never did find the coursework and Dr Jenkins never got it. Colin was almost dismissive when I tried to find out what he had done with it. Colin initially blamed Dr Jenkins for losing it, telling me how much he disliked Dr Jenkins. When I said I had spoken to Dr Jenkins, Colin mumbled about putting it in his pigeonhole or maybe he had handed it in to the office. I was furious but he was so vague and defensive there was nothing I could do. Colin was not contrite; he never apologised. I had never known anyone so inert and insensitive. Luckily my handwriting was so poor that I tended to write out my coursework in rough and then copy it into neat for submission. Dr Jenkins was surprisingly understanding when I took my rough notes to him with my explanation. I did not want to blame Colin but Dr Jenkins almost scowled when I explained that Hipgrave must have put it in the wrong pigeonhole. Dr Jenkins joked, but it seemed heartfelt, that, 'Hipgrave is in the wrong pigeonhole.' I forgave Colin, minded that I had never bought him a Stella Artois in three years, so maybe I was being too harsh on him.

*

As we were in our final year, all the flatmates, Colin, Dave, Pete, Steve and I, were making job applications. I had written to a road construction company and they had sent me an application pack. I had mentioned it to three of the others. Steve was really interested and asked if he could apply as they seemed to need at least five trainee engineers. Dave was not interested as he hated the idea of being a civil engineer and wanted to be 'an adventurer'. Colin feigned disinterest. I say feigned as subsequent events were to show he was very interested. I was excited to be invited to Leeds for an interview. Steve was not called but was quite philosophical about it, probably because his father had a job lined up for him. Steve was just anxious to show his father that he was exploring all possibilities before taking the job in the family firm.

My interview was scheduled for the following week at 1130 on Otley Road, Leeds. I had purchased my first interview suit. It was a chalk-stripe, which in the shop looked quite sharp but, in the cold light of day, made me look like a gangster. It was quite a heavy weave. I now know it was a winter suit but then it was just the right price and seemed to fit. I had never been to Leeds and wanted to be early so was dropped off at Darlington Station by Dave, my obliging flatmate. I was early, far too early for my train, but Dave was off to Cumbria climbing so I was grateful. The result was that I was in Leeds for 0830 prompt, ready for an 1130 interview. There is a large shopping centre in Leeds and most of the shops opened at 0930 so for the first hour I was happy wandering round. I watched the Rotary Club of Leeds set up their charity raffle. The prizes were cuddly toys. I bought the first ticket they sold that morning from a friendly, smiley girl who made much of my being the number one and having orange ticket number one. I did not win but joked that I would come back to buy the last ticket. I walked out to orientate myself as to where Otley Road was so that I knew where I would be heading some two hours hence. Killing time was painful. I must have had five coffees and read the paper cover to cover but it was still only 1000. I went for a walk round the cemetery, and that was a distraction foreshortened by an urge to go to the loo. I had definitely had too many coffees. I had to almost run back to the shopping centre and only just made the public toilets before I would have had an accident. I was somewhat dishevelled but after combing my hair and washing my face I felt better. I decided I had better head to the interview and walked back through the centre towards Otley Road. I found myself retracing my steps past the charity raffle. It was probably the twentieth pass I had made that morning but on impulse I bought a second ticket. It was from the same friendly girl. I tore open the ticket and it showed ***WIN***. The girl shrieked with glee telling me I had won the first prize. It was a huge orange 'Mr Man'. It was four feet in diameter and had two long arms. The girl was delighted for me and we had some photos taken. I still had the first orange ticket that I had bought earlier so the girl, the Mr Man, the 'number one' orange ticket and me posed for at least twenty photographs. I glanced down at my watch and realised it was creeping up to 1100 so I had to go. I walked, with my new orange friend, down to Otley Road. I thought the Mr Man would be a great present for my young sister. It was not the ideal companion to take to an interview but I guessed I could leave it in the reception.

*

Otley Road goes from Leeds to Otley some thirteen miles, of which three miles are probably in Leeds. In my ignorance I assumed the offices would be on the Leeds side of Otley Road, how wrong I was. I started briskly walking and then had to break into a run. Despite killing four hours in Leeds, I was in danger of being very late. My running was not helped by the Mr Man and the heavyweight suit. I arrived at the office block in a sweat and presented myself to reception. I tried to compose myself but the receptionist was giggling and that unnerved me. I asked for Mr Hollingsworth and said my name was Crawford, Harry Crawford. She asked who my friend was. I laughed and said that he was a raffle prize and I was going to leave him with her in reception. She said no and insisted I take him up in the lift to the third floor where there was a second reception. So Mr Man and I took the lift. The doors opened on the third floor to a corridor. A man was standing at an open door before the reception. 'Mr Crawford and his friend I presume?' I was beckoned into the room where there was a chair. The man said, 'Don't worry, I will arrange a chair for your friend.'

*

The interview went remarkably well. I could not be nervous with a large orange toy in a seat beside me. Mr Hollingsworth was a Rotarian and showed me the small round badge in his lapel. He explained he was with a different club and was delighted I had supported the Leeds club's efforts by buying a raffle ticket. He wanted to know whether I would join Rotary at some stage in the future. I was happy, as all interviewees would be, to say how keen I was to join.

As I left Mr Hollingsworth's office and walked to the lift, the door into the reception was open at forty-five degrees and acted like a prism. Just as I stepped into the lift, I thought I saw the reflection of Colin Hipgrave through the door. I dismissed the notion but was wrong to do so.

*

Some two weeks later Colin and I both received similar letters on the same day in the same post offering us jobs as trainee engineers starting on 9th October on the Parkway Bypass project. I was not sure what to think. It did seem strange that he had not said anything. I just put it down to his insecurity, if he had not got the job, he would probably never have mentioned it. As it turned out, Colin was quite upbeat and whilst he did not apologise for his secrecy, he did congratulate me and said he knew I would 'nail it' because I was always going to succeed because I was a 'good man'. I repaid the compliment with similar sentiments but he said, 'No, you and I are different. You wait in turn and work hard for what you want. I am not a good man; I am a queue jumper and a grifter, everything I have gotten has been grabbed or stolen.'

I laughed and patted him on the back but he froze and looked me in the eye.

'No,' he said 'I mean it. I am not a good character.'

*

We were all still thinking of how we could make money over the summer when Dave Wilson told us of his plan. Colin had worked the previous summer in a department store but had left under a cloud. He told us he definitely was not going back to any 'crap shop'. I was open to any ideas. Dave told us we were all going on holiday to

Dorset for two weeks and would be paid for doing so and there would be a £200 bonus at the end if we all enjoyed it. I thought Butlins or Pontins! We were going to be 'Redcoats'. Dave smiled, 'Yes seventy years ago it would have been Redcoats but now it's camouflage.'

All we had to do was sign a couple of forms and spend a fortnight playing at soldiers in Dorset. Pete laughed at the suggestion saying that nothing would get him into uniform. He became quite animated until Dave told him that he was not being conscripted and it was entirely voluntary.

Perhaps I should have thought about it more but after Pete's outburst I found myself backing Dave's suggestion and was drawn into the plot. I had nothing planned for the summer but even if I had, I had absolutely no money to do it with. This seemed like the perfect solution. We were all invited to read the handout that Dave had picked up from a stall in the town centre and which he distributed. The note was clear; enrolment would only take two evenings and one of those evenings was for the medical and it would take place at the Army drill hall in Borough Road. Pete scoffed and went off in a huff.

*

The two evenings were two Tuesdays, one week apart. We four all attended the first Tuesday evening in jeans and t-shirts, a sort of student uniform. We stood apart from the soldiers who were dressed in proper uniform. The uniformed men had a short parade and then went off to a lecture. We four joined several others who were in 'civilian clothes' and mingled quietly until told to 'form up'. There was no shouting, as I had anticipated, we were just herded into three rows. We were then shown how to move from standing relaxed and idle to some semblance of order when called to attention. We were then taken off to a side room where we watched a film on the British

Army presented by a young officer. He could not work the projector, so we only saw the first reel. We then filled in forms and more forms. It was explained we would learn all that was needed on the recruitment camp in Weymouth. The evening ended with everyone on parade including we rabble in civilian clothes. We were brought to attention and then 'fell out' Those in uniform turned to their right and saluted. We just drifted to the door of the drill hall and back to the student house.

*

The second Tuesday was the medical. I was strangely nervous as I had heard dark tales that they made you bend over for one investigation and so I was apprehensive. It probably accounted for my first mistake. The young nurse who was planning to take my blood pressure and temperature told me to strip to the waist. She then had to shout 'waist up' as I proceeded to remove my trousers. The doctor who was a local GP was highly amused and certainly did not maintain any patient confidentiality as he told everyone of my error.

*

It was three days later that I received my joining instructions for the trip to a camp in Dorset for my two-week basic training. Dave Wilson, our ringleader, who had stirred us into action, had failed the medical. This was a major achievement as the Territorial Army were desperate and seemed to take anybody. Dave was devastated but seemingly being blind in one eye and having poor vision in the second would make marching up and down a parade ground being shouted at almost impossible. Dave was consoled by the fact that he could not be an RAF pilot either but may be suitable for the Pay Corps. Steve, the second enthusiast, was thwarted in his plans to serve the colours by a veto from his mother. We agreed if he could not stand up to his own mother, he was unlikely to confront a Soviet special force soldier.

*

So, it was Colin Hipgrave and I that assembled at the drill hall at 0530 in the morning with almost two hundred others to climb on the five coaches that would take us to Darlington to catch a specially chartered train to King's Cross. Just as we were about to step on the coach, Colin was called back by an officer and told to bring his kit. I was launched alone. The trip south was an abject lesson in rushing to wait. The coffee shop and newsagent were out of bounds. Everyone had to sit on their bags until the train arrived, which in the event was an hour later. I was in the back row and had my back to a pile of newspapers in a cage which were dated the previous day. I presumed they were being returned as unsold. I managed to extract a *Times* through the cage. I was told to put it away by the chap who had been in charge of our group. He told me it made us look scruffy, I did as bid and shoved it into my bag. I was at a loss to work out why my reading did anything to detract from the sprawling bodies and bags strewn over the platform. The train journey was slow and uneventful. I was in a carriage with a card school playing five card brag. Whilst I was encouraged to join in, I decided it best not to; not least because I did not know the rules and the stakes were getting higher by the hour. I took to filling in the *Times* crossword. I did get one clue but the rest of the grid was filled in with words of the correct length that fitted. I managed, 'Wheelbarrow' and 'Umbrella'. The Corporal in charge of our group said nothing but I could see he was impressed, thinking I could rattle off the *Times* crossword. Little did he know what a fraud I was. From the train we were driven in the back of green Army four tonne trucks into Dorset. We climbed down from the back into beautiful sunshine. My seaside vacation had begun.

*

The camp was on the side of a gently sloping hill to our front. There were lines of tents up the slope and at the bottom were corrugated-roofed Nissen huts and wooden sheds that were probably ablution huts. Soldiers were crawling all over the vista. On first sight the whole scene reminded me of a Victorian painting by Horace Vernet that I had seen in the National Gallery. As we stood by our kit bags, having disembarked from the trucks that brought us from the station, I mentioned my observation to the chap beside me. He did not seem to hear me so I repeated the remark. He grabbed me by the ear and lifted me up and shouted to the whole group, 'Meet Horace, he's a frigging artist.' My eyes were watering with the pain but I fought back actual tears marvelling that my ear could carry my weight. The chap slapped me on the back, which may have been an act of friendship but felt like it had cracked my clavicle. Needless to say, in that moment I became 'Horace'.

*

We were allocated two to a tent and I found mine quite easily as they all had a wooden board outside and two names were chalked on the board and the boards were in alphabetical order. Each tent had two camp-cots, two wooden wardrobes, a broom, a bucketful of sand and a shovel. There was a shared table and two chairs. A single light bulb dangled from the middle of a wire running through the tent and to the tents on either side. The light was on, even though it was 1630. The light would go off when the camp decided it was lights out, not when we wanted. I had not been issued any kit and only had a small suitcase bag which I had thrown on the chair. The mattress was stuffed with horsehair and there were two sheets, a blanket and a pillow all folded inside a pillow case on the bed. An orderly marched in and shouted at me. I have no idea what he said but after I signed his clipboard, he seemed happy and stormed out. He returned seconds later to shout again even louder. I signed the board again against the name of Eric Cruddick and the shouting stopped.

We had been told to report to the armourer at 1700 to collect weapons so I seemed to have either fifteen minutes to lie on my mattress and relax or fifteen minutes to make my bed. I chose the latter but had a false start as I made up the bed before finding the mattress cover in the bottom of the wardrobe. I had to strip the bed and struggle with the mattress cover before making the bed again. I dropped onto the newly made bed with three minutes to spare. As the sun was dropping in the sky, it was beaming in through the tent door which must have been facing southwest. Suddenly the sunlight went. The door was filled with a figure of a monster. I sat bolt upright and faced this gorilla of a man. I said, 'Are you Eric?' lamely.

He grunted 'no' his voice was at least two octaves lower than mine; mine was probably higher through fright. He spoke slowly to tell me I was on his bed and that he was 'Eddie'. Seemingly, Cruddick and he had swapped as Eddie wanted to share with 'Horace'. At the mention of my new name, I broke into a mild sweat. The tent was already baking and my wrestling with the mattress cover had increased my body temperature but the presence of Eddie and mention of Horace made me feel quite faint.

A shout from outside brought the blood back to my brain. We had to collect weapons from the arms kote. My new tentmate slapped me on the back and I was propelled through the air into a group of men heading down the sloping ground to the hutted headquarter area.

*

At the armoury, I joined a queue of clueless individuals being issued with weapons. I signed a register for what I now know to be a Self-Loading Rifle (an SLR), a cleaning kit, a strap and two magazines. The storeman cocked the weapon as he handed it to me and said 'clear'. I had no idea what I was doing but took the weapon. I put on the strap to make it easier to carry. I watched a couple of others doing the same to make sure it was right and then headed back up the hill. Eddie was back before me and was lying on my bed aiming his SLR at the lightbulb. He had unpacked, or should I say thrown, his clothes into my wardrobe. I thought it best to just make the other bed as this was not a hill I wanted to die on. I had the benefit of making the second bed once, as I knew to put the mattress cover on first.

Eddie said nothing and I had not wished to prod the bear so I too had been silent. He growled, 'You're smart, aren't you, Horace?'

I hated the open question as any answer could be wrong. I tried to avoid the question by asking if there was anything I could help with. Eddie sat up and swung his feet off the bed. He stood up and towered over me. I was 5ft 10" but he must have been 6ft 5".

He grabbed me by the shirt. I could feel the small number of chest hairs that I had rip from my skin. 'Read this.' He was just too close and I could smell his breath.

I replied, 'Yes of course, what is it?'

He thrust a small pale pink envelope into my hand. It was addressed to what appeared to be Eddie Spanswick but the handwriting was so bad it could have been any number of names. Like an idiot I said, 'What, the envelope?'

'No, you friggin boff, the letter!'

I moved back from him and sat on the chair and removed two flimsy sheets of paper from the small envelope. I initially struggled to work out which was the first page, which way was up and what language it was written in. It seemed like a child's writing and it could have been hieroglyphics as there were small squiggles and hearts on top of certain letters.

A cry from outside saved the situation. We were summonsed to stand outside our tent with our weapons. Eddie took the letter off me and despite his bear-like hands, delicately put the letter back in the envelope. We assembled outside. A corporal introduced himself to the four tents in our row and we could hear other corporals shouting similar cries to their rows. We had to follow instructions that were shouted at us as to how to put the carrying strap on the weapon. It did not seem a complex task and of the eight of us listening, five had already fitted the strap. Eddie and I followed the instructions to the letter and I felt quite content, especially when Eddie nodded at me in approval. We now had to return the weapons to the armoury before heading for the evening meal. I never quite fathomed out why we could not just take out the weapons, put on the strap and then hand them back, but then I was learning my first rule. You must never think! We had to queue in alphabetical order to return the weapons and this caused utmost confusion as very few people knew each other. I did get to meet Cruddick with whom I was meant to share the tent. He was next to me in the line as I was Crawford. He explained that 'Big Eddie' told him he was swapping tents and no one, least of all he, would be stupid enough to argue. I asked why Big Eddie chose our tent and he thought it was because 'Big Eddie' wanted someone clever to play chess with and he heard that 'Horace' was a student. I was sure Big Eddie did not play chess but went along with the fiction as I too was not planning any confrontations.

*

The evening meal was worth waiting for. As a student I lived on pasta all week and Chinese takeaways when the grant cheque arrived. The Army food was just piled on to the metal tray: three courses and a roll. Each course had a separate indentation in the tray, but the cooks were so slapdash that custard and gravy both mixed and covered everything. I sat with Cruddick and another chap called Radison on long tables with benches. Radison had a pronounced stutter. I had some sympathy for him as my cousin had the affliction and I knew how hard it had been for him. Indeed, once Radison knew I was prepared to listen and wait to hear him finish his sentence, he relaxed more, his stutter abated and by the end of the meal it was manageable. Radison said he had heard I was called Horace and asked if he was he okay calling me Horace?

I laughed and said, 'Yes.'

Radison said he had been renamed Ra-Ra Radison after arriving in camp, and whilst he was embarrassed at first, he felt better because I was also given a nickname. Ra-Ra told me that he was called Ra-Ra because he stuttered; as if I had not noticed. I feigned surprise and told him that I was Horace because 'Horace Vernet' was an artist. He looked at me as if he was familiar with Vernet and so I said, 'Have you been to the National Gallery?'

'Ye...Ye... Yes,' he said. His dad had taken him to 'Ain...Ain... Aintree' the year before and he had a winner.

I told him that many creative people had stutters. He asked me who and I said 'Henry James' but he had never heard of him and asked if he was in the *Carry-On* films. I said, 'Maybe.'

He asked if I knew any other people who stuttered. I offered Lewis Carroll but Ra-Ra had never heard of him, nor *Alice in Wonderland*. I mentioned King George VI and Winston Churchill, both of whom got a glimmer of recognition. I had run out of names but made a mental note to ask my cousin for some others.

Meals had to be eaten in haste and there was no post-prandial chit chat. Trays and 'eating irons', I was picking up the lingo, had to be washed and placed in a rack before everyone had to assemble for the evening roll call followed by the issue of uniform.

*

The roll call was abandoned as the sergeant major responsible for the recruits had not arrived in camp and no one seemed able to stand in for this complicated task. The hapless young corporal who had organised the tents ordered all the recruits to form a queue to collect the uniforms. He shouted that if any item of clothing fitted properly, it was you that was misshapen.

Everyone, including me, had filled in a form with all their sizes at enrolment, but the individual forms had not reached Weymouth. All the forms had been centralised; the sizes needed were ordered and so all the correct items were in the store but no one knew who needed what. The problem was solved in sensible Army fashion. The storeman simply issued all the clothing that was needed to each recruit and then they tried them on and swapped until something fitted. The scene was set. Seventy would-be soldiers, standing in the twilight of a summer evening, in underwear, trying on smocks, trousers, shirts boots and other apparel. Big Eddie had found me and told me to be quick as we had the letter to read. He had the right idea. He just stood back and waited for someone to bring him the largest sizes available. He told me he was in a hurry to listen to the contents of the letter. I said I would try and get my uniform arranged as soon as possible. He smiled and told me he would sort it. This meant he just walked up to various people of my size who were usually standing smug having acquired the correct size item. He told them to 'swap with Horace'. I tried to protest but Big Eddie was having none of it. I did feel that I was not making myself popular but most just averted their eyes and gave me the item.

Big Eddie and I were first finished. Eddie asked the Corporal if we could leave. After pausing and checking his notepad he just nodded and we walked back to the lines, laden with a kit bag stuffed with clothing and carrying two pairs of boots. Eddie did seem calmer than when we first met but he had a simmering unpredictability and I felt anxious. We sat in the tent, he on the bed, me on the chair under the lamp. I reopened the letter and found the start. The opening part of the letter was easy as it was telling Eddie how much Jacqui was missing him and how pleased she was to have met a soldier and she was pleased that his haircut had been so successful. Eddie smiled and told me that the letter was from his girlfriend who he had met the week before coming to Dorset. She was called Jacqui and she had cut his hair at a friend's house and this was how they met. He had taken her out twice, once to the pub and once for an Indian meal. The second part of the letter was telling Eddie what 'favours' she had in store for him when he came home. I struggled to understand, never mind read, some of her suggestions. I was quite embarrassed to be reading her intimate thoughts but Eddie seemed completely oblivious. Having read, reread and read again the letter, Eddie grabbed it back. I sighed with such relief that the ordeal was over. Unfortunately, the ordeal had just started. I now had to draft his reply. Luckily, I said I should be happy to do so just before he had a red rage. He went from soft, melancholic company to a raging, eye-bulging, growling beast. I was terrified as he grabbed me.

'Never! Never tell anyone what we are doing!' he spat at me and then calmed down, almost as quickly as he exploded.

It was clear that Eddie could neither read nor write. I was no authority but I would have put money on the fact that this was the reason for his temper. It was sheer frustration. Jacqui was going to write every day and Eddie was going to reply every day. My role was clearly defined.

Eddie had come equipped with a set of three Bic pens and a notepad. I sat poised awaiting his instruction. The first part of our letter of response was easy: thanking Jacqui for her letter and explaining how we had arrived safely and been issued with rifles and uniform. I persuaded Eddie that she would be interested in his description of the accommodation and his first impressions of Dorset. I suggested that he could mention 'Horace', his tentmate. It was the second part of the letter that floored me. Eddie tried to dictate what he was going to do to her when he got back. Most of his comments were simply lost on me but even in my innocence I understood the sentiments. Many reflected back on Jacqui's plan for Eddie that she had described in her letter. They were not a surprise, but still difficult to put down on paper. I did tell him about military censors and I made up some fiction about a Postal Communication Act that made some content illegal. I also made up some nonsense about how the best romantic heroes were sensitive and subtle. I explained how the best writers could make things more erotic by use of language. Eddie was not convinced but agreed we could quote other romantic people as he did not think Jacqui would recognise that someone else was helping with the letter. I wanted to broach the subject of handwriting and how mine would be different to Eddie's, but could not think of a way when the young corporal interrupted us. 'You two left without signing for your kit!' he shouted. He thrust a clipboard at me and I signed in two places. He took it off me and gave it to Eddie. Eddie took the board off him and the pen off me. I was intrigued as to what would happen but was pleased to see Eddie take the pen in his left hand and rotate the board to a strange angle before signing a rough squiggle twice. The Corporal took the board, did an about-turn and left without further comment.

I sat back down on the chair and picked up the letter. My brain was working overtime. 'Will you shoot your weapon left-handed?' I asked.

He did not reply but looked puzzled.

'When you box, are you a south paw?' I added. I stood up and adopted a boxing pose raising my fists.

Eddie grinned and stood to face me lifting his fists. I had a sudden cold shiver wondering if he would jab or throw a haymaker. He was a south paw and I explained to him how we were each leading with a different hand. I stood beside him to demonstrate more and this helped me relax. I dropped my pose and grabbed the broom. I showed how I would hold the rifle, being right-handed. He took the broom. He wanted to know how I knew he was left-handed and how it would affect his shooting. I could answer the first question as I had seen him sign the form but I struggled with the second as I had no idea. I did tell him it would not matter as shooting was more about the dominant eye.

The dominant eye raised further questions and so I had Eddie standing with his arm stretched in front of him with a raised finger opening and closing one eye so he could establish that his right eye was dominant. Eddie was fascinated and I was able to discuss ambidextrous traits and the term 'sinister'. The latter probably went too far as

Eddie started to glaze over and said, 'Let's get the letter sent.'

'When Jacqui reads this, she will know it's not your handwriting because you're left-handed and I'm right-handed. Why don't you try and write with your other hand and tell her you sprained your wrist on the assault course?'

Eddie growled, 'And why would I do that?!'

I was on shaky ground but I pressed on telling him that I would help by writing in pencil and letting him go over it? I could tell he was trying to stay calm to see where I was going. His natural response was to flare up. 'Eddie,' I said, 'Leonardo Da Vinci, the cleverest man who ever lived, was left-handed and struggled to write to such an extent he wrote back to front.'

Eddie smiled and surprised me by saying Leonardo Da Vinci was the Mona Lisa man.

I continued, 'Left-handed people write over what they have just written and that is why they often turn the paper.'

Eddie seemed to be coming onside when the lights went out. Eddie cursed and asked if I had a torch. I did not. He went outside. I heard raised voices and then he came back with a flashlight which darted all over the tent until illuminating my face, making me close my eyes. Under the handheld light I wrote out the response to Jacqui in pencil and Eddie carefully traced over in pen. I use the term carefully as Eddie had huge hands and nothing he did had any delicacy or precision. My final task was to rub out the pencil. The rubber was inadequate as it was a hard lump on the top of a pencil, but the finished missive served its purpose. I covered some of the more obvious areas of collaboration with hearts and squiggles just like Jacqui had done and Eddie was delighted. Eddie grinned as he took a stamp from his wallet and put it on an envelope that was too small for the sheet of notepaper we had written on. I wrote out the address. He stood up and went out of the tent. I heard voices and then he returned without the torch or the letter. As he undressed and climbed into bed, he told me that Campion, from the next tent, had taken the letter to the post box.

*

Morning came too soon. I had slept well but was awoken by shouting and movement. Eddie was up and dressed and struggling with a puttee. He had been to the ablutions and had shaved. He warned me that I had better get cracking as they were getting crowded. It was 0445 and first light. We were to be on parade for breakfast roll call at 0630. I was trying to work out why with so much time I was roused so early. I was to find out that I would never have enough time. I would always be running and I would never have time to think. I was able to have a shave because Ra-Ra already had a basin. He was happy for me to push in beside him and use his water. What was particularly helpful was that Ra-Ra had a plug. Everyone else seemed to be using running water or had stuffed the plughole to try and build up the water. Everyone was cursing and growling. Ra-Ra whispered to me that he had two plugs and that he would let me have one later. I wanted to ask why anyone would have one plug, never mind a spare but kept quiet as plugs were clearly an essential asset.

*

Back in the tent Eddie was still struggling with his puttee. A puttee is a long strip of cloth wound round the ankle for protection and support. It was a Hindi word meaning bandage. I only knew from watching an episode of *It Ain't Half Hot Mum*. I had no idea how they were to be worn but helped Eddie and then dressed, putting on my puttees in a similar manner. If Eddie was wrong, I would be wrong too.

I mentioned bath plugs to Eddie and he grinned and tapped his nose. Eddie clearly had one and was aware of the importance.

*

The 0630 parade was the start of what was to be days of mayhem. The first parade showed just how much of a rabble had been assembled. We were, however, introduced to Sergeant Major Busty Burton. It was his parade, and we were his victims. There were only seventy recruits, we were divided into two platoons of twenty-three and one of twenty-four and each platoon had three sections of eight. I was in one section of Seringapatam Platoon. We were given a handout explaining the name Seringapatam and how it was a battle honour following the battle of the same name in 1799. We were told to learn all the information as we would be asked questions about it. Anyone failing to answer correctly would be on guard duty on the Saturday night. There was a collective groan when this was explained as everyone seemed to want to be off on the Saturday as it was the most popular night in Weymouth. The Seringapatam Platoon was immediately renamed Spam by all and sundry. Tangier and Inkerman Platoons got off lightly. Each platoon was given a colour shoulder flash. I was pleased to note Ra-Ra had blue like me, but less happy that so did Eddie. On the other side of the parade ground there were eight or so men having a parade and I was sure one was Colin Hipgrave from my student house. I had seen nothing of Colin since arrival. He did not travel down by train but I was told he was probably on one of the three mini-buses that left the drill hall and came directly to the camp. I had assumed that being 'H' he would be further down the tent lines. I was still hoping he would be in the platoon. I could not be sure it was Colin but was sure they had white shoulder flashes. There was obviously another platoon being kept separate.

I am not sure I want to remember the rest of the day as it was all shouting and confusion. I was grateful for the evening meal. That was rushed and, even though we had finished by 1830, we still had an hour polishing our boots and half an hour learning about Seringapatam. I was expecting trouble from Eddie when I finally arrived back at the tent but he was surprisingly relaxed lying on his bunk looking at Jacqui's letter. He asked me to read the letter to him again. He also wanted me to read the story of the platoon and then test him. I only needed to read it a couple of times for him to know all the relevant dates. I asked him how he was so good at the dates and he told me he knew his numbers from the dartboard and 1799 was seventeen, treble three, treble three. He then reeled off another sequence. 1799 was embedded.

We wrote another letter to Jacqui in which we 'compared her to a summer day', telling her she was more lovely. I had a vague recall of the sonnets. We told her that 'so long as Eddie could breathe, and his eyes could see, so long lived his love for Jacqui'. Eddie was delighted. I was no scholar of Shakespeare and I was worried I did not set the bar too high for future letters. I had read *Romeo and Juliet* for 'O' level English Literature and just wished I had remembered more of it

*

I did not have much contact with Eddie during the following two days. He had been in an altercation with a cook serving the evening meal. There was cauliflower cheese on the menu. Ra-Ra told me that Eddie looked at the dish and asked the cook what it was. The cook told him it was 'recruit brains' but not to worry, they did not need Eddie's as it would be such a small portion. Eddie's response was to push the cook's face into the cauliflower cheese. Eddie was held in the guard room overnight and the cook was sent to hospital to have some minor burns dressed. Ra-Ra, as the principal witness, was able eventually to tell the commanding officer that the cook started it. As it was so early in the recruit camp, and discipline had not been drummed in, Eddie escaped with a warning and a growing reputation.

Eddie had received a new letter when he had been released from his cell and he was keen that I read it to him. I was no expert but this letter was different. It was definitely from Jacqui, but it was on writing paper and it had been folded so that it was neat in the envelope. There were the usual squiggles and hearts but the letter was well composed and easy to read. Eddie was oblivious to the changes. He was thrilled by the kind words explaining how he was missed, how the parting was such sweet sorrow and how she had a thousand images of him in an hour. I was sure that Jacqui was also using some outside assistance. This was confirmed by the postscript after Jacqui's serpentine signature. It said that she wanted to 'keep their love hotter than a pepper sprout'. Eddie asked me what a pepper sprout was and whilst I was tempted to tell him to ask Johnny Cash, I just said, 'A hot chilli.' He was none the wiser. I was going to have to up my game if 'Team Eddie' were to triumph in the letter-writing contest.

*

There were six police forces in Weymouth, all poised to arrest we recruits for any misdemeanour. That was the message of the hastily organised lecture on behaviour on the Wednesday morning. It had been planned for the Thursday, before we were allowed out of camp, but because of the 'Eddie incident', it was brought forward. The first police were our 'regimental police', they had armbands with RP on their arm and were in camp but would be checking up on us in town. The Military Police wore red berets and they were all over the area in cars and would be happy to pick us up if we looked drunk or walked whilst chewing gum. The Ministry of Defence police, called MOD plod, guarded the MOD buildings and the naval dockyard. There was the usual Dorset constabulary, the boys in blue and, last but not least, were the Royal Marine shore patrols. The latter wore Royal Marine dress and carried long staves. Anyone they picked up would be delivered to the next ship leaving Portsmouth. It mattered not whether you were a soldier, sailor or marine. If they grabbed you, they would crack your head and you would wake up on one of Her Majesty's warships halfway to Gibraltar.

As I left the briefing, I bumped into Hipgrave. He was with a group of men with white tabs on their lapels. I asked him where he had been. He was circumspect and took me to one side. 'I'm an officer cadet, I'll be training separately during the camp before going to Victory College at Sandhurst to get a commission.' He blushed.

I was not sure what to say and mumbled, 'When did this happen?'

He said that he would explain when he had a chance and then departed. I was left dumbfounded and felt betrayed but had no idea why. I think it was because of his embarrassment at not having told me. The rest of the day was drill, drill and more drill. The sun was permanently on our necks, ears and noses and we pale-skin folk soon started to burn. Anyone who has had military service will appreciate just how mindless drill seems when it is being taught. The trick is to simply not to think. Act on the commands and never try to anticipate. I was lucky that the platoon was full of people worse than me so whilst I had my fair share of abuse, ridicule and derision, it was nothing compared to Hughes and Ingram. Hughes was nicknamed 'Dolly' and Ingram 'Parton' as the Sergeant Major said they were the two biggest tits!

The usual scream was that if anyone was not enjoying this, they could catch the 1500 train home. I would regularly expect one or two to take up this offer but there was a collective defiance, and no one did.

I was singled out by the Sergeant Major as we were dismissed for the evening meal. He screamed at me to come to him and I ran over and stood to attention before him expecting to be admonished. He was surprisingly calm and spoke softly. He knew I was a friend and tent mate of Spanswick and wanted to warn me that he had caused trouble and I had to keep Spanswick under control. I ran back to join the queue under no illusion that keeping my distance was my preferred option. Big Eddie had other ideas. He singled me out to tell me that we were going into Weymouth to get 'wasted' on our first opportunity which was the Thursday night. I smiled weakly when Eddie gave me this news.

*

Luck would have it that the next day, despite the usual mayhem, I had a moment to reflect and pause. Cruddick went down with heatstroke and we were given ten minutes under a shaded loading bay for cold water and rest. Whist lounging there, Ra-Ra told me that Dolly and Parton were upset because they had been told they were on fire picket duty and could not leave the camp. I was eager to find out more. Ra-Ra explained that, because the tented camp was a major fire risk, a team of six had to patrol throughout the night. The team, led by a corporal, had to make sure there were no naked flames and man the ubiquitous fire buckets if a fire broke out. These were full of sand and stood beside every tent. It was armed with this information that I was able to dodge the night out and could do so with Eddie's full sympathy. It did cause confusion with the Fire Picket Corporal, who could not understand why he had an extra man turn up on his parade. Both Dolly and Parton explained to the Corporal that they had been told by the Sergeant Major of their fate and Dolly added that he had seen me talking to the Sergeant Major too, which seemed to provide the appropriate explanation so I did not need to lie. I am sure there are more mindless ways to spend the night but, if so, I would never experience one in my lifetime. Two hours walking up and down the camp followed by two hours resting in full kit ready to man a bucket. The highlight of the evening was the arrival back to camp of those who had an evening of drink. Eddie's crowd were the loudest and most boisterous but in the most part good humoured. The Thursday curfew was 2100 so they had had little chance of mischief. I was a little annoyed that I had played the fire picket duty one night early as I should have saved it for the Friday or maybe even the Saturday.

*

One good benefit of being on the fire picket was the tub of 'After-Sun'. My neck was badly burnt by the sun and I was losing skin off my ears. I was not the only one. Mclean who had the nickname 'Ginge Jock', for reasons that were easy to work out, had translucent skin which looked as if it had been blowtorched where it had been exposed to the sun. He had been to the medical centre and they had given him cream which either he was allergic to, or was designed for in-growing toenails, as it made his skin flare up. He gave me his tin and it was working for me. It was the first respite I had from the constant urge to scratch my own head off.

*

The escape from a Friday night out with Eddie and his

gang was easier than I had anticipated. Twelve recruits were selected to provide the camp guard. Hitherto it had been carried out by the 'trained soldiers' who occupied the main part of the camp. To give them the weekend off we 'new boys' were stepped up for the task. Ginge Jock had been selected. He was still suffering with what I would consider heatstroke as he had headaches and had been sick. I suggested to him that I did his duty making out that it was because of his illness. He shook my hand vigorously and told me I was better than his brother. He went to hug me but I pulled back. He told me he 'owed me one'. I smiled back weakly.

*

Guard duty was surprisingly good. When the camp was not being used, which was 80% of the year, it was watched over by a civilian nightwatchman. He had a television in the back room. When we were not on the gate or patrolling the lines, we simply watched television. There were no incidents when the camp inmates returned. They were loud and boisterous, but we just checked their ID and moved them on. The guard was paraded at 0300 by the duty officer. I was awake and standing on duty on the gate when he appeared. He was accompanied by Hipgrave, resplendent in his white tabs. I saluted the officer who asked me to call out the guard. I had no idea what he meant but went to the guardroom window and told the guard commander, a corporal who was snoozing on the reception desk. The corporal leapt up and shouted for everyone to get on parade. There was a delay whilst sleepy soldiers in various stages of undress assembled in front of the guardhouse. The corporal called us to attention and the officer, closely followed by Hipgrave, inspected the two lines of six. Having been on the gate, I was the only recruit fully dressed. The officer told Hipgrave to take my name as he wanted it noted that I was well turned out. Hipgrave asked me my name! I replied, 'Judas Iscariot.'

*

Saturday was a sports day. The day started with a cross-country run over a five-mile course. I was back in the first ten and was delighted. I was able to sit under a tree in the shade and just relax until the stragglers that included Eddie came back. A tug-of-war followed. As a lightweight I was in the platoon third team. We out-pulled, or whatever the term is, two other third teams but lost to Tangier's first team so were knocked out. Eddie was in the platoon first team and almost singlehandedly helped them win, beating Tangier first in the final. I was staggered by his power. A football tournament followed. Football was not my sport but I tried to be enthusiastic. After everything was finished and the Sergeant Major explained some complicated scoring system which was marked on a blackboard, Waterloo Platoon were told they were winners. This was the officer cadet platoon. There were mutterings of discontent as Seringapatam had won the cross-country, tug-of-war, and football. Even Eddie, who could not read the blackboard, thought there was skulduggery.

Eddie was calmed by the knowledge that we had won the tug-of-war and he told me how we were going to celebrate that night. He was keen to tell me what I had been missing and how he would make sure we would make up for it tonight. He also reminded me that he had a letter to write. I resigned myself to my fate: a night of heavy drinking with Eddie. I knew it was going to end badly.

The letter to Jacqui was dashed off in moments as sports day was news and Eddie's tug-of-war triumph was perfect padding. Eddie was getting more dexterous with the daily handling of the pen and so even the period of anger and cursing that followed the drafting was foreshortened.

*

Eddie had attracted all the worst characters as his entourage. I felt unbelievably overeducated and I hated myself for thinking it but I also felt 'superior'. There were very few brain cells amongst those that gathered and all seemed ready to drink heavily at Eddie's bidding. Ra-Ra and Ginge Jock, who I might have enjoyed a more interesting evening with, were 'excluded' from the group. I was definitely the odd one out and was struggling to find any point of contact, save that we were all training together. I tried to show some gusto and enthusiasm but I was going through the motions. I was reacquainted with Badger, the thug who had christened me Horace. He kicked off about why I was joining them but a growl from Eddie soon shut him up. He did not like me and the feeling was reciprocated. The evening started on the outskirts of Weymouth at the first pub that was 'in bounds'. There was a cordon of restricted pubs around the camp to protect the locals from any 'trouble'. Most of the publicans were happy to turn a blind eye and serve anybody as they valued the trade. The reality was that the senior ranks and officers used these pubs and did not want the 'soldiery' crossing their paths socially so the restrictions were in place to protect their privacy.

I was able to keep pace with the early drinking. As a student we often had an evening where I could down two or three pints over the course of the night. I was not so comfortable doing it in less than an hour. There were ten in the group and it was an unwieldy size as it moved into the centre of the town. We spilled into the road and several cars honked their horn. I thought one was particularly stupid as he slowed to complain. He was punched on the nose through his open window for his effort. The incident did sharpen me up to the potential dangers of the evening and I decided to stop the alcohol intake as best I could. This proved easier than I thought. There were usually ten or more pints on the table and so I would just keep moving mine nearer a glass with slightly less in and then swapping with this glass. The owner would then pick up mine and be none the wiser. I was picked up only once during the rest of the night and then just simply thanked the fellow for his keen observation. It did mean I was probably doubling Eddie's intake as he was usually next to me. I was hoping to slip away before hitting the notorious Victoria Bars which were the final destination. This plan was thwarted by Eddie who now, increasingly drunk, wanted to tell everyone that I was his best friend and, as this was my first night out, they had to make sure I enjoyed it.

*

The Victoria Bars were not well named. There was no Victorian façade and there was only one bar. The entrance was over a raised veranda and through swinging doors as seen in every Western saloon. This was a wild west movie set. One huge long bar dominated the room and if the barman had slid the beers from one end to the other, I would not have been surprised. As a site of social observation, it was marvellous and I was pleased to have had the experience. The place was crowded but not excessively. We followed Eddie to the very centre of the bar and the three men standing there moved to one side as I anticipated. Eddie had adopted a wide body gait as he took long strides forward. I imagined Eddie saying, 'Set 'em up, barman, and ten shots of red eye.' He did not. It was ten beers and I found myself paying. In fairness it was my round. I was staggered by the cost, especially as I had no plans to drink my pint. There appeared to be a hen party at some tables beside the far wall and a small table free beside them. We had been standing all evening in every bar, but the lure of the hen party was too much. Eddie led us all over to the spare table where there were four chairs. There is probably no law of physics but any large powerful group moving into a small space will soon have ten chairs and a weaker group will disperse. In this case the weaker group were four or five sailors who were less than happy with the change in the balance of power. We knew they were sailors as one of the hen party was urging them to dance a hornpipe and, had we not rained on their parade, they may well have done so. I could feel the hostility from the sailors but that is because I was still alert and sober, the rest were oblivious. The hen party were happy to engage in the banter and they certainly brought out the best of Eddie and his crowd. Sadly, as the relationship with the ladies improved, it deteriorated with the sailors on the flank. It was still just growls when I upped and went to the bathroom. I crossed a floor that had sawdust sprinkled over it and had to pause as the bar staff were loading barrels through a back door and down into the cellar. I was tempted to just slip out the back door and back to camp, but thought I needed the loo and would go there first.

*

I walked into a cavernous 'Gents' with the longest row of urinals that I had ever seen. It was a work of art and a fine example of Victorian architecture. I was sure that it was where Marcel Duchamp would have found his inspiration. As I left, I felt somewhat uplifted and of course relieved. My contentment was short lived. The hen party were all standing at the bar and had been joined by Eddie and a couple of the others. I returned to my seat wondering whether Eddie would be mentioning his new friends to Jacqui in his next letter. The sailors had been joined by two or three others and had retaken at least three of our chairs. Our group had divided. I was no tactician but I felt vulnerable. I am not sure what happened next, even though it seemed to happen in slow motion. A scuffle in the middle of the floor turned into a bar-room brawl of Hollywood proportions. The barman pulled down shutters to protect the optics and the sailors next to me grabbed chairs and waded in. It was a free-for-all with flying glass and broken chairs and no doubt broken bones. I watched in horror and awe. Everything seemed to be almost rehearsed. I saw one of the girls, her face contorted with a snarl, urging on the fight. I saw Badger held by two men and being thumped by a third. Badger was smiling. He pulled his two assailants forward into the centre of the room where most of the fist swinging and kicking was at its greatest. There were not two sides fighting, just everyone having a free-for-all. There were shrieks and growls. One man was lying down with his head in his hands being tended by another. I was probably the only person in the room that had not waded in to throw a punch. All of the hens were fighting and seemed to be more excited about it than some of the men. I was snapped out of my observer status by the movement under the swinging entrance doors. I could see very shiny boots, very white gaiters and the bottom of the long staves carried by the Royal Marine Police. They were paused outside ready to burst in. I did not stop to think, I headed straight to the back door. As I crossed the floor, Eddie came flying backwards towards me. I grabbed him and held him up, just as two sailors advanced onto him. He swung a haymaker and took out the first who went down like a lift. As he pulled back his elbow to strike the second, he caught me on the jaw with his elbow. I was out cold.

*

I came round across the back of Eddie's shoulders. I was

bouncing up and down and was disorientated. Eddie was running and breathing deeply. As he slowed to a walk, I remembered the fight. My mouth tasted of blood and my tongue played with a gap in my teeth. I had lost a side tooth. I wriggled and Eddie felt my change of posture and put me down. He was grinning. There were only two of us. He clapped his hands and said, 'We've outrun them, the south paw and the other paw won!'

I put my finger in my mouth and felt the hole where a bright white molar had once sat. I asked where the rest of the posse were and Eddie told me that he had no idea but that they may have been captured by the Bootnecks.

*

We walked in silence back to camp. I had no idea what you did about a lost tooth. Would I report to the Medical Officer or ask to see a dentist? In the end I did nothing and have a gap to this day. The battle of Victoria Bars was to be talked about in the regiment for decades after it took place. If everyone who claimed to have been there that night had actually been there, it would have been bigger than the battle of Seringapatam. I was there and as a result had gained this strange reputation as the only chap standing next to Eddie in taking down at least ten sailors. Eddie did not stop telling anyone and everyone that he could not have escaped without me at his shoulder, out-punching him.

*

The second week of camp was easier than the first as there was less drill and more soldiering. I found that Ra-Ra and Ginge Jock, who were in the same section as me, wanted to do everything for me. They did make life easier as they competed to be my most helpful assistant. Eddie was convinced that I had been the only one of his friends to stand with him when he had been attacked by the ever-increasing number of sailors. Badger went out of his way to tell me he was sorry he had mistaken me for someone else when we first met. I asked him if he had many friends called Horace. I found I had this strange superpower and, whereas seventy-two hours ago I would have recoiled in fear if Badger had come over to me, here I was standing up to him. The numbers of those we fought increased with the telling as did the beauty of the girls whose honour was being defended. The Sergeant Major must also have heard a version of the battle as he was quick to praise me no matter what I was doing. No one was more surprised than me when at the end of the week on the closing parade I was awarded the prize as the best recruit. Horace the weedy nerd had lost a tooth but gained a reputation and a silver-plated tankard.

Eddie had received another letter. It was signed by Jacqui but it was definitely written by someone else. It started with what was Jacqui's trademark description of what she was going to do to Eddie when she saw him. This was clearly dictated but then it went into an interesting anecdote about a cat that had adopted the salon. I found it quite amusing. It was well written but Eddie had lost concentration. We had much to write about in our reply as Eddie made much of the fight. It came as no surprise that Eddie did not mention the hen party. Eddie was happy that I drafted the letter. He had stopped telling me what to write and so now he just waited until I had finished. He then wrote over what I had written. I did persuade him to ask about the cat.

*

I had only ever heard of Major Tomey as the officer commanding the recruit cadre but it was he who took the parade and handed out the trophy. He told me how high the standards were and that I should be proud of myself. He also asked if I wanted to stay an extra week at the camp as he needed a driver. I immediately said yes without thinking that I did not have a full driving licence.

Billy Connolly, the comedian, had served in the Territorial Army and had written a song which was a written to amuse those who thought it was a gathering of would-be soldiers. Rather than shun such ridicule, the TA embraced it and sang it with gusto. The last night of the recruit cadre rang out with:

'And yes, I am a weekend soldier and the world is scared of me. I fought a million battles but I am always home in time for tea.'

CHAPTER 2

I received the cash bounty of £200 over a table set up in a corridor. I had to salute for my pay and sign in front of the officer. Step back, salute again and then head back to my tent to pack. I was relocating to a different part of the camp for the 'extra week'. I stopped when I heard the Sergeant Major shout my name. I ran back to him as he stood adjacent to the makeshift Sergeant's mess tent. He was as softly spoken as when he had last addressed me. He told me that I was staying the extra week as the OC's driver and he asked me who else from the platoon would be interested in an extra week's pay. He needed three 'gophers'. I had no idea what a gopher did, nor who was available, but suggested Radison and McInnes. He asked for a third name and unthinking I said Spanswick. He dispatched me to find them and have them report to the Company Administration Block. As an afterthought he told me to bring them to him. I found Eddie immediately as he was at the tent packing for the trip home. Eddie was torn between Jacqui and an extra week in Dorset. He settled on Dorset provided that I agreed to help him write to her every day. I got the impression that Eddie quite liked the attention he got from Jacqui who was obviously missing him greatly. Ra-Ra and Ginge Jock were thrilled and assumed it was all down to my careful negotiations on their behalf. They kept thanking me profusely and Ra-Ra wanted to shake my hand. Hipgrave and the rest of the campsite trooped to the train station and went back to civilian life. Several of the white-tabbed platoon remained for the extra week as they were involved in the exercise.

*

The week was surprisingly quiet. Major Tomey was a man not given to excess. He was a primary school headteacher and his summers were spent soldiering. Dorset was his holiday and he spent a week as an umpire for the exercise that was being played out. My driving was coming on a treat. I had failed to mention my lack of a full licence but I was always with a passenger, Major Tomey, and I presumed he had a full licence so all was well. I took the precaution of hiding two 'L' plates in the back of the Land Rover. I was planning to tell anyone that pulled me up that I had forgotten to show them. It seemed a good safety net, but, in any event, it was not needed as no one was any the wiser. I still shared a tent with Eddie and now had so much more time to work on his education. He was reading better. I had managed to find fourteen books that had been discarded by the departing soldiers at the end of the training. They were an eclectic mix from Sven Hassel's *Legion SS* to George Orwell's *Animal Farm*. Eddie was a restless beast with probably the shortest attention span of anyone I had ever met. I think he just avoided anything he could not do. Once I had him engaged and could show him, he could do it, I gained more time. I had a couple of setbacks and almost had a broken nose to show for it but, at the last minute, Eddie calmed down and it was to be his last ever anger directed at me. The letters continued from Jacqui but she had now handed over full control to whoever was her ghost writer. Eddie had pretty much done the same by handing over to me. Bizarrely, I had a new pen friend and once we had written a paragraph to each other about Eddie and Jacqui's sex life, we could then write about life at either end of England. In one telling piece my 'pen-pal' talked of her idea of a romantic evening. She said it was sharing a shepherd's pie, listening to the *Carnival of the Animals* by Camille Saint-Saëns, and reading favourite poetry out loud to each other. I asked Eddie if Jacqui liked poetry, and classical music, but the look he gave me said it all so I did not quiz him any further.

*

Eddie was seconded to the regimental police for the week which was perfect for him. I had worried it would ignite his brooding anger but he was perfect for the role. Ra-Ra and Ginge Jock were allocated to the cookhouse and, despite moaning about cleaning pots and pans, they both thought it could lead to a job in a restaurant when they went home. The nights out in Dorset were restricted to the local pubs and no one ever questioned us. Eddie had suggested one last trip to the Victoria Bars but we all persuaded him that it would be a fight too far.

*

At the end of the week Major Tomey told me that he and the officers were having the Officers' Mess Dinner night and invited me to join them. It was in mess kit for the officers and he would introduce me as one of the officer cadets. He felt that I had been overlooked on the enrolment and I should have been with Waterloo Platoon for training. He added that I was just the sort of chap they were looking for. The Major knew that I would not have black-tie with me but said I should drive into Weymouth or Poole and pick up a black-tie suit from Moss Bros. He told me to take his Land Rover.

I realised that my blossoming career could crash if I took the Land Rover without someone beside me. Neither Ra-Ra nor Ginge Jock could drive so I drove to the guard room and asked for Eddie. I had to spin a yarn to the regimental police sergeant who gave me a list of jobs that Eddie was involved in. I had to use the well worked line that I would go back and tell Major Tomey what he had said. Rather than drive Eddie, I had Eddie drive me. I felt quite important as Eddie dropped me off outside the suit hire and I told him to wait.

*

The fellow in Moss Bros was really helpful, unlike the vacant, disinterested man who had sold me the chalk-stripe interview suit. I learned about shirts, studs, cufflinks, cummerbunds, silk hankies, white cashmere scarves, double-breasted, single-breasted, cheese-cutters, pre-tied, self-tied and a whole lot more. I came out laden with items I had either hired or bought. I hoped that the evening was going to be worth it. My happy disposition soured when I saw a traffic warden leaning into Eddie's window chatting to him. I feared exposure but as I approached the vehicle Eddie jumped out and walked round to open my door. He said to the traffic warden, 'Here is my officer now.'

The traffic warden touched his yellow brimmed hat and said, 'Sorry I have to move you on, sir, only doing my job.'

I thanked him and apologised for putting him in a difficult position and I would not do it again. Eddie and I drove back to camp. Eddie confided in me that he always knew I would be an officer and furthermore so did Badger. He confided in me that Badger had wanted to beat me up before I had gotten too big for my boots but he had stopped him.

*

I was so pleased with myself as I dressed for the Mess night. Ginge Jock sat on Eddie's bed and Eddie sat on the chair. Ra-Ra behaved like my valet, opening the shirt from its wrapping and helping me put it on. Ra-Ra put in the cufflinks. The big surprise was how helpful Eddie was. He knew how to tie the bow tie which was just as well because the instructions on the slip were incomprehensible. Eddie had been a doorman and in one job they had to wear bow ties. His fingers were too big to do mine but he was able to scare a trembling Ra-Ra into follow his exact instructions. What Moss Bros had failed to include, or remind me of, were the shoes. I stood beautifully attired and all I had to put on my feet were my brown suede student 'brothel-creepers' or black Army boots. We all laughed, me with some mild hysteria. Eddie said, 'What size are you?'

I told him nine and he left the tent saying leave it to me. He took my brown suede shoes with him. I had plenty of time and the Officers' Mess was only on the other side of camp but I was anxious. I need not have been, as Eddie returned quite quickly with some black brogues. They were slightly too big but that was better than being too small. I found myself saying 'I owe you one' to Eddie and I swear he blushed.

He said, 'Check out the shoes on the Mess waiters tonight and see if you can spot the odd one out.'

*

I will say that I was awestruck by the splendour of the Mess. Even though it was temporary, for the regiment's period in Dorset, they had brought the Mess silver and all the trappings accumulated over hundreds of years. Major Tomey, who I was to call Alan, introduced me to every one of the twenty or so officers present and I can safely say I did not remember one name. I met the colonel who was called Colonel so I was happy that his title was the only name I needed to know anyway. I met the three Officer Cadets who had trained with Hipgrave and they were all curious as to why I had not been with them. Major Tomey shut them up by telling them I was too busy being the top soldier on the camp.

I did spot one of the Mess waiters who stood out as he was wearing brown suede shoes. They did look scruffy and I worried he would be in trouble. I had to check myself for being less worried about his fate than mine. Up until that evening, as I sat there in my 'posh attire', I used to find those brown shoes acceptable.

The meal with the officers was a far more sober affair than the night out with Eddie, until after the loyal toast and the Mess rugby started. The object was to simply get a rugby ball from one end of the room to the other. Two indistinct teams with little access to the ball, but access to a scrum of people, simply fought a pitched battle until everyone was bruised or broken.

I tried to do my bit without ripping my hired trousers or losing a stud but that was hardly the qualities needed in the melee. After the Mess rugby there were some other boisterous games mostly led by the Training Major, who I was told was the regular officer, and he tried to make all these schoolteachers and civilians bond in group violence.

I sat out with a glass of Port chatting to Marcus. He was the son of a farmer but was about to launch a new venture that he could run until he took over the farm. He was very drunk but still eloquent and interesting. He had been the officer commanding the Waterloo Platoon the week before. I asked him what he thought of Hipgrave. He leaned over and said in a stage whisper, 'Didn't like the cut of his jib, hopefully Sandhurst will sort him out but not sure he's one of us.'

I wish I had not asked but felt reassured that at least I was 'one of them'. Whatever 'they' were.

*

On the Saturday I had hoped Eddie could drive me back to Poole to drop off my hired suit. Major Tomey's Land Rover had not been available when I went to the vehicle park to collect it so I went to the Mess to find him. He wasn't there but the Colonel was, sitting in a high-backed chair in front of the regimental colours. He beckoned me over and asked if I wanted a coffee. I declined and apologised saying I needed to go into Poole and had come to seek Major Tomey's permission to take another

Land Rover. 'No problem,' he said, 'have a coffee and then my driver will take you there.'

I sat with the Colonel discussing soil mechanics and somehow got onto Bernoulli's equation before I left. The Commanding Officer's driver took down the regimental pennant from the front of the staff car and I am sure he growled when he let me into the back seat. I did not blame him. I felt a fraud but it did mean I got the hire suit back to the shop. It was the same helpful chap who had dressed me initially and he wanted to know how the night had gone. He seemed to get genuine pleasure if his suits had a good time. He told me that they had just released a batch of pre-used suits that had been for hire and were now for sale. He told me that if I was going to events, now was the time to buy one. He explained that over the years I would thank him for this advice. He was right, I have worn the suit I purchased countless times, albeit at the time I was spending my rent for the rest of the summer. The Commanding Officer's driver was confused when I came out with a suit and wanted to know why I had not left it. I just growled loud enough so he could not hear.

*

I wrote one last letter for Eddie before we left. In it he told Jacqui that the letters had brought them so close together that he was going to spend the rest of his life with her. I cautioned him about being too committed but he just laughed. I was minded about telling him of the tale of Cyrano de Bergerac but thought better of it.

CHAPTER 3

Back on Teesside, life had changed somewhat. Dave Wilson had a job at a water sports and leisure centre and was now working some very odd hours. Pete was spending a disproportionate amount of his time at his girlfriend's flat and Steve's mother had arranged for him to fly out to the family house in Spain. Steve had moved out and left the house but had given his share of the rent up to September to Colin. Colin told me he had put it in his account so it would be safe. I found myself distrusting Colin now but tried not to let it show as we would soon be work colleagues. Colin was keen to sub-let Steve's room but I discouraged him, although I got the impression it would not matter what anyone else would think. When the rent was payable, almost a month later, Colin wanted a quarter from me and I said it was a fifth. He told me it was split between the four of us now and even when I reminded him that Steve had paid upfront, he claimed Steve only paid up to the end of the last month he was there. I knew that was not what had happened but was too weak to pursue the matter further. I made a mental note to check what Dave or Pete knew. It was largely Colin and I that rattled around until the September, except for a strange week in late August.

*

About ten years earlier my father had been a bursar to a youth club. It was not a paid post but by doing some of the basic administration and book-keeping he took the pressure off a much put-upon family friend who was the youth leader. The youth leader had paid out some of the youth club funds to pay for a week's stay in a youth hostel for a troubled young girl. I was never party to the full story, but it was clearly a misuse of funds and social services and the local authority and the police became involved. As I understand it, my father acted as a peacemaker and mediator and the technical funding issue was resolved. It did not solve the issue with the girl. The upshot was that the girl, Dawn, came to stay at our house for what was intended to be a week but ended up being over fifteen months. I called Dawn my foster-sister as I already had a sister. Dawn called me brother as she thought she was an only child. Dawn was later settled with her aunt in Loughborough but she kept in touch sporadically.

*

It was a fortnight before I was due to start work. I came back from Presto the local supermarket to find Dawn sitting on the steps of the house. Her eyes were hollow as if she had been crying. She looked scruffy and she carried a small satchel but no other bag. I played really pleased to see her and gave her a big hug. I told her how good she was looking and she smiled. Dawn had dropped in occasionally but had never stayed, but then we had never had any spare room. She once came with a boyfriend, Earl. He looked so shifty I jokingly asked her, in a moment when she and I were alone, if he was on the run. Dawn's face had turned so pale at this suggestion that I presume there was a hint of truth. Needless to say, they left soon after and she had promised to come back for longer next time.

I guided Dawn in through the porch to the sitting room. I went in and I made us both a coffee. I knew Dawn would take a little while to start any meaningful dialogue, so I opened by telling her all about the house and what my flatmates were up to as she had never met any of them. I did bang on too long about the TA camp but I deliberately did not dwell on her situation and I started to notice her relax. I put on a Joan Armatrading LP which I remembered she had played non-stop for a week when she had first arrived at my parents. It had put me off the record forever but she was thrilled and stood up and hugged me again. She said, 'Actually I've gone off this album, I think I overplayed it.'

We both laughed.

'Can I stay for a couple of days?' she requested and I said there was no problem as she could have Steve's room as he had left.

I took her by the hand and led her into the corridor and then to Steve's room at the back. I said, 'Why don't you have a lie down for half an hour whilst I put away the groceries?' I added, 'Maybe you want a bath or a shower?'

*

Dawn did not reappear until almost nine that night. She told me she had had a bath and then fallen asleep on Steve's bed. She came through wrapped in a towel and asked if I had any sweatshirts or something she could wear as she had no change of clothing. I left her in the sitting room whilst I went up to my room to find something or anything that might be appropriate. This took me slightly longer than I anticipated as I had never dressed a five-foot girl and was anxious not to give her anything I might not get back. When I came down, Colin and Dawn were in deep conversation, which I clearly interrupted as they both went quiet. I joked that they had clearly met and neither said anything. I handed Dawn a new Adidas sweatshirt which had been too tight on me and some Ron Hill running trousers. She pulled on the trousers under the towel and then shocked me by dropping the towel before pulling on the top. I was more shocked that she did it in front of Colin, although it would still have been weird before me.

We made some small talk before Colin said 'chow', waved and went up to his room. I decided not to ask any questions about her circumstances. I said, 'What do you think of Colin?' I explained I had lived with him for almost three years and he had been to TA camp with me.

She just shrugged. She was not in a mood to talk yet, so I said nothing. I asked how the shower was and she said she had soaked in a bath. I asked her whether the bath had been hot. She answered with a quizzical, 'Yes, why would I have a cold bath?'

I suggested we watched the news but she declined and said, 'I'll turn in, I have a book I'm reading.'

*

Our bath heating system was designed by Heath Robinson. In the whole three years he had lived at the house, Steve had never worked out the sequence of taps and switches that had to be applied to get hot water to the bath. The house heating boiler was separate from the immersion heater. Had Dawn told me she wanted a shower, it would have been straightforward; but for a bath you had to turn on two red valves, switch off the immersion and switch on the water pump. If Dawn had a hot bath, she had either just qualified as a plumber or she had had careful instructions. She and Earl may have had a shower or two but if she had remembered how to work the bath, she was a genius. I went to bed puzzled, but planned to ask her in the morning.

*

I did not see Dawn the following day as I had an early driving lesson before my driving test. It was my second test, the first had been 'discontinued' after I hit a bus. Actually, the bus hit me, the bus cut the corner. The long bus broke my car indicator cluster as it swung in front of me. The examiner did not apportion blame but I did not pass and I did not get a refund. I felt more confident on this test having driven Major Tomey for a week. My confidence was well placed and I returned home triumphant. I did not have a car so it was a hollow prize in the short term. I saw Dawn briefly on the Thursday. She was looking so much better. She gave me my top and Ron Hills back and thanked me. She whispered, 'Things have worked out, please don't judge me.'

I said, 'Did you wash my top?'

She replied, 'No, okay you can judge me!' And she was gone. I never did find out how she worked the plumbing.

CHAPTER 4

What they do not teach you at polytechnic is the sheer size of everything when you are building a road. The plant, the volume of materials, the different disciplines, everything is vast. Even though Colin and I were on the same contract, we could have been on different planets. Colin was sent to join a team of office-bound engineers at one end of the bypass where the suite of offices were. His first task was to extract from a series of cross-sections of the road the soil to be cut out from the terrain. He then had to work out from another set of drawings where the soil that had been cut had to be dropped to fill what would be voids. The object was to construct the road with minimum cut and fill. He tried to explain to me what he was doing and I got the idea but it sounded dreadful and I thought he had drawn the short straw. The road was eight miles long. It had five two level interchanges and one single level. There were two road bridges and one railway bridge. There were eight pedestrian underpasses and three footbridges. It was designed to take 73,000 vehicles a day but the estimated initial flow was 50,000 vehicles.

*

I was initially placed with a setting out engineer as his chainman. I carried an extendable staff marked like a ten-foot ruler. The engineer, Malcolm, looked so old and frail he reminded me of my grandfather. It occurred to me that I had spent the summer with fit young men so maybe I was being a little harsh. I was not. Malcolm was so decrepit he could hardly lift his wrists. I carried anything that needed carrying. Malcolm smoked black cigarettes non-stop and could only walk twenty paces without a pause to either catch his breath or light another fag. He knew everything about road construction and I realised if I wanted to learn anything from him, it would have to be fast as he was dying a little more each day.

*

My degree was in Civil Engineering so I could reel off Bernoulli's equation and other fancy formulae, but I had no practical experience. I could not even set up the theodolite. Malcolm taught me after watching me struggle. I was getting ever more frustrated and angrier. He calmly stepped up and demonstrated; you had to level two legs of the tripod in one plane and then when they were level the third leg could be adjusted so the little bubble was in the centre of the spirit level. I could then twist the theodolite onto the tripod and adjust the three wheels in the same manner I had adjusted the legs. Finally, I could move the beautifully levelled theodolite over the marked point in the ground over which I had placed the tripod. It was all so easy once it had been demonstrated and I had practised. I was so grateful for Malcolm's patience. I had presumed Malcolm was self-taught because he never mentioned any training. He did know all the shortcuts which was just as well as he could not do anything for long. I had to hammer in all the batter rails: these were the two wooden stakes along the side of the road with a cross rail showing the incline and depth that was to be cut by the excavators.

*

We had a white van but as it was the early days of the construction, we really needed one of the fleet of Land Rovers. The Land Rovers seemed exclusively for the use of the agents and construction managers who would drive up onto the high ground so that they could gaze at we ants working below transforming the landscape. Malcolm did teach me pretty much all I needed to know about setting out. I learned where all the trig points and datum level points were along the proposed road route and I could plot the centre lines using the theodolite. Malcolm wore a gold ring with a crest on the little finger of his left hand. I admired it one day whilst we sat so he could have a cigarette. He told me that his family was descended from Robert the Bruce and his ring had been matriculated by his father from some coat of arms by Lord Lyon. Heraldry was not a subject on which I had any knowledge so he could have told me that the ring was from JRR Tolkien and I would have believed him. One day the road was dry and the wind so strong we sheltered behind a pile of wooden stakes to avoid what I called a sandstorm. Malcolm told me that he had worked in South Africa and had been in a sandstorm and this was not a sandstorm. I was able to keep Malcolm amused by tales of the TA camp. He especially liked the fight in the Victoria Bars as it reminded him of some of his experiences on construction sites in South Africa. Malcolm told me that he had started life as Aquarius with his water on his back and as he had got older the water had flowed away. He just followed the flow. He wished he had been strong enough to plough the path in front of him so he could follow the water down a path of his choosing. Malcolm spoke in such a quiet tuneful way that whilst I had no idea what he was talking about, I found it easy to listen.

*

I was sad we never made it to the culvert construction that was on our patch but that was for later construction. Many of the road staff lived in caravans down by the main site. They travelled from one construction site to another and so it made sense. Some had fancy trailer caravans, others more modest affairs. Malcolm told me that he deliberately lived in the smallest and the oldest caravan as it was part of his penance. I tried to question this but it was clear Malcolm had said everything he was going to on the subject. I never actually went near his caravan but he had pointed it out from the top of the road near the bridging site where it was visible in the far distance. I never found out anything about Malcolm's private life, I did not even know his surname. We did talk of work he had done in the past and particularly South Africa but nothing of his more recent work for this firm. When he did mention the current job, it was all superficial. He told me they used him for the specialty work. When I questioned him on this, he told me I had a lot to learn. I did say I wanted to learn but nothing further was offered.

*

A week later our van was in for a service and so Malcolm and I walked out to the exposed upper end of the road. The walking had been too much for Malcolm and it had been a long day, Malcolm was struggling to breathe and coughing incessantly. I told him I was going to run down to the bridge site to phone for an ambulance. He held my arm and said, 'No just pass my fags, they'll calm me.'

I went over to collect his jacket and brought it over to him. I rummaged and found a packet in the inside pocket. They were fancy black cigarettes with a gold band. I commented on how fancy they were. He told me that they were going to kill him so they might as well look like assassins. He added that they were his last pleasure and so he might as well have the crème de la crème. He dropped his jacket down behind the rock he was sitting on. After a few drags on the elegant cigarette, he calmed down, even if I had not. 'Do you know how much this road is costing?' he said, when he had gained his breath.

'Five million two hundred and sixty-five thousand was the tendered figure.' I answered, as I had read the original specification.

I thought Malcolm would be impressed but he went on without answering the question, 'If you just take 0.1% you could be very rich.'

I nodded and wondered if he was getting a little infirm. In my head I was working out the 0.1%.

Malcolm went on getting louder, 'If you take the middle slice of the loaf no one notices. If you take two slices no one notices but if you take three, too many will notice.'

I wisely said nothing.

'The problem we have is that we specialist engineers have been too good and everyone wants more bread and I am too old to provide it.'

There was a long pause so I ventured a question about what were the specialist engineers providing.

I was not sure Malcolm knew I was there as he gazed into the ground. 'I've told them I'm out and no matter what they say they're on their own on this one,' he said, before having another coughing bout. He mumbled on that the water was almost all gone and he had failed to clear the path.

I asked him if he wanted some water but he waved me off. A white van was passing and I flagged it down. It was one of the plant fitters with a full load and he was reluctant to stop but I did not move from the track. I told him Malcolm was feeling poorly. I persuaded him to drop Malcolm off at his caravan as he could never walk back and he needed a rest. Malcolm did not resist as I put him in the front and put his seat belt on. No one wore seat belts on the site and so it was difficult to unravel it from amongst the debris behind the seat. The fitter was impatient but helpfully asked if he should drop Malcolm at the first aid safety station and I said that, 'Yes, that would be a great idea.' I watched Malcolm leave and felt better that it was to get some help, rather than the cold draughty caravan.

I went back to get my stuff and noticed Malcolm had left his jacket. I thought that it was my fault as he was in no state when he left. The jacket was a tweed donkey jacket that was dusty and old and surprisingly heavy. It had clearly been expensive when purchased. There was a tailor's label which I read and it seemed to my untrained eye to suggest it was made to measure for Mr Aiden D Malcolm. Malcolm was not even his first name. I was curious as to what was in the pockets but resisted the temptation to look. I would see him in the morning.

*

The morning was a Saturday. I really did not want to be working as it was a TA weekend and I had hoped to be off but I knew the 'proper job' had to take priority. I managed to get a lift in, which was usually hard on a Saturday, so was pleased to be at the crew hut early. Malcolm was usually sitting having a coffee and a black fag reading a newspaper but he was not. I assumed it was because I was early and so took over the position, coffee, paper but no fag. By nine I was concerned and thought I would ring the main office to check with them. The phone rang for ages before being answered by the most unhelpful person on site. They had never heard of Aiden Malcolm and he did not work for them. I tried to explain but they just hung up. Rather than hang about I grabbed Malcolm's coat from my locker and decided to find him to give it back. I walked all the way to the head office complex, only grabbing a passing van for the last two hundred metres. I passed the prominent first aid point and on impulse put my head round the door and asked the nurse about Malcolm. She was happy to check the previous day's diary. It was empty. No mention of Malcolm. She had not been on duty and explained that because Malcolm had come in so late the entry may not have been recorded yet. I did say Malcolm had probably refused any help. Head Office staff were just unhelpful. The fussy clerk asked me why everyone was interested in this Malcolm character, so it was clearly him that I had spoken to. He said, 'From what you tell me the chap is probably an agency engineer, he will not be on my list.' He added, 'They are self-employed so if he is sick, he loses money, not us.'

My last effort was to walk down to the caravan park. I had never been, but remembered where it was after Malcolm had pointed his little home out to me once from one of the vantage points up on the hill. I may have been disorientated but there was no caravan where I expected to find it. There were more people about than normal, as it was Saturday, but no one could help. One vaguely remembered an old white caravan in the corner but no one, absolutely no one, knew Malcolm.

It seemed so impersonal: I had known him for a couple of months but when I tried to think what I knew about him, it was absolutely nothing. I did not even know where he hailed from. Back in the crew room I inherited all of the equipment but had no one to hold even the end of a tape measure. I had two days borrowing people such as the excavator driver who helped me to set the angles and depths, he, the excavator driver, would then have to grade with his excavator. The machines were costing more than the driver and I together, so they could not be idle. I spoke to Gregg Carol, our agent. I asked him about Malcolm. His reply was, 'When things get busy the agency do send some characters, don't they?'

I asked where he had gone and he said, 'How would I know? I didn't know the fellow.'

I told him I was struggling and asked for some help. He asked me if I knew anybody that was not very bright but could lift heavy weights.

So that is how Eddie joined me as my chainman carrying all the tools and hammering in all of the posts and pins. The main problem was that Eddie thought he worked for me and not the company. He was about 6ft 4" and everyone wanted him on their gang. If anyone tried to tell him what to do or asked for his help, he would tell them to check it was okay with his boss. Gregg the agent was so amused by the situation that he called me Don from *the Godfather* as I had this tame gorilla that was only answerable to me. The road work came easy to Eddie and it came at just the right time. He had asked Jacqui to marry him (when he found she was pregnant) and he needed a steady job. He started reading and writing again with me as we sat waiting for transport beside the land that we would one day turn into a highway. I still had Malcolm's coat in my locker and every time I saw it, I was angry. This old fellow had just vanished and no one had noticed but me.

*

My first real change came in late March. The road construction that had been reduced by the short days and wet weather of winter was starting to burst back into spring activity. Eddie was moved to the concrete mixing station as there was going to be a blitz on two bridges and a number of culverts. I had no support but had set out most of the important tasks that had been allotted. I was in the crew hut waiting for my lift when Eddie arrived. He was flustered having just run what must have been the four miles from the concrete station. He had panicked when he was given a series of cards with concrete recipes on. Without stopping, he had run to find me. I sat him down and we slowly went through each card. He memorised the quantities in seconds with his old darts and gambling skill and this calmed him. Once calm, he realised that he could actually read the ingredients. He was delighted and annoyed in equal measure. Annoyed that he had interrupted me when he had not needed to, but delighted that he could have read them if he had only tried. It was such a breakthrough. Eddie caught my crew bus I was taking home but jumped off at the concrete plant. He later told me that he had told his supervisor that he had been to see me so I could second-check the figures as I was a concrete specialist. This white lie gained some traction and several of the trainee structural engineers would seek me out to make sure their figures were correct before some major concrete pour.

I was plucked from obscurity by Gregg. He said I was getting a promotion. No extra money, no extra power, but loads of extra stress. I was to oversee the build of an electricity sub-station construction. This may not sound much but I was thrilled. It was my first project that I would control from start to finish. I was delighted to accept. I had to go into the head office for a couple of hours to be briefed and then I could launch the project by ordering the materials with the quantity surveyor and I could set out the ground.

*

I had not had much to do with Colin over the previous months. He was well embedded in the head office. He knew everybody and everything and was becoming a bit of a bore. He had purchased a new fancy Rolex watch which he wanted to show me every time we met and every time, like a fool, I showed my admiration. In all fairness, Colin did show so much interest in the sub-station that I forgave him his hubris. He was helpful in co-ordinating my meeting which was held in a lecture room in a building that was due for demolition. The buildings stood on what was to be an access road. The building was used mainly for storage but it was practical and there was less clutter than in the portable cabin complex. I met with Colin, John the quantity surveyor and Rhino, the bricklaying boss. He was called Rhino by everyone but me. He had a huge growth between his eyes. Rhino took one look at the plans and the various elevations and smiled. He did not need to say anything. I knew he knew I was the last person he needed to disrupt his teams' building of what to all intents and purposes was a square brick box with a roof. I was given one plan. I asked for a second so I could have one out on site with me and one kept clean. Colin said it could be arranged. I was told the site had been flattened and fenced and my cabin awaited me.

*

The site area cleared was huge and neatly fenced off. There was a shiny white cabin which did not have electricity but had a three-bar fire powered by a gas cylinder. There was a table with an electric water boiler, which would be useless without electricity, two mismatched chairs and a locker. Under the step into the cabin was a small tabby-tortoiseshell cat. I presumed the cat would disappear when I entered the cabin but it did not, it came in with me. I had a ham sandwich planned for lunch but offered the ham to the cat. The cat liked ham, eating it firstly from the floor but later from my hand.

Shame that my work was not as impressive. I did not get off to a good start. I spent the first week on my own, save for the cat. I had used the datum point and set the levels for the ground work. I marked out all the corners and a centre point. I was rather pleased with myself, especially as I had done so by grabbing Eddie when he was available. I was punctured when the drainage team came to dig the channels. They asked me if the structure had a cellar or was it going to be a sunken pill box? They told me if they followed my instructions, it was to be dug three feet underground. I checked and double-checked my figures and all seemed right, but they were correct. If they started using my measurements, they would be digging far too deep. The JCB driver climbed out of his cab and in an Irish brogue asked if he could help. I bit my tongue feeling slightly undermined but politely said, 'I hope so.'

He grinned and walked over. 'Did you take this from the right datum point?' he asked.

I unfolded my part of the road drawing master plan that had been prepared for the whole road contract. I showed him my mark.

'Easy mistake to make,' he said. 'There are two parallel sets of datum, you're using the road, we're on the higher level here.' He strolled back to the cab. I refolded my master map. I unfolded the map provided for the sub-station. He was right. I was so used to the road levels that it did not occur to me that there were other levels up here on the higher ground. The fix was easier to sort than the error exposed as I simply cut one metre off the 'T' bars that the banksmen were using. I gave the JCB driver a double hand clap over my head, did a little dance and waved thank you. He just got on with digging a precision ditch.

*

Over the next few days, the bricks started to arrive. Truck after truck after truck. I had no involvement with the quantities but I knew that a six-metre square box did not need the number of pallets of bricks being delivered. I was also surprised by the quality and variation in the types of brick delivered, some were pale yellow, others almost white. These were speciality bricks. I was signing for each load and I calculated that I had a thousand more bricks than I needed. Rhino and his team were due next morning so I wanted to get things sorted. I walked down to the nearest site office on the road and rang head office. I spoke to the quantity surveyor. He just told me his job was to give the numbers, not to check the delivery nor the quality, that was my job. I pleaded that the numbers looked wrong at which point he angrily told me something like to 'go forth and learn to multiply'. I rang again and tried to speak to Gregg but his wife had just delivered a baby boy and he was on two weeks holiday. I rang again for a third time and spoke to Colin. He told me not to worry, he would have the bricks lifted and the correct bricks delivered.

Colin seemed so calm and helpful. It dispelled all my concerns over him that had been brewing since the soil mechanics coursework misunderstanding. I went back to the site just in time to see the roof trusses being delivered. I signed for them but I was surprised that they had been delivered so early and they did seem huge. The ground workers had all gone. The JCB driver was still sitting in his cab. I asked him if they were finished, he said, 'Almost.' He was waiting for the low-loader.

I thanked him for saving my bacon. He shrugged his shoulders. He looked me in the eye and said, 'Make sure the mistakes that you make on this job are capable of being fixed with a pencil or a power tool.' It sounded like a warning. I wanted to ask what he meant but he was so clear, it did not need any clarification. When the low-loader arrived, the JCB was manoeuvred onto the back. The driver gave me a thumbs up as they left.

I stood alone, save for enough bricks to build Wandsworth Prison.

*

Rhino and his team of four arrived on site at exactly 0830. They did not come over to me but stood in a huddle looking at the piles of bricks on the pallets. One chap had a notebook and was making notes of what Rhino was saying. It was out of earshot but it all looked serious. I presumed at some point Rhino would stride over and blame me for the 'cock up'. My cabin now trebled up as an office, a cat room and a lock up. It did not have a phone nor a toilet. A portable toilet was on order but seemed a low priority. I toyed with walking over to the group or retreating to the office. It was a Victoria Bar moment. I plucked up courage and walked over. I raised my hand and said, 'Good morning.' I detected no hostility but just slight indifference.

A couple acknowledged me and Rhino said, 'Hi.'

I told Rhino that the specialty bricks had been delivered in error and he said he knew. He asked when they were being uplifted and I said I hope as soon as possible. Rhino pointed to the man who was, by a decade, the youngest of the group and said, 'I'm leaving "Notso" here with you. He'll help with the foundation level. We'll shoot off to sort out the other thing.' Nothing further was said and Rhino and the three bricklayers departed.

'Well, Notso, it looks like you and I are building this on our own today.'

Notso said, 'I'm actually called Ian Bright but everyone calls me Notso.'

I told him I was Harry but my nickname was Horace and that we would get along fine. We were interrupted by the arrival of a truck that was loaded with what appeared to be bricks. I could not believe it. As it got closer, I saw that these bricks were red and looked more like those that may be used on a sub-station. The truck had its own forklift sort of plugged into the back. It was clever engineering. The site area that had been levelled for the sub-station was huge, thank goodness. If it had been a sensible size, appropriate for the small brick box we were building, the over-ordered bricks could never have been delivered nor recovered. The truck made three journeys and picked up certain loads. I asked Notso why the driver was not just taking the nearest and easiest first and he told me that they had been delivered in the wrong order. I asked why they were delivered at all, but he had no idea.

No actual bricklaying took place for ten days. We did pour the concrete footings and I knew that these had to set, but Rhino, who called in twice to check, kept telling me that the concrete was too green. I was amazed, I told him we could build the Eiffel tower on that base. He replied, 'Yes but with your record to date, we would get the one from Pisa.'

*

Notso turned out to be good company. He was a birdspotter and added to my education on the subject. He was also keen to learn about building and road construction so I was able to bore him about soil mechanics. I tried to engage him in the problem with all the bricks but he genuinely seemed to have no idea where they came from or where they went. He did say that Rhino worked on a Sunday and that he assumed bricks were needed.

I kept going over it in my head. The sub-station was approximately 6m square and 3m high. I knew this was 108 cubic metres. It had an area of 6m x 3m x 4m = 72 square metres. There were approximately 60 bricks in a square metre. I would need 4,320, say 5000, allowing for wastage to build my modest building. I had 50 pallets still neatly stacked in the yard and they were being collected as and when needed by somebody for something. They were colour co-ordinated. I had 20 roof trusses. No matter how I tried to view this situation, I was being taken for a ride.

*

An average bricklayer can lay four to five bricks per minute, almost 240 an hour or 1900 a day. Each pallet had 500 bricks. My empire had three brickies and we had not even thrown a brick in anger. My main concern was that no one cared. I was beginning to wonder who knew what was going on. Notso was chosen for his ignorance, maybe I was too. The JCB driver tried to warn me. Malcolm tried to warn me. I went for a strong coffee and I needed to feed the cat. I thought I would ring Colin as he would know what to do. I did not fancy the walk down to the bridge site phone immediately as the rain started coming down in sheets, but would do so later.

I started to look at the only site construction plan I had been given. I compared it to the road drawings that I had worked with on the road construction. They were the same size and print but all the information in the bottom right-hand corner was different. The site plan had no named architect nor designated plan number. The datum point I had for the sub-station was not recorded on the road plan. I wondered when it was built, how the electric cables entered and how it was maintained. I knew nothing about what it was used for and the plan told me nothing either. I could only have one conclusion. My plan was a special project. I was the new Malcolm. This was a loaf of bread.

*

On the Saturday night after work when I arrived home, Colin was dressed ready to go out. I told him I needed to talk to him urgently. He said to make it quick as he was rushing out as his parking was a bit dodgy. I had not really thought out what I was going to tell him about my fears so I just blurted out, 'I think there is something fishy going on at the sub-station.'

He laughed and told me it was my sub-station, what could happen without my knowledge?

I said, 'But all the stuff delivered, all the bricks, all the brickies.'

He looked me in the eye. 'Horace, you doughnut, the sub-station had been given the same code number as an office block in Harrogate. Harrogate have been screaming at Leeds for bricks for three weeks now. If you find any sensible evidence, give me a ring on Tuesday, this has the makings of a long weekend.' He tapped me on both shoulders, picked up a holdall and headed out. I watched from the front window as he climbed into a Golf GTI parked facing the wrong way up our one-way street. I could see him fiddle about and then he climbed out to remove his jacket before getting back in again and driving off. He was wearing driving gloves. He had not mentioned the new car but I was sure he would at some stage, if only to brag. Had Colin settled my concerns, no, but he had brought me back down to earth. I was annoyed that he had taken to calling me Horace. It was fine for Ra-Ra, Ginge Jock and Eddie, and even Notso, but Colin was using it to gain advantage and put me down.

*

Whilst I had planned a quiet Sunday, I was spurred into action by Colin. I went down to the drill hall. I did not go in uniform as I just wanted to find Ra-Ra. Ra-Ra was working in a British Rail works canteen and had bought himself a Yamaha 175 trial bike which was his pride and joy. Ra-Ra had worked Saturday night and so, like me, had missed the formal weekend training and was just hanging about chatting to a couple of others when I arrived. I told him I needed a favour. He was delighted to oblige, especially as it involved taking his beloved bike. I did not have a motorcycle helmet but was able to sign one out of the store. It was military green and had a leather inner. I did not look at the date of manufacture on the stamp, the fact that it had WD (War Department) was sufficient.

I rode pillion giving Ra-Ra directions up to the road construction site entrance. It was blocked to traffic but I knew the route round the back of the building to be demolished, where I had my brief. We then went cross-country, much to Ra-Ra's delight, until we were just short of the sub-station. I explained to Ra-Ra that I had no idea why we were there but I was hoping to find where the bricks in the yard were being taken to. Ra-Ra did not need any explanations from me, he was just happy to await instructions. Luckily it was a spring morning and we were able to lie on some high ground and look down on the site. I called the spot the grassy knoll and often wandered up during the day to take in the views. Ra-Ra had some chewing gum and polos. I was happy with the latter and he the former, so we were both content.

Just after midday an empty truck arrived. The driver was accompanied by one of Rhino's men who jumped out, undid the padlock and opened the gate. It was obviously a well-practised manoeuvre as within half an hour the forklift was off the back, the bricks were loaded and the forklift was back on. Ra-Ra was fascinated by the whole show but I told him, 'Now the fun starts, we have to find out where they are going.'

The loaded truck could not move fast but strangely that made tailing it difficult. We did not want to lose it but did not want to look as if we were following it. Ra-Ra understood what was needed and when a couple of times I was worried that we had let them get away too far, he reassured me, and he was right. The truck went back down the hill, over the road construction site and in a loop back up into the hills. The route would be significantly shortened when the buildings were demolished, and the access road built. The lorry laboured up the hill. We did not follow. We agreed that if we left it half an hour it would be unloaded to come back and we could ride and see the delivery destination. We were right. Some forty minutes later we were up on the hillside. There were two building plots with two half-built beautiful buildings. One building was faced in yellow bricks, the other a pale white. There was much to do to finish them but it would not take long judging by rate of the men working on the scaffolding. Between both plots was the material storage area. I thought, actually that was only the summit store, most of the materials were at my special base camp. Ra-Ra and I headed home. I had the evidence that Colin requested and it was clear there was no one screaming in Harrogate.

CHAPTER 5

Ra-Ra was a good man. We had had some time to chat whilst waiting on what I called the grassy knoll. He told me he was pleased with his nickname because he could always say it. With his own name, Graham, he stuttered. He was embarrassed when meeting someone thinking they would ask his name. He hated his stutter and of all the words he had to say, his own name was the hardest. Ra-Ra rolled off his tongue. It meant he could start any conversation without a stutter. It seemed such simple logic and I told Ra-Ra that I would tell my cousin of the solution to see if it may help him. Ra-Ra laughed and said one Ra-Ra was quite enough. I told him he was lucky that his nickname was not based on Graham or he would have been Ga-Ga. Ra-Ra had allowed his stutter to dominate his life and it occurred to me that all his conversations he had with me usually ended in discussing his speech impediment. I realised I was the only person he could open up to and discuss what was to him the most important issue in his life. The irony being that, with me, Ra-Ra was relaxed and his stutter faded so much that he and I hardly noticed. Ra-Ra dropped me back off at my house. He insisted in taking the helmet from me to return to the drill hall. I was glad to see the back of it as it was ill-fitting and had given me a red burn across my forehead. I was pleased that Colin was away on his long weekend so I did not have to face him. This would also give me some thinking time.

*

I was sitting in the front room reading through the accumulated junk mail for about twenty minutes when Dave came back full of gusto. He was always good company and would help distract me from my concerns. He laughed at my red band across my forehead. He had much to tell me about his sailing and his future plans. We decided that we would walk down to the White Rose for a lager. Dave joked that he would only come with me if I wore a hat to cover the red helmet mark. It was whilst standing buying the drinks that I told Dave how I had never bought Colin a Stella but just a Heineken in a dimpled glass. He laughed and said I had made his day. It turned out he could not stand Colin and he went on to tell me some of the reasons why. I had no idea there was any animosity between them so it was quite a shock. Most of his gripes were that Colin always let him down and he did not trust him. I thought to mention Steve's rent but thought that might throw petrol on the fire. Dave was also annoyed that Colin borrowed his car, without asking, for almost two days to take some girl on a trip to Harrogate. Dave was going away for four days and put his car in for an MOT whilst he was away. He asked Colin if he could collect it when it was ready and Colin was happy to do so. Dave was not so bothered by him using it but felt any normal person would have asked. I mentioned that Colin had a new car and that he had taken to wearing fancy driving gloves. Dave laughed saying, 'More dodgy merchandise that he pilfered from that shop.'

I asked what he meant and he said that Colin always had small leather wallets, lipsticks, perfumes and stuff that was easy to nick. Dave claimed it was accumulated when Colin had worked in some big store the previous summer. Dave assumed I knew. Colin always claimed the goods were paid for, saying he had a big discount, but Dave said it was obvious, by the volume, that they were trousered. There were loads of other incidents but chatting about them would have ruined our night. I had gone from feeling quite upbeat to now worrying about work. Dave had helped in one way. I decided to delay telling Colin about what I was now calling the yellow brick road. I too did not trust Colin, and Dave had helped remind me why. I was going to ask Dave's advice on my problem, when we were interrupted by two girls who were delighted to see Dave. One gave him a hug and the other kissed him on both cheeks. Dave introduced me to Sarah and Carole. Sarah was a tall athletic type with short bobbed hair and an enormous smile. She gave me a hug too, which did make me blush. Carole was dainty, petite and seemed almost as shy as me as she just lifted her hand to wave. Sarah asked if they could join us and Dave said, 'Sorry no!'

I was taken aback and so were the girls. Dave continued to say that I had arranged two beautiful women to join us for a wild party and they, Sarah and Carole, would cramp our style. I cut in and said, 'But, Dave, these are the two beautiful women I mentioned.'

Sarah and Carole joined us and, whilst it was not a wild party, it was one of the best nights I'd had since freshers' week. The conversation was about what we did and mutual acquaintances, as would be expected, but we covered cinema, religion, philosophy and a host of other topics. The conversation was not dominated by any one person and never stopped. We all agreed to buy a Chinese takeaway on the way home and eat it back at our house. I found myself walking back with Carole. She told me that she had spoken more in the two hours in the pub than for the previous six months. I knew from the earlier discussions she worked for the local authority and asked if it was because her working environment was quiet. She told me it was partly that, but partly because she was having an increasing loss of confidence. I told her that I could not understand why, as she had so much going for her. I mentioned her charm, the good looks and the brains. I realised it was probably a delicate subject and was careful not to say the wrong thing. I said, 'I would like to talk to you again, that's for sure.'

Carole never replied. We had a great takeaway. I never had a chance to say anything further to Carole. I did get a hug from both of them before they left. I offered to walk them home but they did not have far to go and declined.

*

Monday was the wettest day since records were kept. The site was a washout, the hut leaked and a lorry laden with roof tiles became bogged down on the track. The cat was waiting outside under the step to stay dry. I let her in and scraped some cat food into her bowl. The lorry was moving up to the unloading area. I felt like telling the driver to go straight up the hill to cut out the double handling, but I held my tongue. I held my tongue, that is, until he asked me to help him unload. I am not sure what he expected me to do but I apologised and said I had an urgent meeting, grabbed my coat and walked down to the bridging site. He shouted after me to sign for the delivery. I increased my pace and pretended the rain had washed out his cries. Walking in the rain was therapeutic. Carole was not the only one losing self-confidence. Here was I, running from a crime scene. Who on earth could I tell of my concerns? Gregg was due back at some point from his leave but he must have known what was going on. I wondered if indeed there was a crime. No one was getting hurt, everyone was being paid, the road was being built and two families would have beautiful homes. But it was hurting me, that was for certain.

*

The bridge site was almost deserted. The rain was just too heavy for any activity and pools of water were everywhere. I noticed the fitter who had helped Malcolm on the day he left, sitting in his white van reading a paper. I knocked on his window and he jumped. It was all steamed up but he wound it down a couple of inches. I thanked him for driving Malcolm to the first aid centre. He nodded and wound up the window. I knocked again and he wound it down half an inch. I asked if he had seen Malcolm go in to the medical centre but he just said, 'I was his bloody taxi, not his bloody carer, sod off.'

I was disappointed but not surprised by his response, but at least I was not going mad. Malcolm had existed.

There was no one else I recognised and I had no reason to be hanging about so I headed back to the sub-station with only one task to do that day and that was to let the cat out of the cabin. On arrival I was disturbed to see Rhino waiting. He was not given to small talk or pleasantries, so I was surprised that he said hello. He was waiting for some window frames and doors and he wondered where they were. I said that there were no windows on the plan and the double metal doors were padlocked down between the white and yellow speciality bricks. I chose my words carefully and said, 'I'm not a fool. When will people stop treating me like one?'

He bade me unlock the cabin and ushered me in, in silence. 'You are no fool, Mr Crawford because a fool would have spoken out before now. A fool would have told someone that all was not what it seems. A fool would not have known that a multimillion-pound road contract is employment for three hundred men directly and thousands indirectly. A fool would jeopardise everyone's livelihood and a fool would jeopardise the award of the next road contract or school contract that this company has fought for and why? Because a fool would not keep his mouth shut.'

'Mr Crawford.' He moved very close to me. 'I do not take you for a fool but if I did…' Nothing further was said as Notso arrived at the door.

He spoke directly to Rhino to tell him the road was too wet for the window truck and they were going direct to the top. Rhino looked at me and said, 'You are correct, Mr Crawford, they are not on the plan.' And he left. I had thought rain had leaked through my coat as I was soaking wet but it was sweat and I was shivering.

Notso bounced back into the cabin shouting, 'Horace quickly, quickly.' I grabbed my coat and followed him to what I presumed was an accident. After running up hill past the parking area, he pulled me to a crouch and pointed out a bird sitting on the edge of the copse. I asked what it was and Notso told me it was a cuckoo. Whilst they were quite common, they were rarely seen and it was a first for Notso and for me. I cheered up. It was the only possible bird that was relevant to me and I would have it on my coat of arms. I was the cuckoo in this nest of thieves.

I made a pact with myself. I would keep my head down and just get my sub-station finished. I was not active in whatever laws were being broken. I was just doing was I was told. I knew this was the so-called Nuremberg defence and did not feel happy with myself. The day dragged on and there was no let-up in the rain so I went home early.

I needed to talk to someone and I would have liked it to be Carole. I had not been brave enough to ask her for her number but I hoped Dave could assist. I could not sleep that night, and Tuesday was another washout, but at least I had the evening at the drill hall.

*

Wednesday evening was the first time I had seen Dave since the drinks. He suggested we repeat the exercise on the Friday but then remembered he was away until the Sunday. I mentioned how much I had enjoyed Carole's company. He agreed she was lovely but cautioned me against rushing in. I told him that I was not brave enough to rush and, if anything, it would be downright hesitancy.

I asked why the caution. He was not certain but he recalled that Sarah had mentioned that she was down to be Carole's bridesmaid for a wedding in the autumn but it had been called off. I asked various questions but Dave had no further information to offer. Dave did not have their house phone number but he encouraged me to go to see her as the worst that could happen would be she would not wish to go out with me. He did know the address where Sarah lived, and they lived together. I grabbed a piece of paper and said shoot. He said, 'It was the road with the reproduction furniture shop on the corner where Andy Harris worked.' He went on, 'Halfway down on the left, no right, no left, there is an old people's home and next to it is their house. The house is obvious because there are rose patterns in the glass window above the front door.'

I had no idea who Andy Harris was, nor where the reproduction furniture shop was but it was the best I was going to get. I asked Dave how his yacht navigation was coming on and he told me he was a day skipper. The irony was wasted on him.

*

On the Wednesday the weather had abated but I had not noticed. I poured through the *Yellow Pages* to find where one buys reproduction furniture and scanned the *A to Z* to see where there were shops near old people's homes. The other helpful factor was the road I was looking for that matched the two search options had to be walking distance to my home.

Armitage Road ticked all three boxes so Thursday evening I plucked up courage and set off. I found the road very easily but soon lost the recently plucked courage. I went backwards and forwards to the top of Armitage Road three times and started walking back home for a fourth when I saw Carole walking towards me. She was with a man. He looked older than she did by some margin but I assumed the worst. 'Fancy seeing you here,' she said and introduced her friend. 'This is Arthur, he is walking me home.' Arthur offered his hand and we shook. 'Where are you going?' Carole inquired.

I was dumbstruck and could think of nothing to say. The silence was so embarrassing and Carole just waited. Arthur stepped in by saying, 'Well we're almost home now, Carole; I'll leave you with your chum.' He patted my arm and walked off. Carole shouted bye and waited.

I took a breath and said, 'I was plucking up courage to come and see you.'

Carole giggled, telling me that she was hardly that frightening. I asked if I could replace the gallant Arthur and walk her home and she agreed. There were no roses over number 27's door and 27 was at least three houses past the old people's home on the opposite side of the street. I made a written note of the address but it was already etched into my brain.

*

Carole and Sarah lived in a clean and cosy top floor flat of a Victorian House. The ground floor was a greengrocer's shop. The middle was where Arthur lived. He owned the whole building and Carole told me his son ran the shop. Arthur was in his seventies so Carole was even more amused, or should I say bemused, when I told her I thought that from a distance I feared he may be her boyfriend. Carole asked me what I had planned to say to her when I had found her flat. I confessed that the evening was not really planned any further than having the courage to knock and that had just deserted me before I had bumped into her. She was planning a pasta on her own as Sarah had a night class and she invited me to join her. We stood in the galley kitchen and chatted whilst she made the meal. The conversation flowed just as it had in the White Rose. I relaxed and stopped thinking about bricks. At around ten o'clock Sarah arrived home. She did not seem surprised to see me but after giving me a hug and kiss on both cheeks she took an envelope from behind the clock on the mantle shelf. With a dramatic flourish she pulled a piece of paper from the envelope and read out the statement on it. It read: 'Sarah Beaumont, the white witch, confirms that Handsome Harry will call on Carole before the next full moon!' Carole and I both had to read the note. I asked who Handsome Harry was. Carole wanted to know when Sarah had made the prediction and whether she had cast any other spells. I asked Sarah if she could predict when I could next meet Carole. Sarah raised her hand and she told me it had to be on the night of the full moon. I still had no idea when it was but agreed to call at seven on the Friday and this time I would book a table so we could eat out. I hugged Sarah and hugged Carole. The hug with Carole was just long enough to be meaningful and she kissed me on the lips.

*

Dave had helpfully left a note for me on the kitchen table when I arrived home. It said, 'The house I sent you to was Andy Harris's, not Sarah's, sorry. Hope Andy could point you in the right direction.' He also added that Colin had packed all his stuff and left the house but had not left a forwarding address. Dave asked if the rent was up to date.

I was not bothered about Colin, we were all due to leave the house within the next month and I had the two-week course at Sandhurst confirmed. I was going to get my TA commission. I was anxious that I had not arranged any accommodation when the lease ran out. My absolute fallback position was an offer from Ra-Ra to stay at his mother's house as a lodger. I knew I had to get something sorted.

*

Electricity is distributed over a large network of power lines and underground cables by the national grid. Electricity sub-stations are used to reduce the 400kV supply to manageable levels. My sub-station was needed to supply all the road lighting and bridge lighting for the length of the bypass.

The 400kV would be reduced to 132kV at what was called transformation level sub-stations and bulk supply point steps the voltage down from 132kV to 33kV. The primary sub-station drops the voltage to 11kV. I was building the box they would put the primary sub-station equipment in for onward distribution. It would have a function and it would have to be finished so I decided to push for early completion. Once the nightmare was over, I could focus on the preparation for Sandhurst and Carole. In my brain I was saying the 'loves of my life' but that sounded premature and both seemed so far off.

*

The next few weeks went quickly. I had noticed a pile of rolled steel joists (RSJs) had been dropped in the corner of the compound. I had mentioned to Phil, who was Rhino's right-hand man, that they were not needed for the sub-station. He told me that they were for the temporary support when the generator was installed. He said that if I was any engineer, I would have known that. He scoffed and strode back to his van. I felt stupid as Phil had been one of the better characters in a pretty miserable bunch. The pile of RSJs was getting bigger and were joined by steel that must have been left over when they reinforced the concrete on the bridge. I was minded to ask Eddie why there was so much left over as there did seem to be a fair pile in the compound. I knew none of the metal would be needed for the houses but had stopped caring.

The brickwork was eventually completed, and the proper roof trusses were fitted. Proper because the original roof trusses delivered were too long and there were twice as many as were needed. I turned my usual Nelson's eye. A small tracked vehicle, with a 'drot' four in one bucket on the front, landscaped the approach before being whisked away to do the 'special landscaping'. I thought I had done just enough to avoid any trouble and, although my conscience was shot to pieces, the nightmare would soon be over. Carole and I had been out for two meals and the cinema. I had a couple of weekends away with the TA. I was now formally 'tabbed' as an Officer Cadet and had received all my joining instructions for a course at Victory College Sandhurst in the October. The landlord had also given formal notice that we had to leave the house in early October as he was refurbishing it before accepting new students, at a higher rent. Colin had paid the rent up to the departure day which was a weight off our mind. I had borrowed Dave's car and taken Carole to the beach and we had strolled hand in hand for an hour before sitting eating fish and chips. I felt so content and relaxed. Carole rested her head on my shoulder at one point and, although nothing was said, I felt I was in love. When we returned to the flat, she invited me for a game of chess. It was such an unexpected suggestion that I found myself saying yes. We both sat on her bed and moved the bedside table halfway down the bed and set up her board. It just seemed so romantic sitting in close proximity and locking our minds. Carole was very good and, whilst I thought I was a fair player, I realised that if I wanted to stay in the game I had to concentrate. Just when I thought I was one move from checkmate, Carole moved a knight and put me in check. In one move the whole game had changed. I leaned over and kissed her clumsily and we rolled to our sides on the bed. I am not sure what would have happened next had we not been interrupted by Sarah coming in and shouting, 'Hi.'

Carole looked me in the eye and said, 'We'll have to leave the mating until some other time.' She had such a glint in her eye and we both laughed. We went through and had coffee with an animated Sarah who was proudly showing off the finished piece of pottery from her night class. I then made my excuses and walked home. I was singing that tune from *My Fair Lady* about being on the street where she lived. I tried to jump and click my heels but the pavement was wet and I ended up falling. I was not hurt but felt such a fool.

CHAPTER 6

I never really used the gas fire to heat the hut but it was great for toasting bread. When the gas bottle ran out, I was not going to bother changing it but Notso mentioned he was going to a meeting at the head office. On a whim I asked Notso to swap the old bottle and collect a new gas bottle from the store. Notso was happy to oblige. When he came back later that day, he apologised for not bringing one back. He told me that the storeman had shouted at him as he did not have a requisition. I said, 'No worries, it's not essential. I'll sort it out at some stage.' The rest of the day was uneventful. The sun came out and Cat was particularly attentive and that calmed my spirit.

*

The next day I had a visit from Mr Clough, the bridging agent. He parked as close to the cabin door as was physically possible and his van door almost restricted the opening of my cabin door. He burst in and he was incandescent with rage. I had never met him before, but had nodded to him on a couple of occasions. I tried to ask him what the problem was but he was not in the mood for listening. I was totally perplexed by his rant. It was something to do with me piggy-backing on the bridge build. I had absolutely no contact with the bridge except to use their phone and I apologised if this was the issue. This was an act of desperation as I had only used it twice in the previous two months. I could not imagine what I had done wrong. Mr Clough ended by saying that he hoped his message was crystal clear because if not the next step would be ugly. I tried to explain my ignorance but he was having none of it and stormed off. He had one of the fancy Land Rovers and he drove straight across the newly landscaped approach leaving two track marks across the seeded grass area. He was one upset man and I had no idea why. I was longing for this special contract to end. I spent the rest of the day waiting for the next turn of events. I did not have long to wait.

*

I spent a sleepless night trying to think what I had done to upset Mr Clough. I was not looking forward to work. My only consolation was that every day that passed, the nearer I got to completing the cursed sub-station. On arrival on site, I was surprised to see the cabin door swinging open. I had definitely locked it so I ran over. The boiler was on the floor in the middle of the room and on top of it was a bright shiny new gas canister. I smiled but then heard high-pitched squeaks. I lifted the gas canister and lifted the top off the boiler. Cat leapt out at me and in shock I threw the boiler top across the room. Cat darted out of the door. I was shaking, shocked by Cat and even more shocked that someone would find trapping Cat funny. I looked out of the door but Cat was long gone. I sat on the chair and saw there was a delivery note on the table for the gas bottle. Written in pencil was an added note. It said, 'Follow the script and no one or no thing will get harmed.' It was written in an educated hand so I discounted Rhino and his team. I paced up and down and walked around the site most of the morning. For me, as warnings go, this was 'a horse's head in my bed'. I was scared that I was falling into a situation that was going to swallow me up. The longer I did nothing, the worse it was going to be. I wanted to speak to Mr Clough. He knew something and was blaming me. In truth I wanted to speak to anyone. I wondered if I could find Mr Aiden Malcolm. I had kept Malcolm's jacket in my cabinet and now took the opportunity to go through the pockets. One was full of books of matches. They were from the Blue Bell, a local pub. Malcolm obviously grabbed a handful of them from the bar. I kept one and threw the rest away. There was a receipt for a car service. It gave the car registration and make of car but no address. I thought I could visit the garage so kept the receipt. There was a betting slip and I wondered if it was a winner. The rest of the pockets were full of pencils, bits of string, elastic bands and tobacco and paper from broken black cigarettes. I was not sure what I would ask Malcolm even if I found him. All I wanted to do was escape from this toxic environment.

*

I was agitated when I eventually arrived home. I had missed my lift and had to climb in the back of a transit van which bounced me down to the far end of the road to catch a bus. The bus was slow and a diversion, caused by the road build, meant it was even slower. Sitting on the step was Dawn. This time she had a small blue case and was crying. She was angry with me for being so late and angry because she was cold and hungry. I steered her into the cold front room and put on the gas fire. I went into the kitchen cursing myself as I did so, as I knew I was out of coffee and tea. I found a hot chocolate sachet and made Dawn a hot chocolate with a huge spoonful of sugar. She cheered up with the drink. She started by saying how sorry she was and could she stay. She did not wait for an answer but blurted out, 'I am pregnant.'

I sort of said, 'Congratulations.' But her wail made me realise this was not what she wanted to hear.

I tentatively asked if Earl was the father and she bit back sharply saying, 'That loser? No, I haven't seen him for years.' There was a long pause and having already put my foot in it twice with only two statements I was not ready to say anything else. 'Colin, Colin, Colin,' her staccato voice was higher each time she said the name.

'He has left the house,' I told her.

She replied, 'No not left, he has run away.' Dawn went on to tell me that she came to see me ages ago, but I was down in Dorset with the Army. Colin had just returned as he had finished his camp before me. He had been really kind and she stayed for the week leaving the night before my return. Colin had told her that he and I had fallen out so best not to mention their time together. Dawn had returned to see him a week or two later but he had been really beastly to her and that was when she had left him and was sitting on the steps the first time I had found her. She and Colin had rekindled their relationship after he had apologised. He had given her a small but expensive handbag as an apology. I could not help an internal grin when she told me he had been stressed at work and that was why he was beastly to her. They had made up and Colin had taken her for a long weekend away in Harrogate in Dave's car. More recently they had been back to Harrogate for the weekend in his new car. They had stayed an extra day because Colin had a work meeting. When she had told him she was pregnant he would not believe he was the father. He refused to see her any more. I was dumbstruck but went over and put my arm round her shoulder whilst she gently wept.

Dawn's plight did put my position in context. I tried to make her feel wanted and said I would chat to Colin if that would help. I put her in Steve's old room but there was now no bedding so I had to give her my second set which I had to retrieve from the laundry pile. I smiled to myself whilst making the bed, making beds for other people was becoming a habit. Once she was in bed, she called me back in and I sat on the corner of her bed. She only had a small holdall but the contents were everywhere. She was one untidy girl. Nothing much further was said and after twenty minutes of silence I went back to my room telling Dawn she could stay as long as she liked. I gave her Steve's keys.

*

Carole was in the local government department that dealt with democracy. She was working overtime in preparation for the municipal elections and so I knew she was putting in the hours. I did not wish to burden her with my issues. We met on the Thursday evening later in the week after she finished work. I knew her birthday was coming up and I wanted to know if she was free to do something special. Marcus, the officer in the TA who was the farmer's son, had opened a parachuting course at Bridlington Airfield. You could train on the Saturday for a static line descent on the Sunday. You stayed in a bunk house on the Saturday night and received a certificate after the jump. It was not something I could organise as a surprise without asking her, as there were various consent forms that needed completing. I was quite excited about the prospect of a weekend away with her. I met her outside the municipal office complex beside the Town Hall. She did look drained and tired. I thought she had been crying but I said nothing and tried to be upbeat. I decided to wait before mentioning the weekend away. It was almost 2130 and she just wanted to go home. We walked back most of the way in silence. We went in for a coffee. I told her I would not stay late but it was nice to see her, even if it was for a moment. I helped her make the coffee in the galley kitchen. I enjoyed the close proximity and felt really happy. The chessboard was still set up in the position we had left it. I half wanted to suggest we finished the game but it did not seem right. I left after the coffee. Carole gave me a hug but turned away from a kiss. I put this down to my clumsy head angle rather than anything sinister. 'You are such a nice man, Harry,' she said and kissed me gently on the cheek.

I cheered up and skipped home. I had not mentioned the weekend away but it did not seem the right time.

*

I had a quiet morning marking out the site access fence which was almost cosmetic as it could be crossed in one bound. I watched the tilers finish tiling the roof of the building and then was surprised by a visit from Gregg. He wanted to walk round the almost-finished project. We chatted about his new baby briefly. I tried to say as little as possible so he could do the talking. He was pleased with how good the sub-station looked. He was confident that building control would 'sign it off' over the course of the next few weeks. He asked me what I wanted to do once the sub-station was finished. He knew of Rod Clough's visit and apologised for his outburst. I told him that I had no idea why it had occurred and he laughed. His explanation was that, 'The old bugger thought you had tried to bill the gas bottle to the bridge contract.'

I replied that the gas bottle was less than five pounds and that the bridge was millions. I added that I had nothing to do with it anyway as I just asked Notso to change the one we had. Gregg's response was that Clough was 'just another old man who wanted to keep his hands clean'. In my head I analysed this remark because he said 'another' I wondered if Malcolm was the first and he mentioned the clean hands. He recognised that what we were doing was dirty. Gregg seemed to assume that I was comfortable with what had happened with the sub-station. My head was screaming to tell him what I really thought. I told him that putting the cat in the boiler had upset me. He claimed he had no idea that it had happened, but rather than sympathise, he told me that I would have to 'man-up' as construction sites were not for the fainthearted.

*

There had been a note pushed through the door addressed to me on the doormat when I arrived home. I did not get a chance to open it because Dawn met me in the hall. 'I've done something silly,' she said. She was holding a little brown medicine bottle. She turned it upside down to show it was empty.

I said, 'sit here' and sat her on the stairs. I went straight next door to Mrs Anderson who I knew had a phone. I explained I needed an ambulance. She kept fussing over me asking what was wrong with me. I tried to explain that it was not me. I rang 999, thanked Mrs Anderson, but she insisted on coming back with me to help. Whilst we waited, I explained that Dawn was pregnant and had accidently taken a tablet and we were worried about the baby. A pale Dawn sat all forlorn and did not contribute to the conversation, so my little white lie was unchallenged. I was so impressed by the speed and efficiency of the ambulance crew. They whisked Dawn and I off to Accident and Emergency at the hospital, and within an hour of Dawn's revelation to me, she was in a cubical and I was in the waiting area. Whilst I waited, I opened the note.

It was from Carole. It said something like, 'Sorry, Harry, but I have to be straight with you.' I do not really remember much of the next twenty minutes because I went from calm warm love to rejection, dejection and crying in such a short period. I was being spoken to by a nurse but hearing nothing. My girlfriend was fine and so was the baby. My girlfriend had dumped me. She was not my girlfriend; it was not my baby. My girlfriend's old fiancé had been to see her begging her to take him back. No, he was not the father either. I was confused but not as confused as the poor nurse. The nurse told me I had no need to cry as everyone was well. So, the old boyfriend had realised what he had lost and had spun Carole some old bollocks that she had believed. The upshot was that I was unceremoniously dumped. Dawn wandered through from the cubicle. She was contrite. The medicine bottle had contained iron tablets and, whilst unpleasant, would not harm her or the baby. Dawn was upset that I was crying and assumed it was because she was fine. She hugged me. I went to the hospital reception with her and we took a silent taxi ride home. My initial upset and tears on the way home turned to anger, not with Carole but with the lowlife that had rejected her and then bounced back when he realised he had lost such a diamond. When we pulled up outside, I paid the taxi and noticed Mrs Anderson waiting. She wanted to know that Dawn and the baby were well. I reassured her they were. She mentioned that I had missed a girl who had called but that she had explained to her that I had taken my pregnant girlfriend to hospital.

*

Luckily Dave was lounging on the sofa when we came in. He was somewhat helpful with his soothing support for Dawn. She went through to Steve's room to lie down. I told Dave that Carole had finished with me. He was sympathetic but spoiled it by reminding me that he had warned me not to rush in. He went on to tell me of his rejection on graduation day. I had heard the story so many times from him, whenever he had been drinking, but I listened again. It was a sad end to his studies and each time the story became slightly more maudlin and darker than the time before. Dave also managed to forget that we had lived with him during the last two years of his tumultuous relationship with her. He became quite tearful and it had the effect of cheering me up and we both started laughing. I mentioned that Mrs Anderson had said that a girl had called whilst we were out but Dave said that he had not heard anyone knock.

*

I had not slept as I was wondering how to deal with Carole. I felt guilty for not being as bothered about Dawn as I should have been. Carole was so good for me. Part of me wanted to fight for her but I knew that would end badly if she was committed to this long-term lowlife. Carole had never mentioned him in the short period we were together. I tried to paint him as the villain but I had no idea about the circumstances of their split. I recall his name was Craig but that was only because Carole wore some Whitby Jet earrings and when I admired them, she told me they were a gift from Craig's parents. I took him to be the former boyfriend, I have no idea if that was right. I consoled myself that, as we both liked Carole, we may both be similar. I went to work feeling dreadful. I am sure a broken heart would justify throwing a sickie but went in anyway. I knew that I would do nothing about Carole, just like I had done nothing about the situation at work. I felt spineless, gutless and inadequate.

*

After Gregg's visit he had given me food for thought. I wandered down to the bridging site. Rod Clough was striding over to his Land Rover and I walked between the two. He took large purposeful strides and I thought it would be more dangerous to be hit by him than the Land Rover. 'What do you want?' he shouted, even though he was feet from me.

'Your advice,' I shouted back. I was far louder than I expected and he stopped suddenly.

He grinned. 'No need to shout, only I shout!' He told me to jump in and I could talk on the way. I had no idea where he was going but jumped in.

I opened with, 'my girlfriend dumped me last night.'

He was driving towards the bridging site exit. He stopped the vehicle and looked at me. 'I'm not a flaming agony aunt, son.' He started the vehicle again and he was laughing. He went on to say how lucky I was and that I should only be worried if I had got her pregnant.

I did not say anything but thought I would rather it be Carole than Dawn. I waited until we were clear of the congested bridging site and then told Rod that I understood he had clean hands. I used the same term as Gregg, hoping it would mean the same thing to Rod.

'Yes, I have,' he explained that he had been in the industry for decades and wanted a pension, not a prison sentence, at the end.

I asked how I could escape from being tainted with anything that was unethical. He sucked his cheeks in. 'You are probably too late,' he murmured. My stomach went tense, and my throat felt dry. 'You could report all you know; you could take full responsibility and maybe as a first offence you would be out of jail within five years, still young enough for a career as a janitor or traffic warden.' He laughed. 'I'm joking, keep your trap shut, get back on the road contract and, next time, don't agree to anything you've not sounded out first. This will blow over like it always does. No one will get hurt, stop trying too hard to sort out other people's problems.' We arrived at the Blue Bell pub. 'I have a meeting here which will take an hour, take the Land Rover back and leave it at the bridging site. I'll cadge a lift back later.' Rod jumped out, his Parthian shot was to say, 'Oh, and I'm sorry your girlfriend ditched you.' He strode boldly to the entrance.

I walked round to the driver's seat which needed serious adjustment so I could get comfortable. I did not drive straight back but parked so I could watch the carpark arrivals and departures. I wondered who else would be at the meeting. It was a work meeting as several Land Rovers were already there. Gregg arrived and I slid down in the seat so he did not see me. Colin arrived in his own car. He looked so stupid in his car coat and driving gloves. I was in two minds whether to confront him about Dawn but decided it was best not to. I had only seen him fleetingly once in the previous three weeks at work. I had no idea what he was up to and did not really care. I would confront Colin at a time and place of my choosing. The only other surprise was the arrival of a smart Jaguar. Mr Hollingsworth climbed out of the back. He was wearing a suit and his Rotary badge glinted in the sun. I was sure he would not recognise me without my big orange Mr Man but took no chances. I drove back to the bridging site, parked up the Land Rover, leaving the keys in the ignition, and trudged back to the sub-station. I poured some tea from a flask and was joined by Cat. I had been forgiven by Cat who, although now more cautious, always came to eat the food I placed by the door.

*

I was quite proud of the sub-station and wandered up to the grassy knoll to take some pictures with my Zenith 36mm Russian SLR. This SLR was single lens reflex as opposed to my SLR at TA camp which was a Self-Loading Rifle. I had picked up the camera in the Camera Exchange which was a shop next to the one selling reproduction furniture on Armitage Road. It was in the window and seemed a bargain, albeit it was second-hand and had some scuffs on the body. I walked down in front of the double blue doors when one of the tilers shouted, 'Don't you dare take any photos of me, son!'

I shouted back that I would not. He seemed agitated and was in heated discussion with his mate on the other side of the structure who was out of sight to me. The other chap soon appeared waving me away with his arm gestures. 'Sod off you, we don't need pictures,' he shouted.

I reassured him that neither he nor his colleague were in any shots and I could not understand why he was being so sensitive. This did not go down well. He muttered about how he had heard I was a 'dick-head' and trouble and now I had demonstrated those qualities. He wanted me to give him the roll of film. I told him to where to go in a no uncertain way with a phrase I had not used for decades. I went back to the cabin. I think that this was the first time I had used this phrase since using it to my younger sister when I was sixteen and she was six or thereabouts. On that occasion I had done so in front of my mother. Had it been my father, I would have had a clout round the head. Mother was just sad and she cried. She said she had hoped I was a gentleman who treated all girls with respect. She thought I was mature and could argue sensibly, like a gentleman, without using anger. She thought I was well educated enough that I did not have to use bad language. The more mother cried, the more my bad behaviour seemed to hurt me. I vowed never to use the phrase again and I told her so. I had kept my word until today. This cursed job had changed me and it was for the worse.

*

I muddled through the rest of the day. I had nothing to look forward to in the evening. Dawn had had a carry-out but had not thought to include me. She had left the mess everywhere. There was a note saying she would sort the kitchen when she came back from the cinema. The bread was stale in the kitchen and the half tin of beans in the fridge had gone. My planned beans on toast idea was aborted. I ate a dry cracker but then dunked the rest in the leftover Chinese sauce. I struggled to set up the bath so it was working properly. The result was that I soaked for less time than I hoped in the lukewarm water before heading to bed hungry, sad and alone. I did think that, with everything going on, taking photographs of the crime scene was probably stupid. Maybe I was a dickhead. I heard Dave or Dawn or someone downstairs and then a knock on the bedroom door. I said, 'It's open' and Dave stuck his head round the door. He admonished me for being in bed at 2130 and proceeded to sit on the edge of the bed. I sat up and asked him if everything was alright. He said he was fine but was worried about me. He felt that, when I had been upset, he had 'gone off on one' about himself and that he should have been more helpful. I told him I was fine and then he launched into telling me that as a result of our conversation he had phoned Heather (the longstanding girlfriend who had finished with him on graduation day) and was going down to see her at the weekend. He thanked me and told me when he married her, I would be his Best Man. He asked if I wanted to borrow his car whilst he was away as he was going by train to see her. I eagerly said, 'Yes.' It would give me some freedom. He also told me that his driving was becoming harder because of his eyesight. The Army medical had shocked him as his eyes were worse than he thought.

Once he had gone, I laughed out loud. I was fit, healthy and my problems were insignificant. Dave was going blind and Dawn was having a baby, I might be at a low point in my life but I thought, as long as I could laugh, things could not get much worse. How wrong I was.

*

Next morning, I struggled to get to work as my usual lift was not available and I ended up thumbing a lift. I had a note waiting for me to say there was a new project in the offing and to familiarise myself with the 'spring site'. The road contract had been developing at a fast pace whilst I had been distracted in the hills. The road from the head office to the bridge was now covered in hard yellow dolomite stone. They were well on the way to having the road from the bridging site to the end ready for the dolomite too but for the discovery of a spring. The last thing that you want under the road when it is covered in tarmacadam would be water. This would undermine the soil and the dolomite and the road would fail. The water source had not been revealed during the original survey and there were some red faces when the remedial work had to be initiated. The note went on to say I was required to set out a culvert which was being retrospectively prepared. Attached to the note was the culvert drawing. I felt so pleased that I was heading back to the real world. I was disappointed that the note was not signed and presumed it was from Gregg. I did wonder if the meeting at the Blue Bell had been to deal with the delays occasioned by the discovery of the spring. I had so little to do during the rest of the day that I walked down to watch the bridge concrete pour. I was joined by Eddie who had, as he told me, been the mastermind behind the concrete mixture. He was a different man to the monster I met in Weymouth. He was anxious for me to meet Jacqui. They were going to get married and he wanted me at the wedding. I also saw Rod Clough, he did not speak but gave me a friendly wave and the thumbs up which I presume was because the concrete pour was going so well. Just as I was leaving the bridge site I saw Colin over by a cabin. He was standing smoking. This was obviously a new habit to go with his style change. He did not seem too happy to see me. I made small talk asking him about how life was at the headquarters but he just said, 'Fine.'

I asked him where he was living and he said, 'Local.'

I then said, 'What are you going to do about Dawn?' I had not phrased it in any elegant way.

He was quite aggressive and told me, 'It's sod all to do with you.'

I told him that on the contrary she was my sister and I had to look after her. He stood up to his full height and faced me. I thought he was going to swing a punch as he clenched his fists and a vein on his forehead started pulsing. I did not flinch but I felt my heart racing. He relaxed his shoulders and sighed. 'If the kid's mine, if, I'll sort something out,' he whispered.

I told him that it was his and this was not something Dawn would lie about. I told him that she had been to A&E as she had tried to commit suicide. I was unsure it was helpful to bring this up, but he flinched and asked how she was. I said that he should sort this out, not for my sake, not for Dawn's sake, but for his own sake. He turned on his heel and walked away.

*

Eight in the morning was not an unusual starting time. It was made easy because I had the luxury of Dave's little Hillman Imp. During the summer the plant and machinery worked from first to last light and during some of the bridge activity they worked all night to minimise any road closures so as not to disrupt the public roads. I managed to get up at 0645. I had to tiptoe about so as not to wake Dawn. She could not sleep at night but I presumed that it was because she spent most of her day sleeping. I did not take Dave's car up the road as it was too rough and I did not want to damage the tyres. I parked at the far end of the road and then I planned to walk back to the spring site. I had taken a level and staff home with me the night before. The staff was in the back seat and poked out of my driver window. It was a cold drive. I did feel stupid but at that time in the morning most people were oblivious to a car with a red and white pole sticking out of it. The spring site was about a mile up what was now a soil road without a topping. It was dusty and I had not gone far before my eyes and mouth were dry and gritty. Despite carrying everything I might need, I did not have any water. I was not sure who I was meeting but knew that in the worst case I could drink from the beck that was fed from the spring. The thought of fresh spring water gave me a lift. I arrived at the spring at two minutes to eight. I was pleased that I had Dave's car. I sat on the box containing the level and retrieved the plan. I could see the culvert and it looked perfectly fine. I wondered why they wanted me to set up for a culvert that was already finished. I tried to orientate the position of the proposed new culvert, assuming I was wrong, but the culvert was already there. I walked along the route and it looked as if it had been there for some time as the water was clear and the culvert well bedded in below the road. I walked back over to my equipment lying in the middle of the wide road. I thought I had been away from the road for too long and I was pleased to be back. Everything was so silent that I could hear the water gurgling through the culvert and the noise of birds. I heard a mild rumble which gradually increased. I heard the powerful engine of the Volvo big wheel dump truck before I saw it. It stood three metres high and had an articulated arm between the two-wheeled cab and the eight-wheeled trailer. It was thundering down the centre of the road. It started to make the earth rumble beneath my feet. It was lifting too much dust for me to see the driver clearly but I thought there may be two people in the cab. My initial thoughts were that whoever was meeting me had cadged a lift off the Volvo. I stood up as the vehicle was bearing down on me. I knew that they had the ability to turn on themselves due to the articulation but I was disturbed that it did not seem to be slowing down, indeed it seemed to have increased speed on seeing me. Initially I went to grab my level and run but I had left it too late as the Volvo was on me. I threw myself to the ground, rolling to my left because that was the way I was falling. I could almost taste diesel and death as the two huge wheels passed over me. The vehicle seemed to swerve over me and I missed, or I should say the two banks of two wheels of the trailer missed me. The vehicle had not touched me and I looked back through the dust cloud. I could not see the vehicle but could hear that it had turned or was turning. It was coming back. This was not a random accident but a deliberate act. I was scared but there was enough blood in my brain to be indignant. I stood up and ran for the culvert. Despite the dust I had the direction in my mind's eye. The Volvo had turned and was bearing down on me. I had no idea how close it was nor where the culvert was but I put down my left foot and threw my body forward so I was long-jumping into the dust cloud. I landed on a downward slope which broke my fall and I tumbled forward and down the slope. The shadow of the Volvo surrounded by a wall of noise accelerated above me. My left wrist was aching and I held it in my right hand. I stepped forward and fell again, this time into water. I was in the culvert and was sitting in two feet of water. I heard the rumbling vehicle above me. I turned over and went with the water flow under what would be the road. I kept my mouth just clear of the water. I took a couple of sips which were refreshing and dunked my head to clear my dusty eyes. The culvert was dark and I knew it would be at least twenty-five to thirty metres long. I wondered whether to continue through or head back. There were at least two people interested in my fate so they could cover both ends. I chose to go on for no other reason than that the water was cold and it kept me alert. My left wrist was tender to the touch and I could not put any weight on it. It seemed like a small wound compared to what could have happened or indeed still might.

*

At the far end of the culvert there was a fabricated frame to stop children entering. It did not stop me exiting so there was obviously a design fault. I kept going downhill and into the scrub at the edge of the road boundary where the water entered a stream. This was the first time I had looked back. I could see up the slope to the road but was too low to see the road itself. I decided to walk back up to the road after first following the perimeter for several hundred yards. I had left the level, staff and my rucksack in the middle of the road. There was nothing I could not replace so I decided to abandon them. I presumed they would have been flattened. I did not hurry back up to the road. I was learning more fieldcraft from this job than I was in the Army. I was in the most part soaking wet but where I was beginning to dry on my back, the dust had begun to harden, chafing my shoulders. My wrist was aching. I kept stopping to massage my wrist and listen. I did hear a car up on the road and waited until the noise had gone before exposing myself. The road was deserted. I crossed over and headed up the hillside so I had a greater view. I started the long walk back to the car. No one would associate me with the car unless they had seen me arrive and that seemed unlikely. I was wondering whether to drive to the police but discounted this plan. They would never believe me. They would say I was mistaken, and the driver probably had not seen me for the dust. I was absolutely covered in crusty dust so that would have supported their assessment. I could drive to the plant park to see who had been out in a Volvo dump truck at 0800. I rejected this also as I would have no idea what to do with the information even if I obtained it. I could drive to the cabin, collect my kit and leave the job for good. I sat in the car for ages wondering what to do. I chose the easiest plan and that was to drive home. I struggled to drive because of my wrist. I had to change gear with my right hand and so had to steer with my knee whilst doing so. Despite the difficulty, I managed to get back to the sub-station. On arrival I made sure no one was about and slipped in to collect my jacket and notebooks. I also picked up Malcolm's jacket. I made sure Cat was out of the cabin before locking up. I threw the key into the trees in an act of defiance. Even though I threw with my right hand, the act of throwing shook my left, which made me scream out. I cursed myself but realised that this was my first act of defiance against this cursed company.

I walked back to the car to find Cat sitting by the car door. A page of a comic was beside the cat and the face of the Lone Ranger, fully masked, looked up at me. On a whim I picked up the cat and said, 'Okay, Tonto, you're joining me on this adventure.' I rested Tonto on Malcolm's jacket on the back seat, shouted, 'Hi Ho Silver' and drove home.

CHAPTER 7

When I arrived back at the house it was only 1400. I had to drive with one hand and changing gears meant using my knees to keep the wheel straight as my left wrist was in agony. My crotch was wet and my underwear had chafed so I was going to need some cream round my nether regions or I would be walking with bow legs for weeks to come. Tonto climbed from the back seat and sat next to me in the front seat. I parked as best I could, using my single hand but I knew it would not be good enough for Dave. I made a mental note to come back and straighten up the car, once I had straightened myself. I put Tonto in my room and lay down some magazines in the corner. Tonto was subdued and prowled around seemingly content. The bath hydraulics did not let me down and eventually I was soaking in a hot bubble bath. I presume Dawn had provided the bottle of bubbles as there had never been a bottle in the bathroom for the three years I had lived there. But for my wrist, I felt quite content. Someone had tried to murder me but since they had failed, I had much to be pleased about.

I was worried that if the wrist was broken it would scupper my plans for Sandhurst. I wrapped my wrist in a tea towel and then fashioned a sling from an old belt. This meant I stopped trying to use my wrist as it was immobilised.

I went up into the box room at the top of the house. It was really a glorified cupboard under the attic stairs and I had not been anywhere near it since shoving in my suitcases several years earlier. It was full of rubbish and I wished I had gone in before my bath as I was getting covered in dust again. I retrieved my two suitcases and a sports holdall which I remember had belonged to Steve and which he had clearly forgotten. At the back was an old bike. It had been jammed at the back and we had all agreed that it would be a renovation project and when complete could be used by the whole house. Singlehandedly I took the three bags and the bike back down to my room. It took three journeys up and down the stairs, it was perfect fitness training for Sandhurst. On my third and final descent I was met by Dawn. She asked me where I was going and I told her I had jacked in my job and was going back to Essex. She said, 'And what about me?'

Her eyes were hollow and pitiful and so whilst I wanted to say 'you are not my problem', I found myself saying, 'You're coming with me, get packed.'

Her eyes lit up and she said, 'Give me twenty minutes.'

Dawn was packed before I was and stood in my door holding her small blue case, whilst I rammed the last of my clothes into Steve's holdall. The kitchen was full of knives and pots that I had accumulated but I had decided to abandon everything to travel light. I realised that three bags and a bike was anything but light and I was now hindered by a damaged wrist and Dawn. My initial plan was to take a taxi to Darlington Station and catch a fast train to Peterborough where I could change for the East Coast, but the more I thought about it, the worse it seemed. I also had the problem of Tonto. Dawn and Tonto were the perfect match and whilst I mulled over my options, Dawn just lay on the floor beside the cat stroking it. Mum and Dad would be pleased to see me, but any stay would have to be short. They would be pleased to see Dawn too but it was quite an imposition expecting them to put us both up in their three-bed semi. Tonto was an inconvenience but my real anxiety was that I would be so far from the TA drill hall and, even though it was a long shot, I would be too far from Carole.

I told Dawn I had a change of plan. We were taking Dave's Hillman Imp to Long Benson. Aunt Gladys would be pleased to see us. I would drop off Dawn and all the baggage and drive back to drop off Dave's car. I would then ask Ra-Ra to drop me back at Long Benson after the TA. The only potential problem would be a surprised Aunt Gladys.

*

Dawn could not drive but was able to change the gears for me, albeit not necessarily in the correct manner. We did have some kangaroo jumps until we learned to work together and, more importantly, hit the dual carriageway. In all fairness Dawn was also hampered because I put her seat as far forward as it would go to fit in the cases. She had to crouch under the bike forks which went over her head. I had removed the bike front wheel. She had Tonto on her knee.

Aunt Gladys was actually Dad's aunt but we called her Aunt. She was far older than Dad and had lost her first husband during the war. She had mourned for far too many years but had remarried late in life to Alf but sadly he had died shortly thereafter. She still lived in a reconditioned pre-fabricated house. It was one of many pre-fabricated temporary homes built in the late 1940s when there was a shortage of houses. They were meant to last a decade, but with the refurbishment and updating, they had lasted forever. Aunt Gladys was thrilled to see us. She had just returned from the hairdressers and was feeling particularly well and fussed about her unexpected visitors. Gladys had met Dawn on one occasion when she and Alf had been down to Essex but it was only a vague recollection; nevertheless, she told Dawn she was one of the family and most welcome. I left Tonto in the car. I thought Dawn and I were enough of a surprise in the short term. Tonto crawled into the back and seemed content between the bags.

*

After tea and beef sandwiches (which Aunt Gladys explained contained beetroot as the bread was not fresh), we moved from the kitchen table and sat in the front room. Aunt Gladys wanted to hear all our news but not before we listened to an update on the life of Aunt Gladys. Neither Dawn nor I knew any of the characters that were prominent in Aunt Gladys's life and so we just had to sit and nod when appropriate. Eventually I was able to explain that I had walked out of my job and was homeless. Aunt Gladys initially disregarded the homeless comment which caused me some concern but she wanted to hear about why I had left the road contract. I explained to Aunt Gladys that the company I worked for seemed to be corrupt and I was being asked to do, or ignore, things that were being done that were probably illegal. Aunt Gladys came over to me and held my hands together in her hands and she said: 'Harry it is never the wrong time to do the right thing.'

She went on to tell me that she had told my father the same thing thirty years ago when he walked out of his job with Vaux Brewery. I had never heard my father mention Vaux Brewery but noted the situation so I could use it in my defence if my father did comment adversely on my action. Aunt Gladys was sharp and she asked if I had reported my concerns to anyone. I told her that it was easier to do nothing and she seemed disappointed. She then went on to ask why I was homeless. I explained that the lease had run out on the house and about my planned trip to Sandhurst if my wrist was better. After my interrogation, Aunt Gladys turned to Dawn. Aunt Gladys managed to extract more information from Dawn in five minutes than I had since the moment I found her on my doorstep months ago.

*

Dawn had been living in Loughborough with a lady she called Aunt but who was no relation. She had found work in a fitness club behind the bar where she met Earl who was a fitness trainer. She had moved in with Earl but he was arrested for supplying drugs and went to prison. Aunt had allowed her to move back and all was well until Aunt had a stroke. Dawn looked after Aunt when she was discharged from hospital but then Aunt's nephew came back from New Zealand and wanted to take over the house and, more importantly, Aunt's finances. Dawn had gone back to live with Earl's flatmate but he was also involved in drugs and had assaulted Dawn which is why she had escaped and come to see me. I had not been at home when she first arrived but Nicholas, my flatmate, had let her stay for a week.

I interrupted her and said that the flatmate was Colin. 'Yes,' she answered, 'but he liked me to call him Nicholas as that is a jumble of "Colin has" and Colin has me; it was his special name for me!'

'What an anagram?' I said.

Gladys cut in saying how nice. I was sure Colin was spinning Dawn a yarn but tried not to burst her bubble.

Dawn skipped over the intervening month and did not mention the baby so it left Aunt Gladys assuming that Dawn had been staying with me for the duration. There were lots of gaps in the tale but it had at least confirmed my suspicions about Earl.

Aunt Gladys told Dawn she could stay in the guest bedroom and told me I would be in the shed. I assumed she was joking but she was not. 'Look out the window.' Aunt Gladys beckoned.

I moved back the net curtain. The shed was a solid structure in the garden which I recalled from previous visits but had never anticipated making my home. Aunt

Gladys advised me that the brick lean-to was a toilet with a tap. Gladys explained that it would be good training for my Army life. I asked if I could share my accommodation with my cat. Aunt Gladys wanted to see the cat and Dawn took the keys off me and went to get her.

I had to get Dave's car back and so left Dawn and Aunt Gladys, who had decided to busy themselves sorting out Dawn's new bedroom. They were also going to organise a litter tray for the cat. They explained that Tonto would have to stay in the shed for a week to get acclimatised before being allowed out. I left Tonto in capable hands.

*

After a fraught journey, where changing gear was becoming almost impossible, I arrived at the house. Luckily there was a huge parking space and, by mounting the kerb, I could park without reversing. Dave was delighted to see me. He had finished a course early and was anxious to collect his car. He too had packed and was ready to hand over the keys. I asked if he could drop me at the TA centre as I was hoping to get a lift from Ra-Ra back to Aunt Gladys's house. He offered to take me back as he was going up to Sunderland. He was meeting up with Heather. At the mention of her name, he smiled and slapped me on the shoulder. I instinctively lifted my arm and he caught my wrist. He was apologetic for the pain he caused and asked if he should take me to A&E to have it x-rayed. I told him that all it needed was rest. He was anxious to have Aunt Gladys's address. He was staying in the North East and he wanted to keep in touch, especially if I was to be a guest at his wedding. I seemed to have been downgraded from Best Man to guest but I was fine with that. I had no idea how long I would be at Aunt Gladys's but was happy to oblige.

*

Dave dropped me off back at Aunt Gladys's. I was quite pleased to escape from him as he talked non-stop about Heather for the whole journey and whilst I was pleased for him, it just made me think of Carole. He also kept saying, 'Can you smell cat?' and as I had not mentioned Tonto, I kept saying, 'No' and that he was imagining it.

Dave wanted to get away so I just said farewell at the car door. I knocked on Aunt Gladys's door before stepping in. I found that Dawn was in the kitchen being taught how to make shepherd's pie. She was dressed in an apron and seemed thrilled with the whole idea and proceeded to explain what she had done so far. Aunt Gladys was standing behind her admiring her pupil. The scene was quite moving as both Aunt Gladys and Dawn were so engaged by the whole experience. My bags were still piled up in the hall and the old bike was in the front garden so I started ferrying them through to my new accommodation. The 'shed' was actually quite substantial and had clearly been Alf's retreat. It had a sofa and a standard lamp in front of a work bench. There were rows of tools neatly attached to the back wall, all marked and in size order. Whatever else I knew about Alf, I now know him to be very efficient and organised. There was a large metal cabinet similar to the one in the crew hut. I unlocked it with the key that was in the door. It had a shelf and a rack where I could hang clothes. The door was plastered with magazine cuttings of naked women. I was quite unsure what to think about these but explained them away to myself as having probably been already attached when Alf purchased the cabinet.

I was so pleased that I had brought the old bike. I now had the tools; all I needed was some inspiration and the 'ghost of Alf' to instruct me. Tonto was curled up on a towel on the workbench and did not even lift her head when I entered.

*

When I was called in for supper, I was expecting shepherd's pie but was disappointed to be served a lamb chop and boiled potatoes. I did not wish to seem ungrateful and after praising the food, asked about what Aunt Gladys and Dawn had made earlier. Aunt Gladys was happy to tell me it was shepherd's pie. I was none the wiser and no further explanation was forthcoming, so I ate in silence. Dawn and Aunt Gladys talked about making chilli con carne the following day. Aunt Gladys had never heard of it but Dawn had tried it in Loughborough and thought it was really great. They were going to try and find a recipe as both were excited about trying to make foreign food. Aunt Gladys then stopped and said, 'But will George want to try it, maybe we should ask him?'

I asked who George was and was told that it was for him they had made the shepherd's pie. I felt quite envious of George and asked about him. Seemingly George was Aunt Gladys's elderly neighbour who had recently had a fall and was confined to a wheelchair. Aunt Gladys and three friends were taking it in turns to prepare his evening meal. Dawn was a natural carer and was enthusiastic about helping Aunt Gladys and now George. I felt enormous relief that Dawn was no longer going to be only my problem. I hoped that she would mention the baby to Aunt Gladys. I was sure Aunt Gladys would be pleased but I had no way of knowing. It was up to Dawn to break the news, not me.

*

I spent two days working on the bike. It was tricky with one hand but I was determined to rest the sprained one in the hope that I would make Sandhurst. I had spoken to my mother and father and explained where I was and what had happened. Both were subdued which I interpreted as being 'disappointed'. The fact that I was going to Sandhurst pleased them and the news that I was with Dawn keeping Aunt Gladys happy was also welcome news. My wrist was not getting any worse, so with it strapped up I went for a run. This helped to clear my head and for the first time I started thinking about the Volvo. I had dismissed the incident, almost from the point that I entered the cold water of the culvert. I had blocked out the thundering black monster that flattened me to the earth and would have crushed me to dust but for my roll. I was also questioning my memory of events. It had run me over; of that I had no doubt. But did it turn and try and finish me off? Was it an inattentive driver running straight down the middle of an empty open road or was it a homicidal maniac trying to murder me? Maybe the cat in the boiler was just a joke; maybe I was becoming hyper-sensitive. The more I thought, the faster and longer I ran. I returned to the pre-fab exhausted. Aunt Gladys only had a handheld shower over her bath and she only had one bathroom and it was occupied by Dawn so I had to have a wash down in the lean-to basin. I could not find the plug and found myself thinking that Ra-Ra was far better organised than I was.

When Dawn finally emerged from the bathroom, it was to tell me that we were all eating with George tonight and that she was unsure whether there was any hot water left. There was no hot water left.

*

George was a wonderful character and I struggled to work out his age. He was probably in his mid-seventies but had a young fresh face. He was presently confined to a bulky wheelchair. He was eating well, thanks to Aunt Gladys and her team, and by his own admission, did not want to recover from his fall anytime soon. When he found out I was going to Sandhurst he was thrilled. He had spent two years in the Army after completing his two-year National Service. He would have made a career of the Army, as he loved it, but his late wife persuaded him to leave. He joked that she gave him a choice of the Army or her; he did not finish the punchline as both Dawn and Aunt Gladys went 'aaah' indicating that they thought he made the right call. George winked at me and gave a knowing look. I was pleased to hear his Army stories, but Aunt Gladys and Dawn were less so.

George had fought in Suez and had kept a diary which he told me he would dig out for me to read. I was telling George that I was trying to fix a bike because of my transport issues. He agreed to help me if I could manhandle his wheelchair into Alf's shed. I told him it would be my pleasure but because of my wrist it would be a struggle. Dawn offered to help but I told her it was not right in her condition. That cut the table talk. Aunt Gladys picked up on the comment immediately and during the 'pregnant pause', so did George. Dawn started to cry and Aunt Gladys put her arm round her telling her that she should be happy. George asked if I was happy, assuming I was the father. Dawn stepped in and told George that she was my sister and the baby's father was a friend of mine. I did not alter the description but felt it was now wrong. Initially, Aunt Gladys sat down and cried and I feared that she was unhappy with Dawn's situation but, far from it, Aunt Gladys was thrilled. The news of the baby made Dawn and Aunt Gladys even closer. Aunt Gladys wanted to teach Dawn how to knit so they could prepare clothes for the baby. George and I agreed that we would work on the bike so everyone would be occupied.

I had one drill night and a weekend before reporting to

Sandhurst. My wrist was getting better but I was unsure whether this was because I was not using it or because I was telling myself it was better.

*

George had been receiving physiotherapy to try and help him walk again and it was not really working. From having been fit and healthy, George was immobilised and it was making him frustrated. I wanted to take him out for a walk but, with my wrist, I knew pushing his wheelchair would be a struggle. George and I were both able to laugh at our situation. George then said, 'But you can drive, can't you?' and I told him I could.

After a morning on George's telephone, I was able to find an insurance company that would insure me to drive George's Vanden Plas Austin Princess. George insisted on paying the premium as I was to be driving for his benefit. I was covered to drive him down to the insurance broker where they would accept a cheque. The Vanden Plas was automatic. It had a wide front passenger door and I was able to swing George in. I could also get his wheelchair in the boot once I had removed the footrests. George and I were mobile. The insurance brokers were in a parade of shops. I was able to park outside a bookmaker and then assembled the wheelchair and dropped George into it. Dropped was the correct term as I did not have him held very well and the wheelchair moved slightly back as I turned. Luckily, we were both able to laugh but I made a note to be more careful. I had not been driving long enough to make getting insurance easy or cheap but George seemed willing to pay whatever was needed just so he could be liberated from his home.

We took the opportunity to walk round the Co-op. George put a basket on his knees and we soon filled it with cakes, chocolate and crisps. There was nothing substantial but George was not cooking for himself so had few needs. He did pick up four bunches of flowers to distribute to his helpers. On the way back to the car I noticed that the bookmaker was next to a tailor's shop. I recognised the shop name but had no idea why. I thought back to the broad chalk-stripe suit and the black-tie experiences but could not put my finger on why I knew this particular tailor. There was also a bakery with a selection of cakes in the window and a seating area. We were tempted by the cakes but decided we had better head back. On the way we passed a garage and we filled the car with petrol. George was anxious that we were all prepared for our next trip. The garage had a service area and that was when my head cleared. The garage was where Aiden Malcolm had his car serviced. The bookmaker was where he placed his bet and the tailor had made the coat sitting in my cupboard. Aiden Malcolm was George and Aunt Gladys's neighbour. I would have to seek him out.

George insisted we went back to Aunt Gladys as he was trying to stay out of his house as long as possible. He feared another long period without liberation once he was home. I gave him my assurances that I would free him even if I had to tie sheets together and lower him from his window.

*

Aunt Gladys was delighted by her flowers and set about finding a vase. When she came back Dawn had made a cup of tea and we sat and admired the flowers. George was so pleased to have a story to tell that was from outside his four walls. He described in detail and with significant exaggeration how I had dropped him. He told the tale with such gusto that I enjoyed the story, forgetting that I had been there. After the tea I took him home and we agreed another trip the following day.

Dawn also had news. She had been to the local

doctor's surgery at Aunt Gladys's insistence and had registered. She had seen a nurse and was now 'on the books' so they would watch her progress. I caught Aunt Gladys's eye and she smiled at me and nodded.

I went straight back to my shed after delivering George home. Aiden's jacket had been made by the Long Benson tailor, the bookmaker ticket was from the bookmaker and the petrol receipt was the same garage that did Aiden's service.

*

The next morning, I planned to cycle back into town. The bike tyres had been changed and the gears worked on the back sprocket, if not the front, all that needed attention were the brakes. The front brake was fine but the back needed serious squeezing which would work if you had a good wrist, but I did not. My eagerness to find Aiden was almost fatal. I took the back road to avoid the main road but had not realised it meant cycling down Long Benson Hill and under the railway bridge. The lady driver that helped me out of the hedge was very sympathetic but the terrified postman less so. I had tried to slow down over the brow of the hill but had gained too much momentum. A road entered from the left just before the railway bridge and a postman chose this exact location to walk across the road. The helpful lady had slowed up and then stopped to allow him to cross. I was following her, anticipating that my ever-increasing speed would be just less than her slowest pace down what was a straight road. It was not. I could not run into the back of her so chose the hedge to her offside. I reached the pavement at almost the same time as the shocked postman. He shrieked and stepped back but my handlebar caught his swinging bag. My bike was snatched from under me and I rolled onto my left side into the hedge. The bike was catapulted into the hedge, slowed only by the post sack which luckily had been ripped from the arm of the stunned postman. I had a flashback to my roll away from the killer truck. My left wrist was fine and, apart from scratch marks on my forehead, I felt remarkably good. I had been wearing Aiden's jacket as it was the best way of carrying it. The jacket was unmarked even though it had actually been pushed through the hedge backwards. I helped the muttering postman to gather his bag and the letters that had been sprayed over the pavement. He wanted to be angry but I could see he was struggling as I had taken such a fall. The lady offered to take me to hospital, but I assured her I was fine. Eventually they both continued on, for what I hoped was an uneventful day. I thanked them both and started the long walk home pushing my broken bike. I decided that Tonto might have nine lives but I did not.

*

When I arrived back at the house, Dawn was dressed in one of Aunt Gladys's aprons and hoovering the carpet. The radio was on loud and she was singing. I tried not to startle her but I could not help it and she jumped when she turned and caught sight of me. She laughed at herself for being so distracted and then noticed my forehead. She started to fuss and went out to get the first aid kit from under the sink in Aunt Gladys's kitchen. She sat me down and bathed my head. I was surprised by how red the tissues were but it must have looked worse than it felt as I had no feeling of pain. When she finished, she sat down and asked me what we were going to do. I noted the 'we' and had no immediate answer so I reflected it back asking Dawn what she was thinking. She told me that this was the happiest period of her whole life. She loved Aunt Gladys and wanted to stay forever. I tentatively asked what Aunt Gladys wanted and Dawn looked crestfallen and said she had no idea but did not think it would be a lodger with a new baby. Almost on cue, Aunt Gladys came in through the front door. She saw all the red tissues on a plate and threw her hands in the air. 'Dawn, is everything okay?' She seemed breathless as she put down her two bags and advanced towards Dawn.

I explained it was me and that I had cut my head. Aunt Gladys calmed slightly and I sat her next to Dawn but she was still breathing heavily. I helped her off with her coat and told her I would make some tea.

Aunt Gladys admonished me for falling off my bike and told me I was too old for bikes. She was going to tell George and he would knock some sense into me. I did feel a fool. I should have been thinking more of Sandhurst which was now only days away. As I was feeling sorry for myself, I was not really following the conversation that Dawn and Aunt Gladys were having about a visit from the priest. I cut in so abruptly that they both sat back shocked. I apologised and asked why a priest would be calling. Dawn told me that the receptionist at the doctor's had asked for her religion for the form. Dawn was a Catholic and the receptionist asked if she could give Dawn's name to her priest. Dawn seemed happy with the arrangement and it was far from my place to comment but I did think to myself that it was a little unusual, not least as Dawn was to be an unmarried mother. Aunt Gladys had pursed lips and was none too keen that the priest was to call, but agreed for Dawn's sake.

*

George kindly let me take his car to the drill hall for the last evening before my trip to Sandhurst so I was able to bring everything I needed back to Aunt Gladys. I was going to take a taxi to the Central Station and then a train to London. I would take the tube to Waterloo and another train to Camberley where a series of minibuses would ferry, we 'victims' to Victory College.

Sandhurst passed in a blur. I could tell tales of the fortnight. It was not unlike the two weeks at Weymouth but with more emphasis on leadership. My drill never improved but it was always better than average. I kept my head down and learned to do just slightly more than was asked of me even at my worst and considerably more than was asked of me when I was given a command task and trying to be at my best. My wrist never seemed to be fully better, but I learned to compensate. My forehead still had a scar from the hedge and the Colour Sergeant called me Zorro initially but then reverted to Horace when someone tipped him off about my 'proper' name.

*

I was absolutely shattered on return to Aunt Gladys, even though I had slept for the whole journey from London to Central Station. I had planned to spend a quiet evening sleeping too but Aunt Gladys had arranged supper with George who was keen to hear about my trip. Dawn and Aunt Gladys sat smiling whilst I gave an eager George a full debrief on my fortnight. Aunt Gladys did say towards the end of the evening that she was sick of all this 'man talk' and was so pleased she had Dawn. She gave her a hug. I could see Dawn's eye and it had a tear in the corner. The following day Dawn walked down to the local doctor's surgery for a scheduled check-up. I took the opportunity to apologise to Aunt Gladys about imposing on her and asking if she was still happy with the situation. Aunt Gladys held my hands together again just like the night we had arrived. She said, 'Harry, the last time I was this happy was when I married Alf. Please do not leave me yet.' She paused and then mischievously added, 'Well, you can go but leave Dawn.'

It was such a great burden lifted knowing Dawn was

safe and secure. I still had to confront Colin but one thing Sandhurst had taught me was that the first principle of war was to 'secure the home base'. I was doing that, and from my base I would plot my strategy.

*

On Wednesday morning I borrowed George's car. He was being taken to his meeting of the Western Front Society by a friend and was happy to entrust me with his car. I drove first to the garage. I waited in a cold reception area with a bench and two oily seats until a fitter who had been changing a tyre came over. I showed him the receipt and number plate. The fitter had huge oily hands and his thumb blackened the receipt as he looked at it. He went over to a drawer and flicked through a dirty diary to match the date of the service to the page in the book. 'You are in luck; Mr Malcolm gave no address but his phone number was...' He read out the number of the bridging site which I recognised immediately. I asked if there was any other information but he shook his head and shut the book. It had been a long shot but at least I knew I was getting closer.

*

I had trouble parking as near to the tailors as on my last trip but walking there gave me a chance to dust down Malcolm's coat. The hedge had deposited thorns and burrs and I picked them off as I walked. When I arrived at the tailors, the door was closed and a sign showed that it closed on Wednesdays. I wondered why shops felt it made business sense to close on a Wednesday. but clearly this one did. The bookmaker was open and so I tried my last card of the day. I had no strategy; I just gave the betting slip to the young man behind the counter. The shop was empty but for a man rocking in front of a TV. There were three TVs all showing racing and two long tables covered in newspapers on either side of the shop with barstools to sit at. The youth left me and went into the back, returning several minutes later with an older man. He looked me up and down and asked me my age. It caught me unawares but I said twenty-six. I was only twenty-five but quite close to my birthday. I had anticipated explaining how the ticket belonged to a friend to try and find out if they had a record of his name but the unexpected interrogation continued. Why had I taken so long to collect my winnings? he demanded. I stayed calm and said I had been away with the Army. This was not a lie and it had the desired effect as the man thrust the slip back into the youth's hand and said pay him. He then exited back through the shop. The youth went to the till and started counting money. I had no idea how much Aiden had won but it was too much for the first till as the youth went to the second till to complete the task. He returned to me and said, 'What a great accumulator, the boss knew it was outstanding, that's why he is so annoyed. He thought you may have lost the ticket.'

I smiled as the youth counted out almost three thousand pounds and then gave me back the ten-pound stake. The wad of money was so large I had to stuff it into the two outside pockets and the poaching pocket in Aiden's coat. I did not ask the bookmaker if he knew Aiden as the last thing I needed was to give him an excuse not to pay. Aiden was going to be very pleased to see me.

*

When I got back to the house Dawn and Aunt Gladys were knitting and bemoaned the fact that I could have collected more wool for them as I had been into town. I promised to go the following day as I was taking George to collect his pension. I went back to the shed where I stashed Aiden's winnings in a toolbox that Tonto had taken to sleeping on. I warned Tonto that if any went missing, he would be held liable. I found a clothes-brush and gave Aiden's coat a good brushing.

*

The following day, armed with a shopping list, George and I went into town. My wrist was getting better so I could easily handle George and I had also perfected getting him in and out of the car. We collected his pension at the Post Office and we immediately went next door into Martin's Bank where he deposited a large portion of it in his savings account. He kept back one note which he used in the tobacconist next door to the bank to pay for a small box of Hamlet Cigars. He explained that this was his weekly ritual. I told him I was surprised as I did not think he was a smoker. He told me he was not but he offered them to his friends at the British Legion who were.

We collected wool from a small haberdashery. It was a shop in a time warp. There was no access whatsoever for a wheelchair and so poor George had to wait outside. Everything seemed to have been on the shelves forever unmoved and unloved. There were racks of sewing patterns and even to my untrained eye, they were for 1950s party frocks. They did have the yarns of wool for Aunt Gladys, albeit they did not have enough money in the till to give me change for the five-pound note that Aunt Gladys gave me. I had to go out to George and he and I had to cobble together enough shrapnel to pay.

*

Our next shop was the tailor. This was another time warp but at least seemed well used and popular. The door was wide so I had no problem wheeling George up to the counter. Mr Radomski came out to meet us. He recognised the coat immediately and stroked the material. I explained that Mr Malcolm had left it with me and I wanted to return it to him but had mislaid his address. Mr

Radomski went to the right lapel beside the zip. I had never noticed but there was a hidden pocket parallel to the zip, beautifully tailored into the lining. Unzipping this pocket, Mr Radomski revealed a white patch with the code number of the garment and a date. There was also a yellow silk ribbon which when pulled out of the pocket was attached to a silver ring with a huge solitaire diamond on the top. The ribbon was tied to a small loop of material sewn into the pocket. Mr Radomski explained that Mr Malcolm had asked for the small loop to be included specifically for the ring. He then went back to his counter and opened his book. George who had said nothing up to this point looked at me and asked was that the Koh-I-Noor? I replied that it was getting on for that size.

Mr Radomski wrote down an address and stapled it to one of his business cards. 'Please pass on my regards to Mr Malcolm.'

We thanked him and, as we were about to leave, he called us back. 'Oh, I almost forgot, give me a minute,' he shouted and he went back through to the rear of the shop into a back room. George and I looked at each other and shrugged. Mr Radomski reappeared with a brown parcel. 'We had some tweed left when the jacket was made and Mr Malcolm wanted a hat,' he added. He thrust the parcel into my hand and smiled. 'Maybe Mr Malcolm can call in and show me how it fits.' I thanked him and George and I left.

*

In the car heading home George told me how much he was looking forward to meeting Mr Malcolm. He told me he had built up a picture of a tall elegant man of some wealth. I had not mentioned Aiden's winnings to George. I had no idea why but each time I was going to raise it, something else distracted me. George continued with his description of Aiden; he assumed he would be of a romantic disposition as he carried an engagement ring beside his heart. George believed that this was the ring returned to him when he was rejected by his true love on the eve of his wedding. George went on to say that Mr Malcolm had a gambling habit, and it was this discovery by his Quaker fiancée that had been the cause of their quarrel. It was such an imaginative story that I just nodded.

This was so far from my memory of Aiden. The small, hunched, consumptive man, old before his time. I did not voice this knowledge as I wondered whether George had visualised Aiden in his youth, maybe at a time he was about to marry. Perhaps Aiden was broken by the 'special projects' as I might have been, had I been drawn in further. My resolve was stiffened. Armed with the address, I would find Aiden Malcolm. My thoughts also went to Carole. I wonder whether she would be about to marry and whether she was sporting a large solitaire diamond.

*

George was keen to tell Aunt Gladys about the ring and the mystery so I trundled him into her house just as a black figure was leaving. I noticed he had a dog collar and some sort of cape. It was a Catholic priest. Both George and I tried to offer greetings but the priest just pushed past and grunted a response. George said in a stage whisper, 'Well that wasn't very Christian.'

I laughed because he did have a point. Aunt Gladys and Dawn were delighted to see us and asked about our day. George was happy to tell them and whilst I wanted to find out what the priest wanted; I was going to have to wait. George did paint Aiden as a dashing figure and the ring on the ribbon was like the sword in the stone or Dorothy's red shoes in his telling of the tale. The girls insisted on seeing the ring and both tried it on. I noticed they both put it on their wedding fingers and held it to the light. I explained that my plan was to return it to Malcolm with the coat. Dawn was curious as to why, with such a valuable and beautiful ring in the pocket, Malcolm was not moving heaven and earth to find it. She was right but I somewhat dismissed it. I was not sure why.

When George's ripping yarn was finished, I mentioned that we had met the priest at the door. Aunt Gladys responded, 'He wants Dawn to have her baby at the mother and Baby Home at St Hilda's.'

I had no idea what a baby unit was and assumed St Hilda's must be a hospital. I suggested that it sounded like a good idea but was shot down by Aunt Gladys. 'They take away the babies,' she growled. I had never seen Aunt Gladys's mood anything but genial so this was a first. She was angry. 'He told Dawn she had committed a sin and that he could help.'

Dawn added, 'He told me that I was a fallen woman but could be saved.'

George laughed but then paused before saying, 'So what will happen, where will you have the baby?'

'Anywhere but that Catholic prison,' said Aunt Gladys who seemed to be getting even more angry.

'He did seem to be leaving in a poor temper,' George added.

'Well, I gave him short shrift and told him to leave my house,' Aunt Gladys explained. Dawn leaned over and hugged Aunt Gladys whose mood was improving. This did seem to calm Aunt Gladys, her taut, tense body relaxed and she smiled. I offered to put the kettle on but Aunt Gladys said, 'No leave it to me.'

CHAPTER 8

George was not getting any more mobile, he knew that, so he did not need his physiotherapist telling him so quite bluntly. George thought the physio was suggesting he was not trying hard enough with his exercises and became upset. The physio did not address this concern but simply told George he was old and that old bodies do not recover as well as young ones. I tried some diplomacy, suggesting that perhaps George just needed more time or perhaps other exercises that I could work with him on, but the physio was adamant that there was little more he could do for George. When he had gone, George called him a 'pompous ass' and we both laughed. I had called to collect George and the car as we had decided a trip to find Mr Malcolm was in order. George had forgotten that he had a physio appointment, and we were just about to leave when he arrived. It took some while for me to get George back into his sitting room and I think this was why the physio started the treatment in a bad mood.

*

The address for Aiden Malcolm attached to Mr Radomski's card was to the north of the city in a hamlet. The address was 'The Bastle'. George had done his research and told me a Bastle was a fortified house and that it was from the same root as Bastille in the French Revolution, as in the storming of. We set off to storm this Bastle. It only took half an hour to reach the hamlet and we had to pass the parade of shops and the garage that had figured in Aiden's life. The Bastle was an imposing detached house set back from the road with an entrance and an exit with a curved sweep in front of the house between. The wrought iron gates to the entrance were partially open and I was able to squeeze in. I noticed that a Land Rover was just leaving through the other gate at exactly the same time. I hoped we had not just missed Aiden. I left George in the car whilst I knocked on the huge door. I had not wanted to manhandle him out if no one was home. In the event, the door was opened by a lady of an age that I struggled to guess. She had a youthful smile and face but grey hair. She looked too young to be Aiden's wife but I had no idea, so I simply asked if I could speak to Aiden Malcolm.

She looked non-plussed saying, 'Sorry, I think you have the wrong address.' I repeated his name but she just shook her head. I asked if there were any other Bastle Houses and she said, 'Yes I believe so, there are several in Cumberland.' I asked if there were any in close proximity and she said, 'No.' I thanked her and walked back to the car.

'No luck?' asked George. I explained what the lady had said. 'It was twenty years ago,' George reminded me. 'Ask the lady when she moved in.'

I went back to the door and knocked again. The lady returned and her smile had been replaced by a scowl. I apologised for my further question but asked if the former owner was Mr Malcolm. She seemed to ponder and I hoped she was going to be helpful but she just said, 'Sorry, as I have told you, that name is not known' and she closed the door.

George said, 'I could tell that she was not going to be helpful from the sour face; ask that gardener if he knows him.' George pointed to a man with a wheelbarrow clipping the outside hedge.

I pulled over and asked the chap but he waved me off in what appeared to be a foreign language. We drove back and I noticed a parking space outside the bookmakers and pulled in on impulse. 'Time for coffee and cake in that baker,' I said. George and I passed the next thirty minutes thinking of nothing but Chelsea buns and apple tarts.

*

Aunt Gladys and Dawn had been baking when we returned and the house had an aroma of lemon. Dawn was excited to tell me of the lemon drizzle cake she had made and wanted to show me the finished article. The creation was covered by a tea towel on a wire frame in the kitchen. She made a 'dah dah' sound as she pulled back the tea towel. I tried to be enthusiastic but having had two slices of Victoria sponge earlier with George I clearly was not as enthusiastic as Dawn wanted and she asked why I was not impressed. Despite my protestations that it looked wonderful, Dawn was crestfallen. Aunt Gladys picked up the thread and put her arm round Dawn's shoulder. 'It's the baby,' Aunt Gladys whispered to me at a volume that Dawn could hear but suggested a conspiracy that only we three were party to.

 I asked if I should call the doctor but Aunt Gladys explained there was nothing physically wrong, just that Dawn was getting anxious about what to do. Aunt Gladys asked me outright, 'What's going to happen?' I so did not want Dawn's problem to be my problem but she seemed helpless. She looked at me with a distant look in her eyes and told me that she was scared. I walked over and put my arm round her and that of Aunt Gladys so we were all in a huddle. I found myself saying that everything was going to be fine and the baby would be born into a happy family. I asked Dawn what she would want if Aunt Gladys had a magic wand and could grant her a wish. Dawn paused and looked pensive. I had no idea what her answer would be but was still surprised when she said, 'A healthy baby.'

 I said, 'But your wish could be that you weren't pregnant?' I was unsure what line I was taking but wanted to try and find out more of Dawn's thoughts.

Aunt Gladys picked up my thread. She held both Dawn's hands and said, 'Do you want this baby?'

Dawn looked at me and in a slightly high voice replied, 'My life has been so rotten so far. This is the first time I have ever had to think of anyone else but myself. I am surrounded by love and I want my baby to be loved.'

I found myself adding, 'And do you want Colin in your life?'

'Definitely not,' she responded and laughed. 'It would be good if he helped to pay, mind you,' she added.

'Then all is decided,' interrupted Aunt Gladys. 'Dawn will have the baby and Colin can pay.' Dawn looked at me with those puppy dog eyes and asked if I would go and see Colin. I nodded, Aunt Gladys smiled and added reassurance to Dawn that I had everything in hand and she need not worry. I felt a cold shiver run down my spine.

*

Next morning, I took George at his word and borrowed his car without asking. I immediately felt guilty so scribbled a note on the back of an old card telling him I had it and I would be back within a couple of hours. I drove straight to the head office complex of the road works. I was going to confront Colin. It had been less than a month since I had walked out and I was shocked by just how much more work had been carried out. The caravan park had gone and was now sculptured and covered in new trees. The back road was open and the old buildings where my briefing had taken place were demolished. The carpark was smooth and the Land Rovers appeared to have been replaced by BMWs, judging by the carpark. I had no idea what I would say to Colin or even if he would be there but I was mindful that he had to be included in any decision regarding Dawn's baby.

As I stepped out of the car, I bumped into Rod Clough. He was striding towards the building too. He slapped me on the back. 'So, lad, how's your pregnant girlfriend?' he shouted, even though he was standing next to me.

'Still pregnant,' I shouted back and he laughed.

'Where have you been?' he added. 'You haven't been annoying me for weeks.'

I mumbled that I had 'moved on'.

He turned off to the left and just as we parted, he shouted, 'If you do need any help, lad, just ask, I like the cut of your jib.'

I raised a thumb and said, 'Cheers.' It seemed like the correct response.

In reception, rather than ask for Colin, I purposefully said, 'Which is Colin's office? He is expecting me.' I was shown down the corridor by the same unhelpful clerk who knew nothing of Malcolm when I was last there. I continued my bold advance and burst into what I believed was Colin's office. He was bent over a planning table beside two others. All stood up and stepped back. I found myself saying, 'Thank you, chaps, can you give me two minutes with Colin?' They both nodded and passed me as they went out through the door. Colin stood still, caught in the headlights. I kept the initiative by saying, 'Right, Colin, you've had almost six weeks, what are your proposals for Dawn?'

I had clearly caught Colin off guard as he mumbled about sorting things and feeling bad. I had kept reminding myself on the journey to the office that I had to keep control of the meeting. When he started to reproach me for bursting in and causing a scene, I gave him no chance to either change the agenda nor the nature of the discussion. I simply told him that if he could not sort out the problem, I would. I said he could start by paying Dawn £30 a week towards her rent and preparation for the baby. I had plucked this figure from the air as I had no idea what Dawn needed. He nodded in agreement. I said that she needed a lump sum to buy prams and cots and told him £400. He again nodded. Emboldened by my apparent success, I said we would need the deal in writing and the cash payment by the end of the week. Colin seemed deflated but I showed no emotion. I wrote George's address on the pad in front of Colin and told him he could contact me there. I was anxious that he did not try to talk Dawn into some other arrangement or see Dawn without her agreement.

I turned to leave and as I did so Colin said, 'Tell Dawn I'm sorry.'

I replied, 'Yes,' and left.

*

As I left the building I shivered with cold. My shirt was wet with sweat and I was shaking. I thought that the confrontation with Colin had been scarier than the meeting with the Volvo. I was rather proud of myself.

I parked the car outside George's house and went to return the keys but he was not in. I found him sitting in Aunt Gladys's kitchen with Dawn eating lemon drizzle cake. They were both pleased to see me. Dawn had collected George and they were awaiting Aunt Gladys who had gone for her weekly trip to a neighbour to have her hair styled. 'Styled' being a peculiar description as it never changed from week to week. I was not sure whether it was appropriate to mention my meeting with Colin in front of George but was rather ambushed when George asked where I had been. I explained I had been back to my old firm to sort out some matters and whilst he was content with the response, Dawn asked if I had seen Colin and so I had to confess that I had.

I thought it right to pass on Colin's message that he was sorry. Dawn bit her lip. She did not reply. I went through the payments agreed by Colin and Dawn nodded. I had no idea if I had sold her short or if I should have asked for more or whether it was a reasonable agreement, but Dawn seemed content. George commended me for sorting it out, adding it would make Dawn's life easier. Dawn asked if Colin wanted to see the baby when it was born. I told her that he had not raised the matter and I thought it best to say nothing. We all agreed that if Colin was as good as his word, this was a satisfactory arrangement. Aunt Gladys reappeared at this point and after we all complimented her on her hair, I proceeded to repeat what had happened with Colin. Aunt Gladys was pleased that we had sorted the money but still insisted that she did not want rent and that the money should be spent on the baby. I found myself thinking that no one, not even Aiden Malcolm, knew of the three thousand pounds stashed in the toolbox. So money was not a problem and it was ready for an emergency.

CHAPTER 9

Eddie's wedding was hard to describe. I had not been to many weddings, so in all fairness I was unsure how they should be but I instinctively knew Eddie and Jacqui had not got it right. Eddie and his entourage met in the Mitre pub before the ceremony for a couple of drinks and I agreed to join them there. Eddie had chosen his brother as Best Man but the brother had been offered a job offshore a week before. Eddie then promoted Badger, who had been one of his ushers, to the role. When I arrived, it was clear Eddie had drunk enough beer and Badger had drunk too many. I took Eddie for a walk round the Garden of Remembrance explaining to him he just needed air to settle his nerves, not alcohol. He was pleased to see me and said he had wished I had been his Best Man as I always looked out for him. We were joined by Eddie's cousin, Eric Spanswick, known to everyone as 'Spanner'. Spanner was of similar mind to me saying that we had to keep Eddie moving to clear his head. I had borrowed George's car and as it was a miserable, rainy, overcast day he made me take a brolly. I cursed myself for leaving it in the car. I thought carrying it would make me look stupid but it reminded me that I should never let vanity cloud my judgement. I was going to get wet as the forecast was that a storm was brewing. At the last minute I had grabbed my camera as I was still learning how to use it. I had it slung over my shoulder. Eddie thought it was a handbag and kept telling me I was a 'poof'. We perambulated once more round the garden and then straight to the Registry Office, Spanner on one arm, me on the other. Our timing was perfect and Eddie was ready and waiting when Jacqui and her bridal party arrived. I was still at Eddie's side with Spanner but there was no sign of Badger. I introduced Eddie to the Registrar before moving off to the side, leaving Spanner to support Eddie. The Registrar was more interested in telling me that I could not take photographs inside the Registry Office than she was in briefing Eddie.

*

There were more guests than I had anticipated and I squeezed on the end of a row. Jacqui was beaming from ear to ear as she marched down the centre of the rows of chairs to join Eddie at the front. She was flanked by two identical girls who I understood to be her sisters. Her father followed behind. They had arrived in the wrong order and, at Jacqui's bidding, her father tried to join her. He struggled to get forward to take his place beside the bride, ready to escort her to the front. Jacqui reprimanded him and scolded her sisters. Jacqui was very heavily pregnant and, in the tussle to pull her father beside her, she dropped her bouquet. Both sisters bent forward together to pick it up, clashing heads whilst doing so. They both tumbled backwards in a fall that could not have been choreographed better. Jacqui continued to berate them. Jacqui's father and Spanner helped the hapless girls to their feet. They both looked dazed. One was wearing flat shoes but the other had huge heels and as a result was struggling to stand. It took Jacqui, her father and Spanner to prop up the sister on her shoes. It was obvious that there had been no rehearsal and neither Jacqui nor Eddie seemed to have any idea what was happening.

Everyone seemed to settle down under the control of the Registrar and matters progressed until the ring was needed. It was then that the missing Badger was noticed. An enterprising Eddie took a silver ring with a skull off the finger of a surprised Spanner. Despite Jacqui's disquiet, all the formalities were concluded and the whole wedding party moved to the square opposite the Town

Hall for photographs.

I took my newly acquired Zenith SLR out of the case and slung it over my shoulder ready to take some pictures. I saw that there was a photographer taking pictures of Jacqui. She was wearing high heels and seemed as uncomfortable on them as Jacqui's sister. She obviously saw me looking at her as she tottered over to me. I almost had to take her arm as she stumbled forward. She asked if I had a spare film. She told me that she had used too many in the morning. Jacqui was a hairdresser and the photographer explained that she was one of her staff. The girl had spent the morning with Jacqui and her sisters, getting shots from every angle. She only had twenty-four more exposures for the actual wedding. I did have one reel of twenty-four which I was happy to donate but the poor girl still looked desperate. She asked that if any of my photos came out, could I send them to her to add to the collection. I said I was happy to do so. I suggested she take my camera as it had a new roll of thirty-six. She gave me a hug and a kiss. This was not missed by Eddie who shouted that I should put her down as I did not know where she had been. The recharged photographer gave me another hug and staggered off to snap the bridal party with gusto. I wondered why a girl would wear shoes that were so hard to walk in but then reflected that it was my vanity that made me leave the brolly. At one point during the photoshoot, she called me over. As her new best friend, she wanted me to be photographed with Jacqui, Eddie and the bridesmaids. I presume I was singled out as she was using my camera. It would have been rude to decline, so I walked over.

*

Running parallel to the Town Hall and across the end of the square was a bridge walkway joining the old Victorian Town Hall with the square, bland, sixties municipal building. The walkway constructed was to shorten the walk by staff between the buildings. As I gazed up, I could see a girl walking along the bridge. As I walked to stand next to Jacqui the girl stopped and stood in a window gazing down at the wedding. Jacqui put her arm round me and pulled me close and her two sisters flanked the pair of us. Eddie had wandered off. We made a perfect four as we smiled for the camera. As I looked up at the window, I had a dawning realisation that the spectator was Carole. I broke free from Jacqui and waved but the figure in the window had gone. I was only fifty yards at most from the walkway so decided to try and catch Carole, if indeed it had been her. I ran across the square to a door which turned out to be a fire exit. The door was on the ground floor and I could see through the window that there were steps down from the bridge above. I waited, hoping that Carole would come down the stairs. It was a long shot. There did not seem to be any other way of accessing the bridge except by going into either the Town Hall or municipal building. I stood waiting but it was to no avail and I wandered back to join the wedding party. Most of the guests had started the short walk to the Old Comrades working men's club where the reception was to be held. I walked over and joined the queue to meet the bridal party. Jacqui, Eddie and the two bridesmaids were in a line at the entrance to meet the quests. I thought Jacqui was trying to get her father, who was at the bar, to join them but Eddie corrected me by saying Jacqui had sent him to the bar and was trying to change her order. I told Eddie I would convey her request. Eddie thanked me and added, 'If Badger doesn't show up, will you say a few words?' I found myself suggesting Spanner but Eddie was adamant that I was his best friend.

There is nothing like knowing you are going to have to

say something in public to ruin a function. I cursed myself for agreeing to attend and cursed myself for being so helpful. I had no idea what the bridesmaids were called. Apart from Eddie and Jacqui I did not know anyone there, save for a brief meeting with Spanner and the photographer. This cheered me up as it meant if I did cock up anything I said, no one would ever know.

The food was laid out as a buffet and there was no semblance of order so the first to the table were best fed. Even though I had been promoted to guest speaker, I received no preferment and just had to join the queue behind the photographer and an old man who had two sticks for support. His walking arrangement meant he could not hold a plate so it was the photographer and I who had to assist in organising his meal, and seat in the bay window. Sandra, the photographer (we had exchanged names), manhandled the chap into his chair. He was remarkably ungrateful and moaned at us that we had not collected his trifle. Sandra was laden down with two cameras, her camera bag and her own bag. I was carrying her hat so we had failed to pick up much food for ourselves but the old curmudgeon was oblivious. He told Sandra he wanted a pint of 'heavy', but offered no money nor pleasantries. I told him he could wait until Sandra and I had eaten and then we would get him a drink. He opened his mouth but said nothing. Sandra squeezed my hand and thanked me. She added that she really liked me. Sandra was engaging me in conversation but I was only paying part attention. I think she said she was not a fully qualified stylist and she explained how she spent one day a week or something at college. I was quite pleased by the distraction afforded by listening to her explaining the intricacies of hair colouring and the chemistry knowledge she needed for the hair dye. I was trying to seem interested by asking questions. I was saved from too much useless knowledge by Eddie calling the room to what sounded like attention. He bade everyone listen as Horace, his Best Man, was going to speak. My last recollection before standing up was Sandra reminding me that the twins were called Amber and Jade. I do not remember what I said about Eddie, Jacqui, or the bridesmaids but I do recall asking everyone to stand for a toast and the loud applause. It was mission accomplished. Eddie's new father-in law followed and mumbled incoherently about Jacqui and Sunderland Football Club. He never really finished but sat down whilst rambling and faded out. I was ready to leave at that point but, as Eddie explained, I could not leave before dancing with the bridesmaids, and Sandra added that I had to dance with her too. I had presumed that Eddie had organised a DJ but a band arrived that consisted of a keyboard player and a singer. They travelled light. The man plugged his keyboard into a single speaker and the singer plugged her microphone into the same speaker. The opening music was a Carpenters number and Eddie and Jacqui took to the floor. Eddie was light on his enormous feet, Jacqui less so. It was painful to watch as Jacqui bounced and bumped and Eddie tried to follow. At Eddie's beckoning, Sandra took off her ridiculous shoes and grabbed me. Before I knew it, we were moving to a slow ballad and Sandra was pressing herself closer and closer to me singing 'we've only just begun' into my ear. Eddie gave me a knowing wink. I realised that I had unwittingly 'scored'. Sandra was pleasant and had a rather pleasant singing voice but I had no designs on her. I felt bad as, whilst we danced, I was thinking of Carole. Sandra was being far too responsive and we ended up having three dances. I worried that this was going to end in tears. When we sat down, I used the chance to go to the bar to buy the old man his pint of heavy. Sandra wanted to come with me but I prevailed upon her to sit with him as he had been watching the cameras and he needed a bit of company. At the bar Badger had reappeared and was holding court about how he had thought the Registry Office was in the Old Shipping Office and had gone off in the wrong direction. Eddie seemed to have forgiven him and explained to Badger how I had stood in. Badger gave me a withering look. He knew I knew his story did not bear scrutiny but he also knew I would say nothing. I also knew from his look that he wished he had beaten me up when he had the chance.

I managed to get the old man his pint of heavy and I also bought two Bacardi and Cokes for Amber and Jade who had joined me at the bar. Both wanted to dance with me. I had never felt in such demand. I bought myself a pint of Stella and Sandra a vodka and orange. Badger offered to help me carry them over but I declined as I only had three drinks and could carry them all. Amber followed me back and insisted I join her for a dance. Amber had the sensible shoes and I said she was better prepared for the dancing. She laughed and said that she had pinched Sandra's shoes as she could not walk in the ones she was supposed to be wearing for the wedding. It was another slow country and western number and Amber was also keen to hold herself against me. She confessed to me that she and Jade always liked the same men. I said it seemed reasonable as they were so much alike. She went on to tell me that they had a wager to see who would get the first choice when they both wanted the same man. She explained that they tossed a coin at the beginning of the reception. I was grinning and said, 'So you won the wager?'

Amber said, 'No, Jade did.'

I was deflated but smiled to myself thinking it was presumptuous to assume I would be the attraction. Amber further punctured my ego by adding that, 'We both wanted Badger.' I was second choice but it made it easier to extract myself at the end of the dance. I told Amber that she was beautiful but sadly, like her shoes, not my first choice. I smiled and headed back to Sandra who was keen to see me as she needed saving from the grumpy old man. I was mindful that whilst Eddie was an acquaintance, I did not want to become too close to him or any of his cohort. The idea of Amber and me and Eddie and Jacqui all out together sent a shudder through me. I was also alarmed by Sandra's intentions. She was a colleague of Jacqui and although a sweet girl, certainly not my type. I felt such a snob but I thought it best to try and cut this off at the pass. I had earlier offered to drop Sandra back at her house as I was being gallant. Sandra had loved the idea that I had a car as she explained her previous boyfriend did not and they had to catch the bus. I should have seen this as a warning as she was putting me in the 'boyfriend bracket'. The Old Comrades club was now filling with the regular members who had been excluded from the main room during the wedding period. The band were still playing. The tempo had not changed and seemed unlikely to do so as the new wave of dancers were all pensioners. Eddie and Jacqui had cut the cake and were walking round the room handing out small pieces. Jacqui told Sandra off for failing to take any pictures of the cake-cutting. I explained it was my fault as Sandra had been with me and was looking after the old man. Jacqui asked me who the old man was. I said I had no idea. Jacqui went off to ask Eddie. I could see her asking him at the other side of the room. He looked over and shook his head. He raised a thumb when he saw me looking. I waved back.

Sandra had smiled beautifully, through gritted teeth, when she was being admonished for not taking the cake-cutting photo. Sandra knew which buttons to press with Jacqui and changed the subject to say just how attractive Jacqui was looking. I grinned; I liked Sandra's style. I do not know why but I asked Sandra why she had covered over the tattoo on her shoulder. 'Tattoo,' she barked! 'I do not have a tattoo; it is a bruise. I was hit by a golf ball, thank you.' Despite my apologies, she was indignant. She then told me she had a headache. I asked if she wanted to leave as it did seem the right time. I gathered the camera equipment and Sandra's hat; she had taken off her shoes and I presumed she was going to put them on but she said, 'Not likely.' She walked over to Amber and rescued her flat shoes. As we walked to the car, Sandra said something like, 'I know you look down on me but I never planned to be a hairdresser.' I was somewhat taken aback and assured her that the world would always need hairstylists. I tried to upgrade the title for some reason and that I did not look down on her. I asked her what I had done to make her think that. She said, 'Well nothing in what you said but I can tell that you think you're superior to Eddie, Jacqui and everyone at the wedding.' I told her I was Eddie's and Badger's boss in the TA and that is why it may seem that I was superior to them but that did not mean I was better or more important than anyone.

Sandra insisted she was not like Jacqui, she said, 'In fact I cannot stand her or her sisters, they are all such trollops.' I chortled; it was such a good word. Sandra laughed too and then went on to tell me that she had not wanted to be at the wedding and had only done so when Jacqui begged her to be the photographer because she knew Sandra had a fancy camera. I confessed to her that I wondered why I was at the wedding and why I kept up any relationship with Eddie. I was thinking to myself that perhaps I did need it to boost my ego and I was just arrogant. I did not need to share this with Sandra as Sandra seemed to have seen right through me.

*

I drove her home in what was now driving rain. She lived on a hill and even though she was pointing out the house, I overshot. I turned round and tried to park outside but I was facing the wrong way. She told me she lived with her mother and invited me in. I declined but she looked disappointed so I said, 'Well maybe for a coffee.' It was only eight thirty but it had been a long day. I was about to lock the car when Sandra remembered she had left her hat in the back. As I was going back to the car, I decided I had better turn it round. It felt wrong to be so badly parked on such a dreadful night. Sandra stood in the rain whist I took what was an inordinate length of time to do such a simple manoeuvre. Sandra was dripping wet by the time I walked her to the door and I was almost as bad. The steps to the door had been replaced by a wheelchair ramp. I noticed them all the time now I was pushing George about. Sandra introduced me to her mother who was in the corridor sitting in a wheelchair. She seemed old but not in the Aunt Gladys sense. I guessed that she must have had Sandra late in life. I had no idea how old Sandra was and it was not an easy subject to broach. Sandra went upstairs to dry off and Mrs McGregor bade me go into the downstairs loo to grab a towel and dry off my hair. I then sat alone in the front room with Mrs McGregor having coffee. There was an open fire and Mrs McGregor asked me to put on a log and it blazed up. I spoke politely about the wedding. I explained how the Best Man went absent and I had to step in. Sandra rejoined us dressed in a dressing gown. She told me it was too late to get dressed and she hoped I would not mind her new ensemble. She did a theatrical twirl. She looked beautiful. Her hair that had been all tight and curly for the wedding was now yellow and flowing. We all giggled when Sandra described the scene in front of the Registrar when the bridesmaids fell over. Mrs McGregor then excused herself as she was going for a bath and then to bed. Sandra pushed her mother out of the room and said, 'I will just get mother sorted and will be straight back.' I should have used this as my cue to leave but did not. I had no idea what I wanted; there was a lustful part of me that so wanted to hug Sandra but I was still thinking about Carole. In all of my turmoil the last person I had been thinking of was Sandra. Sandra deserved more than I could offer. Sandra was better than me and deserved better. Sandra had seen through me.

When Sandra returned, she explained that apart from sherry there was no alcohol she could offer me. I said that I was not a drinker. I was sitting on the sofa. Sandra went to sit on a window seat in the bay but then paused and came over and sat next to me. I instinctively put my arm round her and she snuggled in close. Sandra then swung her left leg over me so that she was straddling me. As she did so I saw her white cotton knickers with a small yellow flower on them. She was facing me and put her arms round my neck. I instinctively put my hands on her bottom. Sandra hugged me and her nightdress stuck to my still damp shirt. I had no blood in my brain and yet as we embraced, I was thinking of 'Porphyria's lover'. Sandra felt so soft and comforting and our kiss was deep and warm.

The rain set early in tonight,
The sullen wind was soon awake,
It tore the elm-tops down for spite,
And did its worst to <u>vex</u> the lake:
I listened with heart fit to break.
When glided in Porphyria; straight

She shut the cold out and the storm,
And kneeled and made the cheerless grate
Blaze up, and all the cottage warm;
Which done, she rose, and from her form
Withdrew the dripping cloak and shawl,
And laid her soiled gloves by, untied
Her hat and let the damp hair fall,
And, last, she sat down by my side
And called me. When no voice replied,
She put my arm about her waist,
And made her smooth white shoulder bare,
And all her yellow hair displaced,
And, stooping, made my cheek lie there,
And spread o'er all her yellow hair,
Murmuring how she loved me – she
Too weak, for all her heart's endeavour,
To set its struggling passion free
From pride, and vainer ties <u>dissever</u>,
And give herself to me for ever.

I was desperately trying to focus on the poem. I so did not want to take advantage of Sandra. I was thinking of the trouble Dawn and Jacqui were in. I had to fight my own desires. I thought more of Browning's poem.

So, she was come through wind and rain.
Be sure I looked up at her eyes
Happy and proud; at last I knew
Porphyria worshipped me; surprise
Made my heart swell, and still it grew
While I debated what to do.
That moment she was mine, mine, fair,

My brain was screaming and I tried to think of another Browning poem. I started reciting in my head:

137

Hamelin Town's in Brunswick,
By famous Hanover city;
The river Weser, deep and wide,
Washes its wall on the Southern side;
A pleasanter spot you never spied;

By drowning their speaking
With Shrieking and squeaking
in fifty different sharps and flats.

I was unsure what was going through my head but I was hearing screeching followed by an enormous bang. I stood up with Sandra still clinging to me. She said, 'What on earth was that?'

I went into the hall. Mrs McGregor was shouting, 'Sandra, Sandra.'

I looked out of the front door and saw a light from a motorcycle pointing in the air. I shouted for Sandra to phone 999. I went towards the bike. The back wheel was up in the air and the front wrecked. A body was draped over the front and there was a strong smell of petrol. Whilst it was still pouring with rain, I was worried that the bike could go up in flames at any moment. The rider was still alive as he was moaning. I went to him shouting words of comfort, explaining that the ambulance was on its way. The man was twisted into the mangled bike. I was trying to remember the breathing, bleeding, brakes, and any other first aid mantras that I had been taught. The man was breathing but was trapped under the front of the bike by one very broken leg. The petrol was pouring out of the tank and he was covered. I knew that to move him would be dangerous as he would clearly have neck and back injuries but any spark would ignite him. Sandra was right behind me telling me that the ambulance was on its way. I said, 'Stand back, I am going to move him from the bike.' This was easier said than done as the man's leg was trapped.

Sandra proved to be strong and resourceful. She took a broken fence post and with a brick from the wall levered the front wheel up so I could roll the man away. She helped me drag him to the front lawn. His breathing seemed steady and, despite the atrocious condition of his leg, I could not see or feel any blood. Mrs McGregor came to the front door in her wheelchair. She shouted that she had a brolly. Sandra went to collect it from her and came back to hold it over the poor motorcyclist. I was feeling anxious that we had moved him but should not have, as suddenly the bike burst into flames. The heat was searing even though we were some twenty yards away. The whole area was lit up and it was then that Sandra shouted, 'Look he had a passenger!'

There beyond the broken fence was a prostrate body. I could not run directly to him because of the burning bike but managed to climb the fence near a fruit tree. The figure seemed lifeless but I found a pulse in the thin delicate wrist. It was a female but she had a full-face helmet and was face down so I was just working off the wrist size. I had no idea what to do with this casualty but knew that I should not remove the helmet or turn her over. She was breathing as I could see her back moving in the light or the burning bike. There was another explosion as a tyre burst. This did signal the arrival of an ambulance closely followed by a police car. The ambulance crew did not really need to ask about what had happened as it was obvious. One man came to me whilst the other went to Sandra. I explained that Sandra and I had to move the man onto the lawn but they were full of praise for this action. Sandra and I were ushered back into the house by the policemen. They came into the front room with Mrs McGregor and Sandra and I explained what we heard and what we did. They took my details. The policeman suggested that we went back to bed as they would sort matters out. Sandra showed them out. Mrs McGregor asked if I was leaving too. She corrected herself saying she wasn't driving me out, indeed I could stay if it had been too traumatic and I did not want to drive. Sandra was dripping wet for a second time. I had never really dried from the first. We both grinned. 'What a night,' I said, 'I do hope the couple will be alright.' Mrs McGregor asked Sandra to take her back to bed. She bade me farewell for a second time.

When Sandra came back, she took off her wet dressing gown and stood in her nightdress that clung to her. It was clinging so tight that I could see the full outline of her body and even the little yellow flower on her knickers. I gave her a hug and lingered as she held onto me. 'We have some unfinished business,' she whispered in my ear, 'perhaps we can find another night?'

'Yes indeed,' I said. I was desperate to stay longer but thought that if I did, it would be for the wrong reasons. We stood on the doorstep for several minutes holding hands. There was still commotion outside. The ambulance was leaving but a fire engine, two police cars and a police motorbike were still blocking the road. I was wet and the cold air made me shiver. As I surveyed the scene, I was mindful that a couple of families' lives could have been changed forever tonight. I gave Sandra one last kiss and walked to the car. The police motorcyclist shouted something to me so I walked over to him saying, 'Sorry.'

He shouted, 'I was just thanking you, the lad on the bike was one of ours.'

I said, 'Sorry, I don't understand.'

He said, 'The lad on the bike was a copper.'

'Is he going to be okay?' I asked.

'Well, he's still alive, thanks to you.'

I said, 'No, thanks to Sandra, she levered up the bike so I could move him.'

He patted me on the back and said, 'Well, both of you.'

*

I drove home feeling very tired. All the adrenaline of the Best Man's speech, through to the casualty evacuation had wrecked me. I swear it was only by thinking of that little yellow flower that I could stay awake.

I woke with the light shining in my eyes in the shed. I had never been woken by sunlight from that angle and realised that it was almost 1130. I had never slept that late. I did not rush to get up but lay thinking of the day before. It had been so eventful. I wondered how the casualties were and then I thought of Sandra. Or should I say, I did not know what to think of Sandra. She had certainly taken over my head. I tried thinking of Carole but could not. I jumped out of bed, threw on some shorts and a singlet, found my trainers at the back of the cupboard and went for a run. I passed Aunt Gladys in the hall. I kissed her on both cheeks and told her I would be back later. Her Parthian shot was, 'Not too late, I'm making a roast dinner.'

*

Running had been my escape at school and at Polytechnic. Mindlessly pounding the miles made me think straight and helped 'get all my ducks in a row'. My priorities were to make sure Dawn was settled, get a job, find Malcolm, get somewhere to live and expose the scam on the road contract. I knew that the last one was just my sense of fair play eating at me and the fact that they had tried to kill me.

My head started to clear and was no longer the 'mince' that it was at the start of the run. I was deliberately not thinking about Sandra or Carole as they were the 'spaghetti'. I passed under the railway bridge where I had had a run-in with the postman. I was further from home than I had planned. I also had the long hill to face. I had not run for some time and cursed myself for being distracted. I had a long lie-in but still felt tired and by the time I was back at Aunt Gladys's, I was whacked. I was also late. Dawn, George and Aunt Gladys were sitting at the dinner table beside my mother and father. The roast was waiting to be carved. I could tell from the look on Aunt Gladys's face that she was not best pleased. I hugged my mum and shook hands with Pa. He said, 'Grab a shower and then we can find out what's been happening.'

*

I showered in record time and was sitting with them within moments. It was moments for me but I was not sitting looking at the food. Once I had been contrite enough and everyone had started eating, I was able to tell them of the bike crash and the wedding. Dawn asked what the other guests did when the bike crashed. I had to explain that the crash was at the home of a guest that I had taken home. George scoffed, 'Running a taxi service in my car.'

I explained it was the photographer I drove home as if that made it different. Mum asked if the photographer was female and once I had said yes, the inquisition began. George joking that his car was not some vehicle for my dates and Mum asking whether I would see her again. I could not believe how quick the conversation had gone from my trip to the wedding to dissecting my love-life. But then my mother had always expected me to settle down after university and have a family. Pa wanted to know about what had happened to my job and whether I had any interviews. Auntie Gladys had known of the planned visit of my parents but had kept it quiet and I teased her for surprising me. They were only staying one night and George had been happy to provide a bed at his house so there was no need for Dawn to vacate her room. It was whilst we were eating the rice pudding that Dawn looked to Aunt Gladys and asked if now was a good time. There was a pause and Aunt Gladys said, 'Well it's not something that can be kept secret for long.'

Dawn looked down and whispered, 'I'm going to have a baby.'

Mum was offering congratulations and Pa was nodding and muttering agreement but I could tell they were embarrassed and not sure what else to say. Luckily Aunt Gladys seemed to have discussed the disclosure with Dawn and stepped in. She almost gave a speech which indicated to me that it had been rehearsed. She said, 'I'm sure you have lots of questions but perhaps I can help. Dawn had a short relationship with a colleague of Harry this summer. She has fallen pregnant and is going to have a baby. The boy is no longer on the scene but will support her financially. Dawn has considered all her options and wants to stay with me here and have the child.' Both Mum and Pa seemed to relax. I knew they both treated Dawn as their own when she had been with us, so the idea of Aunt Gladys helping would have been a great comfort to them as they were so far away. Dawn said that she had seen the midwife and as it was her first baby, it would be born in the Long Benson Maternity Home. She added that the priest wanted her to go to St Hilda's but that Aunt Gladys had objected. Aunt Gladys looked down at her hands and I noticed Mum put her hand on them. George caught my eye and frowned. I responded by lifting my eyes. George and I had only seen the priest leaving the house so it did all seem dramatic.

*

Dawn's revelation completely derailed the rest of my parents' stay. After lunch we went for a walk in Long Benson Park. I pushed George and chatted to my father mainly about Aiden Malcolm and work, as it turned out. I explained about the special project and was able to get the whole sorry saga off my chest. George had sat in silence. Pa was anxious to know that I was not implicated in any way and had not done anything illegal. I had not mentioned the cat in the boiler nor the Volvo incident and was careful to keep the whole matter far less of an issue than it had actually been. Pa uncharacteristically put his arm round my shoulders and said, 'You've dealt with things well.' This was praise indeed from my usually taciturn Pa. We had walked almost half a mile ahead of the girls as Aunt Gladys had limited mobility so we turned round and headed back. Ma and Pa were visiting old friends in Newcastle that evening and so it was not until breakfast that we had a chance to speak further. Pa started on about my career and how if I was ever going to be a chartered engineer, I would have to get on a career path. I was nodding and agreeing with him using a well-rehearsed coping mechanism I had used when younger to 'listen out' his advice. I was adamant that I was never going to be an engineer and whilst I did not tell him, my mind was already made up. The TA pay was keeping me from poverty and, with Aunt Gladys refusing rent, living was quite cheap. George refused to accept payment for petrol and so I had transport.

When it was time for my parents to leave, Dawn, Aunt Gladys and I bade farewell to them. Mum hugged Dawn and said she would be back after the birth to be the perfect grandmother and there would be a room and a nursery in Essex whenever it was needed. Pa shook my hand and said, 'I am pleased we have sorted out your career.' I just smiled and thanked him.

I had not decided what my next plan would be regarding any of the problems that I had.

I was desperate to see Sandra but was not sure of my motive. Well, actually, I was sure of my motive but just not sure that the motive was right. I could not do nothing, that would drive me to distraction. I had lost too much sleep thinking of Carole and that had come to nothing. The weather had picked up and the sun was threatening to come out. I went next door to George's with a bucket and sponge and told him I was going to give his car a valet. He replied, 'Well that's the first good thing to come out of your new relationship, I hope there are many more.'

I remonstrated saying it was only right if I was using the car, I should keep it in good condition. He replied that he was young once, but all he had was a pushbike to impress the girls. He stayed outside whilst I cleaned the car and chatted. George had lived an interesting life and I wanted to know more about him than I had gleaned about Aiden Malcolm. The car came up really well and George had some chrome polish so I did all the chrome. George was getting a little cold by the time I had finished so we went in. George asked me if Aunt Gladys was Catholic. I told him I had no idea but that if she was, she had clearly lost her faith.

CHAPTER 10

On the Monday whilst I was out, Dave dropped a note through Aunt Gladys's door. He and Heather were having an engagement party at the White Rose on the following Friday and I was invited. Written on the outside was, 'Sorry I missed you, see you there, Stellas on me! Bring Dawn if you want.'

*

Dawn was thrilled with the idea of a night out and spent all week deciding what she was going to wear. I was less fussy but perhaps I should have been because, without the planning, I did not have a clean shirt in my makeshift wardrobe. I only discovered this when I was changing to leave. I had to put on the white shirt that I had last worn at the black-tie dinner. It had a plain front so I covered the problem by wearing a sweater.

Dawn was looking striking in a sparkly dress which she had bought on a shopping trip with Aunt Gladys. We borrowed George's car and he insisted on giving me £5 for petrol and the first drink. The White Rose had a car park but it was full so I parked in the road and we entered through the bar. The party was in the 'back room' but all the guests were in the bar. Dave came over and hugged Dawn and slapped me on the back. Heather was beside him. Dawn handed her a small wrapped parcel and said, 'An engagement present,' she added, 'from Harry and I.' Heather thanked Dawn and gave me a rather dismissive grunt. It was not because she realised that I was surprised by Dawn's present, even though I was.

As she turned to greet another guest Dave said, 'She still blames you for leading me astray on the geology field trip.' I reminded him that I had missed the field trip but he laughed. 'Just keep schtum then.'

I was going to claim my Stella but Dave had gone. At

the bar a man was doing a monkey impersonation. He was dangling his arms and then bringing his hands up under his armpits whilst walking on shorter bowed legs. The crowd round him were in convulsions of laughter. Dawn and I had no idea what was going on but found ourselves laughing at his antics. A girl at the bar explained that he was Andy Harris and he was working at the Safari Park. I remembered the name. He lived near Carole and Sarah. I wondered if they would turn up. I started to feel uncomfortable. What would I say to Carole? The sweater was not a good choice of party wear. I was burning up and needed a drink. I elbowed my way nearer the bar and ordered drinks for Dawn and I. I left Dawn on the fringe and she went towards the party room and I lost sight of her. I eventually got served and struggled through the group being entertained by Andy. I was touched on the arm and as I turned the person said, 'Congratulations, stranger.' It was Carole. My first reaction was to hug her but the two full glasses stopped me. I was already sweating with the jumper but her presence made me go even redder.

'Congratulations are for Dave, not me,' I was saying when a man pushed between us. I was going to remonstrate with him but realised he was joining us but in a passive aggressive manner, as he had half his back to me. He positioned Carole by moving her shoulders and then asked her who I was. I could feel an anger rising but tried to stay calm.

'This is Harry,' Carole replied. 'I was just congratulating him on his marriage.'

The man's shoulders relaxed and he turned to me with a smile. 'Oh congratulations,' he said adding that he would buy me a drink but could see I was already loaded. He pushed through the group to the bar leaving me standing with Carole.

'That was "Crught", you remember I mentioned him?' I was not really listening so I missed his name as I was so anxious to say I was not married. Carole said, 'But I saw you from the window.' I explained I was the Best Man. Carole went on to say but the girl was pregnant. I countered telling her that was nothing to do with me. She asked me who the drink was for and at that point the boyfriend reappeared. He asked me why I was still here. It was half in jest but as I had already decided I did not like him; I made no comment. Carole had gone silent again.

I smiled at her and spoke, 'I still have that parachuting weekend in mind, I will contact you.' The man looked perplexed, as did Carole. I could see he wanted to question me but I turned on my heels and went to find Dawn. It was then I remembered I had never got round to asking Carole to go parachuting so no wonder she was as perplexed as her man.

I was pleased that I had not made a fool of myself in front of Carole. I felt a deep sense that the man was not good for her but content that I had cleared up her confusion over my situation. I could see Dawn was at the back of the room talking to a chap with dark hair. As I got closer, I could see it was Colin. Dawn was smiling and holding a drink. I delayed heading back to her. Dawn was a big girl now and I was not her keeper. I looked round and saw a seat near the bay window. I sat on my own and waited. I could see glimpses of Carole's lower legs through the crowd in the bar. I wished I had invited Sandra. I was daydreaming and was awakened from my thoughts by Sarah and another girl who asked to sit with me. I was delighted to see Sarah. She too thought I was married and tried to congratulate me with a hug and a kiss. I presumed she had heard from Carole. Sarah had been to the races at Redcar with her friend all day and was therefore fairly drunk. She was telling me what an arsehole Carole's boyfriend was and that I, Harry, should be with Carole as that was written in the stars. Dawn came over and it punctured Sarah's rambling. Dawn had removed her jacket and she did look pregnant. It was the first time I had noticed and the bump was not lost on Sarah. Sarah started to apologise but I calmed her down by introducing Dawn as my sister. Sarah asked who the girl was that I took to hospital. I explained it was Dawn. 'But that's why I didn't leave Carole's letter,' she said.

I was non-plussed. Dawn added that it was just a scare and that she was fine now. Sarah explained that when she found out that Carole had ditched me by letter, she had made her write another letter of retraction. Carole ran around to the house to deliver this second letter to me but was met by the neighbour who explained I had taken my pregnant girlfriend to hospital. Sarah started crying and was comforted by the friend. Dawn looked at me and frowned. 'What is retraction?' she mouthed.

I whispered that I would explain later. Whatever Sarah had been drinking kicked in and so, together with her friend, we walked her outside for some fresh air. We left by a back door into the carpark where Sarah proceeded to throw up into a flower planter. I left her friend tending to her and returned to Dawn who was sitting with Dave's parents in the quiet corner of the bar. The bar had mostly decanted to the party room which was getting louder and rowdier. I could not see Carole but did see Colin dancing with two girls. He looked in his element. Dawn was ready to leave. I had missed the toast to Dave and Heather that had been given by Dave's father whilst I had been out with Sarah. Dawn suggested one last dance. It seemed like a good idea. I took off my sweater and led her into the party room. I am not sure what my shirt was made of but it was captured by one of the DJ's lights and I lit up like a Belisha beacon. I was this glowing white figure that dominated the dance area. People around me moved back as if my shirt was toxic. Even Dawn was dancing as if she was with someone near me. The track seemed to last forever and I was so pleased when it ended so I could escape from my own self-inflicted embarrassment.

*

Dawn slept in the car going home so I could not ask her about Colin. I just spent the whole journey wondering about Carole and whether she was happy.

When we arrived at Aunt Gladys's, she was sitting in the kitchen. She had been worried that Dawn was out so late and could not sleep. Both Dawn and I admonished her in a joking way but I could see that Aunt Gladys had become an anxious 'mum' to Dawn. She worried just like my own mother did when my sister was out. It did give the three of us a chance to talk about Colin. Dawn said that he had been polite and rather gentlemanly with her but it had served to remind her just how two-faced he was. He had apologised and had hoped she agreed that the deal he had struck with me was good for both her and the baby. He had said that the first payment would be made before the end of the month. I was sure that the agreement was for an immediate lump sum but thought it too late to discuss the finer points as I was tired and was sure that Dawn and Aunt Gladys were too.

*

I spent an administration Saturday at the drill hall. Both Ra-Ra and Ginge Jock were in and so I was able to get twice as much work done as I had planned. As ever they were attentive and keen to do whatever my bidding was. They had the strange effect on the others in their section who also seemed motivated. I had been given responsibility for new recruit induction and training. I had planned to completely clean and reorganise the training wing so I knew just what we had. It was called a 'wing' but it was three classrooms and two store cupboards. The main classroom was where I had seen half a film when I first joined. I found the projector and ran the second half of the film as the room was being cleaned. It gave a soundtrack and background activity to the work. The curmudgeonly Colour Sergeant, who had never looked me in the eye, nor spoken to me, put his head round the door at one point. He saw me and saluted. I was not wearing a hat so I could not salute back but acknowledged him with a nod. He asked if I needed any stores. I half joked that a couple of tins of paint would not go amiss. He asked, 'What colour?' It turned out that the section Lance Corporal, Jarvis, was a decorator by profession and so under his guidance we changed tack. Cleaning was changed to washing down the walls and paintwork and then painting commenced. Painting was so therapeutic. When the recruiting film ended, I found another reel of tape marked *Tunes of Glory*. It was the second reel of a feature film starring Alec Guinness and John Mills. The plot was about a highland regiment and a strict officer. The section laughed and compared me to the John Mills character who spoke in clipped tones. The reel only lasted thirty-five minutes but everyone insisted that it was played again when it had finished. Two of the cooks and the Colour Sergeant and his storeman came and joined in so we had quite a labour force. The work went so well that two men went over and painted the Officer Commanding's ceiling and two walls which dramatically brightened up what had been his drab office.

*

On the Sunday morning I went back and was able to inspect the work. I was shocked by how much we had achieved in one day of activity. The paint on the walls was dry and, save for some of the woodwork, we were able to put everything back by the time the rest of the company came back from the weekend away. I had expected the OC to be pleased but he was dumbstruck. He walked round the whole wing and walked back without speaking. At one point I thought he had stopped breathing as he just stood and gawped. He eventually said 'Harry this is fantastic, remind me to give you more Friday nights off.'

*

Despite my ever-improving career prospects with the Territorial Army, it was part-time work; it was not for real. My dad was right. I had to start thinking long term. I resolved to start my new career search first thing Monday morning.

My plan was delayed by George. He needed to attend an outpatient appointment and could not do so without my help. It took all morning. On our return, Aunt Gladys had made a large lunch and so I did not get any time to do anything until gone 1400. I went back to the shed armed with a blank sheet of paper and a pen. I had no sooner fed the cat and sat down when Aunt Gladys put her head round the door to tell me the police wanted to see me. I cannot describe how this put me into a cold sweat. Why had I not dealt with Aiden's money and jewels? Why had I not reported the sub-station scam? My brain was in full 'guilt' mode. I would have confessed to the great train robbery, if pressed, when I stood in front of the leather-clad motorcycle policeman in Aunt Gladys's front room.

'Harry Crawford?' he asked.

I replied 'yes' expecting him to read me the caution but he smiled.

'I have a note from the Chief Constable. He would like you to meet him at the hospital tomorrow at 1100.' I must have looked clueless as he went on to say. 'You and your girlfriend saved PC Over's life and both he and PC

Over would like to thank you and your girlfriend.' He handed me a note.

I said, 'I'm free tomorrow and should be delighted to attend but I can't speak for Sandra.'

He replied, 'I've just been to see her at her work and she'll be there too.' As the policeman was leaving, I asked how the pillion passenger was. He told me that she was fine and had been discharged the following day.

My note was handwritten by the Chief Constable. It thanked me for my quick thinking and hoped he and I could meet at the hospital. It gave a time and a name to ask for at the hospital reception.

It was quite short notice but George was accommodating and I was able to take the car. I was becoming too dependent on it and I set off late assuming a straight journey but there were roadworks and these delayed me. The hospital car park was full as an area had been cordoned off for resurfacing. I drove into the adjacent housing estate where all the roads near the hospital were 'No Parking' as, I presumed, they wanted to deter hospital overspill. I eventually found a wasteland with parking adjacent. I had to run to the hospital and I had a flashback to running up Otley Road. That seemed a lifetime ago. I arrived at the hospital reception with moments to spare.

I did not need a name as there were a number of uniformed police in the reception and one had met me on the night of the crash so walked over to greet me. I was thinking that if the police were all in the hospital, who was guarding the streets? But realised that the thought was disingenuous. When Sandra came in down a long corridor to our left, all of the policemen turned to watch her. I heard one say to his colleague, 'Wow, what a looker.' He was right. Sandra had her hair down and she did look striking. I smiled at her and raised my hand slightly. She walked right up to me and kissed me on the cheek. I did feel special. I sort of introduced Sandra to the group but was cut short by the arrival of Rowan Connor, a *Gazette* reporter and his photographer.

The photographer knew Sandra. He explained to the group that he lectured on photography and Sandra was in his night class. The policeman who had earlier commented on Sandra asked if she was his model. Sandra blushed and I moved towards her. I was unsure why but I felt slightly protective of her. Rowan also knew Sandra. They shook hands and he kissed her on the cheek. He asked her how the fundraising was going. She replied that it never stopped. We all went up to the third floor. Sandra nipped into the ladies' loo and I waited for her. As we walked to the ward, she said, 'Thank goodness you were there, I dread walking into crowds of people and especially men.'

I said it was my pleasure and thanked her for the kiss. Without thinking I stopped and kissed her on the lips. It was a spasm reaction. I had not planned it and shook my head in disbelief at my uncharacteristic action. Sandra laughed. 'And thank you too!' she exclaimed.

'So, you're learning to use your camera,' I said.

It sounded rather lame and Sandra obviously noticed, as she said, 'Yes, I'm sure that even someone like me could pick it up.' I found myself apologising for being 'me' as we entered the ward.

*

PC Over was in the centre of a large room. He was almost a comic book patient. He had one leg in plaster, one arm in plaster and a large bandage on his head. He raised his good hand to Sandra and me. The Chief Constable was flanking the bed with four Constables on one side. Rowan, Geoff (the photographer) and medical staff were on the other. Sandra and I stood at the foot of the bed. The Chief Constable said we were waiting for one more person and then he would start the introductions.

The one person arrived. It was a petite blonde female. I presumed it was her wrist I had held on the night of the crash. I was correct. She was introduced as Eleanor, PC Over's girlfriend. The meeting was really a photoshoot for the Chief Constable to thank Sandra and me but we did get heartfelt thanks from PC Over and Eleanor. The meeting took a twist when PC Over asked everyone to step back. With his good arm he extracted a box from his bedside cabinet. He asked Eleanor to help him open it. She did, to reveal a ring. Eleanor cried and so did the two nurses. I welled up, as did a couple of the policemen. PC Over asked Eleanor to be his 'pillion passenger for life'. Someone said, 'Well you'd better improve your driving.' Sandra and I were side-lined as Rowan recognised that he had a far better 'human interest' story.

*

Sandra was not due back to the salon until three. She had no idea how long she would be at PC Over's bedside so had erred on the long side. It meant we could walk into town for lunch. I suggested we went by car but Sandra said we would avoid the one-way system if we walked. I had no idea where we could go but Sandra knew a café halfway to town where she often went for a sandwich. The café was on the main road and was a stopping point for people grabbing a sandwich. It was busy so we had to wait for a table. I asked Sandra about her fundraising. She was quite dismissive and said it was just helping a charity. I asked which charity and she said one that helps MS. Sandra could tell from my blank expression that she would have to explain further. 'Muscular sclerosis, the disease that is killing Jacqueline Du Pré,' she added.

'Elgar's *Cello Concerto*,' I replied. I loved it and so

knew the Cellist even though she was probably the only classical performer I did know.

A table came free and we grabbed it before a couple of lads who had designs on it. Once seated, Sandra smiled. 'I knew you would know Jacqueline Du Pré, you are so predictable. I bet you didn't think I would know her, me a mere hairdresser.'

I found myself apologising again saying, 'Sandra, I admit I had you typecast when we first met, but that would have been my loss.'

She laughed, again admitting that she had not expected to see me anyway. She then added, 'And it did take the Chief Constable to get us together again.' I found myself apologising again but was cut short when Sandra stood up, kissed me and then said, 'Sorry I have a living to earn,' and walked out.

I tried to follow but an old lady and gentleman saw the table was being vacated and closed the gap between me and the door. Sandra waved as she passed down the street. I decided not to chase after her but would walk towards the town to see if I could spot her salon. I had no idea where it was, nor its name. It reminded me just how little I knew about Sandra. She had absolutely replaced Carole, I thought, but there was still a 'but'. I was also minded that Sandra may not be that bothered. That definitely brought out my insecurities. I was surprised just how far it was into town and more surprised that I had not caught Sandra up or seen her in the distance. At the top of the high street there was a covered parade of shops and the first shop was a hairdressers called 'Head Quarters'. I walked past trying to see if it might be where Sandra worked but it seemed to be for men, although it did say unisex. I walked out of the end of the parade which rejoined the high street. There seemed to be a barber or hairdresser on every corner. I had never realised just how many could be viable in any town. I started one of those maths puzzles in my head. I was working out how many haircuts I had in one year, how many people lived in the town and how many hairdressers in each shop. All the variables kept changing and my maths was shocking so I ended up walking back to the car with my head full of numbers and only a vague recollection of where I had parked. It started to rain so I picked up pace. The faster I ran, the harder the rain fell. By the time I was near the hospital I was soaked. I tried to retrace my drive into the housing estate but was totally disorientated. I had lost the car. The whole area was deserted, no one would be out in the rain unless absolutely necessary. In any event I was unsure that I could ask them to help me find the blasted car. All I had to go on was that it was ten minutes' walk into the estate and near wasteland. I would like to say I found the car within a few minutes but I did not. It was almost an hour of systematic trawling up and down the estate before I noticed a track between two houses that opened onto the wasteland. There, parked in beautiful isolation, was George's precious car. I could have kissed it. Heaven knows what I was thinking when I parked it but it was a lesson learned.

Dawn was in the shower when I returned home so I took my now preferred option and imposed myself on George. After a warm shower and a hot tea, I sat down and amused him with my tales of incompetence.

*

I am never sure whether we dictate events or events dictate us. Aunt Gladys was the first to call me but she was joined by Dawn; they had the *Gazette*. They were less interested in the front page, which had a picture of PC Over, Eleanor and the Chief Constable with a headline of 'Let's be marrying you', than the article and pictures on page 3. There was the story of the bravery of

Sandra and I in making the whole bedside engagement story possible. Both Aunt Gladys and Dawn were drilling down further as it stated that Sandra was my fiancée. I joked that they must not believe everything they read in the papers. Aunt Gladys was telling me just how beautiful she looked and how we made a handsome couple. I was slightly bemused but thought the *Gazette* error was hardly going to change my life so I was not too bothered. George was as enthusiastic about Sandra as Aunt Gladys was, telling me that he did not mind his car being used for such a beautiful girl.

*

Tuesday was the TA drill night. The *Gazette* was pinned on the notice board so anyone who had not known of the incident did now. Eddie was back from honeymoon and was first to see me as I entered the hall. He was standing with Badger, Ginge Jock, Ra-Ra and two others. He brought them to attention and saluted. I saluted back. They were all grinning. 'Well, sir, congratulations' was the general consensus. I knew it was more about the fiancée statement than the rescue but just nodded. I thought it would blow over faster if I said nothing rather than trying to explain. I was heading to training wing when the Colour Sergeant, who a week ago would have just kept his head down and ignored me, caught up with me. He said, 'Saved the man's life with the rescue, sir. All the MOW are impressed. Oh, and the OC would like to see you in his office.' The MOW were the 'men of war' a strange collective term used by some of the senior ranks to refer to the soldiers.

The OC told me he had called me into his freshly painted office to delve further into my fame. He was delighted that Sandra and I were to get the Chief Constable's commendation and told me it would be noted on my military record. He asked when we were planning to marry. I explained that the fiancée statement was incorrect and how my relationship with Sandra had simply been one lift home. He smiled and said, 'Well, she's an attractive girl, so don't let the grass grow.' I ventured that she worked with Spanswick's wife. He frowned and told me that as long as she was not Spanswick's wife and I kept a professional distance from Spanswick, I would be fine. 'No double-dating,' he added. 'What about a job?' he asked and I was worried he was going to start a lecture like my father. 'You could "go regular".' He was suggesting I join the Army full time.

I thanked him and said, 'maybe.' I nodded, saluted and went back to the training wing. Tonight, there was arms drill, followed with, by popular demand, the reel from *Tunes of Glory*.

CHAPTER 11

How do you find somebody who nobody thinks is missing? I thought I had probably left it too late to go to the police to report Aiden. If I went now, it would really be to report the ring, the money and the jacket, and would be more of a 'found property' issue rather than a lost owner. I sat with the blank sheet of paper and discussed my thoughts with a decidedly disinterested Tonto. I went over and held Aiden's jacket. I wanted it to talk to me. It had given so many gifts, was there anything more? I started to list out on a piece of card what I knew. There was his ring, I recalled, he said he was a descendant of Macbeth or someone but that could not help. The book of matches from the Blue Bell. Not one but several, maybe a trip there and a chat to the barman could be helpful. His fancy cigarettes! Yes, he smoked those black fancy cigarettes. I jumped up and startled Tonto who jumped at the same time. Where do you buy black fancy fags near where Aiden shopped? I put my running kit on. I could not find any socks so decided to run without any. Neither Dawn nor Aunt Gladys were in the house so I locked up, hoping that one of them would have a key. I ran to the tobacconist in Long Benson. The shop was two doors from the Post Office where George picked up his pension. It was where George bought his cigars! The shop was in a time warp, it had pipes and smoking paraphernalia in the window and only sold cigarettes, cigars and smoking equipment. The shopkeeper was old and yellow and of indeterminate age. He smelled of tobacco and his smile was tainted by brown teeth. He was quizzical, telling me that his usual customers did not run to buy their cigarettes. I explained that I had a friend who only smoked fancy black cigarettes and I was hoping to see him and surprise him with a packet. The chap's face lit up. 'Marlboro do a vintage and Dunhill have a range but the best by a country mile is Sobranie Black Russians. As a matter of fact, I do have five hundred. My regular smoker never collected his order.'

I said, 'Do many people buy them here?'

The man replied, 'Not now, my one regular customer, King Malcolm, hasn't been in for months. It was him that didn't collect this batch.'

'King Malcolm?' I exclaimed! 'Is that Aiden Malcolm, descendant of Macbeth or someone?'

'Well descendant of Robert the Bruce actually,' he answered.

'That's who I'm trying to find,' I shrieked. I had suddenly become over-excited and apologised as I calmed myself down. 'Do you have any idea where he lives?' The shopkeeper went on to tell me that Malcolm lived in a caravan on a construction site. He used to call in once a month to collect his five hundred pack of Black Russian. We were interrupted by a man buying a tin of gold flake tobacco. He moaned about the cost and claimed the tin was smaller than he was used to. The tobacconist reassured him that the price had remained the same for over a year and the tin was the 2oz size. The customer scoffed and muttered under his breath before paying and leaving.

The tobacconist told me that Malcolm had not collected his last order. He bent down under the counter and brought out a ledger book. Malcolm had paid for the five hundred but did not collect them. He smiled and added, 'So in theory, if you are going to see him, you could take them to him.'

I explained, 'I already had his coat and other items and was looking for him.'

He coughed as he said to me, 'I do have a telephone number beside his address at the construction site.' He gave me the number and I expected the bridging site but it was a number I did not recognise. I took the big packet of Black Russian cigarettes and the tobacconist's number. I told him that I would have Malcolm call him when I had found him. As I was leaving, the tobacconist told me how much the packet I was carrying was worth.

I said, 'You are kidding me!'

He said, 'No, only the cocktail Sobranies are more expensive.' I ran home thinking Aiden was one rich man. I was also cursing myself for neglecting to wear any socks as I was getting a blister on my heel.

*

Back at Aunt Gladys's house, there was still no one home so I tried the telephone number I had been given. A lady answered. I asked for Aiden. She said no one of that name is known here and hung up. I tried again apologising that I should have asked for Mr Malcolm. She was curt and said, 'You have the wrong number' and hung up again. I could not be sure but it could have been the lady from the Bastle House. I had a warm shower and put some cream on my heel as it was chafed. I dressed and I went next door and related the story to George. He was not particularly interested as he was too distracted by the cost of the Black Russians. He was trying to work out the cost of each individual cigarette. We agreed that if we did not find Malcolm, he could take them to his Western Front Association instead of the cigars.

I felt an enthusiasm for pursuing the matter further. I had been distracted and losing interest but the spark was reignited. I would find out who lived at the Bastle house. I had planned on just going back and interrogating the lady but thought a visit to the library may be easier. I felt sure they would have some sort of public record or would know how to find out the information I sought.

*

The library, being a municipal building, was not far from the Registry Office where Big Eddie was married. I parked in the same spot and walked to the entrance which was behind the Town Hall. I was adjacent to the front of the Town Hall where Carole worked. On a whim I walked in. There was a long reception desk with a girl sitting to one side. She smiled and asked if she could help. I said I was trying to find out who lived at a house. She said. 'Oh, you want to see the electoral roll?' I had no idea what it was but nodded as if I did. She continued by saying that there was a copy in the library but if I waited, she would see if a colleague could help me. She went to the phone and started to scroll through a list of names and numbers on a rolling file system. I mentioned that I had a friend working here as a passing comment. She asked who, and I told her Carole. She smiled again and added that she worked in the right department so she would phone her. I said it was not necessary but she insisted. I felt a cold sweat and my chest was heaving. It was anxiety and I tried to regulate my breathing to stay in control. I was not listening to what the receptionist was saying down the phone but recall her suggesting I wait by the door on one of the seats. I moved towards them without speaking, mindful that I should be thanking the girl but no words would come out. I sat down wondering what on earth I would say to Carole. I did not have long to think as she appeared across the open reception area smiling and waving. We exchanged pleasantries and I did not have to say anything more. Carole was holding a map which she said gave the electoral districts so once she had the address, she could look in the appropriate electoral roll. I calmed down and gave her the information. The Bastle House was not in her area but she had access to all the neighbouring constituencies and was happy to go up to her office to find the information. I was left standing in a far calmer disposition. I walked over to the receptionist and apologised for my ignorance in not thanking her earlier. She just smiled.

When Carole came back, she was brandishing a slip of paper she had taken from an open envelope. She had written down all those on the electoral roll at the Bastle House. I thanked her. She had not asked why I needed the information and I did not tell her. She asked me about the parachuting which she reminded me I had mentioned to her and Craig at Dave's Party. I explained that I had planned to invite her away to an airfield near Bridlington for a wild weekend. I told her a TA friend had just set up a private parachuting school. I went on to explain he was running weekend courses and I had hoped she might fancy the challenge. She said she would love to go but would need to ask Craig. I nodded and said, 'Well if you are interested give me a ring and I'll organise some dates.' I wrote Aunt Gladys's number on the envelope that had held the Bastle house information.

She kissed me on the cheek saying 'got to go' and skipped back over to the access door to the lifts. I thanked the receptionist one more time and headed back to the car.

I had no idea what Carole was thinking. Was she going to come with me skydiving or was she coming with Craig? If she was bringing Craig, did I really want to be there? It all seemed a little weird. I looked at the paper she had given me. It had three numbers and three names listed Albert G Cattermole, Amelia J Cattermole and Amy G Cattermole. At least I had solved one problem.

By the time I had arrived home I had resolved to invite Sandra skydiving if Carole was bringing Craig. It did seem cynical but I was not playing gooseberry. She had explained to Craig that I was married and even though I cleared the confusion up with her, I had no idea whether she had cleared it up with Craig.

*

On the Tuesday at the TA centre, I spoke to Marcus who had set up the parachute school. He told me that if I could get six people, I could go free or knock a fifth off everybody's fee. The school was in its infancy and so most weekends were free, save for the bank holiday. I suggested the following weekend and he agreed. Marcus asked me who I was planning to bring. He assumed it was some of the soldiers. I mentioned that I was minded to invite Carole and Sandra. He was surprised and spluttered. He asked me with some incredulity as to whether women would want to jump. I asked why would they not. He pondered and then said, 'Well I can make over the double room for them and they could use the staff shower.' He seemed quite happy with his plan. I told him that by appealing to women he could double the number of potential guests to his centre. He strode off somewhat pleased with himself.

I thought about asking Dave and Heather but decided that there was no point complicating matters, especially if the accommodation was uncertain and until I was sure what Carole was planning.

I was to find out the following night, just as I was leaving Aunt Gladys to take George to his British Legion meeting. The phone rang and it was Carole. She and Craig were free for the weekend and what were the plans? Thinking on my feet I suggested that she and Craig meet us at the aerodrome at 1800 on the Friday. They needed sleeping bags and tough walking boots. Carole asked whether they were in tents and I said, 'No we'll all be in a former Air Force block.' She asked if the women were in separate accommodation. I was pleased that I had raised this with Marcus and was able to say yes. I had not mentioned Sandra to her as I had not asked her and I still needed to clear the use of George's car. George was a bit grumpy that the phone call had delayed me. I was not sure it was the best time to ask about borrowing the car but I ploughed in. George, surprisingly, was more than happy that I used his car but he wanted to come with us. I tried to explain that with his dodgy leg walking was a danger, never mind dropping from 2000ft. He asked if he could just be on someone's back. I explained that there was the small matter of the parachute. He laughed but still said he planned on jumping one day.

*

Sandra was a different story. I called round at her house on the following evening before heading off to the TA centre. I was careful to park very close to the edge pointing in the right direction. I rang the bell and heard what was probably Mrs McGregor shouting to Sandra. There was a long wait until Sandra answered the door. She was wearing her dressing gown and her head was wrapped in a towel. I had hoped that she would be pleased to see me but she just said, 'Yes.' There were no pleasantries, nor hint of surprise.

I apologised for not being in contact and received no response so just blundered in to, 'Please will you come parachuting this weekend?'

There was a pause and she said, 'You may as well come in.' I followed her into the sitting room where her mother was sitting in the same chair as the night I met her.

Mrs McGregor was pleased to see me and told me so. I explained to Mrs McGregor that I wanted to take Sandra away from her for the weekend. She laughed and said, 'Just for the weekend, surely it can be far longer than that?' Sandra told her not to encourage me as I was in her 'bad books'. Sandra sat at the dropleaf table behind her mother and started painting her nails. I sat opposite Mrs McGregor. I explained that a colleague had just started a parachute school and I wanted to take Sandra. I found myself explaining that we were trained on the Saturday and jump on the Sunday morning, weather permitting. Mrs McGregor seemed more enthusiastic than Sandra. She asked about the height we jumped from and who did the training. She mixed questions about the parachuting with those that were to protect Sandra such as whether there were any other women and were we insured? I answered as best I could. I gave reassurance that I would look out for Sandra. I explained that the only clothes that were needed were some strong boots. Sandra asked her mother where her boots might be as she had not seen them for months. Mrs McGregor tasked me with going through to the garage and looking on the top shelf of some drawers. I was happy to do so. The garage was very neat. Every tool and garden implement had its own space. All the garage was dominated by what appeared to be a low sports car covered by a fine dust sheet. I was tempted to look underneath but just found the boots and returned to the front room. I showed them to Sandra's mother who held them and checked they were all serviceable. She said to Sandra that the last time they were out were for the university field trip.

Sandra replied, 'Mother,' and Mrs McGregor apologised. She suggested that Sandra try them on. She could not turn round to see Sandra as her mobility was so restricted so she gave them back to me. Sandra stuck out a bare foot and said if the glass boot fitted, she would go to the ball. I knelt down and after slackening the laces put the left boot on. Sandra lifted her leg and rested the boot on my shoulder. She smiled as I stumbled back on my haunches. I was somewhat shocked by the flash of white knickers and thigh. 'What about the right foot? They both have to fit,' she teased me.

I bent back down and eased on her right boot. I held the back of her leg and even when the boot was snuggly on her foot, I did not move my hand. 'Sandra looks perfect,' I said to Mrs McGregor as I continued to stroke Sandra's leg.

Mrs McGregor replied, 'Is there anything else she will need?'

I stood up and walked back to the sofa. 'Just a sleeping bag,' I added. I explained to Sandra and her mother that I was off to my TA night and had to leave. Mrs McGregor said, 'Well Rowan is picking Sandra up at seven so she had better get her skates on too.' Sandra smiled but said nothing. As I stood up my head was dizzy; I had a tightening of my chest. I felt hot and my mouth went dry. I thought I was going to faint but wiggled my toes and shook my shoulders. It must have looked odd but I was determined not to react. I was simply jealous. I so wanted to hug Sandra and scream undying love to her but stayed calm. 'I will pick you up at six thirty on Friday,' I casually added. 'Sorry you had better make it eight as it is late night salon and I am meant to be working until nine. I will escape at seven thirty.'

I was totally distracted at the TA thinking of Sandra and Rowan out on a date. I wanted to ask Big Eddie what he knew of Sandra's recent activities but, luckily, he was not in, so I was saved from myself. I had Carole and Sandra with me for the weekend and had no idea what was going to happen.

Most weeks rush by but I was listless and distracted thinking of Sandra and whether I actually wanted to jump from a perfectly sound aircraft.

CHAPTER 12

The aerodrome had been an RAF station that had been transferred to private ownership after the war. The housing was sold off and the perimeter redrawn to leave an airstrip, small control towers, several small hangars and an administration block. Sandra and I arrived last and the gathered group were in the makeshift Mess room when we arrived. Marcus came over and said he would show us to our rooms. I grabbed both of our sleeping bags and both bags and followed him across the internal courtyard. 'You're in here with me,' he said as he pushed open a room with two beds and a wardrobe. I dropped my bag and sleeping bag and followed Marcus with Sandra further along the corridor to another double room. 'This is where Sandra is with the other girl,' he explained. I dropped off Sandra's bag and threw her sleeping bag on the bed. As we stood at the open door Marcus pointed out the showers and ablutions. Sandra said she needed a couple of moments to unpack and would meet Marcus and I in the Mess room.

There were only ten on the course and two instructors. Marcus did the administration and was qualified to pack parachutes. The pilots came on the Sunday morning to fly the planes. Saturday was all learning. I suddenly felt apprehensive. I had never been in a plane before and worried that I was going to be too scared to jump. Craig was surrounded by several men round an open fire. Carole was sitting in front of a chessboard and, as I walked over to her, I saw that it was set up just as the game we had left in her bedroom some months earlier. Carole stood up to give me a hug. 'We have a game to finish,' said Carole as she pointed down to the board. I feigned terror saying that the parachute jump would be easier than beating her. I sat with her. I looked at the knight that had put my king in check. I had been so close to victory. I had not given the game a second thought. I had a chance to relook at the situation and it did not look promising. She told me that the board was still in her room and she considered the position every night so was confident she would get the better of me. I was not sure the game she was playing but I was concerned that it was not chess. I asked her if she was ready for the jump telling her that I was apprehensive when we were joined by Craig. He was a rather 'jolly fellow' slapping me on the back. I was going to try and like him for Carole's sake but it was going to be difficult. He was dismissive of the chess and clearly did not play, as he called it Carole's foolish pastime. I caught Carole's eye and she raised them. I was able to escape when Marcus beckoned me over. He had two forms for Sandra and I to complete. Everyone else had sorted their administration earlier and he was anxious that our disclaimer form was complete. I briefly read how I would not blame Marcus and his company for any mistakes. I did not dwell too deeply as it made me think of what I was signing up to do. I took Sandra's form and went to find her.

She was not in her room and so I walked towards the runway where I saw a figure standing gazing at the night sky. I did not sneak up but when I spoke, she jumped. I apologised for startling her. Sandra started talking quietly, 'My dad used to race his Triumph at an airfield near Darlington. I don't remember the cars nor the races but I do remember watching the sky from my small bed in the back of the car. I was only a toddler but the stars have stayed with me. I was only five when Dad died. He had MS too.' Strange that it was such a dreadful illness that brought them together. I put my arm around her and she snuggled in close. I thought silence was appropriate, although I had a burning desire to show off my knowledge by identifying, Cassiopeia, Sirius and the Pleiades. I was so pleased to be away from Carole, she had made me feel uncomfortable.

Sandra mentioned our early start and we walked back to the block in silence. I am sure we could have kissed as I felt strangely close to her but it did not seem right. Marcus was already in his sleeping bag and we chatted briefly when I returned from the bathroom. I did not sleep; I was anxious about jumping out of a plane but also worried about where my life was going.

*

After what could be described as a camping breakfast, everyone was kitted out in green overalls and given a helmet and goggles.

Marcus gave an hour-long introductory talk that started with a question: If our main chute did not open and our reserve chute did not open, how long would it take for us to land from 2000ft? I tried to remember my physics and the equation. The answer was 'a lifetime'.

We all groaned but it did remind us that things were getting serious. He included the history of parachuting and the history of the airfield, him and his company. We had a break for coffee and then the first lessons on parachute landing falls. The lesson was taken by the other instructor, Kurt. He had obviously recognised Craig as 'the big I am' and used him for one of the early demonstrations. Despite his bravado, Craig could not co-ordinate the bending of the knees followed by a fall forward down onto the thigh and then a rollover bringing the legs up and over. It was simply a controlled fall but the more Craig tried to think about it, the more ridiculous it looked. It came to a point where Kurt got us all up and we started falling and rolling for the next thirty minutes. Carole and Sandra were particularly good and, whilst I was not perfect, I felt confident that it was coming naturally. The next lesson was on the parachute. We learned that it was opened automatically as we fell from the plane by a static line. The line was attached to the plane and to the parachute. As we fell, the line would open the chute and we would fall to earth, approximately 2000ft. We learned that as we left the door of the aircraft we had to shout, one thousand, two thousand, three thousand, four thousand, check canopy. The check would make sure that the 80ft wide canopy had opened above us. If it had not, we had to pay particular attention to the next lesson with Marcus. We had to learn to discard the chute that had malfunctioned and cast the reserve chute from its position on our stomach. This spare chute would save our lives. We practised this manoeuvre until it was second nature. Whether it would be as easy when falling at terminal velocity was another question. I think this was the first time I started to realise that I was justified in being apprehensive. In fact, justified in being scared. We stopped for lunch. I should have had an appetite but was just thirsty. I went to get a glass of water and was joined by Carole. 'I think this is just so exciting,' she said. I told her that I did not mind admitting it but I was scared. She laughed and told me that it was my fault they were here and I had better lead by example. It was perhaps the pep talk I needed as I went back after lunch with more steel in my backbone. After lunch we moved over to an area where there was a series of steps getting gradually higher. We took turns running up the steps, jumping off and doing a parachute landing fall as we landed. It was all going so well until a huge chap stumbled and crashed over onto his shoulder. I just assumed he must have broken a shoulder as he had fallen so hard. He was surrounded by Marcus, Kurt and two others so I could not see what was happening. Then the casualty stood up in the group saying in a stage whisper, 'Tis nothing but an inconvenience.' He was clearly hurt but explained to Marcus he had suffered far worse rugby injuries. Marcus made him sit out the next few jumps despite his protests. It did make everyone more cautious. The crunch of the Rugger Bugger's fall from six feet reminded us of what could happen from two thousand.

*

We had a visit to the parachute packing shed as the last activity of the day. We watched a demonstration of how the chutes were packed and then watched whilst Marcus packed our own chutes in front of us. I did feel ready to jump. Whether I would feel as keen in the morning was another question. Sandra had her chute packed first by Kurt, and had waved as she went back to the block. She had said that she wanted a shower before the water went cold. On my way back to the room I was caught up with by Marcus. He told me that he had done what Craig had asked and swapped rooms. I had no idea what he was talking about. He told me that Craig had said he was my best friend who had invited him for the weekend and he had hoped to share a room with me. I laughed and told Marcus I had only met Craig twice and he was hardly an acquaintance, never mind a friend. Marcus said that it did not matter anyway. He was happy to move into the bunk above the chute shed which he was going to convert to an office or bedroom anytime soon.

I had visions of Big Eddie. Would Craig want me to write his love letters? I thought I would tread carefully as I did not trust Craig. I was right to be on my guard. When I got back to the room, he was sitting on the bed. There was no acknowledgement he just said, 'Your girlfriend is being a bitch.' I did not like his language and told him so. He raised a hand and said, 'Sorry.'

'What's the problem, has she taken all the hot water?' I offered.

'No,' he replied. 'She won't change rooms with me.' I could see where this was going. I felt quite proud of Sandra for not agreeing to his plot, although sharing a room with Sandra that night did seem fun. 'Why don't you swap with Carole?' he asked.

I said, 'If Sandra doesn't want me with her in this room, why would she want to be with me in her room?' He resigned himself to sharing the room with me. I was seething. He had such a nerve. I went for a shower and then, after hastily dressing, to the Mess room. I ignored Craig throughout. The Rugger Bugger wore a sling to supper. He told the gathered throng that his shoulder would be fine by morning. Supper was rather muted. Carole arrived late and left early. She and Craig were clearly on different flight paths. This was not me saying that but a direct quote from Jerry who was sitting next to me who had noticed. Jerry was one of the group who had spent his first evening drinking with Craig.

*

After supper I asked Sandra if she wanted to look at the stars. She giggled and so did Jerry. It did sound corny when they made fun of me but I had been earnest. We wandered over to the back of the sheds as it was darker because the security light did not cover the area. We both lay on our backs and gazed to the firmament and chatted about space, the moon missions and the stars.

Sandra said something about turning me into stars and forming a constellation in my image. She said my face would make the heavens so beautiful that the world would fall in love with the night. It sounded Shakespearian and I guessed she was paraphrasing Juliet so I asked if we were 'star-crossed lovers'.

Sandra sat up and said it was so nice to have someone who recognised Shakespeare. 'You truly are a clever and lovely man.' I smiled as I remembered drafting Big

Eddie's love letter and my half-baked illusions to culture. 'Is Carole your Rosaline or your Juliet?' she asked. I did not have enough knowledge of the play to answer and had no idea who Rosaline was but replied that Sandra was my Juliet and that I loved being in her company. It was clearly the right answer as she leaned over me, hugged me and we kissed. We lay entwined for several minutes and then Sandra sat up again.

She told me that if she had not liked Carole so much, she would have swapped rooms. I joked that maybe it was me that Sandra did not like. She told me that she and I would have plenty of time together when we wanted, but this was neither the time nor place. I found myself agreeing. She went on to say that Carole had not expressly said that she did not want to swap, but Sandra felt Craig was being a bully. I told her how proud I was of her. Almost on cue we both shrieked as we saw a shooting star. It was the perfect backdrop on a calm and stress-free night. Then I remembered we were jumping out of a plane in the morning.

*

As we walked back, I asked Sandra how she was so knowledgeable about Shakespeare and she told me she had played Juliet in her school play. She also mentioned almost in passing that she had planned to read English Literature at university but that was on hold. She added, 'It has to be about mother.' I was being truly surprised by this photographer/hairdresser.

Craig was a noisy sleeper and it took me ages to drop off. I was anxious about the jump but also anxious about where Sandra and I were heading. I was pleased that the work and Malcolm issues now seemed so long ago.

*

Everyone but Rugger Bugger started the day with some parachute landing falls. We then walked over to the two aircraft. I was told that one was a Cessna and one a Piper Cherokee. I never knew which was which as we did all our practice sitting in a mock-up plane door. In the mock-up we looked over our right shoulder into the plane ready to push out when told by the jumpmaster. Each plane only held five so we were put into three sticks of four. We were joined by two others who had done the training on an earlier weekend but had not jumped due to the high wind. Both were nervous and it showed. Marcus tried to reassure them that they would remember everything when the time came but they did not look convinced. I felt anxious just watching them. I prayed that I would remember everything, mindful that I had learned it the day before. I am not sure if it was planned by Marcus, but Sandra, Craig, Carole and I were all in the same stick and sent together to the nearest parked plane. We were all crushed in and shown our positions. This was just a rehearsal and we did not have our parachutes and the plane engine was off. The pilot gave us his briefing. I confess that there was such little blood in my brain that I did not take anything in. He talked of wind and the like but it was lost on me in my small bubble. Sandra and I held hands and she kept squeezing and that did keep me partially alert. Craig was in the door. He was looking miserable. I could not work out whether it was the prospect of jumping out of a plane or his missed night with Carole that troubled him. He would jump first, followed by Carole, Sandra and, finally, me.

*

The first plane took off whilst we were fitting our chutes. We watched it climb. We were meant to go out to the second plane but Marcus called forward the third group. They were all ready to go and I presume he wanted to save time. They went out to the plane we were anticipating being on. It delayed matters for us but did allow us to watch the first descent. We counted them all out and watched the canopies open. It all seemed so perfect in slow motion. We watched the second group fly out just as the first group were landing on the other side of the airfield. Kurt took a Land Rover to go and collect them. I lost track of time but was brought back down by a shout from Marcus. The first plane was ready and we had to walk over. My heart was beating and I was hot and uncomfortable. I grabbed Sandra's hand; it was just the support I needed. It was clammy and we both looked at each other through frightened eyes. I tried to smile but it was weak. Carole was struggling to bend to tie a bootlace because of her reserve chute. I struggled to bend down but was just able to help her. It put our arrival at the aircraft door in the wrong order. I planned on waiting at the aircraft step so we could climb in in the same order that we had practised. As I stood at the door, I realised that the plane door configuration was different. I shouted to the jumpmaster. He pulled a face and said you just climb onto this strut and drop away. 'It is easier than you have been shown.' I was staggered. 'Climb onto the strut!' I was only feeling brave because I planned on looking into the aircraft and being pushed out when I was told to go. I was feeling cheated. I would never have the nerve to step out onto the strut. Sandra seemed unconcerned. Craig was put in the plane first, then Carole, followed by Sandra and me. The order was reversed. I had to go first. I wanted the plane to take forever to get to 2000ft but it did not. I was terrified as the jumpmaster tapped my shoulder and checked my static line. He pointed to the wheel strut and urged me forward pushing my elbow. I remember grimacing at Sandra. She pointed to my disco leg. It was vibrating with fear as the jumpmaster manhandled me to the strut. I do not remember much. The air rushing past my face distracted me just enough so I did not see down as I dropped off the wheel strut. I remember the counting, one thousand, two thousand, and looking up seeing the huge canopy open and then the silence. I did not finish counting. I was hanging in the air. I could see the sea, the town and the Yorkshire Wolds. It was heaven for what appeared to be moments. The knowledge that I was safe was comforting. I then tried to switch back on in readiness for the ground-rush and hitting the earth. I do recall the ground coming to meet my feet but I just crumpled into a heap. Had I done a parachute landing fall? I had no idea. My canopy was billowing and pulling me downwind. I was losing control of it and, as it pulled me over, I faceplanted in the grass. When I stood up, I was able to collapse the chute and gather it in. I had the first chance to look around. Carole was only three hundred yards from me and I saw her land beautifully. I could see Sandra, off to my left, had already landed and was gathering her chute. I felt a sense of euphoria. It was a mixture of excitement and relief. I wanted the sensation again but without the exit from the aircraft. I wanted to hug someone and it could even have been Craig. I looked about for him but he was nowhere to be seen. I wondered whether he had been blown back towards the other side of the airstrip as it was slightly in dead ground. It had been where Kurt had picked up most of the first stick. I could see the Land Rover arriving to pick up Sandra. I stopped walking and decided to wait. Carole was waving and I waved back. Sandra was sitting in the back of the Land Rover. She had removed her helmet and had shaken down her hair. She jumped down and hugged me, thanking me profusely. I shook Marcus's hand as he helped me off with my pack and into the back of the vehicle. We collected Carole who was also buzzing. She hugged both Marcus and me and Sandra. We expected to drive over to Craig but Marcus was driving straight back to the block. Carole asked where he was. Marcus said, 'Oh he took a more conventional route back.'

There was a pause before Sandra said, 'Did he jump?' Marcus tried to play it down by saying that the wind may have picked up so he would have to await the report.

No one spoke. Back at the administration block we handed back our parachutes and watched them being carefully inspected. We then had a sandwich lunch followed by the presentation of certificates. We had all been bonded by the common thrill of the jump and there was much hugging and back-slapping. Rugger Bugger had jumped against Marcus's advice and was planning a trip to A&E if he could get there driving with one arm. He had my sympathy. 'Been there, done that!' I told him. Craig was nowhere to be seen. Carole went to look for him and came back incredulous telling everyone that he had just upped and gone. He had abandoned her. Jerry told her she was well rid of him. Rugger Bugger asked if she could drive.

Marcus presented the certificates and explained how we could train to do freefall. He explained how the aircraft were taking up parachutists that very afternoon and that on future weekends if we joined the British Parachute Association we could jump whenever we liked. I had done my jump and, despite the euphoria, was not too bothered about doing it again. Carole gave me a hug as she left to drive Rugger Bugger to A&E. She thanked me for the experience and thanked me for helping her to see what a poor judge of character she was. I wanted to say more but was sure I would have just made matters very complicated, so I just hugged her again. There was a tear in her eye, and had I not bitten my lip, there would have been a tear in mine.

Sandra slept in the front of the car as we drove over

the North York Moors. I was quite pleased as it gave me time to reflect on the whole weekend.

CHAPTER 13

Sandra woke up as we were leaving the moors. She scolded me for letting her sleep. She complained that she missed what was one of the most beautiful roads in Britain. I asked if she was always grumpy when she woke up. She put her hand across my shoulder and squeezed my neck. She told me that it had been a wonderful weekend and she was only sorry that she had not been able to sleep beside me on the weekend. She added that I could then have found out how grumpy she was first thing in the morning. I was unsure how to respond but found myself blushing which was definitely not right. Sandra laughed. 'You are such a strange one,' she told me. 'I'm usually trying to beat men off with a stick but you are at best disinterested and at worst, preoccupied with something or someone else. Are you interested in me?' she asked. She leaned towards me and stared at the side of my head. I tried to pick my words carefully and deflect the question. I said that she had some nerve challenging me, given that she had been out with Rowan at least once that week. 'Are you jealous?' she inquired.

'Insanely so,' I replied. I was not joking as I remembered how anxious I was when her mother mentioned their date.

'See,' she said, thinking I was being cold. 'You weren't the slightest bit curious when Mum told you that he was picking me up.'

I wanted this conversation to continue, not least so I could find out more about Sandra and Rowan but I was distracted as I had just missed the junction. I cursed my bad driving as I did not know where I could get back onto the road we needed. Sandra was no help as she did not drive and seemed clueless as to where we were, never mind where we were going. We moved on to talk about her driving lessons that seemed sporadic and then onto the sports car in her mum's garage. Sandra did not know much about it, save that it was her father's pride and joy. Her mum did not want to sell it but could not drive so it sat in the garage gathering dust. Sandra told me that her father wanted to drive Sandra to her wedding in the car and that her mum still harboured the notion that it would be kept for that purpose. Sandra had tears in her eyes as she told the story. I lightened the mood by telling her I would drive her to the church, but only if she promised not to marry Rowan. I took what I hoped was a left turn and started trying to concentrate on getting back on track. I had driven too far east and found myself approaching the southern end of the bypass. I was suddenly orientated. I could drive over the yellow brick road and up past the houses on the hill. My heart started racing and my pulse quickened. Sandra put her hand on my thigh. I reciprocated and put my hand on hers. The car had a bench seat in the front and Sandra moved closer to me. 'Do you mind if I show you the road I built?' I asked her.

'Gosh you sure know how to charm a girl!' she groaned.

I pulled off the slip road and onto the newly completed bypass. This was the end where I had parked Dave's car when I walked up to the culvert. We would be driving over the point where I had been almost killed by the Volvo dump truck. I felt a slight anger. Sandra squeezed my thigh and asked me if I got excited when I saw the road I built. I squeezed hers and said that she excited me more. 'Right answer,' she replied.

*

We drove over the bridge and along towards where the offices had been. There were still some residual cabins as the landscaping and remedial work continued. I headed off left and onto the road up the hill. I pulled over opposite the two beautiful houses. Sandra said, 'This is a bit exposed if you are planning to take advantage of me.' I agreed with her. I leaned over and kissed her. She was warm and sensuous and snuggled up close. I broke off the clinch as a car was leaving the drive of the left-hand house. It was a Jaguar. It looked similar to that driven by Mr Hollingsworth but as he was the only person I knew with one, it was hardly surprising. I wanted it to be his but could not see the driver. I made a note of the numberplate. Sandra was sitting back with a frown. 'You should be trying to get my bra and knickers off, but you're more interested in cars.' She started laughing but there was some truth in her statement. I found myself apologising again and told her that I was trying to solve a mystery. Sandra shook her head. 'You're trying to solve a mystery; try sitting in my seat, you are the man of mystery!'

I told Sandra that I would tell my story from the beginning on the drive home. I said that I did want to ravish her but not on the front seat of George's car parked outside a villain's house. Sandra was particularly pleased that I used the term ravish as it sounded fun. I secretly hoped I was not going to disappoint her. Sandra was like no other girl I had met and she was making me nervous.

Sandra stayed quiet for the rest of the trip as I recounted everything from my interview in Leeds right through to walking out with Tonto. Each time I paused and asked if she'd had enough, she said, 'No, go on.' When I had finished, she asked me two things, the first was what was I going to do next, and the second, which gave me a warm glow, was how could she help.

*

Mrs McGregor was waiting in her armchair when we arrived back. A nurse had been in to see her and she explained it had disrupted her day. She apologised for the mess as she had had no time to tidy up. The room looked clean to me but Sandra busied herself taking out plates and generally tidying up whilst I gave her mum a summary of the weekend. Mrs McGregor asked if I would stay for tea and I was happy to do so.

Sandra wheeled Mrs McGregor to what was clearly her side of the dining room table. There was a mat on the floor and a mat under the plate which seemed to be non-slip. Mrs McGregor had to drink out of a cup with a lid and she did not have the full use of her right arm. Sandra was at pains to tell me that it was nothing fancy, just what she had prepared before she went away for the weekend. She added that it was a stew and her mother would be sick of it as she had had it every meal that weekend. Mrs McGregor did not correct her but said, 'Well, beggars can't be choosers.' The stew was excellent. There were only two baked potatoes as I had not been expected. I tried to decline but neither mum nor daughter would back down so I took the smallest and the other was divided in two. I realised just how Mrs McGregor relied on Sandra and just why Sandra had been obliged to stay at home. There was clearly some help for Mrs McGregor but not enough to release Sandra. I wanted to ask so many questions but it was easier to just enjoy the meal. There was an apple crumble for pudding and Sandra opened a tin of custard. I told Mrs McGregor about George and how he had three helpers cooking for him and how everything had to have gravy or custard. Mrs McGregor asked if he needed a housemate. This raised Sandra's hackles and mother and daughter had some banter about how helpful Sandra was and if her mother was not happy, she could leave. I was probably being a bit too keen to ingratiate myself with Mrs McGregor but I asked what had made the crumble so spicy and she replied, 'Oh that's the cinnamon, it makes it hotter than a pepper sprout.'

I said, 'So it's a Johnny Cash recipe.'

'Of course,' she replied and Sandra added 'married in a fever'. I suddenly realised that Sandra was my Roxanne. She and I had both been writing love letters to each other and neither knew. I kept quiet but could not wait to find out if it was true.

I offered to help with the washing up but Sandra told me that she would sort it. Mrs McGregor reminded Sandra that she needed a bath and I took this as my turn to leave. It had been a long weekend and I was shattered. Sandra walked me to the car. We did not say much and the kiss was cursory. She thanked me for a great weekend. I wound the window down and blew her a kiss and her Parthian shot was to shout, 'When are you going to ravish me?' I am not sure she could see my blush. I had not arranged to see her again and felt that had been stupid.

*

There was one development back at Auntie Gladys's house. Someone, who I presume to be Colin, as I had given him George's address for contacting me, had delivered two letters to George. One was for Dawn and had contained a cheque. There was a short note hoping she was well and telling her that money would be dropped in monthly as agreed. Dawn was pleased but as she had no bank account, had no idea what to do with the cheque. Aunt Gladys was happy to help her sort it out for which I was grateful. The second letter was to me from my old employer. As I had left without notice and without a forwarding address, they had not settled my outstanding pay. Enclosed was a brown packet with £75 and some loose change. It was dated almost a month earlier and I wondered how long Colin had held onto it and whether he had been tempted. I went through to put the notes with Aiden's stash but whilst doing so stopped.

I did not wish to mix the money so I untwisted a jar that was fixed by its lid screwed to the underside of the shelf. Albert must have used the jars to store small items. I shoved six ten-pound notes into the jar and replaced it. I kept the rest in my wallet.

*

I went early to the drill hall on the Tuesday. Marcus was already there and was keen that I tell everyone what a marvellous facility he was running up near Bridlington. Big Eddie was in. He saluted and asked how the weekend had gone. I told him of the training and the jump but he was clearly wanting to know about Sandra and I. It was my worst fear. I told him she was a super girl and she and I discussed Shakespeare just like he and Jacqui had done. Eddie was confused but I added nothing further. I did use the opportunity to ask Eddie the name of Jacqui's salon and he told me it was 'Good Hair Day'.

*

Next day I parked George's car just down from the hospital making a careful note of where. It was just past 1100 and I walked for twenty minutes to 'Good Hair Day'. It was a typical town salon and it needed a coat of paint. My plan was to take Sandra to lunch. I could see Jacqui by the till near the entrance and what appeared to be one of the twins but I could not see Sandra. It was early so I walked past and into town where I bought a newspaper. I got back to the salon; I heard the Town Hall clock strike noon. It was still too early but I plucked up courage and walked in. Jacqui was delighted to see me and asked if I had come to see Sandra. I smiled and said, 'Yes.' Jacqui grinned and told me that it was her day at college.

Jacqui told me it was not far and gave me vague directions through the town and onto the Dundas College Campus. I presume Jacqui thought I was taking the car and on reflection I should have done, as it was quite a trek. Some hour later I found the entrance. The area was mobbed with students having their lunchbreak. I saw a girl with blue-dyed hair and on impulse asked where the hairdressing department was. She gave me some abuse as she thought I was suggesting she need to have her hair sorted. She called me a stuck-up prick and called over some of her friends. They were all girls but their demeanour reminded me of the sailors in the Victoria Bars. I smiled and walked away continuing to apologise as I did so. I found a crowded, noisy reception and an unhelpful receptionist. The acoustics were shocking and I struggled to hear what the receptionist was saying. She thought I was trying to enrol on a hairdressing course. In the end I accepted the college brochure from her, smiled and started the long walk back to the car. I was sure that Sandra would think I gave up trying to find her too easily so I drove back via her mother's house with a bunch of roses that I picked up at a florist on my walk back to the car. I had planned on giving them to Sandra but when her mother called me in, her eyes lit up so much that I gave them to her and thanked her for feeding me on the Sunday. Mrs McGregor asked me to stay for a cup of tea and, as I had nothing better to do, I did.

CHAPTER 14

I was making myself at home in the shed. Aunt Gladys kept telling me to throw out anything that was not useful to make more space and to make it more homely. I had cleared out all the old rags and clothes that Ted had accumulated and I had filled a dustbin with various bits of wood, metal and broken tools. Amongst the debris was a wooden chess set. I was thrilled with this find but was disappointed to discover that a white pawn and the black queen were missing. George had suggested that I make new pieces on the lathe. I had no idea where to start. I could recognise the lathe on the bench at the back of the shed but that was the extent of my technical knowledge. The result was that I had to manhandle George into the shed so he could supervise the operation. Whilst he did make it sound easy, the reality was somewhat different. The lathe was old and dirty so the first task was to make it serviceable. We then had to select the wood. I had not helped matters by throwing out all the accumulated off-cuts that would have been ideal for the job. The lathe was also too big, an explanation that George only offered after the destruction of the first twenty or so attempts at a pawn. The morning spent shredding wood was useful as it meant George and I could chat. I explained to him how I seemed to be falling into a predictable routine. I did not have a full-time job and, whilst I was not short of money, I was growing anxious that I had yet to join any rat race that my parents desired. I had no career and no career path. I knew what I did not want. I did not want any more studies and I definitely did not want to be an engineer. George laughed and said that I should be enjoying the time as 'something would turn up'.

I confessed to George that I was somewhat distracted by my unplanned passion for Sandra. I tried to convey to him how she was having such an effect on me. He told me that it was love and that was a subject that neither he nor mankind could explain. I said that I had thought I had fallen for Carole. I tried to describe how high I felt the night I danced back from Carole's flat and contrast it with the anguish I felt when I read her rejection letter. Yet now I had almost forgotten her. I had a strange protective feeling for Carole but that was because I had met Craig. George did agree that I should forget Carole, he gave a good explanation to support his advice but I was not listening as I was thinking about Sandra.

Sandra was so much more complex than I had imagined. I had started by being indifferent to her and now could not get her out of my mind. It was weird that Sandra had been my surrogate pen-pal. I wondered if she knew it was me writing Eddie's letters. 'Would I have written anything different had I known?' I was sitting in the outhouse half talking to George and half to a disinterested cat. George had taken over on the lathe. It was so noisy that I could not hear a word I was saying. I marvelled at how oblivious Tonto was to the dust and noise. I went through to the house to get a coffee for George. Dawn and Aunt Gladys had taken over the whole house cutting out a maternity dress. The floor was covered in dress material and the dining table had a sewing machine and sewing detritus everywhere. I made coffee for George and tea for Dawn and Aunt Gladys and then returned to the shed. George was proudly holding up a black pawn and a white queen. I did not have the heart to point out his error as they were such a close match, save for the colours, to the missing pieces. George asked to be taken home as he was going out to lunch with one of his ladies. I manhandled him back through the house and into his wheelchair before pushing him home. It was pouring with rain when I headed back so I had to run.

Tonto had left his perch and had been out. He had returned via my seat and deposited a film of water which I had proceeded to sit in. Sitting uncomfortably, I decided to write Sandra a letter. It was far harder than I anticipated until I tried to write as if I was writing for Eddie. Then the prose flowed. I found that I could be riskier. By the time I had finished the second page I realised that I had completely gone off track and I was thinking more about Sandra's body and the small yellow flower than I was about Sandra. I folded the half-finished letter and stashed it under the somewhat indignant cat. I decided to drive into town and kill time before meeting Sandra from work. I would buy her some chocolates.

*

I grabbed a coat and, having made excuses to Dawn and Aunt Gladys, went to borrow George's car. I had a set of keys but always put my head round his door to tell him where I was going. I assumed he would be out at lunch but he was not. He was in a particularly grumpy mood as his trip to his 'second helper' for lunch had been curtailed by the rain. He explained that she would normally come and collect him and push him to her house for lunch. Today she had simply dropped in a pre-heated pie and chips. They had been wrapped in foil and were lying open on the table. I did have to agree with George that they looked limp and stodgy, like something that Tonto might have dragged in. My plan to meet Sandra from work was amended. George and I would go to the cake shop in the parade near Aiden's tailor.

Parking was easy and I managed to get George and the wheelchair united, without hitch, in record time. We were becoming like a well-oiled racing team. The café had a note on the door saying it was due to close the following Friday as the parade of shops was being redeveloped.

I had not eaten lunch so was happy to join George in

devouring two fresh cream cakes. When we had finished, we had a second cup of coffee and sat in silence. We had exhausted all conversation when trying to turn the chess pieces.

I had noticed a man in the corner who had looked over a couple of times. I had thought that on the first sight he had waved but had not really noticed. After he had paid at the counter he walked over and introduced himself. It was Rowan Connor, the *Gazette* reporter. He reminded me of our meeting at the hospital. I reminded him that he was friendly with Sandra. He said yes and told me he was seeing her tonight. I was speechless and felt a tightening in my chest. George, ever mindful of my moments of stress, asked where he was taking her; adding, 'Anywhere nice?' It seemed so innocent coming from George. I could have hugged George. I was desperate to know more but could not be so bold. I was unsettled by Rowan's reply. She was going to his flat. It was a punch to my solar plexus. I needed water as my mouth was so dry. Rowan spoke to me. Through my clouded brain I could hear him saying, 'You should come too.'

I was dumfounded and blurted out, 'Me?'

'Yes,' he went on, 'we have set up a charity committee and we always need new blood. I'm sure Sandra would be delighted to see you, she always speaks so highly of you.' I dropped back down into my seat as Rowan handed me his card. 'Here's my address, see you at seven if you can make it.' I found myself limply raising my hand as he left.

'What a nice chap,' said George. 'Why did he cause you so much stress? What happened at the hospital?' I needed a drink of water as my throat and mouth were so dry. George called the waiter who was cleaning a table and asked him to get me a glass of water. The waiter rolled his eyes, I presumed he was going to tell me to go to the counter but he did not, he just did as I asked. Once I had a gulp, I told George of the hospital meeting and he correctly guessed that that was not the cause of my stress, so I had to disclose my fear that Sandra was seeing Rowan. George punched me on the arm and said, 'So you were jealous of him?' He was laughing and, whilst I was embarrassed by my explanation, I could not be angry. We both laughed. George, despite his age, was my best friend.

As we left the cake shop, I noticed that both the bookmaker's and the tailor's shop were vacated. Both had notes on the door and had I not been pushing George, I would have read them. George pointed out that the parade was built before the pre-fabs so must have been due for a major facelift.

*

I dropped George off and returned to a cheer at Aunt Gladys's house. Dawn was standing on a stool and Aunt Gladys was trying to pin the hem of a dress that Dawn was wearing. Neither Dawn nor Aunt Gladys had the flexibility to carry out the task as neither seemed able to bend enough at the waist. They were both thrilled to see me. I had never hemmed a dress before but it is easy to pick up when in receipt of clear instructions. I had clearly impressed Aunt Gladys with my dexterity, as she went and made me a cup of tea whilst I finished the hem and gave me a piece of pork pie that she had kept for me. I then headed off for a shower wondering what one wears to a charity committee meeting.

*

I had worried what Sandra would say when I arrived at the meeting. Was it too presumptive of me to join her group without speaking to her first? I was getting anxious again. This girl was having such an unexpected effect on me. I parked near Rowan's flat. I could have parked outside as there were a number of spaces but I wanted to walk in. I remembered my first walk to find Carole's flat, my nerves and apprehension. This seemed the same and I was minded to simply drive home but, as happened on the walk to Carole, I bumped into Sandra. She was clutching a file of papers across her chest and briskly striding down the street. She stopped in her tracks as I climbed out of the car. 'Harry?' she exclaimed. 'What are you doing here?' I smiled and said that I had come to carry her homework for her. She dumped all the papers into my hands and said, 'How thoughtful.' She then proceeded to kiss me on the cheek. I had the car keys in my hand but could not use them as my arms were full. Sandra took the keys off me and locked the car. As we started walking, Sandra asked me where I was going. I said that I had a confession. I was insanely jealous that she kept meeting with another man and I simply could not let it continue unless I was there to watch her. Sandra stopped. 'You know where I'm going?' she said.

'Yes,' I replied, 'and I know who you're meeting.'

'Mother!' she exclaimed. 'She's a traitor.' I corrected her and told her I had a personal invite from Rowan. She kissed me again on the cheek, telling me that she was happy because I could give her a lift home.

*

Rowan's flat was a book depository or a library, it was not a living area. Five people were crushed in when we arrived and two arrived moments later. There was a fug of cigarette smoke and a stench of musty parchment. It felt like the steering cadre of a revolutionary cell. If Rowan had been wearing a black beret, he could have been Che Guevara. A strange girl in dungarees handed out an agenda that had been copied from a hand-turned Gestetner machine. The ink was still damp and I smudged the sheet she gave me. I marked my fingers in black ink and I had to blacken my hanky to remove it.

There was a garden chair wedged between two bookcases and Sandra suggested that I sat in it and she would sit at my feet. I said, no, she should sit in the seat and I would sit at her feet, and that was how we proceeded. The garden bench on the side of the room was filled by a couple that were smoking. They were arguing and it did not seem very friendly but Sandra assured me they were married and so were expected to argue. I was not sure if she was joking but I laughed anyway. Rowan asked everyone to introduce themselves. The couple said 'Jo and Frances' and nothing else and this set the tone for Sandra, Harry, Rowan, Oli, Steph and Edward. Within seconds I had forgotten them all, save for Jo and Frances, but did know which was which. Sandra rested her notepad on my shoulder and I found my head was moving back further between her legs. She kept squeezing my head between her knees which was a very pleasant distraction but did mean I could not hear anything that was being said. I am not sure Rowan knew we had an agenda because he darted from one topic to another and it took the girl in the dungarees to keep him on track. She actually ran the meeting, if the truth be told, but no one bothered to tell Rowan. It was all rather uneventful until Jo and Frances had a row. He answered a question for her and she objected to him assuming he knew her answer. It was all a little dramatic with raised voices and embarrassed spectators. Eventually the girl said that they were leaving. The chap added that they would continue their disagreement when they got home. The girl reminded him he would not have time as he was writing his novel which he was going to call *Belittle Women*. This broke the tension and everyone gave a nervous laugh. Sandra squeezed her thighs. Steph reminded Sandra of that huge row that Jo and Frances had at the Dwile Flonking weekend. At this Jo laughed and added, 'If only I had known.' Once the warring couple had left, another two made their excuses and went too. Rowan offered to make us all coffee if we agreed to help with his urgent project for his newspaper. I was keen to know about Dwile Flonking but the moment had passed. I presumed Rowan wanted us to help with some sort of survey but it was anything but. Things were to get even weirder. The paper received its horoscopes in bundles that were syndicated round all the newspapers in the group. The bundle had not arrived and so Rowan had to write them for the next five nights. There were twelve signs of the zodiac and so we, the four volunteers left, had to write fifteen separate horoscopes each. They were only to be five lines long so it would not take long.

It was hardly surprising that no one had written a horoscope. Steph wanted to know whether we should be consulting some astronomical charts. Rowan laughed, he said that he often had to step in when they had not arrived and no one had ever noticed. I found it quite easy to write the bland, vague platitudes that meant all things to all men but Sandra was being quite specific. Steph had found a book on astrology which must have been an act of divine intervention as the books in Rowan's flat were well shuffled. Steph was at pains to tell us that there were thirteen signs of the Zodiac and the various meanings of the signs. It was most unhelpful and Rowan told her so. This did not please Steph who insisted that if she was going to give people predictions about their futures, they should at least be based on fact. Sandra rolled her eyes and Rowan sighed. I asked Steph her star sign and she said Sagittarius. I suggested that she wrote all the Sagittarius entries and so at least she would be happy that the correct procedures had been adopted. I had no idea whether there were procedures but Steph seemed content with this compromise. It did not take us long and Rowan was soon able to compile entries for the rest of the week and, as there was no paper on the Sunday, he had two days into next week.

*

I drove Sandra home. She asked if I was still concerned about what she got up to with Rowan and I admitted that I was more relaxed now. She had a piece of paper, she told me it was my Horace scope for the Friday if I wanted to hear it. I said, 'Yes.'

'Today you should abandon any thoughts of jealousy and stop always planning everyone's future.' She then paused said, 'Oh, sorry, that's today's Horace scope, Friday's is more important. "Today is a good day to organise a meeting with a friend. If you choose the correct friend, her mother could be away and the date could last all weekend".'

I was unsure how to respond but said that as today's Horace scope was spot on, I had no doubt Friday would be just as accurate. We were approaching Sandra's house and so I said, 'Do you have any plans for Friday?' Sandra told me that as a matter of fact she was free because her mother was going to her sister's for the weekend. She went on to tell me that she would be lonely and scared in the house on her own and did I have any suggestions. I said that I was happy to protect her and that my suggestions were that we had a shepherd's pie, a bottle of wine and sat listening to some music, whilst reciting poetry to each other. I did not hear Sandra gasp but she certainly took an intake of breath. 'What music will we listen to?' I asked and she said 'you can choose'.

'In that case it will have to be *The Carnival of the Animals*,' I said.

I walked Sandra to the door in silence. I was sure she had put two and two together but she was deep in thought. I kept quiet. We kissed on the doorstep. I was not invited in and strangely did not want to be. Sandra had cued me up for the Friday night and I did not want to spoil it. As I left, she whispered, 'Do not forget the protection you promised me for Friday.' I smiled and squeezed her hand.

*

The rest of the week was strange. I had nothing in particular planned but I busied myself with everything from washing George's car to taking Dawn shopping for baby clothes and a pram. Aunt Gladys had planned the trip and wanted to come too but had suffered a dizzy spell and the doctor had told her to have a quiet week. My main preoccupation was trying to buy condoms. I had never bought them before and had planned to just get them from the machine at the railway station, but that had been vandalised. I was left with no option but to boldly walk into the chemist and ask. I made sure I had enough change and that I knew exactly what I wanted as I could not face a long drawn-out ordeal with a queue building up behind me. In the end the apprehension was ill founded as the girl behind the counter just grabbed a box, put it in a white packet and gave it to me without any expression. I presume that she had seen too many men like me and their discomfort. At least I was now prepared for the weekend.

CHAPTER 15

Friday was a beautiful sunny day. I went for a run but made sure that I knew my route and did not overdo it. I had a hearty breakfast and helped Aunt Gladys vacuum the house. Since her dizzy spell I had taken on as many household chores as possible. I was strangely nervous and was hoping I was not building myself up for a fall. I hardly knew Sandra and the next twenty-four hours could have an impact on my whole life. I had no job and I was living in a shed. I was definitely overthinking the issue. I told myself to relax and look forward to a fun night with a charming girl. Dawn wandered in from the kitchen. Dawn was a changed woman from the pre-pregnant girl that I knew. She was organised and helpful but was increasingly restricted by her ever-growing bump. I had bought flowers for Sandra and two packets of jelly beans as she had mentioned how much she liked them. They had been spotted by Dawn who also liked them so I gave Dawn one packet. She was delighted.

Seeing Dawn happy brought me back to reality. I left her with the jelly beans and went back through to the shed to have a shower. I had just taken off my sweater and watch when Dawn called me. I went back to the house and was confronted by three policemen. One said, 'Mr Harry Crawford, we have a warrant to search your house and we want you to come down to the police station to assist with our enquiries.' I was speechless and just nodded.

Aunt Gladys asked if everything was alright and Dawn went to her and said that there was nothing to worry about. They both sat on the sofa. I asked what it was about but they were leading me out. I asked if I could grab my sweater and watch but they said, 'This will not take long.' This was such a different departure from the last time a constable had called for me. I shouted back to Dawn to ring Sandra and tell her I might be late. One policeman was putting on gloves and asking Dawn to show him my room as I was bundled out.

*

I was pushed into the back of a police car. I was being treated like a criminal. There was no explanation nor civility. The drive was far longer than I expected and I had no idea where we were heading. I was taken from the car and led by an arm on my elbow through a series of doors, the first being the entrance on the side of a huge red brick building. Nothing was said until I was pushed into a room without windows, at what I presumed to be a police station. The room was bare, save for the table and three chairs. I had not gone up or down any stairs so I presumed I was on the ground floor. I had no idea how long I waited as I had no watch but it must have been an hour. I was then joined by two of the three policemen that picked me up from the house. They were both holding mugs of coffee and they sat opposite me. I knew that there was no coffee for me so this was not a friendly chat.

'Mr Crawford, why did you just up and leave your last job?'

The question was direct and I was keen to come clean so I said, 'Because they were all villains and they tried to kill me.' I knew as soon as I said this that it was wrong and I had just opened the biggest bag of worms.

I could tell from their body language that they smelt blood. 'So how much did you make from your enterprise?' This threw me as they were not probing what happened to me but were on some tack about making money.

'Nothing,' I said, 'absolutely nothing.'

'We have found a stash of ready notes hidden in your bedroom, are you telling us you do not trust banks?'

'That's not my money,' I protested.

They did not ask whose money it was but pressed on with, 'Who did you pay for the goods?'

'I did not pay anyone for any goods,' I explained.

They then asked where all the goods came from. I tried to explain that the bricks, roof trusses and tiles were all ordered by the head office and was going to explain further but was cut short when one said, 'Not the building stuff, the scrap metal.'

'What scrap metal?' I asked, I had no idea what they were talking about.

At this point one said, 'You clearly need more time to think,' and they both upped and left the room.

They had only been with me ten minutes. I wondered if I should be asking to see a lawyer. It did seem a little dramatic as I had done nothing wrong. I wondered what scrap metal they were asking about. I was left waiting another half hour. It seemed longer because I was thinking about Sandra and how I had been waiting all week to see her. The two policemen came back into the room but, rather than sit down, again they asked me to follow them into the next room. It was the same as the previous room but on the table was a large tape recorder. I was told to sit. I needed to go to the loo and asked if it was possible. The taller of the two, who seemed to be the lead, told me I could wait as this would only take ten minutes if I told them everything they wanted to know.

This interview had far more structure, they told the tape who they were; Detective Constable Feathers and Detective Sergeant Dolby. The latter was, as I suspected, the lead. They asked me for my full name and address and I was minded that this was how it was done on the television. I was having an out-of-body experience as I was almost watching the performance. I did not feel I was the criminal that was being put through a grilling.

Feathers told the tape that I had been responsible for what he called the sub-station scheme and was responsible for the buying of stores and equipment. I tried to correct this but was told I would get my chance to speak and to shut up. He went on to say that the scheme was an ideal storage site for stolen scrap metal that was accumulated before sale to a dealer. He went on to say that I ran the site and had voluntarily agreed to explain how the operation was run by villains. He took the term I had used in my very first answer. I was not sure why they had made this inaccurate summary and I told them this. The constable leaned forward and switched off the machine without looking up. He called me a 'smart arse' and said, 'Tell us your version of what has been said.' I asked why my version was not to be taped and he shrugged and told me that they were trying to make it easy for me but were happy that I could cock it up.

I tried to start with the nature of the job and my 'promotion' from the road contract but they kept interrupting and telling me to get to the point but it was not that straightforward and I had no chance to even mention Aiden Malcolm before Dolby stepped in telling me that I had had my chance. I had not corrected their supposed inaccuracies that I had claimed needed addressing so they were going back to the theft. He leaned over and pushed a button on the tape. It was clearly the wrong button as Feathers had to move quickly to stop whatever had been started and reset the tape.

Eventually they were ready again and Feathers started the tape and asked me to explain how the scrap metal got to the site. I again said I had no idea that there was scrap metal on the site. He then grunted, 'What about the rolled steel joists?'

Suddenly I had the 'scrap metal' in my brain. I could see the pile of joists where they had been dumped in the corner of the yard. I said they were needed to act as roof joists when they lifted in the generator and that was nothing to do with me. I had no idea where they came from and no idea where they went after they had been used. They asked if I had seen them being used and I had to confess that I had not. They then asked about the reinforcing steel that was there. I had no answer as to why it was there, nor where it went to. I did feel woefully ignorant of what was happening on my watch and I told them this. I changed tack and said how I was just the partially qualified junior engineer. I assumed everyone was honest if they stored stores in the compound, why would that be unusual as it was a storage compound? This logic did seem to have the effect of making them pause to think. 'But what about the bundle of cash hidden in the jar?' spurted Feathers with a triumphant flourish.

That, I paused, was my wages from my last pay day. They had not mentioned the money under the cat but I thought it best to come clean. I said, 'The other money was not mine; it belongs to Aiden Malcolm who will vouch for it if you ask him.'

I was delighted that this answer elicited the response I hoped for which was, 'Who is Aiden Malcolm?' I told them it was a long story and if they let me go to the loo, I would be better placed to tell them. I stood at the urinal and thought there was a slim chance that I could be out of police custody before nightfall and meeting Sandra but I was wrong.

Feathers and Dolby were only doing their job but I did think they were making such a meal of it. When I went back, they had clearly spoken and had agreed that they were leading the interview and they were not going to let some smart-arse young thief distract them. The questions started with whether I knew Philip Agnew. I did not. Maybe I knew him as Phil? I thought not but asked, 'In what context might I know him? Who was he?'

They said he was the steel fix ganger from the bridging site. I recalled the chap that I had questioned over the RSJs and thought he may have been a Phil. I related the conversation I had had with him and how he had called me an idiot or something. I was open and honest about my recollection of the fleeting meeting but this only gave them ammunition. So, I did know him! Why did they have to prise it out of me? I was feeling that they were grinding me down. I needed a drink and cursed myself for not drinking some tap water when I was in the toilet. I tried asking for some water but, as I anticipated, Doyle said that they were not running some fancy café. Doyle tried to stop the tape but again hit the wrong button so Feathers had to step in and reset the machine. They both stood up and told me I could have a break next door. I was shoved back into the original room. I caught site of Dolby's watch and it was either seven or eight. They said it was a break but it was not a break for me. I had to stay in the zone; I was a commissioned Army officer, even if it was only in the part-time Army. I was an engineering graduate. I had a great set of friends and family and I had met a lovely girl. I was determined to stay positive. I had done nothing wrong. My crime was that of omission because I had not done anything when I should have.

I have no idea how long I was left. There were no windows and nothing to give any indication of time. I felt like a hostage. My mouth was parched and I was feeling hungry. Initially I dreamed of shepherd's pie but, as the time dragged on, I would have settled for raw carrots. I was clearly not an escape risk as the door was unlocked, I opened it a couple of times to look up and down the corridor but no one was about. It did occur to me that maybe they hoped I would try and bolt as they would have the criminal they desperately needed. I settled back to try and sleep with my head on my hands over the table. I did drop off but was awoken by a commotion in the corridor. I resisted the temptation to have a look. It sounded as if someone else was being taken into the tape room. I wondered if it was Phil. I had already forgotten his surname.

Bizarrely it was a cleaner that next interrupted my fitful sleep. She poked her head round the door and asked me if she could mop the floor. I said, 'Be my guest.' I was pleased with the distraction.

The cleaner had a name tag 'Connie', so I introduced myself. She was from a contract cleaning company and she only had two hours to do the whole floor. I thought she meant my small room but she meant the whole complex. She had a Lucozade bottle on her trolly and she clearly saw that I was desperate for a drink. She offered me the bottle which I took with unreserved gratitude. She also had a pasty and offered it to me. I almost hugged her. When she had gone it occurred to me that had Feathers and Dolby offered me a pasty and drink, I would have admitted to murder. My blood sugar levels were boosted by the drink and the food so sleep was not an option. I wished I had a ball like Cool Hand Luke or maybe a finch like the birdman of Alcatraz to pass the time but I only had a Lucozade bottle. I had no idea what time Dolby returned but it was to apologise for the fact that I had been left. They had been called out to a serious incident. I was in a slight trance as I was led through a series of corridors that I had not recognised from my arrival. Dolby told me they were letting me go but would be calling me back. I was led to the side of a building and shown the door. It was pitch black outside. I did not even know which police station I was at. I was at my lowest ebb ever. I did not think to ask where I was or how I was supposed to get home but the door locked behind me. I walked round to the front of the building. It was a police station and was bathed in bright lights. My eyes ached and I struggled to keep them open as I stumbled into the reception. Reception was manned by a uniformed policeman who was smoking. He did not look up. I saw slumped on two fixed chairs in the corner two interwoven bodies sleeping on each other, wrapped in what appeared to be a drab horse blanket. It was Sandra and Dawn. I did not want to cry but I could not stop myself. I gently woke them. We all three just cried and hugged. I asked how they had found me. Sandra said she would tell me later. They had come by taxi. I went back to the uniformed policeman on the counter and asked how we could call a taxi. My impression was that he was going to be unhelpful but I pointed out Dawn was eight months pregnant and if she had any more stress, we would need an ambulance. He made some excuse about rules and regulations but then rang a taxi firm who agreed to pick us up in ten minutes. I still had the remains of the Lucozade so the three of us shared it until the taxi arrived. Nothing was spoken. We took the taxi back to Sandra's. I sat in the middle and both girls snuggled up beside me. The taxi driver sensed that silence was appropriate. Dawn did say that Aunt Gladys would be fine as she had told her she was staying at Sandra's. That cleared one of my concerns.

*

It was 0330 when we arrived at Sandra's, and luckily Sandra had money to pay the fare as I had nothing. Sandra suggested that Dawn sleep in her bed. I should sleep in her mother's and she could sleep on the couch. Dawn nodded but I protested. I would sleep on the couch. I hugged Sandra and lay down on the couch. She kissed me on the forehead and I remember nothing else until I woke up at nine.

Dawn and Sandra were both in the kitchen and I could smell bacon and hear giggles. I felt grimy and dishevelled. My mouth was dry and my teeth furry. I dreaded to think how my breath smelt. I tried to be jolly as I walked into the kitchen. I found myself apologising but both were telling me that it was not my fault. Sandra thrust a mug of tea into my hand. I will never forget the feeling of wellbeing that swept over me as I said, 'Thank you.' She hugged me and I broke down crying.

It is amazing how a good meal lifts the spirits. Sandra confessed that she had been looking forward to cooking me a hearty breakfast but had not planned that I would spend the night before in a police cell. Dawn told me that after the police had left and I shouted for her to tell Sandra she was in a quandary. She did not have Sandra's number, nor her address. She did not even know Sandra's surname. She looked in the shed, which was wrecked by the police search, and the only number she could find was a card in my wallet with a Rowan Cowan's name on it. In desperation she phoned the number, telling Rowan that she was my sister. Rowan was happy to help and gave Dawn Sandra's details. Dawn then told Aunt Gladys she was going to tell Sandra what had happened and would try and stay with Sandra if possible, as she did not want to leave Aunt Gladys any more anxious than she was already.

Sandra then picked up the story. She wanted to look her best for me but was disappointed that Jacqui had 'overdone' her hair and make-up. Even before I was due to arrive, she was worried that she looked like a Geisha girl. When I had not turned up, all her insecurities flooded in. All her emotions went haywire. She had felt anger and not a little pain. She had thought she had been too forward and that I had been scared off. She had a shower and washed off all her make-up, changed into her dressing gown and played the *Danse Macabre* very loud on the record player. She had read that red wine and chocolate were not the answer but she opened the bottle and it helped. She was angry and was going to have an early night when a taxi turned up. She had thought it was me and had been prepared to send me away. It turned out to be Dawn. She was shocked to be told the reason for being stood up. Dawn had no idea where I had been taken so Sandra had phoned the main police station but they refused to give out any information. She then made a list of all the police that were at the hospital when we went for our 'thank you'. She then rang them back. Each time she asked for a different name and after the fourth unsuccessful attempt she asked for PC Over. Remarkably he was on shift and came to the phone. He could not give specific advice but suggested that most people taken into custody were taken to the regional police station. So, this is where they went. It was a Friday night and the girls watched all manner of life being dragged, frog-marched, staggered and strutted into the reception. Many accompanied by uniformed police, many drunk, most angry and some frightening. The two early-evening desk officers refused to say whether I was being held and kept telling them to go home. Sandra thought that it was only Dawn's pregnancy that kept them from being physically removed. Dawn's pregnancy also caused them some concern and they did bring two hot coffees and the smelly blanket. They also let slip that I was being held when they told them it was highly unlikely that I would be released before morning. This strengthened their resolve. They were both convinced that I would have spent the night there if they had not been there. They had heard the plain-clothed man, who brought me out, scold the desk officer for dragging him back from Hartlepool to sort me out.

I told them my tale of woe and how I had been saved by a cleaner called Connie. Dawn asked if Connie was like a fairy godmother.

It was mid-morning on a spring Saturday so after we washed up all the dishes we went for a walk in the park. We did not mention the previous night, we just strolled to the duck pond and sat watching the birds in silence. I felt strangely content.

CHAPTER 16

Strolling through the park and woodland would have been fine if I had a sweater or jacket but I did not and I was starting to freeze. Dawn and Sandra were deep in conversation about Leicester for reasons I could not fathom. They seemed oblivious to my plight. My pride would not let me mention my discomfort so I gritted my chattering teeth. I had the same clothes on that I had worn the previous day and I felt scruffy. I was also starting to worry about what the police would do next. I was sure that whatever respite I had was going to be short. Any police record would scupper my Army plans. I felt there was no one I could turn to that I would not worry. I could not confide in anybody close without doubling my stress. George was fond of telling me that a 'problem shared is a problem doubled' and he was right. Eventually we left the woodland and re-entered the edge of the town and I recognised Sandra' house. We had done a large circle. At the back was a cleared area with a hardstanding. Sandra paused and said, 'My dad used to park the yacht here, it seems strange without it.'

I was not really paying attention as I cursed my poor sense of direction and wondered what the Sandhurst Colour Sergeant would have said had he known. Despite the huge breakfast I was feeling hungry and, as it turned out, so was Dawn. Sandra said that she had shepherd's pie that she had prepared for last night if we were interested. Dawn declined saying that she would be happy with a slice of toast. I just walked over and hugged Sandra. Dawn giggled and asked, 'What is it with you two?' I said something about Sandra being very special and that Dawn better get used to her being around.

Sandra hugged me close and whispered in my ear, 'I hope so.' I suggested that we could all get a taxi back to

Aunt Gladys's house as she would be worried. Sandra said that there was a bus at 1130 which went straight to Long Benson and it would be quicker to catch that, rather than ringing for a taxi. We had ten minutes to make the bus so there was no further talk of food. We made the bus stop with two minutes to spare and that was speedwalking a pregnant Dawn. As it turned out, the bus was ten minutes late. Sandra was correct, it was a direct route but it did not go up Benson Hill and dropped us at the parade of shops. The tobacconist and the betting shop had gone but the café was still open. I told the girls to have a coffee and I would run and get George's car and come back to collect them.

*

I ran up Long Benson Bank and despite wearing brown loafers I felt good and I started to warm up. I was reminded of my run down Otley Road. All I needed was a big orange Mr Man. When I came into the house, I startled Aunt Gladys. She was putting her hand down the side of her chair. She seemed distressed. I asked her what she was looking for and she mumbled something. She then, using the chair as an aid, climbed onto the floor to search under the chair. I dropped down beside her and told her if she told me what she had lost, I could help her find it. I helped her back to her feet and into the chair. She looked anxious. I could tell she had been up half the night and all morning. She looked worn out, her eyes were dark and puffy. I hugged her and explained that I was going to collect the girls from the bottom of Long Benson Bank. She did not seem to respond but slumped back into her chair. I changed my plan. I put the kettle on and made her a strong tea. I also put a crust of bread in the toaster. It was the last slice of bread or I would have had a slice myself as I was starving. Once I had Aunt Gladys settled, I asked what she had lost and she said the baby comforter. I presumed it was something she was making for Dawn. I had a look round and there on the kitchen table was an embroidered square. It seemed old and worn. I took it through to Aunt Gladys. Her eyes lit up and she hugged the piece of cloth to her chest. I felt that as Aunt Gladys was settled, I could get the car keys.

*

The shed was upside down. It was ransacked. I could not for the life of me work out how this could be a systematic police search. It was wanton destruction. All the tools were off the wall and mixed with strewn clothing and paperwork. It was not confined to the bed but also the floor and windowsill. It looked like an attempt to cause as much damage and disruption as possible in one small room. Tonto was lying on her blanket oblivious to the carnage. I could not find the keys but I did see my camera. It was out of the case. I took some photographs of the scene as I was sure no one would ever believe the mess. The keys were usually on the edge of the workbench near the vice. They were nowhere to be found. The jar with my £60 was unscrewed and on the bench empty. Tonto stretched and walked onto the bench to be nearer me. I took the opportunity to look under Tonto's blanket. Aiden's money was untouched. Hidden in plain sight but missed by the observant plod. I did not count it but just laughed to myself. I am sure Tonto was grinning. Tonto my Cheshire cat. I went back through and checked on Aunt Gladys but she was sound asleep and I did not want to wake her. I went to see George. He was delighted to see me. I tried to give him a summary of what had happened but he kept asking too many questions. I did eventually get his spare keys but it was on condition that I took him with me to collect the girls. I sorted his wheelchair and got him to the car and we set off down Long Benson Bank. I knew the girls would be worried as it was now around an hour and a half after I had left them. I did not find my watch in the mess and George had not wound his up so it still said 0930. I tried to explain what had happened but George was just getting confused. I snapped at him and immediately felt bad. I was tired and anxious but I had lost my temper. It was definitely uncharacteristic. I could not remember the last time I had. Even when Colin lost my coursework, I never got angry. George was understanding, which made it worse. I kept apologising and was pleased that we eventually arrived at the parade. The girls were standing outside the café and when Dawn saw the car they came over.

I could see they were annoyed, but when they saw George, they both smiled. Once in the car everyone relaxed and I drove the whole party back to Aunt Gladys's house in silence. Aunt Gladys was still sleeping and only awoke when I knocked George's wheelchair against the sideboard and a photo of Ted fell off. Aunt Gladys had not eaten the slice of toast I had made her. She said she was not hungry. I offered it to Dawn and Sandra but they had both had a cheese sandwich in the café whilst waiting and declined. George was happy to accept but wanted me to see if there was any marmalade. George also added that once we all had drinks I could sit down and tell everyone 'what the devil' I had done.

There was a strange silence whilst I collected the jar of marmalade and it made me relax.

George told everyone he was going to chair the meeting and that he did not want interruptions. He then said, 'Over to you Harry.'

I laughed and apologised to everyone for the stress I had caused. I explained that, despite the circumstances of my arrest, the police had not charged me. I explained that whilst being the site engineer on the sub-station there had been scrap metal stored in the compound. Seemingly this was stolen goods that were later sold to a scrap dealer. As I had access to the compound I was implicated. I assured my silent audience, as I had assured the police, that I had absolutely no knowledge of the crime that had been going on under my nose. George interrupted, 'But what about missing Malcolm and the dodgy houses?'

I explained that I had tried to raise this but the police were not interested. Sandra asked if I had told them of my run-in with the truck. I replied that I had not as it still seemed so surreal. I tried to explain how the police seemed to have such a preconceived idea of what had happened that no matter what I said they did not seem interested. George started to mutter that he never trusted the police but was interrupted by Aunt Gladys. She told him that apportioning blame was not helpful. It was Aunt Gladys's first comment. She paused and then added, 'I don't trust the authorities, mind you.' Aunt Gladys was staring into space and not talking to anyone in particular. She went on to say that she had suffered a terrible wrong and would never get over it. Dawn moved over to her and put an arm round Aunt Gladys's shoulder. Aunt Gladys started crying. George suggested that we adjourn the meeting for a 'nice cup of tea'.

I volunteered to make it and Sandra stood up saying, 'I'll help.' Aunt Gladys was dabbing her eyes with the small embroidered handkerchief that she had been so anxious to find earlier.

In the kitchen Sandra put her arms round me and kissed me. 'Oh, for some time together,' she whispered.

George spoiled the moment by shouting through, 'Stop canoodling and make that tea.'

We sat and drank the tea in silence. Aunt Gladys went back to sleep. George, in a stage whisper, reminded me that I was taking him to the Western Front Society that afternoon and he needed to get back to his house to change. Dawn used the lead to give Sandra, George and I a kiss and said she needed a lie down. She kissed Aunt Gladys on the forehead as she left. Sandra and I took George home. I was surprised how easy it was. Sandra instinctively knew the problems with wheelchairs. She opened doors and gates with ease, always on the right side. Her skills were second nature, whilst I was still a relative novice. George had never moved so effortlessly. As he wheeled himself through to his bedroom to change, his parting shot was that we could now canoodle for ten minutes or make him a ham sandwich. We made him his ham sandwich.

I was shattered, and whilst Sandra offered to catch the bus home, I would not let her. Her mother was due back from her aunts and so George and I just dropped her off. I then deposited George at the Old Comrades Club and drove home. After sorting my room into some sort of order I collapsed into bed.

CHAPTER 17

Marcus, who ran the parachute training course, was at the entrance to the TA centre when I arrived on the Tuesday evening. He met me as I climbed out of George's car. After the usual 'how's it going?' banter, he told me he had come down to see me specifically. He had bought two portable cabins and he needed a team to help him move them. He knew I was not working so presumed I would be available for the next ten days. He wanted me as his project manager. He told me that he did not have any money to pay me but he was getting £200 to clear the site and I could have that and keep any money left over after the trucks and skips had been paid for. I could give myself a fancy title and it would look great on my CV. It did not seem like an attractive proposition but it was at least a proposition and so I found myself saying rather weakly that I was free.

I did not see Marcus for the rest of the night. I was running a pipe range in the cellar and did not surface with my platoon until the final parade. He grabbed me again and steered me to the training room as he wanted to make sure I was well briefed. He was looking for a cabin for the airfield and had seen a dozen or so on an old site that was being cleared for housing. The site foreman was planning to demolish the cabins but Marcus offered to buy two. Marcus explained that such was the confusion, that whilst he was offering to buy them, the foreman was trying to pay Marcus to remove them. I was getting confused so I could understand the foreman's problem. I eventually unwound the position. The foreman would give Marcus the two cabins he needed and a further £200 to remove the rest provided they were cleared within ten days. I had become so paranoid that I asked Marcus if the foreman had permission to sell them. Marcus looked at me quizzically and said the foreman wanted the site cleared and planned to demolish the whole lot unless we acted fast. Marcus had sealed the deal on the Saturday and it was now Tuesday so we had to do it in the next six days. I grabbed a pad of paper and started to question Marcus on where they were, how big they were and where were they going. He stopped me. 'Horace, my man, you're the project manager. They're in Loftus; you'll need to do a recce.' He gave me the site address. He went on to say that he wanted the best two for the airfield. He said he only needed two so I could arrange for the rest to be smashed up and taken to the tip if that was easy. I was minded to grab Big Eddie and Ra-Ra as it seemed like a job they would enjoy but I said nothing. I could not make any plans until I had seen the size and scope of the problem. Marcus had confused me with the arrangements so I carefully recapped. Marcus was getting £200 and two cabins provided he cleared the site by Monday. I could have the £200 provided I cleared that site and arranged for two cabins to be delivered to the airfield. In my head I was wondering where there was anything in this for me except hassle. It could end up costing me more than the £200. Why I was agreeing to it, heaven only knows. Marcus was selling it to me like it was some great deal. I was too stupid to decline.

*

Sandra had the Wednesday off so rather than a trip to the Yorkshire Dales, that she had suggested, we went to Loftus. I had to explain the deal to Sandra at least three times. Each time I told her it seemed even more stupid, but if she was thinking that, she was not saying it. In fact, I was surprised by her enthusiasm. Sandra and I both took wellies as we were expecting a muddy site and I also took my yellow hardhat. I thought I needed to look the part. Sandra had thoughtfully brought her father's 60ft tape and a notepad and pencil. The site was easy to find from the directions given by Marcus and the site foreman who was very helpful. He was having the first groundworks team arriving the following week which is why he wanted all the cabins off the site. He said that if I wanted, he could have his dozer crush them, if that was easier. He thought it would be such a waste as one or two were in good order. I agreed with him. There were seventeen cabins including five that were more like sentry boxes and had been used on the access roads to a local quarry. Two cabins were immaculate with fitted kitchens, another had carpet and still had desks and filing cabinets inside. Others were in different states of repair, many had broken windows and poorly hanging doors. There were three single toilets which looked serviceable but I was not sure I wanted to lift them. Sandra was gathering data on them all. She had had the presence of mind to bring a black marker pen so she was able to mark every cabin. Whilst the foreman had been involved in the siting of the cabins, he had no idea of how they were lifted or manoeuvred. He directed us to Aaron who was the man on the gate. I had a double-take when I saw Aaron as he was the double of Malcolm. He was coughing just like Malcolm and stooped just like Malcolm and if it had not been for his off-white ginger hair, he could have passed for Malcolm. Aaron had retired but was earning some extra money, making tea and helping on the gate. He started to begrudgingly impart his knowledge to me but was suddenly animated when Sandra came over. He was happy to show off his considerable knowledge to Sandra so I let him get on with it. He showed her the lifting points and points of balance. He crawled underneath to show the legs, props and, on some, the wheels. He explained the vehicles that were needed and the preparation required at both the pick-up and drop-off. In short, Aaron wrote my project document and Sandra carefully transcribed it into a working plan. We did need at least three people, together with probably two or three flatbed trucks. We would need drivers and cranes at either end, unless the trucks had cranes like the ones that used to deliver the bricks. The memory of bricks gave me a cold shiver. I was trying to weigh up just how much debris would be left if we did smash up the cabins and whether the debris would be as hard to dispose of as complete cabins. I was starting to curse myself for agreeing to help Marcus. I was wondering if Marcus had just stitched me up. I walked over to Sandra who was checking her notes. I said, 'Sorry for dragging you into this, you could be in the Dales.'

Sandra furrowed her brow and said, 'But this is brilliant. I think you've pulled off a masterstroke, my super hero.' I said that the toilets would never be of any use and we could smash them up but Sandra disagreed saying that it was a shame there were not more. Our discussion was interrupted by the foreman asking for confirmation that the site would be cleared by the following Tuesday.

I replied rather nonchalantly that we would be back before the end of the week; I had my fingers crossed behind my back. Sandra seemed so excited and gave me a lingering hug as we stopped walking, upon reaching the car. 'You were quite the expert,' I told her and she enthused about how much she enjoyed proper work. We headed back up to the Whitby Road that we had last driven on when coming back from the parachute weekend. We chatted about how we could clear the site. We both felt destruction of the cabins was a waste. I saw a pub and on impulse we pulled in for lunch. The carpark was tiny as half was closed off for building works. I ordered a 'ploughman's' and Sandra had the soup and a roll. We wanted to talk about our plans but the landlord engaged with us so we passed the time of day with him. He quaffed a pint of beer as he explained how he had recently bought the pub and had a great scheme for its development. He was explaining how busy the Moors Road was and how he wanted to capture the passing trade. Sandra asked him if he needed a temporary cabin for the builders or maybe an outside loo. He laughed saying he wished he could afford such luxuries. Sandra said, 'But just hire one cabin for say a couple of months, £25 per month with a loo thrown in.' The Landlord asked what the catch was and Sandra said, 'We like your lunch, your scheme, and your location. Advertise our company on the side of your hut and we can give you this one-off deal.'

The Landlord said, 'I'll drink to that' and pulled himself another pint. We left the pub with £90. Three months' rent for a standard empty cabin and a loo with £15 delivery fee. Collection fee to be agreed at the end of the hire. It was all done on a handshake between Sandra and Len, the landlord.

*

Sandra and I had another hug by the car. 'Let's go back via the trading estate,' Sandra suggested. I smiled at her and did not even ask what she was thinking. I was playing catch up. The trading estate Sandra had in mind was not the same one that I had in my mind so we had some initial confusion. It was not wasted as we did drive round the first one and noted potential customers. At the second at Portrack, Sandra pointed me into the entrance of a road haulage contractor. I parked in a bay marked 'visitors' outside a pre-fabricated building. I followed Sandra in, like an obedient puppy. The girl on reception jumped up and came round the desk to hug Sandra. 'Yvonne, this is Harry my boss, Harry, this is Yvonne, I cut her hair.' Yvonne laughed. 'She's also my favourite cousin.' The girls continued to hug and Yvonne asked why we were there and Sandra said to see Uncle Tommy if he was free. Yvonne giggled and said he would be for Sandra and both walked through the door to the rear, Sandra beckoning me to follow.

*

Uncle Tommy was not what I expected. He was a small man with glasses and a small moustache who looked more like an accountant than a haulier. He was delighted to see Sandra and there was much talk of Sandra's mother and other family members before Tommy too asked why we were there. Sandra said, 'This is my boss, Harry, he has a proposition for you.'

I shook hands and said that actually Sandra was my business partner and that she was best placed to explain. I also had no idea what Sandra was planning to say. Over a tea, that Yvonne made, Sandra explained to her Uncle Tommy that in exchange for a rent-free luxury cabin for the yard and an outside loo, would Tommy collect and deliver the first ten cabins free to our chosen destination and thereafter at commercial rates? Tommy was pensive and said nothing. Sandra asked if, in the short term, would he allow two cabins to be stored on the site? Tommy looked at me and said that if I had put that proposal, he would have thrown me out. I agreed with him that Sandra was driving a hard bargain but there was some mutual self-interest as of course, in the future, Sandra would soon be one of his best customers and a quality cabin would give him additional space. I think I saw a tear in Tommy's eye as he hugged Sandra. He said, 'The apple does not fall far from the tree.' He asked if I had ever met Sandra's father and I shook my head. 'Fine man, fine man,' he mumbled. 'I am minded to have a canteen for the drivers and an outside toilet may be useful.'

Yvonne came back with a schedule and she and Sandra arranged for the lift of two cabins to the airfield, one cabin and a loo to the pub, and three cabins and a loo to the hauliers. Tommy and Yvonne walked us back to the car. As one last spasm, at Sandra's suggestion, Tommy was agreeing that the two stored cabins could be double stacked so that we could store four on the same footprint. He had one proviso and that was that his forklift was able to lift the cabins. He would check with his yard manager. Sandra was quite a girl. Tommy said to me, 'What is the name of your company?'

Sandra said, 'At the moment "Horace & Co" but we've not crossed the "T"s and dotted the "I"s yet.'

After Tommy and Yvonne said farewell, I did not start the car immediately but just sat and gazed at my remarkable partner. Eight of the cabins sorted and two loos. We had £290 in hand. 'I have plans for the luxury cabin too but we need to chat to Mum first.' We did not speak on the drive back but we both kept smiling at each other.

*

Mrs McGregor had had a wonderful weekend of respite care and seemed to have benefitted from her break. She seemed more mobile and her speech was clearer. I did feel annoyed that Sandra and I had missed that chance to be alone together but knew that there would be others. Mrs McGregor did not even ask if I was staying for supper, she just assumed that I was. I was becoming part of the family. She was surprised when Sandra asked if she minded whether we could place the headquarters of our new company on the hardstanding where 'Dad's boat' used to stand. Mrs McGregor was thrilled. 'So you will be working from home?' she added with some concern that Jacqui would not like her taking business.

Sandra laughed. 'I won't be cutting any more hair.' Sandra said that the business was portable cabins. It did take some explaining, not least because Mrs McGregor kept asking what qualifications we had and what did we know about cabins. I was thinking that half an hour with Aaron was hardly an apprenticeship. Mrs McGregor was suddenly on side when Sandra explained the help we were receiving from Tommy and Yvonne.

*

After supper Sandra and I went and stood on the patch of garden that was the home for this mad joint venture that she had launched. I was quite excited but mindful that I had not lifted a finger nor used a brain cell. Sandra was the super woman. Sandra explained that her dad had electricity down to the garage and so we could run an extension cable into the cabin. We would have to use her mum's housephone until a line was fitted by the GPO. Tomorrow night she would go to see Rowan to use his copier and get him to put an advert in his paper. I was speechless and apologised for my lack of input. Sandra stood and put her hands on her hips. 'The pick-up and delivery of all our assets will go without a hitch, won't it?!' She laughed and we hugged again.

*

I could not sleep that night; my brain was so active thinking of everything we had to do. We still had two cabins, one loo and five sentry boxes to store and we still had to dispatch the rest without incident. I phoned Marcus at his father's farm at 0800 and was lucky to catch him. I briefed him on the delivery of his two huts. I did not go into details about what else we had done as he was not interested. He was delighted that his cabins were sorted. I asked him if we could store anything else at the aerodrome. I said we had five sentry boxes, a loo and two cabins. He said he could hide the sentry boxes and loo in the hangar but not the cabins as he only had landlord permission for the two he had organised. I rang Yvonne and asked if we could add the extra sentry boxes and loo for the aerodrome delivery. She explained it would need an extra truck. I offered to pay as it was such an imposition. She rang me back and said that she had spoken to Tommy. He was happy to just send the allocated truck back for the second load as it was not too long a round trip.

*

Ra-Ra was working at an Italian restaurant in town and even though he mainly worked evenings, he would often be there during the day so rather than drive straight to his mother's house I called at the Diner. Aldo his boss told me he was there, as I anticipated, but he told me he had been sent on a short errand. I should have drilled down as to how short but Aldo just shrugged his shoulders when I asked. I waited hoping Ra-Ra would be back quickly, but in the end, I hung around for over an hour and a half. When he eventually turned up with a parcel for Aldo, he was pleased to see me and anxious to know why I had to find him. I explained that I needed him for the next two days. He explained that he was working from 1700 both days but was happy to assist during the day. Aldo was eavesdropping and wanted to know who I was and why I was taking his staff. Ra-Ra told Aldo that I wanted him to look after my cat and it was no problem. Ra-Ra agreed to be at Aunt Gladys's house at 0800.

*

When I got home Dawn had taken down a message from Sandra: could I collect Sandra at eight in the morning as she was coming with me? She had taken two days holiday. Dawn was not sure about the second half of the message, save that I had to phone Ernie or Arnie who wanted a portable toilet. Dawn had written down the number but was convinced that she had taken down the message wrong. I reassured her that all was well. I explained that Ra-Ra was calling at 0800 and he would be punctual so could Dawn make him a cup of tea or breakfast until I got back with Sandra. Dawn said it was a little early for her but was happy to assist. I rang Ernie who was actually called Alby. Alby had slept on the idea of a toilet but had changed his mind. I thought we had lost this lead when he said I need the cabin as well. 'No point in having one without t'other.' Alby was a farmer and he needed an old cabin for winter storage and the last loo.

I slept better knowing at worst we were two cabins left over but confident that Sandra would have the answers.

*

Sandra had had a busy night at Rowan's. She had printed off headed paper, invoice blanks, with compliment slips and lists of cabins. She had placed an advert in the *Gazette* for the next three Friday nights. Seemingly it was the best night for adverts and Rowan was not going to charge. I said, 'To think I was jealous of that man' and Sandra replied, 'Well you should be, he's been great.' She had put her mother's phone number on the advert and at the last minute added the haulier's too so she would have to speak to Yvonne and Tommy to warn them and apologise.

*

Back at Aunt Gladys's house we were puzzled to find Ra-Ra and Dawn dancing in the front room. Aunt Gladys seemed to be teaching them to waltz. The record player which usually blocked the back of the under-stair cupboard was standing on the table and churning out music that I recognised but could not name. I grabbed Sandra and we sort of pivoted on the spot as there was no room to dance. Aunt Gladys lifted the arm off the record.

I found myself saying, 'Blimey, I didn't expect this.'

Dawn was saying, 'But Ra-Ra is such a good dancer.' Ra-Ra seemed embarrassed and said nothing.

'We've all had bacon sandwiches, would you like one?' asked Aunt Gladys. Whilst I was tempted, I declined as I was anxious to crack on.

*

My plan was to drop Sandra off at the Loftus yard. I was hoping Aaron would agree to help her with the loading. If he did not, I would also leave Ra-Ra. I would go to the airfield to meet Marcus and Kurt. Again, I was hoping they would assist with the unload once we had agreed the positioning. I would then go to the pub to make sure the landlord had cleared the space for the delivery. I was explaining my plan in the car when Sandra stopped me. 'Don't worry, Harry, I've printed off the plan. It's almost the same as yours but Uncle Tommy has agreed a second truck so we can do twice as much.' I put my hand over and onto Sandra's thigh. She put her hand on top of mine and lifted it saying, 'You're very quiet, Ra-Ra.'

In chatting so much about the plans I had forgotten he was in the back. 'Ju… just listening to the arrangements for today,' he said and went quiet again. There was a long pause and I felt guilty that I had not told him anything about the day. I apologised for keeping him in the dark. I was quite taken aback when he asked, 'Is… is Dawn your wife?'

'Heavens no,' I said. 'She's my sister.' We all laughed. 'Dawn and I live with my Aunt Gladys. Sandra's my girlfriend.'

Ra-Ra laughed and said, 'Of course she is, we read about your fiancée in the *Gazette* at the drill hall. When are you getting married?' Sandra responded by telling Ra-Ra that I did not know because Sandra had not told me yet. Ra-Ra asked if Dawn was married and I explained that she was not and that the baby was due next month. Ra-Ra seemed non-plussed. 'Whose baby?' he asked.

'Dawn's,' I replied. 'Did you not notice how big she was?' Ra-Ra said that he had not but he thought she was very lovely. Sandra squeezed my hand that she was still holding.

*

Aaron was delighted to see Sandra. He offered her a cigarette but not Ra-Ra nor I. Aaron was more than happy to assist with the loading as he was the only person on the site that day. The two trucks were due at 0930 and arrived exactly on time. Both drivers seemed to know Sandra. One was Yvonne's boyfriend, Trevor, and the other was her boyfriend's brother, Josh. We did seem to be getting the full family treatment. Sandra joked that I had better get on with them as they would all be at the wedding. She then said, 'That was just a little joke.' I was mindful that I had not laughed, nor commented. It was just that it did seem so 'normal'. I could not imagine life without Sandra.

*

Whilst Sandra, Aaron and the two drivers loaded the specific cabins that Sandra had selected, I made a note of the truck sizes and times to load, size of access and any other information that would be helpful as we became more commercial. I did get a chance to ask Sandra about Alby. She explained that he was the wholesaler who provided the salon with most of their supplies. He worked out of an old warehouse. Sandra had made an excuse to visit him and persuade him that by having offices on the side of his building he would have more space for stock. I confessed that it had never occurred to me that a hair salon would need stock and also confessed that I had not agreed any price with Alby. Sandra raised her eyebrows and said, 'Well it's just as well that I did.'

Ra-Ra and I had to go before the trucks were loaded. We left Sandra helping to put a strap on the side of a cabin.

Ra-Ra was very subdued and so I asked him how they ended up dancing at breakfast. He explained that the *Blue Danube* waltz was playing on the radio and Dawn had said how much she would love to be able to waltz. Ra-Ra confided in her that he had gone to ballroom dancing as a child but that he had never told anyone. Aunt Gladys made him get the record player out as she had an LP of waltz tunes and she wanted Ra-Ra to show Dawn. Ra-Ra asked if I minded. I said, 'Anything that makes Dawn happy makes Aunt Gladys and I happy.' Ra-Ra then pleaded with me not to mention his dancing to anyone. I assured him that his secret was safe with me.

*

Marcus and Kurt were both well organised. They had the plots marked and had cleared access and egress so it seemed as if the delivery would be without hitch. Some half an hour later the two vehicles arrived and because of the preparation, the drop-off was smooth. Marcus was thrilled with his new office. I noted that the two cabins were not the best ones. I presumed Sandra had the best one lined up for our office. Ra-Ra and I left a very grateful Marcus before the unloading was complete as we were heading to the pub.

Len was more of a talker than a doer and nothing was prepared at the pub. Len, who was standing holding a pint of beer, looked like the archetypal landlord. He waved his spare hand over the rough idea where he wanted the cabin but no specific area was prepared. It was very short notice so I tried to be tolerant but he simply could not make a decision and the cabin would be arriving within a couple of hours. Eventually we decided that the flat area at the back of the car park would work with the loo behind. It meant moving three cars and a skip. The cars were no problem but the skip almost impossible. It was Ra-Ra who spotted the fence posts. He suggested we levered the skip forward but, as they were tubular, it was not working. He suggested we used them as rollers and that ended up working. We were able to push the skip clear of the plot like the stones used to build the pyramids.

I told Ra-Ra that he had saved the day with his bright idea but he was still subdued and I asked him what the problem was. I thought it was because he had revealed he was a dancer. I assured him his secret was safe. He said it was not the dancing, it was Dawn. I told him his secret would be safe with her but he assured me that was not the issue. His stammering was becoming more pronounced so I knew he was anxious. I tried to keep him relaxed and he finally said, 'She's so lovely.' I was not quite sure what to say. In the end, nothing was said.

Len offered Ra-Ra and I a pint of his new cask ale. He was disappointed that both Ra-Ra and I declined. He had pulled himself a second and said he was looking forward to his third. Ra-Ra and I gave each other knowing looks. I was not sure that the cabin would last long on the site if Len was drinking away his profits.

We had only been standing half an hour when the vehicle arrived with the cabin and toilet. I could not tell if it was Trevor or Josh driving but I did recognise Sandra in the front. She explained that she did not want to be left alone with Aaron as he was a bit creepy so she had decided to help at the pub. She and Trevor declined Len's offer of a pint of his new cask ale. The drop went better than I had hoped. We moved the loo at least three times as Len was never happy with the location. He seemed content with the position of the cabin once I explained that the door was on the leeward side which would make access and egress easier if there was a high wind. Sandra had prepared a receipted invoice for the £90 and Len tried to pay her again. Sandra declined, explaining he had already paid. Ra-Ra gave me the knowing look again.

Ra-Ra jumped in the lorry with Trevor, to spare Sandra from Aaron and because it made good sense for him to travel to the wholesaler after collecting a cabin and a loo. Meanwhile Sandra and I would go back to her house to await a cabin. The final lift of the day would be back to the haulage yard with two cabins. Josh was going to make two lifts to include the sentry boxes to the airfield so the bulk of the removals would be complete.

I went over to say farewell to Len but he had gone. Sandra was sitting in the car making notes. When I got in, I leaned over and kissed her. She said, 'What was that for?'

I said, 'Because you're such a diamond.'

She replied, 'That's a rough diamond because you haven't polished me yet.' She then added that being 'polished' sounded quite fun. As usual, I had no clever retort but just blushed.

*

Driving back to Sandra's I plucked up courage and told her that I hoped I would not disappoint her, but that I was pretty inexperienced in the art of love. It was such a cliché that we both laughed and that made it sound less cheesy. Sandra moved beside me on the bench seat and held my hand. 'Harry,' she whispered, 'any experience is more than mine.'

'What, you're a virgin?' I blurted out. It seemed such an inappropriate thing to say and I immediately regretted being so blunt. 'But what about the letters?' I added as an afterthought.

Sandra moved back saying, 'What letters?'

I realised I had never disclosed that I had recognised her as the author of Jacqui's letters. 'Jacqui's,' I answered. Sandra fell silent. She looked uncomfortable and shuffled in her seat. She started crying. For the second time that day I had no idea what to say.

Sandra sobbed, telling me that I had been deceiving her all along and she had been right from the beginning, I was just using her. She cried that the letters were not from her and that she was just the scribe. She shrieked, 'Curse Jacqui, curse Amber and curse Jade.' I remonstrated and said that I was going to mention the letters but I had been overtaken by events. I explained that I loved her letters. It was just like *Cyrano de Bergerac*, not all the sex nonsense. I told her I loved the tales of the cat and the culture. Sandra said 'sex nonsense,' and giggled. Sandra paused. 'But *Romeo and Juliet* at the parachute jump, shepherd's pie and *Carnival of the Animals*, you were using my letters to take advantage of me!'

I was able to respond emphatically. 'Well, I have done a lousy job so far in taking advantage of you.'

'I agree,' she replied, 'you have singularly failed to seduce me, despite knowing more about me than I do!'

We pulled in at Sandra's and she said, 'Harry will you get your act together? I have selected you for some "sex nonsense".' I gave a hollow laugh; the pressure was back on me. As we walked up the path Sandra added, '*The Tales of the Cat and the Culture* would make a great film title.'

CHAPTER 18

The cabin in Sandra's mum's garden seemed so large. I was sure that either the council or neighbours would complain but we pressed on regardless. The cabin was by far the best of the batch and I made a mental note to never let Marcus visit. The cabin had carpets throughout, two desks, three filing cabinets and window blinds. There was a kitchen area through an internal door with fitted cabinets, a sink and taps if we could fix up any running water. Sandra had taken the extra desk and cabinets from another cabin. On the whiteboard on the wall Sandra had listed all of the cabins, sentry boxes and toilets. She had tabulated their locations, date on hire and other details so she knew everything about our stock.

Rather than a step up to the cabin, Sandra had placed a ramp so our first visitor could be her mother. Mrs McGregor was thrilled. Sandra explained what we had and where they were. She explained that Uncle Tommy had been invited over as we were keen to let him know just how professional the company planned to be. Mrs McGregor squeezed my hand and thanked me. I was able to put my hand on my heart and say, 'Mrs McGregor, it's all your daughter's work. I'm just the errand boy.'

Sandra had only taken two days' holiday and was due back to work on the Friday. 'Mum,' she said, 'you know I only took the job with Jacqui so that I could be close to you? Well, now I cannot get any closer, I am giving up my apprenticeship and am going to work for Harry.' She added, 'Harry and I have earned £290 in five days. If my share was just £50, it would be the equivalent of three weeks at the salon.'

Mrs McGregor interrupted and in a slightly hesitant voice whispered, 'Sandra, I have complete faith in you and Harry and you have my blessing.' Sandra hugged her mum and I walked out from behind the desk and hugged them both. I was so minded that everything had happened and yet I had been a spectator. Sandra was the driving force and I had a feeling of inadequacy.

CHAPTER 19

I had a TA weekend which started at the drill hall on the Friday night. We were off to Otterburn until the Sunday. I felt badly prepared and was sure I had not packed half of what I was going to need. Sandra was going to write down all her thoughts about the business so we could meet on the Monday at 0900 prompt for our first working day together in our office. Sandra was also taking her mother to yet another relative in Appleby so would be away on the Sunday in any event. I had hoped the weekend would give me a chance to unwind from what had been a frantic week. I was collared by Eddie on arrival. He saluted and tried to be deferential but I could see he was angry. I did not have the fear that I once had but I was cautious. He did not mince his words in telling me that I had stolen Sandra from the salon and that Jacqui was livid. Jacqui had trained Sandra and given her the start she needed and Sandra had betrayed her. I calmed Eddie down by saying that Sandra was a strong woman, just like Jacqui, and I had no control over Sandra. I added just like Eddie had no control over Jacqui. Eddie paused and just like in days gone by he calmed and said, 'You're right, boss, you and I are on the same side on this, our girls are too tough for us.' I found myself agreeing and both Eddie and I walked into the drill hall. We were on the same side. I put my tongue into the gap in my teeth and thought thank goodness. Marcus was also pleased to see me. His landlord had seen the sentry boxes and wanted to use three around the airfield perimeter to give the illusion of security as there had been some petty theft. I had assumed that this meant that he was happy with the storage but Marcus told me he had negotiated a fee of £60 per month which was to be knocked off Marcus's rent. Marcus told me he would pay me £50 per month so we all made a killing! It sounded like another typical confusing Marcus contract. I shook his hand. I knew Sandra would be pleased with yet another deal she could add to her list.

*

The TA weekend went particularly well. Major Tomey had asked me to organise a march and shoot competition for the company. This is simply a race by a fully loaded team of men around an eight-mile circuit followed by a short shooting event at the end. On the Saturday morning the Colonel decided that all three companies should take part. There was serious groaning from the less prepared and a significant increase in my administration but it turned out to be a success. Major Tomey took most of the credit but I did not mind.

*

I could not sleep on Monday morning and went to the cabin at just before eight. I parked beside it and noticed that a light was on. Sandra came out onto the ramp to greet me. She looked radiant. Her hair was down and she seemed so vibrant. She was thrilled that I was early and we hugged. I said that I should carry her over the threshold. I lifted her up to carry out my threat and banged her head on the doorframe. Sandra moved her head back abruptly and I lost my balance dropping her through the door. Sandra was unhurt and laughing. She said, 'When you carry me over any threshold in the future, I want to borrow your yellow safety helmet.'

Sandra had run an electric cable from the garage and had connected it to a socket box at the back of the cabin. It was not a normal three pin plug but an industrial cable so it not only gave power to the lights but also the sockets. It was a significantly better cabin than any on the road contract. Sandra's dad had a workshop (as opposed to a garage) and Sandra explained that there was nothing that he did not have. Despite my engineering degree, I was bringing nothing to this party. I told Sandra of the deal with Marcus and she was pleased. She went over and marked the whiteboard with the details. We then had our first meeting. Sandra had helpfully written an agenda. I was nominated and seconded by Sandra as chairman and then she went down the agenda allocating me jobs. I did take notes but at the end Sandra gave me a typed list of all the jobs that I had written down.

I could not believe that my primary role was to source more cabins. I queried this as we had no storage and surplus cabins but Sandra assured me that, once business took off, we would need at least twenty more cabins. Our main priority was to repair the damaged cabins so they would be useable. Tommy had not been able to double stack because of the damaged doors and windows. Sandra was minded that the current telephone arrangement was not satisfactory and that the GPO could take four months to install a phone.

It was surprising just how much we had to do to get the fledgling company organised. Sandra was churning out lists of things to buy, things to do, things to borrow and people to meet. I was playing catch up. Sandra reminded me that I had to take George to his bridge class that afternoon and that she was going to her charity meeting. In the event we closed early and agreed to meet in the morning.

*

George had been persuaded to make up numbers for an evening's Bridge at the house of one of the ladies who had been helping to prepare his lunch. He was annoyed with himself for being, as he called it, dragooned. He was anxious that he had not played Bridge for a decade and he could not for the life of him remember the conventions. I tried to reassure him that it would all come back, but that only made him even grouchier. I asked if he had any books on Bridge and he confessed that he had a flimsy guide which he had been trying to understand. It was in his bedroom so I went through and collected it. I had played as Steve's partner when his parents had come to stay and Steve had taught me two basic conventions. I understood how to work out how many points were in any given hand. With the crib sheet and my limited knowledge George relaxed. All George needed was the comfort of knowing what he already knew. I was able to reassure him that he had lost none of his old sharpness. I had no idea how good his Bridge had been in the past but when I dropped him off, he told me he would be better than Omar Sharif. I just agreed with him as I had no idea why the star of *Lawrence of Arabia* could help him with a three no trumps bid.

*

The next morning just as I left the gate, I was collared by the postman. He was delivering three letters all addressed for me. He remined me that the last time we had met was when I robbed him of his mail sack on Long Benson Hill. I laughed and shook his hand. He was pleased that I was alright and wondered how the lady was that I had shocked so much. He waved me off saying he was going nowhere until I was well clear. I shoved the letters into my coat pocket and drove to my new office. Sandra was in before me and proudly showed me the telephone extension that had been carefully extended from her mother's hall into the cabin. I was suitably impressed. I was somewhat deflated when she told me it had not been connected yet but she hoped that it would be done in a day or two. She went on to explain that she had been to the charity meeting where she mentioned our new venture. The meeting was at Edward's because Rowan was having to work late as there was a major incident. It all sounded very exciting and she was looking forward to hearing all about it. She gave out the business cards which Rowan had helped print. She had confessed that the phone was not up and running yet and why. Edward, who seemingly I had met at the meeting, had an old phone and 30ft of cable which he gave to Sandra. I could not remember Edward. Sandra explained he was with Steph and I could not remember her either. Sandra was exasperated and asked me if I remembered the meeting. I threw my hands up and declared, 'Sandra, I had my head between your knees most of the evening, I could think of nothing but you!' Sandra scoffed and scolded me for bringing up non-business dealings in the office.

Sandra went back to the house to help her mother with breakfast and I took the opportunity to open the letters. The first was from the constabulary. It thanked me for my recent assistance with their enquiries. It seemed to suggest that there would be no further action and that I could collect my belongings from the station. It did not state what the belongings were but I presumed it was the cash. I reread the letter so many times trying to work out whether they were going to pick me up again for a night in the cells. I was both angry and relieved as it seemed to suggest I had been a volunteer helping them. I decided that anger was a wasted emotion. The second letter was from the polytechnic. Dr Jenkins was gathering some hand-picked alumni to assist with a recruitment drive and I was his chosen graduate. I was invited to a meeting some fortnight hence when all would be revealed. There was a tear off reply slip and a helpful stamped-addressed return envelope. The third was far more curious as it was addressed in a beautiful italic blue ink. The envelope was addressed to 'Handsome Harry'. It said, 'Dear Handsome Harry, this is just a short missive from Sarah, Dave and Carole's friend.' It was written in almost copperplate handwriting. I read the opening line and I instinctively knew it was going to cause me anguish. I did not read it but for some inexplicable reason put it back into my jacket to read later.

Sandra bounced back in and noted the two letters on the desk and I invited her to read them. I was so wishing that I had left the other letter with them. I had an urge to pull it out from my pocket but knew if I did so, it would look as if I was treating it separately. I had not even read the letter but felt it was burning into my chest. I obviously looked distressed as Sandra asked if I was alright. I mumbled about heartburn and Sandra went through to the kitchen and brought a jug of water and a glass. I drank slowly as she was holding the police letter saying 'I suppose this is good news?' I was nodding. She suggested that I drive to the station that day when I went to visit the trading estate. I was due to go and check that Alby was happy with his cabin and wander round the area asking if anyone else needed extra capacity. She also went and marked my polytechnic date in the diary. I had not planned to accept the invite but Sandra wanted me to go as it would be a good marketing opportunity. Sandra was so vibrant and full of life it was making me feel inadequate. She opened her drawing pad and showed me her ideas for our sales campaign. It was quite brilliant. 'Space: the final frontier' was our strapline straight from *Star Trek*. Sandra had sketched some cabins at sharp angles and the sentry box to look like a rocket and she was going to take her camera and try and turn the sketches into photographs. Her enthusiasm was infectious and I gave her a cuddle. She had written a piece for the *Gazette* about offering space as a solution. It was so well written and I foolishly asked if she had written it herself. She stood up and adopted the hands-on-the-hips pose that I had seen before. 'Do you still see me as that floozy?' I apologised.

I did not tell her that it was me that was the fraud. Sandra had all the cards; I was going to have to up my game if I was going to keep her. I did say, 'Floozy, trollop, my goodness you have such a wonderful vocabulary.'

*

After a cup of tea with Alby and a guided tour of his hairdressing wholesale warehouse, I sat in the car and read Sarah's letter. It was initially an apology for her 'overexuberance' at the engagement party. She thanked me for my assistance in helping her friend in helping her. I had forgotten just how drunk Sarah was so I was quite amused by her recollection of events. The third paragraph was telling me how much Carole had enjoyed the parachuting weekend and that she, Sarah, wished she had been and could I provide details? The last paragraph was the one that I had dreaded. Sarah explained that Carole was 'not in a good place' and how a visit from me would be the perfect tonic. It explained how we were such a perfect match and how sorry Carole was that she had not given me a chance.

I stopped reading. My heartrate had increased and I found myself looking round to see if anyone was watching me. I was feeling a strange guilt that I was misbehaving behind Sandra's back. I got out of the car and briskly walked round the carpark to calm down. I was telling myself that I had done nothing wrong. I thought I had no feelings for Carole but I could not understand my urge to go and see her.

Alby had suggested I spoke to Ron who had a car repair yard on the Boundary Road, as he was always looking for extra parking. It did not sound too promising but it would be a distraction and something to report back to Sandra. The businesses on the Boundary Road seemed less 'organised' than those in the trading estate. There were various car breakers and tyre fitters and a scrapyard. Ron had a bespoke specialist car-tuning garage. Ron was a pleasant enough chap who was happy to show me some of the cars that were currently under his wing. I was distracted by thinking of the letter and that helped as Ron had an encyclopaedic knowledge of car trivia. My apparent interest put him in overdrive as he showed me an engine that was in pieces and how he and his team would have it ready for Brands Hatch. I managed to extract myself when Ron was told his wife was on the phone. I cannot remember if I even told Ron why I called but it had killed thirty minutes and I had put the letter behind me for the moment.

*

Luckily, I had taken the police letter to the police station with me, as even with the letter they were reluctant to help. I was the only person in the cold reception where Dawn and Sandra had spent the night. The desk officer took ten minutes even to acknowledge my presence. Eventually he read the letter and suggested I came back when they were less busy. I thought he was joking and laughed. On reflection this probably was not sensible because it put his back up, but it did reflect the absurdity. I gave a staged look up and down the empty reception. It was not lost on the officer who went out of the back. He returned several moments later with a brown envelope and a form that I was invited to complete. I had a pen so was able to comply. I think even this annoyed him as I could tell he was not going to offer me a pen.

I left the police station and returned to the cabin with my cash in one pocket and a problem in the other.

CHAPTER 20

When I got back to the cabin Sandra was not there. She had left a short note that her mother was poorly and she had taken her to hospital. Sandra had said that her mother had been unwell following her trip to Appleby but I had only noted the situation. I now felt that I should have been more attentive. I was not sure what to do. I knew that Edward was coming either today or tomorrow to try and install the phone so someone needed to be around but I was also keen to get to the hospital. Sandra must have gone in an ambulance so may have been stranded at the hospital. I decided that the family emergency took precedence. I locked up the cabin and drove to the wasteland where I knew I could park near the hospital.

*

I found the wasteland entrance easily and thought back to the hours searching the estate for it, only a matter of months ago. I had a moment of doubt when it occurred to me that Mrs McGregor could be in another hospital. The hospital reception was full but eventually I was able to ask a flustered but helpful receptionist where I might find Mrs McGregor. She was on an observation ward in the west wing. The WRVS ran a small flower stand in the entrance and so I grabbed a bunch of flowers and headed off to the west wing. The west wing had its own reception and the chap manning the desk was less helpful than the main reception. They should have given me the number and name of the ward and he had less access to the information than they did. I did not want to get involved in what was some internal dispute. I said I was the son-in-law and that Mrs McGregor was on an observation ward. Eventually he suggested I tried Roseberry Ward on the fourth floor. Sandra was sitting rather forlorn on a single chair in the corridor. She had her head in her hands and did not see or hear me approach. I startled her and she went to stand up. I swung my hands round to hug her but as I brought the flowers round, I clonked her on the head. 'Harry,' she exclaimed, 'what are you doing here?' I replied that I had some flowers without heads for her mother. Sandra held me for far longer than I anticipated but I just let her. It felt warm and comfortable and I was determined to ignore Sarah's short missive.

*

Mrs McGregor had picked up an infection and, given that she had a degraded ability to fight it off because of the MS, the doctor was concerned. They had put her on some sort of drip and they wanted her to rest. They had suggested that Sandra came back for the evening visiting but Sandra was reluctant to leave her. I suggested a compromise that we went and ate and then came back. We walked into town just as we had some months earlier. I was able to put my head into the ward to leave the flowers which looked better than they should.

*

The first café was just closing so we went over the road to a pub that was just opening. There were only bar snacks so we made do with nuts and pork scratchings. Sandra was clearly anxious. Her mother's illness was gradual but not in a linear manner. Each time there had been an episode she had recovered but was significantly worse. Sandra had not remembered her father's decline but had only heard about it from her mother. Sandra had seldom mentioned her father. I mentioned to her that Uncle Tommy had said he was a fine man and that I would have liked him. This made Sandra smile. We sat in silence for a little while. 'I will be very lonely tonight without mother,' she whispered.

    'I would be happy to be your knight in shining armour and keep you safe in your bed,' I replied.

'Not too safe, I hope,' she added.

*

Mrs McGregor had been sedated and so was not very responsive. Sandra and I talked at her. The flowers were in a cardboard vase and I kept wondering if eventually the water would leak out. I was doing this to try and stop thinking about the night with Sandra. I so hoped that I would not be a disappointment. I also had to get George's car back as he had booked it in for an MOT in the morning and I had agreed to take it. I could not believe the bad timing. In the event we went back via George. We told him of the situation and I said that I was staying at Sandra's so there was transport to get her to the hospital if it was needed. George said he was happy that I took the car and sorted out the MOT. We called in to see Dawn and Aunt Gladys who were very anxious to see us. Dawn had been having some contractions and was clearly in some distress. Dawn was worried that the baby was on the way. Aunt Gladys was reassuring her that everything was fine, and now that Harry was home, he could drive her to the maternity hospital. Dawn had spoken to the hospital at lunchtime but they told her that because her waters had not broken, she was fine. The waters still had not broken but Dawn was looking grey and in some discomfort. Sandra went and put her arm round Dawn. Sandra made no mention of her mother. She looked at me and nodded, I nodded back.

I either had to call an ambulance or get Dawn straight in the car. I chose the latter, not least because Aunt Gladys insisted on coming. We all piled into the car. Dawn was in the front seat and it was at that point her waters broke. I now learned that the term was well described. Aunt Gladys had a towel which she produced from her huge bag and, whilst Dawn wanted to go and change, Aunt Gladys assured her she had a change of clothes and her nighty in the bag. I joked that Aunt Gladys was clearly no stranger to these emergencies. I said nothing further as Aunt Gladys was crying. I drove into the 'Ambulance Only' bay at the maternity hospital and Sandra rushed over to grab a wheelchair. She was stopped by an officious porter who brought it over himself and insisted in pushing Dawn to the entrance. Whilst I went to park the car, the other two went with Dawn.

*

On my return, Sandra was waiting in the waiting room. Aunt Gladys had, with Dawn's full agreement, gone to be with her. Sandra and I sat in reception watching the moon rise through a skylight. I squeezed her hand and said, 'Someone up there is playing us along.' I was mindful that the car had its MOT in the morning so I was going to be stuck in Long Benson unless I could get a lift. I thought Ra-Ra might be the answer. I knew he would be working at the Italian so I went down the corridor to the phone box to phone him. There was a queue for the phone. I picked up a discarded *Evening Gazette* that was on one of the chairs. It was not opened at the front page so it was some moments before I got to the headline. 'Dead Body Found Beside Busy Highway.' It was a report by Rowan. The body of a man had been exposed by a dog digging near a road bridge at Lower Nab. A dogwalker could not get his dog to come back to him and it was because the dog had exposed a buried corpse. There was little further to report at the time the *Gazette* had gone to print. I was so transfixed by this that I missed my slot in the telephone queue. Lower Nab was the bridge built by Rod Clough's team where Eddie poured the concrete. I kept telling myself that the chances of it being Aiden Malcolm were very slim, but I was not convincing myself.

I managed to speak to Ra-Ra at the Italian but not before being grilled by a suspicious Aldo as to why I needed to speak to him. Aldo sarcastically asked whether it was a problem with my cat. I had no idea what he was talking about but said it was because I was at the hospital and needed to organise a lift. This was true and seemed to satisfy Aldo who summoned Ra-Ra from the kitchen. Ra-Ra was more than happy to help. He would meet me at the MOT garage at eight and drive me home. He would bring a spare helmet. I said that I probably would not want to go home, but to the hospital as Dawn may have had her baby and I would need to organise a taxi for her and my Aunt Gladys. Ra-Ra wanted to know why Dawn was at the hospital and was she well. I explained that the baby was on its way. He wanted to know which hospital. I gave him a brief background and told him I would tell him all about it in the morning.

*

Sandra was still sitting in the maternity reception. There was no news from the ward. I suggested she went and phoned the General Hospital to see how her mother was. Sandra declined saying that she would go and see her mother tomorrow. I put my arm round her and we just sat for what seemed to be the next hour with no distractions. I had always assumed that there would be a flood of people going in and out. Expectant fathers pacing the floor and anxious relatives shrieking with excitement but, on this evening, there was nothing. Sandra and I were the only people. I asked a passing nurse why it was so quiet and she told me that babies came when they were ready, not when the hospital asked for them. There was some commotion when a leather-clad biker came in through the double doors and dropped a crash helmet. It was Ra-Ra. He had a box that was not fully closed, a bunch of flowers and a helmet in his arms. He had dropped a second helmet. I went over to unburden him asking why he had come. He was clearly nervous as he was in full stutter mode. Sandra sat him down and gave him a glass of water. He explained that Aldo had been angry with him for taking phone calls at work. Ra-Ra was fed up with the job anyway so he had told Aldo what he could do with his pasta and walked out. On the way home he stopped in the convenience store for some Polos and chewing gum. They had flowers and fruit so he made up a 'makeshift' hamper for Dawn and on impulse came straight to the hospital. His impulse was delayed when he remembered he had to go home first for the second helmet. It was typical Ra-Ra. I asked if he had put a bath plug in the hamper and he smiled. Sandra looked quizzical but I said, 'Don't ask.'

During the time we were distracted by Ra-Ra the reception area was filling up. There were suddenly at least two expectant fathers and a host of anxious in-laws. At least three very large ladies came through. They were all waddling and holding their backs as if the nurse had briefed them for my benefit. I was feeling quite 'the calm' spectator. My calm was broken by the arrival of Aunt Gladys and a nurse. I could see from Aunt Gladys's beaming face that it was good news. I was flanked by Sandra and Ra-Ra as she hugged me. 'You are an uncle; Philip Arthur was born ten minutes ago, 6lbs 3oz, mother and baby are beautiful.'

The nurse, realising I was the uncle, turned to Ra-Ra who was holding the flowers and his box and said, 'So you must be the proud father.'

Ra-Ra tried to respond but his stutter was such that he could well have been saying yes. The nurse took him by the elbow and led him down the corridor. Sandra tried to remonstrate but I told her to let him go. Dawn would be delighted with the presents and we had nothing to offer.

Both Aunt Gladys and Sandra told me off. Aunt Gladys sat down muttering, 'What a night!' She asked me if I would tell my mother and father. As an afterthought she added, 'And, I presume, the baby's father.' I replied I would, all in good time. Aunt Gladys looked exhausted and I told her to rest whilst Sandra and I went to see Dawn.

*

Dawn was partially sitting up and looking radiant. She had Philip swaddled on her left arm and a bunch of flowers on her right. Ra-Ra was sitting in a chair close to her side. Sandra kissed the baby on its head and then Dawn on the cheek. I followed suit as it seemed to be the protocol. Ra-Ra said he would leave but Dawn told him he could not. Ra-Ra seemed as radiant as Dawn. Sandra and Dawn chatted about what had happened and the discomfort Dawn was feeling. Dawn had lost some blood but all was well. I tried to feign interest. Dawn was in a private room but was being moved onto the ward once a porter was free. She would probably be allowed home in thirty-six hours as it was her first baby. I told her that Sandra's mum was in the General Hospital and the car was in for a service and MOT tomorrow. Ra-Ra offered to pick up Dawn and the baby. I laughed and said, 'Are you getting a side car?' But he assured me that he could borrow his mum's boyfriend's car for such an important journey. Our planning was cut short by the nurse saying that they were moving Dawn onto the ward and only the father could stay as it was past visiting time.

Dawn waved to Sandra and I. She said to Ra-Ra, 'You can stay for a while, can't you?' He was nodding and nodding and nodding.

*

Sandra and I helped a very tired Aunt Gladys to the car. I offered to get a wheelchair for her but she was having none of it. I had Aunt Gladys on one arm and the bike helmet on the other. Sandra was on Aunt Gladys's other arm and we practically carried her to the entrance. I then went and got the car and drove over to her to save her walking any further. Aunt Gladys was dozing in the car and Sandra and I were surprised when she suddenly said, 'Why doesn't Sandra stay with us, she could have Dawn's bed?' I looked at Sandra who was nodding like Ra-Ra.

'Great idea,' I replied. We made sure Aunt Gladys had retired to bed and I suggested a small nightcap. Aunt Gladys had a bottle of Harveys Bristol Cream which we occasionally opened when there was something to celebrate. Sandra agreed it was just the moment. A new baby and a night to ourselves. I was standing by the sideboard when the phone rang. I answered and heard the stuttering Ra-Ra. Dawn had had a bleed and been taken to the General Hospital. He was frantic. I told him that Sandra and I would head straight to the General.

I was so pleased that I had not had a drink. Sandra and I hardly spoke as we drove through largely empty streets. Sandra said, 'Isn't it ironic that my mum may be in the next ward to Dawn?' I found myself reassuring her that both would be well and out of hospital soon. 'My mum will never get any better but I am sure Dawn will,' she quietly responded.

*

The General Hospital car park was far fuller than I expected given how late it was. We walked briskly to reception. I was resisting the urge to run. The reception was helpful. Dawn had been in the Emergency Ward but had now been transferred to the Thorpe Ward on the fourth floor. Sandra told me it was the ward next to Roseberry where her mother was. The receptionist said that we would not be able to visit either ward as it was too late. I asked if we could go up and ask the ward how the patients were. The young lady smiled and said it is worth a knock but please understand if you are sent away.

The hospital was deserted and the lift to the fourth floor groaned so much that Sandra and I got out on the second floor and walked the rest. The last thing we wanted was to be stuck in a lift. We both felt vindicated when we arrived at the fourth floor and the lift had not. We first went to Thorpe Ward as it seemed busy. I caught the eye of a nurse through the window on the locked door. She acknowledged me and came back some five minutes later. I explained that I was Dawn's brother and next of kin. She seemed surprised and told me that, 'Dawn's husband is next of kin and he is with her now.' She assured me that Dawn was well and that they would continue with the observation and I should come back in the morning.

I thanked the nurse and she locked the door behind her. I shook my head and said to Sandra, 'Ra-Ra's danced with Dawn once over breakfast and he's now her "next of kin".' She replied that it was 'a kind of love story'. He cared so much about her despite her unusual circumstances.

*

Roseberry Ward was dark and silent and even though we waited outside for twenty minutes, there was no movement. We were both shattered and decided to return in the morning. We would go back to Aunt Gladys's so she would not be worried in the morning. I looked at my watch; it was almost morning.

It was freezing outside so I gave Sandra my jacket to put over her shoulders. She was very grateful. As we got in the car, she removed my jacket and Sarah's letter fell onto the floor. Sandra joked that it looked like a love letter. She read the envelope in the light of the open door.

When the door shut, the light went off. Sandra sat in silence. I do not know if it was just because I was tired or Sandra was tired but I said, 'It is, sort of.'

She said, 'Can I read it?'

I said, 'Perhaps in the morning when we're less tired.' I was trying to be helpful as I did not mind her reading it, but it sounded as if I did mind her reading it. She carefully put it back in the jacket pocket and said please drive me home. I tried to insist that she read it, but the moment had passed. I tried to explain that Sarah called me 'Handsome Harry' but she put her fingers in her ears and went la la la. It was a cold uncomfortable journey. I kept trying to explain that Sarah was Carole's friend but Sandra was not receptive. I even told her about the body being found on the bridging site but there was not a flicker. I stopped the car outside of her mother's house. She climbed out and ran to the front door. I called after her but she slammed the door and I heard her apply the three locks.

I cried all the way home.

CHAPTER 21

I do not know why I got undressed and climbed into bed as I did not sleep. It was 0545 and I was taking the car to the garage at 0800. Tonto was making a strange sound in the corner. I presumed it was because I had disturbed her too early but she persisted. In the end I walked over to find that she had brought me a present of a half-dead shrew. Tonto was unusually proud of herself. It was just another brick to add to the wall of disappointment that was being built around me. I dispatched the poor shrew with a lump-hammer. There was no easy, humane way I could think of but at least this method was quick. I wrapped the small corpse in a piece of hessian and dropped it in the pedal bin. I had a shower and dressed and, as I was coming out of the shed, Aunt Gladys shouted through to me. I went to see her, she had had breakfast and wanted to go and see Dawn and Philip. She knew I was going to drop off the car and had risen early so I could take her on the way to the garage. Without sounding dramatic, I explained that Dawn had been taken to the General Hospital but everything was fine and I had been there to see her. Aunt Gladys bombarded me with questions. She wanted to know what time I had been, who was there, why Dawn had been moved, where was Philip, had I seen Philip and had the priest been? I tried to reassure her but she was putting on her coat and demanding that we left. I had never seen Aunt Gladys so animated and agitated. She was ready to go and then paused. 'The blanky, I need the blanky.' I had seen the same anxiety from Aunt Gladys when she thought she had lost the square of material. I pointed to the sideboard and sure enough the blanky was the said piece of cloth.

I was not sure that the hospital would allow Aunt Gladys in so early but I thought it easier to argue with the hospital than Aunt Gladys in her present state. Aunt Gladys asked if Sandra was still in bed. I explained that after visiting Dawn, I had driven her home. Nothing further was spoken.

*

I had to take Aunt Gladys up in a service lift as the one that Sandra and I had chanced the night before had an 'out of order' board outside. Aunt Gladys would never have made the stairs. The ward was busy serving breakfast and whilst the charge nurse was reluctant to allow access, he agreed that Aunt Gladys could slip in. I bade farewell and headed to the garage. I was running late but the garage seemed indifferent. I was looking for Ra-Ra on his motorbike. I had remembered to take the crash helmet from the car. I was thinking that I could have checked on Mrs McGregor but it was early and Sandra may not have taken kindly to the gesture given her mood when I left her. A car in the car park flashed its lights and a man waved from the driver's window. It was a bright red Golf. Ra-Ra had borrowed a car. He was as good as his word. He wanted to know where to take me. He was keen to get back to the hospital to see Dawn. I asked him how she was and he explained that she had given everyone a fright. 'When they took her to the post-natal ward she collapsed when she stood up out of the wheelchair. She had knocked her head and has a "shiner",' he added. They were concerned that she had some internal bleeding as her blood pressure was very low and so they had taken her to the General Hospital by blue light ambulance. Ra-Ra had followed on his bike after ringing me. They had let him see her again after about forty minutes because they thought he was the dad. He kept getting jobs to do. He had fed Philip a bottle and changed a nappy with the help of a nurse. Ra-Ra was relating this tale without a hint of a stutter. He was chatting as if he was the father. I was so hoping that Dawn was happy about this unfolding situation.

*

Ra-Ra asked where I wanted to go. He was surprised when I said I had no idea. There was no point going to Aunt Gladys and I did not want to be stranded at the cabin. The reality was I did not know what to say to Sandra. I had to make up with her soon, as any delay would only prolong my agony. He suggested we went to see Dawn although visiting was not until 1000. I asked if he minded driving to the café on the way into town as I needed a big breakfast. Ra-Ra was, as ever, happy to oblige. Filled with the fullest 'full English' that even included a lamb chop, Ra-Ra and I headed back to the hospital. I checked I still had the cursed letter in my pocket. I felt ready to do some penance and whatever other punishment I deserved to make Sandra understand. Ra-Ra chatted throughout the journey but I was oblivious, just nodding and agreeing with whatever he was saying at various points. He had stopped stuttering and whilst I wanted to mention it, I knew that would be the wrong thing to do. I was just thinking of what I could and should say to Sandra. On the fourth floor, Ra-Ra strutted off to Thorpe Ward and I hesitated before quietly strolling down to Roseberry Ward. I asked at the nursing station if Mrs McGregor was taking visitors. I was told that someone was with her and I could go down and join them. I had assumed it would be Sandra so braced myself. At the bedside was Uncle Tommy. He was delighted to see me and asked where Sandra was. I mumbled about her coming later. Mrs McGregor was smiling and, although she was struggling to speak, wanted to grasp my hand. She held it tightly and continued to do so as I sat down and perched on the very edge of a seat. Tommy said that Sheena could hear and understand everything but was struggling to talk. I joked that Mrs McGregor knew that I could do enough talking for everybody. Tommy told me that he and Sheena had been talking about the business; he added, 'Remember, Harry, that a business partnership is worse than a marriage if it fails.' He hoped that Sandra and I would have a partnership deed drafted by a lawyer, as they were essential business tools.

Mrs McGregor still had a hold of my hand and she pulled me to her. She was struggling to speak but whispered, 'Never mind the business partnership, please look after Sandra. I want you to have a marriage partnership.'

I blushed and Tommy said something like, 'Sheena, give the man a break.'

I said, 'Mrs McGregor, do I have your blessing if I ask her to marry me?' Tommy, Sheena and I then all sat crying for several minutes. I had no idea why I had asked, especially as, at the present time, Sandra could have been sticking pins into my effigy.

She was not, she was standing by the door. She looked at her mother and Tommy and asked if there had been bad news. 'On the contrary, Sandra, great news and congratulations.' Tommy beamed. He stood up and hugged a bemused Sandra. He offered her his seat but she declined, moving over to her mother and kissing her.

Mrs McGregor said, 'Congratulations' in her daughter's ear.

Sandra stood up saying to the room, 'What for?' I offered an explanation and Sandra replied that it had better be a good one. She said it just softly enough that I felt confident in proceeding. I explained that I had just sought Mrs McGregor's permission to marry her daughter and that Mrs McGregor had consented. Sandra started crying and collapsed into the seat Tommy had vacated. She looked at me and said, 'And what has Mrs McGregor's daughter to say about this?'

I confessed that, 'I could not confront Mrs McGregor's daughter with the proposal until I had Mrs McGregor's permission.'

Sandra responded, 'And now you have tricked Mrs McGregor into giving her permission, when will you be making your proposal to Mrs McGregor's daughter?'

'Well,' I replied, 'that's not public knowledge yet as there has been a procurement issue and such events require serious scene-setting. It's not something that can be rushed or taken lightly.'

Tommy gave Sandra a hug and kissed Sheena on the head saying, 'I'm leaving this happy family for now, but expect to see you all soon.' He shook my hand and patted me on the shoulder saying, 'Welcome to the family.'

I walked round the bed and gave Sandra a kiss on the head. 'Bye, potential mother-in-law, bye, potential wife. See you both later, I'm off to see my nephew.' I left hurriedly with a spring in my step. I needed to phone my mother and father, there was so much good news to spread.

*

I paused outside the Thorpe Ward to reflect on what I had just done. A wave of anxiety flooded over me. Had I just irrevocably planned my future just to resolve a petty argument? I sat down on one of the three chairs. I had to chat to someone who would be pleased with my decision and remind me how lucky I was to have found Sandra. I was almost twenty-seven. I did not even know how old Sandra was. This last thought alarmed me. I knew so little about her. I suddenly calmed and laughed out loud. Sandra was wonderful, she filled my every thought and I was missing her company already. I stood up with a new resolve, but thought, just to be certain, I would speak to George.

*

Aunt Gladys was holding the baby and Dawn and Ra-Ra were in deep conversation when I walked in. I had been reminded by the nurse that only two visitors were permitted and so someone had to leave. All were pleased to see me. Ra-Ra dropped Dawn's hand that he was holding and stood up inviting me to take his seat. I passed on the nurse's message and I asked if Ra-Ra could wait in the corridor. He was happy to oblige which was quite helpful as I wanted to check that Dawn was comfortable with his constant presence. Dawn looked the healthiest that I had ever seen her. In my head I compared the waif that I had found sitting on the steps some ten months ago. Dawn was thanking me. I was not sure why. I asked her how she was and she said, 'It's the happiest time of my life.' I asked if she was comfortable with Ra-Ra being ever present. I wanted to be subtle but there was no easy way to find out except by being blunt. Dawn smiled telling me he was the kindest and most wonderful man she had ever met and that she wanted her and Philip to spend the rest of their lives with him. I felt quite tearful. I was minded to mention my recent good news but held my tongue as I did not want to spoil Dawn's moment. I asked Aunt Gladys if I could hold Philip but to my surprise, she declined. She told me that I would have years with Philip. I would watch him grow to be a man. Aunt Gladys only had a short period with him and she was going to fill every moment. Aunt Gladys was crying and Dawn started crying too. I was unsure what had happened but could not stop my eyes filling up. Philip had the 'blanky' pinned to his baby gown. I decided to ask Dawn about it when Aunt Gladys was no longer there.

I did not have much to say to Dawn and I let her recount the birth and the subsequent drama. I asked about the name and she told me that Philip was named after the Prince and Arthur was, she paused and whispered, 'I'll tell you later.' I suggested I could go and ring my parents with the good news and was there anybody else I could tell. Dawn pondered and replied that at some time, but no hurry, Colin. I nodded and left the three of them. In the corridor I asked Ra-Ra if he was not a bit premature in ending his job so abruptly. He reminded me that I had done the same. He told me that he was off to do a Heavy Goods Vehicle course with the TA and, once he had his licence, he fancied a job driving. I was going to ask about Dawn but he beat me to it adding that he wanted to spend the rest of his life with Dawn and the baby and would I object. I smiled and patted him on the shoulder. I did not need to reply.

*

I did not have any change for the phone so bought a paper at the kiosk. I wanted to see if there was any further news about the body. There was no queue at the phone box and I had a seamless connection to mother. She was absolutely thrilled with Dawn's news. She asked how Philip was spelled. I had no idea. I did not realise there were different ways, but told her it was like the Prince. She told me that she and father would drive up the following day and would bring Karen, my sister. I did not mention my news as they had not met Sandra yet and actually Sandra had not said yes, as I had yet to ask her!

I had no car so felt somewhat restricted. I could get the bus back with Sandra or wait for Ra-Ra. The garage had not given any specific time to collect the car. On impulse I decided to ring them. I found the number in the *Yellow Pages*. It took ages for the phone to be answered but it was worth the wait as the car had passed the test and was ready for collection. The service was more than George had been told as they had to put a new tyre on the front offside. I told them I would come over as soon as possible. I nipped back into the Roseberry Ward. Sandra was reading and her mother was asleep. Sandra put her finger to her lips to say 'shhhh', but I knew and just kissed her. I whispered, 'I'm off to get George's car and will be back in an hour for you.' I then went back down to Thorpe Ward. Aunt Gladys still had the baby on her lap but seemed to be sleeping. I was mildly concerned that she would drop the baby. Dawn and Ra-Ra were back in deep discussion and seemed unaware of the baby's plight. They looked up and Dawn smiled. I asked if baby was secure in Aunt Gladys's arms and Dawn suggested I could try moving him but I would need a crowbar. I explained that the car was ready. Ra-Ra kissed Dawn. They did seem such an attentive couple. He suggested that we take Aunt Gladys home first as she needed food and sleep. I gently woke Aunt Gladys who begrudgingly agreed to the plan. Dawn had to stay an extra day on the ward for observation but we promised we would bring Aunt Gladys back. Aunt Gladys slept in the car, and when we got home, she went for a lie down. I made some hot buttered toast for her but when I took it through, she was in a deep sleep so I left it on the bedside table.

*

Once I had picked up the car I drove back to the hospital. I suggested Ra-Ra followed me so he could park on the wasteland. We both went up to the fourth floor together. He turned right, I turned left.

Sandra stopped me coming fully into the room as her mother was still in a deep sleep. She packed her book and we walked all the way down the four flights of stairs and back to the car in silence. I found this rather disconcerting but Sandra seemed fine. Sandra's first words were something like, 'I hope you will not be neglecting our business in the future by rushing off to seduce innocent girls and help expectant mothers.'

My response was that if the innocent girl that I had seduced became the expectant mother, I would definitely neglect the business. Sandra held both of my hands; it was an action that she did when sitting down, rather like the hands on the hips when she was standing. I knew I was in for a lecture.

She told me that my approach to her mother was the only response she had not expected. She had planned a thousand ways to reject my apologies and a thousand ways to thwart any acts of contrition. She had not slept. Her insecurities were in overdrive and she felt so angry. It was only because of her anger that I had a glimmer of hope. She told herself it was because she had loved me too deeply. She had planned to try and get back all of Jacqui's letters from Eddie to recall exactly what she had unwittingly exposed. She had thought me a cad and a bounder. I laughed at the 'Woosterish' language but she narrowed her eyes and I knew to keep listening. In short, she loved me and if I was ever minded to propose, she would probably accept.

She let go of my hands and we embraced. The kiss was soft and warm and lingering. We were parked on a piece of wasteland, and had I not been parked right next to Ra-Ra's red Golf, heaven knows what might have happened. We took the car back to George who was delighted to see us. He was getting 'cabin-fever', he told us, stuck in his 'cell'. Sandra briefed him about the baby. George told us he had a bottle of Champagne on ice ready for the occasion and that perhaps we could open it tomorrow. George asked how the business was going. I did not demur when Sandra invited him over. She said we had fitted a ramp for her mother so access was easy. George jumped at the chance.

*

Back at the cabin Sandra showed George all her wallcharts in detail. If George was not interested, he did not show it. George seemed full of questions and ideas. We were interrupted by Edward. He had kindly supplied the old phone and cable and was now going to try and join it to Sandra's mother's connection. He explained that he was an electrical engineer by training, not a GPO engineer, but he would give it a go. Sandra took him through to the house. George asked me what the baby was called. I said 'Philip' and he said 'is that all?'

I said 'Philip Arthur.' He nodded knowingly and I asked, 'What do you know that I don't know?' After securing my promise not to mention it to anyone he told me that Aunt Gladys had given birth to a baby son some seventy years ago. She had called him Arthur. She was a single unmarried girl and her parents insisted she gave him up for adoption. The Catholic church arranged the whole thing and Aunt Gladys had suffered ever since.

I asked about the blanky. George dabbed his eye with a hankie, as he said, 'That was the only physical item she had to remember him.'

Dawn told Aunt Gladys that if it was a boy, she would name him Arthur so that Gladys's 'Arthur' would never be forgotten. I felt so sad but it helped to explain so much. I asked George how he had found out. He told me that one of the ladies who brought him food, who he did not really like, told him. He had no idea how she knew but presumed Aunt Gladys had confided in her.

We both sat silently until interrupted by the phone on the desk suddenly ringing. We both looked at it as if we had never heard a phone ring. George made a face at me and picked up the receiver. 'Horace & Co, how can I help?' It was Sandra's surprised aunt from Appleby wanting to know how she was. Sandra cut in on the house phone and George hung up laughing. At least the phone was working. Edward came back to the cabin and shook my hand saying, 'Not bad for a first dabble.' He could not stay and refused any payment but did add that if he needed a cabin, he would want a big discount.

Horace & Co had also taken on the first member of staff. George was not just 'more than happy to man the phone', he insisted on doing so.

When Sandra came back, she had a tray of teas and sandwiches. She was thrilled that George was on the team. I was unsure how much Sandra knew about Aunt Gladys so thought I would mention George's revelation when we were alone. I did mention that my parents and sister were heading north tomorrow to see the baby and I was hoping Sandra could meet them. Sandra pretended to bite her nails. She mentioned that her mother was being delivered back later that day. She had been stabilised and was clear of the infection. Her MS seemed worse than before her illness. George said that he would 'man the fort', as long as I could deliver him and pick him up. Sandra said she could leave George sandwiches and that maybe my mother and father could come to meet her, rather than Sandra leaving her mother. I said that mother and father were going to be taken up with the baby but that was a possible solution.

*

I took George home. Aunt Gladys was on her knees trying to plug a vacuum cleaner plug into the wall. She was struggling and was grateful for my help. She was trying to tidy the house before her guests arrived and Dawn and the baby came home. I stood her up and steered her to her chair. I quite firmly told her that she had not to worry about such things. She had to stay fit and strong for Philip Arthur. I added the second name, now I knew the significance. I asked if she had eaten but she had not. I made her a beef sandwich. She asked that I put beetroot in as the bread was dry. I told her the bread was less than a day old but she insisted. It had been a long day, I had a shower and crashed out on my bed.

CHAPTER 22

If Tonto had not walked over me at 0830, I would have slept all day. I felt so content and happy. Tonto had no food in her tray which is why she had uncharacteristically woken me. Even though I had showered the previous night, I did so again. I wanted today to be a fresh start. I chose a new shirt which I had bought months ago but never taken from the packet. I found my Harris tweed jacket in the back of the metal cabinet. I hung up the old jacket after removing Sarah's letter. I put the letter in the vice so I could reply at some stage. I had no intention of seeing Carole but I would give Sarah details of the airfield. I put on my regimental tie. It was so long since I had worn a tie, it took me ages to get it right.

George was wearing a shirt and tie. He and I were both thinking alike. He said it was his first day at work and he wanted to impress his boss; he added, 'Sandra.'

I said, 'Of course.'

Sandra too looked stunning. Her hair was down and she had a flowery frock. Both George and I tried to outdo each other in our admiration of her until she told us both to grow up. Mrs McGregor was not home as the hospital were struggling with transport so she was due to be delivered this morning. Sandra said she was going back to the house to wait. I wheeled George behind the desk and almost on cue the phone rang. I left George to it. Sandra and I hugged in the hall. 'I am so nervous I can hardly think,' she said. I comforted her by saying she had to concentrate on her mother and not let my folks be a distraction. This was a different Sandra, more like the slightly anxious photographer at the wedding. She said, 'I hope your parents like me.' I reassured her that they were typical parents, but if there was ever a choice, I would always choose her.

*

I drove to the hospital for no other reason than that I had no other way of finding out what was happening. I did not know whether Ra-Ra would still have access to the car and it may be that I would have to drive Dawn and the baby home. I got to the Roseberry Ward to find Dawn all packed. She was holding the baby and a grip and Ra-Ra had both a Moses basket and a cradle for a car. Neither had a spare hand so I took Dawn's grip and walked with them back to the car park. Ra-Ra had the presence of mind to park both in the hospital carpark and to bring a selection of beds for the baby. He had never even held a baby before Philip, he confessed to me. I was looking for the red Golf but Ra-Ra led us to a rather old Hillman Minx. I did not ask about the provenance but said I would follow them back. I was worried that the old beast would break down as it had seen far better days. Back at the house Aunt Gladys had erected makeshift bunting and written cards saying, 'Welcome Home Dawn, Philip and Graham.'

I was wondering who 'Graham' was when Ra-Ra said, 'And even I get a welcome.'

*

George had left his bottle of Champagne with orders for me to open it when my folks arrived. He had told Aunt Gladys that there was a second bottle that he would open at Sandra's when we all came over. I helped Ra-Ra take the grip and the Moses basket through to Dawn's bedroom. I asked about the car and Ra-Ra said that it belonged to Ginge Jock and he had it for two days. He said that once he was back working, a car would be top of his list. I wanted to tell him that if he was taking on a family his list was going to be long and regularly shuffled. Mind you, I had no reason to know. Ra-Ra had borrowed a cot that needed putting together. He went through to my shed to get a screwdriver and a spanner. I heard a commotion in the hall and went through.

Mother and Father arrived laden with gifts and food. Karen was carrying the big orange Mister Man. It made me shiver and laugh in equal measures. I had a flashback to Otley Road. Mother immediately took the baby off Dawn and started interrogating the poor girl about her health and that of the baby. I was unsure how to introduce Ra-Ra, when he appeared at the door. Dawn picked up and said, 'This is my best friend Graham, but please call him Ra-Ra or he won't know who you're talking to.'

Everyone laughed. My father leaned over and shook Ra-Ra's hand saying, 'Well done.' Ra-Ra started stuttering something very badly. Luckily my father was well used to my cousin, so smiled and waited. The effect was almost instant. Ra-Ra calmed and gradually his voice modulated and he was able to welcome my parents and ask them if they had an easy journey. I assumed that my father thought Ra-Ra was the baby's father but I said nothing. Aunt Gladys suggested, as he was near the door, that Ra-Ra should put the kettle on. I had not realised quite how small the living room was. Karen wanted to hold the baby and mother wanted the loo so there was a series of moves which included passing the oversized orange Mister Man from person to person.

My father was right next to me and immediately asked how the job hunting was going. I swept his feet from under him by casually saying, 'Rather well.' I added, 'I've set up my own company and I'll be taking you and mother to my office this afternoon, if you're interested.' It was the first time in my life that my father was speechless. I did not let my father gather his thoughts but threaded my way to the kitchen to help Ra-Ra.

Ra-Ra had the same wide smile that he had carried for the previous two days. I asked him what his plans were after he gave Ginge Jock the Hillman back and he just shrugged his shoulders. I had a slight worry that in his enthusiasm to keep Dawn happy, he may not have inquired too much about the car. I told him to check it was insured for him to drive as I would not want Dawn and the baby being driven in a car that was not roadworthy. He nodded and reassured me that he would do nothing to put Dawn in any danger. He was earnest and so I added nothing further. I was becoming my own father. I took the tray of tea and coffee through to the front room. Aunt Gladys had the baby. Mother was beaming and deciding what she would be called; was it to be Nan, Grandma or Ga Ma, which was Karen's name for our late grandmother. Dawn thought Ga Ma was right as it would be like Ra-Ra. I hoped Dawn was not allowing the happiness of the birth to cloud her judgement. Then I remembered I was almost betrothed to a girl because I was not man enough to open a letter in front of her. My father interrupted my musing. He wanted to know about the business. I suggested that he and I went to the office where I could explain fully. I asked if anyone else wanted to join us but there were no takers. Father quizzed me for the whole journey but I gave nothing away. He tried to counsel me against any 'get rich quick' schemes and anything that involved selling. I liked the fact that I was taunting him but he was getting very tetchy.

*

We were welcomed by George who had had an eventful morning. I am not sure if it was just to impress my father but George gave me a full report. We laughed when he said he had been run off his feet, as he banged the wheels of his chair with his hands. He had arranged for two more cabins to go on hire to the Boundary Road Industrial Estate on the recommendation of Alby. They were on the same terms as the one that Alby had. There was also a query for a loo but as we did not have any available, he was going to go back to them. I sat father behind Sandra's desk so he could see her wallchart. I was about to brief him when she came in. She did not see my father, as she had her back to him or she probably would not have given me a hug and kiss. She said she had seen George's car arrive and wanted to make sure all was good and that my folks had arrived. I turned her round and said, 'Well, meet my father.'

Father stood up and shook Sandra's hand rather formally. I told Sandra that I was just about to brief my father but it was better if she did as she was fully up to date. Despite some initial hesitancy, Sandra gave a faultless presentation that resulted in applause from George. George said that he was so lucky to be working for such a great company. Sandra asked my father if he had any questions. For the second time that morning he was speechless. He thanked Sandra who proceeded to invite him through to meet her mother. As we followed Sandra down the path, Father asked in a whisper who she was. I did not respond, although I had the urge to say the girl I am planning to marry. Mrs McGregor was in her chair near the fireplace. The introductions were quite formal. Mrs McGregor could only whisper and her head was increasingly bent towards her left shoulder. She looked rather uncomfortable and I asked her if she needed a cushion. Sandra smiled when she said that a cushion might help. Sandra scolded her mother in a warm manner telling her that she would accept the help from me but not from her. Mrs McGregor added, 'But he is going to be family soon, then I can be horrid to him too.' Whilst it was said in a whisper, it was not lost on my father who gave me a quizzical look.

Sandra said she would make some coffee. My father sat on the sofa and I sat in the bay window. I explained to father that Mrs McGregor was just out of hospital. Mrs McGregor invited us to call her Sheena. Mrs McGregor said calling her Mrs McGregor made her feel old. She started telling father that she had MS and it was getting worse. Sandra cut her off and told her mother that she had to stay positive and that her time in hospital had taken its toll. Mrs McGregor asked about the baby and my father filled in all the details. He said he was sure Dawn would bring the baby over soon. I took a coffee out for George so missed the conversation whilst I was out. It was clearly about where Sandra and I met as Sandra was taking about Eddie's wedding when I came back. Sheena was getting a little tired and so Father and I went back to the cabin whilst Sandra took her to her bedroom. I suggested that we close the office earlier today so I could take George home. Sandra agreed. She would man the phone from the house. I would see her tomorrow. At the cabin, George was back on the phone. He was trying to source portable toilets. When he had finished, he told me he could not believe just how expensive they were to buy new; he was going to work out whether we could assemble our own. George was unsure we should close early but I assured him that Sandra would be monitoring the phone.

*

I took George back to his own house. He had a shepherd's pie waiting and I suspected he needed a rest too. Back at Aunt Gladys's house Dawn and the baby were having a sleep. Ra-Ra had gone and Karen and Mother were watching TV.It was clear that Father wanted to set the agenda. His opening words to Mother were not that he had seen my new office or heard about the company, but that he had met our new in-laws. Luckily Mother just scoffed; telling him she would hear everything from me without his hyperbole.

Karen was definitely interested in where the conversation was going as she stood up and turned off the television. It was easiest to start with Eddie's wedding. They all recalled I had met the photographer. Mother even remembered thinking I had glowed when I mentioned her. I did not remember glowing, whatever that was, but pressed on. Karen asked if she was the hairdresser and I said, 'Yes.'

Mother made one of those faces which made me realise where I had got my snobbery from. I did not dwell, save to say that Sandra and I had set up business together and I wanted to spend the rest of my life with her. Father came to my support saying she was a 'good looker' and had a business brain on her head. Karen asked when would we meet her. Mother went off on a ramble about everything coming at once 'what with the baby'. I reassured her that my plans were at a steady pace. I explained that I had not asked Sandra to marry me yet but had asked for her hand from her mother who was quite poorly. I would rather have not gone into too much detail. Father added that Sheena had MS. Mother still in her protective mode wanted to know if it was hereditary and would Sandra and any of her children catch it. Again, I reassured her that it could not be caught and that I loved Sandra and that she would too when she met her. Karen came over and hugged me saying that she was happy. She added, 'Can I be a bridesmaid?' Which slightly detracted from the sentiment.

'Maybe we can have a double wedding,' my increasingly annoying sister continued. I just wanted to escape. I told them I was going to get out of my work clothes and have a shower. Mother, Father and Karen had booked one night at the Five Bridges Hotel. It came with an evening meal. They had booked Dawn and Aunt Gladys and I to join them. I really did not want to go but felt compelled, not least as they needed two cars.

*

Dawn had her hands full with the baby and did not want to eat out. Aunt Gladys wanted to stay with Dawn and the baby and Karen was not too keen on either option, she just wanted to watch TV. I asked Karen if she would be happy to watch TV with my girlfriend's mum, so Sandra could come out and meet Mother and Father. Karen's response was if that was how she could get to meet Sandra, she would be happy. I phoned Sandra and, after she had consulted her mother, the evening was sorted. Well, almost sorted, as we would need to take two cars and I would have to do a double journey to return Karen to the hotel.

Karen and Mrs McGregor were a perfect match as they both seemed to want the same TV programmes, although I suspected Mrs McGregor was compliant as she was just happy for new company. Karen had told her that she would tell her everything about me.

*

Sandra and I made our own way to the hotel. Sandra was still nervous. I could see why. My father had been affable with Sandra and Mrs McGregor but Mother had been strangely cold. I knew that she too would have been nervous but she was acting uncharacteristically. I was not looking forward to the meal.

The hotel restaurant was dimly lit. There were very few people eating and it seemed cold. Father was drinking beer and my mother had a Babycham. I was driving and so had a ginger ale and Sandra just had water. Most of the first course was my father telling my mother about our business. Mother never asked Sandra or I to comment on what he was saying, so it was almost as if we were not there.

Whilst waiting for the main course there was a long

pause. I asked Mother if everything was alright. It was said in a genuine attempt to lift the tension but it had the wrong effect. Mother launched into a tirade about my hair-brained scheme that could not pay for me, never mind a family. Why was I rushing off to get married to a girl I hardly knew and she then she exclaimed, 'Is she pregnant too?!'

Sandra stood up and said, 'Excuse me,' and she went from the table. I followed her and stopped her just before the ladies' loo. I hugged her and tried to kiss her but she turned away, she was weeping. I was apologising for my mother and offering to drive her straight home. My father appeared at my shoulder; he too was apologising to Sandra. I told him it was Mother, not he, that should be apologising. He was agreeing and begging us to return to the table as the main course had arrived. Sandra declined saying she had lost her appetite. I had not, but found myself saying the same. Sandra and I walked slowly back to the car. I had already apologised for my mother but found myself doing it again.

Sandra stopped and adopted the hands-on-hips pose. 'This isn't going to work is it?' she said.

I laughed, replying, 'Of course it is, but not until you've produced loads of grandchildren for her.'

She said, 'fat chance of that, you never come anywhere near me.' I grabbed her and told her that it was not true and we were going to skip to the car. So that is what we did, oblivious to the group of people waiting in a nightclub queue and the two policemen on the street corner.

*

Karen had a great night. Mrs McGregor had let her roast marshmallows in front of the fire. I left Sandra, telling her I would be in the office at 0800 because hair-brained schemes do not run themselves. Karen was telling me about the fun Sandra used to have as a child. Her dad raced a sports car. Much of what she said I already knew so I just nodded. Karen then mentioned 'Dwile Flunking', at this I asked her to repeat the story. It was some wild drinking game that Sandra played at university. I asked about the university and Karen told me that Sandra had only spent two years there because she had to come back to look after her mother. Mrs McGregor was really sad about this and it used to cause arguments between them so they both agreed it would never be mentioned. I found myself asking what course was she reading and Karen was puzzled. She asked me whether I knew anything about Sandra and I said clearly not. Sandra had read English Literature and she had a deferment. Karen did not know what a deferment was but had guessed. Sandra only started the hairdressing so she could be flexible and work from home and around her mother's needs as they got more demanding. Karen asked how the meal had gone with Mum and Pa. I just said fine, I did not mention the scene. She was growing up into a perceptive young lady and was going to be a good ally in the rocky family times ahead.

I drove back to the tranquillity of Aunt Gladys's shed.

CHAPTER 23

George was up and ready in his work attire, a shirt and tie, when I picked him up. He wanted to try and walk to the car. He was feeling invigorated by using his brain and he wanted to get his body back in shape. He had so much purpose and determination that he did get to the car but was shattered by doing so. I tried to counsel him, saying, 'Little and often' but he just waved me off. I told him of my mother's behaviour at the meal. He was not surprised saying that no mother wants to lose her son. He did think that my mother should have been more subtle and that this was her Achilles heel. I was intrigued by his logic and he explained Mother had exposed her hand at the outset so I knew the score. It would have been more dangerous if she had been all sweetness and light because then I would have been lured into a false sense of security. Wise words from George but no solution to what was a serious problem.

*

Sandra was pleased to see me. She was more than the anxious, needy Sandra of the wedding. She demonstrated her insecurity when she told me that she wondered if I would turn up. I hugged her and told her that she would be sick of the sight of me when she had to spend the rest of her life with me. George went straight back on his quest for the cheapest portable loo. It was a quiet morning until about 1130 when Rowan Connor called in. He had been invited by Sandra to see the operation and assist with the next week of advertising in the *Gazette*. He was not involved with advertising, as such, but was happy to assist. I casually asked him where he trained. His undergraduate degree was at Durham, he then did an extra year for his masters. I also asked him about the body. He was still covering the story. The police had no idea who the body was and were still following various lines of enquiry. He confessed that the police had no further lines of enquiry but planned a press release the following Thursday inviting the public to assist them. They were trying to get the names of any missing persons over the last twenty years. I was incredulous when he told me that the police did not keep any records of missing people. I asked him what the procedure would be and whilst he did not know for sure, he presumed it would be a phone line where names could be offered. I asked if they had released any information about the body and he said that it was male but as it had been undiscovered for a long time they had little further to go on. He moaned that it was not a particularly good story but he was pleased that I was interested; it meant other readers would be too. I confessed that I was only an occasional reader but promised to order delivery to the cabin for the next few months. George, who had picked up the last threads of our conversation, added that he would like to scan the *Gazette* as it would tell us where there were potential new works that may require cabins. Rowan added that if we bought it for the business, it would be a legitimate business expense and could be written off against tax. I had not even started to think about accounts and tax. I was not going to let this 'hair-brained scheme' fail and I knew that I had to switch on. I was not going to let my mother or any dead bodies distract me.

Sandra had a coffee with us. She was relaxed in Rowan's company. She gave him a hug as he left. He shouted back, 'Don't forget to bring the diary on Wednesday, Mac.'

Calling her 'Mac' made me feel jealous. I wanted a pet name for her. I chided her and said 'Mac?' She explained that there were three Sandras on her course. One was Sandy, one was Sandra and she was 'Mac'. I asked, 'And what course was this?' She blushed and paused and so I continued. I asked if it was the advanced Dwile Flunking or maybe the school *Romeo and Juliet*. I went over and hugged her again. George groaned and told us that he was trying to run a business. He added that it would have been worse if Sandra was called Smac. Sandra laughed and went to smack George. She checked herself and told us to get working as she was going through to help her mother. George and I were alone for the rest of the day. We both agreed that when the police asked for information to assist their enquiries, we would tell them about Aiden Malcolm.

George insisted on walking to his door and, despite a stumble by the step when I had to catch him, he moved well. He said he was going to the Western Front meeting the following day and so was taking a day's holiday. I was pleased that Mother, Pa and Karen had left; I was fed up with petty family matters. Ra-Ra had been and left. The scene was of contentment. Aunt Gladys was knitting in her chair and Dawn was doing a jigsaw puzzle. Philip Arthur slept soundly in the Moses basket. I sat down and enjoyed the peace.

*

It had been an uneventful week. I had gone away with the TA all weekend. I had missed two calls from my father and had not returned them. Sandra's mother was requiring almost hourly assistance and, save for the occasional coffee, I had not seen much of Sandra.

The Thursday *Gazette* headlines were, for a small provincial paper, dramatic. 'Body Mystery Deepens.' The police had, despite extensive investigation, failed to identify the body found by the Nab. They were asking all members of the public who knew of any missing people to contact a phone number. They also wanted anyone who had visited the Nab in the last five years to remember if they had seen anyone or anything suspicious. It did seem a tall order but I presumed it might just trigger a memory. The police were also using local radio and a stand in the high street and had a noticeboard erected at the Nab to spread the message.

I sat and wrote a statement that covered my first meeting with Aiden right through to putting him in the white van. I then wrote a further note on my subsequent attempts to find him. It was a comprehensive recall and I was pleased with the result. I was going to ask George to read it and suggest any amendments but I then realised I had never mentioned the winnings to him. It was too late now. I had not touched the money but it would still seem odd to George. I kept the details of the betting shop visit but removed the accumulator win. I read through one last time. I had to make two adjustments. The first was to mention the Black Russian cigarettes and the second was the Blue Bell matches. I was also careful to omit any suggestions of crime, theft, misfeasance, and special projects. I did not want anything that would draw me into any further police investigation.

George was impressed by my memory. He had nothing to add but suggested he put his name to the second part where he had been involved. Armed with the document I tried phoning the 'Police Body Mystery' line. The line was engaged and would be so throughout the day. I could not imagine that it was blocked by thousands of people phoning so presumed it was a technical glitch. The glitch seemed to continue the following day, so I said to George we would go down to the High Street kiosk. It was just as well we went down that afternoon as it was being taken down when we arrived. I had expected to speak to a policeman but the kiosk was manned by a young girl. I tried to give her my notes but she simply asked me to complete a form. It was one side of A4; it asked for my details and the details of the missing person I was reporting. It included their address and family connections. I filled in what I could but the form was pretty sparse. I was unsure that the police investigation was as thorough as I expected. George was annoyed that we had made such an effort and that it would amount to nothing.

*

We had left Sandra manning the phone from her mother's house. Mrs McGregor seemed more demanding than ever and Sandra was spending more time with her. Sandra gave me a list of phone calls she had taken. She also reminded me that I was going to the alumni meeting the following week. I had ignored the letter so she had replied for me. I had forgotten all about it and told her I had not planned to go but she reminded me that it would be a good opportunity to sell cabins to all the engineers who were now working all over the country on engineering projects. George took the list of phone calls from me and said he would walk back to the cabin. George was getting increasingly more mobile. He was talking about having a go at driving. If he did start driving, I would lose access to the car. I was also minded that Sandra was also quite depressed. I knew she was worried about her mother but I think that my mother had also unhelpfully clouded matters.

I had to visit the haulage yard as I was meeting a joiner who was going to repair the windows and doors on the damaged cabins. The joiner seemed reasonable and could start the following day. He presumed I worked for the hauliers so did not ask for any deposit. I had taken what I hoped was enough cash to pay him but kept the money in my pocket. I took the opportunity to call in and see Tommy. Yvonne made a cup of tea for us and we chatted about how the business was going. Tommy was

Sandra's father's younger brother. He told me what an action man his brother had been what with the car racing and how he was sadly struck down with such a debilitating illness when so young. He liked the fact that I was in the TA and had taken Sandra parachuting as he saw much in me that he missed in his brother. I explained that I wanted to 'pop the question' to Sandra and needed to take her away for the weekend to do so but was struggling to get the time. He suggested I send Sheena to her cousin in Appleby. I explained that she was not long back. He picked up his phone and called Yvonne through. Yvonne was tasked with getting Auntie May on the phone. Yvonne asked if he was sure and would he not rather she spoke. Tommy grimaced and said that sometimes he had to do what a man's got to do. Yvonne rang a number that she knew from her head from Tommy's phone. She handed him the handset when the number rang. She told me in a stage whisper that her dad was useless. Tommy and Auntie May chatted for ages. Tommy clearly did not phone often as he had to give Auntie May chapter and verse on all family matters. He eventually got round to finding out when Sheena was next due to visit. I could not hear the response but I think I had put in train a family gathering. Tommy, his wife, Yvonne, and her fiancé and a host of others were invited to Auntie May's. Yes, Sheena and Sandra could stay with her but Tommy and family would make alternative arrangements. It would have been Auntie May's ruby wedding anniversary, if Frank had been alive, so we were all going up to raise a glass. Tommy eventually put the phone down after saying goodbye almost constantly for five minutes. He put his finger in his ear and shook his head. Yvonne, who had listened to the whole conversation, laughed saying, 'And that's why you always tell me to phone.'

'We have a fortnight and then Sheena is back to Westmoreland,' said Tommy, 'Just one problem and that is that Sandra is with her.'

'And everyone else,' added Yvonne. Tommy had a meeting at 1000 and so I was ushered out with him apologising but promising to sort something out. I did not go straight back to the office. I went to Northern Goldsmiths. George had told me to give Aiden Malcolm's ring to Sandra. I explained that not only was it not mine to give but what would happen when Aiden turned up? George was not convinced but I was.

*

Northern Goldsmiths was the best jewellery shop in the region. I knew any ring would be expensive but, never having bought a ring, I did not realise just how much. I had a pocket stuffed with cash for the joiner. I had taken it from my TA earnings.

The demeanour of the jewellery assistant on the counter changed from cold efficiency to warm empathy when I asked to look at engagement rings. I was taken to a chair in front of a small table and offered a cup of tea. I was joined by a lady who sported a shiny name tag saying Clarissa. Clarissa wondered whether my fiancée would be coming in to confirm my selection and have the ring sized. It had not occurred to me to invite Sandra as it would spoil my surprise. I had no idea of her finger size but had supposed the ring could be resized later if it was wrong. Clarissa produced a selection of diamond rings when I explained I wanted just diamonds. I did not realise that any number of stones could be included. I wanted to keep it simple but Clarissa was already confusing me. Did I want a solitaire, three stones for 'I love you' or five stones for 'I will always love you?' I narrowed it down to a solitaire thinking just how good Aiden's ring looked. Clarissa then started on the diamond. Cut, Colour, Clarity and Carat was her mantra. It was like an Army briefing. I was expecting an overhead projector to be wheeled out. I was adding an extra 'C' to the explanation 'Cost'. This was all going to come down to what I could afford to pay. I suggested this to Clarissa who, whilst not crestfallen, did seem deflated. The large solitaire, that was a fraction of the size of Aiden's, was twice what I could afford to pay. I was taken by a smaller lozenge shape. Clarissa was concerned that it lacked clarity but it was within my newly decided budget and I agreed to buy it. Clarissa carefully gift-wrapped my precious purchase. I was unsure why, as in all the films I had watched, the man goes down on one knee and offers the girl the ring in an open box. I was paying a king's ransom so I was happy to wait. I was feeling well organised and went straight next door to a branch of my bank. I opened two accounts in my name and one in Horace and Co. Our finances had been all over the place and Sandra had urged me to have them sorted. One of my accounts, the savings account, I named H Crawford (Morning). I was going to put all the Aiden Malcolm winnings in so they would start getting interest. The morning was AM. The other account was SM which would be for Sandra and I and the future. I put the balance of the joiner's money into the Horace account.

*

When I eventually got back to the cabin, George was annoyed by my prolonged absence. They were demolishing an old school near Thornaby and George had been advised they had an outside toilet block. I had to go and see it and make an offer. I was not going to argue with George as he was putting so much effort in.

The school was not being demolished but two temporary classrooms were being replaced by a brick building that would include toilets. The two temporary toilets were being removed. The classrooms, which were made of two cabins joined together, were separated ready for collection. The toilets had been used until the last minute and were now ready for removal. The cabins themselves looked serviceable but the toilets were filthy. The school janitor told me that they were kept spotless when the children used them, but they became dirty when left for the construction team. The girls' loos were serviceable but I was unsure about the boys'. Both units had one sewage outlet each and plumbing for hot and cold water. The janitor advised me that the water had been switched off. I agreed to collect them the following Tuesday. I had no idea where they were going. I had to pay the school £75 but it could not be cash, it had to be a cheque. The school clerk gave me all the details.

*

George was in better spirits when I got back. When I told him that we were the proud owners of two toilet blocks he punched the air. He picked up the phone. I went through to the kitchen to make some tea. I was minded to go down to the house but thought I would spend some time with George. I made George a coffee. George came off the phone and moaned that he wanted tea. I gave him mine. I did not particularly like coffee but I made do.

George was grinning and telling me that we made a great team. He went on to say, 'Those toilets need to be spotless because they're off to Victoria Park for a music festival. We're getting £260 per week for the three weeks.'

'Wow,' I exclaimed, '£780.'

'No,' he said, 'each, £1,560.' I was not wishing to sound negative so I carefully asked about whether there were any sewage pipes we could connect to or piped water on the site. George had no idea but he did say that there was more money in toilets than anything else.

Everyone needed them and we had to be able to supply. I had to agree the money did sound great and would give us plenty of headroom. I phoned Aunt Gladys and as I thought Ra-Ra was there, I told him I could employ him for a couple of weeks if he was interested. He was worried that he did not have a car but I explained his bike would be fine. George set about finding out if a water bowser and generator would provide the running water we needed to flush the loos and provide water for the basins. I set about finding out about how to dispose of raw sewage. My first port of call was Marcus. He once mentioned how the toilets at the aerodrome were an issue but they had been sorted out by an effluent engineer he knew. I left a message with Kurt for Marcus to phone me. I then walked down to see Sandra.

*

Sandra had been crying and looked dishevelled. I put my arms round her. She felt limp and vulnerable. She said nothing and I led her through from the kitchen to the front room. It seemed cold. There were only yesterday's embers in the hearth. Mrs McGregor was spending longer in bed and so Sandra had not been lighting the fire. Sandra was shivering and so I put my arms back round her and held her close. She was apologising to me for letting me down and not living up to my expectations. She could understand my mother's concerns. I found myself being rather dramatic saying, 'Sandra you are my destiny. You and I will spend the rest of our life together. We will grow old together and we too can enjoy our ruby wedding anniversary.' At this Sandra asked who had a ruby wedding. I said, 'Aunt May and Frank.'

'But Frank has been dead for a decade,' she responded, 'and anyway how do you know about Aunt May and Frank?'

I smiled and told her I knew everything, including all her darkest secrets, especially Durham and the Dwile Flunking. For the first time since the meal Sandra laughed. Not just a laugh but a snort. This made us both laugh even more. Mrs McGregor shouted through asking if everything was fine. I shouted back, 'Yes Sheena, it's only me.'

Sandra said, 'If you wanted a name for me, it could be Cassie.' I asked her to explain. She held up the Companies House form she was completing. In forename she had typed Cassandra.

'Cassandra,' I read the name out loud, the girl who can foretell the future but no one believes. Sandra went on to tell me that only her father had ever called her Cassie, everyone else, including her mother, called her Sandra. 'I will henceforth call you Cassie,' I exclaimed.

*

Everything is possible for a price and effluent engineers do not come cheap. We managed to lift the toilets thanks to Uncle Tommy but delivering them was a challenge as they were to be sited in a country park and access was difficult. The water solution was an expensive plastic header tank that required its own dedicated scaffolding. The sewage was drained into a holding tank with the other grey water from the basins and the urinals. The holding tanks needed emptying every two days by an expensive small tanker. A large tanker could not gain access, if it could, we could have emptied every week. All the add-on costs were eating into the hire charge. Sandra was able to spend more time in the office because Dawn and the baby came over to help Mrs McGregor. Ra-Ra was working for me and Dawn was pleased with the change of scenery. Mrs McGregor also picked up as she had the baby and Dawn to fuss over.

Sandra did the accounts and the toilets were a money-spinner, especially once we knew what we needed to do. George could rent them out ten times over and so started to put up the price and extend the hire periods. George organised for the spare sentry box to be converted into a loo and this was always in demand. He did rather hope we could recover the others from Marcus as they were easier to transport in batches.

I had paid Ra-Ra on a day rate and tried to do the same for George. Ra-Ra was delighted but George less so. George said that he was not doing it for the money and I had to save any money that he was earning so we could employ proper staff when he was gone. We did have jobs for Ra-Ra every day but his great strength was that he did not care what he was doing. I found cleaning the toilets almost impossible and often wanted to retch but Ra-Ra just cracked on without a care in the world. George kept saying 'where there's muck, there's money.' He was right but he was not cleaning the muck.

CHAPTER 24

I was unsure why I was going to Dr Jenkins' alumni meeting but Sandra had assured me it was important. I put on my ghastly chalk-stripe suit and regimental tie. I grabbed a pocket full of business cards thoughtfully provided by Sandra. George told me the Japanese protocol for presenting them. I had to hold them in both hands and point my name towards the recipient. He seemed earnest but I told him that there would be no Japanese there. He then told me the protocol if I was given a business card. If I liked the person, it went in my right jacket pocket. If I did not like the person but might at some point want to do business, it went in my left jacket pocket. If I met a real pillock, I should put their card in my breast pocket. In the future if I met another pillock, I would give them the card from my breast pocket. It amused me, but Sandra told me off, not for the first time, for encouraging him.

Dr Jenkins may have drafted the invite so we felt it was a small gathering but there were at least twenty-five people in the room when I arrived and I was exactly on time. I saw Colin, of all people, so I knew that Dr Jenkins had not vetted the guest list. I picked up a glass of what turned out to be elderflower cordial from a tray. Colin saw me and came over. If he gave me a business card it was going straight into my breast pocket. I had rung him at his office a couple of weeks earlier to tell him of the birth. He had asked to meet the baby but Dawn had said, not at the moment. Colin was anxious to hear about Philip and I was able to say that mother and baby were well. He asked if the baby looked like him. I was emphatic that he did not. Thankfully we were joined by Sam Ademalui who had been on our course. Sam had never attended lectures but only involved himself with the student union. It did not surprise me that he was working for a Trade Union. He was interested in Horace and Co and wondered if we had any employees. I thought it easier to say no. Various sausage rolls and pieces of quiche were passed round and then there was an introduction from Dr Jenkins. There was a poor sound system and so I could not hear what he was saying clearly. The gist was that they wanted our money but also our help in expanding the reach of the polytechnic and especially the Engineering Faculty. Dr Jenkins handed over to a younger girl who then ran a short film repeating what Dr Jenkins said but in more detail. The girl then repeated the message at the end of the film. We were given a proforma to fill in but there were no pens. I had one which was in great demand when I had completed my form. I never did get the pen back as it passed into the depths of the room. I had finished my drink and decided to slip away. I had not given away any business cards. As I was leaving, Dave was coming in. He was so pleased to see me. I told him it was over but he insisted on dragging me back in as he was taking me to the White Rose afterwards for a drink. Dave was in his scruffy sailing kit. He spotted Sam and Colin and I followed him over. He greeted Colin like his long-lost brother and pumped Sam's hand. They were planning to leave and were happy to stop at the White Rose at Dave's suggestion.

*

I reprised my role at the bar by buying four pints of Carling but having the fourth in a dimple glass. I made sure Dave heard when I said, 'Here's your Stella, Colin', handing him the dimple glass. I was unsure why I was there. I was fond of Dave but had nothing to say and I was not really interested in what they had to say either.

I decided to finish my pint and go when someone put their hands over my eyes from behind me and said,

'Guess who?' It was Sarah. Why had I not replied to her letter? She knew Colin and Sam.

Sam wanted to buy Sarah a drink but she deferred as she was waiting for a friend. My heart pounded and I felt hot and uncomfortable. Sarah joined us and asked whether Dawn had had the baby. Dave was interested too. I was unsure whether Colin realised that babies made people the centre of attention or not but he butted in saying, 'I am the father.'

It was an awkward revelation but he got the congratulations that he sought. Sarah whispered to me that he was such an 'arse.' She clearly knew Colin. Dave promised that he and Heather would be sending invitations out soon. Colin added that Dave would soon have lots of babies. Sam seemed indifferent but stood up when Sarah's friend arrived, it was Carole. She looked striking. The first time I met her in the White Rose she had been bordering on inconspicuous. Tonight, she was made up and wearing a tight top and leather trousers. It seemed like a different girl; in fact I was grateful when Carole introduced her to Sam as it confirmed it was Carole. Colin was first to give up his chair and almost manhandle Carole into it. He took Sam's chair next to her, oblivious to the fact that Sam had vacated it to buy the drinks. Carole had been invited to appear in the local authority film about voting. She had just returned from the filming. She was embarrassed by her outfit. This last statement was drowned out by the approval of Sarah, Dave, Sam and, most loudly, Colin. I was still stunned and she asked me. 'And you, Harry?'

I mumbled about her scrubbing up well. I wanted to leave but Sam had brought me a half so I stayed a little longer. Carole asked how Sandra was and had we been back to do any more parachuting. I did not get much chance to respond as Colin was bombarding her with questions about the film. I took the opportunity to finish my drink and stand up. I waved farewell and backed off towards the door. Both Sarah and Dave tried to stop me. Sarah wanted details about the parachute course and Dave wanted me to organise his stag night. I told Sarah I would drop her a line and asked Dave to phone me at the office. I gave him a business card. Sarah asked for one as well. I escaped before I was trapped further. Carole had unsettled me and I did think that I had run away somewhat. Was I running because I was somehow attracted to her or was I being genuinely honourable? I focussed on the recent laugh I had with Sandra and I calmed down. The nearer I got to home, the more I was missing Sandra. I still had a ring in my pocket and the sooner I got it on her finger, the better.

*

I took Sandra flowers the next morning. I had no guilt, as I had behaved well, but I wanted to cheer her up and devote more to time to her. I gave her a potted summary of the evening. I mentioned meeting Colin and Dave and going back to the White Rose for a pint. I mentioned Sarah and Carole arriving. Sandra seemed to slump before me and sat down in tears on the mention of Carole. George came in from the kitchen carrying a tea for me but he gave it to Sandra. He put his hand on her shoulder saying something like, 'You're both putting yourselves under too much pressure and if you're not careful, something will burst.'

Sandra apologised and agreed she was just feeling exasperated with her mother who was gradually getting worse. She told George that she and her mother were off to Appleby for a long weekend and if she could cope until then, she would feel better. Sandra looked at me and added, 'You've been invited too but I don't suppose you'll want to come.' I did not want to show my hand too early so said I would check what the TA had planned. Sandra seemed resigned to a trip with her mother but I had other plans.

*

On the Tuesday I asked Major Tomey about climbing in the Lake District. It was Major Tomey's passion when he was not soldiering. I explained I was taking my girlfriend and wanted a 'climbable' peak that we could do in a day. He told me of the excitement of Helvellyn by Striding Edge, of the views from Catbells but he confided in me that his most romantic weekend was staying at a hotel in Bassenthwaite and walking up Skiddaw with his wife-to-be. He even kept the hotel number in his Filofax.

I phoned the hotel and booked the Saturday night. I would drive Sandra and her mother up to Appleby on the Friday. We would stay the Friday night and then, once her mother was settled, I would whisk Sandra to Skiddaw. I confided in George who thought my plan perfect. He was happy to lend me the car but told me not to lose the keys on the mountain or my plans would be buggered. He wanted to see the ring but I said he could wait for Sandra to show him.

*

Aunt May lived in an old farm house on the fringe of Appleby. It was clean and tidy but in a state of gradual decay. There had been no paint on any surface for at least a decade and there had been nothing new introduced to the house for the same period. Sandra and her mother had warned me that I was heading back in time on the journey up but I had not realised how accurate their description was. Mrs McGregor thought it an excellent idea that Sandra and I escaped on the Saturday to climb a mountain.

Yvonne and her mother were already in residence. I was introduced as Harry, Sandra's friend. Yvonne's fiancé was driving up on the Saturday evening with Tommy as he, the fiancé, had a football match. No excuse was given for Tommy's late show. I was shown by Yvonne to a very cold bedroom above what she described as the boot room. It was an appendage to the house and had no heating. I was pleased it was only for one night. I had my woollen hat and gloves for the climb up Skiddaw but had not anticipated wearing them in bed.

May, Greta (Yvonne's mother) and Yvonne had made a huge stew with dumplings for the evening meal. Sandra talked about the parachute jump and the new business venture, Yvonne about her wedding plans and Aunt May about her late husband, Frank. It was a pleasant evening. Luckily, I did not have to say much but it was just as well as I was strangely nervous of my plans for the next day. Tommy knew that I planned to take Sandra off on the Saturday but I was not sure if he had mentioned it to his wife and daughter. I did sleep rather well even though my breath was white and the window was frosted on the inside.

*

We left Appleby on the Saturday morning before anyone else was up. I kept checking the ring. I had taken it out of the box and put it in a small red felt pouch with a yellow draw cord. I was wondering if perhaps it would have been safer just leaving it in the box.

Sandra chatted about her family on the journey. I was just thinking about how I would ask her. I was worried it was too soon. I was worried that my mother was yet to be convinced. I was worried that the business would not prosper. It was probably too late in the year to have a leisurely stroll up Skiddaw and I was worried that it was too tough.

I parked in the layby at the bottom of the climb; there were three other cars parked there so it was quite tight.

Sandra was well wrapped up but was wondering if she needed an extra layer. In the end we put extra sweaters in my backpack and started the climb. After a few steps I went back to the car telling Sandra I was just checking it was locked. I quickly attached the ring pouch to the car keys and put them in my inside pocket. It was a beautiful frosty morning. What would have been muddy tracks were frozen and made walking easy. I was surprised how quickly we reached the first of the two hills that give a false impression of just how high Skiddaw was. We stopped for a drink of tea from our flask. It was not a clear day but we could see down to Bassenthwaite and the lake. I felt in my pocket to make sure the ring was still safe.

We pressed on and made the second hill very quickly. As we started the long drag up to the summit I heard a commotion ahead, before I saw it. As we pressed on, I could see a group of people: one was gesticulating, another was bending over someone on the ground. We increased our pace and closed with the group. There were five people and the one that was gesticulating came towards us. It was an older lady in some distress. Her brother had collapsed. I ran towards the group. One older man was lying on the ground and three others were clustered round. Two seemed to be teenagers and the third, a middle-aged lady, was unfastening the prone man's collar. The man was almost sitting up but slumped forward. I could see the man was a grey colour and not breathing. He was heavily overweight. I careful laid the man down and started pumping his chest. I had one hand on top of the other. The chap was wearing a scarf and fleece so I was getting little traction. I pulled off his scarf and opened the fleece. When I started the pumping again, I felt movement in his chest. Sandra was comforting the lady. I asked the group if anyone could drive. The middle-aged lady said that she could. I told Sandra to take my keys from my pocket and run down to the car with this lady. I checked my self and said, 'Do not run, it will be dangerous, ring 999.' I was breathless.

I could not believe how hard it was to keep the pumping going. Sandra put her hand inside my pocket. She took out the keys and she and the lady set off. I saw that the young girl standing over me was looking pale and distressed. I told her to go with them. She needed no telling and set off with Sandra. The young boy seemed alert and I asked him if he could take over as I needed a rest. He immediately took over. His hands were too high at first and he was having no effect but I repositioned his hands and he started having a better effect than I had. There was definitely some colour in the man's cheek. His grey pallor had gone. I told the older lady to get my flask out of my backpack. It was more to keep her occupied as she was starting to shiver and was looking poorly herself. I introduced myself to my co-worker. He was John and it was his Uncle Bill that we were helping. John asked me if Bill was alive and I said, 'Well he's not dead.'

John nodded towards the lady pouring the tea from my flask saying, 'That's Aunt Jessie.' Aunt Jessie gave me a mouthful of tea and then I took over the CPR again from John. I was grateful that John was such a fit young man. He was able to continue with a steady rhythm for long periods of time. Uncle Bill was definitely not dead but I could see very little signs of life. After what seemed like an eternity, four men came over the brow of what I was calling the second hill. They were from the Mountain Rescue. I do not remember the next few minutes as I collapsed onto my back absolutely shattered. When I sat up, I saw that the chest pumping was being continued by one of the men. John was lying on his back. We were joined by another group of men from the Mountain

Rescue. Aunt Jessie, John and I were ushered away from Uncle Bill. Aunt Jessie wanted to stay but we were all led off down the mountain. One of the men insisted on carrying my backpack.

*

Sandra was at the car. She gave me a hug and asked how the man was. I said I had no idea. The Mountain Rescue had set up a control where there was a vehicle and an ambulance. I had to go over to answer some questions. Aunt Jessie and John were already there. I explained who I was and what I had done. I asked if it was okay to leave. They asked me if I needed any medical attention but I said no. They asked me where I was driving to and I said only the hotel in Bassenthwaite. They seemed content but told me that often even those who helped at an incident could deteriorate so if I started feeling poorly, I should not feel bad about seeking help. I assured them I was fine. Aunt Jessie and John shook my hand and thanked me. Sandra had anticipated a drive back to Appleby. She asked if I was okay to drive. I reassured her that I was fine. I added that I could not be so sure about the patient as he did seem in a bad way. Sandra told me she had practically ran down Skiddaw with the lady and the girl. The lady was able to drive and they went straight to Bassenthwaite. Sandra gave me back the car keys as she explained what had happened. I noted that the small pouch was still attached. Sandra had run into a fancy hotel and reception had called the ambulance. I drove to Bassenthwaite and pulled into the hotel. Sandra exclaimed, 'This is the hotel we came to for help.'

I grabbed my bag and the extra bag that Yvonne had packed for Sandra and said, 'Come on, this is where we're staying.' The receptionist recognised Sandra and asked how the chap on the mountain was. I told her he was on his way to hospital but we knew nothing further.

The receptionist reminded me that our table was booked for seven and gave me the room key.

*

Sandra was saying nothing. She followed me up the stairs. The room was far bigger than I anticipated and had a sofa as well as a huge double bed. Sandra walked round saying, 'Wow.' Sandra went into the en-suite bathroom and came out saying, 'What a bath.' She then wondered out loud, what my room would be like.

I dropped the bags and dropped onto one knee. I took my car keys from my pocket and opened the little pouch that was still attached. It was empty. I shook it and put my finger in but nothing. I stood up and turned to check my pocket. I was cursing myself for changing it from the box. I turned back and Sandra asked what I was looking for. She said that if it was a ring, it was hidden about her person and if I wanted it, I would have to find it. I asked what if it was not a ring. She said, 'Then in that case just take the keys and close the door as you leave.'

I am pleased to report that I found the ring.

CHAPTER 25

The latest time for checking out was 1130. Sandra and I missed breakfast and signed out at 1129. We had briefly considered climbing Skiddaw but agreed it was better saved for our next trip to the Lake District. Sandra gazed at her third finger left hand for much of the journey back to Appleby. She marvelled that I had the ring size just right and loved the lozenge shape. I felt so content and happy but at the back of my mind I kept hearing my mother. I resolved that Sandra and I would head south as soon as possible since the quicker the problem was addressed, the quicker it would be sorted.

*

Everyone at Aunt May's were thrilled by our news. Sandra did not mention the poor man on the hill, nor that we did not reach the summit. It made good sense as that would have detracted from our good news. Tommy had arrived and was keen to open a bottle of Champagne. Aunt May was distressed that she did not have any in her cupboard, but Tommy told her he had brought some in the car. Tommy's wife asked how he knew about our plan. She was less than pleased that both her daughter and husband knew and that neither had mentioned it to her. She asked Sheena if she knew and was told only that I had sought Sheena's permission but not when I was going to ask. This seemed to calm her but I suspected Tommy had not heard the last of it.

I only had a sip of Champagne as I was driving and it was just as well as Sandra and Yvonne were finishing off both bottles. After a late lunch I drove Sandra and her mother home. They both slept soundly for the whole journey. I kept gazing at the profile of Sandra and thinking how lucky I was. I was wondering when I would next get to spend the night with her. I could not take her back to the shed. I had to sort out my living arrangements. Aunt Gladys had a full house with the new baby and Ra-Ra, an ever-present figure.

*

Monday at the office was quite depressing. George had sat on two letters from the previous week as he did not wish to upset my weekend. The first was from a law firm in Doncaster. They had a client called H Race & Co who were building merchants. George told me it was what the Americans call a 'cease and desist' letter. They thought our firm's name was too similar to theirs and wanted us to stop using it as it could cause confusion. George called it 'poppycock' and thought we should just ignore it. George had asked a retired court clerk who was a member of the Western Front Association what he would do and his advice was to ignore it too. I was not sure if our legal advice was as sound as H Race & Co's but agreed that we would do nothing. The second was more concerning. The local council were claiming that the cabin on Sandra's mother's land was in contravention of a local planning law. A council officer was to attend the site on the following Thursday. George did not have any suggestions so we agreed to await the visit. George tried to reassure me that 'we could not have rainbows without a little rain'. He also remembered that he had been given a note from Dawn to give me. It was a message that Dave had phoned and wanted me to attend his stag weekend which was being organised by his Best Man, Robby. I was to phone Robby to find out all the details. There was a number which was written in a different colour by a different person. I could imagine Dawn asking Ra-Ra or Aunt Gladys to write the number because Dawn always got her numbers mixed up. The last thing I wanted was a lads' drinking weekend but at least I did not have to organise it for which I was thankful. Robby was Dave's friend from the sailing club and was a sensible guy.

*

Rowan called in after lunch. He wanted Sandra to help with some charity work. I explained she was spending more time with her mother as we walked down to the house. The search for a name for the body continued. Rowan asked whether Horace & Co might want to offer a reward for information. He explained that it was easy publicity. I was not so sure. I did not think being associated with what could be a murder or something was right for the business. Sandra was pleased to see Rowan but I could sense she was reluctant to take on any more commitments. Looking after her mother was taking it out of her and it was not lost on Rowan. After a tea and chat he departed. Sandra and I sat in the front room. There was no fire and it was cold. Sandra's mother was in bed. I told Sandra about the two letters and the invitation to the stag night. She was concerned with the letters but quite phlegmatic agreeing that we would just wait and see what happened. She did point out that we had not received an invite to the wedding so the stag night did seem presumptuous. I cleaned out the hearth then put paper in kindling onto the grate. I took out the ash and returned with coal. I suggested that, once the fire was roaring, we brought her mother through. Sandra hugged me and said that she felt very lucky. She added that she only ever wanted the extra reel of film for her camera and look what she had got.

    I rang Robby as instructed by Dave. Robby apologised for the short notice but Heather had refused to allow Dave to have any stag event unless it was at least two months before the wedding. Dave was only left with the upcoming weekend or he would run out of time. Robby had arranged for us all to meet on Saturday lunch time. I needed, football, squash and swimming kit. I had to wear a hat. We were staying at the Saltburn YMCA on the Saturday night. He added one further apology and that was for taking over my role as Best Man. I scoffed saying I was never in the frame. Robby insisted that I was with Dave, but Dave was overruled by Heather. I asked if it was because of the geology field trip and Robby said yes. I did not tell Robby that I missed that trip but I was curious as to what had happened.

*

Thank goodness George was running the office. The landlord of the pub where we dropped our first cabin had rung to say he needed the cabin and toilet picking up. He gave some implausible story about relocating to Spain but George was not convinced. George asked me if he could sort it as he already had a site for the toilet. I was more than happy to oblige. I did tell George that I was going over to the coast on the Saturday if he needed me to visit the pub. In the event, it was not necessary. I put my hard hat in the car just in case. I also remembered that I needed a hat for the stag night so that would sort that.

*

Robby was waiting at the five-a-side pitch carpark when I arrived. I was last so he was anxious I got changed and met the rest on the pitch. The pitch was on the other side of the building and I could see and hear people playing. The dressing room was quite small and all the benches were covered by abandoned clothes. I cleared a space and quickly changed. There were only eight of us and I was on Dave's team with a man called Rob. Also on our team was Colin. I was surprised to see Colin as I knew Dave did not like him. I just shook his hand and nodded. The other team was led by Robby and had Sam, Steve, and Pete. All came over and we had the usual banter until Robby told us that it was game on. I had not realised how poor Dave's eyesight was until I saw him trying to kick the ball. Football was not my game and whilst Rob was fine, he was no match for Sam and the other three. We were being trounced. Colin was getting angrier and angrier. His anger was not directed at our poor performance but at Sam who was metaphorically and literally running rings round him. Robby eventually stepped in and we rebalanced the sides. Dave went in goal and Rob and Sam swapped sides. Colin grumbled on and was still angry at Sam but the match finished without incident. It was December so Robby knew we would lose the light quite early. We went for a short run along the beach. The plan was for us all to have a swim but the cold wind and very unsettled sea made it stupid, even for a stag party. Colin wanted to tie Dave to the pier stanchion and then leave him until Heather came to rescue him before he was drowned by the rising tide. Everyone laughed but in a strange way I felt Colin was serious. Colin asked me how Dawn and the baby were. I gave him a brief summary. I knew he was desperate to ask further about his son as he asked me to remind him of the baby's name. I said Philip Arthur and I swear he had a tear in his eye. I went on to say how he was fit and strong and was a content child. Colin seemed calm. He asked me what I was doing and I told him I was running my own cabin hire company called Horace & Co. He asked nothing further and feigned disinterest. It reminded me of the time I was making the job application when he showed no interest. I asked him what he was up to and he said 'no change', tidying up the road contract and planning the next. I took the opportunity to ask if he had much contact with Gregg Carol, Rod Clough or Aiden Malcolm.

I added Aiden as an afterthought. 'Gregg still runs the show,' he replied, 'Rod has a bridge to build in the middle east and I still do not know this Aiden Malcolm you always mention.'

He seemed irritated and so I pushed by adding, 'Well we both worked with him.'

He turned to me. The vein was pulsing in his forehead. 'I only know one Malcolm and that's Malcolm Hayden and he owns the company.'

I was dumbstruck. At last, a 'Malcolm' I thought. 'But the name in the jacket was Aiden,' I mumbled rather to myself.

Colin stood up and as he left he said, 'Your girl's called Samantha but I bet she has St Michael in her knickers.' He then walked off.

'Samantha,' I thought, 'no my girlfriend is Sandra. Cassie.'

*

The next sport was squash. It was a simple knock-out tournament. I played Dave in the first round but it could well have been a walk-over. Dave simply could not see the ball. I tried to make it competitive without looking as if I was helping him, but he played on bravely. When we shook hands at the end, he told me that these were probably his last ball sports and he would be sticking to sailing and chess. My next opponent was Colin. His opening words were that he was seeing Carole. I knew he was just trying to unsettle me as he could have mentioned it during our earlier chat. I just smiled and said, 'Fine.' Colin and I were evenly matched but he was obsessional about winning. In his desire to dominate the court he always obstructed me. He was happy to catch me with his racket or shoulder if it gave him position. Robby, who was watching over the top from the stand, even warned Colin that his play was such. He told Colin that he would be losing points if he were the umpire. Colin snarled back that he was not. I am sure that I could have won but I almost felt better letting him win. I knew he would be smugly arrogant, but I did not care. In the other side of the draw on the second court Sam had won through so the final was between Colin and Sam. It was brutal. We all watched the delicate and light touch of a nimble Sam against the power and aggression of Colin. It was clear they despised each other as they were having arguments during the warm up. Dave stepped in and appointed Robby as umpire. He knew Colin would not disagree. Colin tried to say an umpire was not needed but Robby had already found a coin to spin.

The match started well for Colin as he had the opening serve but gradually Sam gained the initiative. Colin could not use his favoured obstruction technique as Robby simply called, 'Let.' It became clear to the me that Sam was going to win and it did to Colin. He crumpled onto one knee clutching his back. Neither medication nor rest could solve Colin's issue and so Sam was victorious. They did not shake hands.

*

We sat in the bar before changing. I noticed that there was a sauna and asked if anyone wanted to come with me to try it. I had never been in a sauna and it sounded fun. No one was interested. Colin called it some fancy 'Swedish nonsense'. I went to collect a dressing gown and towel from the girl on reception and changed into my swimming shorts. I walked over to the sauna and realised that there was a loose coin in the dressing gown pocket probably used for the lockers. I was turning the coin over in my pocket as I passed the payphone on the wall so on impulse phoned Sandra. She was so pleased to hear from me. I pretended I was giving her the sports results with updates on the football and squash. We chatted until the money ran out. I then walked down to the sauna but was disappointed to read a sign on the door saying 'Sauna out of use for maintenence'. I noted that maintenance was spelled wrong.

I went and had a shower and then went back to the bar. It was getting rowdy. Several of the squash club members and other guests were gathering and the lager was flowing. I did not see Colin but recognised his leather jacket on the back of the chair and the beer in a dimple glass.

We were suddenly interrupted by the young bar manager. He wanted Robby but we all followed him as there had been an accident. Sam was lying on a bed in the first aid room and we crowded round the door. Sam sat up on seeing us. His arm was bandaged by the shoulder and he looked shattered. He was drinking a large glass of water. The manager explained to Robby, and all of us listening behind him, that a broom had fallen and trapped Sam in the sauna. Sam had tried shouting and banging but eventually had to use the metal water spatula to break the small window. He was able to put his arm through and with the spatula dislodge the broom. Sam was grinning as we applauded his ingenuity. I interrupted by telling the manager that I had gone to the sauna but was stopped by the sign saying 'Sauna not in use for maintenance' or something like that. The manager asked if I was joking and I repeated exactly what I had seen. I even mentioned my phone call to Sandra. There was a pause broken by Sam saying, 'So someone tried to kill me!'

Dave told him he was being dramatic but the manager said, 'Well it was a bloody foolish prank and whoever did it will have to pay for their tomfoolery.' The manager asked me where the sign was now. I said I had no idea as I just read it and followed the instruction.

He asked if it was a proper sign and I said, 'Well it worked as I did not go into the sauna.' He corrected himself by asking if it was a proper printed sign and I said, 'No, as it was misspelt.' The manager then addressed the whole group. He advised us that the sauna door was damaged and the glass did not come cheap and someone had to pay. He was calmed by Robby. Robby was apologising saying that we would pay for the damage. Sam was still saying 'you bastards' or something similar.

I went over to him and said, 'You're obviously feeling better if you are cursing.' He told me he had been on the mend, until I mentioned the note. He said being stuck in that wooden box was frightening. He had had a moment of blind panic where he struggled to breathe and the heat seemed unbearable but once he calmed down and realised he had the spatula, he was emboldened. He laughed as he told me he had taken on the Zulu warrior spirit of his ancestors. He used the spatula like an assegai, nothing was going to stop him.

*

Everyone headed back to the bar. Sam and I said we would join them after Sam had had a shower and dressed. I went back down to the sauna and retraced the steps from the door that had the sign attached. I was sure that whoever had put the sign on the door must have returned to remove it. There were only two routes and one passed the phone box I had stood in; I walked back down the second route which went straight to the bar. As I walked past the stairwell, I saw the crumpled paper. It still had the electrical tape attached. I put it in my pocket. I only wanted to show Sam. He could decide what to do next.

In the bar, the stag party was several drinks ahead of Sam and me. I was in no hurry to catch up. Colin was starting to dominate the conversation. His back had recovered enough for him to offer an arm-wrestling challenge to Steve who sensibly declined. Robby had planned a sports quiz but there was little take up on the offer. There was a prize-giving for the squash tournament. It was two squash balls in a sack. There was writing on the sack saying 'you do not need these as you have shown you have them. Champion'. Sam gave a graceful thank you speech thanking Dave and Robby for the organisation and everyone for the sportsmanship. Colin thought this was a dig at him and said something about 'next time' as a stage whisper. It was a curious comment. Dave made a joke about one stag night being enough and Robby seconded him. Colin turned on me saying, 'Well you're next, Horace. You were rejected by my Carole and are now marrying some townie on the rebound.'

I felt the bile rising in my throat. I was not sure which of the inaccuracies I wanted to address as I stood up. Sam was at my side and turned me towards him, away from Colin. He was calmly saying, 'Don't get into the gutter with him.'

Colin was telling Sam to 'Keep his black face out of it.'

Sam asked him what the colour had to do with it. Sam was happy to be black and not yellow. At this, Colin launched over the edge of the table at Sam and I. We stepped back in harmony and Colin fell at our feet. Robby jumped on his back and subdued him. The young manager came over and told us we all had to leave. I for one was pleased. I had only had one pint so was well able to drive. Sam too had had enough and so we both thanked Dave and Robby and headed to the car. On the way I showed Sam the note. He stopped and stared at it. He asked me why I had it. I think for a moment he thought I was part of the prank. I explained that I had gone to find it. He was incredulous that someone was out to endanger his life. He then wondered if it was meant for me. I asked why and he reminded me that I was the only person who was interested in having a sauna. I was dumbstruck, but maybe he was right. I tried to make light of it saying it was probably Colin's idea of fun. Sam called him a bastard. Sam said Colin was the reason Sam did not join our student house in second year. Colin refused to live with Sam who he, Colin, called a 'darkie'. I was quite shocked. I recalled to Sam that Dave had organised the house-share but that I had no idea he had even been considered. Sam explained that he faced the injustice every day so nothing surprised him. We both agreed that only Colin could have come up with such a nasty prank. We agreed to meet again, maybe for a game of squash, but if not, we would see each other at Dave's wedding. I dropped Sam off and then drove home with my brain racing. Malcolm Hayden. Aiden, Hayden. It could be the same name spoiled by a loose thread.

CHAPTER 26

It was an unexpected shock for Ra-Ra when I came home late on the Saturday evening as he was asleep in my bed. I offered to crash on the sofa but he was adamant that it was his problem. He was contrite and sort of blamed Aunt Gladys who had insisted that I would not mind. Armed with my Army sleeping bag he decamped. As he left, he asked why I was back early and I joked that someone tried to kill me. Unsurprisingly Ra-Ra had no answer but went on to ask me if he could ask me a question. I said, 'Yes, of course.' It was whether I would object if he asked Dawn to marry him. I said that I was not Dawn's guardian but if Dawn was happy, I would be happy. He smiled and went off to the sofa.

*

I slept surprisingly well but woke to those aches in muscles that were seldom used except in certain sports. I wondered how the rest of the stag night went. Robby would have taken no more hassle from Colin and I suspected they all had a quiet night in the YMCA. I was disturbed that Carole had picked up with another loser, but she was not my problem. I could not remember the insult he had for Sandra, but I know it had annoyed me.

*

I did not see much of Sandra the following week. We were busy moving cabins for the first three days. Ra-Ra was working non-stop but each time our paths crossed he apologised for taking my bed and I asked him if he had popped the question yet. I did think Ra-Ra was a good prospect for Dawn as he was devoted to Philip Arthur and Dawn. It was not until the Wednesday that I had a chance to chat to Sandra. I told her about the stag night and the prank. I made it quite light-hearted, as if it was the sort of thing that might happen on any lads' night out. Sandra said it was not to happen on my stag night. I told her about Colin and Carole. She went quiet and asked if I was jealous of Colin. I reassured her that I loved her and if I could not have Sandra, I would rather die. She told me not to be so melodramatic. She wanted her Romeo, not the Romeo! We harked back to the pen-pal letters and our night at the aerodrome. I wanted to sleep with her and suggested that I give up my room to Ra-Ra and move in with her. She loved the idea and said she would raise it with her mother. She added that I could just marry her now. It did seem a solution. I did not press the issue as I wanted to have my mother and father on side.

*

On the Friday just as I was about to close the office the phone rang. George was not working and so I answered. It was the facilities manager to the managing director of Bindens, the department store. It was a really bad line and I offered to ring the man back but he ploughed on, 'Could you provide, at short notice, a cabin for our roof repairs?' I asked about the location and was told it was the roof. I wished George was about as he would have known all the questions to ask. The man asked if I could meet Mr Binden on the roof at 1930 that night. It was late night Christmas shopping. If I went to the gold card member lounge on the top floor, I would be shown to the roof access. I mumbled my agreement. I tried to get the man's name but the line went dead. I wondered if the problem was at our end and I jotted down a note to George to have it checked as it was fitted by Edward as a favour. It was past 1730 and I had no time to go home. I was wearing my steel-toecap safety boots and looked ready for a site visit so I grabbed Aiden Malcolm's tweed coat to make up the full ensemble. Do not ask me why but I took out the diamond ring from the inside pocket. I was going to put it in the box that had once held Sandra's ring but I had second thoughts and put it back into the pocket. Sandra and her mother had gone to Yvonne's to try on bridesmaids' dresses. It was Friday night so I picked up fish and chips and a newspaper and ate in the car before setting off on the thirty-minute drive.

I took a notebook and tape measure. I decided to wear the hard hat that was still on the back seat of the car. We had to take hats to the stag but I had no idea why. I presume I would have found out if I had stayed to the end. I would wear it once I got on the roof. It just seemed more professional.

I parked in the multi-storey car park and walked over a pedestrian bridge to the high street. It was cold and I stuffed the notebook into my pocket. I had left the measuring tape in the car as it was too dark to do any measurements. The High Street was winding up for Christmas so there were lights and trees and a feeling of goodwill. I almost felt like skipping to Bindens. The store was the last vestige of beauty on what had become a concrete high street. It had a Victorian façade and beautifully dressed windows. I entered through a rotating door just for the hell of it as the doors on either side were open. I climbed the stairs to the top floor to get my heart pumping and it would put some blood in my brain.

*

The Gold Lounge reception was just a desk. I gave my name to the young lady and she gave me an envelope with my name on it and with a Bindens' gold card lounge card in it. She explained that there was a sheet in the envelope with all the advantages of being a gold card member. I explained I was here to meet Mr Binden. She looked slightly perplexed but motioned to the door behind her. I went through; it was furnished like a hotel lobby with a variety of tables and chairs. It looked as if coffee and tea were provided from self-help tables and there were queues at both. Late night shoppers were strewn throughout, mixed up with bags and boxes. I found a helpful but harassed waitress who had been asked many things but never the way onto the roof. She assumed it was the door over the stairs. I put on my hard hat and set off. The door was a metal fire door and I initially assumed it was locked as it did not budge. After a bit of muscle, it smoothly glided open. I climbed a flight of stairs, through another door and was on the roof. The roof was pitch black. I could see two figures thirty paces to my left so I walked towards them. I was grateful for the hard hat as it was quite windy. As I approached the figure, I realised it was in fact just the top of an air conditioning duct. I felt such an idiot but then someone shone a light in my eyes and I lost all perspective. I cursed and turned only to be unbalanced by someone grabbing me and pushing me past the duct and over a small retaining wall. I was falling. My brain started counting one thousand, two thousand, I was grabbing for the parachute cords and trying to check my canopy. I felt some wires, I was still falling but hearing smashing and seeing flashing lights. I hit what appeared to be a glass dome with my back and neck, it smashed and threw me forward and I lost my hard hat. I was getting ground-rush. As I hit the earth, I was smiling; I was doing the perfect parachute landing fall.

*

I woke up in a hospital bed. It was a strange room as I could see a blurred Sandra and her mother hugging through a window and Father was standing with a policeman. A nurse was sitting at my arm. I felt nauseous. I remember the nurse putting a silver dish under my chin. I tried to sit up but the nurse told me not to and I lay back. I asked what happened and she said, 'All in good time, Harry.'

I came round fully several hours later. No one was at the window but the nurse was still at my side. I had no idea if it was the same nurse. I asked her what happened. She said, 'You've had concussion after a fall, we've kept you sedated just to be on the safe side. You may have a broken wrist and you do have some bruising.' I asked where and she said it was easier to say where there was no bruising. I laughed but it made my ribs hurt. She added that I may have broken a rib too.

I asked if I could sit up and she said, 'Yes.' She would adjust the bed but I had to be careful to move slowly. I did feel bilious and the moving bed made me retch. The nurse puffed up a pillow behind me and I felt quite comfortable. I asked what happened next and the nurse told me I was seeing the duty mental health nurse. I was surprised by this and asked if they thought I had a brain injury. She tactfully told me that not all brain issues were injuries but it was not her speciality. I thought I would ask whoever came. I asked if my girlfriend had been to see me and was told that there had been lots of visitors and they would be back at 1400 when visiting started again. I was going to ask about how long I had been in hospital when a man in a white uniform came in and introduced himself as Duncan. I could see his lapel badge also said mental health team. The nurse stood up and told me she was leaving me in capable hands.

Duncan asked how I was feeling and I confessed that I felt very well but somewhat confused. He then rambled on about taking time to reflect and recover. He had a long diatribe about the body being in harmony and how I needed to reflect. It all seemed rather banal and eventually I interrupted and asked what tests he was going to do on me if he thought I had brain damage. He said that it was not damage as such but that the brain was out of sorts if it wanted to self-destruct. I was more confused than ever and asked him what they thought was wrong with me. He smiled at this and said, 'That is what we're trying to establish. Why were you in such a state of mind that you would jump off a building?'

'Jump?' I gasped. 'Jump? I was pushed! I want the police here not some shrink.'

Duncan put his hand on my arm. He started saying, 'Sometimes it takes some time to admit …' but I cut him off sharply.

I asked what time it was and he said almost lunchtime. I said, 'No what actual time is it? I need to see my girlfriend.' Duncan tried to suggest I was getting anxious because I was tired. The truth is I was getting apoplectic because someone had pushed me off a roof and they thought it was self-inflicted. I asked Duncan if there was a phone box on the ward and he claimed to have no idea. I decided to find out for myself. I tried to push back the blankets but my left wrist had no power and I also felt bilious again. Duncan came round to the side of the bed, I presume to stop me climbing out. He looked unsettled.

He adopted a more conciliatory tone asking why I was not happy to discuss my state of mind. I explained that I was happy to discuss it but that his premise was based on a false narrative. He asked if this had been a cry for help or an attempt to kill myself. I explained that his line of questioning would only be relevant if I had jumped but, as I was pushed, it was the state of mind of my would-be killer he should be addressing.

I closed my eyes and focussed. I needed to know what had happened from the point I was collected from the street where I had landed. Duncan probably had no idea but I tried asking. He had no idea. He recognised that I had all my faculties. The balance of power shifted from him to me. I had the questions, he had brief notes. He thought I had been in the hospital for thirty-six hours.

The police had spoken to my office who had confirmed that there were business pressures. The police had spoken to friends who said that I had been involved in an altercation over a woman. My girlfriend had disclosed that in my last conversation with her I had told her I could not live without her but she never dreamed I was the sort to do something stupid. He added that everyone thought it was uncharacteristic. He was only going on what he had been given. He was looking a little disappointed. I had so much misinformation to dispel. I asked Duncan if I could have a pen and paper as I wanted to write down my version of events. I told him he had been fed erroneous information. He was not sure if I was allowed a pen. I laughed asking him if he was joking; I asked whether they thought I was going to stab myself. My problem was that Duncan was serious. The body of opinion was that I had jumped from the roof of Bindens.

Duncan stuck his head out of the door and summoned the nurse. She returned and he left saying that he hoped we would continue our chat soon. I just grinned. The nurse told me that the lunch trolley was on the ward and, as I had been out cold when the choice was made, she had chosen for me. I did not feel hungry but asked what she had ordered; she had no idea. I tried asking her about the circumstance of my arrival but, if she knew, she was saying nothing. I asked why I had a permanent nurse when most wards did not have enough. She shrugged her shoulders so I asked if I was on some suicide watch. At this she did say that sometimes it is a precaution and that as I was getting all my faculties back, the decision could be changed by the doctor.

Lunch was a colourless liquid that was lukewarm. I dipped the white plastic slice, that may have been bread, into it. It felt as limp and lifeless as I did. The main course was a pasta with grit and lichen. I was too well for hospital food. I could not wait until 1400 when I hoped to be flooded with visitors.

I felt sorry for the poor nurse. I did try humour, irritation, anger and every other emotion to get her to leave her post but her orders were orders. I am not sure she was even allowed to pass the time of day with me in case she turned my mind to dark thoughts. She was unwilling or unable to engage, no matter the subject I raised. I am sure she was almost as pleased as I was when at two minutes past two Mother, Father and Sandra burst in. I naturally hugged Sandra first, albeit her and Mother each came to a side of the bed at the same time. Mother was slightly miffed but I knew she was going to have to get used to it. I offered my dad my good hand to shake. He was at the bottom of the bed. There was a moment's silence which I broke by saying loudly and deliberately, 'I did not jump, I was pushed.' Both Mother and Sandra broke into tears and tried to hug me again. I once again favoured Sandra. This time Mother hugged us both. My rib started to hurt so I extracted myself.

Father, ever the most direct, told me that I should have died from that height. He said that the Christmas light cables that I swung on helped break my fall but not as much as the Victorian glass canopy that covered the window. He added that my hard hat was found in two pieces so that must have worked and the jacket I was wearing absorbed glass shards that would have diced fresh vegetables.

I butted in to remind everyone that if I was planning to jump, why would I do so in a hard hat? Sandra was still crying and came over for another hug. I said I really needed a cup of tea and father volunteered to get one.

Sandra was still sobbing and mother looked decades older than when I had last seen her. I realised just how scared they must have all been. Sandra told me that the police had found my name on the business card in my wallet and visited the office in the early hours of the morning. Sandra had seen the police car and gone out and spoken to them. She explained she was my fiancée and after that they were happy to talk to her. They had said there had been an accident, that I was injured but it did not seem life threatening. They asked her about our last conversation and whether we had had a row. She explained, through tears, that this caused her to break down as it seemed as if I had done something stupid. She was able to give the police my mother's address and Aunt Gladys's. Sandra had phoned her Uncle Tommy and he had taken her to the hospital. I had been in A&E but they had moved me to the mental health unit when it was clear I was not critical. I was still shocked that everyone assumed I had jumped. The door opened and it was George. He had a stick but was walking steadily. He had a flat cap which he doffed to me in a dramatic gesture and slightly bowed whilst doing so. I smiled and his first question was, 'What have you done with my blessed car?'

I told him it was in the multi-story car park and I would collect it when liberated from the bed. Seemingly the police found the car keys in my pocket but could not find the car. He asked me what I had been thinking about. I admonished him saying that I could not believe that George would think I jumped. I spelled out I was pushed. George had nothing to say. His mouth moved but nothing came out. He hobbled over and shook my good hand. He then said, 'Thank God.'

George had received a visit from the police who were given his name by Aunt Gladys. They had probed him about the business and asked him if there were any difficulties. To be helpful he had mentioned the two recent letters. The police wanted to know if the letters had caused me stress and he said they had not. He also confessed to the police that he had no idea why I would have gone to Bindens and it was nothing to do with the business.

It was clear that a man falling off a building was more likely to have jumped than be pushed. It was also clear that it would take some time to get the facts straight.

Father came back with the tea and the nurse came back at the same time to check I was still fine. George asked her when I would be released. Her stock answer was 'all in good time.'

Once the nurse had left, Sandra told me that a policeman had been with me for the first hour or so and that he would be coming back. She presumed he would need a statement or something. Conversation was drying up. I was pleased that Mother and Sandra seemed to be getting on. I asked about Sandra's mother and about my sister but there was not much else to say. Father suggested that he take George and Mother back to Aunt Gladys's house and he and Mother would return tonight before heading back south. George was not ready to leave but agreed as it meant he had transport. George had taken three buses to come and see me and it had taken him all morning.

I was grateful for some moments with Sandra before we were interrupted by a policeman.

The young constable seemed amiable but I was determined to be on my guard after my last experience. He asked me about my injuries and how I was feeling and then he asked me to tell him what had happened. He took out his notebook.

I started with the phone call from Bindens and the actions I took thereafter. I tried to recall every single detail, even where I purchased the fish and chips from. The constable was not the fastest writer and I could see he was itching to get to the point where I 'jumped'. He was increasingly not writing everything I said such as my conversation with the girl on Bindens' gold card reception. He did sit up when I opened the door to the roof. I told him of the two figures but as I got to them, it turned out that one was an air conditioning duct. I mentioned the bright light and then the push from the side over the small wall. The time from door to wall was the shortest part of my story. The policeman stopped writing. I could see that he was troubled by my explanation as it did not fit his instructions. He ventured that I was blinded by a light and could have stumbled. I corrected him saying that I was pushed. He suggested that having had a blow on the head, my recollections were cloudy. I suggested that being pushed off a roof was not something you forget. He changed tack and asked me who would push me and then added why? I shook my head as this was what puzzled me. I told him I had no idea. In all fairness to the young constable, he had done some homework. He had spoken to George and yes there were issues at work. He had spoken to Sandra and he had spoken to Sam. I asked how he had contacted Sam and he explained that Sam's name and address were on a piece of paper in my pocket. Sam had mentioned the prank and the confrontation with what he called my old girlfriend's new boyfriend. I conceded that out of context anything could be cobbled together to suggest a reason to jump but I countered by saying, 'If you checked my business phone records you will see I received a phone call from Bindens. You will have found the gold card they gave me. You will note that when I fell, I was wearing safety shoes and a safety helmet.' I went on to say that I was told that I had grabbed Christmas decoration wires and this was hardly the action of a suicide attempt. This was the first time since I had come round that anyone had mentioned that word.

The constable was probably now out of his depth. If he believed what I was telling him, it was attempted murder. If he did not, he needed more evidence that I was temporarily 'off my rocker'. I said nothing further. Sandra asked him if he believed me. He did not answer. He told me I was very helpful and he would digest the information and come back to me. He nodded to Sandra and left. We both laughed but it was a nervous laugh. I was thinking that someone out there was trying to kill me and I suspect Sandra was thinking the same.

*

I was desperate for the loo and did not want to use a bedpan so I was escorted by the nurse. Sandra stayed in the room. Walking was more unsteady than I had expected and my back, shoulders and arm ached. There were no locks on the doors and the poor nurse had to stand in the entrance. It was most embarrassing, probably more for her than me. I asked her when the doctor would be visiting and she told me he had been requested by the ward as he did not do conventional rounds. It reminded me that I was on the ward for the headcases. I did not see any other patients throughout my stay.

Sandra was worried as her mother was being looked after by Uncle Tommy and his wife, and she was minded that she had to relieve them. She had no transport. She had been dropped off by Tommy. I asked her to wait to see what the doctor said about my release.

The doctor looked younger than the policeman. He asked that Sandra leave but I wanted her to stay and so, after some hesitation, he agreed. He wanted to talk about how I might be thinking so differently now that I was safe in a hospital bed, as to how I was feeling walking onto the roof. I stopped him and told him I categorically did not jump. I explained how I had given all the details to the police right down to my invitation to the roof. The doctor did try to suggest that if I followed his train of thought, it may cast doubt on some of my more strident statements. I reassured him that the only strident statement between what he believed and what I believed was 'that I was pushed'. If my statement was true, I did not need his intervention. He smiled and agreed. He believed me and he would recommend my discharge to a medical ward. I asked why it could not be a discharge to the home of my fiancée.

*

The much-suffering nurse was no longer required to watch me and Sandra and I had a half hour when we discussed our wedding plans. She had put some thoughts on paper but had not wished to raise them with me until I started showing some interest. I did confess to being mildly indifferent but that from now on I would focus. Our chat was interrupted by a figure I recognised but could not think where from. It was Detective Constable Feathers of the night in the station fame. If he recognised me, he did not show it so I let him believe it was the first time we had met.

He too had a notebook and his ability to gather information was worse than his uniformed colleague. He started by explaining that whilst the constable had all the information, some of the facts needed clarification as there was some suggestion that I had not jumped off Bindens' roof. I stepped straight in saying it was not a suggestion, it was a fact. I did not jump. Feathers adopted the same 'well let us wait until I have the facts' demeanour. I then started my story again. This time I dwelled on the call from Bindens explaining how it was a bad line and conversation was difficult. I explained my preparation for the site visit. I dwelled on the conversation at the reception. I wanted Feathers to be crystal clear that I neither had the inclination nor motive for jumping. Feathers did more writing than talking so he did gather all my story. He also asked the same questions about who would push me and why. I was able to reassure him that I was asking myself the same question. Feathers seemed satisfied with my explanation, telling me that he would do some digging and I would be hearing from him.

    I was discharged that night. As I was leaving a nurse gave me a black plastic bag which looked like a rubbish sack. She explained it was the clothes I was wearing when I was admitted. She cautioned me about how they were handled as they were covered in glass. Father took the bag as he and Mother had just arrived to collect me. Mother and Father dropped us off at Sandra's before heading back south. Mother's last words to Sandra were that she had to keep a closer eye on me.

CHAPTER 27

It is not a statement I ever thought I would make but my wrist took longer to heal this time than the last time someone tried to kill me. The rib annoyed me when I laughed or tried to lift anything so I avoided both. I had some nightmares and flashbacks but increasingly spent my nights at Sandra's so she was next to me and able to comfort me. I had plucked up courage to empty out the black bag given to me as I left the ward. The safety boots had lived up to their promise and seemed unmarked. My trousers were shredded and covered in blood. Aiden's jacket was in strips. I had seen a sniper's jacket hanging on a locker at Sandhurst and it looked very similar. It had no discernible outline. The left arm was ripped off and hung down, held by a thread. I could see all the shards of glass embedded in the fabric. I could see why the nurse had cautioned me. I could see where the jacket was cut from bottom to top by scissors. Presumably this was done by the ambulance crew. I tentatively looked in the inside pocket. I pulled out the ribbon; there was a silver band attached but the diamond was gone, torn from the mounting. I gathered all the glass and put it in a bowl. I would try and sift through at some stage to see if the gem was there but it was no job for the present. I wondered if the person sweeping up the glass from outside Bindens would ever know the value of one of the small pieces they were shovelling into a bin.

*

Rowan had been attentive. He wanted to write a story about what happened to me but the police would tell him nothing. The official line was that a contractor working on the roof had fallen. There was reference to the Christmas decorations being pulled down by the falling man and it fed into a narrative of an accident. The man, me, was never named and he had recovered after a miracle fall, and in the best Christmas traditions the story had a happy ending. I was not keen on being 'newsworthy' and Rowan respected my silence. I had gone to the TA centre and told Major Tomey of my injury. He asked what I had done and I told him I had fallen over a wall which was partially true. He thought my reluctance to tell the full story was because I had been drunk and he tapped his nose knowingly. He was happy that it was over the Christmas period and so I would be missing nothing.

*

Sandra and I were somewhat tied to looking after her mother for Christmas so we declined my mother's offer to go south. In the event we had a splendid meal at Aunt Gladys's house. Dawn and Ra-Ra were there, as was George. We took Sandra's mother to Uncle Tommy's on Boxing Day. Dave's wedding was set for 14th February and Yvonne was marrying in March so our futures were being planned around us. Sandra wanted to marry in the autumn but was mindful that her mother was in gradual decline and so we could not leave it too long. I was happy to fall in with her plans. I was spending most of my time at the office. Ra-Ra was often out on the ground and we were increasing the number of toilets as they were the most lucrative part of the business and always in demand. We had been granted a six-month temporary permission to keep the cabin at Sandra's mum's, provided we made a retrospective planning application.

*

Sandra had arranged care for her mother three days a week and it meant Sandra was able to man the office with George and to take some of the administration from me. She was also able to escape to go shopping and on one day even arranged to meet Yvonne for lunch. I chided her as a 'lady who lunched'. It was on her return that she was excited to tell me that she had bumped into Rugger Bugger. His shoulder was better and he was in rude good health. I presumed that this was the extent of the news but Sandra had that gleeful look that told me there was more. Seemingly Rugger Bugger should have been at Dave's stag weekend as he was, and still is, dating Carole. I was confused but not as much as the Best Man Robby had been. Heather had allowed Dave to invite Carole's boyfriend as they were both being invited to the wedding. Colin told Dave he was dating Carole on the back of having only met her once at the White Rose. Dave told Robby who, knowing no different, invited Colin on the stag. It took me a few moments to take in what Sandra had recounted. She added that she could not believe that Colin had the brass neck but I assured her that he had.

*

Several weeks later I had almost forgotten what Sandra, George and I called 'my trip to Bindens' when I had a visit from DC Feathers. He was circumspect but wanted to update me on his investigation. He started by saying that there was a record of the phone call from Bindens to the office. There was no Mr Binden as he had died in 1934 and there was no facilities manager to the said Mr Binden. Bindens could only imagine that the phone call was to tell me that the gold card was ready, albeit they had no record of me having made any application. He seemed satisfied that I had been lured to Bindens and therefore unlikely to have jumped. He also conceded that a 'jumper' was unlikely to wear a hard hat and safety boots. He had no idea who would have pushed me as no one else was on the roof. He did think that it sounded to him like another stag night prank that had gone wrong. He said that Sam could have had serious injuries in the sauna and he wondered if Sam could have invited me onto the roof to get back at me. I was incredulous. I asked whether he thought Sam pushed me. Of this he was not so sure. He annoyed me by saying that Sam was foreign, as if this could be relevant. I rebuked him and said that Sam was from Lincoln. I explained that I was the only person who intended to go to the sauna. Sam came as an afterthought, and, as I was delayed by a phone call, maybe I was the target of that prank too. This was outside DC Feathers' narrow explanation and he dismissed it.

His conclusion was that I had stepped out onto a dark roof, a bright light, maybe from a flashing Christmas decoration, blinded me and, whilst disorientated, I fell over the balustrade. He and his colleague had been onto the roof and tested the theory and, whilst no one fell, they both felt that had they had been closer to the edge, they could well have done so. He said that the air-conditioning duct was only two paces from the wall. I shook my head. I did so recall being pushed. I could see that the matter was as closed as DC Feathers' mind, so said nothing further.

DC Feathers explained that the investigation was not over and, if anything further came to light, it would be reconsidered. He snapped shut his notebook then added, 'We have met before, have we not?' I nodded wondering where this would lead. 'Yes,' he said. 'I never forget a face.' it was such a cliché. He added that I had helped them sort out the scrap metal case. He was pleased to tell me that, thanks to my help, they had a result. The villain would soon be facing up to seven years at Her Majesty's pleasure. I asked who and he said I could read about it in the papers next week as it was going to trial. He wanted to tell me more but also maintain his control of the dialogue. He said it was a young engineer from the south working at the head office of the road contract. He paused. 'Actually the chap was working on the road that ran below the sub-station where you were working.' I tried to explain that it was all the same contract but Feathers was not listening. He added that the chap had his fingers in too many pies and had been in Feathers' sights for a few years as he had been given a caution for theft from his employer the previous summer. DC Feathers rubbed his hands as he explained how he had followed his hunch from the outset. It was all about DC Feathers and I was content that this would be our last meeting. Sandra popped her head around the door and asked if we wanted tea. I had not asked him, having remembered how I was treated when at his establishment, but I know I was being churlish. He declined saying he had to go. As he left, he paused and asked one last question.

'Who is Aiden Malcolm?'

I asked, 'Why?'

He said that the name was in the jacket that was shredded in the fall.

I replied, 'I have no idea' and I meant it.

After Feathers left, Sandra said, 'I'm not sure we have heard the last of the law,' and she handed me a white envelope. It had Harbour and Co Solicitors on the back. The letter wanted me to urgently provide a character witness statement for their client who was due in court the following week on various charges, including theft and handling stolen goods. Their client was Colin Hipgrave. Sandra asked me if I would help him. I shook my head. Colin was the last person on earth that I felt like giving any assistance to. I did not think him a good character and could not lie to the court. I added that he would not have done it for me. She hugged me and asked, 'What are we going to do now?'

I said, 'Grab your coat as I'm taking you to my gold card lounge in Bindens for tea.'

Sandra stood with her hands on her hips and said, 'That sorts out the short term but what about long term?'

I replied that it was no problem, if she gave me a pen, I would write out her Horace scope.

About The Author

Bryan Campbell Johnston was raised and schooled in North Yorkshire, having returned with his wife, Wendy, to live in Richmondshire in 2020. Bryan has three children, two step-children and he and Wendy have two grandchildren.

Between leaving North Yorkshire and returning, Bryan had both a military and legal career. His military career started at Royal Military Academy Sandhurst and ended as a major commanding an infantry company during Gulf War I. In between he served in Germany and Northern Ireland and other outposts around the shrinking globe.

His legal career started at The University of Westminster and the School of Law, and ended as a Solicitor and Managing Partner of a law firm. In between Bryan was involved in the arts as a Director and Trustee of a regional theatre for six years. He has been, among other appointments, Chair of a charity and Chair of a Chamber of Commerce. Bryan is a trained mediator.

Bryan wrote articles for a business magazine for several years; he had a play performed at Brentwood Theatre and his adaptation of Northanger Abbey was performed in over thirty-one locations by a professional touring troupe. Bryan's hobbies include writing, theatre, horseracing, sailing, golf, trekking and skiing.

Bryan writes under the name Campbell Johnston and *Horace* is his first published novel.

www.blossomspringpublishing.com

Printed in Great Britain
by Amazon

Contents

Preface		i
Chapter 1	Family and Child	1
Chapter 2	Mill Hill School	51
Chapter 3	The Furniture Bu	77
Chapter 4	National Service	105
Chapter 5	Social, Family and Married Life to 1973	134
Chapter 6	Travel Interludes 1961 – 7	167
Chapter 7	Malawi 1973 – 6	224
Chapter 8	Kenya 1977 – 84	262
Chapter 9	Lawyer	321
Chapter 10	Gathering the Threads	359
Epilogue		407
Appendix I	Selected correspondence sent from abroad	410
Appendix II	Exodus from Liberia	434

To Dani.
Best regards

NOW I COME TO THINK OF IT…

Recollections of a life

By

Roger Rose

Roger Rose

Published by New Generation Publishing in 2017

Copyright © Roger Rose 2017

First Edition

The author asserts the moral right under the Copyright, Designs and Patents Act 1988 to be identified as the author of this work.

All Rights reserved. No part of this publication may be reproduced, stored in a retrieval system or transmitted, in any form or by any means without the prior consent of the author, nor be otherwise circulated in any form of binding or cover other than that which it is published and without a similar condition being imposed on the subsequent purchaser.

www.newgeneration-publishing.com

 New Generation Publishing

Dedicated to Irene, who has shared most of the journey, and to our children and grandchildren, for whom above all this account is written

Preface

From an early age I have thought rather vaguely that "some-day" I would like to be able to look back on my life and tell my children and grandchildren about it. Happily that day has arrived. Though I do not make any claim to have led a life that is extraordinary, I like to think that it has involved an interesting variety of experiences and that this will become apparent from the chapters that follow.

It is said that our past is the only thing outside our bodies and minds that we ever truly own. But inevitably the further back we attempt to probe into that past the more unreliable is the memory of the events we try to recall. It is very easy to persuade ourselves that a particular event happened in a particular way, but subsequent research (assuming it is even possible) may show that the event has been recalled erroneously or even that it never happened at all, our perceptions having been influenced by hearing things from others or by converting mere supposition into fact. And when we attempt to set things down at a fairly advanced age, those who might have been able to correct facts and perceptions are in most cases long dead. Indeed occasional errors of memory have been pointed out in the course of writing this account and corrected. I have nevertheless done the best I can to faithfully recollect the persons, events and situations described.

Inevitably a decision has to be made as to which memories and events would be likely to be of sufficient interest to warrant inclusion, and I have had to take a subjective view on this. I have been lucky in that records exist, mainly in the form of contemporary correspondence, relating to some periods of my life (in particular the travels and general life recounted in chapters 6 and 8), but otherwise I have had mostly to rely on my memory. Sometimes correspondence that I know existed (e.g. that written to my parents during my time in Nigeria on National Service in 1959-60) seems unfortunately to have been lost or mislaid.

In order to flesh out this account a little I have sometimes added topographical information, and some background historical information, either directly in the text itself or, where it seemed less directly relevant to it, in footnotes. Obviously in the case of historical notes I could not have been aware of some of the events at the time, e.g. those existing at the time of my birth and early childhood; or the exact timings of some of those events (e.g. the great freeze in the winter of 1947). Again, the variety and extent of these bits of background information will disclose personal interests and preferences, but I hope they will make the little side-tracks concerned worthwhile.

Roger Rose
London, December 2016

Chapter 1

Family and Childhood

1. Family
   - First things 1
   - My mother and her family 4
   - My father and his family 10
2. Childhood
   - Edgware 18
   - The War Years 19
   - Nanny 23
   - Aspects of life in my childhood
     - *Keeping warm* 25
     - *Food and shopping* 26
     - *Toys and pastimes* 30
     - *Clothes* 32
     - *Friends* 33
     - *Entertainment* 34
   - Education
     - *Kindergartens* 36
     - *Belmont* 38
   - Religion 44
   - Transition 48

1. Family

First things

My earliest memory is, I think, being at the London Zoo with my parents, watching polar bears. I must have been about 3 years old, so that would set the scene probably in 1942. I cannot say whether or not I was particularly taken by these, or indeed at that stage in my life any animals, but in view of my later interest in natural history this is a particularly appropriate first memory.

Or it would be if I could somehow be sure that it was really my earliest, for I cannot be entirely sure that the Zoo recollection predates the other very early, and painful, one of being in a nursing home to have my tonsils and adenoids removed (removal of both at an early age was considered advisable in the medical fashion of the period). I remember that I was lying in or on a bed before undergoing what I now know to be the quite minor operation involved. My mother was sitting by my side wearing a beige check dress that I liked. But when I "woke up" after the event she was not there. Suddenly all I wanted in the world was that she should be there, exactly as she had been before. I well remember that, with all the unreason of a 3 or 4 year old, I screamed and screamed in fear and fury; and to such an extent that, I was later told, I had to be sedated.

To this day I have no clear idea of the true context of this little scene. I think I had to stay overnight in the nursing home, but it could be that the whole episode lasted only a few hours and my mother had slipped out to do something and I had "come round" earlier than expected. Whatever the true situation, the anguish I felt was very real. I can also remember the sense of anti-climax when eventually my mother, or it may have been both my parents, came to collect me and take me home. It was my first lesson in life: things are not usually as bad as they seem at the time.

But, first memories apart, it is appropriate at this early point in the story to recall my mother. She was to die at a comparatively young age on 30 August 1961, just over a month after her 48th birthday, in the London Clinic of complications brought on by asthma. As this was some nine months before I was to meet my future wife, there would over 50 years later be no-one close to me, except of course for my brother and sister, who even knew her. And as my father remarried some three years later (in what actually I believe to have been in many ways a more successful marriage than his first), my children would always know his second wife Suzanne as their paternal grandmother. They knew of course that she was not my natural mother (especially as she was a mere eight years or so older than me), but obviously my own mother could be only a "theoretical" ancestor for them.

Though I was 22 at the time of her death, my memory of Mother and her qualities is not as sharp or perceptive as I would like it to be. She was mild-mannered, intelligent and usually approachable, but she was actually not a very "motherly" person, and could quite easily get irritated by us children. Indeed, raising children was not at all a vocation for her and, as she could afford to do so, she preferred to leave the task to a nanny, although as it happened this course of action was not possible during the middle period of the Second World War (when my nursing home experience had taken place). That huge series of events and the atmosphere they created on the "Home Front" was a constant background to my early childhood.

My vagueness about Mother arises from comparative lack of close contact with her (what today is sometimes fashionably, and to me rather irritatingly, called "bonding" or "quality" time). From the summer of 1943 onwards I, then aged 4, was (along with my 18 month old brother Clifford and subsequently my sister Sarah) put into the charge of Elizabeth O'Leary, always known to us and the family as Nanny, and to her own family as Lily, and to whom I will refer more fully below. Apart from that, between the ages of 13 and 17 I was mostly away from home at boarding school, and was at age 19 called up for 2 years of National Service in the army. So the periods of my life spent entirely based at the family home from age 13 onwards were not continuous, and even then the time I spent in Mother's sole company was in practice quite limited. Added to this, for most of the period from about 1954 she suffered to a greater or lesser degree from the asthma that began taking her breath away and cutting her off from much in the way of a social life, eventually leading to her early death some seven years later.

But, to go back to the beginning, I was born on 15th April 1939 when Europe was in the shadow of the impending Second World War. Most people fervently hoped that it would not come about. Memories of the "Great War" (as the First World War was then still called) and the appalling loss of life on the battlefields of Flanders were fresh in peoples' minds. Though the attempted appeasement of Germany at around the time of my birth is today regarded with some derision, this is to have the benefit of hindsight. At that time most people recalled with grim horror those dreadful battles, of which the Somme in 1916 and Passchendaele the following year were simply the most terrible among many, and thought that *anything* would be better than to have to face all that again.[1] Indeed this was the view of our then Prime Minister, Neville Chamberlain, and most senior politicians. Added to that everyone foresaw, after the Zeppelin air raids of the Great War, the widely reported frightful experience of aerial bombardment in the Spanish Civil War (which had ended only in the early part of 1939), and the obvious potential that now existed for aircraft-borne gas attacks, that any future war would be too horrible to contemplate. Next time, civilian as well as military casualties would almost certainly be enormous.

My maternal grandparents, Archie and Anne Abrahams, were great admirers of Chamberlain. This was especially so after he had flown back from Munich the previous October and, on landing, had famously waved a sheet of paper that was signed evidence of the supposed desire of Britain and

---

[1] In fact my maternal grandfather's younger brother, Robert Abrahams, only recently commissioned into the 4th Battalion, the Yorkshire Regiment, was killed in Flanders in September 1916.

Germany never to go to war with each other[2]. "I believe it is peace in our time!" he famously stated. This admiration for him was echoed by my parents and was, I was told a little sheepishly later on, the reason why I was given the middle name Neville.

My mother and her family

Mother was born Peggy Abrahams on the 29th July 1913. Peggy was, and is, an unusual name in Britain (though much more common in the USA) and when it was used was often as a diminutive of Margaret; but not so in Mother's case (she actually also had an aunt, my grandmother's sister, of the same name, which was passed in her particular family to my second cousin Peggy Sherwood). The Abrahams family had been quite well off. My great grandfather Abrahams (I never discovered what his first name was) had emigrated from, I believe, somewhere in the pale of settlement in eastern Europe (always referred to in the family as "Russia") in the latter part of the 19th century and either brought with him, or started or enhanced in England, a flourishing fur business. His family of 7 children, of whom my grandfather (actually named Isaac, but always known as Archie) was the eldest, lived in a large house in Hackney, north London. But my great grandfather was an inveterate gambler, especially in the way of backing horses, and I was told that over a period of time he gradually frittered away most of the family assets in this way.

My great grandfather died in 1944, presumably some time after his wife, of whom I don't recall even a mention, let alone a name. I remember as a 4 or 5 year old being taken to see two of Mother's maiden (or possibly widowed) aunts, my grandfather's sisters, who had lived with my great grandfather and must have looked after him before he died. They told me, and seemed to make a great play of this, what a pity it was that I hadn't been able to see him "before he went on his holidays". I remember wondering why they were so concerned, as surely I could see him when he returned, not realising of course that, as was the practice in middle class families in those days, death was not even to be spoken of in front of children.

---

[2] This was actually true for Hitler as well as Chamberlain, although in the former's case not for altruistic reasons. He wanted Britain, with our enormous potential manpower resources in the Empire, out of the way so as to give him a free hand in Eastern Europe. Too many senior British politicians, including Lord Halifax (who very nearly later became Prime Minister after Chamberlain resigned in May 1940) this was a desirable course of action. Winston Churchill was one of the few prominent politicians at the time who thought that Hitler would eventually turn on Britain anyway, probably after attempts to impose limitations or unacceptable conditions on our interests in the Mediterranean, the Middle East and beyond.

My grandfather, Archie Abrahams, c.1930

The loss of the family assets was well before my time. By the time I knew them, my maternal grandparents earned what must have been a very modest living running between them a social card-playing club in Maida Vale, and lived in a very ordinary semi-detached 3 bedroom house at 4 Meredith Avenue, off Anson Road, Cricklewood, in north-west London.

My grandfather Archie died suddenly of a heart attack in his 50s in January 1946 when I was 6 years old, only a fortnight or so after my sister Sarah was born. Though I do just remember him the memory is not a strong one[3]. My grandmother, whom I always called by the slightly bizarre name "Windy" (probably from my first efforts as a baby in saying "granny"), was however a strong presence in my life, as indeed she was on the lives of my mother and her younger brother Robert (always known as Bobby) and those of my own younger brother Clifford and sister Sarah. Though named Annie as a child, she was known to most people as Anne (slightly more classy, that!). Her extended family, the Aarons, were at least in part long established residents in England: she told me rather proudly that a branch of her family had been "Cheltenham people" although exactly how far back the English connection went I never discovered.

Windy was the youngest of, I think, six children. I actually had little or no contact with her brothers or their families and some of the extended family were a little odd (although that was not, I think, the reason for non-contact!) But I did know her two sisters. The older of these, Sadie, was married to Sidney Seymour and they had an only son, Phillip, who was very deaf from birth, spoke as a consequence in a barely comprehensible squeaky voice, and was gay[4]. The family owned two or three "chemist" shops in the Soho area of London which mostly dealt in objects and appliances that concerned contraception and sexual aids. As for Auntie Sadie, I always disliked the

---

[3] He actually died less than 2 years after his own father. He had been, I was told, a chain smoker of cigarettes, something that may have contributed to his early death.
[4] In those days that word was not used to mean homosexual. It actually then meant happy in a lively sort of way, and its later transformation in meaning is hard to understand. And as "practising homosexuality" was actually against the law, gay relationships tended to be hidden or disguised, although Phillip, I was told, lived with "his friend" Arnold.

fact that, doubtless out of genuine fondness, she used to pinch and poke us children with her fingers with their (to me) disgustingly red-painted nails.

The only other great aunt Aarons sister, whom I saw very little, was Peggy, the second youngest sibling already mentioned. She was married to Louis Sherwood, a wiry man of medium height as I seem to remember him in old age, who had made a fortune from money-lending; indeed they lived in a flat in Park Lane, one of London's very smartest addresses (as those who have played the UK version of Monopoly will know). Great Uncle Louis came from a family whose name had originally been Scher and were probably originally from Germany, but they were among the very few Jewish families to have settled in Cork, and in consequence Louis spoke with a southern Irish accent. They had two children, Phillip, a solicitor by the time I knew him, whom I always thought of as eccentric, and Fay, an ungainly single woman with a voice like a foghorn who, like her cousin Philip Seymour, was also probably gay[5]. Fay was, appropriately enough, an announcer over the loudspeaker system at one of the London mainline railway stations (I think Waterloo). Uncle Louis' younger brother, Bernard (Bernie), was the family dentist. We children dreaded for some time in advance the regular visits we had to make to his surgery in Devonshire Place[6] in the school holidays, as he nearly always found cavities in our teeth. His Irish-accented assurances that what was about to happen would be over very quickly were of little comfort, as he proceeded to drill and fill them without using anaesthetics.

Windy's was a marriage of a youngest to an oldest child in a family (as subsequently, in reverse, my own was to be). Though she did not usually speak about the fact directly, it was not difficult to infer that she somewhat resented the fact that the family had come down in the world. She would tell me wistfully how she and my grandfather had lived in a much larger house in Cricklewood when they were first married. Indeed for their honeymoon in 1912 they were well enough off to be able to make a kind of grand tour of part of Europe. During that honeymoon she had been allowed to cut flowers from the Kaiser's garden in Berlin, which she subsequently pressed into a book. When war with Germany came 2 years later she had, she said, impetuously thrown the book of pressed flowers into the fire.

---

[5] Phillip Sherwood's wife, Joyce, was however delightfully "normal". Their daughter Peggy is the only remaining member of the whole of my mother's side of the family with whom I have kept contact.
[6] Situated in that part of Marylebone where many of the medical and dental professions had (and still have) their surgeries and consulting rooms.

Mother & Bobby with my grandmother, c.1920

The house in Meredith Avenue, though built in the 1920s did not have any of the household appliances that are considered standard today; indeed, it did not even have an ice-box, let alone a fridge. Windy had always managed without one and most of the time this did simply not constitute a problem for her. If there were a hot spell in the summer she would simply stand bottles of milk, and the butter, in a tub of cold water. She was finally encouraged to get a little up to date when she and Bobby moved to a flat in Sandringham Court, Maida Vale, in 1960.

Doubtless because in his early life the family had had money, Mother's brother Bobby was accustomed to dress in smart well-made clothes. Though a stock-broker, he was merely an employed half-commission man, and thus not particularly well off by city standards. He nevertheless to the end of his life always had his suits tailor-made, and he always bought expensive shoes, shirts, ties and even underwear, usually from shops in the Bond Street area of London. "The trouble is", Windy would say, "he has champagne tastes and a beer pocket". But he never married, lived with his mother until her death in 1972, and so did not have to face the costs of buying or renting his own home and bringing up his own family.

Actually Bobby had wanted to marry his then girlfriend Barbara just before the Second World War, but my grandparents had for some reason opposed the marriage and Barbara married someone else. However, quite fortuitously a short time after Windy's death Barbara's husband also died, and for a few short years she and Bobby got together again, though they did not marry or actually live together. It was a tragedy for him that she died prematurely in 1982. He himself died of a heart attack at our house, shortly after our return from Africa, in November 1984, a few days after his 68th birthday.

But, going back to Mother herself, I see in retrospect what a pity it was that in her comparatively short life she had in a sense missed out. She had had an adequate but unexceptional education at Clark's College in Cricklewood, and had then gone on to a job as a secretary in the civil service (she actually worked at the Admiralty). But in those days the civil service, in common with most employers, did not employ married women, and she had to leave her employment when she and Dad married in 1935.[7] Even if the family could have afforded it, the idea that a young girl should go to university was widely thought of as a waste of time and resources

There was in fact little expectation placed on middle class women, and it took one of extraordinary determination and ability, assisted by a supporting family, to buck the trend. In Mother's case there was no-one who could encourage her to get out of the rut that marriage created and go and do things, and as she employed Nanny to look after us children when we were at home, there was in fact too little for her to do. Reading apart, she had no particular interests, and she was a bit ashamed, as she implied to me on more than one occasion, that the many hours she spent reading was mainly of novels.

Mother had met Dad at a Jewish charity function in the spring of 1935 (in fact the song *Easter Bonnet*, by Irving Berlin, was popular at about that time and she always regarded it as "their" song). It's not difficult to imagine that he was very much attracted to her – she was good-looking, though in a quiet, low-key way, and intellectually bright, and she came from a family whose life-style was what he, with his working class background, aspired to. Not least of her attraction for him was, I believe, the fact that she came from an

---

[7] It was assumed in middle class circles that it was the husband's duty to provide for his family, and the wife's to look after the family home and raise the children. This social convention was a strong one, and to the end of his days Dad would not hear of either woman he married working – it was usually only in the working classes that this happened. I'm sure that for either of them to have worked would have induced a sense of shame in Dad, and although he never actually expressed it in these terms, his fear would have been that in such a case "people will think I can't afford to support my wife and family".

Mother and Dad shortly before their wedding. Summer 1935

assimilated English Jewish family (in contrast to his own, with, as will be seen, his *very* foreign father). For her, on the other hand, here was a handsome young man with an engaging, strong and dynamic personality, who though perhaps not quite her social equal[8], was perceptive, intelligent and doubtless fun to be with. They married on 8th September 1935 when she was 22 and he was just two weeks short of his 25th birthday.

The two people who were now closest to her, her husband and her mother, were both strong personalities. Given the social attitudes of the time, the fact that she was not a particularly maternal type of woman, and that there was always going to be a problem of how she occupied her time, it was Mother's tragedy to be caught, indeed "trapped" might even be an appropriate word, between these two dominating people[9]. I believe she was in a sense gradually suffocated by the situation, and it is thus not surprising that she eventually succumbed to, and later died from complications relating to, asthma. This is not to blame either Dad or Windy for what happened; each in their own way certainly loved her[10], and both were distraught when she died.

---

[8] This was something that would matter more to her parents than it did to her. I am convinced that the somewhat strained relationship that existed between Windy and Dad, which became considerably worse after Mother's death, was due in part to this apparent social inequality.
[9] Unless she was away on holiday, Mother felt obliged to speak to Windy on the telephone every day. While this might not be exceptional today, in those days daily contact of that sort was, I believe, unusual.
[10] Dad would sometimes, *a propos* of nothing in particular, put his arm around her shoulders and say to us in a jocular manner, as though presenting her for the first time in a new light, "Our Mum!" This always slightly embarrassed her and she would protest feebly by telling him not to be so silly.

My father and his family

Dad's family could hardly have been more different from Mother's, and indeed was much more typical of the mass of London Jewish families in the early twentieth century. His mother, born Sarah Lippman in London in 1886, was the eldest of, I think, 7 children of parents who had emigrated from somewhere in the pale of settlement. His father, the only one of my grandparents who was not born in England, had come to London from Lithuania in the early years of the 20th century, one of many thousands of Jews escaping greater Russia in those years from poverty and persecution. It is possible that, like many of those refugees, he thought he was emigrating to the "land of promise", the United States, and indeed Dad understood that my grandfather had a sister who had gone to that country. How the two became separated was never made clear[11].

The exact circumstances of my grandfather's emigration or arrival I never knew. I seem to remember my grandmother saying that he had lived for a while in Germany beforehand. Even his name was something of a mystery: before his arrival in England he had adopted the surname Rosen (which my father as a young man later changed, without having taken any formal steps to do so, to Rose) but his original surname, to the best of the recollections of the extended family some time later, was probably Lebelski or something similar. Part of the mystery lay in the fact that my grandfather spoke English with a thick accent, and never learned to read or write in English. He was anyway obviously not interested in discussing his origins; the most I ever got from him about his life before England was that it had been "very hard". Whether or not it was his original first name, he was known as Louis, or Lou. He thus ended up with a name, Lou Rosen, that could not have more obviously placed him as one of the Jewish immigrant masses in the East End of London at the beginning of the twentieth century[12].

Lou was a cabinet-maker by trade. The most common trade learned and brought with them by Jews from eastern Europe was that of tailor, which is

---

[11] It was probably typical of my grandfather that information on the subject of his sister was vague. Dad made efforts to find her on a visit he made with Mother to the United States in 1949, but such information as he had as to her whereabouts was out of date and he failed to do so. He must, incidentally, have been able to persuade the authorities that the visit in question was a necessary one for business purposes, for at that time travel was expensive and foreign currency, which was tightly controlled by exchange control legislation, was simply not available to the ordinary traveller. This was especially so in the case of American dollars which were ordinarily hoarded by the Government to help pay back to the US the enormous war debts Britain owed it.

[12] In the way that things happen, my grandmother Sarah, who was intelligent and shrewd, would have been able to fill in many of the blanks about his life. But she died in 1986, at the age of 100, before I developed any real interest in these matters.

why so many of them were in what was colloquially known as the *"Schmutter"* (from the Yiddish for "rag") business, especially in ladies' clothes. But there were also a good number of cabinet-makers. My grandfather was not an entrepreneur, or if he had ever tried to be his own boss he had failed: Dad used to tell how one of his earliest recollections of the family was his mother crying one Friday evening when his father had failed to bring home any money at all. However, the "family" trade being what it was, it went almost without saying that Dad and his older brother Alf would also be apprenticed as cabinet-makers. His younger brother Bertie was apprenticed in an allied trade, upholstery.

Dad was born Davie Barnet Rosen on 22nd September 1910 in Whitechapel, in what was known as London's East End[13]. Although that was the name on his birth certificate, as far as I can remember it was only ever my grandmother who called him "Davie", everyone else, partly depending on their social background, called him either Dave, or (particularly Mother and her family) David. For some reason Barnet (and its diminutive Barney) was a common English Jewish name at the time[14], but as far as I know Dad never subsequently recorded it as one of his given names. And as previously indicated he simply and unofficially changed his surname to Rose.

Quite unlike the circumstances of Mother and her family, it would not be an exaggeration to say that he was born into poverty. At best his family were only a working-class step away from it. This fact, together with experiences like that already referred to, made him determined above all things that he was going to do whatever it took to get out of it.

Dad was in his youth good-looking and physically well-built and well-co-ordinated. He performed particularly well at sports and was a good ballroom-dancer; in fact when a young man he was a good enough dancer to have entered (alongside his brother Bertie) the Star Ballroom Dancing Championships[15]. At school he had played soccer and cricket, the former at left-half (today's left midfield) and the latter at wicket-keeper, and, presumably in his senior year (he left school, as did most children of poor

---

[13] The poor side of London. By contrast the West End contained, as well as the most fashionable shops, much of the very best London residential property (as indeed was that of my mother's uncle Louis Sherwood).

[14] Probably most famously in that of Cecil Rhodes' one-time financial partner, Barney Barnato.

[15] The Star was at that time a London evening newspaper. In my youth it circulated alongside the Evening News and the Evening Standard, but the Star ceased publication in 1960, doubtless as a result of competition from television, and the other two merged in 1980, eventually to become the Standard. This became, in spite of new rivals appearing from time to time, the only consistently available London evening paper.

Dad (seated right) and family, c. 1919

families, at the age of 14), he captained both teams. In adult life he performed well at tennis, and also learned to ride a horse. However, having taken up golf with a passion shortly before the Second World War, he never rode afterwards, and played tennis only very occasionally with Clifford and me when later we as a family had our own tennis court. In spite of total lack of practice, he usually managed to beat each of us without much difficulty.

Golf in fact became his main activity outside work (for many years he played to a handicap of 9, for a short time as low as 7) and he played every Saturday and Sunday, leaving Mother as a "golf widow". In fact, other than in the early morning and the evening, we saw him at home only if the weather was too bad to play golf. He finally retired from the game at the age of 89. He had been playing only half a round once he was in his eighties, but knew it was time to retire, he told me, when he found that he was looking forward to "coming in" more than to playing. His only other serious interests outside his work were playing bridge, and following movements of shares on the Stock Exchange.

But most of this was later. After his apprenticeship and during a short spell working as a qualified cabinet-maker, he met a young man in similar circumstances, Isadore ("Jack") Angel. Jack, a good-looking and rather elegantly dressed man to the end of his days, had a flair for drawing and design, and the two of them decided that they would set up a furniture-making business on their own account. Dad recognised that although, as a paid employee on a bonus system, he had been what he called "a fast man" and hence able to earn comparatively well, Jack was the better craftsman. On the other hand it became increasingly obvious as time went on that Jack had no real business sense and that the entrepreneurial drive would have to be Dad's alone. But for the time being the business, which they named "Supersuites"[16], operated initially from the Brick Lane area of Shoreditch.

Dad (right) with brother Alf (2nd right) & friends, c. 1928

Supersuites made bedroom furniture, consisting in those times mainly of suites comprising a large lady's wardrobe, a smaller gent's wardrobe and a mirrored dressing table. These were made mainly from walnut-veneered plywood, later to be superseded by chipboard. After some time, as the business began to get established, and possibly also as all three sons began contributing to the family income, the family finally moved out of the East End to Gants Hill, Ilford, sometime in the early 1930s[17]. At about the same time Dad and Jack Angel moved Supersuites to a new industrial estate adjoining one of the canals into which the River Lea is channelled near Edmonton, North London[18].

---

[16] In some ways this was an unfortunate name as it was constantly misquoted or misspelt, and post used to arrive at the factory addressed to "Super Sweets", "Super Suits" or "Supper Suits", among other variations.

[17] Dad told me how the modest semi-detached house at 26 Southview Crescent had seemed to him at the time almost as a mansion of unimagined luxury. I remember that the downstairs front (dining) room had stained oak panelling (which I think the family men had installed), that to my eyes made the room dark and depressing.

[18] For a fuller account of Supersuites, and the furniture business generally, see chapter 3.

Dad was very much his mother's son. He was a man of ability and shrewdness with an immense capacity for hard work, and as was necessary in the career path he had chosen he was determined and focussed. There were two short maxims that he often quoted (he didn't of course invent them, but made them cornerstones of his life). The first was "If a job's worth doing, it's worth doing properly" (he always pronounced the final word "proply"); the second was "If you don't do anything, nothing will happen" (actually, in the cockney vernacular of his youth, he would say "if you don't do *nothing*, nothing will happen"). He lived by these and encouraged us children to do the same. He also very much disliked what he called the "something for nothing" culture in which people were, as he saw it, encouraged to be spongers on the State, and he despised the practice, encouraged towards the end of his life by the legal profession, of bringing law suits on the flimsiest of grounds in the hope of gain.

Dad and Jack Angel, early 1930s

Yet he had a really good sense of humour, and when he was in the mood loved nothing better than to recount stories and experiences and roll around laughing about them, as he did so slapping the person he was talking to on the shoulder. These bouts of hilarity were infectious. Another thing he did to amuse us as children was to place the plate with his three or four false teeth half out of his mouth, leer at us and wave his fingers about, pretending to be a hideous monster. He was a tactile person, and loved to hug and kiss us children. I still feel a little ashamed that (partly influenced by Nanny's insistence that "boys don't hug and kiss") I did not always respond to this side of his personality.

Dad was very fond of music, and had built up a small collection of what were then called gramophone records[19], mostly popular vocal and instrumental pieces by singers and bands of the 1930s and 40s. Though he had never really developed a taste for classical music, this did not mean that he was totally ignorant of what it had to offer; in fact in about 1952, soon after so-called long-playing records[20] began to appear, he bought three of them containing music he really liked: a series of operatic arias by Maria Callas, Rimsky-Korsakov's *Scheherazade*, and a record containing Chabrier's *Espagna* and Tchaikovsky's *Capriccio Espagnol*. For him, music had to have what he thought of as a melody, which was the reason he gave for not being able to enjoy the subtler sounds in most classical music, or indeed jazz. As Mother was, or seemed to be, somewhat indifferent to most music, I undoubtedly inherited my own love of it from him.

I also inherited from him, though in a less absolute form, his left-handedness. However, though I am predominantly left-handed, e.g. in writing and painting, I have for many purposes the ability to use both, a useful attribute when it comes to carpentry or decorating.[21]

Dad had considerable concern for his appearance and was to the end of his days always well dressed and turned out. I remember him reprimanding me at the age of 17 for looking scruffy: "At your age" he said "I was always spick and span". He usually had his suits made to measure by a Jewish tailor, Cyril Castle, in Conduit Street, near Saville Row, and I remember him on one occasion on holiday trying on a new light grey one with patch pockets of which he had just taken delivery and was particularly proud: "How do you like me new whistle[22]?" he beamed as he paraded, pleased as Punch, in front of the mirror.

But Dad was also opinionated (at times bigoted) and domineering. This meant that any opinion on almost anything which did not coincide with his own, or indeed any statement that he considered foolish or ill-thought-out, was liable to be dismissed by him out of hand, sometimes contemptuously[23].

---

[19] These were so-called "78s" (because they revolved 78 times a minute): breakable shellac discs, usually 10 inches in diameter, but occasionally 12 inches (especially in classical music) which came in paper or cardboard sleeves with a hole in the middle so that one could read the centrally placed label.
[20] Made of vinyl and not easily broken, though they could bend or go out of shape if not well cared for.
[21] This attribute meant that though I was predominantly left-footed at soccer and rugby, in playing cricket I batted right handed and bowled (and threw a ball) with my left.
[22] Cockney rhyming slang: whistle and flute = suit.
[23] As often as not he would refer to the person holding the differing opinion, or making the statement, as having "only half a brain", or by the contemptuous Yiddish word *schmok* (a

Though he undoubtedly loved us children, these last characteristics sometimes made it difficult for me in particular to get really close to him, let alone (as I was later to find out) to work under or with him.

There had been, as he saw it, one blight on his life: his lack of education. This, he believed, prevented him from really being on a level with those that had been well educated, and part of him felt inferior and disadvantaged in their company. I say "part of him", because he was well aware that "well-educated" people were not by his standards necessarily wise, or even particularly intelligent; but even so, what they had was in his opinion something of value that gave them a particular kind of self-confidence he considered was lacking in himself. He would, for example, refer to lack of it as the reason why he felt distinctly uncomfortable if he ever had to speak in public.

One particular occasion illustrating his supposed disadvantage stays in my memory. We were as a family staying one summer holiday at Saunton Sands Hotel, near Barnstaple in Devon when I was 11 or 12. The hotel had, naturally, a golf course attached to it on which Dad played daily. Also staying at the hotel was Lady Spencer, the Marchioness of (I think) Northampton, unaccompanied by her husband but with her three children, the oldest of whom was about Cliff's age, and whom we got to know as holiday playmates. Lady Spencer was another very keen golfer and said to me on more than one occasion that, having seen Dad playing, she was eager to have a round with him; I think she had told him as much. When I asked him why he did not do so (I think Mother was rather amused by the idea), his rather sheepish response was that he wouldn't know what he should call her. What he was really saying was that he would have considered himself socially totally out of his depth in her company.

His disadvantage was of course largely his perception, but it ran so deep that he was determined that he would do all he could to make sure that we, his children, would have the best education he could afford so that we did not "suffer" as he did.

Dad's determination to rise as far as he possibly could from the environment of his birth drove him almost inevitably also to seek the usual status symbols of the *nouveau riche*: a suitably impressive car and, above all, an impressive address. His tastes were always, however, slightly subdued (never what

---

stupid or derisorily incapable person). This latter word was considered in some Jewish circles (though clearly not Dad's) as unsuitable for use in polite society, especially as it had come colloquially to mean "penis". Even so, it passed from Yiddish into American English (and hence to British English) in the rather lighter form *schmuck*.

might be colloquially termed "flash"), and though he did not aspire (at least until later when he worked for Great Universal Stores) to a Rolls Royce or Bentley, he drove what was perhaps the next best thing in cars, an Austin Princess. But the crowning glory that announced his social "arrival", at least to those whose estimation he sought, was the purchase of a house in The Bishops' Avenue. This road, well known to those living in north-west London, was almost in a class of its own: neither Hampstead, nor Hampstead Garden Suburb, nor Highgate, nor East Finchley, with all of which it was contiguous, its name alone was sufficient to locate it. It contained many vast mansion-type houses.

In fact "Fourways", the house he bought there (actually from a man by the name of Sam Peskin, who had a very similar Jewish furniture business background to himself, but who had clearly "arrived" earlier) on the southern junction with Aylmer Road, though quite large, was one of the smaller ones in that road. But apart from its location, its special features included a tennis court in the garden[24] and a full-size billiard table in the large room at the top of the house that must have originally been assembled *in situ*, for it was far too large and heavy to manoeuvre in one piece.

Almost from the start Mother hated it.

---

[24] A subsequent owner hived off the tennis court, and probably a slice of the back garden as well, and built another substantial house on the space.

2. Childhood

Edgware

But I need to go back in time a little.

For the first 14 years of my life we lived in Edgware. Until the mid-1920s Edgware had been a small and largely unremarkable Middlesex village whose High Street was part of "Watling Street" or the Edgware Road (the original line of the Roman Road that went northwest from London) which it straddled. In one respect the original village was however a little unusual: it had, as can be partly confirmed from old postcards and photographs, at least nine pubs.[25]

Some added importance had been given to the village when in 1867 it had become the terminus of the Edgware, Highgate and London Railway, soon part of the Great Northern Railway[26]. That railway is not to be confused with the Northern Line of the London Underground ("the Tube"), whose Edgware terminus[27] was constructed in 1926 on a site some 200 yards to the northwest. We knew the former as "the steam train station" and the latter as "the Underground station" (though it was actually at this point above ground). Very quickly competition from the Tube made the steam line uneconomic and it ceased carrying passengers in 1939 and ceased functioning altogether in 1964, when the station was demolished and the site redeveloped[28].

---

[25] There may have been one or two more. According to my memory and reckoning, from south to north these were: the White Hart, the White Lion, the Red Lion, the Chandos Arms, the Mason's Arms, the Boot Inn, the Beehive Inn; also, at Stonegrove just to the north, the Leather Bottle and almost at Stanmore on the junction with Spur road, the Corner House. By the Second World War the Chandos Arms had disappeared when the High Street was widened, but the Railway Hotel had by then appeared in Station Road.

[26] The route had been via Mill Hill East and Mill Hill. The GNR was subsequently in the 1920s subsumed into the London and North Eastern Railway (LNER), one of the big four railway companies, the others being the London, Midland & Scotland Railway (LMS), the Southern Railway (SR) and the Great Western Railway (GWR) that were nationalised into British Railways – subsequently British Rail – in 1948. BR itself was denationalised in the 1990s.

[27] In fact it had been planned that the Northern Line would extend northwards beyond Edgware via Brockley Hill and Elstree to Bushey Heath, but there were issues around the "Green Belt" that was brought in as a town planning measure to stop continuous expansion of Greater London in the late 1930s and the extension was never built (though some preliminary viaduct work was begun and the remains of this can still be seen just off the A41 near Spur Road leading to Stanmore).

[28] All that remains of those days is the Railway Hotel (itself rebuilt in a mock Tudor style in 1931) which adjoins the site of the former station.

Edgware was served by a number of motor bus routes, and also by the electric trolley-buses that were a feature of transport in London during my childhood. These had by the 1940s largely replaced the electric trams that had originally run through the village in the early 1900s. Trolley buses had the advantage over trams in that they did not need tramlines; they were also very quiet. However, they had some considerable disadvantages: they needed to be powered by overhead electricity lines that were unsightly, and they were less manoeuvrable than petrol engine buses. From time to time the trolley poles that connected the top of the bus to these power lines became disconnected and the bus was immobilised until the bus-conductor could reattach the trolley pole using a long connecting pole carried for the purpose. From the late 1950s they were phased out in favour of motor buses and withdrawn altogether in 1962.

The extension of the Tube virtually guaranteed that the surrounding land would be developed into a typical London suburb with shops, offices and houses. What became known as Station Road was largely constructed in the mid-1920s at the same time as the Underground station, along with large tracts of adjoining land for streets of residential housing. Edgware effectively became part of Greater London from this time.

My parents, with some help from my maternal grandparents, bought one of the newly built houses on the Canons Estate[29] at the time of their marriage in 1935. And so it was that my childhood was spent in a typical 1930s suburban house with two living rooms, four bedrooms, kitchen, bathroom and garage situated at 12, Dorset Drive. It had small front and back gardens. In the front garden was a box hedge and two lines of cultivated rose trees (I thought as a child that roses grew on small trees rather than bushes); in the back Dad had planted apple, pear, plum and cherry trees, as well as gooseberry and black and red currant bushes.

The War Years

The Second World War (always referred to in my generation and the one before as "the War") dominates all my earliest memories. On some of the street corners there were large concrete blocks that, I understood, were

---

[29] This was actually a small part of what had been the grounds of "Cannons", the stately home first developed by the 1st Duke of Chandos in the 18th century. Confusingly "cannons" and "canons" seem to have been to an extent interchangeable. The words refer to monks, not guns, as the estate had been owned by the Augustine Priory of St Bartholomew until dissolution of the monasteries in the 16th century under Henry VIII. In 1929 the stately home and immediately surrounding land was bought by North London Collegiate School, as a girls' Public School. Part of the remaining land was turned into a public park (Canons Park), and the remainder sold off to developers for building houses, including our own.

meant to impede the progress of German tanks, should an invasion occur. And no-one who lived in London (or any city) at that time could forget the head-piercing wail of the air-raid warning sirens. The initially rather frightening crescendos of sound (as the siren was switched on and off) foretold the approach of enemy aircraft (or, later on in 1944, the dreaded unmanned V1 flying bombs known universally as "doodlebugs"); and then, when the danger had passed, a long continuous wail of about 20 seconds signalled the "All Clear".

Dad in AFS uniform with me aged about 9 months, early 1940, Dorset Drive

Dad had a brick air-raid shelter built in the garden at the beginning of the War, but as it was separate from the house and unheated and unlighted, it was a damp, airless and miserably uncomfortable place at any time of the year. We probably used it for the purpose for which it was built for a while, but I have no memory of this, and in my consciousness it served only as a shed and storage space for fruit that we grew in the garden and wrapped in newspaper. In fact my earliest memories of taking shelter from air raids are being told to sleep with my brother underneath our substantial dining-room table (doubtless we followed this procedure for daylight raids too). Towards the end of the war Dad had a second air-raid shelter constructed which was directly attached to the dining room, but although it was for the adults (including Nanny) as well as us children, I don't recall my parents ever sleeping in it.

In fact at the beginning of the war Dad had arranged for Mother and me to be evacuated out of London, to a large house in Hassocks, near Brighton, along with his parents and the family of his brother Alf (then consisting of my Aunt Sophie and cousins Maureen and Jacquie – respectively about 6 and 3 years older than me). But a combination of being on top of Dad's family (with most of whom she had little in common), missing her own family, and the fact that it was the period of the "phoney war" when the expected bombing of London had not yet materialised, led to a return to London after only a short period of months.

Dad was exempted from military service as being engaged on essential war work (the Supersuites furniture factory had been requisitioned for manufacturing parts for military gliders). He stayed in London for his work and joined the Auxiliary Fire Service for evening and weekend duties. In that capacity his station (a temporary one in Stonegrove, Edgware) was often called to fires, especially in the Dockland area of London that were very badly hit in the intense aerial bombing of London from September 1940 that became known as "the Blitz".

In fact it was during the Blitz that Mother and I (together with a maid or nanny called Kathleen – I know that she existed only from a photograph taken of her and me at the age of about 18 months) were once again evacuated; this time (I was told) to Cheltenham. This absence also did not last long and I of course do not remember it, but I think it was during the final drive back from Cheltenham to London that Dad (probably in trying to avoid something in the road, and possibly in the blackout) jammed on the brakes of his car so hard that Mother was thrown against the dashboard, knocking out her two upper front teeth and requiring her to have to wear a bridge with replacement false ones thereafter. There were no such things as seat belts (or indeed tooth implants) in those days.

In fact use of civilian cars was severely restricted during the War, as petrol was rationed and available at all only to those who could persuade the authorities that they needed it for essential purposes. Dad was able to run a small Austin on the basis of his war work. He had actually bought an American Dodge saloon just before the war, but this was laid up on bricks in the garage of our kind neighbour, Mrs Austin (a quite co-incidental name) "for the duration". He sold it soon after the war, when cars were at a premium, without ever running it again.

On the 14th December 1941 my brother Clifford was born. Because that particular date was the birthday of the King, he was given the middle name George. I must have been jealous of him, and was not very nice to him at times. I recall Mother telling Dad on his arrival home one day how good I had been towards Clifford (this must have been an event that was in itself noteworthy), and can still remember how this prompted me to make up for

December 1941, aged 2 years 8 months

my praiseworthy conduct by rushing to his cot as he was being put to sleep and pinching him.

Though I can still see each room clearly in my mind's eye, both our house and the furniture in it were frankly unremarkable. The one item of furniture that I particularly liked, in fact it fascinated me, was the oak bureau that, somewhat oddly, stood in our hall. It had been made by Jack Angel as a wedding present to my parents, and as usual it had a fold down desk flap at the top with drawers underneath. Behind the flap were two small drawers, one of which contained various pencils whose smell I loved and which I often "sorted", and a number of pigeon holes in which Mother kept stationery and papers of all sorts (but not paid bills; these were kept on a spike in the larder). I loved the smell and feel of stationery, and always have done since.

There was also in the bureau a conical shape pot of glue, of the kind that had a brush inside attached to the lid. One day, to amuse myself, I decided that the pot would look more attractive if decorated, and I carefully pasted a numbers of Mother's best envelopes overlapping each other diagonally around the conical pot. I was rather proud of my work. I was duly chastised by Mother, but could sense that she was a little amused by it.

The only other interesting piece of furniture was the store cupboard, not for itself but for its contents. It was a low brown-painted cupboard about 5 feet wide by 3 feet 6 inches high that stood upstairs on the landing, and in it were tins of food that Mother had hoarded from the days before rationing, most of which became unobtainable afterwards. From time to time a tin was taken from the store cupboard for a family treat. One of my favourite occupations as a child was to "tidy" this cupboard by removing all the tins (there may have been some packets too) and stacking them neatly back again.

Mother, late 1940's passport photograph

Actually I was probably ill-disciplined and often badly behaved. Dad (who was anyway not inclined to be a disciplinarian) was not very much present and I was, I see in retrospect, largely beyond Mother's control. I used to play out in the street in spring and summer with other children in the neighbourhood. All of that was, however, to change abruptly in the summer of 1943 at the age of 4 years and some months when Nanny arrived back on the scene.

Nanny

She had in fact been employed by my parents to look after me when I was a baby, but her mother in Ireland had fallen ill in 1940 and Nanny had gone back to Wexford to look after her; so she was in fact returning to us in 1943. She came from a family of, I think, four daughters and three sons, but (as was typical with many Irish families) all but two had come over to make their lives in England.

Interestingly I can even remember the occasion of Nanny's return: I was out riding my tricycle and had reached the pillar box at the end of our street when an unknown woman appeared and in a kindly voice said "Hello, Roger". How, I thought, does she know my name? I think I glared back and turned and rode away.

From now on the discipline that I at first hated and resented, but doubtless needed, began to be instilled. I was forbidden from playing in the street, and Cliff and I were regimented in all the ways that would be expected at the time of properly brought-up middle class children: in particular we had to sit properly at the table, eat our food correctly, sit on the lavatory to do what she called "ugh-ughs" after every breakfast and lunch (surprisingly we usually performed as required) and generally do what we were told. Disobedience or failure adequately to comply led to the use of "the stick", a thin garden bamboo pea stick with which we were beaten ("got the stick") on the bottom or thigh. I don't remember if this hurt (and thus it probably didn't much), but it was more the indignity of the punishment that did.

Being older and possibly hence to a degree wilder, I was the one who usually got the stick. But I remember on one occasion witnessing my brother getting a beating for having wet his pants (Nanny referred to the action of peeing as "doing pippies"). At each stroke of the stick she intoned "pippies Nanny!" to forcibly remind him of what he was supposed to say if he wanted to pee. Far from feeling indignant on his behalf, I (horrible little boy that I doubtless was) rejoiced, probably with a smirk, that it was he and not I that on this occasion was being punished.

Part of the discipline process involved us children having to go to bed at what seemed to me (and still does) the ridiculously early hour of 6 pm; this practice was insisted on just as much by Mother as by Nanny. It of course meant that we were awake early in the morning, and although it was annoying for me in particular at all times, it was particularly irksome in the summer months when it was still broad daylight outside. No satisfactory reason was ever given for the requirement (except the feeble one that we "needed sleep") and my belief was, and is, that part of it was to get us out of the way, for it was only "brats" who were allowed to "stay up till all hours". This requirement applied even on holiday, except that by a certain age we were allowed as a treat once a week to stay up and have dinner with our parents.

But I do not want to leave the impression that Nanny was nothing but a harsh and unmitigated disciplinarian. She undoubtedly cared for us children and was doing her duty by us as it was seen to be in those days. She would spend hours preparing meals for us, and made in particular an Irish soda bread that I loved (Mother disliked cooking and I don't remember her ever baking). Nanny took us for walks, played card or board games with us, and if we were ill she was an excellent and sympathetic nurse. This latter attribute drew her especially close to my sister Sarah, who developed whooping-cough when about 18 months old sufficiently badly for it to be life-threatening.

Nanny had very fixed views on, for example, some people. Black people, or "darkies" as she would call them, were definitely lesser beings, as were most "foreigners", particularly if German. It was however an article of faith for her that "Indian people" (i.e. those from the Indian sub-continent) were consistently the most good-looking in the world, and she always liked or respected "Jewish people" for some of whom she had worked before us. She also considered that most food that was not plain British (or of course Irish) cooking was "foreign muck". She smoked quite heavily, mainly I seem to remember the popular brands of the time: Wills "Gold Flake" and later Players "Navy Cut", and particularly if she were doing house work, and she had a smoker's cough until the end of her life. She also had the by then slightly outdated view that it was unacceptable for a woman to smoke in the street or in public, and never did.

Nanny with Sarah, 1953

Nanny never married. She had a boyfriend in the early days, Larry, who in spite of being Irish was in the Royal Artillery when I first knew him (though southern Ireland was neutral, there were quite a number of southern Irish volunteers in the British Army in the War) and drove a 3-ton truck. But the relationship obviously ended and gradually I became aware that he no longer visited us.

I found as I got older that some of the views she expressed on life in general were to say the least questionable, and that I was growing out of what I began to see as her rather narrow ways. But that didn't prevent me from continuing to be fond of her. She stayed with the family until Dad remarried and moved out of Fourways in 1964.

Aspects of life in my childhood

Keeping warm

My childhood was well before the days of central heating, at any rate in private houses, and most houses needed to be heated by open coal fires. In fact we had these in the downstairs rooms, gas fires upstairs and a coke-fired stove in the kitchen which warmed that room and heated the water in the hot water tank. Over the stove was a pulley operated clothes-drying rack that I enjoyed being allowed to raise and lower. The lack of central heating, a facility that is now taken for granted in homes in the richer temperate climate nations, meant that in winter it could often get cold enough for frost to form on the inside of the bedroom windows.

Fuel, in the form of coke (processed coal) for the boiler, and coal for the open fires, was delivered from time to time by the coalman. These were brought by horse and dray in heavy duty bags, which the coalman carried from the cart on his back (wearing a one-piece leather hood and back protector in the form of an apron that reached down the back to the waist) and tipped by him into the appropriate coal bunker outside the kitchen. This was dirty work, and with the coal dust created when the substance was moved, by modern standards almost certainly unhealthy. The coal or coke then had to be brought as needed into the house by us, using a small shovel and a coal scuttle or container that was placed by the fire.

There was one memorable period of time when almost no-one was able to keep warm: the winter of 1947. From 23rd January until 10th March Britain was locked into a weather system that created sub-arctic temperatures and conditions (in February the thermometer did not rise anywhere above 5° Celsius): snow drifts were common on the roads, the River Thames froze and for part of the time there was even pack ice in the English Channel. Movement of coal, whether for power station, industrial or domestic use, was severely restricted owing to the frozen roads and railways and eventually power supplies were in danger of failing altogether. As a result electricity supplies were limited to certain hours of the day. Gas supplies too must have been affected, for I remember my mother attempting to boil water on a bar electric fire laid on its back.

There were wide economic effects of that terrible winter, including rationing of staple foods like potatoes that had not been rationed during the War, but of course we three children (my sister Sarah had been born in January 1946) were largely sheltered from them. It must have been difficult to get to school (I was at Belmont, Mill Hill, by this time) but I have no specific memory of this.

Food and shopping

I say we were "largely" sheltered from the effects of the winter because of course no-one could avoid the limited choice of food that was available, especially in winter and "out of season" (unless after shady deals on the "Black Market" where rationed goods and those in short supply were sometimes bought and sold illegally). Everybody was issued with a ration book containing coupons that had to be surrendered when rationed goods were bought[30]. Bread and margarine were staples, and hot meals often consisted of "stew" that was essentially a mixture of boiled vegetables (potatoes, carrots, swedes, turnips and parsnips – the last three of which I disliked then and have continued to dislike since unless very well prepared) and which occasionally contained bits of what was usually rather rubbery and/or gristly stewing steak. As compensation we did sometimes get desserts of stewed fruit, mainly from dried apples, apricots and prunes (which were welcome) and dried figs (which in my case were not)[31].

There was of course other food available, but most of it was rationed and had to be home caught or produced: for example herring, especially in the form of kippers; sausages; bacon – Dad would for some reason happily eat this last, although not pork in its un-smoked form which early on we never had in the house; some rationed cheese – the choice at the grocers was always "cheddar, Kraft (processed cheese) or Dutch (Edam)", and not much of any of it. Flour seemed to be available and so cakes were occasionally made, although these needed a lot of sugar, which was rationed; and there seemed to be no shortage of things like jam, breakfast cereal (the one I most remember was Shredded Wheat, which tasted like I imagined wood shavings must taste, and surprisingly is still sold today) and of course home grown fruit in season including cucumbers and tomatoes. We attempted to preserve, by wrapping or bottling, some of the fruit that grew in our small garden. I think Mother did have a go at bottling, but gave up after the first or second year. A kind of orange juice was available on official distribution for children, along with the occasional bottle of cod-liver oil. These had to be collected from the Ministry of Food office situated next to Canons Park underground station[32] on presentation of a child's ration book and it was often my task to do so. Both tasted disgusting.

Much of the food we today take for granted was in very short supply or not available at all. Eggs were hardly ever available in the shops, and so people often kept their own hens. What could be obtained was powdered egg, which most people had to settle for, but which many found unpalatable. Fruits that could not be grown in Britain (typically oranges and other citrus fruit, bananas, pineapples, apricots, peaches and pomegranates) were hardly ever

---

[30] This applied not only to food, but also to clothing, fuel (especially petrol for cars), soap and, though it didn't affect us directly, paper (newspapers were limited to 25% of their pre-war consumption).

[31] In fact a disgusting liquid substance called Syrup of Figs was sold as a sort of laxative tonic and general panacea for children and administered to us children by Nanny. I always took the proffered spoonful with my breath held and, for some reason, my eyes shut.

[32] The other station serving Edgware, which was on what was then a branch of the Bakerloo Line (subsequently the Jubilee Line) from Stanmore.

available, and exotic fruits and vegetables never. In fact fruits like avocadoes were virtually unknown until well into the 1950s.

Milk (also rationed) was a commodity that was delivered to the house by the Dairies (the United and Express Dairies were the usual ones in London). In my early years this was by horse and cart, but later by the electric milk floats that replaced them and which can still occasionally be seen today. In fact it wasn't until the 1980s, when supermarkets undercut the dairies and sold milk cheaper (by which time most people anyway had cars and didn't need home deliveries), that this service (which included delivery of other grocery products as well) began to tail off and gradually cease.

Sweets were also rationed. Cliff and I were allowed 2 squares of chocolate each from time to time after meals (and certainly no more than once a day). So much was the pent up demand for these items that when they were first "taken off the ration" in 1949 there was a run on the sweet shops as demand far exceeded supply. I remember seeing our local sweet shop (Maynards, next to the Ritz Cinema in Edgware) completely empty, having been stripped bare of all its stock to supply eager shoppers[33]. Sweets had to be "put back on the ration", and in fact it was not until February 1953, when sufficient stocks of sugar had been built up, that the government decided they could be permanently de-rationed.

As an exception to the general non-availability, Dad had managed somehow to obtain a turkey one year at Christmas. Exactly how it had been delivered to our house I never knew, but I came home one day with Mother to find a large dead bird, black feathers and all, dumped in the porch behind the front door. Mother nearly had a fit, as she disliked animals and avoided contact with any form of animal life that had not been pre-prepared by a butcher or fishmonger. Dad had to arrange to have the thing plucked and trussed ready for cooking.

As there were no medium term facilities for storing perishable food (we had a fridge but home deep-freeze units did not exist) shopping had to be done on a regular basis. I can't remember what age I was when first given the responsibility of a shopping basket, shopping list and money; presumably it was during the school holidays when I was eight or nine. One of the regular tasks was to take Mother's library books back to W H Smith which at that time operated a lending library and obtain in return the latest available novel on the reading list she left with them. As with most Smith's shops at the time

---

[33] Sweets were at that time sold mainly by weight from large jars, and given to the customer in a paper bag.

it had a newspaper and magazine counter at one side of the entrance, and inside one needed to weave one's way around tables of book displays.

Other regular visits would be to Sainsbury's, which in pre-supermarket days had counters round three sided of the shop where meat, dairy and other produce were sold. Cheese was cut from a block with a wire, and butter weighed and patted into shape by small wooden flat spade-like implements known as butter pats. Woolworths still advertised that all goods it sold cost either 3d or 6d (1¼ and 2½ pence respectively in modern money; for some reason the letter "d", standing for denarius – a small Roman coin – was used to denote old pence rather than "p"). However, by the end of the War inflation had effectively put an end to the possibility of selling exclusively at those prices.

But the shop that we most used was named, appropriately, Pedlars (run by Mr & Mrs Pedlar and, after demobilisation from the armed forces, their two sons Cyril and Ken). This was a corner shop opposite Canons Drive, and hence only two or three minutes' walk from our house, of the kind that is today mainly run by Asians, and was basically a tobacconist, though it sold other things such as sweets, packaged cakes and various odds and ends – almost a general store. It was as well to be on good terms with the Pedlars (as we of course were), because they were in a position to keep back for their favoured customers things that they got into stock from time to time that were desirable and difficult to obtain. This was a common practice in those hard times and such goods were known generally as "under-the-counter" goods[34].

Mother used to tell the story of having been in Pedlars one day when the air-raid siren went off. There was no cover in the shop and people tended to lie on the floor. The natural place for maximum protection from e.g. flying glass was behind the counter, but Mr and Mrs Pedlar made sure (on that occasion as they always did) that none of their customers took advantage of the extra protection thereby afforded, for they might then have seen any hoarded stocks of under-the-counter goods.

The shop also had a window with sheets of collectors' stamps for sale; these soon enticed me, and I spent pocket money, plus odd pennies I had sometimes saved illicitly from bus fares, on adding to my stamp collection. Cyril and Ken started a chauffeur-drive car service that they ran from the back of the shop, and occasionally the family made use of this service to take us to, or fetch us from, school.

---

[34] Sometimes, but by no means always, these were illegally obtained "black market" goods.

The café that Mother sometimes patronised was called the Almond Tree, and she occasionally took us there to eat rock cakes[35] (which was about all there was in the way of children's food) and drink lemonade, but my personal favourite shop by a long distance was Cresta, which sold toys and model-building kits and was situated in the same parade as the cinema. Its windows were a magnet for most small boys, especially as they usually displayed a variety of model aeroplanes constructed from kits, and later on a working model railway display.

Toys and pastimes

The earliest toy I can remember was a stuffed rabbit that I had named "Bunny Gro" (Cliff also had a different kind of rabbit, which I had named "Bunny H"). Bunny Gro was a constant bedtime companion until I either "growed" out if him (he was definitely male) or he was taken away when it was decided by the adults that I was too old for such nonsense[36].

Toys were of course not readily available in the late 1940s, as their production during the War had been given very low priority. Along with most little boys at that time, I prized my collection of Dinky cars: model cars, made by the Meccano Company that was best known for the eponymous construction sets of parts, and of course for Hornby and Hornby Dublo[37] model electric trains. None of these products had been made at all during the War. The Dinky cars were quite crudely made by today's standards but were eagerly wanted by us, especially as they were comparatively difficult to obtain. Mother would tell us how she had to queue in Cresta's to be allocated one car, and organised her friends to do likewise so that she could obtain two or three for us for Christmas or birthday presents[38].

Dad had visited Switzerland on business in 1946 or 1947. This was a country that, having been neutral during the War and largely avoided its consequences, had a standard of living at that time that was the envy of most

---

[35] Pyramid shaped cakes of the very heavy dough consistency that gave them their name.
[36] Though I don't think I have ever written it before, I have always thought of my rabbit's name with this spelling ("Gro" rather than "Grow"). My ability to find odd or original names for pet things was to be echoed many decades later when my grandson Ollie decided to call one of his pet guinea-pigs "Tratta" (the other one had the quite ordinary name "Olive", although they were both male).
[37] The name came from the very small 00, or double 0, gauge of the tracks.
[38] Cliff and I used to "race" them between our beds in the early mornings. Perhaps because she considered we were making too much noise, or not getting enough sleep, Nanny decided she had to get this activity to cease, and confiscated some of the offending cars.

of the rest of Europe, if not the world. He was always generous to us children, and liked to bring us back presents if he had been away. My recollection of his return that time was of him giving me three things: a three-dimensional wooden picture of the inside of a Swiss chalet, a flat tin of Caran d'Ache coloured pencils and a small Meccano set. All were of a kind or quality unknown in England at the time, and I considered the last two in particular immensely desirable.

In fact that was the beginning of an infatuation with Meccano that lasted well into my teenage years. Not only did I love spending hours constructing models from the hundreds of different metal parts, but I was fascinated by the whole new language that was used to denote them. There were numerous different lengths and sizes of strips, plates, girders, brackets, gears, couplings, pulleys, discs, wheels and axle rods; but there were also many parts that had technical engineering names, such as trunnions, bell cranks, bushes, drifts, sleeves, fishplates, pawls, collars, sprockets, worms and pinions. I also got to distinguish parts that were perforated, threaded, flanged, cranked or curved. All the models were constructed with a screwdriver and spanner and 7/32 inch nuts and bolts.

Gradually my stock of parts became larger and more sophisticated and Dad had a wooden box specially made for me at the factory to keep them in. Indeed, sometimes I would spend my pocket or birthday money at Cresta's buying parts that I didn't really need but liked the sound of. Where else would I have found contrate wheels (gear-wheels with teeth set at right angles to their planes, used e.g. in motor car differential gears), or helical gears (those that have the form of a helix, and are doubtless useful somewhere), or eccentrics (*sic*), triple or single throw? But the Meccano highlight of my childhood was undoubtedly when my parents bought me a No 9 set for my eleventh birthday.[39]

It is difficult to adequately describe this envelopment of mine in the world of Meccano, especially after the reception of the no. 9 set. The hours just disappeared as I applied myself to making some of the seemingly grand models now within my capability. And it didn't end with the construction kits themselves: there was the Meccano Magazine, a monthly publication

---

[39] A Meccano enthusiast's apotheosis was to own a no. 10 set. This was more than twice the size of the no. 9 and housed in a wooded cabinet. It was quite outside the price range of birthday presents and in the late 1940s and early 1950s such sets were anyway made mostly for export. Very many years later I bought one as an adult, telling myself that I would introduce my son to it. But he wasn't really interested (things had moved on in a generation and I certainly could not blame him) and it remains in my office to this day, hardly used but a reminder of boyhood dreams and aspirations.

which I looked forward to eagerly during the years 1948 to 1953. Though I did not read many of the articles (for actually, in spite of my happiness in constructing models, engineering and associated subjects never really interested me) I enjoyed collecting the magazines with their coloured picture covers well-attuned to attract boys of my age.

In fact collecting various different things was an interest, at times an obsession, throughout my life. At one point Cliff and I were given a box of cigarette cards by Windy that had been collected randomly by our deceased grandfather Archie (who had been a heavy smoker)[40]. These we shared out between us, although it was frustrating being unable to add to our collections, as the cigarette manufacturers had ceased inserting these into cigarette packets once the War had started and paper became rationed, and they did not resume doing so again afterwards. We collected as a substitute for a time the cards of similar size that were dispensed by weighing machines (one's weight was printed on the card after the machine had been activated by inserting a penny). The nearest machine dispensing these was in Woolworths at Belmont Circle, a good two miles from where we lived, and at my instigation we made the journey (somewhat under duress in Cliff's case) and spent pennies from our pocket money getting on and off the machine, weighing ourselves as many times as the money we had would allow.

In furtherance of this interest in collecting, at various times in adulthood I was to amass (though not simultaneously) very good collections of stamps (British Africa and Middle East), of cigarette cards and of postcards. I even put together a collection (again in adulthood) of an almost complete run of Meccano Magazines from the fifteen years from January 1939 through to December 1953.

Clothes

There were not really such things as casual clothes in my childhood, at any rate for men and boys, and experimentation with design on the part of manufacturers was anyway not encouraged by the fact that clothes were rationed: "make do and mend" was the watchword applying to all clothes until the decade of the forties had ended. Boys wore short trousers until around their thirteenth birthdays, and in our cases the clothes seemed to be uniformly grey: typically grey long-sleeved shirt, grey "pullover" (what today would be called – as are so many things – by the originally American

---

[40] These cards, most of which measured approximately 2¾ x 1½ inches (68 x 36 mm), illustrated and described on the rear a vast number of different subjects, and had been eagerly collected in the 1920s and 1930s (see further chapter 10 under "collecting").

name: a sleeved or sleeveless sweater), grey short trousers and long grey socks (with elastic garters to hold them up); in fact the same as we were required to wear for school uniform.

If a degree of formality were required to our dress (going out to the cinema or theatre, or even to a child's party) then we would add a blue tie and blue school blazer. As a small concession, school uniform decreed that in the summer we could wear light blue cotton "Aertex" short-sleeved shirts, and so we wore these at home too. I think the first suit I ever had (as opposed to a grey jacket that "went" with short trousers) was a navy blue one bought for me age nearly 13 for my bar-mitzvah. In fact there were one or two exceptions to the general rule about grey clothing: there is a picture of me taken in the summer of 1945, aged 6, wearing a corduroy outfit I remember as being navy blue in colour, that had a tunic-type top that I was very fond of; and we did wear light cotton shorts in the garden in summer.

Friends

Once I had been brought in from playing in the street my circle of friends, at least until I went to school, was limited. My parents were very friendly with a family that lived three doors away at 6 Dorset Drive, Harry and Sylvia Griew and their four children. The youngest of these, Jennifer, was actually a couple of years older than I, and we were perforce thrown together as playmates for a time. But the household that interested me more was that of the Reverend Chilvers at the end of the road. He had a son, Christopher, who was about my age, and soon after they moved in I was taken round there by Nanny to ask his mother if we could be friends.

In fact I realised quite soon that Christopher, though pleasant enough, was not really someone with whom I had very much in common (apart from anything else he was most earnestly concerned that I should believe in and love Jesus), but his company was certainly better than none. His father, a non-conformist minister (who did *not* seem concerned that I should believe in or love Jesus), had been a missionary in the Belgian Congo in the 1930s and the lounge of their house was full of African artefacts: drums, spears, wild animal skins, and wooden and ivory carvings, with which we were forbidden to play. Besides it also contained a grandfather clock, the first one I had seen or heard. At the time it was a cause for wonder that what seemed to me to be such a large collection of fascinating and exotic things could be amassed in one place.

There was also a large collection of cigarette cards depicting life in the Congo that we found one day loose in a paper bag at the bottom of a wardrobe. As they seemed to our innocent eyes to belong to nobody, Christopher decided that we should divide them out between us. Needless to say, as soon as I got my share of the booty home I was ordered to take it straight back.

Entertainment

There was no television during my early childhood – an embryo television service had started from the BBC studios at Alexandra Palace in the late 1930s but this was discontinued from the outbreak of war until about 1948. Soon after it resumed Dad bought a set[41], a floor standing model with a small screen, but all that could be watched in the early days was a demonstration film that consisted of clips from programmes that had been shown before the War. I nevertheless found this fascinating. Gradually programmes started to "go on air" including a children's programme that involved a dialogue between a pianist (Annette Mills, sister of the screen actor John Mills) sitting at the piano and a string puppet mule called Muffin on the top of the piano. This I found less intriguing.

Radio programmes were severely limited. In the 1940s there were only two, both put out by the BBC: the Home Service and the Light Programme. Our radio set was run on a "wet-cell battery"[42], a heavy piece of equipment known as an accumulator that had periodically to be recharged (and taken to the local radio shop for the purpose). Doubtless there was more variety than I remember, but the programmes broadcast by the BBC seemed to involve (on the Home Service) mostly news bulletins and (on the Light programme) seemingly endless stretches of light music played on a cinema organ by Sandy McPherson or on the piano by Charlie Kunz. There was also a weekday half hour programme in the mornings entitled "Music While You Work" in which a variety of bands played light music.

Possibly my memory of Charlie Kunz is from records that Dad had bought. These were the so-called "78s" already referred to that we were allowed to play on a wind-up gramophone, inserting a steel gramophone needle into the playing head that served as an amplifier. A number of these consisted of medleys of tunes played in a distinctive soft/loud style by this artist.

---

[41] He had actually purchased a pre-war set that had sat idly during the War; but it had a tiny screen and he replaced it, either because of the screen size or possibly because it no longer worked at all.
[42] As opposed to the standard batteries today, which were originally called "dry-cell batteries".

Inevitably, we read books, although there was nothing like the variety of children's books available that there is today. I had only one book by Beatrix Potter, *The Tale of Johnny Town-mouse* which was read to me often enough for me to know it almost by heart, but I also I liked to have read to me, and subsequently to read myself, the books by Alison Uttley about Sam Pig, his family and their guardian, Brock the Badger. These had a strong natural history background, and I knew early on that I wanted to be able myself to identify the various different kinds of animals, trees and flowers referred to in them. From these I progressed through Rupert Bear annuals in strip cartoon format to the stories of Enid Blyton. We were allowed one weekly comic approved of by Mother.[43]

As I got older I was drawn to a set of encyclopaedias that we had in the family bookshelf: an illustrated series of 20 volumes published in the late 1930s by Odhams entitled *The New Book of Knowledge*. Though poorly produced by today's standards the volumes contained a wealth of information on all sorts of things that I found interesting, and I particularly used to like sitting by the coal fire in our lounge in autumn and winter, reading them against the soothing background noise made by the flames.

The first time I was taken to the cinema I remember being quite overwhelmed by the sensations it produced: the size of the pictures on the screen, the volume of the sound, and the surrounding darkness. The film was called *The Three Caballeros* and I remember nothing about it, but I was enthusiastic for more. In fact there were children's film programmes shown at the Ritz cinema on Saturday mornings, but we were not allowed to go, presumably as that might mean mixing with the hoi-polloi. We were nevertheless occasionally taken to see children's films.

As today, the theatre was generally not a medium of entertainment that catered for children, although the exception was and is the pantomime. Mother's brother, Uncle Bobby, who was an enthusiastic theatre-goer, arranged for me, and later also Clifford and Sarah, to go to one of these in the Christmas holidays each year. I must have seemed ungrateful, for even the first time I went at the age of 5 or 6, I found this form of entertainment to some extent incomprehensible and also (as I suppose it is meant to be) silly. I still do.

There was one adult person who came into the category of an entertainer in my childhood. Nanny had an older sister (in fact the oldest of her siblings)

---

[43] Many of these she probably rightly regarded as unsuitable (possibly too coarse or just bad). However, the Beano and Dandy were permitted, as was later the Eagle.

Eleanor, known to her family as Nell. We of course never called her that, she was always "Mrs Long". Conversely however, her husband we knew not as Mr Long, but by his first name, Bill. They were an odd couple: she had been a governess (a woman employed as a private teacher of children at home), while he was a lino-type setter for a printing firm. They had no children of their own, but Bill seemed easily to get to the level of children: he would tell us jokes, and entertain us with a seemingly endless store of tricks with cards, matches, coins, etc., chuckling much of the time. He also appeared to enjoy playing games with Cliff and me, especially cricket (in the garden or one of our local parks), when he would typically purport to imitate the actions of famous bowlers of the day. Though we were somewhat in awe of Mrs Long, whom we found to be strict and austere, we always looked forward to the company of her husband.

Education

Kindergartens

Today it is more or less standard procedure that children will attend some kind of school from the age of about 3, but it wasn't so in my childhood. Nevertheless it seemed suddenly to me at the age of 5 of utmost importance that I should go to school. I'm not sure what I knew of such institutions (as already indicated, there was no television and very little radio) or what it was that I expected. Perhaps, having been brought in from playing with other children in the street and having, as already noted, few friends, I just wanted to be with other children again.

I remember well the struggle to read and how seemingly suddenly I was able to recognise the words on the page. The process must have been similar to that I have watched more closely in my grandchildren than I did in my children. I must have already started kindergarten when I learned to read, although I have no clear recollection of exactly when this was.

My first "school" was a little kindergarten called Carlton House in The Drive, Edgware, and I must have started attending it in the autumn of 1944 at age 5. It was simply a house similar in layout to our own with the two downstairs reception rooms used as classrooms.

Only a few memories of it stay with me. The first was a board with the letters of the alphabet in different colours that was attached to one wall. The memory is of interest only for the fact that ever afterwards when I have thought of a letter of the alphabet, in my mind's eye I see it in the exact position it occupied on that board: A to I on the top line, J to R in the middle, and S to Z on the bottom line. The second memory was a map of the world on the wall in the other room with the countries of the British Empire coloured red. The third was of being given, along with the other children, small calendars with military scenes on the covers representing the armed forces; I think this was to commemorate victory in the War. My fourth memory is sitting on the stairs being shown how to tie my shoelaces. My final memory is of a little fellow pupil called Neil who had worn leg-irons until one day of celebration when they were able to be removed.

Probably because it was so much nearer, my parents decided after what must have been an academic year to change my school, to Fernhurst School, in Fernhurst Gardens only about five minutes' walk from the house. It was run by a person who seemed to me to be a stout old lady, Miss Elliot (she was probably in her forties or fifties). The first new experience was intoning with the other children the Lord's Prayer first thing each morning. I had never heard this before, and though I quickly learned it I failed (having never previously been exposed to the language of the King James Bible) to understand some of the words. They seemed to me to be:

> Our Father, which art in heaven, Hallo be thy name...
> Forgive us our whisperses, for we forgive them that whispers against us...
> For thine-is-the-kingdom-the-par-and-the-glory
> For ever never. Amen

This was on a par with the other well-known mistranslation (that I wish I could claim for myself):

> Into the father, into the sun, and into-the-hole-he-goes

Though I probably would not recall it except for the fact that a photograph of it exists, it was at Fernhurst that I first went on stage, taking part in the school Christmas play (Cinderella), in what must have been in a local church hall. I think I had a non-speaking part. Mother and Nanny combined to find some material that could be stitched together for the costume, with a bit of old window curtain suitably gathered in front to look like lace.

The teachers (Miss Elliot had one or two helpers) had learned that I had a baby sister in January 1946 and they asked me what her name was. For some reason at the time I didn't think much of the name Sarah Ann (as she was originally called – after both her grandmothers) and so I told them that her name was Sally.

But the big move was to come the following autumn when I was sent to Belmont.

Belmont

Although the kindergartens to which I had been sent were private schools, my real entry into what is always known, confusingly, as the Public School[44] system began with Belmont. It is fashionable today to disparage fee-paying schools as being "elitist"[45] (as though excellence were something to be shunned rather than aspired to) but these schools taught, as they doubtless still do, a culture and system of values that I came to regard as worthy and have tried (not always successfully) to adopt.

Apart from obvious ones like honesty, loyalty and industriousness (that doubtless any schools would at least set out to teach), the Public Schools set a high value on team spirit. In consequence much importance was attached to team sports, and in fact it was those boys who excelled at the major sports, particularly rugby and cricket, who were the school heroes rather than its scholars. Other attributes that were inculcated as being important in all spheres of life were fairness, courtesy, playing to the rules[46] and magnanimity in victory; in fact those things that used to be called the attributes of a gentleman.

At the same time any tendencies to arrogance, brashness or boastfulness were strongly disapproved of. For example, the phenomenon that a player in soccer (we played this until the age of 11) or rugby who had scored a goal or a try would rush around like a lunatic playing to the crowd (let alone cupping a hand to his ear in mock pretence that he could hardly hear the crowd's cheers of adoration), was regarded as completely unacceptable. We were told very firmly from the start that scoring was essentially the result of the team's, rather than a particular individual's, good work. The same disapproval of course applied to "celebrating" the taking of a wicket in cricket, and the concept of "sledging" (oral abuse being exchanged between opponents on the cricket field) would have been an abomination. In the

---

[44] This term was originally coined in the days before education was regarded as a responsibility of Governments to distinguish the schools concerned from church schools or guild schools, and to emphasise that there were no qualification criteria for them on the basis of e.g. religion, occupation or home location. It contrasts in the UK with "state schools" run from public funds by the Government. In most countries the equivalents would be "private" and "public" schools respectively. In fact the Grammar Schools, the upper level of UK state schools, which were largely abolished by a Labour Government in the 1970s, were run on very much the same lines as the Public Schools (for an excellent insight into these see the play and film *The History Boys* by Alan Bennett).
[45] This word (pronounced in the south of England with a glottal stop in place of the middle t) is almost always used as an insult, implying that whatever noun it modifies is undesirable as not being available to those without money or social connections.
[46] For example, in cricket a batsman who knew he had been dismissed would regard it as his duty to "walk", i.e. to leave the field without waiting for the umpire's formal decision. It upsets me to see that this is no longer necessarily so, at least in the professional game.

highly unlikely event that it might have happened, a guilty player would have been very strongly warned by his own side to desist and if he ignored the warning probably dropped from the team.

But it should not be thought that these attributes and disapprovals applied only in sport; we were encouraged to recognise the qualities of those with whom we were in competition or co-operation in any sphere of life. An example will serve to illustrate this, but I need first to explain the concept of the House.

In order to foster team spirit we were assigned to these "Houses", i.e. groups to which boys were assigned for the duration of their school life. Later at Mill Hill the House was literally the place where you slept and spent out-of-school hours, but at Belmont it was simply a more or less random grouping of boys of all ages, known there by the names of peoples in history who had established England – Celts, Angles, Saxons, Jutes, Danes and Vikings. At one point at the age of eleven or twelve I was chosen to represent the Vikings in an inter-House poetry reading competition. Thinking I had done reasonably well I was mortified to find that the visiting judge (a teacher of English at Mill Hill) had placed me fifth out of six. It was at least of some consolation to learn from even my co-competitors that they thought I had been hardly done by.

I don't know how much of all this my parents recognised as being part of the credo of the education they were putting us through, but though I never discussed the matter with either of them, they almost certainly believed that it was their duty to give all three of us children the best education they could afford. For Dad at least this course of action would be offering us the opportunities he considered he had never had.

In fact in the early days after the War sending me to Belmont involved the family in making what he called "sacrifices". I remember soon after the beginning of my first term thinking I wanted, along with some of my classmates, to be taught to play the piano. But individual instruction in music was not included in the school fees; I don't remember the exact words used, but it was made clear to me that my parents were not prepared to pay for such "extras".

Belmont, in September 1946, had just returned from Cockermouth in what was then Cumberland (now Cumbria) where it had been evacuated for the duration of the War. The school building in Mill Hill had meanwhile been leased to ICI[47] (those of the main school had been requisitioned during that time as a military hospital and sanatorium) and all available land previously used for sports had been ploughed for the production of crops. So the school had a rather "make do" air about it until it could gradually expand back into all of its former grounds. There were, however, "the Woods", a wooded area behind the chapel which at that age seemed to be extensive and where we could roam freely, set ambushes for each other and generally behave as little boys are wont to do.

As land began to be reclaimed, lorry-loads of earth and all sorts of waste objects were dumped at the end of the lower fields to extend them. These dumps were supposed to be out of bounds but we used to scavenge bits of stuff that must have been Government surplus material, for among the debris there were things that looked like half-constructed Morse-code machines. And commonly to be found dumped were strips of rubber that seemed to have been cut from tyre inner tubes. We would flick each other with these slightly elastic strips and even tie each other up with them, until finally discipline was asserted and anyone caught with this material was liable to punishment.

At one point a fashion arose of boys "sword-fighting" each other using rulers for swords. Needless to say that had to be outlawed too. Though I did not myself participate, roller-skating was popular too, with the best exponents of it tearing around the school playground at what seem in retrospect to have been dangerous speeds. In fact surprisingly I don't recall anyone being injured in the process. Less unruly entertainment in the playground often took the form of playing with marbles, mainly in the form of shies. From several paces you would try to hit a row of marbles with one of your own; a hit won you the marbles in the shy, a miss forfeited the marble to the shy owner.

The school teachers (always referred to as the Staff) were all men except for those who had charge of the most junior classes (the first and second forms). The female teachers we called by their names (Miss Thorpe and Miss Bowers respectively in my case) but the male teachers, always known as masters, we invariably called "Sir". As with any school, these varied between those who were seen as tyrants and those who were a soft touch. Discipline, at least after I had been at Belmont a year or so, was kept by a carrot and stick system of "Commends" and "Black Marks". Both were slips of paper, coloured blue and red respectively, which were awarded by teachers as they considered appropriate for good achievement or bad

---

[47] Imperial Chemical Industries, the largest company by far in the UK at that time. It was finally sold to the German company Henkel in 2008.

conduct (Commends gained five points for the recipient's House and Black Marks lost one).

But ultimately discipline was upheld by beatings, known as "tannings", administered by the Staff with a flexible gym shoe (then referred to for these purposes as a "slipper" – but what today would be called a light trainer) on the buttocks. The maximum number of strokes receivable at one go was six (known as "six of the best"). I did receive several of these beatings during my time at Belmont, usually for misdemeanours committed in the company of others (though, with one exception referred to below, I cannot remember any of my particular offences), and so in these cases the tannings were administered after we had stood in line waiting our turn outside the masters' common-room, with the sound of the tanning of the boy whose turn it was clearly audible. The sensation of having been tanned was a rather unpleasant and severe stinging, but it wore off after a while. The punishment had at all costs to be borne stoically (even with pride on some occasions!) It was definitely not the thing to be seen to be discountenanced by the experience, let alone (God forbid!) to be seen crying as a result.

Indeed, stoicism was an attribute that needed unofficially to be cultivated in other areas too. Little boys are always potentially cruel (see the novel *Lord of the Flies* by William Golding) and although bullying did not seem to be a major problem, teasing or baiting others tended to take place at the least opportunity. In fact someone who got angry was known as being "in a bate" (although it is quoted in the Oxford dictionary, I have never heard or seen this word used with that spelling and meaning anywhere else), and a boy in this state of emotion was likely to be goaded to further anger. So in practice it was generally wise to avoid such potential trouble: showing anger tended to mean loss of face.

At that time Belmont had probably between 130 and 150 pupils, of whom about 60% were boarders and 40% day-boys (or day-bugs as we were known to the boarders). Boarding school was still very much the fashion among middle class families in the 1940s and 50s and in real terms cost less than it did later on (at Mill Hill School, where Cliff and I later on became boarders, the proportions of pupils were more like 85% boarders to 15% day-boys). Some of the boarders came from as far away as Yorkshire and Lancashire.

For day-boys the school day normally ended at about 4 pm on weekdays or at lunchtime on Saturdays, when we would either be collected or make our way home on the bus. In the first years I was usually collected. On one occasion the nanny of one of my school mates was supposed to collect me along with her charge but forgot. I remember standing outside the school chapel on the misty, darkening autumn evening concerned with the sinking feeling of a seven-year-old that I had been abandoned. As the plan had been for me to be collected I had not been given money for a bus fare. Lacking the confidence to go and ask the Headmaster or one of the Staff to lend me the requisite 1½ pence (less than 1p in modern currency) I finally decided there was nothing for it but to walk home. The distance was about 3½ to 4 miles and it must have taken me well over an hour, but I knew the way intimately and, in following the bus route home, was relatively happy in the knowledge that I was tackling the problem in a practical way. Needless to say Mother and Nanny were frantic at my non-appearance. Nanny had taken a taxi to try to find me, but apparently the taxi had, that misty evening, followed a route different from the one I had taken. It was my first experience of noticing how events can affect different people quite differently; I could not quite see what all the fuss was about.

Though I took part enthusiastically at sports I was, at Belmont at least, no more than a good average performer. And though I was subsequently at Mill Hill always in the school rugby team for my year, at Belmont I did not make the school team (of which there was only one for each sport). Curiously the one sport at which I seemed to do better than most was boxing, although thereby hangs a sad little tale. The two of us who reached the boxing finals one year were probably fairly evenly matched. Before the bout started my opponent (Martin Bunyard, who was a gifted "natural" at all sports, something which possibly made me slightly in awe of him) whispered to me words to the effect that if I did not hit him hard, neither would he me. The result was a pussy-footing around that was severely censured by the gym master who told us in effect to get stuck in. I was now torn between two irreconcilable things: an agreement made, and a contrary instruction given by someone else. I remember thinking "I gave him my word, how can I go back on it now?" The pussy-footing continued, much to the disgust of the Staff present, who having at the end to decide a winner in a non-event, did so with bad grace and in favour of my opponent.

I did show some early promise at painting, at least in the junior forms. I don't remember whether art classes continued after that; if they did I must have lost interest, perhaps as the abilities of others caught up with or overtook my own. It went similarly with drama. I remember taking the lead at the ages of nine and ten in form plays such as the Brahmin in *the Brahmin, the Tiger and the Six Judges* (with my face blacked and dressed in a suitably Indian garb), and in another adventure play about schoolboys and spies the name of which I have forgotten, but after being cast with a very minor part in the school play *Lady Precious Stream* I hardly acted again until I was in my mid-thirties. In music classes during the earlier part of my time at

Belmont, the teacher, Miss Perret, used to place those who could sing on one side of her grand piano to her left and those who couldn't on her right. I was placed mostly on the right, but was from time to time given the honour of joining those on the left.

In short, I had little idea where my abilities lay; I seemed to be about average at everything. But some foundations were being laid, though I didn't recognise them at the time. It was painful having to write an English essay every weekend (I could never seem to find enough to write about), but the discipline must have had some beneficial effect, and introductions at Belmont to poetry, mainly on the part of my sixth form teacher, Harold Alston, sowed a seed of appreciation which lay dormant for many years before beginning to sprout much later in life.

Another way the school had of laying foundations was to require all boys from, I think, the fourth form upwards (those of us who were ten years old and above) to take turns in reading the lesson in the morning chapel service. This was a selected passage from the bible that took probably two or three minutes to read, and the boy whose turn it was had to walk up to the lectern at the front from wherever he was sitting, and begin reading to the assembled school after everyone had sat down following the previous hymn. This was a little daunting the first time round, but it taught us by direct experience how important it was to speak clearly and reasonably slowly in public. It was also a source of wry amusement if, as sometimes happened, the boy concerned miscalculated and arrived at the lectern too early or too late.

In spite of everything, at times I must have been frustrated, or perhaps irked, by school rules. I remember one afternoon after lessons throwing two ripe half oranges at the blackboard and watching with some delight the juice trickling down to the ledge below. Doubtless this was one of the misdemeanours for which I was subsequently beaten.

Belmont was the preparatory (or "prep") school for Mill Hill School just a little way along the Ridgeway, and it was expected that a high proportion of its students would go on to what was called the main or senior school at the age of 13. As the decision that I should after all go to Mill Hill had been delayed (while I was, as will be seen, busy failing the examinations to Haberdashers) it was for some reason found to be necessary for me to start there not with the traditional yearly intake, which in my case would have been in September 1952, but in the previous summer term of that year. To this end I had sat and passed the Common Entrance examination (the one set for all prep schools) only the previous January. Being the sole candidate at that time I was assigned an individual invigilator, a retired (and I believe very popular) teacher from Mill Hill, "Buster" Brown. He fell asleep while I was writing one of the papers and I could easily have gone over time. But, bearing in mind the school credo, I didn't; I just coughed and shuffled papers around a bit at the end so that he could wake up "in the nick of time".

Religion

Both Belmont and Mill Hill schools had been founded in the Christian non-conformist religious tradition. Although you did not have to profess that particular faith to attend, it was made clear that all pupils would have to follow the religious practices of the school (basically attending a chapel service every day) and that there were no concessions in this regard to be made to other denominations of Christianity, let alone other religions.

In fact in the 1940s and early 1950s the senior school operated a quite small quota of Jewish boys it was prepared to take, but there was in the autumn of 1946 under the headship of Arthur Roberts no such quota at Belmont[48]. My parents, along with those of other Jewish boys, accepted the terms. Mother was lukewarm about religion anyway (she did not to my knowledge ever attend a synagogue unless socially for a wedding or bar-mitzvah) and, though he would probably have denied it if confronted with the question, Dad was too. Later on, especially immediately after Mother's death, he occasionally had bouts of religious observance, but I was sure he was doing what he did because he thought he ought to and that his heart was not in it.

So it was that chapel services became a daily routine for Cliff and me throughout our school days. As we entered the chapel in the mornings, the music master, Maurice Lanyon, was normally playing a "voluntary" (organ solo) and it was there that I first heard a number of pieces that captivated me (the first of these I later identified as pieces from Handel's Water Music). Though school chapel never really got me nearer to belief in God (such exposure as I had later to Judaism even less so), I enjoyed listening to some of these pieces and singing the hymns and psalms. And though my exposure to any sort of religious service in later life has been confined to weddings and bar-mitzvahs, to this day I still feel much more at home attending a service conducted in a structure and a language I understand, and I still enjoy singing hymns.

---

[48] Doubtless the Mill Hill quota extended to other faiths too, including Catholicism, although I was never aware of any Catholics at either school, and cannot remember anyone who might have belonged to another faith. Because many Jewish families had moved into the suburbs of north-west London in the 1920s and 30s the percentage of Jewish boys at Belmont was thus quite high (at a guess around 20%).

Because of the quota of Jewish boys applied by Mill Hill, it was obviously risky to assume that there would be places for Cliff and me, and anyway the fact of there being a quota made the prospect to an extent unattractive. The answer was for me, as a nine or ten year old, to sit the entrance exam for Haberdashers Aske's School (at that time situated in Westbere Road, Cricklewood) where there was no quota. I duly failed the exam. Disappointed but undaunted, my parents entered me for the exam again the following year, and as an incentive Mother promised me a prize of six Dinky cars if I succeeded. This time I passed the exam but failed the subsequent interview[49]. Though I usually came at or near the top of my class at Belmont, a brilliant scholar I clearly wasn't. Luckily for me, by the time I was ready to attend secondary school, Mill Hill had anyway dropped its quota.

Actually at some point the headmaster arranged for the then rabbi of Edgware Synagogue, the Rev. Saul Amias, to conduct classes in reading Hebrew and basic religion for Jewish boys at Belmont, and I was duly enrolled in these. However, as far as I was concerned not least of the problems about them was that they took place on a Wednesday afternoon, the only "free" afternoon for those of us not involved in organised sports, and the only time in the summer term when we could use the swimming pool for play. The temptation was too great, and I began to cut the classes and soon ceased going altogether. Sometime later Dad saw the rabbi (probably at the synagogue) and in answer to an enquiry as to how I was getting on in his classes, received the diplomatic reply "I don't see him there very often". Dad related this conversation to me afterwards with a barely concealed smirk on his face; I got the message.

For me the question of religion had always been confusing from two standpoints. Firstly there was the concept of an invisible but omniscient, all-powerful and ever-present God. In short I never got it. I heard people say that they knew "in their hearts" that God existed; all I can say is I never did (actually, in the early days I thought there must be something missing in me). When on one occasion I attempted to explain my agnosticism to Dad he (clearly out of his depth, or weary of the subject, or both) simply retorted "cleverer people than you find no problem in believing in God".[50]

Secondly, though I would not have phrased the question in that way as a child, there was the issue of what God? As already noted, I became

---

[49] Nonetheless, Mother gave me one Dinky car (a Post Office van, I can still remember) "for having tried hard". Prior to this second attempt I had actually been sent for a while to a tutor, Miss Chick, who lived nearby, in what turned out to be a vain attempt by my parents to secure my entry.

[50] For a fuller examination of this non-belief see chapter 10.

conversant with Christian services and beliefs. At home we always kept Christmas, albeit as an entirely secular festival (with great excitement we decorated a Christmas tree on Christmas Eve and gave and received presents to and from our parents on the day itself), and it did not enter my head probably until I was in my teens that Jews (at least observant ones) did not celebrate it. It also interested me at about the same time that Jews did not accept Jesus as the Messiah and believed that his arrival was yet to come. It struck me even at that early age that in the context of the modern world this belief was slightly ridiculous.

But quite apart from my individual belief or non-belief there was of course the question of anti-Semitism. This was something I recall better from my days at Mill Hill though it unquestionably existed at Belmont. Usually it took the form of insinuations that one was of a class of people who were tight-fisted and avaricious (the qualities imputed to Shylock in Shakespeare's *The Merchant of Venice*) and there were sometimes nasty little accompanying physical signs: rubbing a forefinger and thumb together to indicate the feeling of banknotes, and/or stroking a nose, apparently to indicate the hooked noses that Jews were supposed to have[51].

But, unpleasant though they were, I was aware at the time that the taunts were usually skin-deep; little boys are always looking for things they can use with which to attack others and will say and do things that they do not necessarily really mean or even understand. One had a choice of responses to the gibes: to ignore them; to laugh them off; to answer in kind (though that was in practice difficult as there were no parallel insults for non-Jews in general, and one had to find something personal to the tormentor); or ultimately to fight, for one's "honour". Actually it was rare that this last recourse was needed, and I don't want to leave the impression that I was constantly taunted; I certainly wasn't. In fact the most uncomfortable thing for me was to have to be associated, at least for a short while, with a minority of Jewish boys who were unattractive weedy specimens with whom I had absolutely nothing in common.

Attendance at synagogue did not begin for me until I was about 9, and then only in the company of Dad on one or two days each year. In the orthodox synagogue to which he belonged, men and women sit separately (women at the back of course![52]). My first reaction was one of apprehension. The

---

[51] Paradoxically (and *almost* to the point here) it was Windy, my grandmother, who occasionally came up with the humorous doggerel:
>Aaron said to Moses, "all Jews have got big noses";
>But Moses said to Aaron, "that's the way they wear 'em".

[52] That is not the case in the Reform and Liberal Synagogues where all sit together.

congregation was standing the very first time I entered and all I was aware of was what seemed like a wall of white: rows of men wearing the white *tallit* (the prayer shawl worn by men) and making what sounded like a sort of droning noise. It was puzzling and not in the least welcoming. As I continued to be taken on those thankfully infrequent occasions, it became increasingly puzzling to me how people could sit (or stand, I could never work out when one needed to do one or the other and simply – as probably most did – followed everyone else) apparently for hours, listening to a service conducted in a language none of us understood[53]. Of course in reality they didn't listen most of the time, and there was a constant background murmur of people talking to each other.

Yet I accepted that I was to have a bar-mitzvah, the ceremony that marks the end of childhood at the age of thirteen and introduces the celebrant to the fact that he is thenceforth of an age when he qualifies to be called up to read the *Torah* (the five books of Moses) in the synagogue service[54]. Having skipped the classes of instruction made available at Belmont I needed, starting some months beforehand, to learn to read Hebrew all over again and learn to recite my *paresha*, the relevant small portion of the *Torah*, from a parchment scroll known as the *safer torah* (literally "book of the law"). My teacher was the rather fat, kindly *chazan* (cantor) of Edgware synagogue, the Reverend Fagin. Dad, who used to refer to him as "Old Fagin", could not resist, with a twinkle in his eye and much to Mother's disapproval, the occasional ribald reference to the anti-hero of the same name in *Oliver Twist*.

Rev. Fagin had an ability that astonished me at the time. While I was reading aloud (stumbling through the Hebrew words would be a more accurate description) in the dining room of his house, he sometimes needed to answer the telephone which was situated out of sight in the hallway. In such a case he would always tell me to continue reading, and if I made a mistake while he was so engaged, he would call to correct me from the hall with barely a pause in the flow of his conversation with the person on the other end.

Thus it was that my childhood so to speak officially ended on 26th April 1952, shortly after my thirteenth birthday, as I chanted the *paresha* in the ugly temporary building (it seemed to me rather like a small warehouse) that

---

[53] In fact most prayer books had an English translation of the Hebrew text on the opposite page, but most of it consisted of praising God in a seemingly endless variety of words that I found soporific after a sentence or two.
[54] In actual fact, after his bar-mitzvah, any reading of the Torah that a man is called on to do is normally done on his behalf by the rabbi, the *chazan* or a keen congregant, the "reader's" task being confined to saying or reading the required ritual blessings before and afterwards.

was serving as the Edgware synagogue until a new building could be funded and built a few years later. The portion of the Torah assigned to me to read was from Leviticus, and dealt with edifying matters such as treatment for boils, or it may have been leprosy, I can't recollect exactly.

The ceremony that morning was unusual in that three of us were "bar-mitzvahed" at the same time. The other two boys, whose names I have remembered as one of those pieces of useless information one's brain retains (for I had never met either of them before and never did again afterwards), were Michael Morris and Michael Musicant. The latter (I presume that was how he spelled his name) asked me if I was a Cohen, a Levi or an Israelite (at least I think that was what the third option was; I didn't quite hear it). I didn't know what he was talking about, but thinking that I should have done, and thus not wanting to ask him to repeat, let alone explain, the question, I took a guess and muttered "the third". This seemed to satisfy his curiosity; he was apparently that too.

The following day my parents had arranged the conventional (in those days) dinner party for family and friends (mostly theirs of course) in honour of the occasion, which was held at the Trocadero Restaurant, near Piccadilly Circus. I remember being impressed by the fact that Windy arrived in a spectacular pink dress she had, I was told, originally worn for my parents' wedding; and also that one of Dad's business associates (a cultivated Jewish Frenchman, Eric Adler, who dealt in veneers) had come all the way from Paris for the occasion. I duly gave a speech, most of which Mother had written, leaving out the conventional thanks to her and Dad ("we did what we did because we wanted to, not because you asked us to" she had said). I was told I spoke well.

Transition

The bar-mizvah was not the only transitional event leading me out of childhood. A few days later I began as a boarder at Mill Hill School; a few months previously I had started wearing long trousers (in those days another transitional mark of entry into adolescence); and then about a year later the family moved from my childhood home in Edgware to The Bishops' Avenue.

With Cliff & Sarah, Swanage 1952

In fact the country as a whole was in transition. Throughout the summer of 1951 there had been a large exhibition on the South Bank of the River Thames known as the Festival of Britain. This was in part to mark the centenary of the Great Exhibition of 1851, but a century later large areas of London and other main cities were still in ruins as a result of enemy aircraft action in the War[55], and the Festival aimed to give people in the UK a sense of recovery and progress and to promote quality and design in the rebuilding of towns and cities. Even today pictures of the buildings that were put up for it are a source of wonder, and the experience of visiting it, as I was able to do twice, was like being pitched into a magic and slightly unreal environment. There was just too much for a 12 year old fully to take in[56].

There was a change of Government in the October of the same year, as voters finally got tired of the Labour Government's post-war austerity measures and voted Winston Churchill's Conservatives into power. And then, in February 1952, King George VI died at the age of fifty-six and his

---

[55] I have photographs I took myself of St Paul's Cathedral in 1955, surrounded by bomb-sites. The fact that the Cathedral itself emerged from the War largely unscathed was regarded as little short of miraculous, although it is possible that the German bombers had done their best to avoid it.
[56] The Royal Festival Hall, though it has had face-lifts since, is the sole building that remains from that time (as was intended should be the case). Interestingly, Dad told me how, at a similar age, he had had a similar experience in visiting the British Empire Exhibition at Wembley in 1924.

daughter Elizabeth became Queen.[57] Time was also running out for what was then still called the British Empire – India, Pakistan and Burma had become independent in 1947, and Ceylon (later Sri Lanka) in 1948 – and nationalist movements were gaining ground, particularly in Africa. The Queen's Coronation in June 1953 was effectively its last pageant.

Finally, the rationing that had been so much a part of life for twelve years was being phased out, ending altogether in July 1954, by which time reconstruction of the country was well under way. It was only five years afterwards that the then Prime Minister, Harold Macmillan, could assert, in the sentence with which he will always be associated "Most of our people have never had it so good". My childhood had neatly fitted almost precisely into that period of war and austerity that was passing as I entered adolescence.

---

[57] The King actually died of a heart attack in his sleep, but he had been in bad health, including suffering from lung cancer (he had been a heavy smoker), for some time. Almost certainly his accession to the Throne on the abdication of his brother, Edward VIII, in December 1936 (for which he had been totally unprepared), coupled with the experience of the War, had worn him down both mentally and physically. At the time Princess Elizabeth (as she then was) and Prince Phillip were just starting a Commonwealth tour that the King and Queen were originally supposed to have undertaken. They were famously staying at Treetops Hotel in Kenya when news of his death reached them and forced their immediate return home.

Chapter 2

Mill Hill School

The School itself	51
Social structures at the School	54
Academic work	58
Discipline	60
Food and dining	63
Bullying and anti-social behaviour	64
Sport	65
The CCF	68
The Winterstoke Library	70
Leaving school	71
Home life in the school holidays	74

In my experience we are often not particularly conscious at the time that major changes in our lives are taking place, but I certainly was so aware at the time of the transition from day to boarding school. I was now on my own in a way that I had not been previously; and from this point my parents would play an important but much reduced part in most of my life.

Though I had visited Mill Hill School once or twice when at Belmont, it was then simply "the main school" (or as it was still rather oddly often called "the GC"[1]), and as such more of a concept than a reality and I had very little idea of what it was really like.

The School itself

The school could hardly have been set in more beautiful surroundings. Its grounds cover around 120 acres from its centre on the Ridgeway, sloping gradually down to the south west, so that its playing fields are set out in a series of terraces. The larger part of them originally constituted the grounds of the home of Peter Collinson, a well-known 18th century botanist and fellow of the Royal Society, who made money as a cloth merchant but whose passion was plants (he planted many different species of trees and shrubs

---

[1] This reputedly stood for Games Committee, probably originally a committee of the Board of Governors of the school responsible for sports and games, and hence equipment and property. In time the initials had become synonymous with the school itself. In my time the expression was gradually fading out of use.

throughout the grounds, including the first ever hydrangeas in Britain). His house, known as Ridgeway House (not to be confused with the more modern school boarding House of that name situated in Wills Grove), adjoined the road of that name but was later found to be unsatisfactory as a school building and demolished[2].

The school's educational and other facility buildings gradually accumulated over the period since the foundation in 1807, the best known of which is the handsome School House building with its striking porticos at the front and rear[3]. Others included the Science Block[4] and various other buildings named after benefactors or famous persons associated with the school: the Marnham Block[5] (containing in those days the school auditorium and theatre as well as classrooms), the Winterstoke Library[6], the Murray Scriptorium[7] (where we could read newspapers and magazines), the McClure Music School[8], and of course the school chapel[9]. There was also a tuck-shop and, in an unobtrusive building beyond it, presided over by the school's own somewhat diminutive professional soldier, Sergeant-Major (retired) Crouch, the armoury. Here were kept the rifles, Bren (light machine) guns, ammunition and general stores for the Combined Cadet Force (CCF)[10].

Apart from its playing fields, which were adapted according to the season for rugby, hockey, cricket or athletics, the school had a gym, tennis, squash

---

[2] The school boarding House named after Peter Collinson was completed later (see below).

[3] Designed by Sir William Tite, who also designed the Royal Exchange in London, it was completed in 1825.

[4] Completed in the 1920s, when it was formally opened by the then Prince of Wales (later King Edward VIII).

[5] Named after Herbert Marnham, a former pupil and benefactor.

[6] Named after William Wills (of the tobacco family), later 1st Baron Winterstoke, a former pupil and major benefactor of the school who in the 1890s purchased and made over to the school a large tract of land that included the Park and other land adjoining the private road running through the area and named Wills Grove after him (as of course also was Winterstoke House itself).

[7] Named after Dr James Murray and erected on the site where he had begun work as the first editor of the Oxford English Dictionary. Dr Murray's name was also given to the House for day-boys.

[8] Named after Sir John McClure, a former headmaster.

[9] Designed by Basil Champneys (a well-known architect of his time who designed many buildings in Oxford and Cambridge Universities, and Bedford College in Regent's Park, London) and completed in 1896.

[10] This was the successor organisation to what had been up to 1948 known as the junior division of the Officers' Training Corps, and was set up in many public and some state schools to provide a disciplined organisation in a school to develop leadership and promote the qualities associated with it. A subsidiary goal was to encourage boys to become interested in careers as commissioned officers in the armed forces. The name derives from the combination of army, sea and air cadet corps.

and Eton fives[11] courts and two swimming pools: the outdoor Buckland pool[12] and, in a building containing the changing-rooms, an indoor pool[13]. Neither pool had modern filtering facilities and simply had to be emptied when the water became too disgustingly filthy and refilled. When in its "just filled" state the water in the outdoor pool in particular was freezing cold; I remember having to take my bronze medal life-saving exam in these Spartan conditions and the intense relief I experienced in being able to warm up again after it was over.

In my time at Mill Hill in the 1950s there were around 400 pupils in six boarding Houses and one day House. The boarding Houses consisted of School House (itself divided into two: Scrutton[14] and Weymouth[15]) plus four others set apart from the School and all in Wills Grove (in those days an un-surfaced road): Collinson (completed 1903), Ridgeway (1911), Winterstoke (1924) and Burton Bank (1935)[16]. The one day-boy House, Murray, originally occupied rather unsatisfactory premises in the basement of the Marnham Block, but later moved to what had originally been an indoor rifle range.

For us boarders the House was literally our home during the school term. With minor variations they all contained dormitories (sleeping between six and eighteen boys), a common room for junior boys, studies for senior boys (each of which usually housed three) and a so-called quiet room for reading and studying and where also House assemblies were held, and gardens that could be used in the summer. The housemaster for each House and his family occupied a private section within the same building.

Ridgeway House, to which I (and later my brother Cliff, and much later also my daughters Rachel and Jessica) was assigned, is situated about 200 yards from the main school buildings. This required its inmates to have to make

---

[11] In this variety of hand-ball, 2 teams of two compete in a court roughly the size of a squash court but without a back wall and with, on the left hand side, a "pepper" (a small buttress representing part of the chapel at Eton against which the game had originally been played) and a floor at a slightly higher level at the front. A Rugby fives court does not have these latter features.
[12] Named in honour of Richard Buckland, the Hon. School Secretary from 1899 to 1945.
[13] This last has since been demolished and replaced by a modern classroom block.
[14] Named after two members of the family of that name: Thomas Urquehart Scrutton, a prosperous ship-owner who was one of the driving forces behind the re-founding of the school in 1869, and his son Thomas Edward Scrutton, eventually a Lord Justice of Appeal who had made a name for himself as a particularly difficult judge.
[15] Named after Dr Richard Francis Weymouth, a former headmaster of the school.
[16] Originally situated in Burton Hole Lane about a mile from the main school buildings and rebuilt in Wills Grove after the original one burned down. The occupants of the original House were allowed to ride bicycles to and from the school.

constant short treks back and forth to the school, firstly for meals (all of which were taken there rather than the House), secondly for lessons (always referred to as "periods"), thirdly for changing into and out of games kit and showering or "troughing" (communal washing and soaking after games in long troughs of hot water) afterwards, and fourthly for CCF activities. It became a point of honour in the middle school to leave the House for breakfast at the last moment, and this meant literally getting dressed on the run, one's vest, shirt and tie having been removed as one piece of clothing before going to bed the previous evening.

Social structures at the School

As was typical of public schools at the time, Mill Hill had layers of social status for its pupils. Although the formal prefect structure must have been decided by the educational authorities of the school, other social structures were informal in that there were, so far as I knew, no school rules setting them out. They were merely "the way things were" at Mill Hill and for all I know developed as a culture over time but were clearly approved of by the school authorities. At the very top were the monitors (the small select band of senior prefects of whom there was rarely more than one for each House – hence most were heads of Houses); below them were school prefects; and below them the house prefects whose status, as their designation implied, was recognised only within each House.

At the bottom of the social scale were the "fags". Assuming a boy joined the school at the age of thirteen (which almost all did), for the whole of his first school year he was a fag, and as such required to do all sorts of menial work, either for his fag-master or generally. It was one of the privileges of the monitors and school and house prefects to "own" a personal fag. At the beginning of each term within each House a selection process took place after the first House assembly during which the most senior prefect had first pick of the first year boy who would be a kind of unpaid servant to him for the coming term. Those left over (including me, certainly in my first term) were termed "general fags". Interestingly, I never heard a member of the teaching staff use the word fag; they always referred to "first year boy(s)".

Personal fags were required to do such things as wake their masters in the morning, clean their shoes and rugby/cricket boots, be on hand to cook snacks, particularly at weekends, to sweep, dust and tidy their masters' studies, and to run general errands. I can't remember what our exact duties as general fags were, I think they included sweeping and cleaning the common room and quiet room and other menial tasks that came up, such as shifting furniture, but if personal fags got ill or were for some reason unavailable, we had to be on hand as potential substitutes at a moment's notice. It all sounds a bit archaic, even barbaric, to modern ears, and indeed it was a little antiquated even in our day, but we simply accepted the situation as the way things were; and anyway we in our year were all in it together[17].

Sometimes fags could get their revenge in the smallest of ways against those they felt were unjustly tyrannising them (although in fact this was rare). The informal kitchen (actually merely a gas hob) in Ridgeway House where fags were sometimes required to cook snack food for their masters at the weekend was in the same room as the sink for cleaning boots and shoes. This also had boot lockers and pegs for coats, and was known as "the boot-hole". Just occasionally a little brown shoe polish might find its unobtrusive way into the baked beans.

The school was divided quite rigidly into years (it was known as "the year system"), and unless in the process of playing team sports, there was almost no social mixing of boys between the different years; in fact a fag was forbidden from any but purely formal contact with those in the years above him. After that the social distinctions were still in place, although less rigid. As markers of the system there were what seemed to me even then to be a series of rather idiotic cumulative privileges that were attainable after the first year. Second year boys were allowed to put their hands in their trouser pockets (fags' hands had to go into their blazer pockets), but second-years' blazers still had to be buttoned up; third year boys could wear their blazers open; and most bizarre of all, fourth-year boys could turn up the collars of their blazers. On one occasion during my first term I was reprimanded by a senior boy for turning my collar up in the rain!

The separations thus engendered were easy enough for the regular intakes of boys each September, but I had to start in the summer term, and this meant that, in common with the handful of others in the same situation, I had to straddle the years. As those I was closest to in age and most friendly with arrived in the following term, the system meant that in the following summer term I was already a second year boy. The privilege of being able to put my hands in my trouser pockets did not compensate for the temporary "loss" of my friends.

Actually there was another odd-term (not to say odd) boy, Martin Stern, in Ridgeway in much the same situation as myself except that he had joined the school one term earlier than I had. He was also the only other boy in the

---

[17] The practice in the form described was actually finally abolished in the mid-1960s and replaced with a system of "House Duties".

house at the time whom I knew to be Jewish[18]. I was thus to an extent thrown together with him by dint of that fact alone. He had also been at Belmont, although I had not been especially friendly with him there. In fact I had virtually nothing in common with him at all: he was a rather ugly boy, not at all athletic (he had round shoulders to the point of almost being hunchbacked, though he was actually not bad at tennis), not very bright and, I thought, rather mean spirited.

I have already referred to minor anti-Semitism at Belmont (as indeed there was at Mill Hill – more of which later), and it soon became apparent that both of us were going to have to live down the fact that there had been one Jewish boy in Ridgeway who had apparently been deeply disliked by most of his contemporaries. Although he had left by the time we arrived at the school, the memory of him seemed to be fresh among senior boys. It appeared to be almost a case of our being treated as guilty by association until proved innocent, and this was one of the reasons why distancing myself from Martin Stern was not going to be all that easy. Another, at least for a short while, was his well-meaning parents.

So long as one was not required for sport or some other school activity at the relevant time, the school allowed its boarders to be taken out for tea by parents, relatives or adult friends on Thursday and Saturday afternoons at the school shop, Blenheim Steps, located near the entrance to Wills Grove. My parents (or, more likely, Mother or Uncle Bobby) took advantage of this a couple of times a term, though I have no specific recollections of this, and it probably happened only rarely if at all after my first couple of years. But, to begin with at any rate, the Stern parents came regularly every Thursday and Saturday afternoon. They seem to take something of a proprietary interest in me, presumably as a friend who needed to be fostered for their son, and I was always invited too. Though I had nothing against Mr and Mrs Stern (albeit that the latter was a slightly overbearing lady), I did not particularly enjoy the slightly suffocating atmosphere of these occasions,

---

[18] There was actually one other, who was indeed a good friend throughout our times at both Belmont and Mill Hill: Stephen (later to become Lord Justice) Sedley. But Stephen's "notoriety" was that he professed to be a Communist (his father, a solicitor, had in fact stood as an official Communist candidate in the general election of 1950 or 1951, or both) and I had known him for a few years before I realised that he was also Jewish, or at least that his parents, though professing no religion, were from Jewish families (the family name had been changed from Seletsky). His invariable answer to the question about what he was doing as a Communist at a public school was on the lines that "unfortunately the Capitalist system forces people to have to pay if they want a decent education for their children." Strangely, his political stance did not affect our friendship. It did tend to get between us after our school days when we drifted apart, although such limited contact as we did have later remained extremely cordial.

and very soon sought excuses, real or imaginary, to miss out on them. Eventually the penny must have dropped and the invitations thankfully ceased.

Though I have referred so far to boys by their full names, in fact not only did the teaching staff always call us by our surnames alone, we ourselves almost always did so among ourselves (although occasionally a boy had a nickname that seemed to stick and be used instead). Indeed this had been the practice at Belmont too, and it actually followed the convention of the time (which was just beginning to break down in the outside world) whereby middle and upper class men who were acquainted, even friendly, with one another called each other by their surnames.[19] Unless we knew boys well, we probably wouldn't even know what their first names were.

As for nicknames, mine, though in fact it wasn't often used, was inevitably "Rosy" or "Rosie" (for a while at Belmont, in an amusing misunderstanding of the name of the plant concerned, it had been "Rosydendron"). And the boys, as boys always will, coined nicknames not only for each other but for most of the teachers. Some of these latter were easy enough to understand, although the origins of others were unfathomable. From Mill Hill I recall "Pooch" Bowring (perhaps because of his somewhat rotund shape), "Froggy" Brown (probably because of his widely stated admiration for France and all things French), "Suave" or "Spiv" Baker (actually the rather dapper art master), "Bogs" Duncan[20], "Baggy" Stanham, "Rutch" Turnbull, "Mousy" Vine, "Skyles" McAllister and, most bizarre of all, "Cork" or "Cork-arse" Phillips[21]. Others were merely onomatopoeic, or nearly so: "Mog" Morrison, "The Cronk" Cronheim and, not surprisingly, "Buzz" Bee. The headmaster, Roy Moore, was always referred to as "the Head Man".

---

[19] Social conventions in this area were, and are, complicated, and different ones applied to women. In male working class circles yet different conventions operated, and these still seem to apply today. Such men seem rarely to call each other by their first names but will adapt a surname to e.g. Smithy or Jonesy, or use a nickname or abbreviated form of the surname, as testified by the way professional sportsmen habitually refer to each other. Some of these nicknames seem to have a sort of magnetic connection to the surname, resulting in highly unoriginal ones such as "Chalky" White, "Dusty" Miller or, less explicably, "Nobby" Clarke and "Smudge" or "Smudger" Smith.

[20] "Bog" and "bogs" were the universal terms for the loo(s). Perhaps the man concerned had at some time had an affliction that brought on the nickname, but I have no recollection of it.

[21] The extraordinary myth attached to this (actually very popular) teacher was that he had in the First World War been wounded in the relevant part of his anatomy, and had undergone surgery to replace whatever had gone missing with cork!

Academic work

We were assigned to classes, always referred to as "forms", according to our supposed ability, in each year. These were illogically designated for the five years that most boys spent at the school as the Fourth (the lowest level – there was no First, Second or Third), Remove, Fifth, Lower Sixth and Upper Sixth Forms. To complicate matters, alongside the Fourth Forms and Removes were concurrent "sets" for what were considered the more important subjects: I think these were English, French, Latin and maths. Thus one could be (as indeed I was in my first full year) assigned to the second stream form Remove B, yet placed in Set A for each of the relevant subjects. Doubtless on the strength of that, I was awarded the Remove B form prize for that year, the only academic prize I gained during my school career.

Though considered of above average academic ability (I was one of only 3 boys in Ridgeway in the academic year above that of most of our contemporaries) I was not a particularly dedicated student; the subjects taught were to my mind those that one simply had to learn (that was after all, as I saw things, the purpose of school) and it did not enter my head to question why. At I think Remove level we were required to choose to be put into "Arts" or Science streams. In the former stream students concentrated on English, classics (Latin and Greek), modern foreign languages, history and geography, while in the latter the focus was on physics, chemistry, biology and maths.

I don't recall any of my teachers inspiring me, and in fact it would not be an exaggeration to say that most subjects most of the time induced feelings of varying degrees of boredom. I remember how in maths one year I constantly had difficulty in keeping awake, and lessons in German, taught rather badly by Dr Cronheim, consisted almost entirely of reading aloud passages from set books and then having to proceed to orally translate them. Dr Cronheim was a refugee from Germany. He was probably, like many people in similar circumstances, of Jewish origin, though in fact a practising Christian – as indeed I believe was also Hans Berge, one of our music masters and a founding member of the Amadeus String Quartet, then very well admired. "Fritz" Cronheim was something of an expert in Renaissance art, and I imagine this was where his real interest lay; it certainly wasn't in teaching.

What kept my attention at a minimum level for these kinds of subjects was the knowledge that we would all be required to do out-of-school-hours work that in a day school would have been called homework, but at Mill Hill was known as "prep", and it was thus as well to do one's best to keep up with the what was going on in class.[22]

One exception was history, a subject that in spite of what I see in retrospect to have been largely indifferent teaching, struck a particular chord with me. It was thus an irony that history was only subject I failed at what was then called Ordinary, or "O" Level, School Certificate (subsequently GCSE)[23]. I also become enrolled into the set plays and books our particular year had to study for English Literature O Level, and to this day I can remember liking the plots and counter-plots of Shakespeare's *Henry IV Part I*, and even thoroughly enjoying the descriptions of all the pilgrim characters in the Prologue to Chaucer's *Canterbury Tales* (the opening paragraph to which I can still recite by heart).

I had no particular interest in science at the time and my parents considered that modern languages would at least be useful subjects in which to get a solid grounding. I did not disagree, and so in the Remove I began to learn German, the second modern foreign language conventionally taught in schools at the time[24] (French was a subject taught from prep school days, as indeed was Latin). I was thus eventually put in the senior school into the Modern Language Sixth.

Although this seemed to be a practical course, I was actually not particularly adept at learning languages and anyway in the sixth form the work concentrated more on studying literature than on speaking. We were nevertheless from time to time required to undergo instruction in the latter, and I remember the mortification I felt after having been required to speak for five minutes in German about a play (in English) that I had seen in the previous school holidays. It was a not particularly good thriller called, I remember, "The Love Match" (how on earth, I thought for a start, do you translate *that* into German?) and I found that the necessary words simply would not come. On another occasion I was required to speak for the same amount of time in French, and with equal blank-minded distress, "*au sujet des oreillers, s'il vous plait* [on the subject of pillows, please]"!

---

[22] I wished I had been the one to originate the "epitaph" scratched on the inside of a desk:
This desk is dedicated to the memory of ... who fell asleep here on ...
[23] I had experienced a kind of brainstorm during the exam and chose to answer questions on subjects about which I knew very little. Somewhat mortified by the experience, I applied and was allowed to retake the subject the following term, when I passed with good marks.
[24] In fact most of our German books were then still printed in the Gothic script that was just beginning to be phased out in post-Nazi Germany.

This somewhat brutal approach to oral instruction was, it seemed to me, surely not the way to instil confidence in speaking foreign languages into pupils. It was only in later life, when I ceased to worry unduly about the correctness or otherwise of what I was saying, that speaking French or German became altogether easier (though neither ever reached the standard of fluency that I theoretically would have liked).

Discipline

Unlike the system at Belmont, the general administration of discipline was a task allotted mainly to the monitors and prefects, and although the teaching staff had the power to administer beatings to boys, in my experience they rarely did. Rather they would in appropriate circumstances order a pupil to undergo detention (enforced extra periods of study) for unsatisfactory behaviour. I don't recall ever being disciplined in this way; in fact the nearest I remember to being disciplined academically was one day when sitting in Mog Morrison's Latin class, where boredom had me idly examining the back of my hand. Suddenly I received the wet rag he used as a blackboard rubber splat in the left side of my face. "Interesting from an anatomical point of view as your hand doubtless is", he said to me "this class is more concerned with translating Livy". Mog also had a rule that related to the setting of prep: if he forgot to set it on whatever day it was due to be set, and we in turn failed to remind him of the fact, the next time, if he "remembered he had forgotten", we would have to undergo double the amount of work. It was a good way of ensuring that we reminded him.

The standard means of exacting discipline by the prefects was the "copy". Those of us on the receiving end of this minor punishment were required to copy out in duplicated longhand and within a specified time typically a line of poetry or an epigram in, depending on the severity of the punishment, between one and three pages. As each of the ruled pages of the exercise books we used, contained about 35 lines, this was in itself a tedious chore. But added to that, in so doing we had to make each copied line *exactly* the same as the one above it. Failure to do this to the satisfaction of the prefect concerned could result in having to do the whole laborious task all over again. I remember a particularly nasty line set as a copy in this way (because of the tediously difficult positioning of the letters in each word) was:

> "*Egypt for the Egyptians! Egypt for the Egyptians!! Egypt for the Egyptians!!! – Muhammad Naguib*"

More serious misdemeanours were made the subject of beatings by the prefects. As at Belmont, these were administered by a gym shoe to the buttocks. I think those I received were mainly in my latter years at the school for deliberate insubordination. This was, and is, an attitude usually quite foreign to my nature, but it became increasingly common as I found myself frustrated by what I saw as the pettiness of some of the school rules coupled with (as I got older, and was not, as I thought I should have been, made a prefect) a certain contempt for some of those that had. This applied in particular to our Head of House in my final year; I was not the only one to regard him as a buffoon.

The excuse given to me by our Housemaster, Major Alan Bush, on my very last day at school when I went to say good-bye to him was that I had not been made a prefect because I was leaving a year earlier than most of my contemporaries. This latter was true, for being in the year above most of them, and not intending to try for a university place, there was no point in my staying on beyond A Level. But three of my contemporaries were made house prefects at the end of the previous school year and one the term after, and I had thought that I was no less competent or eligible than any of them. The comparatively short time (actually a whole year) I had still to go had not, it seemed to me, been a valid reason for the inaction[25].

I pretended to myself and others at the time that it did not matter, and taking a long view of life it actually didn't (it would have conferred little if any practical advantage in later life), but it was an early lesson in the fact that life is not always fair. On the other hand there was certain kudos in the fact that a number of us were in a similar position both in Ridgeway and other Houses. We called ourselves rather proudly "the social failures" and lost no opportunity to compare ourselves favourably with those that had been promoted.

One of the most bizarre aspects of enforcement of discipline involved the daily line-up in the Marnham Block prior to going in to meals. The monitors would at the appointed time themselves gather at the far end of the Block and, headed by the Senior Monitor, would then begin to walk in single file down the lines of pupils chanting "STOP TALKING" in a drawn-out monotone as they did so. Anyone who was not in his required position by the time this chant started was liable to punishment. We then had to file into our respective House dining rooms in the main school building, passing as we did so a school prefect with a roll-call clip board and to whom we had to shout out our surnames. Where there were two boys with the same name, these were designated as e.g. Smith major and Smith minor. This was so in my case, when another boy with the surname Rose joined the school the term after I did. And where there were three or more of us (as happened after

---

[25] Perhaps there was one, though. See the extract from my diary at pp. 72-3 below.

my brother also joined the school) we were designated, rather like Dr Seuss' "Things" from *The Cat in the Hat*, Rose one, Rose two and Rose three.

Obviously, being boarders, we were not allowed to leave the school premises without express permission. Nevertheless there were, after our first year, limited though real opportunities to do so. We needed first to obtain an *exeat* (Latin for "let him go out") from our housemaster, and these were granted readily enough on "half days" (Tuesday, Thursday and Saturday afternoons, when there were no formal academic periods) so long as we were not required to take part in organised sports or other activities. We had to satisfy him that we needed to e.g. go to Mill Hill Broadway in order to get a birthday card or present or some other necessity (we were not allowed, for example, to go to the cinema) and the *exeats* specified the times when we were permitted to be absent from the school.

Three times each term we were allowed "Home *exeats*" on a Sunday. In the case of two of these we could be collected by family or friends from school after chapel (about 11.00 am) until 6.00 pm; for some reason the third allowed us to be away only from after lunch. Though I always looked forward to these periods, in fact the situation of being neither at school nor properly at home made the process at times just a little unsatisfactory. As time went on, and particularly after Cliff joined the school, we often arranged to take friends home with us.

Inevitably smoking and drinking alcohol, both of which were obviously forbidden, were looked upon by some (mainly senior) boys who liked trying to push the boundaries of discipline as desirable things to try covertly to do. Indeed occasionally boys were caught smoking and presumably punished, although, in spite of frustrations already referred to, this was an activity that seemed to me at the time to be particularly pointless and I was never even tempted to try it. I do however remember smuggling into school a large bottle of beer in my last term for the purpose of celebrating the end of the season with fellow members of the Gentlemen of Ridgeway Cricket Club[26], that I had been partly instrumental in founding. It wasn't even that we particularly liked beer, as I doubt if any of us had acquired a taste for it by that time, but rather that it was, in the minds of us immature young men, the thing to do. Our misdemeanour went undetected.

---

[26] See below p. 67.

Food and dining

I have forgotten most of the detail relating to the meals we were given, but though I have never thought of myself as a fussy eater it was obvious that the general standard of the food we were offered at Mill Hill at that time was poor. We sat at long tables with a prefect at the head; the rest of us I seem to remember rotated places, and those at the foot of the table were responsible for stacking the used plates and putting the cutlery into a wooden box.

At breakfast there was always porridge, usually full of lumps, and bread with margarine (butter was still rationed at the beginning of my time there, and I remember that we were given it only for breakfast on Sundays). I suppose I must perforce have eaten the porridge at least some of the time, but I cannot remember what my standard breakfast consisted of. Lunch was the main meal, and usually to supplement whatever was the main dish there were in the middle of the tables bowls containing apologies for mashed potato (again full of lumps) and cabbage. One had to be very hungry indeed to want to eat either.

Inevitably there was the tuck shop, where we could, if we had the money to do so, buy tastier things like filled rolls or, once they came off the ration, chocolate and sweets or ice cream. I seem to remember that I rarely did. Though we were given an allowance of pocket money by our parents which had to be banked with the housemaster and could be withdrawn in limited amounts at appointed times, these bits of cash never seemed to last long in my pocket.

At the beginning of each term, and also after home *exeats*, most of us were given small amounts of food for our own consumption such as fruit, biscuits and sweets which we kept in our personal tuck boxes (again, my personal "tuck" never seemed to last that long). These were small plywood boxes, approximately 18 x 12 x 12 inches (45 x 30 x 30 cm) in size on which we had to have clearly painted our name, initials and school number, and in which we kept not only food but (before we qualified to reside in studies) also other personal items.

A boy needed to be circumspect about the contents of his tuck box. Thefts were known (even though most of us used padlocks, these were sometimes mislaid), and sometimes younger boys were bullied into parting with their food to those who had no compunction in using "persuasion" to achieve compliance.

Bullying and anti-social behaviour

However, bullying did not play a significant part in life, although it was certainly true that anyone who did not for any reason fit in easily was likely to find life difficult.

As the school represented a cross-section of middle class middle England, it was not surprising that anti-Semitism was present, though it was not pervasive[27]. As had been the case at Belmont, Jewish boys had to face the fact that they were regarded in some minds as being automatically in the Shylock mould. But now as we became older even worse characteristics seemed to be additionally attributed to us, more by inference than directly, and it became clear that the idea existed that Jews were generally potentially untrustworthy people, even swindlers. It was also a fact that they tended to be intellectually brighter than average, and given the mild anti-intellectualism that existed, and still exists, in middle Britain, this fact did not help their cause either.[28]

All of this, as previously at Belmont, had to be lived with and lived down. But the situation needs to be seen in its proper perspective, for in fact it was not difficult to do this, and indeed it was very easy if one were good at sports, for any such boy was a potential hero whatever his background[29]. But it was less easy for a boy if, like my contemporary Martin Stern, he was not good at sports and did not readily fit in.

Although anti-Semitism was something that I was particularly aware of, in fact it was not only Jewish boys who were potentially to be singled out for disapproval or as the targets of ribaldry or teasing, and obvious differences in anyone could be seized on. Though I do not have much personal

---

[27] Indeed, though Germany and Eastern Europe generally had been obvious examples of where this prejudice had been pursued to extremes through persecution to death, there were (and still are) in Britain and other countries in Western Europe too, particularly France, a good number of people who regarded Jews with dislike. There were at a guess around 40 Jewish boys at Mill Hill at the time (roughly 10% of the total pupils) most of whom were in Murray, the day-boy House.

[28] The roots of anti-Semitism are complex, and this is not the place to examine them. Suffice it to state that I believe that anti-social traits are no more likely in Jews that in any section of society. Jews as a whole have tended to do better than average at many things, and in a small percentage of cases these have been bad things involving unscrupulous, anti-social or even criminal behaviour. This has caused those anyway inclined to dislike them to focus on these negative aspects and disregard the positive ones.

[29] A good example was Joe Grimberg, who came from a Jewish family in Singapore, where I met up with him many years later (though he had an Ashkenazi Jewish name inherited from his paternal grandfather, his family were predominantly Sephardi Iraqi Jews). He had left Mill Hill shortly before I joined it, had excelled at all sports and was unreservedly held in high esteem by all who remembered him.

recollection of this at Mill Hill, I recall the author Salman Rushdie (born in Bombay of a Kashmiri Muslim family) stating in a television interview how he had suffered at an English public school (Rugby), where he had had the misfortune to be, he said, foreign, clever, and bad at games. He considered that he could have got away with any two of these attributes, but that all three of them present in one person more or less guaranteed that his life at school would be made difficult, even at times unpleasant.[30]

In this regard it is relevant to recall, as I do with some shame, one boy by the name of Peter Hendrick who arrived in Ridgeway the term after me. He disclosed early on that his mother was German. This, for reasons which are today almost incomprehensible, seemed to make him the butt of all sorts of teasing, taunting and general unpleasantness, eventually to such an extent that an outwardly happy boy gradually became withdrawn and depressed. Unsurprisingly he did not come back after the end of his third year. Though I disliked what he was subjected to and certainly did not take part in it, I still to this day feel an acute sense of discredit, even of cowardice, that I did not do more to befriend him, or at the very least to let him know that I deplored what he was forced at times to undergo.

Sport

To be good at sport, especially to be in the school first team at one or more of the major sports, was to set a boy up to be revered as a god. This was especially so in the cases of rugby and cricket; hockey – played in the spring term – though important, did not carry quite the same cachet as the other two. Even excellence at so-called minor sports (principally squash, tennis, fives, swimming, athletics) endowed considerable prestige. Set against this on the other hand, academic excellence did not even rate in the eyes of most boys.

In fact rugby was regarded as the king of sports at Mill Hill. The 1st XV had been unbeaten in the three seasons 1948-50 (having won every single match in that period except for one that had been drawn) and from that era the school had produced two England internationals in the mid-1950s to early 1960s[31]. So much importance was attached to the sport that it was

---

[30] It is ironic that in later life, after publication of his novel *The Satanic Verses* in 1988, he was the subject of a *fatwa*, a legal opinion expressed by the leaders in Iran (mostly clerics) that he should suffer death for blasphemy against Islam. This was seen as an open invitation to extremist Muslims to attempt his assassination and led to his having to live secretly in undisclosed places under British police protection for more than a decade, until finally the Iranian Government partially relented.

[31] Johnny Williams at scrum half and Jim Roberts at wing three-quarter.

compulsory in my time for all boys to watch the 1st XV playing at home unless we were playing concurrently for one of the other rugby teams. Not only that, a monotone chant of MILL HILL (similar to the "Stop Talking" of the monitors) was required from us all in the way of encouragement to the team from the touchline. If they won, either at home or away, the convention was that every boy walked into supper clapping.

Sports were played not only at inter-school level but also constantly within the school between the different Houses. Indeed, rather in the way that civil wars are said to be the most violent and ugly kinds of strife, inter-House matches were often played with a determination and intensity that surpassed inter-school ones. A range of trophies was available to be won each year (mainly for inter-House sports, and at various different junior or senior levels, but also for other activities such as chess and the annual CCF competition) and in the summer term when the formal House photographs were taken, these cups and shields would be lined up on the ground at the front. The reputation of a House depended to a large extent on the silverware it was able to display in this way.

The recognition of merit at any inter-school sport senior level was by the award to the player concerned of "colours". These were awarded at 1st and 2nd team levels for major sports, and at senior level for minor sports, and entitled those on whom the honour had been bestowed to wear appropriate caps (on the cricket field), or blazers and ties (off the field). The ties could be worn anywhere in the school on designated days (Tuesdays, Thursdays and Saturdays) and the blazers while taking part in the relevant sport (including teas and receptions afterwards, though obviously not on the field) and in school or house photographs. In practice, as blazers were expensive, and during the wartime and post-war austerity period subject to clothes rationing, not many of those entitled to wear them did so, and those that did possess them had usually received them as family heirlooms.

Within Houses themselves the system was that a House tie could be awarded for meritorious play at any sport (each House had a different pattern with its distinctive colour appearing together with the chocolate and white of the school – Ridgeway's colour was purple). There was also a House scarf that could be awarded for exceptional merit, but in practice normally only the Head of House was awarded one.

As I was to leave a year earlier than most of my contemporaries, and thus had only one as a senior, my own school colours were limited to 2nd XV ones (for which I don't remember there being a tie). But my best sporting memory was at the age of 14 of the award of my Ridgeway House tie. This happened after a junior rugby House final that Ridgeway won, very much contrary to expectations, against Burton Bank who were strongly fancied to win the tournament. I had had the good fortune to be in the right place at the right time to be able to initiate the move that led to the only try (indeed I think the only score) of the match. It says something about the school values, and what I in particular aspired to at the time, that this match and the subsequent award is still one of the strongest and proudest memories of my time at Mill Hill.

As a special concession, those who had just been awarded school or house colours for the first time were allowed to wear the relevant tie the following day, even if it was not one of the appointed "colours" days. In fact the day in question for me was a Wednesday on which the CCF was to go on an out-of-school exercise; but though I was dressed in battledress trousers, I still made sure that I wore the tie (borrowed from an existing owner) with a school blazer into breakfast!

Though I make no pretence that my abilities at rugby were anything special, I was at least always in the relevant school team. But this apart, my abilities seemed to remain at most sports, as they had at Belmont, at good average standard. I played, I seem to remember, some House hockey and cricket, but not at a level or intensity that I recall in any detail. Partly through boredom, in my senior year I and one or two others founded an unofficial cricket team we called the Gentlemen of Ridgeway. We played against a number of scratch sides with more enthusiasm than skill.

In fact I readily took part in all the sports that were available[32], including a particular kind of hockey called "single-handed" that was played with a specially made stick on the school quad and existed nowhere outside Mill Hill School (it was played with a small hard black ball rather larger than a squash ball and there was considerable danger of being hit and possibly injured either by the fast-moving ball or a wayward stick). I particularly liked squash and fives, where one did not have to be of potential school or House team standard to enjoy games with those of roughly equal ability, and I was a reasonably good shot, although shooting was a sport that was mainly connected with military activities of the CCF[33].

---

[32] We were also permitted at senior level, to learn to play golf at the nearest golf club, Finchley.
[33] See note 10 on p. 52 for the origins and purposes of this organisation.

Some of us 15-year old Gentlemen of Ridgeway, Summer 1954

The CCF

Every boy had to be inducted into this organisation (usually referred to as "the Corps", or by wags as "the Corpse") unless he elected instead to join the Boy Scouts[34] (about 20% did so). For that purpose we each had to be kitted out in the army uniform of the time, drawn from the armoury for either the term or the year and then returned. We were required to take part in a weekly muster parade on the school quad and then to disperse to do some kind of military training. These afternoons lasted 2 to 3 hours. A system of promotions to NCO ranks (lance-corporal, corporal and sergeant) existed and one boy was appointed as Under-Officer, effectively the schoolboy head of the CCF. Once a term we went on a "Corps Exercise" to some War Office land where we would attempt military manoeuvres of a limited kind and be issued blank ammunition for the purpose. Once a term also we would go on a route march of five miles or so outside the school, and at the end of every summer term many in the senior school went to the voluntary CCF summer camp, where we all lived under canvas for a week.

The details of the training we actually underwent are hazy. We had of course to learn marching in formation ("square-bashing") and its various moves with and without rifles, how to fire a rifle and a Bren gun accurately, and how to strip and clean the .303 inch Lee Enfield 1st World War issue rifles (universally known as "303s"), and Bren light machine guns, issued to us

---

[34] Founded around 1907 by Robert Baden-Powell; "Boy" in the title was beginning to fall into disuse. Most of the boys who took up this option were already Scouts anyway.

for the afternoon from the armoury. We also had classroom instruction on various aspects of field-craft. As seniors we could elect to join one of the specialist CCF groups (Engineers, Artillery, etc.). Parades were "taken" by Sergeant-Major Crouch[35] and we were assigned to sections and platoons for the purpose. Crouch would give his impressive stentorian parade-ground orders and generally get us to behave with something like military precision. He also instructed us in the art of parade ground drill, something that was later to be elevated almost to the level of an art form in basic and officer training during National Service.

Initially my experience with shooting had been with a .22 inch bore rifle, and in the first competition I found myself in I had come second (having missed only one bulls-eye with my five allocated shots). But the school had a rifle range only for this calibre rifle; if we needed to be able to fire a 303 we had to make a trip to the Middlesex Regiment barracks "miniature" range (25 yards from firing point to target) on Bittacy Hill a mile or so away.

I remember well my first experience of firing a 303. Unlike the smaller rifle, the bullet fired by the 303 was large enough to cause it to recoil slightly, or "kick", when fired. We adolescents were aware of this and before we had experienced it tended to exaggerate to ourselves the supposed effect of this recoil ("It can break your shoulder if you're not careful!" I remember someone saying in dramatically hushed tones). In spite of my efforts to hang around at the back once we got to the range (I was anxious to see whether anyone actually received a broken shoulder before I attempted firing myself) I was somehow, and not for the last time, ordered to be in the very first firing "detail"[36]. More concerned about the kick than the target when the time came I just shut my eyes and pulled the trigger. Needless to say the experience turned out to be nothing like as bad as I had supposed it would, and by the third or fourth shot I was actually taking proper aim.

The CCF was taken seriously enough for there to be an inter-House competition each year for the Newcastle Shield (I don't remember why it was so called). This involved a series of sub-competitions including "turnout" (smartness of dress)[37], parade-ground drill and possibly also field-craft. Regular Army officers would be invited to come to judge the competition. Inevitably some Houses took this more seriously than others, and it was usually won by dint of the keenness of the senior House NCO, and in these cases we did begin to approach true army standards. An offshoot

---

[35] Or, to give him his full title, Regimental Quarter-Master Sergeant Edward Crouch, BEM.
[36] See chapter 4 on my similar experience with an anti-tank grenade.
[37] In this regard, the coating with khaki "Blanco" of belts and gaiters, the shining of brass and the polishing of boots were also jobs that fags were required to do for their masters.

of the CCF was the school bugle and drum band whose parade tended to be a centre piece for the annual school open day, known as Foundation Day, when parents, relatives and friends were welcome; I sometimes wished in retrospect that I had joined this as a drummer.

The Winterstoke Library

The school library contained a good stock of books, and was also the place where we were expected to spend "free periods" (i.e. those to be devoted to private study, especially for exams) when we were in the Sixth Form. While there I often found my mind wandering and myself drawn to shelves of books on travel, and in particular nineteenth century books on exploration in Africa. There were quite a few of these, but I mainly recall being captivated by David Livingstone's *Narrative of an Expedition to the Zambesi*, and Henry Morton Stanley's *How I Found Livingstone*. They were leather bound and illustrated with beautifully executed line drawings and the paper had a particular rather pleasant smell. Rather than reading them through I merely dipped into them from time to time, but they worked on my imagination in a way that would have consequences later on in my life.

In view of the fact that Dr Murray had undertaken much of his early work as editor of the Oxford English Dictionary on the site, the library also had a full set not only of the complete dictionary [38] but also a leather-bound set of what was called "Murray's English Dictionary" running to about the same number of volumes (possibly an earlier edition of the same work). I found the size of both to be so intimidating that I don't think I ever referred to either.

The school collection of team photographs was kept there, and it was from these that we could literally get a picture of school sports heroes of the past. The library was also usually the site for the display of photographs entered in competitions. In the winter term of my last year I had entered a photograph (actually of Nanny with Cliff and Sarah in the rear of a speedboat on Lake Lucerne in Switzerland taken the previous summer) and then forgotten about it. Much to my amazement, I was reminded of the fact that I had entered it when one day almost by chance I saw it pinned up with others on a display board with an announcement that it had won the prize in the relevant category. I was delighted; I had always believed that this sort of unexpected bonus was granted only to other people, not to me.

---

[38] It had been expected to take ten years to complete and be some 7,000 pages long, in four volumes. In fact, when finally first published in 1928, it ran to twelve volumes, with 414,825 words defined and 1,827,306 citations employed to illustrate their meanings [Wikipedia].

For some reason I recall in particular the person who was responsible for cleaning the library (and doubtless some of the other buildings as well) and who was usually to be found there: a colourful round jolly middle-aged woman we knew as Irish Mary. Mary's problem was that she was obsessed with horse-racing and it was not only easy to get her going on the subject, but difficult to stop her once she had started. She was reputed to be willing to place bets for those who were interested in doing so (not only was this against the school rules, it was actually illegal at the time, as betting on horses could until 1961 be effected only at racetracks), although I never heard of any disciplinary action being taken as a result of such an activity.

Leaving school

There was no plan for me to go to university; actually only a minority of boys did so in those days, and they were usually intending to go take up an academic career or go into one of the professions[39]. I didn't at that stage want to go anyway, and would have had little idea what to study there if I did. That being the case, my parents certainly did not push the idea. In fact their plans for my future were a little vague: both Cliff and I were to go into the family business, Supersuites, but there was talk of my being articled to a firm of chartered accountants, and also a vague idea that I should spend some time in France with a business associate of Dad's studying veneer production.

Thus it was that I left Mill Hill at the end of the summer term of 1956 aged 17 years 3 months. In fact, in something of an anti-climax, that particular school term had ended rather suddenly a day early as there had been a suspected case of polio in the school and consequent need to isolate the sufferer. The planned CCF camp which I was to attend was also cancelled. As I found out when the results came through, I had French and German A Levels to my credit, an achievement that would not rate very highly in modern times when pupils expect to take three or four A levels. Indeed, looking back years later on my time at Mill Hill, I didn't seem to have achieved very much at all. As already indicated, there were the obvious rewards for excellence in sports; academically too there were various school prizes to be won and one could attempt to obtain scholarships or exhibitions

---

[39] Unlike professional requirements in later years, it was not necessary in those days to have obtained a university degree in order to undertake articles or equivalent. In most cases the attainment of two A levels was sufficient for this purpose.

to universities[40]. But my own attainments in both sport and academic life had been very modest.

Arguably of course fulfilment rather than identifiable achievement should be the goal at school, but even on this alternative test would I have been more fulfilled if I had done more? I did join a choir in my senior year that sang choruses from Handel's *Messiah* as part of one of the Ernest Read Children's Concerts at the Royal Festival Hall in London. I auditioned for a part in the school play one year (Shakespeare's *Twelfth Night*) but read the audition piece badly and did not get the part. I could with hindsight have attempted more in these areas (especially in view of my considerable involvement in drama in later years), or have applied to join the school military band as a drummer, and of course regret that I didn't.

The fact was that I didn't think I had much talent. In an ideal world there would have been a member of the teaching staff (for example my Housemaster or his subordinate the House Tutor) who could have encouraged me to do other things. But that would have been going beyond the call of duty for such a person and in any event it didn't happen. Many years later the film *Dead Poets Society* struck a particular chord with me. I had, I thought when seeing it, needed someone like the teacher portrayed there by Robin Williams to grab me by the shoulders and whisper "*Carpe diem!*"

I kept a daily diary in four exercise books during my last term at school and the end of the preceding one. Prior to my retrieving them to do some research for this chapter they had been packed away in a trunk in the loft and had remained unopened for nearly 60 years. Frankly much of the content is trite and immature, even embarrassing, but there are some insights in an epilogue I wrote to it some three months afterwards:

> I will not pretend I have any nostalgic feelings after leaving [Mill Hill] because I have not. I was always quite certain that I had had just enough and whereas one more term might have been acceptable, another year certainly would not...I am certain that I would have maintained while still at school [that] I was never unhappy. Many things are a bind, yes, and one is sometimes attacked by boredom, more especially in the often impossible weather of the spring term.
>
> I always associated with a large group of people – by that I mean that I never stuck to one or two...Our year was a large one and a large year is always prone to causing trouble, especially when [those in] the senior years are weak. Our

---

[40] My brother Cliff won the Hamilton Bailey Memorial Prize when he was in the fifth form for all round achievement. Apart from the minor form prize referred to (p. 58) I never seemed even to be in the running for any other.

Ridgeway year had in fact been the spearhead of the school where not only general infamy[41] but also sport were concerned.

Many people said that in the summer of 1955 I went to the dogs and cooked my chances as far as social promotion were concerned, for I had been told more than just in flattery that I was well in the running with [*my three contemporaries who were made prefects*]...Be that as it may I acted as my fancy bade me and if I cooked my chances then well tut tut [*sic*]...Even though I may have caused much trouble in my last year and a half, which in the last two terms one or two people wrongly asserted to be "sour grapes". I knew I could never have been a good little angel on purpose just for the sake of a "staff drive" [*i.e. aiming for promotion*].

The diary does not make enthralling reading and frankly I cannot all this time later even be bothered to go through it in detail, but nevertheless there is in the above extract a sort of summing up of my Mill Hill experience. I cannot remember what trouble I was referring to in the last sentence, but in any event the "one or two people" mentioned there (presumably other pupils) were almost certainly correct. A perceptive Housemaster or headmaster might have written in my school report at the end of my final term: "Keen on sports but not as good as he would have liked; un-stimulated and frustrated by much else to the point where he felt the need to rebel".

Soon after leaving, by contrast with the view expressed in the diary, I began to regret that I had not set myself on a path that would have enabled me to get to Oxford or Cambridge. There would have been some hard thinking to do as to the subject(s) to be studied there, as modern languages were not, I thought, where my best talents lay, but I probably would have benefitted from the experience, particularly after I had done National Service and matured a little.

I also regretted later that I had had almost no science education, especially in zoology and botany, and my largely latent interest in natural history came to prominence later in spite of this. But the pursuit of such an interest does not of course depend on formal education in the subject. Indeed, the same can be said of my enjoyment of music (I had virtually no musical education apart from what I heard and participated in during school chapel services) or even history (where as previously noted my teachers played little part in inducing a love of the subject). On the other hand, though I did not recognise it at the time, some seeds had been sown at Mill Hill with respect to appreciating English prose and poetry, and I returned years later to some of the poets whose work I had had to read (and of course in some cases learn by heart), and to enjoy reading and reciting it. I was once asked after a recital many decades later how it was that I became interested in poetry. When I

---

[41] I have no idea what I meant by this.

said that I had been introduced to it at school, the questioner was sufficiently impressed to ask me which school.

Perhaps because of my own rather low boredom threshold, another thing that struck me about teaching at school was that it needs to consist of more than merely explaining the elements of a given subject. In my own career, in which teaching adults was later to form a significant part, I have always been conscious of the need to enrol those in my class into the subject matter, and this in turn requires constant awareness of the attention being paid, sometimes called the "energy level".

In any event a new period of my life was about to begin; a period for which in many ways I was ill prepared.

Home life in the school holidays

The family had moved from Edgware to The Bishops' Avenue in the spring of 1953. From many points of view for us children the new home at Fourways was ideal. Firstly it had a large back garden with a tennis court, and though the spaces behind the base lines were a little short this hardly mattered at our standard of tennis. Secondly it had a large room at the top of the house about 40% of which was taken with a full-size billiard/snooker table and in which there was also room for a table tennis table that could be stacked away when not in use. There was even a little room leading off this that had been created as a photographic dark-room and this encouraged me to start developing and printing my own black and white photographs. There was no shortage of things to do.

However, one of the problems about being at a boarding school was that one's closest friends tended to live a long way away and this made contact with most of them during the school holidays virtually out of the question. As school was our main life for the duration it thus meant that in the holidays we had hardly any social life away from home. In Cliff's and my case this was not a particular problem for though we undoubtedly squabbled a lot, we did many things together; if all else failed we could fall back on a game of snooker (a game at which, in spite of the facilities at hand, neither of us achieved any notable degree of competence) or table tennis.

From Mother's point of view too, the new home seemed as though it should have been ideal. Her first cousin, Jean Sadow, had married Ronnie Sadow of the Beautility Furniture family, and they lived in Aylmer Road only 150 yards or so away. Mother and Jean had been quite close when they were growing up (her father had been a brother of my grandmother Windy, although I don't remember ever having met him) and it had been quite reasonably expected that they could spend time with each other again. For some reason this didn't seem to happen. Neither woman was particularly sociable, and it may be that they had simply grown apart. In fact I don't remember seeing "Auntie Jean" more than once or twice at our house. Even given the fact that I was away for more of the year than I was at home, this is in retrospect remarkable.

Those who had lived in Dorset Drive in Edgware had formed quite a close community during the War and the austerity times after it. Local people were drawn together in adversity, and Mother had developed especially close friendships with two of our neighbours, Sylvia Griew and Lucy Cohen. After the move she had of course left both of them behind. Although none of them was working, neither Mother nor her friends were able to drive a car and so this made the distance between them considerable (a bus and train ride for an hour or so). While this was clearly not an insurmountable obstacle, and she probably did visit them (and they her) from time to time, it needed determination to keep up the social relationship. Possibly they did meet occasionally on neutral ground (e.g. for lunch in the West End) but I do not remember ever seeing either woman in our house.

Nanny was of course (except on her days off) always at home, and in the cases of Cliff and Sarah still very much their main carer, at least in Cliff's case until he too joined me as a boarder at Mill Hill. I can only imagine that she filled such need as Mother thought she needed for social contact, and that others gradually faded out of the picture. In fact Lucy Cohen and her husband Henry later moved to The Bishops' Avenue, but things were not as they had been. Lucy was not well, I seem to remember, and anyway in the context of the large houses of the locality the days of talking to each other casually in the street or "dropping by" were over.

Gradually Mother began to suffer from asthma. I don't recall when it started and in the early days when I was still at school her condition did not seem to be anything serious: she just seemed occasionally to bend over, coughing slightly. I think I was aware that this condition was more likely to come over her if she were stressed or upset.

We had summer holidays away, and firstly in 1955 these were taken abroad (in Switzerland). Then in the summer of 1956 I made my own first attempt at independent travel, taking a fortnight or so with a school friend, David Auld, to hitchhike in Ireland, staying in youth hostels. The weather was consistently indifferent to bad and the holiday was not a great success, but during that time we met up with people who had travelled quite widely. I remembered one young man describing his experiences of a bull-fight in Spain. That kind of thing, I thought, was what I really wanted to do: to travel widely and gain experiences of life. Though I did not exactly see myself as an explorer in the Livingstone or Stanley mould, memories of their books in the school library were of course fresh.

Travel, in the way that young people undertook it later, typically during a "gap year" between school and university, or between university and work, was virtually unknown. The predominant idea in middle class circles then was that you had to "establish yourself" in some kind of working career as soon as possible. Apart from short vacations, travelling, besides being much more expensive in real terms than it later became, was seen, certainly by my parents, as a waste of valuable time. I nevertheless began to look for opportunities. For the immediate future they seemed to be frustratingly almost non-existent.

Chapter 3

The Furniture Business

1. Supersuites
   - The organisation and factory personnel 77
   - The despatch department 83
   - The cabinet makers 86
   - The office 88
2. Beautility
   - The organisation 91
   - My duties 92
   - Other tasks 95
   - After National Service 99

1. Supersuites

The organisation and factory personnel

The world of work, while not exactly a shock, was quite different from anything I had previously experienced. It was not that "the factory", as we had always called it at home, was unknown to me for I had visited it on many occasions from childhood onwards, and had in the previous summer school holiday actually worked in the office there for a fortnight (and found out in the process that my abilities as a wages clerk were decidedly lacking). It was rather that I now found myself constantly in a workaday, mainly working-class, world where people's attitudes and actions were often considerably different from those I had been used to.

As has already been noted in chapter 1, Supersuites had been moved from the East End and established in Edmonton in the mid-1930s. Sometime after the outbreak of the Second World War the factory was requisitioned by the Government for the manufacture of military supplies, and as time went on the work consisted mainly of the construction of fuselages and other parts for the Hamilcar gliders that were designed to carry military equipment (including light tanks). When the War ended the company was, in theory at least, free to resume the manufacture of furniture. The demand for new bedroom suites was high, as production of virtually all non-essentials had ceased for the duration, but timber and plywood were in short supply. Thus for the immediate post-war years, Jack Angel designed, and the company put into production, a three-piece bedroom suite constructed from a mixture of metal, plywood and timber, marketed as the "Angro" (Angel and Rose) suite.

It had already become obvious that the entrepreneurial drive behind the business was going to have to be Dad's and his alone. In fact he gradually became more and more frustrated with those he began to see as "hangers-on" who could contribute in only a limited way. It was not only Jack who fell into this category; my grandfather Lou was "employed" in the business (in what actual capacity I never discovered), although by the mid-1950s when he was probably in his mid to late 60s the company paid him off in order to get him out of the way[1]. He had left by the time I joined the company in September 1956.

But, returning to general attitudes and actions, I found at Supersuites that a situation of confrontation rather than co-operation tended to exist between management and workers (or in practice their shop stewards as representatives of NUFTO[2], the relevant trade union). And rudeness rather than politeness was often the norm in business dealings between buyers and suppliers, whether those dealings were between the factory and its timber, plywood and other suppliers on the one hand, or the factory and its retail furniture shop customers on the other. Coarse language on the factory floor was so normal that after a while one hardly noticed it, and even words for some everyday things were different: what I would have called the morning tea break was known as breakfast, what I knew as lunch was dinner, and the evening meal taken at home after work was tea.

But the main difference between this new life and anything I had previously experienced was an obsession with money, at all levels of factory life, and all the time. I had obviously grown up in a sheltered environment, both at home and at school, in which having enough money was, within reason, taken for granted. And whatever the drawbacks of the institution, school had taught me that there were situations in which it was desirable to act without seeking reward. In the factory environment such an attitude would have been thought of as little short of ridiculous. Here, everything was calculated in terms of the rates that were payable for the jobs to be done, the costs of raw materials and overheads, the prices to be charged to customers, the discounts to be offered to them and the times within which payment was supposed to

---

[1] He invested the money he had been paid in a small hotel in Southborough, Kent, that he and my grandmother attempted to run. The enterprise was a complete disaster.
[2] The National Union of Furniture Trade Operatives. This later merged with other unions to form the Furniture, Timber and Allied Trades Union.

be made. Money spent on anything, from machinery down to pencils, had to be justified to the last penny. Life was ruled by the workers' pay packets on the one hand and the company's annual profit and loss account on the other.

It quickly became obvious that some of my ideas about life had been instilled and formed from a wholly middle class perspective; I was now discovering that there were others. In this regard it was obvious that social classes mattered. Today the very word "class" in this context is shunned, possibly because it is thought best to pretend that the categorisation does not exist, or because it might be thought to imply that people have to be seen as being in particular "fixed stations" in life (which of course they are not). But it was (and still is) an important concept in that there were (as there still are) differences in outlook and expectation in different sections of society that needed to be understood. There was for a start a definite social division between those who worked on the factory floor and those who worked in the office.

In the mid-1950s the accepted class distinctions were very roughly as follows: working class (subdivided into skilled and unskilled); lower middle class (generally better educated people including clerical and shop workers); middle class (e.g. shop and small business owners, and minor professionals); upper middle class (e.g. executives in industry, professionals in medicine, law, accountancy, university and some school education, officers in the armed forces); and upper class (the formal aristocracy and those with "old money" i.e. families who, while not formally ennobled, had for some time lived similar lives to the aristocracy).[3]

The workers on the factory floor, including the charge-hands and foremen, were all working class men (no women were in employed in that capacity in Supersuites in those days) and apart from a few labourers, they would have been classed as skilled, having probably served some kind of apprenticeship. The office workers on the other hand were mostly lower middle class people of both sexes (although office cleaners and tea-makers tended to be working class women). However in the predominantly male work environment at the time the office manager was, and would almost certainly always have been, a man. In practice a woman would have been in

---

[3] This personal social analysis neither draws on authorities on sociology nor purports to be exhaustive. The categories were not in practice rigid, and there were of course many exceptions and refinements to those stated. In the 21st century these categories have been redefined a little, more in line with people's skills, earning capacity and property holding, but they still unquestionably exist.

charge of an office or department consisting of only, or predominantly, other women.

The social division applied even to the times of the working day: the factory workers clocked in by 8.00 am for an 8 hour working day that finished at 5.30 pm (the 9½ hours thus represented included an hour's "dinner break" and two 15 minute breaks in mid-morning and mid-afternoon). This made a 40 hour working week. Office workers started their day an hour later at 9.00 am, wore suits and ties (or equivalent formal wear for women), and generally, though they were not necessarily as well paid as the better-paid shop-floor workers, thought of themselves as living in a world that, if not actually superior, was certainly different[4]. Their day also finished at 5.30, but they did not clock in or out and tea breaks were not deducted; their working day was thus 7½ hours.

An interesting aspect of the class division was the way in which the foremen and factory workers referred to and addressed the directors, Dad and his partner Jack Angel. Although the bulk of the factory floor workers would have called them Mr Rose and Mr Angel, the foremen and those on the factory floor who had been with the company for a long time mostly called them Dave and Jack. Such familiarity would however have been unthinkable in the office, even on the part of the office manager. There, though the younger office workers might call each other by their first names, an older person would probably also have been addressed as Mr, Mrs or Miss X (there was no "Ms" in those days); and all of them would have addressed Mr Couchman the office manager[5], let alone the directors, formally in the same way.

The factory workers (although not the charge-hands and foremen[6]) all belonged to the trade union, and this made for a constant tension as the union persistently strove to improve the standards of living of its members by increasing wages in real terms[7], while the management (in this case essentially Dad and his factory manager) struggled to keep production costs down. These two opposing goals meant that from time to time there was ill-feeling and occasionally even strikes or threatened strikes, when the factory workers, led by the factory union shop steward and his committee, objected

---

[4] One of the markers of this was the provision of separate toilet facilities for male office workers; they would not at all have liked the idea of sharing them with the factory workers.
[5] I think, but at this distance I'm not sure, that his first name was Reg.
[6] Once promoted to the "staff", as these posts were collectively known, the man concerned was regarded as a "governor's man". He received a higher salary (at least in theory – it did not always work out that way in later years), was not, as also with office workers, required to clock in for work, and was entitled to receive pay while away sick.
[7] I.e. above the current rate of inflation.

to things that they perceived as obstructing their aims. In practice, however, any strikes there were did not usually last long (a matter of hours at most) and were "unofficial" in that they did not have the formal backing of the union. In fact Dad made a good deal of effort to maintain good relations with the local NUFTO representative (as indeed it was in his interest to do). In the early days this was a grey-haired, bald, energetic and slightly unkempt small Jewish man by the name of Sidney Fineman, who reminded me a little of the then Israeli Prime Minister, David Ben-Gurion.

Reached by an access road that passed alongside a canal fed by the River Lea, the factory was split between two separate premises, one on each side of that road. On the right was the main building with the offices at the front and behind them "the mill" where timber and plywood were shaped by a variety of saws, "four-cutters"[8] and other machines into the necessary parts for the relevant pieces of furniture. Obviously it was a noisy place, as was particularly apparent whenever the connecting door between the mill and the offices was opened. Behind the mill were the areas where unprocessed timber and plywood were stacked.

Across the road were the presses (in which veneers were bonded to plywood), the cabinet makers (the craftsmen who put together the necessary machined parts to construct the relevant items of furniture), the polishers (who sprayed the items with coats of nitro-cellulose lacquer which then had to be "French-polished" by hand), the finishers (who added catches, knobs, handles, etc. as appropriate), and the despatch department (from which the finished articles were loaded on to vans for delivery).

Three individuals stand out in my memory from those days. Firstly there was the factory manager, Eddie Gray. Mother used to refer to him as "Monsewer" (a crude anglicised version of Monsieur), a title that had been adopted by a character of the same name who was one of a group of rough and ready comedians calling themselves The Crazy Gang and who performed for years at the Victoria Palace Theatre in London. Our Eddie Gray however was a straight, hard-working man and the picture that remains in my mind of him is his seemingly incessant rushing around between the office and the various factory departments, bent over his clip-board and with a slightly frowning, concerned expression on his face. He had actually been promoted over the head of the former factory manager, Harry Ross, a stout Jewish man (whose name had formerly been Rosenberg) who had, in company with quite a few furniture workers, lost most of the fingers on one

---

[8] Machines that were capable of planing timber on four sides at the same time. Other machines in constant use in shaping timber and plywood were known as routers and spindles. All were potentially dangerous and needed to have suitable guards to protect the operatives.

of his hands to woodworking machinery. Harry had been all for a quiet life, and had eventually been demoted by reason of this relaxed attitude to become foreman of the presses.

At the other end of the factory social scale was Fred (I don't recall his surname). Although mechanised factory transport, mainly in the form of fork-lift trucks, was available, at Supersuites most goods were moved from the mill across the road to the presses and the cabinet makers' stores on low pallets using a simple hydraulic hand-pulled device known as a low barrow. The person who usually did this was a slightly simple-minded and rather scruffy though hard-working labourer, whose hair was invariably dishevelled to the point where it stood out at all angles. Fred was the butt of good-natured teasing on the part of the factory workers and at Christmas that year they made a present for him: a "vanity set" consisting of a series of nails banged into a large flat brush-shaped piece of plywood and a matching strip with multiple saw-cuts made to look like the teeth of a comb.

The third individual I particularly recall was one of the two joint managers of the despatch department, Johnny Lewis. An affable Jewish ex-salesman with a Groucho Marx-type moustache, it was his job to try to keep the peace between the factory and managers of furniture shops complaining about the late delivery of their orders. While his usual opening gambit "Hello, Sir, what can I *do you for?*" wore a bit thin after a while, there is no doubt that his natural good nature helped on many an occasion to smooth ruffled feathers.

But quite strong memories of others too remain. Bill Proctor, the foreman of the mill, seemed to me to know just about anything there was to know about machinery, and about cars in particular. It was from him I learned how differential gears in a motor vehicle worked, and also some of the finer points about servicing my own car. Tommy Williamson, the foreman of the polishers, with his hands permanently stained from the materials of his trade, would always patiently explain things when asked. And there was Arthur Russell, the jig-maker[9] and finest cabinet maker employed by the company, from whom I learned some of the things that I was able to put to use later in home carpentry.

This, then, was the background against which, aged a little under 17½, I was to start work. Though I received a salary, I would not of course be an ordinary employee: I would always be the boss's son. For the first six

---

[9] A jig in this context is a device that holds a piece of work and guides it around the tools used to cut or shape it (particularly for those machines in the mill known as spindles and routers). The making of these required a high degree of skill.

months or so of my time at the factory my work was to be as nearly as possible on the "shop floor". This wasn't possible in an absolute sense, for the intention was not that I would actually do, even temporarily, any of the jobs the factory workers were employed to do (apart from any apprenticeship that might have been required for this, the trade union would not have allowed it). But I was to "learn the business" by getting as close as I could to the pulse of the factory. For a start this was to be in the despatch department.

Some of the factory personnel at Supersuites, circa 1953.
Seated second row back l. to r. Fred Dickinson, Johnny Lewis, Eddie Gray, Harry Ross, Dad, Jack Angel, Grandpa Lou Rosen, Tommy Williamson, Bill Proctor

The despatch department

This was run by Johnny Lewis and Fred Dickinson, and as they worked from an office their social status was marginally higher than that of the foremen on the shop floor. Their task was to organise and plan the delivery of the bedroom suites that had been ordered by furniture stores around the country by making up loads corresponding to the outstanding orders. This was more complex than it sounded as account had to be taken when planning the routes for the vans not only of efficient distribution, but also of the various mid-week "half-day closings" (when the shops closed at 1 pm) on a Wednesday or a Thursday[10]; these varied in different parts of the country, sometimes within the same general area. It was also much easier to plan loads for the industrial areas of London, the Midlands, Lancashire, Yorkshire, Tyneside and Glasgow, where obviously there was a much greater density of people and shops, than it was for more thinly populated areas like the South Coast, Somerset, Devon and Cornwall, and East Anglia.

An average consignment consisted of a core 3 piece bedroom suite (a lady's and a gent's wardrobe and a dressing table) to which there was also usually added a "bed", in practice a headboard and footboard fitted with metal brackets or "cheals" to which a sprung metal bed-frame (not supplied by us) would be bolted[11]. Occasionally also there would be one or two bedside cabinets (known in the trade as pot-cupboards[12]). All were finished in matching (loosely at least), mainly walnut, veneers.

There was always the potential for tension here too. The furniture shops wanted the merchandise they had ordered to be supplied as quickly as possible, often more quickly than the factory could manage. In practice most of the shops the factory supplied were part of groups of shops, and by far the largest of these was Isaac Wolfson's Great Universal Stores, usually known in the furniture trade, and always at Supersuites, as "The Group"[13]. The shops comprising this conglomerate inevitably had more clout when it came to obtaining quick supply and were thus often able to jump the queue, and this equally inevitably meant that sometimes smaller shops (especially those in the less populated areas) were left frustrated over longer than expected delivery dates. It was part of the job of the two despatch office managers to field telephone calls from upset customers who could on occasions be rude or even insulting.

Once the loads had been made up in the office the suites (together with any odd pieces ordered) need to be loaded on to the delivery vans. I don't remember what I was given to do in the office (filing, I remember, was one

---

[10] Saturdays were normally full days in the retail business but, except occasionally in London, the Supersuites drivers did not normally make deliveries then, and if they did would have had to be paid overtime rates.

[11] However, divan beds (consisting of a mattress laid on an upholstered spring base, usually with its own headboard) were beginning to replace the conventional beds described.

[12] I.e. as in chamber- or piss-pot. There were still many homes without an internal loo, and these utensils were thus still in use there at night-time.

[13] The Group, or GUS, had bought up several smaller groups of furniture shops such as Cavendish, Smarts and Woodhouse in the 1940s. Widely known as "Gussies", especially in institutions like the Stock Exchange, at some point they also obtained a majority interest and then a controlling interest in Supersuites, and in Beautility, the company with which it was later to merge.

of the tasks, and I can't think that I would have been much use in making up loads) but I was certainly called on to help load the vans and memory of my first three or four months of work is dominated by this procedure.

The packaging of items of furniture in "knock down" flat-pack form was virtually unknown at the time, and so each individual made-up piece of furniture had to be wrapped in a specially made and re-usable fitted padded cover to prevent damage in transit and then loaded systematically so that the items at the back would be the first to be delivered. Lack of fork-lift trucks at Supersuites has already been noted and loading was done entirely by hand. This involved wheeling each piece from the loading bay on a metal hand barrow, and then two of us bodily lifting it on to the delivery van and positioning it inside where required. Special care had of course to be taken with the dressing table mirrors, which were removed and packed separately for the purposes of transportation.

In order to get the maximum use from the furniture vans, each was loaded with its tailboard[14] down (a tailboard could hold two ladies' and two gents' wardrobes). It was the loading of the last piece on the tailboard that involved a practice that would today almost certainly be condemned by a factory inspector as unsafe. All other pieces could be lifted into position from the floor of the van or on the tailboard, but for the last top piece on the tailboard there was nowhere to stand and lift it to the requisite height. In the result a short ladder was propped against the lower piece of furniture at the back of the tailboard. While two men lifted the prospective upper piece as high as they could from the ground, the third (usually Johnny Lewis) would take a run up the ladder with his arms outstretched; the momentum thus engendered enabled the piece to be manoeuvred finally into position. It was, as the modern cliché phrase has it, an accident waiting to happen.[15]

Unlike the so-called "country loads", deliveries in London were all capable of being made within a single day and on one or two occasions I was assigned to accompany the driver and help to make these deliveries. Our London driver was an old man (probably in his late fifties or early sixties) whom everybody called "Pop" and my task was to accompany Pop on one of his rounds (actually I seem to remember the occasions I did this as being Saturday "half-rounds" taking just the morning), sitting in the driver's cab while he made the required tour of all the shops on the delivery list and then

---

[14] A hinged metal platform that could when empty be folded up and locked to the rear of the sides of the vehicle.
[15] Although in fact I didn't witness one and don't remember hearing about one.

helping to offload. Our morning naturally included a stop at a workman's cafe (chosen by Pop as being in his opinion clean) for "breakfast".

The cabinet makers

My next factory assignment was to assist Tommy Dale, the foreman of the cabinet-makers, or "makers" as they were usually called. To do this I had to get to know the store of milled parts for all the variety of pieces of furniture that needed to be made, for my main task was to make up pallet loads of the requisite parts for distribution to the bench of each individual maker after he finished his previous job. Not only were there parts for wardrobes, gents' wardrobes and dressing tables (as well as occasionally for beds and pot-cupboards) to be made up, but there were several different designs for each. A maker was given three items of main furniture to construct at one time, and so sufficient quantities of the relevant veneered panels, wooden rails, mouldings and machine-dove-tailed drawer parts needed to be assembled and stacked on his pallet.

Though the job was not very stimulating (and it was beginning to dawn on me that this applied to most jobs in the factory once mastered), somewhat to Tommy's surprise I quickly got to know the requisite parts for each load; and I at least enjoyed being kept busy and slightly challenged by the many different permutations. There were often shortages, and one of my tasks was to go across the road to the mill to try to chase up parts that were needed to make up pallets. One day, as Dad was doing his rounds of the factory and I was occupied as usual making up these pallets, Tommy ventured the opinion to him in my hearing that I was "a smart lad". "What do you expect?" came the half-serious reply "He's my son!"

In practice each maker worked mainly on one of the three pieces of the suite. The largest of these pieces, the ladies' wardrobes (known as "robes"), had to be constructed so that they could easily be taken apart into two halves lengthwise. This was because they could not otherwise have been manhandled up the narrow staircases in most houses. Although delivery to members of the public was normally undertaken by the retail shops, occasionally this was done directly by us, typically where a piece had been sent back to the factory for repair and the householder concerned lived in London. I remember on at least one occasion making the delivery with the driver and going through the process of taking the wardrobe apart in order to do so (and, somewhat to my surprise, receiving a tip for my efforts).

The makers, rightly regarded as the most skilled of the factory workers, were a disparate group. A few of them had been with the company since its earliest days (one of these I recall in particular was a polite, quietly spoken Jewish man, Morry Greenberg, who made robes and talked fondly of Brick Lane days). Newcomers included a couple of pleasant young Greek Cypriots who had recently settled in north London[16].

Some of my strongest memories of the department are the smells emanating from it, the most obvious of which was that of glue. At the time this was made from a derivative of animal hides (it was some time after this that a move was made in the industry generally to synthetic glues) and needed to be "cooked" in pots heated over gas rings. The strong but not unpleasant smell given off from this thick dark-brown viscous substance pervaded the department. And of course there was also the smell of wood.

We used a variety of different woods in construction, but the days of using locally produced timber were long gone, and virtually all of it had to be imported. It came mostly from countries in West Africa and South-East Asia, that were beginning to deplete their indigenous rain-forests, but at the time seemed to be able to supply endlessly. The different woods thus supplied went under a series of exotic names that few outside the furniture industry had heard of, then or indeed since.

The most common all-purpose timber was *ramin*, a straight-grained cream-coloured wood from South-East Asia (we used it for structural rails and mouldings); but unseen rails were usually constructed from a better quality softwood such as *Parana pine* from Central America. For drawer-sides and backs, which because of their more constant use as movable parts needed to be made from solid wood, we used mainly *niangon* (an African mahogany). Large surfaces consisted of veneered plywood[17]. Internally these needed to have a mahogany finish, and for this we used African redwood veneers without obvious grain patterns, principally *makore*, *sapele* and *utile*. Externally in the early days the veneer was almost entirely walnut[18], but experiments were beginning with "contemporary" furniture designs that made use of *tola* (or African cedar, a straight and strong-grained mahogany-type wood), teak and *afrormosia* (another West African timber but with a slightly golden appearance).

---

[16] In fact this was the era in which many immigrants from Commonwealth countries began to arrive in Britain, and we also employed a couple of West Indians as labourers.
[17] The switch to the cheaper and lighter-weight chipboard was just beginning in the industry at this time.
[18] Mainly imported from France. It always struck me as an unsatisfactory wood finish as it quite quickly turned a rather unattractive reddish colour.

The office

After six months or so in the two factory-floor departments, it was decided that I needed experience closer to the running of the business, and that meant being given something to do in the office.

Besides Mr Couchman the office manager, three women and two men were employed there. In view of the small number, there was an expectation that there would be a certain amount of doubling of functions. The oldest of the women, Mrs Jimack, a middle-aged Jewish woman whose husband was a taxi driver, was mainly a shorthand typist, but did a variety of jobs including answering the telephone. "Jim", as she was called by those of us who were her colleagues, had "culture" and would from time to time arrive at the office in the morning dressed to the nines so that after work her husband could collect her and take her off to the theatre or even the opera (their son, who had worked for a while at Supersuites as a labourer, was a student at Cambridge).

Part of Jim's original job had been as a secretary to Dad (not a very onerous task as he didn't like dictating letters very much). But it transpired that he didn't like *her* very much either, and he substituted Anne. There were nevertheless plenty of other people who needed letters processed (e.g. the office manager, the despatch office and the buyer). Anne, aged about 20, was mainly employed to answer the telephone, but in view of her "promotion" to process Dad's letters, I presume she was also a reasonably competent shorthand typist. Otherwise she was completely empty headed. Edna, a single woman who was older, capable and had a sharp and very dry sense of humour, seemed also to do a variety of jobs. She had her eye on the young (married) man in the office employed as a buyer.

Stan Bettel, the wages clerk, had an ability that is almost extinct in modern times: he could run his hand quickly down a column of figures adding them accurately as he did so. There were no electronic calculators in those days (mechanical ones did exist but they were comparatively expensive and slow) and at the time a pound sterling consisted of twenty shillings, and a shilling of twelve pence, making money calculations considerably more complex than they are today[19]. He kept the hand-written wages ledgers impeccably. Stan was rather a large man who always wore a grey double-breasted suit, and seemed to smoke incessantly. He was also very obviously gay, and enjoyed himself hugely making camp catty remarks with the women.

---

[19] The change to decimal coinage did not come until early in 1971.

Ted Hunter was the buyer. He had been enticed away from competitors (Lebus, at that time the largest furniture manufacturers in the country, whose premises in Tottenham were not far away). In view of his age (early to mid-thirties) he was, as with the younger women in the office, known by everybody by his first name. He seemed to reciprocate Edna's attentions. Though he was by nature a likeable man, Ted had developed a manner on the telephone of no nonsense talk, and an especially aggressive attitude to suppliers whose shipments were late (as was fairly often the case). He had also produced an impressive working chart showing the state of all timber and plywood ordered, pending and delivered. In fact Ted was someone Dad described as "a nice boy" (Dad's ultimate seal of approval for a youngish man) and I was to be his assistant.

I quickly mastered the chart, but my efforts at copying Ted's style on the phone sounded patently hollow to myself, let alone the suppliers I was talking to, and I soon realised that my own approach to matters would have to be different. But in reality there was not much for me to do. I found, as I was to do later at Beautility, that my questions to various people about various aspects of the business tended to turn into general discussions on all sorts of things. At times the days passed slowly. Although in these early months I did not for a moment think that one day I might leave the company and do something else, I never seemed to be able to envisage myself as the boss of Supersuites either. Even if I had, bearing in mind his strong views on the business and the world in general, working with Dad was clearly not going to be easy.

In October 1956, soon after I started work, the "Suez Crisis" blew up[20]. The immediate effect, as the Arab world with its crude oil resources sided with Egypt, was a diminution of the supply of that commodity (as was to happen

---

[20] This is today regarded as the series of events that effectively brought the final curtain down on the British Empire and on Britain's claim to be a first-ranking world power. The bare bones of what happened are that in June 1956 Colonel Nasser, the then President of Egypt, nationalised the Suez Canal (shares in which up to that time were owned mainly by the British Government and French private investors). Anthony Eden, Britain's Prime Minister, was certain that Nasser was another Hitler in the making and was determined to do everything he could to oppose him, if necessary by force. The French Government thought much the same. Together with Israel, a plan was formulated under which Israel, which had been provoked into responding after suffering a number of Egyptian-backed raids across its borders, would invade the Sinai Peninsula up to the Suez Canal. Egypt would obviously attempt to oppose Israel, and British and French forces would then move into and occupy the Canal Zone "to separate the warring parties". As the plan began to be put into effect, the Americans, who had not been consulted on the proposed occupation, were furious and threatened financial sanctions against Britain and France unless they immediately withdrew. There was no practical alternative but to do so, and in humiliating circumstances. Anthony Eden resigned shortly afterwards.

again on subsequent occasions). The British Government was forced to introduce rationing of petrol and cancelled all driving tests for the duration (employing driving test examiners to administer the rationing system). Following on from this, they relaxed the restrictions on learner car drivers having to be accompanied by qualified drivers. And so, after taking lessons with a driving instructor who was a friend of Eddie Gray, and being adjudged by the instructor to be ready to take a driving test, I was supplied with a car on the business[21]. For several months I was able to drive it alone on L Plates.

One of my resulting jobs was to drive down to the City with bills of lading for goods imported directly by Supersuites (dressing-table mirrors from Belgium were the main ones) in order to get the goods cleared through customs by the importing agents in St Mary Axe. Another was to go and collect the money for wages from the local branch of Barclay's Bank. This job was usually entrusted to Jack Angel, myself and one of the men in the office. Though we were careful not to do this at a regular time, the risk of robbery while doing this must have been more considerable than we realised, especially as we were "armed" with no more than rolled-up paying-in books! This was before the days of widespread use of specialist security companies for the purpose.

The timing of events that now took place is hazy in my mind, but by about the spring of 1957 an arrangement was concluded (if not actually brokered by GUS, doubtless with their approval) that there would be a "reverse takeover" by Supersuites of the much larger Beautility Furniture. Quite clearly there was more to be learned from the much larger organisation and I was "posted" there shortly afterwards. In fact the whole business of Supersuites was within a short time to be moved to other premises owned by the larger company and the Lea Valley factory vacated. My time at Supersuites had thus been for what turned out to be most of its final year in its existing form. Indeed, as the new premises were to be some twenty miles away at Brentwood, most of the staff employed at Edmonton chose not to continue working with the company.

---

[21] This was a green, 3-gear Ford Prefect, registration number 15 KMC. I actually took and passed my driving test after they had been reinstated sometime in the spring of 1957.

2. Beautility

The organisation

Beautility had been founded in the 1890s by, I believe, Simon and Abraham Sadowsky, Jewish cabinet makers who, or whose family, had come originally from somewhere in the pale of settlement. It had in the 1920s and 30s been greatly enlarged by the sons of one of them, Ronnie and Gerry Sadow (as they now called themselves), and by the time of the takeover the company had become one of the best-known manufacturers of dining-room furniture in the country. These second generation brothers were, besides being business acquaintances, also personal friends of Dad and Jack (and as will be recalled, Ronnie was married to Mother's first cousin Jean).

To what extent the brothers had willingly entered into the takeover arrangement (as opposed to having been put under pressure from GUS to do so) was never made clear. In fact I would not even have suspected anything but a purely voluntary agreement on their part to retire had it not been for Dad's defensiveness (and a certain elusiveness) on the subject if ever it was subsequently raised, by me (and I was genuinely interested to know the details) or anyone else. Whatever the truth of the matter, the financial settlement for the brothers must, I imagine, nevertheless have been an attractive one.

The fact remained that sometime early in 1957 Dad was appointed as managing director of Beautility. Jack was nominally appointed a joint-managing director, but everyone knew that in reality he would play little part in the central management of the business. The only person near to Dad in responsibility for the company's affairs would be George Byatt. George, who had as part of the takeover plan stayed on as Works Director, had risen to that position through the ranks of the company from an assistant buyer. He was an able, intelligent, likeable, rough diamond of a character whose knowledge of the business was vast. In due course I was to become his assistant.

Beautility occupied a large site on the Edmonton industrial estate abutting on to the North Circular Road near the Lea Valley Viaduct, and had a work-force of something like five times that of Supersuites. In fact comparing the two businesses was almost like comparing an amateur with a professional organisation. The somewhat makeshift nature of the production process at Supersuites contrasted with the highly mechanised and efficient plant at Beautility. As with Supersuites, however, the factory occupied two separate but adjoining buildings. On one side the basic manufacture of parts for the furniture took place; here were the kilns (the company kiln-dried its own timber), the mill and the presses. On the other side the furniture was assembled by the cabinet makers, passed to the polishers and fitters, and finally the individual finished pieces were placed on to a continuous railway of flat platforms to go to the loading bay.

In view of the size of the company there were all sorts of jobs, even whole departments, that had not existed at Supersuites at all. Beautility had, for example, a machine tool shop, a design office, a jig-making department, a hardware store, a machine and building maintenance department and even a small printing shop; it also had its own canteen. Instead of one individual there was a small department for buying, and the general office consisted of seemingly dozens of (mainly female) employees. The factory was managed on day to day basis by two factory managers, Arthur Millie and Lou Harris, who sat facing each other in a noisy little office in and out of which trouped a seemingly endless succession of foremen and charge-hands.

But the Edmonton site was not the only one. Beautility also had a large site at Brentwood, Essex, about 20 miles away, which had been used mainly for storing timber, plywood and veneers. It was now reorganised to accommodate the bedroom suite manufacturing operation of Supersuites, which moved there soon after the merger, and also the operations of the newly acquired Bluegate Company which made kitchen furniture. Bearing in mind that Beautility also acquired at about this time William Goodacre & Co Ltd, a carpet manufacturing company situated outside Kendal in the Lake District, it was now a major player in the production of virtually all the important elements of home furnishing. On top of everything else it had a showroom occupying a prime position double shop site in London's West End (actually in Oxford Street right opposite Selfridges).

With his family now living in The Bishops' Avenue, and his appointment as *de facto* chief executive of this group of companies, for someone with his humble beginnings it must have seemed to Dad that he had, at the age of 46, attained his apotheosis. In the late spring of 1957 I was transferred to Beautility at Edmonton. With the potential to direct even a part of this small industrial empire, who would not, as Dad would have put it, have given their right arm to be in the position in which I now found myself?

My duties
It was decided that I should start studying operations at the beginning of the whole process of manufacturing furniture, i.e. at the entry point of timber into the factory. Thus for a week or two I hung around the four kilns, each having an area of about 13-14,000 cubic feet through which heated air was

passed through timber that had been stacked so that the individual planks did not touch each other. George Sumption, an ex-cabinet-maker who had learned most of what needed to be known about the process on a course in Princes Risborough in the Chilterns, was in charge of the operation of loading, drying and unloading the batches of timber. He already had an assistant (Bill, whose surname I do not remember) and so there was not much for me to do except to have the process explained to me and be shown how the levels of moisture in the timber were tested (I think it took up to a couple of weeks in the kilns for the timber to dry out sufficiently to be stable enough to work on in the factory).

After a couple of weeks of this it was decided that I would learn more by shadowing (i.e. trailing round after) Vicky Walker, the foreman of the bag presses[22]. With no actual responsibility it was all rather dull, and I said as much to Dad when he asked me. It was obvious to both of us that there was not going to be much to be gained by my simply hanging around various factory departments (where there would be even less for me to do than there had been at Supersuites). The plan for me was therefore revised: I would, it was thought, better get to know the business if I were to be with George Byatt. And so it was that, for the 18 months or so until I was called up for National Service, my job would be not much more than to trail around after him. As I knew very little I could hardly pose as his assistant; I felt at times a bit like his pet dog.

Generally speaking, the Beautility factory was well-planned with a well-designed layout, and in the early days of my induction into it, ran smoothly and efficiently most of the time. Nevertheless, following George around on his daily tours of inspection, and inevitably hearing the things that were *not* going according to plan, was not my idea of a stimulating time. It took a while even to get to know the machines or departments that were being spoken about. At times I found myself mentally switching off, and developing a technique of making out that I was listening when in fact I wasn't. This was easy enough to do unless and until someone asked me a question! But in the early days that didn't often happen.

From time to time I would be asked to show visitors around the factory. This was actually something I enjoyed doing, and it gradually began to dawn on me that I liked showing and explaining the basic techniques of furniture manufacturing more than I did hearing about (mostly) minor problems of administration. Though I would not have phrased it in that way at the time,

---

[22] In these machines a flexible rubber sheet (or "bag") was forced by compressed air around the piece of plywood on which the requisite veneer had been laid. It was thus possible to create rounded veneered edges or to veneer uneven shapes.

I began to recognise that such talents as I had lay in presentation and explanation rather than in overseeing technical processes.

Another major element in George's work was trade union negotiation. Shortly before I arrived at Beautility there had been a minor revolution in the factory. For some time the management had enjoyed particularly good relations with the factory union representatives. In fact they had been too good, and indeed George had been warned by one of his senior foremen, Jim Oblein, that there was a perception amongst some on the factory floor that the union officials were "eating out of the hand" of management. Trouble was brewing. Sure enough, the union members at a general meeting voted the incumbent chairman and secretary out of office and elected a new pair of officials whose stated aim was to make their presence felt.

Comparative harmony gave way to regular confrontation. Almost daily there were issues raised as to unfairness, as the management were accused of overriding the interests of the workers ("taking diabolical liberties" was a favourite cliché phrase) and more and more of George's time (and hence mine) was spent in investigating and arguing the matters out. Occasionally, as had been the case at Supersuites, there were minor unofficial strikes.

I have never enjoyed arguing (I always thought that one of the last things I could have been good at was being a politician) and did not relish these confrontations even though I was not at that time myself responsible for putting the management's case. Mostly I was of the view that the issues raised were try-ons.

An aspect of the procedure that was particularly resented by the union was time and motion study, by which it could be worked out how long it should take to do a given piece of work and hence what the piece-work rate for the job should be. The study was undertaken by John Sumner, the company's officer trained in the skill, or his assistant. Usually the individual operative being studied in this way was all too obviously dragging the process out so that the time thus recorded would be longer than it really took to do the work, and more often than not disputes with the union turned on these kinds of tiresome "times-on-jobs" issues.

There was a dispute resolution procedure worked out between NUFTO and the Furniture Trade Association (the employers' representatives), that involved two formal stages once a dispute had been registered. I don't remember what the first of these was, but the final one was an appeal to a tribunal (known as a panel) consisting of one representative from the union, one from the employers and a supposedly neutral chairman. I was present during one such appeal on a time-on-job issue concerning upholstery. I don't remember the precise issues involved, nor even what the outcome was (it was probably, as they usually were, a decision that came somewhere between the two opposing sides), but what struck me was how weakly controlled the whole process before the panel was. And though it had not entered my head at the time that I might one day to go into the legal profession, I do recall thinking I could have both presented the case and cross-examined witnesses better than I saw being done.

Other tasks

Three particular tasks were assigned to me during this early period at Beautility in addition to the regular duties described. The first and most regular was attendance on Saturdays at the company's Oxford Street showroom[23]. It was a double shop site consisting of ground floor and basement that was somewhat misleadingly advertised in the London evening newspapers (in their "places to go" column) as "Beautility's permanent exhibition of furniture"[24]. In fact its object was, rather than merely to exhibit it, to try to sell the furniture, not directly to the public (that would have upset retail furniture customers) but by taking unconfirmed "orders" for furniture seen in the showroom and channelling the prospective customers through a retail shop near their home. But it was nevertheless for most purposes like a retail shop, and involved those of us working there in the inevitable long hours of comparative inactivity. For me, these hours were punctuated by tasks that I did not relish in trying to get "sales"; indeed, the whole experience seemed to be a chore that had to be got through.

Another one was the Earls Court Furniture Show. Once a year most furniture manufacturers exhibited their ranges during the fortnight of this event, which was open only to the trade for the first two or three days and thereafter to the public. It was a chance for all manufacturers to show off their latest designs and to see what their competitors were offering, and was naturally a gathering time for all the Beautility salesmen, or "reps" (representatives) from the various areas of the country and a chance for them to meet with the top management and with each other. It was also where Cyril Montrose, the Sales Manager, was most obviously in his element, as most of the bigger customers (and many of the smaller ones) came to the Show. Back-slapping

---

[23] This must have been for half days during the rugby season, as I was playing for the Old Millhillians at that time and games were on Saturday afternoons.

[24] Some people took that literally and were surprised, sometimes annoyed, by discovering the true purpose of the showroom. Today such advertising would probably be investigated by the Advertising Standards Authority (a statutory body that did not come into existence until 1962) and effectively banned.

heartiness and flattery, laid on in the cases of bigger customers by Cyril with a metaphorical trowel, were the order of the day.

Cyril, whose surname had originally also been Rosenberg, though a very good salesman, was one of those people whom Dad referred to as having "only half a brain" (meaning mainly that he did not always agree with Dad or do the things that Dad considered he should do). From a middle class family he had served in the army as a captain or major during the War (for a time, I believe, he had continued to use his army rank as a civilian[25], although not by the time I knew him). Though certainly not a man of grand intellect, he was easy to be with and established the necessary good relationships with good customers. On one occasion I accompanied him for a couple of days to Newcastle (I cannot remember why) and over dinner at our hotel one evening, obviously thinking he needed to give me advice he prefaced his remarks with "I don't know if you have had sexual experience with a woman. I know at your age I had." At that stage I hadn't, but said nothing; it was anyway a statement rather than a question. Unfortunately I have no recollection of what the advice was.

At the Furniture Show, as at the Oxford Street showroom, I passed the time as best I could, listening to the salesmen's seemingly interminable chatter (the telling of jokes featured largely in this) and when required myself attempting to play the part of salesman. At least at Earls Court there were more people around and some of the exhibits were, for a day or two at least, worth looking at. But I had quickly discovered that selling was definitely not what I wanted to do or what I was even remotely good at. Was there anything at all, I often wondered, relevant to the furniture business, apart perhaps from making up pallets for cabinet-makers, that I *was* any good at?

The third task, in complete contrast to those that required efforts at salesmanship, was to assist in veneer buying. Veneers are the thin slices of wood applied to plywood (and later to chipboard) to give the effect of solid wood; they were of both interior and exterior quality. While interior veneers, which did not require any particular wood-grain pattern, and exterior veneers for the sides (or "ends" as they were termed in the trade) were bought in quantity from dealers in London, those required for the fronts of wardrobes and the fronts and tops of dressing tables, sideboards and dining tables needed to be attractively grained. They were considerably more expensive and, especially in the case of walnut, needed careful selection.

---

[25] This was permitted, and was much more common in the post-war years than afterwards.

The manufacture of walnut veneers at the time was done mainly in France and Dad went two or three times a year to Paris with an English plywood and veneer dealer, Lew Hill (actually a second or third cousin of Mother's), direct to the manufacturers in and around that city. Lew (who though only a few years younger than Dad was another of those referred to by him as "a nice boy") had been useful in introducing Dad to the relevant veneer manufacturers. An ex-rugby playing graduate of City of London School he spoke French (albeit with a rather strong English accent), which Dad did not. Nonetheless, after a time Dad did not see why he needed to pay Lew's middleman's profit and came to some sort of arrangement with him, especially as he now had me to interpret with those manufacturers (actually a minority) who did not speak English.

So it was that I began to accompany Dad in regular visits to Paris. In those pre-jet aircraft days the flight was by Vickers Viscount landing at Le Bourget airport, and we invariably stayed at the Hotel California in the Rue de Berry just off the Champs Elysées[26]. There were always a number of veneer manufacturers to visit, and on each occasion Dad (who seemed thoroughly to enjoy the process) would go through his buying routine examining every individual "flitch" or bundle of veneers (of which there could be several hundred) making up the consignment or "parcel" on offer. In doing so he would gleefully throw out any substandard ones (there were a percentage of these – he called them "slingers" – in every parcel) before beating down the price. My job was to observe the proceedings and then to mark up each individual bundle with consecutive chalk numbers so that we could be sure that what was eventually delivered was exactly what we had bought.[27]

The walnut veneer industry was dominated by *Léon Groscot et Cie* of Paris. The eponymous owner was a dynamic, rather ugly little gnome of a man who wore spectacles and had huge hands and stubby fingers that he jabbed in the air when making a point. His surname had originally been Grosskopf, or "big head" in German, so his change of name was understandable[28]. Léon, who spoke good English, drove a large flashy American car, a beige Ford Edsel with press-button gears set in the steering wheel of a kind that I had

---

[26] On one of those early occasions I got to Heathrow with Dad only to discover (to his intense and unsurprising annoyance) that I had forgotten my passport. I had to go back home to get it and catch a later flight. The Hotel California was still there in 2014, although unrecognisable inside as the place I remembered from 50 years and more previously.
[27] That was the theory at least. I remember on one occasion later when a query arose at the factory being embarrassed by not being certain whether or not the marks on one or two bundles were mine!
[28] His brother Sam, who had migrated to Canada, ran a similar business there that went under the name of Société Éléphant!

never seen before and never have since. The experience of being driven in it induced in both Dad and me concurrent feelings of amusement and slight embarrassment. For some reason from the outset Léon got my name wrong (he would always call me Rogers) and particularly later, when I first grew a moustache, he would with a twinkle in his eye liken me to the fictional, Paris-dwelling, caricature Englishman, Major Thompson.[29]

But Léon knew his business; even Dad called him the "King of Walnut". His factory contained huge vats in which logs were steamed before cutting to make them comparatively soft and the resulting veneers pliable. The large cutting machines were of two types. From wood without much grain pattern the veneers were produced on a huge lathe-type machine with a blade that sliced the revolving log into a continuous sheet that needed to be cut and the resulting sheets pressed to make them flat. Attractively grained wood needed however to be cut differently to get the best of the grain, and this was done on huge horizontal guillotines with blades that swung back and forth. Watching either process was mesmerising. The factory was run on a day to day basis by Léon's son André, an obviously capable young man slightly older than me with whom I got on well.

After we had bought a parcel of veneers, I would do my stint marking up with the help of the warehouse workers under their foreman Monsieur Delacasa. I probably would not have remembered his slightly unusual Spanish name (though he was French), but for the fact that Dad would *always* get it wrong. During all the years that we went there he would invariably refer to the man as *Alacazar* (with incorrect stress on the last syllable, to rhyme with bazaar), something that at first amused, but eventually mildly irritated me.

Sometimes at lunchtime, sometimes at the end of a day's work, there was a restaurant meal to look forward to as the guest of Léon Groscot or another veneer supplier. These restaurants tended to be very modest in appearance and were often to be found in out-of-the-way parts of suburbs, but those that we went to invariably offered food of (by UK standards of the time) exceptional quality. The problem was that Dad, though he professed otherwise, did not really appreciate good cooking. He tended to order the same things over and over again, and would look at me in amused bewilderment if I ordered a dish he personally wouldn't touch, all the more so if it were one I had never tried before or even heard of. Such conversation as there was at these meals tended to be about business, and the pity was

---

[29] On more than one occasion he remarked "Rogers is Major Thompson!" This character was the hero of books by the French author Pierre Daninos and a 1955 film *Les Carnets du Major Thompson* (the Diaries of Major Thompson).

that for me the food alone could not compensate for the lack of anyone to talk to at least some of the time about things that interested me.

After National Service

In the autumn of 1958 my call-up papers for National Service arrived and the process began for my two years in the army which formally began at the beginning of February 1959. This period is covered in chapter 4.

During part of a period the sick leave I had been given in the summer of 1960 after recovering from hepatitis contracted in Nigeria, I did spend some time back at Beautility, but I was recalled to the Queen's Surreys battalion at Colchester in September of that year and did not take up employment full time with the company again until February 1961.

It was either during the period of sick leave or shortly after my formal return the following year that I made my first visit to Germany. The sequence of events is hazy in my mind, but I believe that there was at the time an exploration of the possibility of some sort of joint venture between Beautility and the German furniture manufacturers Welle. There were meetings both in Germany (although Welle was based in Paderborn in Westfalen I think the initial meetings were held in Cologne during the time of the big international furniture fair there) and in London.[30]

No-one at Beautility spoke German, and neither Herr Welle the managing director nor his colleagues at these meetings spoke any English. I do not recollect how the initial meetings went, I may have needed to translate at times by use of my school German, but certainly I was so called on to translate at a dinner one evening not long afterwards held at the Savoy Hotel in London. As there were to be three English speakers and three German speakers round the table (not counting "interpreters"), I needed to get two school friends from the former modern language sixth form at Mill Hill to help me out. I remember doing my rather incompetent best, but feeling totally out of my depth in doing so. The excellence of the meal and surroundings did not compensate for this.

One thing that emerged from the first meeting in Germany was my first acquaintance with Werner Welle, the older son of the managing director. At the time Werner was still a student at the University of Karlsrühe, but he was already involved to some extent in the business and it was arranged that

---

[30] There were at the time many Jews and some others who, with memories of Nazi Germany still fresh, would not have bought German cars or other goods, let alone formed business partnerships with Germans. Quite obviously Dad was never such a person.

he would come to London soon afterwards (it must have been the late spring and early summer of 1961) for three months to learn English and to study the manufacturing process at Beautility.

Werner's visit opened my eyes to a number of things. Although arrangements were made for him to stay with the family of Alf Morley, one of the Beautility foremen (with whom he got on particularly well) rather than with us, I naturally saw a lot of him. Not only was he obviously someone with immense ability and intellect, it was quickly apparent that his grasp of the process and the technicalities of furniture manufacturing was considerably greater than mine. To be sure he had an odd lifestyle (at times he seemed to exist mainly on scotch whisky and German *Ernte 23* cigarettes), but it was through him that I began to see more clearly that I was attempting to establish myself in the wrong career.

As he had come to learn English, he was adamant that this was the only language we should speak together (end of that conversation!) and his ability to speak which had not been at all bad at the beginning became very good. Our discussions ranged far and wide and were always stimulating. I remember for example him telling me that agnosticism (in the sense of simply being unsure whether there was a God) was not in his view a tenable intellectual position. Although he would not have used the precise expression, he considered it was simply an abdication of thought: one either believed that God existed or did not exist (interestingly he was of the former view). Our talks also inevitably touched on Germany under the Nazis and what he called "these horrible things" that had happened. He thought it unfair that those in his age group, who were small children during those times, should by association be saddled with any part of the blame. I had always thought so too.

It was also partly because of Werner that, learning as I did from him more about university life, albeit in his case in Germany, I began to regret not having gone to one myself. He went back to Germany and eventually took over and greatly expanded the company his father had founded. We kept in intermittent but constant touch afterwards.

Another young man I had known since joining Beautility and with whom I became briefly associated, was Terry Hart. A year or two younger than I was, he had originally been a trainee with the design office but was obviously bright and energetic and by the time I knew him a trainee factory manager. Suddenly in 1962 it was decided that Terry and I should go to Brentwood to co-manage Beautility's bedroom furniture division (the successor to Supersuites, but with very few of its original employees). For a while the factory had been managed by Ted Jones, an old furniture hand who had been brought in as a temporary stop-gap a year or two previously, but who now wanted to retire. So it was that Terry and I were to take over from him.

Little remains in my memory of the direct process of management in which I became involved, and anyway Terry had a better understanding of the technical problems associated with manufacture than I did. But in the event the arrangement was fated to last for only a few months. It was apparent that the production was slowly running down and indeed the decision was made at board level not long afterwards to close down the Brentwood site. Beautility had made its name as one of the leading manufacturers of dining-room furniture and the recent association of its name with bedroom suites as well had simply not worked.

As to the actual closure of the Brentwood bedroom production, which must have been at the end of 1962 or beginning of 1963, what hit me suddenly and forcibly was the way in which the event was covered by the local press. In fact we had gone to some lengths to try to arrange for alternative employment for the factory workers (and indeed a number went straight to work for the Ford Motor Company at Dagenham who were recruiting at the time), but the local newspaper nevertheless ran banner headlines that went something like "Beautility Shutdown. Dozens thrown on the Dole" and went on to lambast the company. It was my first direct experience of how strongly, even maliciously, a different point of view could be expressed.

But in fact my memory of that time is dominated by quite different and unrelated events. The first was the Cuban Missile Crisis in October 1962 which had seen the United States and the Soviet Union in a head to head diplomatic clash of such magnitude that it is no exaggeration to say that it threatened to provoke a nuclear war. I remember standing on the platform of Brentwood railway station going home from work wondering how, at its height, people could go about their daily business when a possible nuclear strike was hanging over them.[31]

---

[31] Briefly what happened was that there had been an overthrow of the pro-United States Batista regime in Cuba by a left-wing coup led by Fidel Castro in 1959. Castro had reversed that country's previous strong links with the US, and developed links with the Soviet Union. An American trained and assisted Cuban anti-Castro invasion force was landed at the Bay of Pigs on Cuba's south coast in mid-April 1961, but was defeated soon after landing. In response to a perceived threat of further invasion by, or assisted by, the US, Castro arranged with the Soviet Union to have nuclear missile bases set up in Cuba; the nuclear missiles themselves were about to be delivered late in 1962 by Soviet ships. US President Kennedy warned Soviet Premier Khrushchev that the United States would not permit offensive weapons to be delivered to Cuba, set up a kind of blockade of Cuba (which because there

Moving from the grand scale of events to the petty, the second memory is of the event that led to my standing on the train station that October day. When I went to Nigeria during National Service, the Ford Prefect car that I had been given was passed to someone else. On my return I was allowed to choose what I thought of as an obviously "bosses' son's car", a two-seater semi-sports Sunbeam Alpine. This was just the sort of car that the police were looking out for, and I duly obliged them by allowing myself to get three convictions and three consequent endorsements on my licence. Ironically the first and second of these endorsements (for driving without due care and attention, and speeding, arising out of the same event[32]) came about as a result of driving not the Sunbeam but Cliff's borrowed Triumph Herald car. The third (for speeding in the Sunbeam) would automatically lead to a suspension of my driving licence for six months unless I could show undue hardship. I must have been persuasive in court for in the event I was disqualified for only three months.

I don't think I ever drove the Sunbeam again. In the meantime I was part owner of a second-hand Land-Rover that I had purchased together with friends to travel to Greece the year before. But the question of a car did not immediately arise, for in early February 1963 I set off on what was ostensibly a study tour of furniture production in the United States that was to last for nearly six months. The experience is recounted in chapter 6.

Whatever it had done for me, the American experience did not draw me any further into wanting to make my career in the furniture business. In fact the two and a half years or so following my return are at this distance in time, so far as Beautility is concerned, largely a blank.

What was obvious was that working with and under Dad was going to consist essentially of doing what I was told for, as with most people, he seemed unable to see in see me a person capable of making his own decisions, at least as regards anything he considered important to the business. On one occasion he walked in to the office I shared with George

---

was no formal state of war was called a "quarantine") and demanded that the Soviets return all offensive weapons to the Soviet Union and dismantle the missile bases already completed and under construction. Khrushchev at first called this an act of war, but (probably on a hint of what was to be offered) ordered the Soviet ships to turn back. Eventually sense and statesmanship prevailed and an agreement was reached under which the missile bases would be dismantled in return for a promise by the US that it would not directly or indirectly attack Cuba.

[32] Going home one evening at the junction of Colney Hatch Lane with Pages Lane, Muswell Hill, north London, I had cut inside someone who seemed to be taking an age in turning right. As I accelerated away I found myself tailed by a police car!

Byatt (who was not present) as I was in the course of an argument over factory matters with Harry Hearson, the union shop steward.[33] I don't remember any details of the conversation but shortly after entering Dad suddenly rounded on Hearson with "Don't you talk to my son like that!" It was for me one of those highly embarrassing moments when any authority I might have had was completely undermined.

I also found myself in the most profound disagreement with him over a situation that had slowly come about over the years. As the wages of the men on the factory floor had, owing to trade union pressure, increased, those of the foremen and charge-hands had not, to the extent that many of them were now actually earning less than those over whom they were in ostensible authority. These "staff" were key to the operation of the factory and many of them were disgruntled; indeed some of them left in disgust. They were not replaced, and anyway no-one on the factory floor would have accepted "promotion" to the job under the circumstances then existing, and so the pressure on those remaining became greater.

Staff wages were an overhead in the company profit and loss account, and it seemed to me that Dad's obsession with reducing overheads in the interests of end of year profit and loss accounts and his determination to do nothing about this particular problem was breeding a potential source of disloyalty and storing up trouble. But I was absolutely powerless to do anything about it; indeed if I raised the subject I was curtly dismissed or, if I persisted, shouted down. In the end the trade union threatened to take up the cause of these staff, but by that time I was almost on the point of leaving myself.

There is no doubt that he had unusual ability and drive, but it seemed to me that these qualities of Dad's were directed to short rather than long term gains, and that he was more interested in immediate rather than longer term profitability. In other words the interests of the shareholders (principally GUS) overrode the interests of the company in the wider sense of its continuing to be a leading producer of household furniture. Inevitably it was his approach that counted, and as tends to happen when people are in a dominant position of power in an organisation, his manner seemed to become more and more dictatorial, and there were increasing rows even with

---

[33] Formerly the union shop steward at Brentwood who had by now got himself employed, and elected into the same position, at the main Beautility factory. He was actually a wily but likeable man whose preferred way of getting things done was by diplomatic rather than confrontational means if at all possible.

George Byatt, the only other person in management who had in his view something more than half a brain.

I sensed too that the efficiency of the factory was gradually being reduced year by year, not least because of the depletion in the ranks of junior management staff already noted. More and more energy seemed to be spent in improvising production rather than in concentrating on well-planned production flow.[34]

If I had been fired with the idea that eventually I might take over, all of this might have been containable, but far from focussing my mind on central problems of factory production, I found myself wishing for the days to pass and spending more time than was necessary talking with people in small departments about things that interested me but which were not central to the running of the factory: the little printing shop run by George Stafford; the design office presided over by Hector "Mac" MacDonald and Bert Proud[35]; the general supply stores run by Johnny Oblein and Jimmy Bird; and the hardware stores supplying the cabinet makers and fitters run by Ron (whose surname I have forgotten).

I envied those who enjoyed working at their jobs, because frankly I didn't most of the time. I began seriously to question my assumption that my future was in Beautility. Although it is much easier to see this in retrospect than it was at the time, it was becoming apparent that my career had to lie outside the furniture business altogether. But as to what form it should take, and how I was to go about changing course, my mind was blank. It wasn't that I disliked the process of furniture manufacturing: I was and still am drawn to wood and wood products and have always enjoyed carpentry assignments of one sort or another. But for the various reasons noted my mind was simply not in tune with the business; indeed I even feared that part of my brain was beginning to atrophy from lack of use!

However, as will be seen in chapter 5, assistance with resolving these matters would soon be at hand.

---

[34] In fact Werner Welle, in his time at Beautility in 1961, had memorably and quite accurately described the factory production system as "one enormous improvisation". This only got worse as time progressed.

[35] Irene and my wedding invitations were to be produced by a combination of Mac MacDonald's calligraphy and George Stafford's printing.

Chapter 4

National Service

1. Induction — 105
2. Basic Training — 107
3. Mons Officer Cadet School — 115
4. Nigeria — 122
5. Back in England — 128

1. Induction

My induction into the army for two years conscripted service (known universally as National Service) was to land me in an environment that was not entirely new. I had after all spent my days at Mill Hill School in the Combined Cadet Force (always known as the CCF[1]). As the minority of the school who chose the alternative option of joining the Boy Scouts would have said, we "played soldiers". Whatever the truth of the matter, the army had nevertheless plenty of the unfamiliar to offer me.

I was actually keen to do National Service. My routines in Supersuites and Beautility had become humdrum and I think I must have thought on many an occasion that there had to be more to life than I then knew about. I had been officially "deferred" for call-up for a while under a government arrangement that allowed young men to complete a university undergraduate or professional training course before undertaking National Service. My deferment had been agreed because it had been intended by my father than I should undergo articles in a firm of chartered accountants (the name of Russell Tillett had been dangled in front of me on various occasions by him, as though it were some sort of Holy Grail). In the event, however, this didn't actually happen, and mention of Russell Tillett gradually subsided and ceased. I don't remember asking or discovering why; presumably Dad had on further reflection considered that I didn't really need to be an accountant to fulfil my part in his plans for me and my brother, namely that we should eventually take over the business. But I was, then and ever afterwards, very relieved about this change of plan as my interest in

---

[1] See note 10 in chapter 2 for the origins of this organisation, and pp. 68-9 for a brief description of the kinds of things we did.

accountancy was and remained throughout my life next to zero. There was thus nothing to delay my call-up any longer.

At some time in late 1958, aged 19½, I therefore reported for my "call-up" medical examination and interview at a building in Finchley on the east side of Regent's Park Road that has long since been demolished to give way to (actually quite attractive) blocks of flats. The medical didn't seem to throw up any problems (my one recollection of it is either the doctor or an orderly syringing my ears) and I passed on to the subsequent interview to have my suitability for particular branches of the armed forces determined. I had no particular interest in the Air Force or the Navy, particularly because in the former one could not as a national servicemen learn to fly, as the two years was not considered enough time both to do so and to give the Government a reasonable return on its money, and the latter took hardly any national servicemen anyway. And so it clearly had to be the Army. The idea, not entirely without foundation, that we prospective soldiers had conceived about the object of the interview was to find out where and in what sort of unit we would ideally like to serve and then make sure we landed up in something as far as possible from it, both in distance and in kind.

My time in the senior school CCF had been spent in the artillery section, when we lugged around and fiddled with a 25 pounder field gun owned by the school. Though I have no clear recollection of it, I must have airily swept aside any possibility of joining the Royal Artillery, and the same must have applied to the army's various specialist corps – Signals, Engineers, Electrical and Mechanical Engineers, Service, Education, etc. And even at that stage I was aware that the "cavalry" (by then of course mainly tanks and armoured cars) was officered by "chinless wonders" from the aristocracy, or at least the very rich, and was not for me. Besides, if one aspired (as I did) to becoming an officer, presumably one would need in the cavalry at least to be able to ride a horse, which I couldn't (the nearest I had got to it having been an occasional sedate walk on a superannuated seaside donkey). So it had to be the infantry.

I first asked whether I could do my time in a Scottish regiment, having always had a love of the bagpipes, unfashionable though that was among those brought up in England, and having been particularly impressed by soldiers at Stirling Castle on holiday in Scotland the year before. This request, from a young Jewish man from London with no conceivable personal connection with Scotland, was clearly an unusual one to say the least, and after the interviewing officer had got his head round what I had said he shuffled his papers and muttered something that was a polite rendering of "don't be so ridiculous".

I then fell back on my Plan B and asked if I could join the Parachute Regiment. This, coming hard on the heels of the previous request, must have had him wondering if I had spent too much time reading comics or watching war films; but he stolidly pointed out that one could be only *transferred* to that regiment from another branch of the army. That was extremely unlikely to happen in the case of a national serviceman with only two years to do altogether. However, if I had ambitions to a commission, the "Paras" would, if I qualified under their extremely rigorous selection process, take me as a minimum on a short service commission (i.e. three years from the date at which I achieved officer rank). That would have meant serving a minimum of three years and eight months altogether. I was keen, but not that keen.

And so, with my two first choices stymied, I came out with my third crackpot request, namely that I wanted to serve in the infantry but not (and I think I made quite a play on this) in the Middlesex Regiment. Naturally the interviewing officer asked why, as the regiment had a good reputation (it was known as the "Diehards") and with its depot at Mill Hill East it was the overwhelmingly obvious choice for a young man from north-west London. I said something to the effect that I found the barracks of that regiment depressing. They were only about a mile from Mill Hill School, and I had often visited them while in the CCF (mainly to shoot .303 rifles and Bren light machine guns on their firing range).

I find it difficult after all these years to recapture what was going through my mind at the time; possibly it was a notion that I wanted to be "different", though if pressed I might have found it hard to explain quite how. The by now bewildered interviewing officer made a note of my request. In view of where I was subsequently sent he must have said to himself "Right, I'll show him!"

It was thus that I was some weeks later ordered to report, on the 5th February 1959, to the depot of the East Surrey Regiment at Kingston-on-Thames.

2. Basic Training

This depot was a series of buildings first put up in the eighteenth century, that with an appropriate high security fence around it would have been most people's idea of a typical prison. The barrack rooms were ancient, and had minimal provision of bathroom and toilet facilities. It would not have been any sane person's choice of venue for undergoing what I was now about to undertake: National Service basic training.

The induction process for this, on that cold February morning, involved military clerks recording personal details (these clerking jobs were among the postings known at the time as "cushy numbers" and aspired to by those who were sufficiently literate and happy to avoid usual infantry routines). The one thing that sticks in my mind about the process was the question as to what religion we belonged. As most being inducted were (supposing they had given any thought to the matter) Church of England, the clerks each had a rubber "C of E" stamp for the purpose of indicating this on the form. Occasionally a Roman Catholic would present himself, at which the clerk would a little grumpily put down the stamp and insert the information by hand. My turn came. I answered the routine questions, and then:

"Religion?" asked the clerk, his rubber C of E stamp poised.
"Jewish" I said.

Putting his stamp down, pausing and looking blankly at me he said:

"What's that?"

We then had to go to the quartermaster's stores to be issued with our uniform and kit. The uniform of the day must have been about the ugliest the British Army has ever required its soldiers to wear. A hang-over from the Second World War, it was known as "battledress" and consisted of a heavy khaki tunic and trousers (the material of which seems in retrospect to have had a similar consistency to what was later used as carpet underlay). The accessories to this uniform were a khaki shirt and tie, a blue beret with a regimental cap-badge, a canvas belt fitted with buckles at the back (for fixing packs) and canvas gaiters (together known as "webbing") and black boots. We did not of course have to wear battledress all the time, this was reserved for parades and special occasions; most of the time was actually spent in lighter cotton khaki "fatigues".

Although it would probably have been denied by the Army at the time, the object of what was called "basic training" in National Service was seen by those of us who went through it as breaking us in. The process required immediate and unquestioning obedience to even the most asinine requirements. Among the more understandable of these requirements was the obligation to appear at all times in a smart "turnout", but this, taken to extremes as it was, required the process of what was known as "bull". Every piece of uniform and equipment had to be brought to a pitch of pressing or shine or (in the case of canvas belt and gaiters) immaculate coating with a chalky substance called by its brand name "Blanco". The spit and polish "bulling" of boots, the toecaps and heels of which had to shine so that you could see your face in them, the endless meticulous polishing of brass fittings and buttons, and the blancoing of webbing seemed to take up every spare minute of the day and night we had.

We were kept hard at it by the knowledge that any uniform kit worn on parade that was, in the opinion of the inspecting NCO or officer, substandard could lead to random summary punishment, or "jankers" as it was known in army slang. This took various forms of minor torture of which the favourite seemed to be to make the unfortunate individual run on the spot ("get your knees up!") with his 7lb (3 kilo) rifle held in outstretched arms above his head for ten minutes or so (just try it with a pole of equivalent weight!) or, for repeat offenders, being put on a charge to appear before the platoon officer, potentially leading to longer-lasting punishments involving anything from extra fatigue duties to confinement to barracks ("CB") over leave periods.

The army had its own way of dealing with persistent offenders against discipline, and it really took someone who was either a masochist or of sub-normal intelligence to fall into this category. I remember one individual from the regimental battalion (then, as normal, posted elsewhere) whose name was Button, who fell into this category. I never learned what his transgressions had been, but presumably he was a recalcitrant offender as he was seemingly in perpetual "close arrest", being marched at forced-march pace around the barracks to do a variety of menial tasks by the provost or "provo" sergeant and his staff (i.e. those forming the unit military police). The one stage higher (or lower, depending on your perspective) in punishments was to be sent to the army prison at Shepton Mallet in Somerset, a place spoken of by us in hushed tones of fearful respect.

In recent times "past reality" shows on television included a series in which young men were put through what purported to be the kind of basic training that we underwent in National Service. I remember one episode of this series in which one of the "soldiers" lost his temper over something quite trivial while waiting to go on parade and flung his rifle down. I think he was reprimanded. Such behaviour would in real life forty years before have been unthinkable, for the punishment for deliberate insubordination of that kind would almost automatically have involved probably at least a week's jankers of the kind seemingly being suffered on a continuous basis by the unfortunate Button.

The intake of which I was part consisted of about 60 recruits together known as the Training Company, and this in turn was equally divided into two platoons (we were known as "Dettingen" – the one I was assigned to – and

"Gibraltar" platoons, named after particular eighteenth century battles in which the regiment had distinguished itself) each under a second lieutenant, a sergeant and two corporals or lance-corporals. These latter, especially two of the corporals, were our particular tormentors and they got to work on us with relish. All sorts of transgressions were found by them to justify making life just that much more unpleasant, usually taking the form of extra drill or extra fatigue duties. One punishment, the supposed cause of which I have totally forgotten, involved making the whole platoon get out of bed late at night and run in bare feet and pyjamas (it was winter remember) three times round the barrack square.

The worst tormentor was one of the corporals in the other platoon, whose language and manner were particularly crude, and whose name rather appropriately was Oathen. This young man (who frightened the life out of us and seemed a veritable ogre) was however particularly gifted in one respect: he could play musical instruments, particularly the piano, well and entirely by ear (he could not read music at all). In fact the one and only time I featured as a member of a jazz band was at his instigation (probably his command): I played a double bass consisting of a tea chest with a hinged arm and string, in fact a quite effective homemade instrument.

We found it difficult to believe that, though the sergeants were regular soldiers, the junior officers and corporals were in fact all national servicemen like ourselves. We surmised that the corporals must have suffered at the hands of those like themselves in their own basic trainings and were determined to get their own back.

The intake was mainly a group of working class young men from the Dartford area in south eastern Greater London, actually in Kent[2]. Being thrown in amongst them was for me, with my middle class public school background, something of a culture shock. My exposure to working class men had hitherto been of a limited nature and confined to factory workers at Supersuites and Beautility. However, I did not, except in the cases of one or two individuals at the beginning, find it difficult to be accepted by them, and was soon known universally as "Rodge".

In fact there were, as far as I can remember, only four of us in the whole intake who had the education and ability that might have qualified us for a

---

[2] It had in fact originally been intended that all of us should be inducted not into the East Surrey Regiment at all, but into the Buffs (the East Kent Regiment). As Dartford happens to be in west Kent, which at the time had its own Royal West Kent Regiment, this made no more sense than what actually happened.

commission. One of these, Peter Barrett, a newly qualified architect with whom I became particularly friendly (we later went to the same intake at Mons Officer Cadet School and were commissioned on the same day) was later to be killed in a tragic motor car accident in Hong Kong. At the other end of the scale there was a young man of obviously low intelligence named Baker who could neither read nor write. This was a shock to me, for although I knew as a statistic that there were still such people, I had no expectation of actually meeting one on intimate terms. It was an even bigger shock that after a short time he was assigned to occupy the bed next to mine. It must have been hoped that some process of osmosis might leak intelligence from me to him. I occasionally had to read his letters to him, although nothing about their contents has stayed in my memory.

Our training lasted 12 weeks, rather longer I gather then most (9-10 weeks seemed to have been about the norm) and after the first three weeks or so the sadistic elements of our treatment seemed to abate. Or maybe it was simply that we had by this time been broken in, or had at least begun to learn how to avoid trouble. Our days consisted mostly of things physical: the gym, parade-ground drill, stripping and cleaning rifles and Bren guns, cross-country running in Richmond Park, and films on such things as personal hygiene, during which most of us fell asleep. The food provided in the "cook-house" was wholesome, and periodically one of the junior officers would wander around while we were eating and ask if there were any complaints. This, we thought, was merely a matter of form, as we didn't think that it would advance our status with our training NCOs if we did complain (and actually there was no need anyway).

One of the duties that each of us recruits had to undertake was a stint of two-hour "sentry duty" around the Guard-house at night. This was done on a rota basis, and fortunately there were sufficient of us recruits for this unpleasant experience not to have to come round too often. I remember the first time being woken at the appointed hour (I think my particular shift the first time was 2 – 4 am) and dressing to report at the guard house, where I was I think (does my memory play tricks?) issued with a pick-axe handle in addition to my unloaded rifle. This was fortunately an era well before the IRA started their attacks on British Army premises, for I could not to say the least have put up much of a defence against an armed attack. In fact the memory of sentry duty remains only of tiredness, boredom and sheer biting cold (it was February when my first turn came around) with the inevitable relief of being able to get back to the warmth of one's bed, albeit for only a short time, at the end of it.

After a few weeks of basic training, we were allowed to travel to and from the depot at weekends off by our own transport if we had it, and I was one of the few who actually had a car (the green Ford Prefect I had been given at Supersuites). This was a prize possession and occasionally fellow soldiers, even our own platoon NCOs, would sidle up to me and ask if they could borrow it. In fact, lending it was a good way of earning favours and I recall doing so to our platoon corporal on one particular occasion. It was duly returned, and I thought no more about it until one day shortly afterwards I was marched in before our platoon commander, a short fresh-faced young second lieutenant named Cox who looked about 16.

He asked me if I had lent my car to Corporal Hart a few days previously. As this was the incident just described I was clearly implicated, but in exactly what way I was at that stage not sure, and I did not want either to "grass" or indeed to potentially self-incriminate. I therefore muttered:

"You should ask Corporal Hart about it, Sir."
"I am asking you!"

I prevaricated further. The seeming 16 year old went a little pinker and almost barked at me:

"This is the Army, Rose, not a bloody public school! Did you or did you not lend your car to Corporal Hart on the day in question?"

Concerned that, if I were to continue in the same vein, the exchange might descend to ordering me to answer, yet at the same time fearing the worst for myself, I gave in and admitted it.

Only then was it revealed that I was not in fact myself being accused of conspiracy or indeed any misdemeanour, but that the corporal had apparently on the day in question used my car to go absent without leave. I don't know what punishment he was made to suffer, but I did go to some lengths to imply to him that the incriminating information had been dragged out of me, if not actually under torture then under extreme duress!

One centre-piece of training was the assault course, a military obstacle course that involved climbing and crawling. The obstacle most of us had difficulty with originally was the 10 metres or so of single rope strung between fixed points about 3 metres from the ground. One had to position one's legs so as to be able to propel oneself along it with one's arms, not so easy dressed in full kit and with a rifle. The other unpleasant obstacle was a horizontally laid drainpipe of just sufficient diameter to allow passage through it with a pack on one's back; while I never found this difficult some recruits were, at least initially, overcome with claustrophobia especially when as was often the case it was partly flooded with rainwater and had stinging nettles thrown into it by our sadistic training NCOs.

Another centre-piece was boxing, a sport in which we were all required to participate. Somewhat to my surprise (I had not boxed since prep-school) I found myself winning bouts in what eventually became an inter-platoon knock-out (*no pun intended*) competition. Having reached the final for my weight (light heavyweight) I discovered that this was scheduled to take place on the day near the end of training when we were to undertake what was called a "15 mile bash". The "bash" was a forced route march in full battle kit from where we had been bussed (just outside Dorking) back to barracks in Kingston, with a 10 minute rest every hour, and must have taken between four and five hours. At the end of it we had to complete the assault course and then fire off ten rounds on the firing range.

The boxing finals followed that same evening. I won my bout, which was stopped in the third round, and was duly awarded a cup, actually the only silver sports trophy I ever won (though I did later win copper and glass mugs at golf). I remember the roars of encouragement from my platoon, especially as my opponent (a Glaswegian Scot named Lindsay, who had somehow got into the mix of the intake) seemed to have a reputation as a "hard man", but nevertheless realised that near the end of the bout he was not really responding to my attack. I therefore dropped my guard and stepped back slightly in what seemed to me (and I hoped to the officers watching!) to be a gentlemanly gesture, but actually anyway not relishing the idea of punching someone for the sake of it. I later learned that my gesture was misunderstood by my platoon colleagues, for whom the concept of chivalry would have seemed preposterous (even if comprehensible), as one of tiredness! As in civilian life one would have to actively seek out facilities for this sport, I have in fact never boxed since.

All of us involved in the boxing finals seemed to take the physical exertions of the day more or less in our stride, and I remember thinking even at the time that we must have been at a peak of physical fitness which, unless we were to find ourselves in the Paras, the Marines or some such crack unit, was unlikely to be equalled, let alone surpassed, in our lives.

Of one thing I was, throughout basic training, sure: I intended after it to get out of the obvious grind, not to say mind-numbing routines, of "other rank" existence and become an officer. Besides, I fancied the kudos attached to the rank, even though a national serviceman could not hope to rise above the "one pip" lowest commissioned rank of second lieutenant. In order to achieve this there were three hurdles to overcome: firstly the Unit Selection Board (USB) at your depot had to assess you during basic training and recommend you to go, secondly, before the national War Office Selection Board (WOSB, universally called "Wosbee") for a three day assessment and formal sanction for officer training. Thirdly, if you passed that, you were sent to Officer Cadet School for four months' training, successful completion of which led to formal "passing out" as a Queen's Commissioned Officer.

Receiving the Best Recruit shield, Kingston Barracks, April 1959

All I can remember about the USB was that I was required to give a short lecture to the officers assessing us. One of them, a rather physically out of shape captain who had recently served in Malaya, gave me a week or so beforehand the not very original task of talking about recent events in that country. Anyway, my lecture sufficiently satisfied them that I would not embarrass the regiment if I were sent to WOSB, and some weeks later there I went.

At this stage it is relevant to record that each of us national serviceman, as indeed each regular soldier, was given an army number that needed to be indelibly imprinted in our brains, as it often had to be reeled off when formally identifying ourselves (e.g. on pay parades). Mine, I have over fifty years later not the slightest difficulty in recalling, was 23607169. The WOSB assessment comprised various tests of intelligence and leadership which seemed to be reasonably within my capabilities, and at the end we were required to attend an interview with the relevant assessment board. This involved marching in to the boardroom, stamping to attention in a corner of it where a small triangle of the carpet had been rolled back to allow our boots to make a suitably military kind of stamping sound, and shouting one's number, rank (we were all privates at this stage) and name, followed by SIR!

I duly marched in, stamped to attention and bellowed in my most military manner the required formula. A puzzled silence followed; one of the officers looked down at a sheet of paper and asked me to identify myself again. I repeated the rigmarole and realised as I did so that I was giving my number as 23607, without the last three digits. Finally I got out the correct "23607169 Private Rose, SIR!" I must have been nervous, though I didn't actually feel so just at that time, and I couldn't believe that I had made this idiotic mistake right at the end. I had to fight hard to keep it to the back of my mind as I answered the questions put to me. Mercifully, all turned out well, however, and I was passed for four months' training at the Officer Cadet School, Mons Barracks, Aldershot ("the home of the British Army"), Surrey.

3. Mons Officer Cadet School

Even though a commission had become my intended goal since induction into the army, and training to this end should logically have stood out for me more than the earlier months, my recollections of Mons are nothing like so clear as those for the first weeks of basic training.

There were at any given time four companies training in the Infantry Wing (this included artillery and the various Corps, but was distinguished from the Cavalry Wing located in a separate part of the School). These companies were known, with predictable army lack of originality as A, B, C and D, each one beginning its training about a month after the previous one. Those assigned to the first three of these were distinguished by the wearing of respectively red, white and blue lanyards, while, having run out of the colours of the national flag, those of us assigned, in June 1959, to "D Company" were required to wear a green one. We retained the uniform of the regiment or corps from which we had been posted, but to denote our new status to this we added a white plastic disc behind our cap badges, and white tabs attached to the collars of our battledress tunics.

In fact we had all come from a variety of different units of the army. My friend Peter Barrett (and, I seem to remember, one other cadet from our contemporary intake at the East Surreys named Le Mesurier) were assigned to different platoons of D Company, but within my own (known as 19 Platoon) were young men from various infantry regiments (Lancashire

Fusiliers, Duke of Wellington's, Suffolk and Queen's [West Surreys]) and Corps (Signals, REME, Ordinance, Education), as well as from the Royal Marines, the Royal Armoured Corps and the Military Police. We even had a couple of overseas cadets, one each from the Ordinance Corps in Malaya and the Royal Thai Police.

Certain conventions needed to be observed at Mons, largely owing to the fact that we were now officially trainee officers and thus, potentially at least, gentlemen. We were addressed by NCOs as "Sir", though that was often with the kind of intonation that seemed somewhere between indifference and contempt. The NCOs themselves, none of whom was below the rank of sergeant, had to be addressed by us as "Staff" (a designation normally reserved for staff sergeants, but used at Mons even if they did not have the crown above the stripes denoting this higher rank); or if warrant officers (company or regimental sergeant majors) by the usual "Sir". To save the potential tennis match of "Sir" when speaking with one of the latter group, they usually addressed us, if they knew us, as "Mr ..."

There was in fact only one Regimental Sergeant Major, a tall stout ramrod-backed Irish Guardsman of enormous presence named Lynch who put the fear of the devil into us. He ruled parades with a rod of iron, and anyone who moved a fraction of an inch on the parade ground when he was not supposed to would hear the dreaded "Take his name!" order to one of the company sergeant majors on parade as a prelude to summary punishment or a charge.

Actually the army changed the standard rifles issued to soldiers during my time at Mons, from the World War II Lee Enfield (with a hand operated bolt and a magazine that held 10 rounds) to the new semi-automatic Belgian Self Loading Rifle (or SLR) then being issued to all NATO forces. These new rifles were a definite improvement, as they could be fired without having to "re-cock" each time, but they were also of sufficiently different shape to necessitate the formation of a new parade ground drill. This involved the rifle being held in the right hand against the body rather than, as traditionally had been the case, at the "slope" on the left shoulder. And our bayonets, when fixed as they were required to be for parades, glinted an inch or two from our faces (but fortunately pointing away from them).

At some point before the changeover to the SLR we had been taken to a firing range and required to fire anti-tank grenades, not the kind one sees today in films and newsreels being fired from what look like drainpipes (though those "bazookas" certainly did exist) but from an attachment fitted to a rifle. For this operation, the rifle's sling had to be lengthened so that it would pass over the left shoulder and hang at the level of the right hip and the barrel of the rifle had to be grasped firmly with the left hand with the legs braced. We were instructed not to launch the grenade by pulling the trigger in the normal way with the index finger curled round it (for if one did that the rifle's backward kick from such a heavy projectile was said to be likely to break it) but to flick it with that finger in a sharp backward movement of the right hand. In fact I had heard about this somewhat notorious device before and was not relishing the idea of firing one. However, there was clearly no avoiding it; the best I could do would be to position myself at the back of the platoon as we formed up to march off to the firing point so that I would be one of the last up.

Duly formed up, we approached the firing point, where the remains of a tank faced us about 30 yards away. Possibly having anticipated that some of us would attempt to hide at the back, as indeed I had done, the NCO in charge of us ordered the platoon to wheel about so that effectively the back row became the front one. My position at the back left of the platoon thus now became that at the front right, the *very first* to be required to fire. Stepping forward as ordered, with my heart in my mouth, I fitted the grenade (a real one but with no explosive head) to my rifle and waited for the order to fire. As it came I braced myself, held my breath, shut my eyes and flicked the trigger as instructed. In a split second my fear of the resulting explosion and kick of the rifle was quickly overtaken by the mortification of seeing my grenade miss the very large (and not very far off) target, and by some distance! The NCO rolled his eyes and called the next man forward...

I remember being placed on a charge once at Mons, though I cannot remember what for (it was probably for being late for a parade). The procedure involved being quick-marched at about double the normal rate in before the Adjutant (at that time a certain Captain Tollemache, a Grenadier Guards officer of about 6ft 8ins in height) and marking time at the same hectic rate until ordered by the provost NCO to stand to attention ("prisoner, SHUN!"). As far as I can remember, my punishment was (along with one or two others, I think) an hour's extra drill in full kit with rifle "at the double". This was more of a penance than usual that year, as the summer was unusually cloudless and hot.

In fact the long, hot summer of 1959 made all physical exercise that much more tiring, and made it almost certain that we would sometimes fall asleep in lectures that were less than fascinating, and almost always if we were shown a film. There must have been a very busy army film unit for their products were shown to us on almost any subject, ranging from personal hygiene through field tactics to the atomic bomb. This meant, all in all, quite a bit of sleeping time. Another side-effect of the weather was a plethora of mosquitoes that summer, for which we were unprepared and which made night exercises mightily unpleasant at times.

In fact the giving of lectures was something that we ourselves, as trainee officers, were expected to be able to do to a reasonable standard, and various sessions were set aside for each of us in turn to lecture to all the others, including our platoon commander, Captain Jeffrey Howlett of the Parachute Regiment (I saw his picture in the paper many years later as a major- or lieutenant-general) and receive feedback from them. The talk had to be for 15 minutes on any subject we liked.

Many of these lectures were frankly more boring than the official lecturers on an off day, and I realised, probably for the first time, that most people in most walks of life seem to have little idea about their purpose when talking in a structured way to others, which must surely be first and foremost to enrol them into the subject matter. I had recently read an article in the National Geographic Magazine on bees, and I decided that I would lecture on this (in the circumstances) slightly unusual subject. My talk was well received, although I remember being unable to answer a question at the end "Do bees sleep?" And feedback was given to the effect that I tended to cause a slight distraction by constantly shifting about on my feet (clad then of course in heavy army boots on a wooden floor) as I did so. Indeed I am at times aware that I still do this today. The only other lecture I can remember, because it was interesting and well presented, was by one of our number named Thomas Sherry, on Freud's concept of the mind. Most of the others complained that it was "too technical" (by which they meant boring). It was neither. Sherry was from, and on commission returned to, the Royal Army Education Corps which must have been glad to have him.

However, the "prize" to aspire to at Mons was to be the one cadet to be appointed, near the end of the training course, as the platoon Under-Officer. Eventually one of these was chosen to be the one Senior Under-Officer, who would be presented with the Mons equivalent of the Sandhurst "Sword of Honour" at the passing out parade, and another "Junior" UO appointed in his place.

I did not achieve either category of this rank, but I did have a fleeting moment of glory, when I was appointed Parade Commander for the passing out parade of what must have been B Company (two companies ahead of us). The holder of this temporary post was selected from those who were not passing out, as the system was that *all* the training companies paraded at all passing out parades. The Parade Commander's duties included getting formal permission from the general who had inspected the passing out company to march the rest of the School off parade, and then, in a mighty voice, giving the necessary orders. What I had done to impress the authorities of my parade ground talents I don't remember. It was however unfortunate that two days before the parade C Company appointed its Under Officers, and the decision was taken that one of them had therefore to be given the honour that had *almost* been bestowed on me.

Having told my father that I was going to be the Parade Commander, he, never one to miss a chance to embellish a story, and probably having anyway misunderstood the system, somehow got the idea that I was to be presented with the Sword of Honour. To my intense embarrassment, and even though I had not even undertaken the more mundane role originally assigned to me, he passed this story around accordingly, and it came back to haunt me for some time afterwards.

Towards the end of the training we were taken to Battle Camp for field exercises lasting a week deep in the Brecon Beacons in Wales. I remember one night exercise to be undertaken there by the Company in which I was assigned to the leading 3 ton truck, given an ordinance survey map and instructed to guide the convoy to the starting point. Map-reading in the dark is difficult at the best of times, but where there is no moon and virtually no visible landmarks it is a whole lot more so. Fortunately the lance corporal driving the vehicle had done this trip a number of times before and knew the way we had to go. We pretended that I had duly instructed him how to get us there.

Soon afterwards we were all involved in another exercise that for some reason involved sliding downhill on our bottoms for part of the way. As we were resting afterwards, a colleague noticed something of which I had been up to that point unaware: that my fatigue trousers were covered in blood. It transpired that in sliding downhill I had passed over a piece of jagged glass that had given me a deep cut in the left buttock. This required stitches (it's a slightly undignified procedure, having stitches inserted in your bum) and effectively put me out of action not only for the remainder of the Battle Camp, but for some days back at Mons too, as I could not bend or exert myself in any way that might reopen the wound. It was all a great inconvenience as it meant I was unable to take part in some of the end of course festivities.

Our status as (potential) officers and gentlemen was confirmed by the rules for the civilian dress we were required to wear when on leave. This included not only a jacket and tie, to be expected at that time, but also a hat, which was not. Hats as required "about town" items of apparel for men were fast disappearing from contemporary fashion, especially amongst the young, and I myself had never worn one except a school cap up to the age of 12 as part of the required prep school uniform. I bought myself what was termed a "Pork Pie" (a hat that had a round undimpled crown) from Dunn's, the off-the-peg standard hatters of the day. It was greenish in colour; I do not remember wearing it after Mons days.

One of the places we regularly went when off duty, dressed of course in the regulation civilian dress with hat, was the Frensham Ponds Hotel near Farnham. This was a "free house" i.e. not tied to one of the big breweries as the majority of pubs were and therefore able to sell whatever beer it chose. In general, the beer of choice for young middle class men in those days was "bitter", normally sold on draught in measures of a pint or a half pint at room temperature; in fact even most other kinds of beer (with the one exception of Guinness, which I never liked in the slightest), let alone other alcoholic drinks, tended to be looked down on. Frensham Ponds had five different bitter kegs from which to choose and it became a ritual for many of my colleagues to work steadily through a pint of each of the five of them in an evening (some could manage more). Now, in spite of some effort on my part in my late youth to acquire the taste I have never particularly liked bitter, or indeed room temperature beer of any sort, and apart from that I found it anyway next to impossible to get the sheer quantity of liquid involved inside me. I therefore performed somewhat feebly by the standards of the day as it was as much as I could do to get down five *half-pints* of the stuff. And in fact I soon made excuses not to go.

Another strong, if insignificant, memory of Mons days is a bizarre one. There were some food and drink dispensing machines near to the mess hall. On one occasion I had inserted the required money into the machine for a packet of Maltesers or something similar. When I had inserted the required money and pressed the button to release the little trap-door which dropped the packet into the chute, for some reason all of the trap-doors dropped at the same time, filling the chute with the dozen or so packets loaded into the machine. It was the nearest I ever came to winning the jackpot on a one-armed bandit.

I mentioned that my recollections of Mons were not as clear as I would wish, and aids that I might have had in the form of photographs are minimal. Though I shot a whole 36 exposure film during the first three months or so of my time there, I found when I came to remove it for processing that the teeth of the sprocket wheel in the winding mechanism of my 35^{mm} Kodak Retinette camera had, instead of engaging in the holes in the film and advancing it, in fact broken those holes right at the beginning. Thus, when I thought I had been winding on after each shot I had actually not moved the film on at all, and to my mortification after being returned from processing it was a complete blank. I did load another one rather late in the day, and there are a few shots of a group of us at Battle Camp, playing rugby and hockey, and at the Passing-Out Parade, but most of those I had taken were sadly destined never to be.

At the time the "loss" of these photographs mattered a lot, for as a younger man I was very much concerned, some might even say obsessed, with photographing aspects of life I thought interesting, and was careful to meticulously file my slides or mount my prints in albums. And in fact there were to be two further incidents leading to loss of treasured photographs when, each time, my camera was stolen with unprocessed film in it[3]. I wonder at myself that in later life I have almost lost interest both in taking photos and mounting them (I decided to end the taking of slides in January 2010 when my camera jammed while taking pictures on a houseboat on the lake at Kumarakom in Kerala, Southern India).

Mention of photography has relevance here, as during the latter part of the Mons course each of us needed to decide whether, after commission, we wanted to be posted back to our own regiment or Corps or to be transferred or seconded to another unit. Overseas postings, in what my father always referred to as "the outposts of the Empire" were still widely available, for independence was still a few years away for most of the Commonwealth, and I applied to be seconded to the King's African Rifles (as the umbrella designation for the colonial regiments in East and Central Africa was still known), hoping for a posting to Kenya, then only just emerging from the Mau Mau emergency. However, there were no vacancies just at that time in the KAR; but there were postings available in the glamorous sounding Royal West African Frontier Force (which similarly covered Nigeria, Sierra Leone and the Gambia – Ghana having already achieved independence in 1957). I applied for one, and was in due course told I had been successful and would be sent to Nigeria. In speaking to a training officer at Mons who had had experience of that country he said, amongst many other things, "don't forget to take your camera".

---

[3] This happened once on Diani Beach in Kenya, when I had left my camera unattended for a minute or two at the edge of the sand, and once three or four years later in 1986 in Yosemite Park, California, where I had left my camera bag with the camera in it on a viewpoint wall. The silliness was compounded by the fact that I actually saw someone pick it up, thinking as I saw this how funny it was that someone had the same sort of canvas bag that I had.

Thus it was that, after commission in early October 1959 and a few days leave, I left England to report to the RWAFF, in particular the Recce Squadron of the Queen's Own Nigeria Regiment, based at Kaduna, Northern Nigeria.

2nd Lieutenant, Queen's Surreys, October 1959

4. Nigeria

Ever since my schooldays I had been fascinated by Africa. I recalled in chapter 2 how I had spent hours looking through nineteenth century books by famous explorers in the Mill Hill School library: *How I Found Livingstone* by H M Stanley and others. I was captivated (as I still am) by the painstaking line drawings used at the time to illustrate these books. I was also captivated by a television series at about that time called *The Search for the Nile*, although my memory may be playing tricks with me as Alan Moorehead's book of that title was not published until the following year. Here at last was my chance to go.

The flight to Nigeria in those days took rather longer than today as it was before the time that jet planes had come into normal service. Firstly one had to report to the BOAC terminal at Heathrow, at that time a temporary-looking building (I think only Terminal 1 and the Queen's Building – many years later to become Terminal 2 – had been completed). My flight was in a Britannia propeller aircraft which flew via Tripoli in Libya to Kano, northern Nigeria, from where I would need to fly by local aircraft to Kaduna. I forget how long the international flight took, but it must have been around 15 or 16 hours. It was the first time I had travelled outside Europe and I remember being struck by the seemingly exotic sight of an Arab seated on a camel at Tripoli airport. The onward flight from Kano to Kaduna was in a DC3, an old workhorse of an aeroplane examples of which I believe were still in service in parts of the world in the early twenty-first century. I remember the plane had me white-knuckled with anxiety as it shuddered violently when the engines revved for take-off, almost as if it were flapping its wings, but it finally landed without incident on the grass strip that was Kaduna Airport.

My introduction into this new world of the Recce Squadron was actually something of an anti-climax. I was met at the airport by a wiry little African sergeant-major who, it transpired, was one of the party of skeleton staff left behind at that particular time at headquarters (Kalapanzin Barracks, Kaduna) while most of the rest of the Squadron was off in the British Northern Cameroons to the far north west of colonial Nigeria.

This was territory that had originally formed part of the much larger Kamerun, a German colony situated just to the east and south of the great bulge that is the western part of the African continent, that after the First World War was broken up and ceded as League of Nations mandates to France (the larger southern part) and Britain (two smaller parts to the north that became known as British Northern and Southern Cameroons respectively). These were considered not to be viable as either two independent states, or even one, and the British Government had organised plebiscites in both to determine whether at independence (due in just under a year's time) their peoples wanted to join Nigeria or Cameroon.[4] It had been the Recce Squadron's task to assist with the conducting of the plebiscite and to try to make sure that no violence broke out during the process (it didn't).

---

[4] In the event the voting went predictably on tribal lines, the Northern Cameroons electing to join Nigeria and the Southern to join Cameroon. This latter territory formed an English speaking enclave in the independent Cameroon that continued to administer English law, and was a major factor in the country being admitted as a member of the Commonwealth in 1995.

So my first week or so in Kaduna was spent doing almost nothing, rather bored in the heat and the dust, until in great style, the various troops of the Recce Squadron began gradually to return.

The unit was actually formed as a modern cavalry one (hence the term "squadron" rather than battalion, itself divided into four "troops" rather than platoons). The idea was that it should eventually be equipped with light armoured cars, but all that could be managed at that time (and for the foreseeable future) was a fleet of Land Rovers each mounting a Bren gun. Having on induction into the army avoided the cavalry because of its reputation in the British Army of being officered by the rich, it was ironic that here was I posted into what might have been thought of as a poor man's equivalent, the colonial cavalry!

Its Commanding Officer was a British major, Bob Scott, and its other officers were a second in command (Chris Manning-Press, a British cavalry captain), a transport officer, Peter Rodgers, and four troop commanders including myself. One of these, Alex Madiebo, was one of the early batch of Nigerians to be awarded a Queen's Commission, while another, Guy Crossman, a regular officer on a short-service commission was from a family of leading brewers at that time (Mann, Crossman & Paulin). The fourth, a national service second lieutenant like myself whose name I think was Tony (though I can't remember his surname), was a bumptious, immature and irritating young man who quickly got on my nerves and whose company I found I needed to avoid as far as possible.

I enjoyed what to me were, at least at first, the exotic surroundings, but some of this soon palled as it became obvious that when the unit was in base there was not enough to do. I had to rack my brains trying to think of training programmes for my troop to fill in the time. One of the first things I found was that the privates (or "troopers") were constantly coming to my quarters wanting to borrow money, having spent their pay quickly each month. As I was a new European officer, I was obviously seen as a potential soft touch, but I soon got tired of "helping out" irresponsible soldiers, and was anyway discouraged from doing so by my fellow Nigerian officer. The other reason soldiers occasionally came to me was to tell me that they were "sick for here" pointing at their groins (VD) and needed to see the Medical Officer based at the hospital.

The officer's mess was a thatched single storey building with minimal facilities except for a comprehensive military library that had been bequeathed to it by a former commanding officer. It had a record player (in those days called a gramophone) and, so far as I can remember, only two LP records, which we tended to play often. One was Moura Lympany playing Grieg's piano concerto (and to this day I cannot hear the piece, especially that recording, without drifting in my mind back to Kaduna) and the other, by contrast, was Bob Crosby and his Bobcats playing swing tunes. The track we especially liked from this was called "The Big Crash from China"; it was over forty years before I managed to get hold of another recording of this piece, which I had by then almost totally forgotten. However, Guy, being from a rich family, had the almost unheard of luxury of his own gramophone in his room, and it was through him that I was first properly introduced to Bach and Vivaldi.

D Troop, Recce Squadron, Queen's Own Nigeria Regiment, early 1960

As the newest, and therefore the most junior, second lieutenant in the mess I was immediately assigned to the chore that was traditionally that person's lot, namely that of Mess Officer. That involved responsibility for the running of the Officers' Mess and, amongst other things, keeping a check on the bar and food stocks. This in turn meant a good deal of association with the mess corporal. All went well for a while until quite suddenly I found that this man was behaving in a strange way towards me, refusing to speak to me except in sulky monosyllables or to look at me while doing so. I was baffled as to the reason for this, and as it was making such limited tasks as I had around the mess difficult to say the least, I reported the matter after a few days to the Commanding Officer, who summoned us both to his office to get to the bottom of the matter.

What emerged was bizarre, and at the time literally beyond my belief. It turned out that he had seen me talking to Alex Madiebo, my fellow troop commander, some days before and that during the conversation I had pointed at him (i.e. the corporal, who must have been somewhere in the vicinity at the time – I hadn't even seen him) in a way that obviously indicated to him that I had put a spell or curse on him! After he had explained my wizardry, and I had recovered from my disbelief, the CO told him that no-one had put a spell on him and that he should resume working with me. He did so, somewhat warily, and I was never sure that he was entirely convinced.

The biggest event of my all too short time in Nigeria was a journey that the squadron had to make to Katsina in the far north and Sokoto (pronounced soko-*too*) in the far north-west. The purposes of the exercise was to show the flag and help to keep the peace in the run-up to Nigerian independence set for October the following year. The whole of northern Nigeria was, as it remains, predominantly Muslim, and the journey was full of what was for me the newly exotic. The towns seemed to be relics of the Middle-Ages, with crenulated mud walls to most of the buildings, and from time to time we would come across, for example, small parties of Tuaregs on their camels, with faces veiled against the sand and dust. These desert people, whose women I never saw, lived in the far reaches of the Sahara and came to northern Nigeria presumably to trade.

The problem was that the journey had to be made across country on roads that were never very solid and tended to wash away altogether in the rainy seasons. One that we were following disappeared at one point into a moderate sized, albeit shallow, river, and as there was no obvious way round without making a 50 mile or so detour the task was to get my troop and its vehicles, including a 3 ton lorry, down the river bank and across to the other side. I don't remember the details, but we managed to ford the river and eventually to reach our destination. The journey had been far more difficult than anyone had expected and we had seriously wondered at the time if we would be able to get to our destination. The CO came round that evening as we had established our camp to congratulate me. Though I was of course pleased by this acknowledgement, I remember thinking that it was at least as much the tenacity and expertise of my troop sergeant that had got us through.

Much smaller things come to mind from that time. At one point early on in Nigeria we were out on an exercise and just about to have a break for lunch. I had a sandwich that had been prepared for me and to which I was looking forward to eating for lunch. I put it on the ground while I attended for a minute or two to something in the way of administration, and when I returned I found that the sandwich had all but disappeared under the hundreds of ants that were now busy consuming it! I had learned my first lesson about wildlife in the tropics: forget about ants (and termites) to your sorrow.

The other thing I remember was shooting with a .22 rifle (i.e. a small bore weapon I had used previously only on miniature firing ranges) issued to me in Nigeria with a small amount of ammunition for no discernible reason. I still cringe to think that I shot a few doves, even on one occasion a small owl, and a few lizards by way of "sport". Though the birds could have been thought of as food (I seem to remember giving them to the soldiers who plucked, cooked and ate them) there was no justification whatever for shooting lizards. Though I am not averse to killing vermin (i.e. animal life that constitutes a health hazard or a nuisance, and amongst which I later included speckled mousebirds in Africa and woodpigeons in England) or within reason for food, I very much dislike the idea of killing anything for its own sake.

Early in 1960 I bought a second-hand car, a black Opel Rekord four-door saloon I remember, probably from an officer in another unit who was leaving. This was delivered to the barracks, but just at the time we were about to go out on an exercise away from base, so that I could not drive it immediately. In the event I never did.

At some point around that time I gradually became aware that I had lost my appetite. It seemed strange that I, who had always loved food, could not face eating. Things came to a head a short time later during the exercise referred to above, when I found that I hadn't the energy to move. I also suddenly noticed that my pee was very dark. The Commanding Officer, who was clearly irritated by the situation rather petulantly sent me back to report to the base hospital, where the doctor examining me immediately diagnosed hepatitis and had me admitted straight away.

What followed was an extended period in hospital on (when I managed to eat at all) a fat free diet. Hospital food is rarely better than mildly disagreeable, but the imposed fat free element ensured that it was all but inedible. There was nothing to do but read from a poor selection of books in the hospital "library" and attempt to listen to rather poor reception on the radio of the BBC World Service.

One of the things one necessarily has to undergo when in hospital with hepatitis is to have one's blood constantly checked, and this involved a large sample being taken. Firstly a piece of rubber hose was tied around my arm (to make the veins swell) and then the needle was inserted to draw of the necessary quantity of blood. The African orderlies charged with the duty of taking a sample of blood from me were often incompetent: they would for example tie the hose so tight that it felt like my arm was being severed, and on one occasion, just as the syringe had filled with blood, the needle came off the body and its contents emptied over me and the bed.

All of this and the loneliness made inevitable by the situation gave cause for mild depression on my part, especially when I was told after a number of weeks that the authorities had decided to send me back to the UK to recover and complete my Service. I was released from hospital in Kaduna just beforehand so as to be able to pack up my things and arrange for somebody to sell my car, and just had time to pose for a photograph (looking decidedly thin and pale) with my troop.

5. Back in England

Queen Alexandra's Royal Military Hospital lay on the Thames at Millbank just next to and north of the Tate Gallery (now known as the Tate Britain – the river runs in an approximately south to north direction at this point), but it is there no longer. The two of its original four south-facing wings nearest the river have long since been demolished to give way to the Clore Gallery of the Tate, and the remaining two form part of its administration block. I spent nearly two months there recovering and in the charge of a large, bluff and rather masculine Queen Alexandra's Royal Army Nursing Corps ward sister and her staff, and a Royal Army Medical Corps colonel whose face resembled that of a moustached bloodhound. The sister ensured that the ward ran like clockwork, while the medical care extended to me by the doctor consisted merely of ensuring that my disgusting fat (and alcohol) free diet continued. In fact he gave me the impression that he probably didn't know much about what he was doing or, if he did, didn't much care. A bedside manner was something that had clearly never crossed his mind to cultivate.

"Disgusting colour!" roared the sister in a deep alto voice, referring to my jaundiced complexion on first meeting me, while handing me some temporary hospital pyjamas and waving me to the changing room and my allocated bed. She later told me she thought I was an Indian officer.

The ward (which was for officers) was about thirty yards long and consisted of some four dozen beds arranged in groups of four. Naturally there was a good deal of coming and going, and officers from all walks of life passed through. The man in the bed immediately across the corridor from me most of the time was a cavalry captain who owned a string of polo ponies. He tended to pronounce upon things as though from on high when giving an opinion on the world or its affairs, or indeed anything, and was a bit of a joke to most of us lesser mortals. However, he announced himself as a "Today" fan (referring to the BBC morning radio programme of that name that had recently come into existence) and disappeared into his headphones for as long as this was broadcast each day.

A number of the inmates were sadly there to die of incurable cancer of one sort or another. I remember the shock of having seen an apparently fit young officer, probably not much older than I, arrive one day, apparently with leukaemia, and then of seeing the curtains drawn round his bed a few days later as they removed his body. At the other end of that particular scale there was a major who was slowly and surely wasting away, being kept on pain-killing drugs until his time came too. Another such patient down the ward from me who was probably unable to control his natural bodily functions, occasionally let out a fart that was both very long and loud. A plummy voice from the bed next to mine would mutter "I bet that feels better".

As my health improved I began to want to eat more and found a willing orderly who would help supplement my prescribed diet with cake and biscuits at tea time. In fact I discovered to my horror that the first time I was given leave to get dressed and go for a walk outside the hospital grounds I could barely do up my trousers. Apart from overeating, I first took up another unhealthy habit: smoking. In those days cigarettes were smoked widely; not only did most people not think much about the consequences of smoking (which was anyway only just beginning to be associated with lung cancer), but cigarettes were offered round in a social group almost as a matter of course, and it required a determined effort to refuse them. In contrast to what had been the case in Kaduna, there was plenty going on around me, and of course I could get visits from the family and friends.

I decided, once I was able to get out of the ward, that the Tate Gallery, next door and free, might be a useful starting point in attempting to instruct myself in modern art. The first book I owned on art ("Impressionist Paintings in the Louvre") is inscribed by my mother as a birthday present at this time (April 1960), and shortly afterwards I bought further books in that same Thames & Hudson series, on Paul Klee and A History of Modern Painting. However, in spite of these efforts, modern painting, though I understand what it is trying to do, remains for me largely a closed book.

The outside world impinged in one big way at that time, and I remember the newspaper reports that March of the shooting dead by South African police of 69 protesters against the country's Pass Laws at Sharpeville, a little town hardly anyone outside the Transvaal had heard of up to that point, but whose name was to resound around the world. Sharpeville became the first internationally well-known event in the struggle for equal rights in that country which would dominate world news for the following thirty years. It was also the point at which many white people began leaving, or thinking of leaving, South Africa.

Release from hospital in May resulted in an extended, and as far as I could see largely unwarranted, period of sick leave; I was not recalled for duty until September.

It so happened that the very Recce Squadron I had left behind in Kaduna had been invited that year to take part in the Royal Tournament, an annual display at Earls Court by the British Armed Forces, with participation by invited overseas forces[5]. If I had known about this when in Kaduna, I had probably forgotten about it, but I remember attending the show with my brother Cliff and seeing their routines, including some vibrant marching to songs, and going behind the scenes at the end to see the very men I had in charge of a few months earlier. "We cried very much when you had to leave" was the sad testimonial from one of them.

What remained for me of National Service was a distinct anti-climax to all that had gone before. I was required to join "the Battalion", the main part of the Queen's Surrey Regiment stationed at that time at Colchester, and preparing to undertake a tour of duty that December in Aden. As it was obvious that, with only about four months left to do, I would not be going with them the time began to hang a little heavily. The company of the other officers I found mostly dull, but there was one exception.

Bryan Hudson was a "regular" (i.e. not National Service) ex-East Surreys lieutenant who had, for reasons I never fully fathomed, fallen out in a big way with the previous Commanding Officer. His one aim was to get out of the Queen's Surreys altogether and into the Parachute Regiment, and to this end he was busy getting himself as fit as possible for their "P Course", the physical selection process an aspiring entrant had to pass in order to be accepted by them[6]. He was thus, albeit for different reasons, in much the

---

[5] This in fact continued until 1999, when defence cuts effectively put an end to it. It has however since been revived from 2010 as the British Military Tournament.

[6] Bryan did get accepted into the Paras where he was soon made a captain, but was injured a few years later while being air-dropped somewhere in the Gulf States by a transport plane

same situation as myself. I encouraged him in his fitness regime by accompanying him on longish cross-country runs. I also at his invitation joined a poker school in the Officers' Mess (the only time I have played this game; the fact that I won £20 – quite a lot of money then – one evening actually frightened me a bit), and we spent quite a bit of time together on and off duty.

It was possibly my clear association with this renegade that led the Second in Command of the Regiment, a certain Major Beatty, to decide that I too was an Undesirable Type. What's more, I was Jewish. If my apparent misdemeanours were ever explained to me, I cannot remember what they were; I certainly never intended to anger or upset those in authority over me, least of all by insubordination. But, for whatever reason, he decided that I needed to be disciplined and to some extent punished.

Normally subalterns (lieutenants and second lieutenants) did a rota of duty as Orderly Officer. I cannot remember exactly what the duties entailed (I think it mostly involved responsibility for security), but one of them was to "Call out the Guard". The Guard was a rota of other ranks who undertook the duties I had myself been introduced to in that cold first February in Kingston. The Orderly Officer was supposed to descend on the guard-house at any time unannounced and require the soldiers concerned to assemble in parade formation. In theory this had to be done at night, but in practice was usually at some more congenial time for all concerned, and sometimes not at all.

Beatty's punishment took the form of ordering me not only to undertake this duty for a week, but deciding exactly when each day I was required to call out the Guard. This was his special bit of sadism, as he would not inform me of his required time until the day in question and this always involved the activity taking place in the small hours of the morning, so as to ensure that I had to get out of bed to do what was necessary. My one mild satisfaction was that, at any rate once or twice, he himself had to get up at the particularly inconvenient hour concerned to ensure that I had followed his orders! Not content with the punishment he called me to his office near the end of both our times in Colchester and told me that I was "a thoroughly unsatisfactory young officer". By this time, with just over a month to serve, I really didn't care what he thought (I stood stiffly to attention and said "I'm sorry you think that, Sir"), but I had no illusions that, had I an intended

---

flying too low, thus preventing his parachute from opening fully. His injuries were considered sufficiently bad for him to have to be invalided out of the army, and he was thus forced to forego the career he loved and forge a new one for himself, firstly in industrial management and later in teaching.

career in the army in front of me, he could have effectively all but wrecked it.

Summary punishment without charge or trial was a novel experience (and fortunately the only one of its kind I was to experience in my life), but two other "firsts" come to mind also from those Colchester days. One of my duties as platoon officer was to oversee firing range exercises. Normally this didn't involve very much, but in the case of live ammunition that failed to explode it was the officer's responsibility to go and blow it up (this applied in particular to hand grenades). For this I was issued with a kit consisting of a small block of gun-cotton, a detonator, a length of fuse wire and a box of matches. On the day in question it began raining as the platoon lobbed their grenades and, whether or not the weather had any effect on what happened, in due course one of these things failed to explode and remained unexploded by the time the exercise finished. It was by now pouring with rain, but my amateur Guy Fawkes act was nevertheless going to have to go ahead.

I gingerly approached the unexploded grenade, and, trembling slightly, began to position the explosives as I had been previously instructed ("this is what the bloody sappers are supposed to do", I was muttering to myself). As I bent over the assembly to light the fuse I was quickly getting soaked through and the rain was cascading off the peak of my cap in a little waterfall; also, by way of increasing my handicap, the wind was gusting. In spite of numerous determined attempts, and much cursing, I simply could not get a single match to light, let alone set the fuse going. Having by now actually exposed myself to the danger of the situation, I was frustrated and not a little angry at being unable to see the thing through, and feeling (in spite of the extenuating circumstances) something of a failure, I finally gave up. I had of course to report the incident and precise location of the offending grenade back at barracks.

The other new thing did not involve danger (at least in theory). I was for the only time in the army required to go on parade wearing a sword. The Sam Browne belt that officers and warrant officers wear (and is so much a feature of military and para-military uniforms around the world) is so designed, with its strap going over the right shoulder, to balance the weight of a sword hanging from the belt on the wearer's left side. Having not previously had any experience of it, I needed to be instructed in parade-ground sword drill beforehand by the Regimental Sergeant-Major. But this was not difficult to master and I acquitted myself adequately when the time came.

If Colchester had proved an anti-climax, Canterbury, the then Home Counties Brigade Headquarters, where I was required to spend the last month or so, was the nadir of my army experience. It was January 1961 and seemingly incessantly raining. I was given what amounted to a clerk's job, updating the records, kept by an unusually boring superannuated colonel (who offered to sell me his ugly khaki greatcoat), of officers of the four regiments making up the Brigade who were posted to other units. Time dragged, and I finally knew what people meant when they used the expression "time-serving". Demobilisation, on 3rd February, could not come quickly enough.

Yet I had undergone a wide variety of experiences, met all sorts of men I would not otherwise have met, learned at times to be resourceful, and enjoyed the experiences of the Army's pomp and circumstance on the parade ground. I had become a respectably good shot (having won the rifle shooting competition in basic training) and passed out as joint (with Peter Barratt) Best Recruit, for which I received a shield plaque still hanging in the dining room at home. But most of all I had indulged a taste for Africa, which was to lead to other directions my life would take.

Chapter 5

Social, Family and Married Life to 1973

A flashback to childhood	134
After school	136
After National Service	139
Mother's death	140
Frognal Court	143
Irene	145
Her family	147
The summer of '62	151
An absence and a coming together	153
Marriage	155
44 Elsworthy Road	158
44 Temple Fortune Lane	162

A flashback to childhood

Social interaction outside the family had for us in childhood been limited. This applied even to social connection within the extended family, as our first cousins (all of whom were on Dad's side of the family) lived the other side of north London. In our street there were of course children of friends of our parents with whom we were thrown together, and a friend (Christopher) I had made through Nanny's intervention. There were also acquaintanceships with children of our parents' friends who lived further away, and from time to time with more distant cousins (on Mother's side). On occasions, principally birthday parties, we would see all or a good proportion of these children, but nevertheless in general, Sarah being that much younger and a girl, Cliff and I simply had each other as companions.

Obviously we made friends at school but, birthday parties apart, I do not recall more than a handful of occasions on which we invited our school-friends home. We did of course invite them, and were invited back, for our respective birthdays; indeed, sometimes these parties were quite lavish affairs by the austerity standards of the late 1940s and early 1950s.

I recall my very first firework party in November 1946 at the age of seven given at the home of a school friend, Nicky Lane. I had not grown up with fireworks; they were not available at all during the War, were comparatively expensive and consisted at that time to a large extent of "bangers" (fireworks that did nothing else but "fizz" briefly and explode) and "squibs" or "jumping crackers" (ones that jumped about making a series of explosions). I was at the time frightened of loud bangs (I seemed to be the only little boy that was); perhaps they were associated in my mind with the occasional explosions of bombs and doodlebugs heard during the War. Whatever the reason, I still feel embarrassment at having to admit that I cowered for most of that party in the hosts' garage, and I was struck dumb with shame when Nicky's father came to ask me uncomprehendingly what the matter was.

Other school-friends' parties that remain in my memory include one given in the summer of 1947 when I was eight by the parents of Sidney Hornick, a class-mate with whom I was friendly, although not especially so. Sidney's parents were Jewish refugees, either from Germany or somewhere in central Europe, although they must have been able to escape with their money as they lived reasonably comfortably on the borders of Edgware and Mill Hill and were able to afford to send their son to a fee-paying school. At the party we guest children were at some point each given a model Dinky car, a particularly generous gift at that time, as these were comparatively difficult to obtain. I was especially pleased with mine, a blue Wolsley that I had long before coveted but could not possibly afford to buy with my pocket money and had not expected to be able to add to my collection.

The pleasure did not last long. Almost immediately one of the other guest children asked me if I would swap my car for his, a green Riley. I refused as I already had the one he was offering; but he did not accept my refusal, snatched my car from my hand, threw his at my feet and ran off. A little boys' argument and physical scrap now broke out between us, and Mrs Hornick was forced to come and mediate. She took the cars from our respective squabbling hands, held them in hers and without, it seemed to me, paying any heed to the facts of the case pronounced in a strong middle-European accent "*Look, zey're bos ze same. Von is blue and von is green, zat's all*". She thereupon handed the coveted blue Wolsley back to my enemy and the green Riley back to me. I protested, but to no avail and realised, with a burning sense of injustice, that I had no alternative but to accept what I saw as this patently flawed verdict (and doubtless spent the rest of the afternoon in a sulk).

I recall a birthday party at Stephen Sedley's when we were probably 8 or 9 rushing around the host's very large house with his friends like a pack of puppies on the loose (it seemed somehow the natural thing to do) and having to be reprimanded by Stephen's father.

But sometimes birthdays involved activities relevant to the boy concerned or his family: Roger Holliday's father was the editor of *The Motor Cycle* magazine and in I think 1950 those of us invited to his birthday were taken to the Motor Cycle and Cycle Exhibition at Earls Court. The ostensible reason for the visit was the purchase of a new bicycle for Roger, but we youngsters were captivated by the machines on display: famous brands of British motor cycles of the time like BSA, Matchless, Norton and Triumph that were household names before the Japanese began to dominate that particular market; and those of bicycles such as Hercules, James, Raleigh and Rudge that were then well-known to most of my contemporaries. We eagerly collected the free advertising fliers that were available on the exhibition stands[1].

I retain various bits of unimportant information from my childhood. For example I can still remember the dates of the birthdays of both of the last two friends, and also that Roger's mother was Swiss. At least that was what we were given to understand; it was not until many decades later, when he and I met again after something like 50 years, that he told me that she was in fact German; it just wasn't a good idea in those post war years in Britain to declare that fact.

From the age of thirteen both Cliff and I were at boarding school, holiday socialising could be only with those of our friends (actually a small minority) who lived nearby.

After school

Thus it was that when I left school in the summer of 1956, I had virtually nothing in the way of a social circle at all. My parents thought it would be a good idea if I joined a young Jewish group, the Federation of Zionist Youth, to which Patricia Sadow, my second cousin, could introduce me (Patricia was the daughter, whom I actually hardly knew, of mother's first cousin Jean). At the time, Zionism[2], essentially a movement that fosters the idea

---

[1] I was given a bicycle for my 12th birthday. I think it was a Rudge, but am almost ashamed to say I cannot accurately remember the make.

[2] In modern times, owing to constant Arab pressure on the UN and other international organisations, the word "Zionism" has become (along, for other reasons, with fascism, communism, imperialism, colonialism, racism and even capitalism) tantamount to a term of abuse. According to the Israeli ambassador to the UN in 2013, Hamas in Gaza had recently published a textbook for 55,000 high school students in which page after page denied Judaism's historical connection to the land of Israel and described Zionism as racism (UN General Assembly agenda item 18, 25 November 2013). Indeed, the mantra "Zionism equals racism" has been picked up by chanting students and others in frequent anti-Israel demonstrations in various parts of the world in recent years.

that all Jews should go, or at least aspire to go, and live in Israel (in other words to return from the diaspora to Zion) was about as far from my life and thinking as Mormonism. I was to say the least not enthusiastic; but I went.

In actual fact, apart from a few who were really keen, the people I found in the FZY did not really aspire to emigrate to Israel[3] and were not as different from me as I had feared they might be. Minor and temporary friendships developed and I found myself attending the odd Jewish charity dances, mostly rather grand affairs held at one of London's big Park Lane hotels, the Dorchester and Grosvenor House. But rightly or wrongly this social world seemed to me to be an enclosed one consisting mainly of people with narrow social goals (basically finding a partner) and I did not fit comfortably into it. My own acquaintance with, interest in and support for Israel, even a passing flirtation with Zionism, were to come later.

Thinking I might improve my social skills if I were to learn how to ballroom dance properly, I went for a while to a dancing school. I can't remember how I discovered Van's School of Dancing; it was run, not as I might have expected from some sort of studio by a middle aged lady who had taken the name Madame Markova or something of the sort, but from a house in Middleton Road, Golders Green by a middle-aged bachelor Dutchman (hence the name) and his spinster sister. I never really mastered the intricate steps of the fox-trot, but did meet there Barry Marks, someone whom I had known at Belmont School (though he was two or three years my senior) and who now had much the same reason for learning dancing as I did.

Barry seemed as devoid of a circle of friends as I was at the time and we "hung out" together. We occasionally "picked up" girls at dances; one or two even stuck for a while as girl-friends; it seemed socially more interesting than meeting predictable girls at Jewish charity functions. It was Barry, who had done his National Service in the mid-1950s in the Canal Zone in Egypt, who drove me to the East Surreys' barracks in Kingston-on-Thames that February morning in 1959 to begin my own two-year stint.

Another area of social interaction at this time of my life was the golf course. I had taken up the game at school and on leaving it made sense to join a club. Golf clubs were at the time one of the more obvious settings in which a kind of apartheid operated. In London, at any rate in areas where there were significant percentages of Jews, most of them did not welcome Jewish members (or for that matter probably members of other "foreign"

---

[3] The expression Zionists always use is to "make *Aliyah*". The Hebrew word means "ascension" or "ascending" as the idea is that anyone doing it is entering a higher plane of life.

communities either) and, doubtless fearing that they would be swamped with Jewish applicants if they did, at best operated a quota system. While this was doubtless not the only reason why Jewish golf clubs had been formed, it was certainly a contributing factor.

The principal clubs concerned were Potters Bar, in Hertfordshire, Hartesbourne Manor, near Stanmore, Middlesex, and Coombe Hill, situated between Kingston-on-Thames and New Malden, Surrey. Dad, after having been at one time a kind of peripatetic member simultaneously of all three, had finally "settled" at Coombe Hill[4]. Its distance from where we lived made it to that extent an inconvenient club to belong to for it took at least ¾ hour by car to get there. But I enjoyed playing the course and the sporting challenge it posed, although with one exception I did not make any friends there, and then only after National Service.

However, for a real golf challenge in the summer of 1958 Cliff and I joined the family on a golfing holiday at Turnberry in Ayrshire, south western Scotland. On the way up we had attempted to camp in the Lake District, but the weather was foul and we cut our losses.

There were actually two courses at Turnberry. I had never played a links (seaside) course before, and the challenge of coastal winds and long heather "carries" over which one had to hit the ball from the tee in order to reach the fairway (in one case one had to play from one cliff to another across the beach) made me wonder if I would ever reach the kind of standard I had set for myself (in fact I did do this briefly later on in Africa). Apart from regularly losing golf balls my main memory is of slicing a tee-shot on a hole that adjoined the road just as a car was passing. I watched in dismay as it came down and struck the car on its roof. I can't imagine what the driver must have thought; I don't think the car even stopped. Perhaps this was not an out-of-the-ordinary occurrence for the person concerned.

I had a the mildest of holiday affairs with a young woman of about my age staying at the hotel with her family, and indeed later went to visit her in Cheshire where she lived, but by then we had both somewhat lost interest in each other (she more than I, it has to be said).

---

[4] The original club had become insolvent during the Second World War and been bought in 1946 by a consortium of Jewish businessmen. Although not himself a founder member, Dad had joined in the very early days, and his name was the very first on the relevant board in the clubhouse as having won the club's Captain's Prize competition in 1947. It was not untypical of him that when I remarked on this to him at the club ten or more years later, he had almost forgotten about it, having walked past the board on hundreds of occasions without noticing it.

There was also the Rugby Club. At that time there was much enthusiasm for the game amongst those who had been to school at Mill Hill and in the late 1950s the Old Millhillians were a team, if not quite of the first rank, then at least of a respectably good standard. In fact the club ran five teams that all played weekly. To my intense surprise I found myself climbing through the ranks of the C XV, the B XV and the A XV to the 1st XV all in my first year. Then and for the subsequent two seasons I was quite honoured to be able to play with (at times) two England internationals plus one or two more Oxbridge blues and county players.

But the fact was that the club ground at Headstone Lane, Harrow, was of heavy clay consistency and for most of the period from about mid-November until mid-March the pitches tended to be very muddy and retain surface water. This was by contrast to clubs in south-west London where the soil tended to be more sandy and well-drained and which consequently lent themselves more to open running rugby. I simply did not enjoy playing the kind of closed down rugby, much of it consisting of rucks (in those days known as loose scrums) and line-outs up and down the touch-line that the conditions in north London seemed to necessitate.

The social aspects of the club mostly centred round the drinking of beer. Although I have always enjoyed the occasional cold light beer in warm weather, I was never able to develop a liking for the kind of brew, known as "bitter" and drunk at room temperature, that was consumed almost exclusively there. As a result, the combination of rugby that was played for much of the season in less than ideal conditions, and a beer-soaked social atmosphere that was not particularly to my liking, the club did not have much to offer that I really wanted, and I did not continue playing after returning from National service.

After National Service

Perhaps I came back from the army with more confidence, perhaps it was just luck, but from 1961 onwards from a social point of view things began to look decidedly better.

Barry and I had planned to travel overland to Greece and back in course of about a month in the summer of 1961. We had found and bought a second-hand Land Rover and advertised for a companion or two to accompany us and share the costs, but this had come to nothing. Nevertheless, at what I think was an engagement party thrown by the Sedleys for Stephen's sister Michele and her fiancé, I mentioned the plan to someone by the name of

Chris Gane, a contemporary of Stephen's at Cambridge, currently a teacher at Haberdashers School. Both he and his girlfriend Sheila seemed very keen on the idea.

In fact Chris (who a short while later had split up with Sheila) did join us and we did make what was for those days the fairly exotic journey concerned (described in chapter 6). In fact this initial meeting turned out to be much more significant than I supposed it could; indeed it could be said in hindsight to have led to a turning point in my life.

In the meantime, however, significant events of quite a different kind were taking place.

Mother's death

Mother as I remember her, late 1950s

During the time we were away and unknown to me, Mother's health began deteriorating rapidly. In fact things had got so bad that towards the middle of August attempts had been made (unsuccessfully) through Interpol to try to contact me to get me to return immediately home. The day following our return (which had been late in the evening and I had stayed sleeping on the floor at Barry's house) I discovered what had happened and went to see Mother in the London Clinic. Her greeting came as a shock: "You had better make the most of me," she said weakly, "because a few days ago you nearly lost me". My main reaction was of disbelief that things could have got so bad so quickly; I heard but couldn't really digest what she had said.

But apparently she had developed medical complications from taking the cortisone drug prescribed for her asthma. All sorts of remedies for the condition in which she now found herself (even including a faith healer) were tried, but on the 30th August, not long after my return, I answered a telephone call from the hospital quite early one morning saying that she had "collapsed" (I didn't know at the time that this was a euphemism for "died") and asking that we should come as quickly as possible. Dad, Clifford and I did so, with me driving as quickly as I could. We found mother, lying on her back as though asleep, with for some reason a small piece of cloth partly covering the lower part of her face, which had already taken on a kind of waxen appearance. It was actually only then that, owing to my earlier misunderstanding, it finally dawned on me that she was dead. Dad fell on the bed and embraced her body, crying out "Peg!" It was the first of only two occasions that I ever saw him weep. I (and I think Cliff too, at least at that point) just felt numb.

Jewish funerals are rushed affairs, at least in the orthodox synagogue to which Dad belonged. Under a religious law that takes no account of modern refrigeration methods, the body is supposed to be buried as soon as reasonably possible after death. It was thus that, accompanied by Dad's golfing friend Alf Gilbert, I did the necessary chores to make the arrangements. I don't remember getting the death certificate (as Mother had died in hospital this must have been just a formality) but I do remember having to go to the offices of the United Synagogue, at that time in Woburn Square in London's West End, to organise the funeral. For this it was considered at the time that one needed to pay a bribe to the Synagogue authorities to be sure to get a quick slot for the burial, which was to be at the Jewish Cemetery in Willesden[5], and at a reasonable time. Ushered in to see the relevant official, after some formal preliminaries I duly handed over the money (I don't remember the amount but it was probably about £50, a not inconsiderable sum then) as a "donation" to the organisation. I was duly offered a convenient time for the funeral the following day. I felt mildly disgusted with both the organisation and myself.[6]

Little memory remains of the funeral. Dad, Cliff and I were expected to say not only the standard mourners' *Kaddish*, a prayer in Aramaic for the dead (the word comes from the same root as the Hebrew word for holy) which we found we could reasonably manage from the Hebrew script, but also an extended "*Rabbonim Kaddish*" (Rabbis' *Kaddish*) which was more difficult for us. Quite why we had to do this I never discovered, for in my admittedly

---

[5] One had of course to have previously purchased the necessary plot, and this had been done some years before for both parents.

[6] Perhaps this was an over-reaction. After all, as I was later to find out, much of the world operates in some areas and at least some of the time on a system of bribery in one form or another. And the money concerned almost certainly did go to the United Synagogue rather than to the official personally. I believe that these "donations" are no longer thought appropriate. The practices of the Reform and Liberal Synagogues, especially the latter, have always been more open and considerably less dogmatic in many respects. As far as I know the sort of procedure described would not, then or later, have happened in either.

limited experience of such things I have never heard this extended prayer being intoned by a mourner since. Dad was no better at either of these tasks than we were, and in fact I think he quickly decided he could depute the extended *Kaddish* to us. Afterwards at home we underwent the standard "*Shiva*" (old Hebrew for seven, pronounced as in the English word shiver), the standard period of a week's mourning during which the family of the deceased sit around at home and receive visitors, a process known as "sitting *Shiva*". I was bored. I remember trying to get the rabbi of the local synagogue to which Dad belonged (actually a senior rabbi with the title Dayan) to do what he could to convince me about God. He was gracious about it and patient, doubtless thinking he had to make allowances for me and my apparent lack of belief because of my recent loss. But we didn't progress very far.

The second time that I saw my father weep was a few days later. I myself was lying tearfully on my bed in the room I shared with Cliff. Though I was undoubtedly fraught on account of the recent events, the immediate reason for my state was actually self-pity. Dad came into my room at this time and broke down: "We've got to stick together as a family!" he said, somewhat inconsequentially, through tears. I nodded weakly. But actually I was not weeping for the loss of Mother, at least not directly. I had already reflected on the fact that her death had been a long time coming; what was hitting me now was that there was no longer anyone who could intercede between me and my father.

Other things crowded in. Perhaps Dad felt a need to atone for the death, for he quickly got it into his head that he, Cliff and I should attend daily morning prayers at the synagogue (in Norrice Lea, only a short walk away). We had never done anything remotely like this before. Fortunately for her, my sister Sarah was not included in this requirement; females do not count for much (at any rate in these kinds of things) in the orthodox synagogue.

A small group of men attended these morning prayer sessions and the occasions involved a process known as "laying *tefillin*" (the Hebrew word for the set of two phylacteries – little black approximately 2 inch cube boxes containing printed prayers). These have leather straps attached, to enable one to be placed around the head and the other wound around the arm; the idea being that one daily dedicates ones mental and physical strength to God. Although I had heard about it, I had never imagined myself taking part in this (to me) arcane mumbo-jumbo. It continued for some months and I remember thinking at the time "Poor Mother; I'm certain she would not have wanted all this done in her name or even on her behalf". Dad even insisted that we had to attend a synagogue service on Christmas Day that year. But I think soon after that he decided that we had done our duty and the observances described ceased.

Though clearly I could not do so immediately after the death, I thought with increasing urgency that I needed to get away and establish my own home life. In fact an opportunity to do this very thing was just at that time presenting itself.

Frognal Court

Chris Gane shared a flat in Mapesbury Road, Brondesbury (north-west London) with another of Stephen Sedley's Cambridge friends, Nat Joseph, and I had been there on a number of occasions both before and after the journey to Greece. Late in 1961 or early the following year they moved to 34 Frognal Court.

Situated in Finchley Road, adjacent to Frognal, the road which leads to Hampstead Village, Frognal Court was not everyone's idea of comfortable living: it consisted of two three-storey blocks of flats, one along the main Finchley Road with shops on the ground floor, and another just behind it. Built probably in the 1930s the rear of the flats in each block faced inward to a courtyard where cars were parked and to each of the vertical group of flats on the three floors were linked metal fire-escapes. The complex had at first glance something of the appearance of a prison. The flat had nevertheless an attraction for me, and as it had 3 bedrooms Nat, as the holder of the head lease, and with Chris's ready consent, agreed that I could rent the third room. And so, in March 1962, I moved in.

With Nat Joseph & Chris Gane, Frognal Court, July 1962

There are various points in one's life when a watershed is reached and life takes a different direction from then on. This needs to be contrasted with a period of life that is spent in a temporarily different environment (such as had already happened in National Service), but where "home" remained the same. My first watershed had been my departure for boarding school, where I had entered, at least for the majority of the year, a different home environment. This was now the second. Although, much to Nanny's wry amusement, I still occasionally took washing to be done in the machine at Fourways, I had now moved away from the family home, and henceforth would go back to it only as a visitor.

There was an immediate sense of freedom, of being able to organise my life just how I wanted it. I now shed the remaining aspect of my social life that no longer fitted for me and ceased playing golf (I would not take up the game again until Malawi days, more than eleven years later). My little room in the flat had a bed and a chest of drawers, I can't remember whether the table, chair and bedside cabinet were already there or whether I supplied them, and I furnished it with my clothes and a few books and some other simple things, and the flat with my records. Sharing with two recent Cambridge graduates was a little like being at university without the lectures and exams. It was my ideal existence. Friends and acquaintances dropped in from time to time, and discussions ranged sometimes well into the night.

At the time Nat was establishing an independent record company, Transatlantic Records, and artists he had signed up, mostly from the folk music genre, would periodically appear at the flat. I particularly remember Sidney Carter[7], the various members of the Dubliners and the poet Christopher Logue, although Nat was also instrumental in launching the careers of groups that were well-known in their time such as Pentangle and the Humblebums, and individuals such as the guitarist Bert Jansch, the jazz singer Annie Ross, and probably the best-known of all, the all-round musician, actor and entertainer Billy Connolly.

Chris was, by any standards, a character; it seemed then that he was willing to try anything just for the experience. As already noted, at the time he was working as a schoolteacher, but his interests lay in what were then called "teaching machines", effectively the forerunners to personal computers, and had already made contact with people in that embryo business.

My flat-mates apparently found in me a person whose lack of university education gave me what they saw as an interestingly independent and uninfluenced outlook on life.[8]

---

[7] Better known at the time than later, his mournful songs *Putting out the Dustbins in the Gray's Inn Road* ("...*but the bone-white wagon never showed*") and *Down Below* [i.e. in the sewers] are ones I always associate with Frognal Court and that time generally.

[8] Nat was to die prematurely aged 66 in 2005 after a few years of suffering with Parkinson's disease during which time he gradually began to fade out, both physically and mentally. A long obituary in the London Times of 15 September that year described how Transatlantic Records had been a forerunner for other independent record companies such as Virgin (the industry had been dominated up to that time by the recording giants EMI and Decca). Nat later became an impresario of some note; his most successful enterprise *Kipling* being a one-

Irene

I had various girlfriends during that period, the longest-standing of whom, Wendy, broke up with me tearfully shortly after I moved into Frognal Court. She didn't say so, but I think she wanted to get married, and I hadn't seemed at the time to be the marrying type. My flatmate Nat had had a yearning for a one-time girlfriend, Monica Grodzinski[9], but that relationship had been somewhat one-sided and had ceased by the time I got to know him well. But its relevance is that Monica's closest friend was someone named Irene Lyons, who was known to both Nat and Chris, and in whom the latter seemed to be taking an interest: he had recently described with delight her pleasure in simple entertainment and how they had both spent an afternoon enjoying a ride on the top of a bus together. I hadn't met her and had no reason to give her a thought.

We three in Frognal Court often used to go to a curry restaurant for lunch on Sundays; the favourite was the Gulistan in Hampstead High Street, where Chris would often embarrass Nat by going into what the latter thought were embarrassingly unseemly raptures over the food; but we went to others too. In fact one was just across the Finchley Road from the flat, and Nat and I were eating there one Sunday in the middle of May 1962 when he suddenly remembered that "Irene" was coming round with the typescript of the libretto to the musical he had recently composed. We hurriedly paid the bill and dashed back to the flat.

At the top of the stairs was a slim, dark, smiling young woman of medium height in a fitted overcoat with a file of papers in her arm; Nat's rather breathless apology for lateness as we bounded up the last flight was brushed aside. Irene announced cheerfully that she had only just arrived herself, that she had a cold and would not give him a kiss, but that he could have "one of these" (a one-armed hug) instead. Perhaps thinking that I might feel left out she said to me "You can have one too." I thought how nice and friendly she was; but at that point little more.

---

man show by Alec McCowan, with the actor playing out excerpts from the great man's life and reading some of his poetry. Irene and I went to the first night of the show about a week after I had returned from Kenya in 1984.

Chris became a leading authority on computers. After a failed marriage he went in the mid-1970s to live and work in the US where he became respected in his field and at one time quite wealthy. But in spite of academic brilliance he lacked common sense, and with Nat's illness and death he lost the only person with both the ability and will to give him sensible guidance in his day to day affairs. He ran through all his money and needed to live out his days on charity support in New York.

[9] Monica, as with many of her relatives, was involved in the eponymous Jewish bakery family business.

Life continued at the flat as before. Irene was often there too, and for a while we occasionally did things as a foursome. Typical of that time there are pictures of Chris, Irene and me crammed into a photo booth, rather in the style of the film *Jules et Jim* that was currently showing.

Irene had some 18 months before broken up with a serious boyfriend, Matthew Leighton, whom she had wanted to marry, but who did not at the time feel ready for that commitment. While getting over the break-up she had gone to the US in the summer of 1961 to work as a camp counsellor (in charge of groups of 11 year old girls). Her desirability as a partner was still however very much in evidence. When the camps had finished, extricating herself from the attentions of a young woman co-counsellor with whom she had done some travelling and who had wanted to form a Lesbian relationship with her, she went to stay with her sister Monica and family in Los Angeles. There she had been introduced to a young man, Gary Glober. Gary, the captain of his college (American) football team at the time, was an anglophile and in something of a whirlwind romance, at least from his side, he announced to her that he seriously wanted to marry her, a state of affairs that, naturally, Monica was keen to encourage. But Irene had returned to London to think things over; it seemed that the situation was in effect the reverse of what it had been with Matthew the year before, and she appeared unsure what to do.

**With Chris Gane and Irene,
July 1962**

Although Irene's feeling for Gary did not seem to us three men in Frognal court to have been particularly strong, there were nevertheless clearly competing claims on her affections and it still did not enter my head to become a suitor as well. She now had a job as receptionist and "girl Friday" with a small firm of advertising agents, J. Manser Atkins in New Oxford Street, where she was popular with staff, customers and suppliers alike.

Things seemed to change of their own accord towards the end of June of that year. Irene's friend Sarah Brodie was having a 21st birthday party and Sarah had urged her to bring along any young men she knew; Irene duly obliged with Nat, Chris and me. All four of us went (in the Land Rover that we had used to go to Greece the year before, and which I now owned, having bought Chris's and Barry's shares in it) to the rather grand flat Sarah's family occupied in Albert Hall Mansions, next to the Albert Hall.

Apart from the trio I went with, I don't think I knew anyone at the party, and I remember at some point sitting in an armchair and letting the world carry on around me. A short time later Irene, dressed in a pale pink dress with a flared skirt, asked me to dance with her. That was not altogether unusual, although in those days it was still more the custom for things to operate the other way round, with the man expected to ask the woman. It nevertheless struck a chord with me, and I remember there then crystallising in my mind a thought that had been taking shape beforehand "Here's a girl who is not unduly afraid of convention". I liked that. However, presumably thinking back to my very limited success at Van's School of Dancing, I apparently protested feebly that I wasn't very good; but I could hardly refuse. Irene seemed to think my protestations were nonsense.

In today's terms, this would be the point at which a relationship between us could be said to have begun, albeit a little tentatively on my part; it just seemed the natural thing to happen. Nat and Chris made their own way home and left the two of us together[10].

Her family

Irene's background had been somewhat irregular. Her father Bernard Lyons was one of three children of immigrant parents from the Pale of Settlement in Eastern Europe who had arrived in London in the 1890s. The family name had been Arie (*Ar-ee-ay*), which was anglicised either on arrival or soon after to Lyons. Born in 1897, Bernard had grown up in the Finsbury Park area of London and served in the British Army in France in the First World War, where he was able to put to good use the French he had learned at school.

---

[10] In fact it was soon after this that Irene, always one to see potentials for successful relationships, arranged for a date between Sarah and Nat (her considerable understanding of the way people interact might have caused her in another life to have been a formal matchmaker!) In due course they got married.

Irene's mother, a little confusingly for this account also named Irene, had been born around the turn of the century in Krakow in Poland, although the family then moved to Warsaw. In the early years of the twentieth century her father, Irene's grandfather, Jacques Bellau[11], had migrated to Paris and set up in business as a photographer. His wife, Celine Bellau, and their six children followed and for the youngest three of them (including Irene's mother) at least, France became their cultural home. However, a second migration of four of the Bellau siblings led by the oldest son Marjan began in the 1920s to London, where opportunities were seen to be greater for the trade and business skills (millinery and dressmaking) that they possessed[12]. In a foretaste of some of the things that were to happen in the following generation, Irene's grandmother, by this time separated from her husband, moved to London as well.

It was soon afterwards that Irene Bellau was introduced to Bernard Lyons by his younger sister Cissie. Bernard was quickly attracted not only to the lady herself, but also by the fact that she came from France, a country of which he had, as noted, some wartime experience and for which he had a fondness. They married in 1929. They had one child, Monica, born in 1930. Irene then had a number of miscarriages in the intervening time before getting pregnant again in 1939. At the beginning of the War she and Monica were evacuated to Bournemouth where on 4th October she gave birth to a 2-month premature baby girl. Tragically, in those days before the availability of antibiotics, she developed peritonitis and died some 16 days after the birth. The baby, needing to be placed for some time in an incubator, was originally to be named Barbara Ann, but after the death of her mother was given the names Irene Barbara Ann[13].

The difficulties attendant on the War were many. It was not easy to travel around the country and most people, including Irene's father, did not own a car, or even if they did were unable to obtain the strictly rationed petrol to run it. Baby Irene was somehow shunted around different institutions[14],

---

[11] That at least was the name by which he was known in France.
[12] The others were his sisters Rose, Irene and Marie. The oldest of the siblings, Hélène, married a Catholic Frenchman and remained in Paris. The younger brother, Henri, spent some time in England and married an English woman, but the marriage broke up and he went back to Paris, from where during the War he was eventually rounded up by the Nazis and sent from Drancy to one of their death camps. It was a supreme irony that Hélène and her husband, having survived the war unscathed, were killed when the car they were traveling in shortly afterwards hit a land mine.
[13] Jewish law or tradition does not approve of calling a child by the same name as its living parent.
[14] For one of these journeys Irene's father had managed to get the help of his brother-in-law Marjan, who was able to run a car. It was not untypical of this gentleman that he required payment for the services provided.

including the Welgarth Nursery in Hampstead Garden Suburb and a nursing home in Shrivenham, near Swindon, where the staff gave their opinion that unless the little girl were to be given loving care in a family she might die.

So it was that Auntie Rose, an older sister of Irene's mother, agreed to take care of her. But there was also the question of Monica[15]. Rose had by this time two children of her own, David and Lilian Saffrin, but had separated from her husband Phillip and she and her children had been evacuated to Leamington Spa, near Warwick. Rose decided that she would be prepared to take Monica, who was very near to David in age, under her wing as well. Thus from some time in 1941 or 1942 Rose's virtually single-parent family became one comprising four children. She was very capable and truly loved Irene as her own child, but there were problems that were to dog family relationships for years to come.

Firstly, Rose and Monica did not get on at all well; the former saw in the latter a self-willed and (in Rose's words) "naughty" girl who reacted badly to attempts to discipline her, while the latter, already 11 or 12 years old by this time, thought she was treated unfairly and downright badly by her aunt from the start.

Secondly, and perhaps more profoundly, Rose made it clear that she very much wanted to marry Bernard, Monica and Irene's widowed father. She admired him and brought to the situation the weighty fact that she had looked after his children in Leamington until their return to London after the War and was continuing to do so. The problem was that the affection was not returned in the same way. Nevertheless, Bernard, who had developed no attachment of his own in the intervening time, felt obliged to comply with what was not unreasonably expected of him, and the couple married in 1949 soon after Rose's divorce from her first husband had been completed.

But the relationship was less than ideal and the family became to a degree divided, with Bernard and his daughter Monica on one side, and Rose with her children David and Lilian on the other[16]. Irene, who quite genuinely

---

[15] Up to that time Monica had been living with the younger sister of her mother's, Auntie Marie (Grant), and her family who had moved to Plymouth, Devon, where her husband Mark's job with Shell Oil had taken them. Marie and Mark's daughter Judith was near to Monica's age and they also had a younger son, Stanley.

[16] This is not at all to imply that the children themselves did not get on together; they did, both then and later, between themselves and David and Lilian's respective spouses Beverly and Henry. But the disharmony there had been between the parents was bound at times to have at least some effect. Lilian was sadly to die in 1993 at the age of 58 of lung cancer. Although herself a non-smoker, she had worked for some years in an office where some of her co-workers were heavy smokers.

"belonged" to both, was in the middle and grew up in an atmosphere that was at times hostile between the parents, who were unsuited in many ways. Her father considered he had been trapped and resented it. One of Irene's childhood fears was that she had to be "good" so that her parents would stay together.

Monica on the other hand had as she grew up one burning ambition: to get away from her aunt/step-mother. This had taken the form of travelling to California, where one of her father's two unmarried sisters, Jenny, had moved in the late 1930s and was working in Los Angeles as a shop assistant. After an extended visit in 1952 Monica decided the following year that she would make her future there. She later met and married Gunter Markus, a German refugee, in 1957.[17] Their children, Beverly and Miriam, and subsequently their families, were to play quite a large part in our lives later.

Irene had had a less than illustrious school career. With an immediate family who had high academic potential[18] it was a big blow to her and her family that she had failed the Eleven Plus examination that in those days separated those who could go on to the state grammar schools from those who could not. Irene always thought that she had let her father in particular down, and that he considered her to be a dunce. After leaving school at sixteen, encouraged by Rose she had trained as a florist with Constance Spry, at that time the best training of its kind. Though loving the work and very good at it, she found the unsocial hours demanded by floristry (which often required work to be done for functions at weekends) gradually to be a disincentive; hence her move to the advertising agents for whom she was working when I first met her.

---

[17] Gunter had an interesting background. His family had been well-to-do department store owners in Gleiwitz (then part of German Upper Silesia, now Gliwice in south-western Poland). He had a married sister, Ilse, who had gone with her husband Hugo (known as "Huks") to what was then the Union of South Africa in the 1930s. By the late 1930s he wanted to join them there, but could not get a visa. Almost at the last minute in terms of being able to flee Nazi Germany he managed to get one to go to neighbouring Swaziland. There he worked during the war years as a refugee farm and store hand, hoping that when things settled down afterwards he would be able to, so to speak, complete his journey to South Africa. But he had in the meantime also applied for an American visa, and in the random way that things sometimes happen this came up first and he decided he would take the "bird in the hand" and go to the USA. There, grabbing what employment opportunities he could, he made his way in slow stages from New York, via Sioux City, Iowa, to Los Angeles. It was a real thrill for me in particular for us later to be able to help finance a journey by Gunter, Monica and the girls to South Africa and Malawi in 1975 that enabled him to revisit some of the places he had lived in during those war years. He died in 1994.

[18] Her brother David went on to achieve a first-class degree in law from London University.

All this became apparent to me quite soon after I first knew Irene. In fact I was to meet her parents only a few days after that very first meeting, when she invited the three of us from Frognal Court round to her house in Armitage Road, Golders Green, one evening after dinner. Her father in particular was always interested to meet new people, and perhaps, having become friends with young men such as ourselves (although, as I was later to find out, she was certainly not short of friends generally) both parents were happy that their daughter was apparently over her entanglement with Matthew Leighton and possibly considered that there was now less likelihood that she would go back and get married in California.

The summer of '62

But for the moment I was busy with other not very serious affairs. One, with Elaine, a girl I had met working as a receptionist in Torquay the previous Christmas and seen something of between times, had got herself a job at Bouley Bay Hotel on the north coast of Jersey and invited me over there in May. That had led to another invitation for July during the time that Beautility was closed for the summer holidays. However, things were now getting complicated because in the meantime Irene was coming more to prominence in my life. A straggly, bitty sort of holiday now began on the Côte d'Azur, where I joined for a few days some friends who had rented a flat in Juan les Pins. On the first day there I stayed too long in the sun without a hat and for the only time in my life suffered a bout of sunstroke that had me in bed with an excruciating headache for the best part of 3 days. My memory of the Côte d'Azur is dominated by that experience and by the private beaches seemingly full of rich people lying on sun-loungers. It was not what I was looking for.

The next part of the holiday plan was to meet Chris and Irene in Paris, where, by contrast to the luxury of the French Riviera, the three of us stayed at an inexpensive little hotel for students, *L'Hôtel du Commerce*, near the left bank of the Seine run by a lady named Madame Matuzzi. Comfortable was not how you would have described it: it was quite Spartan in the facilities offered and still had "hole in the floor" toilets that you had to flush as you were half-way out of the inward-opening door, as otherwise your feet got wet in the process.

For the three of us it still seemed to me a sort of *Jules et Jim* arrangement. At one point while eating our lunch on the river bank of the Île Saint-Louis, Chris somehow managed to drop his spectacles. They clattered down the cobbled embankment and on to a ledge at just above the water level, but the bank was too steep simply to climb down after them without danger of falling in. Help had to be sought from one or two passers-by and a human chain formed with Irene a not very effective anchor at the top in fits of laughter. But in due course the spectacles were recovered.

The third and final part of the holiday was to be in Jersey, and I had thought that I would need to take steps to end the relationship there. I needn't have worried, for it was immediately obvious that, not surprisingly in the closely confined society of hotel staff, Elaine had now anyway found someone she preferred to me and I was clearly surplus to requirements. We went to see Jersey's Battle of the Flowers (a parade with floats) together for form's sake and then said goodbye. I sent a telegram to Irene telling her I was coming back to London early and that I hoped (though wondered if I deserved) that she would be around. She was, and I suppose we could really be said to have become "an item" as from then, the early part of August 1962.

Gradually I began to meet more of Irene's very wide circle of friends. These had emanated from various sources at various stages in her life: her membership of what was known widely (though not by me) as the "JM", the junior membership of West London Reform Synagogue; her work as a volunteer at the Brady Club (a club for deprived Jewish youth originally situated in Brady Street in Whitechapel, London); her friends from some intensive months spent in Israel in the summer of 1959; and various others either from school or other social activities.

My life by contrast had been almost monastic. I did not have many people I could introduce her to in return, although one occasion does stand out in my mind. In mid-August I was invited by a friend with whom I used to play golf at Coombe Hill, Stanley Marber, to make up a four with his wife Jill to go to the theatre at Glyndebourne for a performance of Donizetti's *L'Elisir d'Amore*. Though the theatre had by then become something of an institution and I had of course heard of it, I had never been there. Indeed, apart from one unforgettable experience hearing Maria Callas at the amphitheatre at Epidavros in Greece the year before, I had never been to an opera. I naturally invited Irene. Memory of the opera itself soon faded but I do recall two things about the evening. The first was our picnic dinner on the grass, Stanley having left a bottle of white wine tied to string in the lake in the garden at Glyndebourne to cool while we saw the first half of the opera; this seemed to be an altogether enchanting life-style. The second, and more significant recollection, was Stanley's earlier whispered remark to me about Irene shortly after we had arrived at his house before setting off, "Jill approves!"

Stanley had ribbed Irene about her name, pretending disappointment when it turned out she was not related to the Lyons Corner House family[19]. "I thought for a moment" he said to her in the droll caricature voice that he often used "that we was all on Easy Street!"

At some point, I think in the early autumn, my driving licence was suspended in the circumstances recounted in chapter 3. On one occasion it was necessary, for reasons I cannot remember, to get to town by car, and Irene volunteered to drive my Land Rover for the purpose. Though the prospect at first secretly scared her, she was determined to overcome her fear and she did well. It was further proof to me, if proof were needed, that this was a young woman who would take hold of life as circumstances required her to do.

An absence and a coming together

It was ironic that just as this relationship began to grow, so did plans and preparations for me to go to America for a while to study furniture manufacturing there. My job at Brentwood had come to an end with the closure of the bedroom furniture division, and links had for some time been forged with a small number of American furniture manufacturers who had visited the Beautility factory and issued invitations for us to visit them. It was decided that we would take them up on the offers and that I would spend short periods of two to three weeks in a number of different factories in the southern and mid-western States.

In those days it was easy to get a visa to go to the USA as an immigrant, for while the quotas of immigrants the Americans were prepared to take from southern Europe were always significantly over-subscribed, those from northern Europe were well under-subscribed. So long as one could prove that one had no criminal record, was in good health and had never been a member of the Communist Party, as an applicant from the United Kingdom one was almost certain to get the relevant documentation. So it was that the rest of the year was spent in the certainty that Irene and I would be apart for a good part of the coming one. I left on a Trans-World Airlines Britannia flight to New York on 7th February 1963.

The time spent in the USA is covered in chapter 6; during that period of five and a half months Irene and I corresponded frequently and took up with each other again on my return on 23rd July that year. We decided to get engaged

---

[19] In fact the principal families concerned were not named Lyons at all: they were the Salmons and the Glucksteins. Some of the businesses in their conglomerate (e.g. tobacco) were in fact run under those names.

at the end of August, a procedure that involved my formal request one Saturday lunchtime to her father at the family home, myself dressed in a suit for the solemnity of the occasion, the women present (Irene, her mother, and her father's sister Auntie Cissie) having made themselves tactfully scarce in the kitchen[20]. Bernard, for whom the request was not exactly a surprise, said that if marrying me was what Irene wanted then he was happy about it too. In fact Irene's parents were delighted, not least in Bernard's case because he (a dealer in precious stones) "happened to have" two very fine ones, a diamond and a ruby, that he had rather hoped to be able to provide to his daughter's suitor to be made into a ring for her on just such an occasion. I was more than happy to oblige.

As has already been noted in chapter 3, the American experience, far from drawing me further in to the furniture business, had had almost the opposite effect. But I now had in Irene someone with a practical turn of mind and with whom I could have serious discussions about the shape of the future and how I might extricate myself from Beautility. I remember in particular walking together with her one autumn day in Richmond Park, when ideas began to take shape.

The first one was in retrospect a little odd, and to be frank Irene never thought it fitted. I would become a medical doctor. Never mind that the study period would last a long time. I applied to, and was accepted by, St Mary's Hospital, Paddington, as a student (the interview went particularly well) on condition that I first of all filled the gaps in my science education by obtaining O Level passes in biology and chemistry. But therein lay the first problem. I enrolled for the necessary educational courses at a night school somewhere on the Harrow Road. It was to be a depressing experience: the building (it was a primary school during the day) was old-fashioned and Spartan, the subjects were not well taught and the other students did not seem at all interesting. The educational struggle seemed as though it would be a long, steeply uphill one.

And then, quite by chance when visiting my friend Stephen Sedley at his house one day, he showed me some of the law examination papers which he had recently been given in his Bar finals. Almost to my surprise they seemed really interesting: the questions were mostly about matters that concerned people's behaviour in everyday life. They seemed to strike much more of a chord with me than did the rather elementary matters of chemistry I was attempting without much success to assimilate at night school. What is

---

[20] The engagement procedure, the point of which I have never quite been able to see, was expected at the time as a prelude to marriage. Somewhat to my surprise the tradition seems to continue, at least if couples are actually going to take the trouble to get married.

more, it was clear from discussion with Stephen that the process required to qualify professionally as a barrister was considerably shorter and easier than that for a medical doctor.

This was something of a relief to Irene, who was convinced that I did not have the right temperament for the medical profession. Impatience and, I'm told, lack of sympathy with those who are ill were cited as good reasons not to take the Hippocratic Oath. My bedside manner was prophesied as being in the style of "There's nothing wrong with you; just get a grip of yourself!" and though I protested that being a general practitioner was not what I would have wanted, the idea stuck that I was not cut out for medicine. As noted, there was anyway clearly an easier and probably more suitable pathway to a profession.

But I am getting ahead of the story, for meanwhile on 1st March 1964 Irene and I got married.

Marriage

The run-up to the wedding had had its own drama: my grandmother Windy was refusing to attend. That meant that probably Mother's brother Bobby would, whether he agreed with her or not, feel obliged to stay away as well.

Dad had by this time established his own relationship with Suzanne, and Windy knew that they intended to marry. Though she never said as much in terms, it was clear that she blamed Dad for her daughter's death, or at least for the circumstances in which Mother had become ill, and her demise in 1961 had brought to the surface strains between the two of them. Dad *might* have been able to allay these if he had "grasped the nettle" and gone to see Windy, possibly a few times over a period, to do his best to convince her that he had done everything he reasonably could. Perhaps he had tried at the beginning; but continuing contrition in the face of resentment was not his style, and the relationship simply festered, with each tending to think the worst of the other. Needless to say, his intention to remarry in 1964 made the situation even worse.

A Jewish wedding involves the marrying couple standing under a canopy (known as a *chupah* – the *ch* sounded as in loch and the *u* as in put) in front of the officiating rabbi. Traditionally the parents of both bride and groom also stand there on each side, or if one parent cannot for any reason do so then another close relative stands there in his or her stead. There was never any disagreement from anybody that Windy should take Mother's place in this way. If she refused, as now seemed likely, there was going to be a problem of protocol. There was no other woman from Mother's family who was close (or who would have anyway been likely to agree to take her place in the circumstances). Suzanne was not my mother and was not yet married to Dad. And yet if Dad stood on his own an unfortunate silent public statement of family rift was going to be made. An impasse had been reached

Typically, Irene regarded this as a challenge that needed to be tackled head on, and she took it upon herself to try to convince Windy to reverse her decision. One thing in her favour was that the old lady really liked her, and so, making a personal visit (on her own) on a late afternoon two days before the wedding Irene spent time explaining patiently how much it would mean to me (indeed to both of us) if she were to come, at least to take Mother's place under the *chupah*, for the synagogue service. In an early demonstration of her powers of persuasion, she managed to turn the situation round.

So Windy and Bobby came and although the former looked more like she was attending a funeral than a wedding, she did take Mother's place for the service. She even attended the wedding reception afterwards, albeit as part of a little breakaway group that stood somewhat apart. A family wedding photograph taken just after the service shows her standing next to Dad. He, never one for holding on to grudges, did his best to be pleasant, but the atmosphere was less than cordial.

For the service formal (morning) dress was required. This is the kind of outfit that improved as time went on, and today's equivalent is generally fashionable and smart, but then the choice was limited and the outfit seemed to me just a little ridiculous and reminded me of the sort of clothes that stage conjurers used to wear (complete with top hat from which to produce rabbits). Irene thought that I had deliberately hired a slightly ill-fitting suit and hat; that was quite untrue (and the few photographs we have of the occasion seem to bear me out), although the only top hat that could be supplied by Moss Bros (the best-known hirers of formal menswear at the time) was a fraction too small. It had of course to be worn during the service itself, and I was nursing a slight concern throughout that if I made a sudden movement it would fall off. Irene looked wonderful, as again the few photographs we have bear out, and a florist friend of hers had made her bouquet. Those things apart, the only distinct memory that remains to me of the actual service, at Dunstan Road Synagogue, Golders Green, that March day in 1964 was that the cantor seemed to have a cold and kept making snorting sounds at inappropriate moments.

**Wedding Day, 1st March 1964.
To left of us: Cliff, Dad, Windy; to right: Bernard and Rose Lyons, Sarah**

We went for our honeymoon via Tunisia and Greece to Israel. Tunisia at the time was just beginning to open itself up as a tourist destination and Hammamet, the place where we stayed, and which was within a comparatively short distance of Tunis, had obviously been where many wealthy French people had had seaside houses of some distinction. The Hotel Miramar at Hammamet was comfortable but unexceptional, and apart from a train ride from and back to Tunis along with people and animals, the fact that our suitcases were snatched from my hands at the station (not theft, the individual merely wanted to earn a tip) and a hotel room in Tunis with a bathroom that seemed almost the size of a ballroom with the bath in the middle of the room, not many impressions of the country remain. We did travel to Kairouan, one of the holy cities of Islam, from where I recall the not particularly attractive Great Mosque and fly-blown cafés, and also to the ruins of Carthage, where French-speaking Arab touts tried to sell us coins that they said were "punique" (i.e. from the original Carthaginian city that had been destroyed by the Romans in 146 BC after the Third Punic War) but almost certainly weren't.

It was my first time in Israel, and there we did establish lasting social contact with a number of people. This and the subsequent quite intense experiences of that country during the 1960s are related in chapter 6.

44 Elsworthy Road

We had bought a flat in 44 Elsworthy Road, a large house that had been converted into five flats of which we owned the lease of no. 1, the one on the ground floor that contained the original front door to the house. A small T-shaped corridor led from the front door to, on the left, a spacious living room at the front with a small kitchen leading off it and the main bedroom behind it (the three rooms together would have constituted the main reception room of the original house), and on the right to a small bedroom and bathroom at the back of the house. The flat had a small garden attached, accessible from the front path and from French windows in the living room, and the house itself was situated almost opposite the entrance to Primrose Hill.

By the time we had returned from our honeymoon either the sale had yet to be completed or the flat (to which I don't remember having to do much in the way of maintenance or decoration before moving in) was not ready for occupation, and so we spent a short time back at the flat at Frognal Court. But it was soon afterwards that plans began to be put in place for my career to change direction, and the memory of what turned out to be six years at Elsworthy Road is dominated by that change and by the birth of our first daughter, Rachel.

With Suzanne, November 1965

Firstly there was the study of law. Amazingly in today's terms, my two A level passes were sufficient to enable me to enrol as a Bar student and to study for and sit the professional examinations (Part 1 and finals) without having a university degree, let alone one in law. I applied for membership of the Middle Temple[21] and, as of course I was still working at Beautility, began my studies out of working hours by correspondence course from the College of Law. Not surprisingly some of the subjects needed to be studied were considerably more interesting than others. Roman law was for some unfathomable reason still a required subject for Part 1, although even that was more interesting than land law, which involved, besides a dreary study of the Law of Property Act 1925 and associated legislation, trying to understand many concepts that I had never heard of before and probably never would again afterwards[22]. But on the other hand I was truly interested in criminal law, contract law and conflict of laws (the study of which law applies when for example a couple from one country marry in a second one and then come to live in England, or where actions under a contract made in one country are performed wholly or partly in another).

Much of the time my Bar studies were undertaken in the reference department at the newly constructed and then rather novel Swiss Cottage Library. In the early summer of 1966 I sat and passed Part 1. It was time to "come out" and tell the family of my plans. I'm not sure how much of a shock the revelation was to Dad, but after an initial silence he seemed almost to welcome the idea. At least I was doing something that he could approve of and not wasting it by becoming, as he seemed to have feared I might, a "hippy".[23]

I could now finally take my leave from the furniture business and concentrate full-time on study for the Bar final examinations the following spring. Irene and I first spent about 6 weeks travelling overland to Israel and back that September and October and then after a winter and spring of slog over the books I sat and passed the exam the following May (1967). Hardly had this been completed than it became clear on the international scene that there was going to be another war between Israel and the Arabs. With my

---

[21] One of the four legal Inns of Court, the others being the Inner Temple, Lincoln's Inn and Gray's Inn.
[22] The mysteries of, for example, fee tail and the law against perpetuities, while doubtless of interest to a few real property lawyers were not exactly likely to hold most students, including me, spellbound.
[23] I.e. those of the jeans and guitars, long hair and narcotic drugs, and an anti-war (though not necessarily passive) culture dubbed by the press as "flower power", that emerged as an identifiable social group in the early to mid-1960s firstly on the West Coast of the USA and subsequently elsewhere. Actually there had never been the slightest chance of my being attracted to it.

finals behind me and a pupillage at the Bar arranged for the autumn, we were free for the time being to travel to Israel yet again, this time as volunteers to respond to a call by the Jewish Agency on behalf of the Israeli Government to temporarily replace, mainly in agricultural work, those Israelis who had been called up to fight what became known as the Six Day War[24].

Return from Israel involved the first stage of a career at the Bar: the process known in other professions as "articles" but there as pupillage. A full year at least of this had to be undertaken before a pupil was eligible for Call to the Bar, as the formal process of being admitted to practice as a barrister was termed.

Some months earlier Irene and I had attended a wedding reception and dinner at which we were seated at a table with a group we didn't know, including Sam and Honour Stammler (I didn't know until afterwards that in fact Irene had previously discovered that the couple were friends of the bride's parents and that Sam was a barrister, and that she had asked if we could be seated at a table with them). Actually Sam was not there initially, and when I explained my own intention to qualify for the Bar, Honour summed up her husband's career to Irene with a wry "You know, you'll never see him!" As if on cue, Sam appeared shortly after that, an hour and a half or so into the evening's proceedings. Inevitably conversation turned to the law, and the Bar in particular, and later in the evening he kindly offered me (assuming I passed my Bar finals) a six-month pupillage with him for the following autumn.

I of course had no notion of what I was about to face, and in fact I was thrown in at the deep end. Sam, a brilliant lawyer at that time in his early 40s, was one of the leading junior barristers (this designation did not refer to age or experience but simply to a barrister who had not "taken silk" to become a Queen's Counsel – in Sam's case this had not yet happened) in the practice of commercial law. I found myself as one of three pupils thrown into the maelstrom of huge briefs and heady conferences (or "cons" as they were known at the Bar) concerning situations and law that I was ill-equipped even to grasp, let alone master. This is not the place to relate the stages of my career in the law, which are covered more fully in chapter 9; suffice it to say that for my second six months of pupillage I found a much more suitable placing in chambers that in due course offered me a "tenancy", i.e. a permanent place as a member of a set of chambers, at 1 Garden Court in the Middle Temple. My name could now be put on the entrance doorway; in the

---

[24] See chapter 6 for a full account of this period.

autumn of 1968 at the somewhat advanced age of 29 my career at the Bar was launched.

Rachel was born on Boxing Day 1968. Irene had miscarried the year before and we had been worried that she had inherited her mother's propensity to such misfortunes, but all would be well this time. We had been to a party on Christmas Eve and shortly after returning that night her labour started. As we arrived at University College Hospital for her admission to the maternity ward in the early hours of Christmas morning it was snowing, and in what seemed for a short while like a Dickensian scene we seemed to be unable to get anyone to let us in. Finally we were able to rouse somebody and the admission process began.

A "Jesus Crib" had been set up for the first baby to be born there on Christmas Day, but it wasn't to be Rachel, who hung on until the following day. I was supposed to have been present at the birth, but the doctors decided after what was becoming a very long labour to effect a forceps delivery and I was excluded from the proceedings, although they brought the baby out to me in the corridor straight afterwards. "Baby Rose" as she was at that time, tagged with a little band around her wrist, was a fine-looking little child (and it wasn't just her parents who thought so, that was the view of the nursing staff too).

The experience of having a little daughter was captivating, especially as she began to take note of things and, as babies do, to wave her arms seemingly aimlessly around. People would sometimes stop us in the street to look at her. For her first few months we would if invited out for an evening take her with us in a little wickerwork cot, and I loved showing her to friends.

One of the other leaseholders at 44 Elsworthy Road (at no. 5 which comprised the whole of the second floor of the original house) was a quiet, dapper little man of German origin named Hans Feibusch (Mrs Elliot, our Irish cleaner, who worked for him too, called him Mr Firebush). We met him soon after we moved in and invited all of the other tenant in for drinks. It gradually became clear to us that he was a graphic artist who was well-known in his sphere: he specialised in the painting of murals, particularly in Anglican churches. Originally a Jewish refugee from Hitler's Germany, he was baptised into the Anglican Church at about the time we first knew him.[25]

---

[25] Although apparently he reverted to Judaism towards the end of his life, dying in 1998 just four weeks short of his 100th birthday. His best-known work is probably "the Baptism of Christ" in Chichester Cathedral. A little research has shown that there is some published literature about him.

I really began a life-long "do it yourself" hobby at the flat. Painting the hall was my first project, during which I managed to knock over a tin of paint whose contents ran from the dust sheet I was using on to the newly-laid carpet. Quick action, accompanied by a screaming fit from Irene, fortunately saved the day. Another occasion on which things did not go to plan was my attempt to plumb in a new washing machine in our kitchen. Having connected up the necessary pipework using some new "fool-proof" copper pipes and joints, I turned on the machine. After a short while there was a loud sort of "fung" noise as my joint in the hot water pipe sprung apart sending a jet of hot water into the air behind the machine. This water had to be directed out of the kitchen window before I could turn off the relevant stopcock and then face the humiliation of calling in an emergency plumber. The day concerned was, Irene recalls, *Yom Kippur*, the Day of Atonement; God was doubtless punishing me for my presumption.

The final memory is of learner drivers. The house backed on to a very quiet road, Wadham Gardens, which was effectively used only by access traffic. This made it an ideal place for driving instructors to take their clients to practice backing round a corner and three-point turns, and anyone trying to concentrate on anything in our back room found themselves doing so at times against a continual noise of revving car engines. This affected both of us (particularly me during my law studies) and it was necessary to take whatever counter-action we could. This included parking our Fiat 600 car on the corner in question and rushing out to remonstrate occasionally with the driving instructors concerned.

44 Temple Fortune Lane

As our little girl grew and became mobile it was clear that we needed to be able to expand; the time had come to look for a house. We had wanted to live somewhere in Hampstead, but quickly found that the prices there were beyond our range, starting as they did at around £20,000 (a price that in the early 21st century sounds difficult to believe, as this would probably translate into over £3 million). This was still the time when, though property prices were steadily rising, there was not the rampant inflation that began at about the time of the Yom Kippur War between Israel and the Arabs in late 1973[26].

---

[26] One of the more significant reasons for the inflation was the jacking up of crude oil prices by the Arabs (soon followed by other oil producing countries) as they reacted to the war, which was soon seen from their point of view to have had an unsatisfactory result. Only the intervention of the major powers through the United Nations had averted the potential annihilation of the Egyptian Third Army that had been surrounded near Suez by an Israeli force under General Ariel Sharon (later to be one of Israel's Prime Ministers). The Egyptian army as a whole had nevertheless achieved some initial successes over the Israelis, to the extent that President Sadat felt proud and confident enough to take the very bold step in 1977

By keeping our eyes on the market (and Irene was particularly good at this) and being ready to move quickly when something new came on to estate agents' books, we found, in the autumn of 1969, the house that became, apart from those periods spent abroad, our permanent home. We bought it for £13,750 from Harry and Wendy Gilmour[27], took possession in the spring of 1970 and after having quite a lot of work done, including the installing of central heating, we moved in there in June.

Home (except for periods in Africa) since 1970.
44 Temple Fortune Lane, Hampstead Garden Suburb, London NW11

At about the time of the move a minor new social network opened up. Under a system in operation at the Bar a "sponsor" had been assigned to guide me in my days as a student. This was a young man, Andrew Urquhart, who explained the ropes when I first joined and when I was attending the Middle Temple Hall to eat the required number of dinners that we Bar students had to consume to signify that we had spent the requisite amount of time in study. This system, a relic of the time when the Inns of Court were residential institutions for students, seemed slightly antiquated even then.

---

to go to Israel, and the following year to negotiate and conclude a peace agreement, brokered by the then US President Jimmy Carter, with the Israeli Prime Minister Menachem Begin. In 1981 he was assassinated for his pains.

[27] The couple were, as we were to become, close friends of their (and of course subsequently our) next door neighbours John & Sonia Woolf. Harry had been a pupil at Mill Hill School some 15 years before me.

Andrew was in different chambers from me after my call, but we continued to meet socially, and in about 1970 he encouraged me to join him and his American girlfriend Doris Goldberg (his subsequent first wife, who was as the same stage of a legal career as I was) as a legal adviser at the Islington Legal Advice Centre which they had been instrumental in setting up in the crypt of a church in Upper Street. Work at the Advice Centre involved attempting to help people who could not afford a lawyer or who possibly did not qualify for legal aid. We advisers were a varied crew of seven or eight ad hoc lawyers. One, John Mummery, went on to become a Lord Justice of Appeal; another was a then slightly built young woman whose subsequent career turned out to be very different indeed as a cook and broadcaster, Clarissa Dickson Wright.[28]

It was to Clarissa's family home in St John's Wood that Irene and I, together with Andrew and Doris and some others, were invited to dinner one weekday evening. Clarissa's father, who was not present that evening, was a well-known surgeon who numbered at least one member of the Royal Family among his patients. Her mother, Molly, an Australian heiress, seemed to us to be a shrewd woman who had cultivated an air of studied dottiness. In this regard her daughter undoubtedly followed suit.

We were admitted to the huge house in Circus Road, St John's Wood by living-in staff and ushered into a large room where Molly (who in fact had no trace of an Australian accent) was pointing out, and holding forth about, various artefacts she had purchased. She announced that when she was in doubt about a purchase she would consult "her saint", Saint Wilhelmina, who advised her what to buy or not to buy. This set the tone for the evening. I don't remember how the fact that we were Jewish arose, but seemingly interested by that fact she asked us if we knew one of her Jewish friends (David Manasseh I think was the name). "Did you know he was asked to be the King of Israel?" she enquired. Playing along with this nonsense we asked why he hadn't accepted. She said that unfortunately he couldn't because he didn't speak Hebrew.

---

[28] Christened somewhat improbably Clarissa Theresa Philomena Aileen Mary Josephine Agnes Elsie Trilby Louise Esmeralda Dickson Wright, she was the youngest woman at the time (1970) to have been called to the Bar. Clarissa later made her name in broadcasting, initially as one of two eccentric women cooks during the 1990s in the BBC's *Two Fat Ladies* series (with Jennifer Paterson). They would appear at the beginning of each programme with Jennifer riding a motor cycle and Clarissa, now grown to a size that fitted the description, in an attached sidecar. Asked about why they had chosen that particular title, Clarissa said: "Well there are two of us. I have a problem with 'Ladies' as it sounds like a public convenience, but which bit do you object to? Are you saying I'm thin?"
She died in 2014 at the age of 66.

Drinks before dinner seemed to go on and on: 8.30 pm came and went, as did 9.00 and 9.30, until finally at about 9.45 twenty or so of us sat down to eat. I was placed next to our hostess. At some point toasts were proposed, I think the Queen and then Prince Charles. "Roger, don't you think that Charles is a darling?" she boomed, apparently to me but in reality to the table at large. Before I could come up with a suitable reply, one of the chinless wonders[29] at the table ventured "Well, I wouldn't say he's a darling, but I'd say he's a jolly good chap!" It was in this vein that the evening continued, with almost anything likely to constitute the next, usually bizarre, twist of the conversation.

However, apparently unlike the chinless wonders, Andrew and I had to go to work the following day and Irene and I must have employed a baby-sitter for Rachel. It was thus with some relief that we finally got away from the whole somewhat surrealistic encounter at about midnight.

My grandmother with Rachel, 1971

Rachel, about 18 months old when we moved house, began to exhibit some of the common traits of childhood, in her case putting everything in her mouth, whether edible or not. Once when Irene was out she had found a jar of chocolate spread; I found her a little while later with chocolate all over her face and couldn't resist taking a photograph of the result. We must have

---

[29] A scornful middle class reference to upper class young men, a number of whom seem perennially to fit the description.

quietly conspired between us that I would clean her up and we would not tell Mummy, because apparently the first Irene knew of the incident was a little while later when the picture concerned arrived in a batch from a recently developed film.

Sometimes things that went in her mouth were less nourishing, and we had a real scare when Irene caught her sucking on the plastic foam head of a small container of liquid black shoe polish and had to rush her to hospital. Fortunately no harm was done, which was just as well, for she repeated the process a short while later. Rachel also began to put us on notice that she was not going to be an easy or compliant child. One day she had a tantrum while with Irene in the bank and lay on her back in the middle of the floor screaming and kicking her legs. "Never mind, darling" one old lady viewing the spectacle said to her somewhat inconsequentially, "you've got a lovely face".

The next big family event was of course the birth, in November 1972, of our younger daughter Jessica, but by then the stage was being set for spending some years in Africa, and that particular story is taken up in chapter 7.

Chapter 6

Travel Interludes 1961 – 7

The lure of travel	167
Overland to Greece July – August 1961	168
The United States 1963	172
Altavista, Virginia, and the Lane Company	173
Other furniture companies	178
A variety of people	178
The Mid-West and westward to Los Angeles	187
Last things	192
Israel 1964	195
Overland to Israel 1966	201
Kibbutz G'vat 1967	210

The lure of travel

The idea of travel abroad had become something of an obsession for me in the late 1950s. It had been present much earlier, and I remember dreaming of far-away places while gazing out of my parents' bedroom window on occasional sunny summer evenings from the age of about 6. But since the hitch-hiking holiday in Ireland in 1956, not itself a particularly adventurous event, I had longed to get somewhere exotic; not because I felt a need to escape from life at home or work but quite simply to experience life in different environments, the more different the better.

A grand opportunity to do so had of course come during National Service in 1959-60, when I had been able to go to Northern Nigeria, but though fulfilling in some respects that experience had been frustrated by my contracting hepatitis comparatively early on and eventually being invalided home after only six months. I had in fact had vaguely formulated plans to drive at the end of my service in Nigeria to what was then Northern Rhodesia (now Zambia) to go and visit a distant relative (Tony Foster, who was a lawyer at that time living in Ndola on the Copper-belt[1]), but for this reason alone they came to nothing[2],

Nevertheless, during the 1960s opportunities for travel abroad in more than a mere short vacationing capacity did indeed arise, and in some ways the decade could be seen as setting the scene for the broader travel experiences that came later.

Overland to Greece July – August 1961

Things started in a small way in 1961. Soon after demobilisation from the army, I formed a plan with Barry Marks and Chris Gane to travel overland to Greece and back that summer. We bought for the purpose and shared the cost of a second-hand motor vehicle that Bill Webber, the Transport Manager at Beautility, had located for us through his contacts in the trade: a Mark II short wheel-base canvas-top Land Rover (registration number 5813 NO). It was a vehicle of which I was as proud and fond as any other I have owned.[3]

Though on nothing like the scale of the dreamed of journey through part of Africa, the trip was nevertheless for those days a reasonably adventurous one and of a kind that not many people from Britain attempted. Once you had reached the Italian border with what was then Yugoslavia and proceeded down the Dalmatian coast (through today's Slovenia, Croatia and Montenegro, including a small enclave of Bosnia Herzegovina) tarmac roads could not be found except in towns. And having reached the southernmost point on the coast road, south of which was Albania[4], and

---

[1] Tony was one of three sons of the brother of my great uncle Jack Foster. Jack was married to Aunt Lily, my grandfather Archie Abrahams' youngest sister (she was very much younger than Archie) and of whom I was very fond. Jack and Lily Foster had no children and were actually, to complicate the picture even further, first cousins to each other. Another member of the Foster family, Ada, had founded a well-known dancing school. I never fully worked out my relationship to them.

[2] In fact the plan would probably have been quite impracticable except with a well-equipped expedition, and in any event the chaos and civil war that ensued in 1960 and 1961 in the former Belgian Congo after independence (it would have been necessary to travel through part of it) would almost certainly have made transiting any part of that country for practical purposes impossible.

[3] Soon after our return I bought Barry & Chris' shares. My fondness for 5813 NO was on a par, in Kenya some years later, with another Land Rover in shared ownership, and afterwards a Range Rover (which was to come to a sad end on the road to Mombasa). I eventually sold it in 1963 or 1964 in Germany to the father of my friend Werner Welle, who wanted it for use in his deer-hunting expeditions.

[4] At that time under a Stalinist Communist regime and almost sealed off from the world – certainly no tourists could go there.

journeyed inland over the mountains of Montenegro you dropped down into what was then part of Serbia (now Kosovo). The predominantly Muslim world you now entered was almost as different from Western Europe as it was possible to imagine. Mosques instead of churches dominated villages and most of the male population dressed in baggy trousers and wore rough white felt hats like large skullcaps. Road transportation was mainly in the form of animal carts.

Hardly anybody spoke English in those parts: the *lingua franca* in Yugoslavia was Serbo-Croatian, and the most widely spoken (or at least understood) international language was German. This was because of the still relatively recent history of the connection of the Balkan world to the predominantly German-speaking Austro-Hungarian Empire, and probably also to some extent because of the Nazi German occupation during the Second World War. The tourist population at that time consisted anyway mainly of Germans (in the divided Germany of the era, in practice West Germans[5]). Though Chris was something of a linguist, neither he nor Barry spoke it and thus it was I, with my school German, who needed to be the communicator. Not surprisingly because of recent history Germans were not then very much liked, and I often needed to preface remarks with w*ir sind Engländeren* (we are English). Even this did not always work, particularly in Titograd (now Podgorica, the capital of Montenegro) which, named as it then was after the well-known Yugoslav Communist leader, seemed to have been set up as something of a model Communist city. At the time we passed through, it appeared to be full of Young Communists, or whatever they called themselves, seriously going about their business and with an apparent dislike or disdain of all foreigners. We were definitely not welcome.[6]

On the way down the Dalmatian coast we had given a lift to two young Englishmen, Roy and Dave (if we ever knew their surnames I have forgotten them) who were spending some months travelling, and the pair stayed for some days with us. They were highly resourceful young working class men

---

[5] It was actually during our time away on this journey that the East German Communist regime began erecting the infamous concrete Berlin Wall, effectively sealing off East Germans and preventing them from escaping to the West, something that quite large numbers of them had done up to that time.

[6] In fact Yugoslavia, like most countries of Eastern Europe, was created after WWI mostly from parts of the former Austro-Hungarian Empire, when the European map was redrawn by the victors at Versailles. It had become Communist after WWII but had broken away from Moscow in 1948 and was not part of the Russian led East European Communist bloc. Even so, when Communism in Eastern Europe generally was finally overthrown in the late 1980s the country split up into its constituent parts, some of the process involving nasty wars. Even today the least homogeneous of the constituent countries, Bosnia Herzegovina, is a potential flash-point.

who were able, amongst other things, to bake their own bread by creating a kind of oven in the ground. The three of us had begun the journey by pitching a tent each night, but Roy and Dave did not bother with such unnecessary luxuries and we soon found that we were happier following their example, sleeping out in the open and on the bare ground (in fact for some nights after my return I found myself unable to get to sleep on a bed and needed to sleep on the floor). Unlike Western Europe, where pressure of population on land meant that there were very few places outside formal campsites that one could stop for the night, places to park and sleep were quite easy to find, and I can still recall the feeling of wellbeing and calmness lying under the sky on land that did not appear to belong to anyone looking up at the stars (something that was not to be repeated until some years later in Africa).

Our Land Rover performed well on the journey, although at first we had big problems with the wheels: we seemed constantly to be getting punctures, and almost got accustomed to returning to the vehicle and irritatingly finding it tilted at a slight angle with a flat tyre. We became frustratingly adept at the regular chore of removing the relevant tyres by hand with tyre levers and extracting and repairing the inner tubes, until we realised that it was the tubes themselves that were faulty or worn out. Somewhere on the journey we located and bought new ones and the problem ceased.

Once in a village we somehow got talking to a group of locals that included a man who had farmed for a while in South Africa and spoke a bit of English, and the conversation got round to political leaders. Tito was obviously one of those approved of (it was best to be of that opinion of the dictator in Yugoslavia at that time), as was our own wartime leader. Both, among others that included Eisenhower (who only early that year had vacated office after eight years as President of the USA), were toasted with a local bottle of wine: "Churchill [etc.] *verr guud*" We did not press for opinions of the then Soviet Russian leaders, but one local stated mockingly that he was "*ein grosser, grosser Kommunist*".

Eventually we made it to Greece. My memories of my first experience of that country are dominated by several things. Catching the first sight of the Acropolis in Athens was one: you can see the imposing Parthenon at the top in the distance as you approach Athens from the west. This was so striking and is still so clear in my mind that I was almost certain that I had taken a photograph of it; but in fact I hadn't. Another memory was of Greek popular music, which we could hear mainly from recorded music being played in cafés. I was and remain captivated by it, and later built up a collection of my own CDs of some of the better known Greek popular singers. A third was the spectacular ancient amphitheatre at Epidaurus, situated about 50 miles south of Corinth in the easternmost peninsula of the Peloponnese.

We had decided to go to this latter place to try to see a production of *Medea* (I think it must have been the opera by Cherubini) that we had discovered was starring Maria Callas, at that time probably the most famous (and of course Greek) diva in the world. However, on arrival we were told that there were no tickets available. This left quite a number of disappointed people besides ourselves. The exact details of what happened next are hazy, but those of us who felt ourselves to be thus dispossessed found that we could climb up to the top and back of the theatre premises where a good percentage, including the three of us, were able to scale the rather flimsy wire perimeter fence. There was a somewhat half-hearted attempt to stop this on the part either of the police or the theatre security authorities and doubtless some would-be gate-crashers were caught and turned away, but it was dusk and there were shrubs or bushes at the back of the rows of seats amongst which we three and many others could hide, and once over the fence we were not pursued. So it was that we were able to watch the whole production (albeit rather far away from the stage) with the added slightly guilty joy of knowing that we were doing so without having had to pay for the privilege.

This was my first ever opera and though, except in the case of Mozart's most popular ones, I never developed a particular love for the art form, the experience against the background of Peloponnesian hills, was unforgettable.

We travelled deck class on a boat to Crete, in the company of people and animals. At one point a row broke out as one man who had decided to pee over the side of the boat without having sufficiently "aimed off", managed liberally to sprinkle his neighbour. Easily the best-known site of interest on Crete is the Minoan palace at Knossos, not far from the capital Heraklion. The excavations undertaken by the British archaeologist Sir Arthur Evans from 1900 for over 30 years include a number of reconstructions of the palace as it was thought to have been. I had recently read Mary Renault's novel *The King Must Die* (her meticulously researched novels set in ancient Greece were very popular at the time[7]) and so had some background to this visit to the supposed home of the Minotaur.

---

[7] Her name (actually a pseudonym for Eileen Mary Challans) is pronounced *Ren-ohlt* with the final LT sounded, and not in the French way as with the cars of that brand. Probably her best-known novel is *The Last of the Wine* set in Athens during the in the fifth century BC Peloponnesian War, whose background is the homosexual relationships that men in ancient Greece habitually established. She herself was homosexual and went to live with her partner

All in all there was a sort of romanticism about Greek ruins, artefacts and remains that struck a chord with me, probably at that time even more than they would today. They represent a civilization that had given an enormous amount to the world in art, architecture, mathematics, science, politics and philosophy, and it upset me (as it still does) when I later heard people say dismissively "Nah! They're just heaps of stones". In my experience this was usually Israelis being dismissive of any ruins but their own (and sometimes those too).

We took a shorter route home, taking a car ferry from Piraeus to Brindisi in Italy through the impressive slice through the isthmus that is the Corinth canal. That journey which we accomplished in three or four days, was long but unremarkable. It was only afterwards that I learned of the attempts that had been made to try to get hold of me to return home early owing to Mother's serious illness.

The United States 1963

The reasons for undertaking this journey are explained in chapter 3. Unusually in relation to my life's events, there is a detailed record of this trip, which lasted just over 5 months, in the various letters I sent, especially to Irene. Re-reading these letters for the first time over fifty years later reinforced memories of some events, but revealed others I had totally forgotten. In some ways it was like having the opportunity (that never comes in practice) of filling in details of a dream of which one can recall only the salient features.

I had been warned that New York in winter can be exceptionally cold. To my surprise it turned out on my arrival in early February 1963 to be about 45° Fahrenheit (the temperature measurement we used in Britain in those days, and they still do in the US) equal to about 6° Celsius, much warmer than expected and I was over-dressed[8]. I found a room in an inexpensive hotel off Times Square and prepared to spend a few days in the city looking around before travelling south to Virginia, where I was to stay on the first leg of my tour of furniture factories. After the comparative warmth that greeted my arrival in the city, the wind veered to the north overnight and the temperature in the city plummeted the following day to 1° F (-14° C). I had never before experienced such a dramatic temperature change, and there was

---

in South Africa where they became active in the Black Sash anti-apartheid movement there. She died of lung cancer in 1983.

[8] Interestingly the winter in the UK had, from Boxing Day to the time I left, been one of the coldest on record.

now a biting wind that seemed to be funnelled down the streets between the high-rise buildings; sightseeing was out of the question, and I needed to ride around in the New York Subway just to keep warm.

At one point I asked a newspaper seller for a copy of the New York Times. I must have passed for a New Yorker, for "Where ya bin, Mac?" came the sarcastic reply: most of New York's newspaper industry had been on strike for some weeks. In stark contrast to what I later discovered about Americans generally: that they are among the most gracious and effortlessly friendly people in the world, New Yorkers I came across seemed often to be sullen and rude. But my first stay there was merely a short interlude before taking the Greyhound bus south to Roanoke, Virginia and onward to my first hosts, the Lane Furniture Company in Altavista.

Long-distance buses were the standard way of getting around by public transport in the 1960s. One could of course fly or take the train, but air travel tended to be used for longer journeys, and the bus networks were considerably more comprehensive than those of the trains, which by this time had lost passengers to planes and were tending to concentrate on freight transport. Of the bus companies Greyhound was the best known and had the widest network of routes (always in the US pronounced to rhyme with *bouts*, not *boots*) and before travelling I had bought in London a season ticket lasting 99 days for $99. Unfortunately, however, Greyhound were not so well represented in the Southern States I was travelling to, and for journeys other than between major towns there I needed to use the rival company Trailways, lessening somewhat the value of my ticket.

Altavista, Virginia, and the Lane Company
The American South was in the final years of its old conservative past. In fact it was in August of that year Martin Luther King led the first really big civil rights demonstration (there had been some others before) that became known as the March on Washington. But Virginia and North Carolina, the two Southern States with which I became passingly familiar, were still sleepily what they had always been: in the main intensely religious, highly conventional, insular and with an Apartheid system towards blacks (known there as "segregation") that was similar to that in South Africa. Indeed, as had been the case in South Africa too, religion seemed to dominate life, and the irony of a Christian view of life that regarded fellow citizens as lesser beings did not seem to strike most people as in any way odd. I confess that on one or two occasions in the South I myself ate at a café or restaurant designated for "Whites only".

As an example of the parochialism referred to, when I was asked where I came from (as because of my funny accent I often was), it was usually assumed when I said England that I meant New England – a part of the world, inhabited by foreigners called Yankees (sometimes "damned Yankees") that was almost as remote from them as Europe. For those who had heard of "London, England" the usual question, doubtless recalling the song made famous by Frank Sinatra and others, was "D'ya'll have fogs there?" Nevertheless innate courtesy made people want to be friendly and hospitable (to me as a white man at least) and the way in which newcomers like myself tended to be introduced to the community was by invitation to attend a Sunday service at the particular church of which the new acquaintance was a member (there seemed to be dozens of churches in the town). I was conscious that I needed to exercise extreme tact to refuse.

My accommodation in Altavista was the Dalton House, a grand house that originally belonged to a rich entrepreneur of that name who had lost a fortune in the depression years, but which had now passed into ownership of the municipality. It was at the time managed as a hotel by Mrs Andrew, a cultivated lady who took the Christian Science Monitor (a respected newspaper) and liked to have the opportunity to talk about the affairs of America and the world with someone different. I was offered accommodation (double room and shared bathroom) at the amazingly cheap rate even for those days of $10 a week. Mrs Andrew and I became good friends for the duration of my stay, I often had coffee and a snack with her, and she introduced me to other people in the town. When the time came for me to leave she expressed the hope that I would return some day so that she could meet "my bride". I still today feel some sadness that this was not to happen, for after leaving the little town I never saw it or her again.

Altavista was a small town, roughly half way between Roanoke and Lynchburg, set in a valley at the junction of two major railways, and one of the strongest memories is of the mournful booming of railway engine sirens as the trains approached level crossings close by (some of them were very long – I counted 205 railway trucks on one freight train). It was the home of two large manufacturing businesses, the Lane Company and a textile mill, that together employed most of the workforce in the town and surrounding area. At that time the former employed about 1100 people.

My recollection of the Lane Company is of a progressive business whose central production was that of cedar chests; they produced other furniture too, but it was these items on which they had made their name. The cedar wood they used not only has a distinctively fine smell but is effective in keeping clothes moths away, and they marketed their chests to a large extent as trousseau storage for couples intending to get married. The company was the first I had seen to operate on a computerised system: the central humidity-controlled computer room was about 16 square metres with several huge cabinets whose capacity would today probably be contained in a single lap-top. Information was produced on hundreds of punched cards of about the size of a modern aircraft boarding pass that were fed through sorting machines and decoded.

But my main recollections are of social events. Occasionally I would join a couple of young men, Peyton Richardson and Frank (I don't recall his surname), working as management trainees at the company for a meal at the rather run-down but pleasant little restaurant known to them ironically as "the Officers' Club". More often I would eat at a working-man's restaurant at a boarding-house known (after the woman who ran it) as "Ms Walshall's", where, for 50 cents, you could eat as much as you liked of the southern style food on offer: bowls of beans and corn, beans and lettuce, beans and potato salad, and various rissoles and stews. For desserts there were the ubiquitous, and delightful, lemon meringue and pecan pies (this was my first introduction to the latter, for so far as I knew pecan nuts were not at that time available in the UK). On one occasion I got talking there with a man who was interested in my accent. Clay Nelson was an engineer (railway engine driver) and an official of his trade union, who later took me for a ride, together with his young son, on the footplate of his diesel locomotive. Though espousing a kind of socialism (with which at the time I was myself in sympathy) he felt he needed to reassure me on more than one occasion: "mind you, don't get the idea that I'm a communist". I in turn reassured him that I had not for a moment thought he was[9].

On various occasions social lunch or even evening gatherings were organised for or around me, mainly by women in the offices. They were always curious to know how I found things ("What d'ya think of us?"), and the young man who organised the company's social events, I. W. Tuck (always known, as many Americans were at the time, simply by the initials of his first names "IW"), made a point of getting me to address their Fellowship Club "about England". Some of the senior staff were there, including B. B. Lane, one of the sons of the founder and the vice-president of the company in charge of manufacturing, and it was to his house that I was later invited one evening for dinner.

---

[9] This was not that long after the McCarthy era of the early 1950s during which the paranoid Michigan Senator of that name had pursued, in the House Un-American Activities Committee, and hounded out of office many people he accused of being communists. Indeed, as already indicated in chapter 5, one of the things one needed to swear in order to obtain a US immigrant's permit was that one had never been a member of the Communist Party.

That gathering was at the house of rich, educated and intelligent (I would almost say patrician) southern Americans. I caused amusement and slightly raised eyebrows by asking for my whisky "straight" and without the conventional serving "on the rocks" with ice. The steaks served for dinner were of a gargantuan size and the accompanying salads, as was normal in those parts, very good. Conversation ranged widely albeit, so far as any reference to politics was made, within a very obvious conservative framework (they were definitely not supporters of President Kennedy[10]). In a letter to Irene I noted:

> I discovered that certain topics just aren't discussed, as when B. B. said something about the negroes not taking their share of responsibilities equivalent with their rights; an attempt to follow up on this on my part was met with a firm changing of the subject by Stuart Moore [*the young and dynamic Secretary of the Company*]

Even so, my hosts, especially BB's wife, had what I discovered to be the American talent of making guests feel at home, and in spite of obvious differences in political outlook (which it would have been bad manners to dwell on) I felt, as I usually did at American social gatherings, very much at ease.

Although the Altavista experience was merely the first of a number in my journey, it was in many respects the richest and most memorable. There was even a kind of natural lead-in to my next stay, with the Drexel Furniture Company in the town of that name in North Carolina: a young couple whose acquaintance I had already made, Leonard and Betty McKeehan, planned to spend a long weekend in Knoxville, Tennessee, from where both came and invited me to join them on the 300 mile road trip there westwards across the Appalachian Mountains. The plan was that I would stay with his parents (and they with hers); from there I could get a bus back east to North Carolina.

Leonard and Betty struck me as a fairly average young middle class American couple. He worked as a trainee manager at the Lane Company and she was a teacher for 3rd and 4th grade children (both had been present at the evening at the BB Lanes). In conversation with Betty previously she had admitted to me something I was to hear implied if not stated by one or two others on other occasions: that she felt a little inferior to European people of her own age and standing. I thought this was a shame and we discussed why

---

[10] Subsequently infamously assassinated in Dallas, Texas, on the 22nd November of that very year.

it should be. Although we came to no firm conclusions it struck me that two things in particular had a bearing.

Firstly there was the fact that those like myself who were in the US from Europe (and thus in practice the only such people she could meet) tended to be for one reason or another unusual and probably unrepresentative of the average back home. Secondly it seemed to me from what I picked up that the American educational environment tended to be narrowly focussed and, as was to become the case later in the UK, education seemed to concentrate more on students obtaining good academic grades than on their becoming more aware of the world around them, in for example the realms of art, nature, events, etc. In other words on becoming what in former times would have been called a "more rounded person".

In retrospect there was probably a third factor that I had not considered at the time: that many Americans were descended from people who had deliberately left, even fled from, Europe in the hope of a better life in the New World, and had turned their backs on their countries of origin. This helped to perpetuate the idea that American values and systems, often referred to as "the American Way of Life", were the only ones that mattered, and this in turn did nothing to encourage an interest in things that went on outside the country.

Typically of the hospitality of Americans, Leonard's parents welcomed me almost as though I were a long-lost relative and went to great lengths to make me feel at home. His father worked for the Tennessee Valley Authority[11], was an enthusiastic protagonist for it and bombarded me with literature about it, some of which I felt obliged to take with me. His only request to me was that I should try to find for him and send him when I finally returned to England, of all things, a shove-halfpenny board[12]. I confess that in the light of all the subsequent experiences in the US I must regrettably have forgotten, for I have no recollection of seeking or sending such a thing later.

---

[11] Set up under the Government of Franklin D. Roosevelt in the depression years of the 1930s.
[12] A once popular English mainly pub game involving a flat wooden board approximately 20 x 14 inches (50 x 40 cm) marked with horizontal lines. A player positions the coin at the front of the board with its rear just protruding over the front edge. Any part of the hand may then be used to shove the coin up the board, and the object is to get the coin completely within two horizontal lines.

Other furniture companies

As my reason for being in the US was to study production methods, there were of course a number of furniture factories that I visited in addition to the Lane Company, and these were located in Virginia, North Carolina, Indiana and Kentucky. My experiences of them were distilled into a report to Beautility, complete with hand-drawn diagrams, that I wrote partly in America and partly on my return. I actually still have the original document and am impressed by my own writing all that time ago in the light of what I know see clearly as the limited interest I had in the details of the technicalities of furniture production.

One manufacturing process I saw for the first time was the "distressing" of finished furniture so as to make it look, if not exactly antique, then at least "mature" (so long as you did not look too closely). Various marks were applied to the tables, chairs, sideboards, etc. (even with black pencil), but the most bizarre part of the process was a kind of light flaying with chains in order to leave small indentations on the surface.

With one exception I was given open access to the plants and treated hospitably and generously, and met a series of delightful people in the process. In one company however, the Johnson-Carper Company in Roanoke, Virginia, it was made clear to me after a very few days that I was no longer welcome. This was one of the few companies in the Southern States that was what they called "unionised", in fact by the (then) mighty Teamsters' Union. I was taken to a sumptuous lunch at the President of the Company's club and the news broken to me:

> [It has] been most politely hinted at that my presence at Johnson-Carper is no longer desirable and that in one week I have outstayed my welcome – I don't know what they have to hide but anyway the President of the Company made it very clear that while he was pleased to have had me "the office is very busy just now and it really would be very difficult to gain any further information regarding administrative procedures". I took the hint – maybe they think I am an undercover agent for the unions (with whom the company has had a lot of trouble recently) – and knew where I was not wanted.

I had indeed talked to one of the union representatives (amongst many other employees at the company), so perhaps a kind of mild paranoia had developed.

A variety of people

But the more abiding memories are those of ordinary Americans I met. There is no pattern to these people and each was representative of no-one but him- or herself. Besides those already referred to in Altavista, there was to start with **Mrs Bristol**, my landlady in Morganton, North Carolina, for the period I spent in that State (there was no accommodation available in the little town of Drexel itself).

Unlike my first landlady, Mrs Andrew, Mrs Bristol, though certainly not from the "blue collar"[13] classes, was not a lady of any great education. She was probably in her mid to late fifties, and her husband had died some 3 years before; I was put in touch with her by the company and was to be her first lodger. She told me how she "just loved" my accent, although at times she found it difficult to understand what I was saying. I in turn found it difficult to understand how a person of her social standing could be, as I put it in a letter to Irene:

> …so abysmally ignorant about anything outside the US, and much inside it. A question like "What sort of money do y'all have over there [*in the UK*]" is one that I would expect from a 7 year-old child.

Her idea of looking after her grandchildren was to stick them in front of the television, and she was not the cleanest of persons:

> I have just had a bath [*in the shared bathroom*] and as usual had to do a major operation in cleaning it out beforehand. Mrs B really is the dirtiest of individuals; I wouldn't mind even if she expected me to keep the room clean (which I know she doesn't) but she hasn't swept it since I have been here [about 3 weeks]. I nearly got choked with dust while looking for one of my pyjama buttons underneath the bed tonight, and the bath is always full of dust and beetles and things.

We nevertheless developed a fondness for each other. She enjoyed showing me off to her family (what I thought of as my "prize animal in the zoo act") and I was happy enough to be invited to spend a weekend afternoon walking aimlessly with her and some of her family around the local shopping mall[14], or in joining her for the weekly invitation for coffee and cake to watch the variety show on Sunday evening television that she enjoyed (the only thing which stays in my mind about that show was that it was sponsored by Pilsbury, which must say something for the power of advertising – I think they made cakes). Mrs Bristol liked to frequent the "Beauty Parlour" every so often to have her hair done, etc. (I had previously heard of such places only in relation to poodles!) and she almost squealed with delight when I complemented her on her appearance afterwards.

---

[13] This and "white collar" were used generally as references to working and middle classes respectively. I believe they still are.
[14] These are now a familiar part of the shopping scene in the UK, but that was not so in the early 1960s.

John Heaton, North Carolina, April 1963

John Heaton was an altogether different type of person. I had been intending one weekend to try to hitch a ride to Jonas Ridge, a little town in the Blue Ridge Mountains about 15 miles from Morganton that I had been told was worth visiting. I was having no luck, when a man I hadn't even signalled passed by on a motor bike, stopped a little beyond me and offered me a lift. I was delighted with this unexpected good fortune, especially as he was also going to Jonas Ridge. I think it was the first time I had ridden, albeit pillion, on a motor bike and was nearly hurled backwards by the tremendous thrust of acceleration as we pulled away.

John, aged 54, had a married son and daughter but he and his wife now kept a household full of seven children (two adopted, four "on welfare" – I presumed foster children – and one granddaughter from his son's first marriage). He was currently working as a meat packer in Hickory where he lived, but had served for a time in the Merchant Navy, as well as having been employed at various times in "cow-punching", sheep farming, agricultural farming, as a carpenter's assistant, and in a host of other kinds of jobs.

All this I learned during the next few hours. Besides enjoying the spectacular scenery of the Blue Ridge Mountains, at his suggestion we stopped at various places along the way to drink at streams, to study stones and rocks, about which he seemed to have a good knowledge, and at one point to taste birch sap, which was very sweet and smelled a little of cinnamon. On the way back he insisted that I should go home with him to meet his family. I agreed, and the experience was nothing if not intense:

> We had just got in to an empty house when in walked Mrs with all the 7 children, the most varied collection you have ever seen. They were all very taken with me, especially the little granddaughter of 11 years who with a glint in her eye ("they'll *never* believe me at school when I tell them we had a visitor from England!") bombarded me with questions. Mrs Heaton meanwhile got some supper for John and myself and before I knew what was happening a plate of vegetable salad with the most gorgeous hot corn bread was placed in front of me while various members of the family trod on one another to get me coffee, cake, etc. After I had eaten fit to burst, talking with all the children as I did so, the whole family disappeared almost as suddenly as they had come, dressed up and went off to a church social event or something, leaving John and me to sit and talk.

In a large shed in the garden of his house there was a boat he was in the process of building, although even he seemed to have run out of steam with that particular project. He begged me to stay the night, but I had a lunch date with some people from Morganton the following day, and I knew that my hosts would be trying to contact me at some point in the morning. He thereupon drove me on his bike the 25 miles or so back to my lodgings and promised that if and when he did a similar trip (he mentioned Cherokee and the Indian reservation) he would call me beforehand and pick me up on the way.

A few days later I received a letter from him (to "Dear friend Roger" and signed "yr friend John Heaton") apologising for the fact that he was not going to the mountains again that weekend but suggesting that he might come and fetch me and "Mabey (*sic*) you would like to come with me to Sunday School". Enclosed in the letter was some English money I had lent the children to show their classmates at school (I had actually thought I had given it to them). I received the letter too late to take him up on his offer, but I did take the bus into Hickory the following weekend and spent another afternoon and evening with them:

> ...the family were delighted to see me and insisted I join them in [*late*] lunch...I can say that I have never met people in whose company it has been a greater pleasure to spend an evening. They are quite poor by our standards but live life to the full and spare no efforts to please a guest. I spent much of the evening discussing with John many things including his secrets on raising children... On almost any subject I was hearing confirmation from experience of things that I had felt to be true, for this man is a shrewd observer whose...wide interests more than make up for any lack of intellectual ability (and I know enough about people to know that this latter quality is not to be underestimated in him either).

As was to happen on other occasions, I was sad to take my leave from them all, knowing that it would be unlikely that I'd ever see them again.

I met **Athas (Arthur) Peroulas** the very first night I was back in Virginia (this time in Roanoke). I had checked in to a modest hotel there that would be convenient as a first stop for my planned visit to the Johnson-Carper Company. An hour or two later I was just going upstairs to my room when I was accosted by a scruffy, emaciated looking man wearing only trousers, who proffered a quarter to me to go and buy him some beer from the Sterling Restaurant across the road and begged me not to say anything to anybody. I didn't know who he was or what he was doing there, but there was such pleading in his eyes that I felt I couldn't refuse. In retrospect I was probably undermining attempts to wean him off alcohol, or even acting illegally, but I got him the beer and told him to keep his quarter.

Athas Peroulas, Roanoke, Virginia, April 1963

I then decided that would go back to the restaurant and have a beer there myself as it was anyway a refreshing change to find myself in a "wet" town where beer, wine and liquor could be purchased in restaurants, etc. There I soon got into conversation with the Greek owner whom I came to know as Athas (his anglicised given name to most people was Arthur, but I took the view that it didn't suit him and preferred his real one). I was full of enthusiasm for Greece from the visit made a couple of years before, and we discussed many things about the country; he was, it seemed, a fervent anti-monarchist. He told me that there was a Greek community in Roanoke and indeed in most of the large towns of the US, but in common with many of them, it was his ambition to return to Greece to retire. He invited me back one evening to drink *ouso* and *retsina* wine with him. In fact I went back there many times subsequently, and he usually insisted on taking less than the advertised price for what I consumed.

Meanwhile, my new lodging was to be with **Mr & Mrs Cumbie** (that was what I always called them, though I later found out that their first names were – rather suitably, I thought – Talmage and Ruby). Mr Cumbie, very much an old fashioned Southerner, with conservative views on such things as the Negro Question[15], worked for the Norfolk & Western Railroad. He had at home a little electric organ on which he played rather old-fashioned music rather badly, but his repertoire was not limited by his ability and I was on occasion treated to murdered renderings of Schubert's *Ave Maria* and one or two Strauss waltzes, as well as a barely recognisable version of *God Save the Queen* played with pride for my benefit. The only thing worse than his organ playing was his collection of records, which seemed to be mainly of polka-type music, one of the very few music genres that I really do not like.

Mrs Cumbie, as with my other landladies, was most taken with my own situation (i.e. with a serious girlfriend back home, whom she wanted very much to meet one day) and adopted a mothering attitude towards me. For her, as with many American women I met, a little romance went a long way. She and her husband had no children; she told me that she had married rather late in life "to the man I always wanted", a poignant situation bearing in mind that her husband had originally married someone else and it was not until the death of his first wife some 12 years previously that she could realise her ambition.

Jeff French was a fellow lodger with the Cumbies. An ex-salesman now newly employed as a chief draftsman at the Johnson-Carper upholstery factory he gave me a lift daily to the factory for the short time I was there and I was to spend some time in his company after I had left the organisation. He had a wife and children but they had not yet joined him. Jeff was a happy-go-lucky, easy to get along with kind of fellow with interesting views on people and the world in general who liked to talk over a few drinks, and on more than one occasion we both spent an hour or two at Athas' Sterling Restaurant.

One evening after work he stopped the car in which he was giving me a lift and offered me a swig from a half-bottle of bourbon whiskey he produced in a paper bag. As I took the bottle out of the bag and went to drink, he grabbed it from me quickly and put it back in the bag, looking around furtively as he did so; drinking liquor anywhere other than at home or in a licensed establishment was apparently an offence. On another evening he

---

[15] It was his view that too much attention was paid to these people (known at that time, in Southern pronunciation, as "nigras") and not nearly enough to people he thought of as more deserving of it: the American Indians. It was certainly true that the problems of these latter people were little heard about. Nowadays social and political correctness requires that these populations are to be known, rather clumsily it has always seemed to me, as African Americans and Native Americans respectively.

came to pick me up already slightly the worse for drink and after a quick meal we decided to go to a symphony concert:

> I had to contend with Jeff who sober is embarrassing with his sociability but drunk is a positive menace. I spent most of the evening apologising to various women he picked on and then keeping him in check while he made odd beer-smelling comments during the performance, nearly falling into my lap as he did so.

But he was generally very good company. He was also a cook of some ability and turned his hand to roasting a leg of venison for a sumptuous meal one evening at the Cumbies'.

After my premature exit from Johnson-Carper, I was travelling by bus one day to meet the management of another furniture company in Staunton (pronounced *Stanton*), Virginia, with a view to a few days' visit later. The bus had hardly pulled out of Roanoke when a rather English-sounding voice from the seat behind me said "Excuse me, but if I'm asleep when we reach Lexington would you do me the favour of waking me?" I looked round and found a well-dressed but unshaven young man. Because of his accent, I asked him where he was from. Thus it was that got into conversation with **Jay Taylor**, a young professor (he was 29) of, I seem to remember, Romance languages and literature, at the Washington and Lee University in Lexington.

Jay was one of a class of Americans I had not yet met, an intellectual with experience of the world outside America. His accent was actually New England, although what he referred to as his "ancestral home" was in Tennessee. He had spent two years in Germany in army service and then a further two years studying in Paris; he was a great wit and a profound cynic about many things American. He invited me to break my journey at Lexington on my way back from Staunton to Roanoke later that day and spend the evening with him, which I gladly undertook to do.

> In what seemed to be the middle of the 'coloured' area is a large house with an old-fashioned outside stairway leading to apartments upstairs, one of which is occupied by Jay. He has a balcony through which one must pass in order to enter the apartment and on this repose a cable drum on its side, a smaller one beside it and a couple of antiquated white chairs. On [the larger drum] repose a variety of plants and stones. The apartment itself is divided into two rooms, each absolutely packed tight with books, paintings, photographs, pottery and various oddities like tin cans, number-plates, Aztec sculptures and odd pieces of twig…Many of the pictures are signed by the artists and in the middle of the dressing table is a large signed photograph of Delphine Seyrig who played the lead in the film *Last Year in*

Marienbad[16] and who, with her husband, a painter, are neighbours in New York [*where Jay also had an apartment*].

Jay seemed to know many people in the theatre and film world. He also had a collection of music records (LPs) that varied from Japanese through to Arabic, as well as language courses in Norwegian and Polish. We spent the evening in conversation on many things, firstly at the apartment, secondly over a very fine steak which he insisted on paying for, thirdly on the veranda of the apartment drinking bourbon in the evening air and finally inside. During the evening he was visited by a couple of his students (actually from the Jewish Fraternity, membership of which, he said, was sought after by gentiles as well as Jews in view of its high scholarship record).

> I think my own views which often accorded much with his own interested him, although I found that in many ways he was much more perceptive than I was. Part of the time we listened to music by Villa-Lobos, the Brazilian composer whose music I had heard very little of before but which I liked immensely.

Finally, in view of the late hour, I accepted his invitation to stay on his couch (he was actually ready to remake his bed for me, but I refused). But we seemed to get a second wind and it was 2.45 am before we turned in, he having lent me some pyjamas. The following morning we rose bleary-eyed and drank coffee without milk or sugar (I forget whether he had run out of both or did not require either; but in fact that is the way I have drunk coffee ever since) and we both afterwards walked down to the bus-station. He invited me back to stay with him whenever I was passing.

The next occasion on which I did so was the weekend some ten days later, on my way to Washington DC, when I saw rather more of Jay in his chosen context and persona – very much that of the outspoken and studied eccentric, who had succeeded in obtaining a kind of awed respect for himself, principally because most of the students at the University could make neither head nor tail of him. As in most walks of life, most people cannot

---

[16] In this unconventional (some said, then and later, pretentious) 1961 French drama *L'Année Dernière à Marienbad* directed by Alain Resnais, a group of unnamed aristocrats interact at a palatial château, resulting in an enigmatic tale told partially in flashback. The male lead character is convinced that he met the beautiful female lead the previous year in the Czech resort town of Marienbad where, he states, they had a passionate affair. She denies this, and states she has never been to Marienbad. The film is full of unanswered questions, as well as photographic tricks like double exposures; I (along with most people) didn't really understand it, but was fascinated by its haunting quality and the beauty, so it seemed to me, of the French language used. It won a Golden Lion award at the Venice Film Festival in 1961. Interestingly it was refused entry in the Cannes Film Festival that year as the director had signed Jean-Paul Sartre's left-wing *Manifesto* in support of the Algerian rebels in the Algerian [*independence*] War that was then at its height.

understand someone who does not conform to an expected pattern of behaviour; Jay delighted in this, and the unexpected became his speciality.

He was for example involved in what were seen at the time as almost dangerous political causes such as the anti-segregationist movement, and would occasionally even be refused entry to a restaurant in town. That very weekend he had organised an inter-racial Saturday evening buffet (something quite revolutionary in the South at that time), and on the following evening he and I went to the home of a delightful black couple (an almost unheard-of thing then for most Americans, let alone Southerners) and discussed, among other things, some of the bitter incidents that had taken place in connection with segregation. In a restaurant earlier he had the students he came across there believe that I was an English newspaper reporter writing an article on segregation (a role I needed to play up to), and he even had inserted a piece in the local newspaper, the Lexington News-Gazette, about himself which began:

> Mr Roger N. Rose of London, Eng. was the guest of Mr Jay Laurence Taylor last week in Lexington.

Jay also ran a film and lecture society at the University that had recently showed Jean Renoir's film *La Regle du Jeu* (Rules of the Game) after which he had produced and read out a telegram he had received from Renoir the previous day; it duly impressed the campus audience (though Jay had in fact solicited it). And that weekend he had arranged a visit from New York by a theatrical friend of his, Richard Barr, an actor, director and producer who was becoming well-known, having recently produced on Broadway Edward Albee's new play *Who's Afraid of Virginia Woolf?*[17] Richard too was staying overnight with Jay and both of us were invited to the mixed-race buffet.

It was clear that Richard (by then in his mid-forties) was not just an acquaintance but a genuine friend of Jay who regarded him as a highly stimulating and entertaining young man, if something of a "naughty boy". Sometimes he would say "Oh, Jay!" on hearing of some excess or other, rather as an amused and very mildly disapproving older relative might have done. Indeed at this length of time it is easy to dismiss Jay as a somewhat immature, egotistical, attention seeker; those things he undoubtedly was, but through it all there was an originality, brilliance of mind and undoubted

---

[17] He had received as a result two 1963 Tony awards, for best producer (drama) and best play. It was a play that I myself later very much wanted to direct, but even if the Garden Suburb Theatre (more of which in chapter 10) had been willing to put it on, the amateur performing rights seemed never at the relevant time to be available.

social conscience that cast a spell over those he knew and liked. I was and am very happy to have been, albeit for a very short time, one of them.

I finally left on the Sunday night/Monday morning to catch a 12.30 am bus to Washington DC, promising to contact him again in New York.

The Mid-West and westward to Los Angeles

From Virginia, my journeys (mostly undertaken hitch-hiking) took me via Washington DC to the mid-West, where I had a number of furniture companies to visit. I stayed for short periods in Louisville (Kentucky), Richmond and Evansville (Indiana), and Chicago, and met a number of people, both connected with the furniture business and generally, but the fact that I did not stay in one place for long meant that I did not gather the lasting impressions of people or places that I had done in Virginia and North Carolina.

As for hitch-hiking, it was often not easy as there were inevitably stories about criminals using this facility to overpower and steal vehicles and property from those who had offered them a lift. I had developed a technique that gave me a small advantage in having a small British flag and a sign stating that I was a British student, both of which I attached to my suitcase (although I was not of course studying in a university as the statement implied, it was in view of my programme actually true), especially on the long stretches of road between Washington DC and the Mid-West. I certainly had some success and enjoyed talking with people I met casually in this way. One man who gave me a lift and obviously felt the need to state his position early on waved in my face a revolver that he produced from beneath a blanket on the seat between us, "just in case I should try anything". But he was protecting himself, not threatening me (at least not directly), and he turned out actually to be both amiable and amusing.

Towards the end of May that year I was invited to be interviewed on the radio. One of the employees at Kemper Bros. in Richmond, Indiana, that I got to know asked me if I would like to accompany him to the local radio station; he knew the people there and thought they might be interested in having me on their "Off the Top" *ad lib* discussion programme around current affairs and general points of interest. As it happened they were:

> …we went on the air at 7.30 pm without any idea of what we (2 of the newscasters and myself) were going to talk about. It was not difficult to get going however, although I must confess I felt just a little nervous at first, and we finished up running nearly 15 minutes over time. This did not really matter as the half hour after the programme was only "padding" [*classical*] music…we talked about the main topics

of the news (the Pope, segregation, Cuba[18], etc.) and I was asked to give my views on all of them. American radio is pretty informal…and I soon found myself talking as if I were at home…

The principal newscaster, who was also part owner of the station, was an ex orchestral violinist, hence the accent on good music (they broadcast a concert each evening). One of the small things that stays in my mind with regard to this was that I was able to tell them how to pronounce the name of the Dutch *Concertgebouw* Orchestra. After the programme I was shown around the station, which occupied the top floor of an office building, and besides watching the announcers at work I was able to see the equipment with which they not only carried out the normal functions of a radio station but also arranged to "pipe" music to local offices and banks.

That was not the only first experience at that time. A few days later I was generously invited by Mr Clements, the President of Kemper Bros., to accompany him and his family to see the Indianapolis 500 motor race. Although not part of the annual Grand Prix programme, it is nonetheless considered one of the most important motor races in the world.[19] I had of course heard of it, and while motor racing is not a sport I was or am particularly attracted to, I enjoyed the experience of being there and talking with those who were, and was able to appreciate the thrill caused by the knife-edge that racing drivers are often balanced on between having control of their cars and losing it.

I later hitch-hiked my way to Chicago, which was not so much a destination in itself for me as a jumping off point for travelling to Los Angeles. Apart from plane, train or bus travel there was at that time a popular scheme for travelling by car: one contacted a "share-a-ride" agency to co-drive and share fuel expenses with somebody who was for whatever reason intending to go. One was put in contact with the person concerned and invited to meet him (it would always be a person the same sex) and see if he and I liked each other sufficiently to undertake the three-day odd journey together in necessarily very close proximity.

Having contacted the agency, the first person I was put in touch with was a native of LA who seemed to me:

---

[18] The Cuban Missile Crisis had taken place the previous October (see chapter 3, pp.101-2) and the death of Pope John XXIII, who actually died a few days afterwards on 3rd June, must have been expected.
[19] Run on a 2.5 mile rectangular circuit with appropriate bends at the corners (i.e. more regular in shape than those of the Grand Prix circuits), this 500 mile race involves completing 200 laps.

> ...a smug and conceited fundamentalist Christian. I found this out because he one of the first things he had said to me was "By the way I must make one stipulation: absolutely no drinking or smoking on the journey." Actually I had very little intention of doing either but...after I had talked to him for a few minutes I decided that 3 days or so in the car with him would send me quietly up the wall.

However, shortly afterwards I made contact with a young man in his mid-thirties, Bob Boozan. He had just finished taking a degree in night school and was going ahead of his family to take up a job in LA. We agreed to share the ride.

In the meantime I put up at the YMCA in Chicago. I needed to visit a furniture market there, renewing acquaintances and arranging some further quick visits to factories in southern Virginia on the way back east. I decided the city was not a place for sight-seeing, although I did spend some time idly watching fishermen at the lake. One evening I somehow got into a cosmopolitan bridge evening. My partner was a cigar-chewing negro: "Man! We gonna eat 'em", was his prediction of our success, based on no evidence at all, especially as the other three turned out to be better players than I was. Our opponents were a 20 stone Japanese Methodist minister (I could not have made up such a character) and an American student. My partner would almost lie on the table uttering wry comments about his hand and everyone else's ("Man! Looks like you got a hard job on from where I'm sittin'") but he certainly knew how to play bridge. We won too.

The acceptance of the ride with Bob meant that I had to leave Chicago slightly earlier than I had intended, but opportunities had to be taken as they arose. My companion turned out to be:

> ...typically Chicagoan in that words like please and thank you did not seem to exist in his vocabulary, and was a bit dull and staid...It was the devil's job to persuade him not to bat through like a lunatic and to enjoy some of the scenery. When I suggested going slightly out of our way to visit Las Vegas his reply was "Well, what would we do there?" I left it at that.

His car was, rather unusually in America at that time, a Volkswagen Beetle. Following what was then known as "Route 66"[20], we crossed the Mississippi River at St Louis (the river is not especially wide or memorable at that point) and made our through the deep red soil of the State of Oklahoma to Oklahoma City. We stopped at truck stops when we could find accommodation. As one progresses westwards the land gets drier and more arid and the temperature distinctly hotter. After crossing the Colorado River

---

[20] It was also actually the title of a song. The designation was officially dropped in 1985; most of the route is now Interstate Highway 40.

at the Davis Dam we entered the bleakest region of all, the Mojave Desert in south-eastern California. It was here that trouble struck:

> Bob was driving and unlike me having almost no interest in what lay before him he was belting along like a bat out of hell. VWs although sturdy and economical little cars are not made for constant pushing at around 70 mph in the 104 degree heat of the desert. There was a muffled grating noise and the car slowed down, soon to begin pouring smoke out of the exhaust. It was obvious that we were burning oil. By good fortune we managed to crawl to a little service station in the middle of nowhere and learned that in all probability we had "blown" a couple of pistons.

We had to get a lift some six miles to the nearest telephone in order to arrange for a breakdown vehicle to tow us back all the 62 miles to Needles on the Arizona border where, we were told, we would be able to find a mechanic to work on the car. It was obviously a lucky day for the owner of the towing vehicle, and we had to wait a short while for his wife to get herself ready for this unexpected opportunity for a shopping trip to the "big town" (Needles). It felt rather inglorious being towed with only our back wheels on the ground and in the opposite direction from that of our choosing, only to find when we got back to our destination that the work would take three days to complete. Apparently the very high desert air temperature and the overtaxing of the engine had combined to cause a heat so great that the rings of two pistons had melted and welded themselves to the piston heads, causing the free burning of oil and no compression.

There was now clearly nothing further that either of us could do; the matter was one for an eventual insurance claim. Bob needed to be in Los Angeles in a couple of days and we thus decided to continue the journey there the following day (he would later get the bus back to Needles to retrieve his car). There was the possibility of hitch-hiking, but we met some would-be hitch-hikers who had been picked up by the police and spent the following night in police cells, so it clearly had to be the Greyhound bus. Thus it was that at the central bus station in downtown[21] Los Angeles I took my leave from Bob and caught a local bus for the journey of something like an hour and a half to Van Nuys, where Irene's sister Monica, her husband Gunter and their two small daughters lived.

After travelling and experiencing new people and places for some four and a half months, arriving as a guest at the home of a family was nevertheless in a sense like coming home, even though they were not (yet) quite "family". Monica said she hoped that I did not mind sharing accommodation with two

---

[21] It was on this trip that I first heard this word. I presume it originated from the topography of Manhattan Island, New York, where there is downtown (the business centre at the southernmost part), midtown and uptown.

little girls, because the house was full of them. That turned out to be an accurate statement.

With Monica, Beverley & Miriam, Los Angeles, June 1963

For the first night I was given a bed in 16 month-old Miriam's room, but she clearly objected to sharing it with me, for she woke during the night and stood in her cot bawling her displeasure. I was offered an alternative bed, the couch in the living-room. This solved baby Miriam's problem, but it facilitated a situation in which I could be woken early each morning by four-year-old Beverly whispering in my ear "Are you awake yet?"

Playing with the children inevitably became part of the scene, and, as is usually the case in families with young children, it was difficult to talk with Monica and Gunter except in the evenings. I was nevertheless introduced to various of their friends and to Monica and Irene's unmarried Auntie Jenny (their father's older sister) who had gone out to the USA in the late 1930s and now lived in an apartment of her own not too far away. Auntie Jenny did not say much and with what little she did say seemed to have the knack of upsetting someone or other, usually either Monica or little Beverly, but there was clearly a family bond and Monica put herself out to include the old lady (who actually died the following year) in family things as often as practicable.

Gunter, whose history is referred to very briefly in chapter 5, was employed as a salesman, actually of medical equipment for doctors' surgeries. It was a job he did not particularly relish and to which he was not ideally suited, having neither the extrovert brashness nor dogged persistence that those in that profession ideally need, especially in the USA. As was and is usually the case with refugees, he had had to find work where he could, for there was neither the time nor the money to qualify in a profession, even if his age and unfinished education in Germany had not been against him. But he made a living nonetheless, and the family did not go short.

I did get to do some of the things all those new to Los Angeles do, such as visiting Disneyland and doing a tour of some of the sites both with Monica and with a widely-travelled LA resident friend of Irene's, Hershel Shorr, whom she had met on board ship when travelling to the USA to take up a summer post as a camp counsellor two years before. Hollywood was of course a place to visit even though it had already for some time passed its golden age and, living on its reputation as the capital of the film world in the 1930s and 40s, was (and indeed remains) a tourist attraction for that fact alone. But for me the most memorable site was the now famous beautifully ugly Watts Towers, designed and built in Watts district during the period 1921-54 by an Italian immigrant, Sabato Rodia on his own plot of land. The towers (the tallest of which is 30 metres, or nearly 100ft, high) have survived various misfortunes, including earthquakes and an attempt by the municipality to pull them down in a strength test to establish their safety (the towers remained intact and the test was abandoned when the crane involved suffered a mechanical failure!) In a nice twist of fate they are now owned by the municipality and have an adjacent "Arts Center".

Last things

I had booked a return passage on the "United States", one of the ocean liners that still ran on a regular service across the Atlantic, which was due to leave New York on the 18th July, but I still had some furniture factories to visit in Virginia. I had actually wanted to drive back the three or four days that it would have taken, on a similar basis to that on which I had travelled from Chicago, but there seemed to be nothing available, and so I booked an unscheduled flight (these were put on in response to need rather than operating a regular service) back to New York. As bad luck would have it the very next morning a call came offering me a shared ride to Birmingham, Alabama, but the hassle involved in cancelling my flight, as well as an impending shortage of time, meant that I had reluctantly to refuse it.

On the flight to New York I shared a back row of seats with, amongst others, 2 film starlets who wanted me to "just talk" because they, as with others I had met, "just loved my accent". Most of the time, however, they talked incessantly between themselves about nothing. My plan was that I would leave my luggage at Jay Taylor's apartment, but I couldn't get hold of him.

A neighbour of his found me sweating on the landing in the steamy heart of New York July transferring into my small case clothes I would need for the following week and agreed to hold my main suitcase for me until Jay returned. That night I took a bus back to Roanoke; I had 2 seats to myself and tried to sleep on my back with my legs up the wall, but I received a sharp crack on the head from the seat arm every time the bus hit a bump in the road.

Having arrived at 4.45 am, I needed to wait some 2½ hours for a connecting bus to Martinsville.

> While doing so I decided to have a shave and found myself being watched by an old boy who begged me to shave him "when I had finished". Feeble excuses were brushed aside and I was soon running my razor over his stubbly face, assuring him that he was going to be very sore, etc. Someone walked in and watching the spectacle with a broad grin declared that now he had seen everything! Finally I got rid of Grandpa, washed my razor [and] dashed outside to the restaurant only to find that at 5.45 in the morning it had just closed for the employees' breakfast. Another hour passed before I could get a lousy cup of coffee.

It took about 3 days for me to make the quick visits I had arranged in Virginia, another two staying at the Washington apartment of a friend, Tony Round, from London and then I arrived back for my last 3 days at Jay's in New York. The apartment was in Coenties Slip almost at the base of Manhattan Island (a number of small roads there are called slips) and from the window you could see barges starting to make their way up the East River. It was spacious but not very comfortable. I sat down to write a last letter to Irene:

> It seems amazing that tomorrow I shall be sailing back to England, for this evening seems just like any other. I am sitting in Jay's one room while he is out doing a summer job which keeps him occupied from 5pm to 11pm each day. It is a huge place with miles of bare floor, no electricity (that was cut off), no gas (that was too) and consequently no hot water. Only Jay could choose such a place – a sort of business premises due for demolition[22] – with rats on the floor upstairs to keep him company. I expect I shall have to finish this letter by candlelight.

And finish it by candlelight I indeed did, stopping every so often in the unpleasantly humid heat to peel the thin air-mail writing paper off my sweating arm. The radio was on and, having almost finished the letter, I was listening to "some dreamy music by Delius" and resisting the need to get myself packed for the voyage home.

---

[22] That area has in fact since been extensively redeveloped since the 1960s.

This time I had done a fair amount of walking in Manhattan, a tiring business as the island is a continuous network of streets, many of which have necessarily to be crossed in order to cover any distance. There are few places other than Central Park, which isn't very central, where one can relax; in fact on one my last few days I was so tired that I slept on a seat there during the daytime. But it was not the "pace of life" in New York that tired me but a combination of travelling, a crowded schedule, and lack of sleep that had been induced by the need to cover large distances on night-time buses. In my experience the "pace" of New York was no greater than that of London or Paris, and the traffic not as bad as in either.

As I had technically entered the country as an immigrant,[23] I was required to register for US army service after six months. One of the things I needed therefore to do was to inform the authorities of my impending departure. It took me most of one day and a lot of queuing, often in the wrong line, to locate the correct department and to hear officially that I did not need to register until my return. As will be seen, this eventuality was not at that time a merely fanciful one.

One of the areas that rather shocked me as I covered the area from Greenwich Village to Coenties Slip was the Bowery, a wide street that runs south from the junction of 3rd and 4th Avenues at around 6th Street:

> Never have I seen such human degradation as here…even in the poorest parts of Africa I didn't see such miserable examples of humanity[24]. Ugly, unshaven, filthy men were lying all over the pavement very often with a bottle in their hands, although quite honestly I couldn't tell whether most of them were in drunken stupors or simply asleep – I fancy the latter.

From this, the lowest level of humanity, to that of "society" I had by living and travelling as I did been able to see a fair cross-section of American people and places. In general I liked what I had seen. Throughout the months there I had been giving serious thought to returning there with Irene. From what I had seen in industry and information I had been given, it is ironic that I had wanted to try my hand in a profession subsequently taken up by my son Jonno, that of management consultant. Whether this would have been with a view to gaining experience in industry generally and then returning to Beautility, or of potentially staying in the USA, I cannot after all this time remember. In any event it didn't happen: after my return I was persuaded, mainly by Dad, to stay put. And that, at least for a short while, is what happened.

---

[23] See chapter 5, p. 153.
[24] At that time my experience of the continent had of course been limited to Nigeria.

Jay took me to the relevant ocean terminal the following day. I don't remember details of the voyage except that time, in the sense of day or night, seemed not to have much meaning, especially in an inside cabin. I met a girl named Cathy from somewhere in Rhode Island, who in other circumstances I might well have wanted to get to know better. After the ship had docked at Southampton I was having tea with an acquaintance prior to disembarking and travelling to London, when a steward brought me a message that someone had come to see me. There, unexpectedly, on deck looking fresh in a pale blue summer dress, was Irene.

Israel 1964

Palestine and later Israel had been of only background interest to me when growing up. My parents believed in Jewish assimilation into British life and were not Zionists at any level of participation, although Dad did make occasional contributions to what was called the Joint Palestine Appeal[25]. Israel's independence in 1948 passed almost unnoticed by me, although I do remember being given at about that time, probably on one of my first attendances at Edgware Synagogue, a booklet entitled *Molodet*, which gave basic information about the embryo State; but I didn't take much interest in either the booklet or the new State it celebrated. And as already recounted, although I had at the age of seventeen joined for a short while the Federation of Zionist Youth, this was intended only as membership of a social rather than a political organisation, and it did not anyway last for more than a couple of years.

An example of my standpoint at the time will show what I mean. The series of events comprising the Israel/Arab war and the Franco British occupation of the Suez Canal Zone in October 1956 had held my attention far more from the point of view of the involvement of, and subsequent humiliation suffered by, Britain than it had from that of Israel, even though I was pleased by the success of the latter in demonstrating that it was not going to continue to be bullied, much less exterminated, by the Arab nations surrounding it.

Irene, coming as she did from a much more typical Jewish family was considerably more involved in Jewish life, though certainly not in a narrow or enclosed sense (for otherwise there would not have been any foundation for a relationship between us); even so, her parents would not have thought of themselves as Zionists. But she had in the summer of 1959 done what many young Jewish people were doing at that time in making an extensive

---

[25] It provided support for Jews in Palestine, and later became the Joint Israel Appeal.

visit to Israel; in fact it was on that trip, in which she had seen much of the country and worked for a short while in a kibbutz, that she formed a number of friendships that were to be lasting. Her involvement and friends fostered in me an interest in the country, and it seemed a good idea to spend the main part of our honeymoon there. As I read up some background to the creation of Israel I found myself drawn into the subject; it remains a fascination to this day.

There had always been a small Jewish population in "Zion", basically that region of the Turkish Empire which after the First World War became known as Palestine and which had always been intimately connected with Jewish religion and history. By the mid-nineteenth century that population numbered about 10,000, mainly in religious communities the majority of whom originated from the Pale of Settlement[26]. Most of these lived in the Jewish Quarter of the old city of Jerusalem but other small populations lived in, among other towns of the region, Safed, Tiberias, Jaffa and Hebron. They existed to a large extent on charity from Jewish communities abroad.

Meanwhile poverty, lack of opportunity and anti-Jewish pogroms in the Pale in the late nineteenth and early twentieth centuries caused a huge emigration of Jews, mainly of course to the United States and to a lesser extent Western Europe. But by the late nineteenth century Zionist movements had fostered the idea of creating, if not a Jewish State then at least a viable and self-sustaining Jewish population in Zion. A small minority of Jews from the Pale and other areas of mainly Eastern Europe were fired by this idea and the need to do something practical about it.

Various attempts were made to create an agricultural society in Zion. Tracts of land, much of it in the ownership of absentee landlords, had been bought with the help of the Jewish philanthropist Baron Edmund de Rothschild. A good deal of this land consisted of un-drained malarial swamp, and some of the early attempts failed, but the immigrants of what became known as the First *Aliyah*[27] were persistent in the face of adversity, and bit by bit viable farming and small industrial communities were established. After the 1896

---

[26] That swathe of territory in what was then Greater Russia in which, with few exceptions, Jews were required to live. It included much of present-day Lithuania, Belarus, Poland, Moldova and Ukraine, and part of western Russia.

[27] The Hebrew word for ascent, the notion being that those who went to Zion were "ascending" to their destiny. Among the first settlements from the late 1870s and early 1880s were Petach Tikva (Gateway of Hope); Rishon le-Zion (First in Zion), both of which are now swallowed up in the conurbation that is modern Tel Aviv; Rosh Pinar (Head Stone); Zichron Ya'acov (in Memory of Jacob – the name of Baron Rothschild's father) and Rehovot (Wide Expanses). Martin Gilbert's *Israel, A History* (Doubleday 1998) is to date the best comprehensive modern general history of the country.

publication of Theodore Herzl's book *Der Judenstaat* (The Jewish State) and his work in forming the World Zionist Organisation, the idea gained wider adherence, and a much larger wave of immigrants in the early years of the twentieth century formed what became known as the Second *Aliyah*. To these communities were of course added many thousands of refugees from Nazi Germany and Eastern Europe in the 1930s and 1940s, and many more immigrants from all over the world after the establishment of Israel.[28]

The armistice that ended the first Israel/Arab war of 1948-9 had partitioned the country roughly along ethnic lines, although Israeli successes in the war (which the Arabs had declared immediately the new State came into being in May 1948 in an attempt to exterminate it) had delivered into its hands areas that had not been assigned to it in the original UN partition plan (especially a large part of the Galilee, and part of the central plain, that were occupied exclusively or predominantly by Arabs). Most of the rest of Palestine, consisting of the hill country of biblical Judea and Samaria and the Jordan Valley to the east of them, except for a corridor to Jerusalem that had been bitterly fought over, came under Jordanian jurisdiction.[29] The Gaza strip came under that of Egypt.

The city of Jerusalem, that had been intended by the UN partition plan to be under international control, was now divided by an armistice line that ran north/south, cutting off from Israel the walled old city with its Jewish Quarter and the Hebrew University and Hadassah Hospital on Mount Scopus. Ugly patches of no-man's land lay between the actual armistice borders in the city, the largest of which surrounded the residence of the Governor in mandate times, and was now the UN headquarters.

Some family research disclosed that I in fact had some distant relatives in Israel from a branch of my grandfather Archie Abrahams' family that had lived in Germany. The contact in London was Aunt Jenny (also of course a

---

[28] This is not the place for more than a cursory overview of the factors leading to the creation of Israel. Suffice it to state that there were other important milestones on the way, most importantly the Balfour Declaration of 1917, in which the British Government had stated that it "viewed with favour the establishment in Palestine of a National Home for the Jewish People". What *exactly* this meant (and it was deliberately vague and subject to a proviso regarding other populations there), was to cause constant wrangling between Jews, Arabs and the Government of (the British Mandated Territory of) Palestine, and the situation generally led to riots and eventually armed struggle between Jews and Arabs. Finally the British Government, unable (and increasingly unwilling to attempt further) to keep the peace, "threw in the towel" in 1947 and passed the problem to the United Nations. The UN General Assembly voted in November of that year to partition Palestine. All the Arabs refused to accept this at the time; many have continued to do so ever since, often violently.

[29] This area eventually became known as the West Bank (i.e. of the River Jordan) and includes the towns of Bethlehem, Hebron, Nablus, Jenin and Jericho.

cousin of some degree to my grandfather, and not to be confused with Irene's aunt of the same name), whom I had not previously met but who was in regular contact with those in Israel. Irene and I duly established contact with her and discovered that these distant cousins, Werner Finkelstein and his sister Lottie, had been involved in the Zionist movement in Germany and both had gone to live in Palestine in the early 1930s.

Werner, as he was still known to Aunt Jenny, had in fact been one of the founding members of Kibbutz Ashdot Ya'akov in the Jordan Valley. He had then or soon afterwards taken the Hebrew name Ze'ev Yaholom, and it was this latter name by which we always knew him. Lottie had married a man originally from Galicia (not to be confused with the area in Spain of the same name) then in Poland, now in Western Ukraine, by the name of Sig Chozner. Sig was an entrepreneur, and by the early 1960s both he and Lottie were successfully running an exclusive and expensive ladies' dress shop in Jerusalem.

There was in 1964 still a pioneering spirit to the country, and indeed almost everything had started from scratch. There were no valuable natural resources and the Arab population there had existed to a large extent on subsistence farming with some minor industry. Very few people owned private cars, which were considered extreme luxury items and taxed very highly, and the standard way of getting around was by the Egged buses[30], which were inexpensive and reliable. People worked long hours, and the weekend, running as it did from about 2pm on Friday until Sunday morning (i.e. the Jewish Sabbath) provided little respite. Consumer durables such as fridges, let alone televisions, were not automatically to be found in homes, and many people did not have a telephone. Food and clothing, mostly home-produced, were simple and not of great variety. Travel abroad for Israelis, unless on official business, was out of the question except for those who were comparatively rich, owing to an enormous travel tax the Government then levied.

On this visit we did indeed take in some of the obvious tourist sites (although, as noted, it was not possible to go to the old city of Jerusalem; the nearest you could get was Mount Zion, abutting the south-western section of the wall). But the main recollections are not of these but of the people we got to know.

Ashdot Ya'akov, where we stayed with Ze'ev for a few days, was my first experience of a kibbutz. These collective farms, that often operated small

---

[30] Egged, which means union, was a co-operative that had been formed from the merger of various different bus companies.

factories as well, were unsurprisingly organisations of the political left, the only question being how far to the left. In fact Ashdot had actually split into two separate communities some years before owing to irreconcilable political differences between the members (I think the split was between those who supported the party known as *Mapai*, as did Ze'ev, and those the more extreme *Mapam*). We were ourselves later to spend some months in a kibbutz, and further discussion of the kind of society we found there will be found below.

On honeymoon, Irene at Ashdod, Israel, April 1964

Ze'ev himself was the man in whose principal care was his Kibbutz' date production. He had recently suffered the loss of his wife at a comparatively young age, but had four children the eldest of whom, Eitan, had married and was living at Sdot Yam, near Caesarea (the kibbutz of his wife Amira's family). Ze'ev had a further son Gabriel (Gabbi) and daughters Ruthi and Nurit, all of whom still lived at Ashdot.[31] Ze'ev prided himself, with some justification, on his spoken English. He regularly read *the Observer* newspaper that was sent to him on a subscription paid for by Aunt Jenny. He was probably in about his mid-fifties when we first knew him, and very interested to find that he had us as relatives, albeit rather distant ones. As with many Israelis of German origin his general manner struck one as being

---

[31] Gabbi was to be killed a short time later, I think when on reserve duty in the army, in what I seem to remember was a cross-border raid by Arabs. Eitan was to serve in the paras during the Six-Day War the following year, where he was wounded in the battle for Jerusalem.

German first and Israeli second[32]: he was rather pedantic and his sense of humour was somewhat laboured by English standards, but he was a kindly man who was dedicated to the kibbutz and did his best to make us welcome. The apartments that *kibbutzniks* were allocated were small, and he arranged that I would sleep in his room, while Irene slept in that of his next-door neighbour, Hannah, who was also originally from Germany.

During our visit Hannah was herself visited by an old friend, Lottie Hofri, whom she had been friends in Germany and with whom she had "made *Aliyah*" to Palestine. Hannah and Lottie quickly took to Irene and we were invited to go and stay with Lottie in her flat in Tel Aviv and to meet her daughter Ruthi and Ruthi's fiancé Gidon, at the time a captain in the Israel Defence Force. Lottie had herself been an officer in the British army during the Second World War, something of which she was justifiably proud, and spoke excellent English. Ruthi was just about to complete her army service; she had met Gidon originally when he was her instructor on a course.

Lottie and Sig Chozner had two sons, Mikki and Roni, aged at that time about 16 and 13. They lived in a fine house in the Katamon district and had their dress shop "Rovell" in what was then still called Princess Mary Avenue (now Shlomzion Hamalka). In fact the shop was located only about 50 metres from the border of the divided city; across an adjoining street called Mamilah was an ugly high concrete barrier necessitated by the armistice line that caused it to be cut in two (as it did with numerous other streets of the city).

These were the people we were to see again on further visits to Israel in the 1960s and in some cases after. With most we subsequently lost touch (we heard while we were living in Kenya from Eitan that his father Ze'ev had died, and from Ruthi that Lottie had too), but Ruthi and Gidon married later in 1964 and their lives were to run in many respects parallel to ours. Their three children were almost the same ages as ours, and they were to live for three years in New York after Gidon had retired from the army.

---

[32] Jews originating from Germany were referred to by Israelis as *Yekkes* (they still are, although in practice the kind of person concerned is fast dying out). As is often the case, different explanations are offered for the origins of this word. One theory is that it is a word derived from the German *Jacke* (pronounced *Yakkeh*) meaning a jacket, the idea being that male German immigrants to Palestine, being western Europeans, wore this type of clothing in preference to the longer coat worn by eastern European Jews. Another is that it derives from *Jäckel,* (pronounced *Yekkel*) which according to Wikipedia is a diminutive form of the German name for Jacob, the name many of them probably had. But the explanation that rings truest for me is that apparently in the Rhineland area of Germany *Jecke* is a colloquial word for a person (as in English – for men at least – with "bloke", "geezer" or "guy"). It may simply be how some German Jews referred to themselves.

Overland to Israel 1966

An opportunity opened up to travel back to Israel two years later. In the late summer of that year I had recently taken my Bar Intermediate exam and formally left the furniture business behind. The exact timetable of prior events is hazy in my mind, but we could afford a period of time away, from early September to early November, before I needed to get down to full-time study for the Bar Finals the following March or April. I also needed to be back in time to eat the requisite number of dinners at the Middle Temple for that Michaelmas (autumn) Bar term. We therefore decided we would use spare time available to travel to Israel, but we would do this the "hard" way, i.e. overland through Europe, Turkey and the adjoining Arab countries. This would mean entering Israel through what was at the time the only available entry point by land, the Mandelbaum Gate in Jerusalem[33].

We kept a joint journal during our travels (it petered out once we had actually reached Israel) into which we tucked various normally ephemeral documents, including brochures, cards, bills, etc. collected on the way, which is why it is still possible to record, amongst other details, the names of hotels.

I had started the journey sporting a beard; there's a picture of me sitting on the ground shaving it off somewhere on the road between Venice and Trieste. For a while I kept the moustache, which was in keeping with male fashion in the Muslim world, although in Israel that year I shaved that off

---

[33] In its time this site was one of the two best-known crossing points between "cold war" nations (the other being Check-Point Charlie in Berlin). The house from which the site took its name was built in 1927 by a Jewish merchant, Simcha Mandelbaum. During the 1948-9 Arab-Israeli war it stood between the predominately Jewish areas under the control of the *Haganah* (the main Jewish armed force until independence, that later became the Israel Defence Force) and the predominantly Arab ones under the control of the Jordanian army. In 1948 Mandelbaum's widow and family were required to abandon the house when it was requisitioned by the *Haganah* as being in a militarily strategic position between the two areas, and occupied as a forward base. The house was in fact largely demolished in a Jordanian attack later that year, but after the armistice the remains of it (part of the front wall with the entrance porch) were retained on the Israeli border. It was to some extent rebuilt and became the official crossing point between Israel and Jordan until June 1967 when Israel captured the whole city from the Jordanians in the Six-Day War. As the armistice lines were not yet recognised as official sovereign borders, on both sides the border posts were technically police rather than immigration posts. After that war, Jerusalem's Mayor Teddy Kollek ordered the demolition of the site (but not the building) which, he thought, had come to symbolise a divided city.
The Mandelbaum Gate is in fact the title of one of Muriel Spark's best-known novels set in Israel and Jordan in 1961. Published in 1965, it won the James Tait Black Memorial Prize for literature.

too. I don't remember exactly when this facial feature became a fixture with me, but it was probably the following year.

In contrast to the vehicle that three of us had used to travel to Greece in 1961, this time it was to be a little yellow Fiat 600 (EMG 58B). The journey across Western Europe was comparatively uneventful (from Italy eastwards in those days the tourists were, at least in Europe, 75% German). The Dalmatian Coast road was now surfaced, making this part of the journey considerably easier than it had been five years before. Skopje, in Macedonia was still partially in ruins after the massive earthquake that had struck it three years before[34], and there we put up at the Hotel Jadran ("roasts and Macedonian specialities vintage Macedonian wines"). As we came to dinner in the great hall of a dining room of the hotel Irene had been thirsty, and to quench her thirst she drank a quantity of the local wine. She must have done this too quickly, for suddenly she felt her legs wobbling (even though she was seated!) and slumped over the table. I had to half carry her through the enormous room and up to our bedroom, thinking it must seem to puzzled onlookers as though I had drugged her. She slept off the effect without further problems.

We eventually reached Istanbul where we booked in to the little Hotel Balin near the university (which according to its card *"Has all confort. Cleanear and cheep price*[35]*. This hotel same like your home"*). The only trouble was that there was a mosque just a short distance away, and the muezzin (or rather a loud recording of one) started the first call to prayer at 5.00 am daily. Although we had come through parts of Yugoslavia where Muslims were in the majority, Istanbul was our real first taste of a predominantly Muslim city. We took in the main sites (by far the most impressive of which was the Blue Mosque) and enjoyed wandering from our hotel through to the Galata Bridge (this spans the Golden Horn, essentially a river estuary running into the Bosphorus). In doing so we passed through streets where many activities were taking place: shoe-making and repairing, carpentry, tailoring, haircutting, etc., and from most shops came the sound of Turkish music being played on the radio.

Driving in Turkey was (as it was to be in most points south) a hazardous affair, especially at night. Many vehicles did not have all their lights, or any

---

[34] On 26 July 1963. It caused the death of 1,070 people, injured between 3 and 4,000 and left more than 200,000 homeless. About 80% of the city was destroyed.

[35] Presumably this meant merely clean and cheap, but we couldn't help speculating on possible alternatives: "cleaner and cheaper price" [no dirty prices there] or perhaps the more sophisticated "clean air and cheap price". The hotel was still there 50 years later, as a check on Google Maps could verify.

at all, and being forced off the road by oncoming overtaking vehicles was not unusual. At one point we saw a horse and cart upside down in a ditch by the side of the road, the dead horse with its legs in the air still harnessed to the cart. We had a brief stop in Ankara with a Jewish family Stanley had met the year before. From there onwards stopping anywhere was a potential hazard:

> On one stop to take a photo we were surrounded by gypsy children (one with a transistor radio playing) demanding cigarettes – one had actually plonked himself on the driving seat. We got rid of them with sweets.

We made for Antakya (Antioch) and thence to the Syrian border.

Before we started the journey we needed of course to have obtained visas to get to Syria, Lebanon and Jordan. Syria was the most difficult; it did not particularly welcome tourists and the slightest suspicion that we wanted ultimately to get to Israel would have led to refusal. More than that, one's religion had to be stated on the application form, and verification evidence of the fact provided. We were, naturally, Anglican Christians for the purpose. My friend Andrew Urquhart, my "sponsor" during my studentship at the Bar, was able to offer the necessary verification assistance: his father was a vicar and was prepared to write a letter "to whom it may concern" stating that Irene and I were his congregants. We had also to supply details of our proposed itinerary while in the Middle East. This we did, on the basis that we were interested in Roman and Crusader sites (true) and wanted to make a circular tour through Syria, Lebanon and Jordan, returning through Turkey (false).

In the end we did get the necessary visas for all three countries. Ironically it was the one for Jordan, the only country through which one could actually cross into Israel, which was the easiest to obtain. King Husain of Jordan had not only been educated in England but had recently married an English woman, and relations between that country and the UK had continued to be good. We did our best to make sure, however, that we would provide no evidence whatever of our intended destination, especially in Syria, even going so far as to cut the labels out of any items of Marks & Spencer clothing we had with us.

To get from where we were to Israel, the simplest route in those days was (apart from some side-tracks) to take the coast road through Latakia to the Lebanese border, on via Tripoli to Beirut and from there to travel inland over the mountains in a south-easterly direction back into Syria and on to Damascus. From there you took the road south to the Jordanian border, on to Amman and thence westward across the River Jordan to Jerusalem. It was not possible to go anywhere in Lebanon or Syria that was near the border with Israel, especially the area to the west of the road south from Damascus that led to what became known after the Six Day War by the Israelis who captured it as the Golan Heights.[36]

We had expected that French would be the principal foreign language in Syria and Lebanon, but while it probably was we were asked, while talking to the polite and cheerful Syrian immigration officials at the border crossing, to speak to them in English. That was not so in Lebanon, where one did need French in order to communicate. Actually we did not find much of particular interest in either coastal Syria or Lebanon apart from one or two ancient sites, principally Baalbek in Lebanon, with its grand ruin of the Temple of Jupiter, in a particularly beautiful setting in the Beqaa Valley between Lebanon's two great ranges of hills. We sat for a while watching the spring at a nearby little place called Ras al Ain, although the peace of the surroundings was disturbed after a while by a man proceeding to slaughter chickens, seemingly using a blunt knife. The result was not a pretty sight and it filled me with disgust. This was where I first came to witness the way in which the body of the bird from which the head had been severed leaps around as though alive. My own experience with handling (though not actually having to slaughter) chickens would come later, at G'vat in Israel the following year.

Beirut was still a city that prided itself on its sophisticated mainly Christian French culture[37]. It was thus ironic that on our first evening there, and for the only time on the journey, our car was broken into. The thief took minor items, including an inexpensive camera in which I had loaded a black and white film and which contained the only shot of the family in Ankara. But the worst loss was of a pair of my trousers; it was not that they were new or of especial value, but Irene had recently spent some hours sewing new pockets into them for me (a difficult job), and I hadn't had much chance to wear them afterwards.

In Damascus we felt somewhat tense, although this was probably due to our paranoia about the secrecy of our destination. There seemed be more of a military presence there than in anywhere else we had visited on the journey, although in retrospect that was not surprising as the country was politically somewhat unstable and had experienced various recent coups to establish

---

[36] This area overlooks and from a military point of view completely dominates the Upper Galilee in Israel. Prior to the Six Day War the Syrians had from time to time shelled settlements in that area.

[37] It was decades later to be the focus of intense inter-religious warfare that destroyed large parts of the city.

the Ba'ath Party rule that became an effective dictatorship well into the twenty-first century.

It was in Damascus that Irene noticed a small pool of oil under our car. Investigation showed that one of the sump bolts had come away and the casing was hanging down slightly. With some difficulty we found the only Fiat agent in town, but the incident led to one of those delightful moments of travel acquaintanceships: the garage owner got his mechanic to work on our car straight away, and while we conversed in French (I recorded his name as Shukri Bamboukian – probably an Armenian) he told me he was intending early the following year to make a trip to Europe. When I went to pay he refused to accept any money for the work; we parted wishing him a good trip.

There was an imposing market, or souk, in the city and it was there that we bought the ivory and mother-of-pearl inlay nest of tables that has been in our lounge ever since its reception at home some weeks later, and also some inlaid cigarette boxes for gifts.[38] Otherwise the scene was much like that in any urban Arab environment: most men were wearing traditional Arab dress; in cafés many were smoking the water pipe known in those parts as an *argileh* (sometimes called a *hookah*); and in the street many men walked hand in hand (no man would have done so with a woman). Letter scribes were in evidence in certain parts of the town and the picture was one I would have liked to record, but any request for permission to do so was met with the slight upward toss of the head and a sort of tutting sound that signifies "no". People generally did not like to be photographed (something to do with superstition about the "evil eye" – at the time I was keen on photography) and did not seem particularly friendly.

But we now faced the much easier stage in the journey; Jordan and its people were indeed friendly and English was widely spoken. Apart from East Jerusalem, the most interesting sites there were the Roman remains at Jerash, and that wonderful (in the truest sense of the word) ancient city carved from the rock, Petra.[39] Of historical interest too in the Jordan Valley near the Dead Sea were Jericho (reputedly the oldest continuously occupied

---

[38] In fact the three tables arrived in a partially disintegrated state, mainly owing to the poor quality of the glue used. They were not otherwise damaged, however, and it was a simple matter to reconstitute them.

[39] The most famous reference to this site comes from a poem published in 1845 by a little-known English poet, the Rev. John William Burgon. Though born in Smyrna (also, as Petra at the time, in the Turkish Empire) he had never actually seen it:
"But from the rock as if by magic grown, eternal, silent, beautiful, alone! ...
Match me such marvel save in Eastern clime, a rose-red city half as old as time."

settlement in the world)[40], and the Qumran caves in which the first of the Dead Sea scrolls were found by chance by a Bedouin shepherd in 1946[41]. It had not of course been possible to get to any of these places during our visit to Israel two years previously, and that fact alone made them even more of interest.

At Jerash after wandering around the site we sat talking in a café to a group of Jordanians that included a tourist policeman. On hearing that we intended to visit Petra he gave us an introduction to a friend of his there who might be able to assist. Petra was indeed a wonder:

> We decided to hire horses for the ride through the Siq [narrow gorge] into the city and were glad afterwards that we had done so. The Siq itself is marvellous and the first view of the gigantic treasury building, probably the best-preserved of all owing to its sheltered situation, did not lose any of its splendour for us through having seen it many times in pictures. Two little boys led our horses (both named Mohammed) which made the business of riding really very simple.[42]

Having been given an introduction to the Assistant Curator of the Petra Museum, we looked him up and talked to him for a while, but decided not to spend the night in Petra in spite of his offer as we wanted to get within striking distance of Jerusalem in order to be able to get there the following day.

The journey took us along the so-called King's Highway[43] (where we thought we saw King Husain driving in a small convoy in the opposite direction), taking a slight detour to Mt Nebo, a vantage point from which it is supposed that Moses first viewed the Promised Land; it was too hazy to see that far, but we did get a first magnificent view of the northern end of the Dead Sea[44]. As you descend to the Jordan Valley the heat becomes intense. The road crossed the Jordan (as it still does) by the bridge known to the Jordanians as the King Husain Bridge (and to the Israelis, who of course had no access to it until after the Six Day War a few months later, as the

---

[40] Dating back to around 9000 BC.
[41] Further scrolls were discovered on subsequent archaeological expeditions to 1956.
[42] But I don't want to give the misleading impression that we had suddenly become accomplished horseman and woman. The pace was slow, the horses old, and we had sore bottoms later.
[43] An ancient trade route, it runs from Heliopolis, just north of modern Cairo, through the Sinai Peninsula, Aqaba, Petra and Amman, and on to Damascus, ending on the upper Euphrates in modern Iraq.
[44] This lake is 394 metres (1,291 ft.) below sea level, making it the Earth's lowest elevation on land.

Allenby Bridge[45]). On the other side the road soon rises quite steeply up into the Judean Hills to Jerusalem. Eventually the buildings at the top of the Mount of Olives can be seen:

> Finally Jerusalem itself and the city seemed to equal all expectations. The extreme heat had by this time made us a little testy but in spite of this the city seemed just lovely. We parked near the Damascus Gate and just paused for half an hour or so to get ourselves oriented and get cooled of, both literally and figuratively.

We decided to stay at the East Jerusalem YMCA, which seemed to be occupied mainly by rather pious groups of Christians. The Armenian barman there told us something of the state of his community in the city (small, close-knit, despising, and in turn being despised by, the Muslims/Arabs); he himself was making for Canada in the near future. From the roof of the hostel you could look right over the city and indeed over the Mandelbaum gate itself, only a stone's-throw away. After dark a red neon *Magen David* shone as though defiantly from the old Hebrew University cut off on Mount Scopus[46].

The procedure for crossing to Israel was slightly complicated, although because the relationship between Israel and Jordan (though on the surface non-existent) was in fact one of guarded respect on both sides[47], things were much easier than they might have been. Our starting point was the British Consulate, from where we needed to get the necessary application forms (and also to collect a number of letters sent from home, including a telegram from Dad and Suzanne offering congratulation to Irene on her 27th birthday that very day). The completed forms then had to be delivered to the Jordanian External Liaison Department at least forty-eight hours before the intended crossing. It was Tuesday; we were told to collect our passes on the Thursday that week for a crossing on Friday.

In the intervening time we took the opportunity to see something of the sites. In Jerusalem one could visit the Dead Sea Scrolls, then housed in the

---

[45] Named after Sir Edmund Allenby, the British general who commanded the allied forces that captured Palestine from the Turks in 1917. The bridge was destroyed a number of times in the 20th century, including during the Six Day War.

[46] The *Magen David* (literally "Shield of David", more often known in English as the "Star of David") is of course the principal Jewish emblem and appears on the Israeli flag. In fact, unlike e.g. the Menorah (the seven branched candlestick), it is actually not an exclusively Jewish symbol. Mount Scopus was then a small enclave of Israeli Jerusalem surrounded by Arab-held territory. Although the Armistice agreement of 1949 granted Israel the right to pass in convoy through to it to maintain the buildings, in fact access was soon denied by the Jordanians (presumably on suspicion that the Israelis might use the area to mount attacks).

[47] The Arab Legion, Jordan's army, was the only Arab armed force which, then and later, Israel regarded as a capable and well led fighting force.

Palestinian Archaeological Museum. We had seen them in London and we compared the seemingly endless queuing there with the fact that here it was possible to walk straight in and wander round at leisure. We eventually found the Wailing Wall[48] (quite difficult to find in those pre-Six Day War times as there were only the odd signs). It actually constituted effectively one side of an out-of-the-way little street. There was hardly anyone around except some children playing; they demanded baksheesh when we requested a photograph. During the period from 1948 to 1966 it was unlikely that many people even visited the spot; it would not have been high on the priority of Christian tourists, as they would have been more interested in the Stations of the Cross and the more obvious sites of Christian interest such as the Church of the Holy Sepulchre and the Mount of Olives. And as for Jews, there would in practice probably have been only a handful of those such as ourselves with non-Israeli nationality who had made the necessarily complex arrangements to get there[49].

At one point we were invited back to the house of the Arab Mayor of the Mount of Olives, to whom Irene had got talking. The house was pretty filthy with people and children all over the place, but we were seated in the living-room, given tea and coffee and talked about nothing for an hour or so (luckily we had with us an Arab boy who spoke good English). The grandmother was presented to us as a person of some note, having recently made a pilgrimage to Mecca. It was then suggested by the women that Irene should dress in Arab women's clothes and pose for a photograph. She did so (although the resulting picture was underexposed and not very successful), but as she came out of the back room she whispered to me that the old man had been trying to paw her during the process and quietly pleaded that we should go as soon as she had got out of the fancy costume. We made our excuses and did just that.

We of course visited places in the city and nearby that anyone would want to visit. We found the Church of the Holy Sepulchre to be a complete mess. The inability of different sects to agree on who should pay for restoration had led to the church deteriorating to a remarkable extent; there was actually heavy and ugly scaffolding all over the place and workmen chipping stone or generally wandering about inside, but it remained essentially unrestored. We began to see the old city as it really was (rather dirty and smelly) as the fascination began to wear off.

---

[48] *HaKotel HaMa'aravi* in Hebrew: part of the western outer wall of the Second Temple, the main body of which was destroyed after the Roman suppression of the Jewish revolt in 70 AD and subsequent sacking of the city.
[49] After the Six Day War the buildings in the area of the Wall were demolished and a large open space constituted.

In Bethlehem the scene at the Church of the Nativity was much the same – ugly, and with the crypt where the birth of Jesus is supposed to have taken place full of 19th century Russian ornamentation which looked hideous to us and gave no sense of majesty or even cohesion. At Qumran in the Jordan Valley the caves where the Dead Sea Scrolls had been found were much smaller than I had imagined, but here at least there was the imposing location, just a short distance from the Dead Sea. A visit to the Valley needed to be made in the early morning or the evening, as otherwise the heat was unbearable. In fact our visit to Qumran was on what was to be our last evening before crossing into Israel and we made our way back up to Jerusalem as the sun was setting behind the Judean Hills.

> It was going to be difficult to sleep as earlier in the day we had been to the External Liaison Office and the Customs and had completed the formalities for crossing the Mandelbaum Gate and we were excited about the prospects for the morning. But on top of this we could hear celebrations coming from the other side for the end of the Jewish festival of Succot. We just sat listening and wishing we could be there.

The border crossing the following morning was a slightly strange experience, for we were conscious that we were about to drive our little Fiat through a gap in a wall that didn't look as though it had any significance, but was nevertheless one through which few people other than UN personnel passed. For their part the Jordanian officials could not have been more pleasant, finishing with us quickly and wishing us a good journey "on the other side"[50]:

> Up went the bar and in we went to no-man's land with the half ruined buildings all around us, and there before us was the Israeli flag and the welcoming notice. In spite of the unimpressive location, the entry into Israel gave a marvellous feeling (of accomplishment as much as anything else).

Formalities took longer on the Israeli side and, somewhat exhilarated by having finally achieved our goal, I eventually drove away into Israeli West Jerusalem. Excitement had made me forgetful however, for when visiting the insurance office where we needed to collect our Israeli 3rd party motor insurance certificate I remembered that I had driven away from the Mandelbaum Gate without my passport and the carnet identification for the car. Back we tracked to find the rather harassed Israeli Customs officer wanting to know why we had driven off before he had had a chance to examine our car. We apologised and after the requisite inspection (which

---

[50] This at the time was the characteristic way in which reference was made by Jordanian officials to Israel, a country which they, in common with all the Arab countries, did not at that time recognise.

could not have been more than cursory as no recollection of it remains) we finally went on our way.

It is there that our journal ends. I made some very short notes for the first few days in Israel, but in fact nothing much particularly noteworthy took place during our stay of some three weeks. I do recall in particular that we drove straight down to Tel Aviv to stay with Lottie Hofri and her amazement that we had come to her straight from Jordan; this was something that hardly ever happened to Israelis and it was memorable enough for her to immediately telephone her daughter Ruthi with the news. We revisited the relatives and friends met and made two years before, and others as well, for Monica Grodzinski was living in Tel Aviv at the time and sharing a flat with two other young women.

Politically there was talk of the likelihood of another war, especially as the situation with occasional shelling and terrorist incursions from Syria were seen as things that could not continue to be endured for much longer.

Towards the end of October we took the boat from Haifa back to Brindisi in Italy. Our overnight cabin was right next to where a noisy band played into the early hours, but there was nothing we could do. The homeward journey by road through Italy and France was memorable for two things. Firstly, as we crossed the Apennine Mountains in Italy it began to rain, hard, and continued raining for most of the rest of the journey[51]. Secondly, as we approached northern France and the Channel to catch the ferry (there was no Channel Tunnel then) the weather turned suddenly very cold. Passing through a village in the Pas de Calais our car hit a patch of ice and slithered completely out of control. It was a moment when we shut our eyes and tensed our bodies, for on the opposite side of the road a large lorry was approaching and a collision seemed inevitable.

Somehow we missed the lorry; it could not have been by more than a whisker.

Kibbutz G'vat 1967

In April 1967 I sat (and subsequently passed) the Bar Final examination. Contingent on my passing, I had been offered a pupillage at the Bar with Sam Stammler to start in the autumn. I need not have worried how we would

---

[51] This was the very same rain that caused widespread severe flooding in Florence in early November 1966 in the course of which 101 people died and countless works of art and rare books were damaged or destroyed. It is thought to have been the worst flood in the city's history since 1557.

spend the intervening period for during the month that followed events were taking place in the Middle East that made another (3rd) Arab/Israeli war virtually certain. The final challenge duly came, not as had been half expected from Syria, but from Egypt.

In mid-May Egypt's President Nasser effectively expelled the UN peacekeeping force from Gaza and the Sinai Peninsula (it could remain only with Egypt's consent), manned the strategic points that they had occupied with his own forces, and ordered the massing of troops on the Sinai border with Israel. On the 22nd May he declared that the Straits of Tiran (the narrow entrance to the Gulf of Aqaba from the Red Sea) which his troops now controlled at Sharem el Sheik, were closed to Israeli shipping. Israel had stated after the previous Arab/Israeli war in 1956 that such an action, which could only be intended to seal off Israel's port of Eilat, would be considered an act of war. A full-scale armed conflict between Israel and all the Arab States now seemed inevitable.

We were caught up in the frenzy of people (by no means all Jews) who wanted to go to Israel and do what they could to help to keep the country going during the war that was clearly coming (agricultural labour would be an obvious area of need). The Jewish Agency in London were almost overwhelmed with volunteers, and such was the pressure of applicants that they were not particularly keen to accept married couples in this capacity (although there was no official ban). However, we knew someone who worked there, and she was able to help to process our application.

In fact the Six Day War, as its name indicates, was over quickly. It began with Israel's pre-emptive strike on Egyptian and other Arab military airfields early on 5th June, destroying most of the planes on the ground and ensuring air superiority for the duration. By a series of very fast and brilliantly executed military operations Israel captured all of the West Bank area from Jordan, the Golan Heights overlooking the Galilee from Syria, and the Gaza Strip and the whole of the Sinai Peninsula from Egypt.[52]

This meant that the war was over before any significant number of volunteers could be transported to Israel. The Jewish Agency decided to continue with the process nonetheless; it would be a while before all the

---

[52] In fact Israel offered after the war to return Sinai and the Golan heights as a quid pro quo for peace settlements with the countries concerned, and to negotiate with Jordan as to what its western frontier should be. However, the Arab Summit in Khartoum that September unsurprisingly resolved that there would be "No peace, no recognition and no negotiation with Israel". For all except Egypt and Jordan (who had most to lose by the continuation of the policy and later reversed it) this is still the position.

reservists in the Israeli armed forces could return to their civilian jobs, and anyway there was an opportunity to attempt to persuade those who volunteered to stay in Israel as immigrants. We ourselves arrived there on an El Al flight in mid-June and after spending the night at a reception centre near the airport at Lod we were assigned the following morning, along with I think twenty-three others, to Kibbutz G'vat, situated in the Jezreel Valley west of a line between the towns of Nazareth and Afula. Our commitment (in order to qualify for free return passage) was to work there for four months.

The sense of euphoria in Israel generally at the time was palpable. Not only had the country won a significant military victory, but now it was comparatively speaking secure: terrorist incursions would be much more difficult and the upper Galilee was now safe from Syrian shelling. After nineteen years the old and most direct road from Tel Aviv to Jerusalem, which had passed close to the hill dominated by the village of Latrun, could now be reopened[53]. But best of all Israelis could now go to the Old City of Jerusalem, have access to the Wailing Wall and re-occupy the Jewish Quarter. In fact they could go to all those places we ourselves had been able to visit the year before. And at last the ugly scars caused by the division of the city, the sandbagged defence works on both sides of the old armistice line and the half-ruined buildings on that line and in no-man's land, could now be removed or repaired[54].

Although volunteers arrived in Israel from a large number of different countries (particularly England, France, the United States, Canada, South Africa and Argentina), all of us in the G'vat group were (with the exception

---

[53] Under the armistice agreement of 1949, the approximately 6 km section of the road running below Latrun had lain inaccessible to both sides in no-man's land. In spite of intense military efforts by Israel to capture Latrun in the 1948-9 war, the Arab legion had managed to hold on to it. It contained two buildings of note, a Trappist Monastery and a so-called Taggart Police Fort built in British Mandate times, and it was possession of this latter that enabled the Arab Legion successfully to defend the village and the spur salient on which it stood. They did so tenaciously, as not only did it give them control of the road to Jerusalem, but they were well aware that its capture by the Israelis would have enabled the latter to advance with comparative ease to Ramallah and thence to attack Jerusalem from the north. Arab control of this section of the road meant that the Israelis were forced rapidly to build another one (which they called "the Burma Road" after a similar structure built by the Allies in similar circumstances in the Far East in WW2) in order to keep open the way to Jerusalem. The combination of this engineering feat and their ability against the odds to keep and defend this route, which passed through mainly Arab land, was one of Israel's extraordinary achievements in that war; but it was costly in terms of casualties.

[54] In particular the Convent of Notre Dame and the buildings on Mount Zion immediately adjacent to the north-west and south-west walls of the Old City respectively. As has already been noted, one of the first structures to be demolished was the crossing point at the Mandelbaum Gate.

of one young American woman) from England, mostly London. The average age was probably around 23 or 24 (Irene and I, at 27 and 28 respectively, were the oldest). In our group we were to the best of my recollection five women and twenty men, mainly young men of the artisan class from East London. The names of most are after nearly fifty years just names, but a handful of them became friends and are referred to later on: Colin Slack, an archaeologist who had been working in Israel for two or three seasons before (he was not Jewish, although he had picked up Hebrew on the job and spoke it reasonably well[55]), two trainee rabbis (one, Harold Vallins, orthodox; the other, Colin Eimer, reform[56]). There was a wide variety of other occupations represented including, a trainee dentist, a hairdresser and a nurse.

The arrangements to receive us at G'vat were efficient, and two of the kibbutz members (always known as *kibbutzniks*) were assigned to look after us and show us what to do: these were an older woman, Rachel (pronounced of course in the Israeli way with the ch as in loch), and after a few days on his return from the army, a younger man, Uri Kelman. We were allocated quarters in Nissan huts that were originally built for air crews stationed at the air base at Ramat David that adjoined the kibbutz. Most of the rooms slept two or three, and Irene and I were given a room to ourselves in the women's hut. These were a little spartan, but we thought they were very reasonable in the circumstances; it wasn't as though we had arrived for a holiday.

Our work regime started straight away and we were up at 5 am each day to get the most of the daylight and the comparative lack of heat. There was tea and a snack at the dining room (always referred to by us volunteers by its Hebrew name, the *chader ochel*) before work, and then we went to work in the orchards until breakfast proper at about 9 am. Afterwards we continued working until about one o'clock when there was lunch and the main part of the working day ceased. In June the work to which we were put involved mainly the picking of fruit, firstly pears, then as the season progressed apples and then peaches. As the harvest passed its peak some of us got to do other things: weeding the cotton fields, later harvesting the cotton and, if we were lucky getting to work with the animals.

---

[55] Later to become Professor of Archaeology at Queen's University, Belfast. He died in about 2005.
[56] Colin later became for many years the rabbi at Southgate Reform Synagogue, north London. Harold, I learned after re-establishing contact with Colin, had gone as a rabbi to Australia where he later converted to Christianity and became a minister of that religion.

Some of the G'vat volunteers, July 1967

If we were less lucky there was always work to be done in the kibbutz kitchen and the *chader ochel*. The women volunteers tended to get assigned this work more than the men, although everyone had to do a regular turn at washing up. Irene had one day been given the task of peeling onions and found that if she did this under running water, the fumes did not make her eyes water; unfortunately it also spoiled the taste of the onions. She noticed that the salt in the salt cellars constantly solidified in the heat and humidity and suggested a simple remedy to the effect that putting a small quantity of rice in the cellar enabled the moisture to be drawn out of the salt. But new ideas were not particularly welcome in the kibbutz (where they already knew everything) and her suggestion was ignored.

In theory there were Hebrew classes in the afternoons, but we were tired from our physical work and most of us found concentration to be difficult. In fact I was assigned after a month or so to assist the man whose task it was to grow fodder for the cattle, Yitzhak Meyer (always known as Itche – pronounced something between "itcha" and "itchy" by the *kibbutzniks*, and by the latter version by us volunteers). Itche spoke no English and I was not making much progress with Hebrew, but he was originally from I think Romania and spoke some German, and so this was the language in which we communicated. He always called me Rogers.

This is the work I did for the longest time and remember best. It mostly consisted of moving and assembling irrigation pipes to water the beds growing lucerne (alfalfa) to feed the cattle. After a while I was trusted to drive the tractor some of the time, and I often needed to repair the pipes, especially where the ends had got out of shape and would not fit easily together. On one occasion in September:

> I was in the process of moving some irrigation pipes when I felt something bite me, and thinking it was an insect I put down the pipe to look at my leg. There were four little holes with a trickle of blood coming from them, and then two yards away I saw a long black snake making into a hole in the ground! It could only have been the snake which must have caught me with a glancing bite (which had not found its mark) as I unwittingly trod on it.

Actually I was almost sure that the black snakes found in the vicinity were not poisonous (I had seen one before, disappearing into an irrigation pipe) and the fact that there were four holes instead of the two that one would expect from snake fangs led to the conclusion of a "glancing bite". I did not seem to be feeling any ill effects, but I checked immediately with the kibbutz hospital just in case. They would hear of no other course than sending me immediately to the hospital at Afula, and I was rushed there in someone's car. There I was told by the hospital authorities that I would have to be admitted and spend 24 hours under observation. Actually I felt fine, but was treated as though I were about to die.

> Meanwhile I had got a message back to the kibbutz for someone to bring me up a book and when the news arrived the story had already got inflated to the point that I had been bitten by a viper. Malcolm [*one of the volunteers*] arrived ...with some books, shaving gear, etc. and walked in with the sort of face that expects to look on a dying man!

The time in hospital passed agonisingly slowly, and I was not able to talk to anyone as no-one seemed to speak English, however eventually I was discharged the following day, none the worse for wear. The hopelessly inefficient hospital clerk who had to formally to discharge me faffed about for what seemed an eternity (I could not even get my clothes back until I had been given my discharge ticket), and I was so relieved finally to get out of the place that instead of waiting for the local bus to take me into the main town of Afula I walked the 30 minutes or so to the bus station to catch the bus back to G'vat.

This was a story I needed to record in a letter to Irene, for she had by that time left and gone back to London. After we had been in Israel about six weeks she had begun feeling tired and somewhat lifeless, even to the extent of falling asleep at the back of one of the more ancient and rickety Egged buses. It was not like her, and one weekend in late July or early August when we were staying in Tel Aviv with Lottie she arranged for Irene to get a medical check-up. The results communicated to us at the kibbutz a few days later confirmed to our surprise that Irene was pregnant. Bearing in mind this fact and the way she had been feeling, it clearly did not make sense for her to stay on in the kibbutz and for both of us to have to worry about her condition and ability to work. The pragmatic course would be for her to go back home to London and for me to stay on and complete the contracted four months before re-joining her for the second half of her pregnancy. The Jewish Agency had agreed that she could go home early.

There thus began between us a regular correspondence detailing, on my side, the everyday life of a kibbutz volunteer. For her part Irene, who was having one or two minor difficulties with the pregnancy, was told in London that it would be in order to travel to the United States in September (she wanted to go and stay with Monica and family and also to visit other friends). For various reasons I myself was at times also travelling around Israel quite a bit and so this meant that we were both moving targets for correspondence, but though there were gaps in reception all of our letters to each other did in fact arrive. It is from this correspondence that some of the detail of the last two months emerges.

My work with Itche Meyer came to an end in September; the growing of lucerne was over, the cows were given other fodder, and I was allocated other work. At first this was picking fruit in the orchards again, where the time passed slowly now that I had developed a taste for more varied and interesting work, but then by chance (because I happened to be in the right place at the right time) I was assigned to work in the chicken sheds. This inevitably involved cleaning the cages and sorting birds in order, for example, to segregate the layers from the non-layers or to separate the immature birds into respective sexes (the males have slightly bigger combs). With mature birds it did not take long to overcome a slight natural dislike for picking them up, a task that was inevitably accompanied by wild squawking and flapping of wings (the method was to grab them by one thigh). And there were things the average non-farmer does not think about:

> I have also had to feed the little balls of fluff which have been newly hatched out in an incubator. They rush around cheeping all over the place tripping over in their anxiety to get away from the human being who has dared to invade their cage. One of the problems with chickens of all ages is that they tend to bunch up in one corner when they are frightened and those in the thick of the crush get suffocated by the others. One of my jobs was to go round collecting the dead ones after a morning's work...The last two days have been very hard work; we have been mainly employed in taking fully grown birds from one series of cages to others and injecting them at the same time – at least applying serum to their anuses. This can be a dirty job, particularly if the birds decide to crap just as you are about to do this.

We were given the weekends (Fridays and Saturdays) off, and so tended to spend the time away from the kibbutz, sometimes with Ze'ev and Hannah at Ashdot Ya'acov, sometimes in Jerusalem with a variety of different people, sometimes with Ruthi and Gidon in Nazareth Ilit, but most often with Lottie in Tel Aviv (I can still picture quite clearly the layout of her flat in Ben Yehuda Street). It was easy and cheap to get around on the Egged buses, and a "direct" bus from Afula got to Tel Aviv in about an hour. Towards the end of my time, after Irene had left, I seemed to be for one reason or another constantly on the move.

One of the reasons for this was that I was chosen to be the representative of the G'vat volunteers to go to a convention in Jerusalem on the theme of the continuation of the volunteer scheme in Israel. I was, and remain, a little sceptical of these kinds of gatherings, as I have it that they tend to be vehicles for a few loud-mouths to show off how clever they are. Indeed in the beginning that is just what happened:

> There is a small but highly vociferous group from South America who are usually at loggerheads with the remainder. Yesterday we split into groups to discuss practical measures to advance the volunteer programme...We sat for hours and passed a few meaningless resolutions. Part of our function was to elect members to a permanent volunteer committee to liaise with the Jewish Agency; this too became something of a farce when those who weren't elected but considered that they should have been tried to reconvene the meeting and pass a vote of no confidence in the chairman.

And so it went on; I was mostly irritated and bored. However, on the last day four of us (2 English and 2 South Africans) decided that we would meet up with the South Americans to try to thrash out some of the difficulties and see if we could get the convention going again. In fact we reached a good measure of agreement and I was pleased with myself at having been instrumental in turning things round, albeit behind the scenes. It was an early lesson in the fact that the most important work in large gatherings must almost of necessity be decided in corridors or private meetings outside the plenary sessions. One thing I did find was that I got on well with the South Africans; they tended to be more congenial, easy-going and matter-of fact than the British or Americans, and indeed for the duration of the conference I mixed socially mainly with them. This association remained at the back of my mind when Irene and I were later considering openings for work in Africa.

My final job in the kibbutz was to assist in harvesting the cotton crop, something I did in the event for only one day, as my being chosen as the delegate to the convention intervened . The work did not actually involve all that much as the cotton-picking was done mechanically, but what was required of those of us assigned to the job was to compact the cotton that had been loaded from the harvesting machine to the transporting lorry to maximise the loads. It was a bit like treading grapes, except that cotton needs rather more of a bashing. After a short while the process was rather like trying to march on the spot in leaden boots, and it made our calves and thighs ache for a few days afterwards. In my case my armpits too were sore from heaving myself up and down on the side of the lorry cage.

Living in a kibbutz was an interesting experience. The communal pattern of life that this entailed had served the settlers extremely well during the building of the secular Jewish agricultural and livestock-producing society in Palestine and then on into the independent Israel. The land was often swampy and unforgiving and people needed to work extremely hard to make it productive. In addition, in the early days there had also been the need to defend the land by force of arms against Arab attacks[57]. These communities were well suited to making efficient use of manpower; work was centrally planned and organised and all able-bodied *kibbutzniks* were assigned to the tasks most needed at each season of the year. A feature of the kibbutzim was the separation of the children, who lived not with their parents but in a separate children's house that doubled as a school, although they would spend time with their parents after work and at weekends. This freed the parents from day to day concerns about them and, in theory at least, enabled them to work more efficiently.

By the late 1960s, although people still need to work hard the pioneer spirit was beginning to fade. Agriculture and livestock raising in Israel had been a great success, indeed most kibbutzim had done well enough to allow their members gradually to improve their standards of living; they had become like moderately prosperous farming villages. They seemed now to be institutions populated at one extreme by political idealists, for whom the concept of communal ownership was almost a religion, and at the other extreme by no-hopers who tagged along doing what was required of them but who would find it difficult to get employment anywhere else. Communal living meant that privacy was virtually impossible (although that would probably be the case, albeit to a slightly lesser extent, in any small community): everybody knew everything about everybody else. Although members could take minor meals in their flats or houses, it was expected that main meals would be taken in the *chader ochel*, the communal dining room.

---

[57] For a fascinating account of the establishment of a kibbutz in Mandate Palestine in the 1930s see Arthur Koestler's novel *Thieves in the Night*, written from his personal experience.

But it was not possible for us volunteers to get a real feel of the "inside" of the kibbutz community; as temporary outsiders who by and large did not speak Hebrew, we could see things only somewhat superficially. It was nevertheless easy for us to fit into the routines that the life required and except as regards work the *kibbutzniks* were undemanding of us. There was a tradition of young people being "adopted" by older kibbutz members who would become their "parents" for the duration of their stay, and we were duly taken on in this way by a couple, Ruth and Avram, who were friends of Ze'ev Yaholom (and also of German origin). It was kind of them, but our Hebrew was almost non-existent and their English was not very good, and so we needed to communicate in a mixture of English and German. We had tea with them at their house once a week or so, but there was no foundation for a close relationship.

We quickly got used to the heat, the hours of work and the work itself. The food supplied was mainly home-produced and generally good, although in the *chader ochel* by our standards the table manners of the members left a lot to be desired. There was a tradition of putting a "slop-bowl" in the middle of the table, into which people scooped their unwanted left-over food; this was not done delicately and further emphasised any lack of any pretension to gentility. Water and soda water were available on tap outside the *chader ochel* and at lunchtime a kind of fruit soup was available for us. I remember that we would come in from work with enormous thirsts and drink large quantities of the latter, which I found delicious. If one smoked (as I did at the time) Israeli manufactured cigarettes, though mildly disgusting, could be obtained on free issue. On the experience generally I wrote to Irene in the last days of my stay:

> You know, in spite of everything, when I look back at life in the kibbutz there was not one material thing that I consciously missed during the whole time of my stay there, not one. I missed friends [*from home*], I was at times annoyed by people, but never did I feel that I needed to run back to so-called "civilization".

It was not only the life that was satisfactory (at least on a temporary basis), the actual kibbutz land and surrounding countryside, with distant views of the hills of Samaria, were picturesque, even beautiful. This was especially so in morning or evening light, as photographs I took at the time testify.

After Irene left I moved in with Colin Slack who was at that time sharing with Harold Vallins (who liked to be known as "Zvi" for the duration"). It was a room that seemed to attract visitors at all hours, but for the only time in my life I found I could if need be happily fall asleep for the night in a crowded room with the light on. One of the walls was decorated with an as yet incomplete mural painting that Colin had originally undertaken with a former occupant of the room, Colin Eimer (known as "Eli" for the duration – who had gone away from the kibbutz for a few weeks on a course with the army, an interesting training for one who intended to become a rabbi, albeit in the Reform movement). I was encouraged to, and did, add my bit to the mural.

Colin Eimer, Diana Fisherman, Colin Slack and other volunteers, G'vat July 1967

The close proximity to each other of the volunteers over a period of nearly four months meant that we got to know those we had become friendly with very well. Apart from the two Colins, the one other person in our group I got to like in particular was the young American woman, Diana Fisherman. It was apparent during our time there that she was getting closer to Colin S. and an affair developed that I truly hoped would become permanent; so much so that I wrote to Irene about its progress or lack of progress. They visited us together in London afterwards (it must have been in early 1968) but we lost touch afterwards. I was subsequently disappointed to discover that they did not in fact stay together.[58]

---

[58] As regards Diana, however, the story has a happy ending. While in the process of recollecting the events of all that time ago I found myself very much regretting losing touch (as I had also with American friends from 1963). Sitting around the dinner table after a meal at the home of Sylvia and David Lewin one evening in February 2016 I mentioned this fact. Sylvia brought an Ipad to the table and using the Google search engine she came up with a name, Diana Fisherman Crispi, an age (71), and a connection with a law firm in Los Angeles whose telephone number was also given. That almost certainly had to be the lady in question. "Go on, give her a call!" was the advice of those present (including Alasdair and Terry MacLeod). Suddenly it was all too quick for me and I was irrationally fearful that I might, by ineptitude, cause the phone to be put down on me and the connection severed. It turned

It turned out that my last night at the kibbutz was at the end of September shortly after my return and from the convention. It was not a particularly emotional leave-taking; a few of our group had already left (for example Colin S. had started working at the British School of Archaeology in East Jerusalem) and new volunteers were arriving and taking over some of the rooms we had occupied. We were each given a copy of the recently published illustrated book "Victory" that chronicled Israel's success in the Six Day War, inscribed by Uri thanking us for our voluntary work. I was eventually notified by the Jewish Agency that my flight back to London had been organised for 10th October.

At her invitation I made my base for those last days at Lottie Hofri's flat in Tel Aviv. While based there I took myself off to see some of the places I hadn't been to before: Masada, Hebron and Gaza. I found the latter two places less than impressive. From Gaza I wrote:

> I write this from one of the more peaceful places in this filthy, fly-blown, in fact typically Arab city. Every time I am in such a place I can't help but feel a kind of wonder that these people can actually aspire to be something great (or at least their leaders). [Theirs] seems to be such a hopelessly static society. I have just taken the bus from Beersheva – by no means a model city by Israeli standards as you know, but compared with this place it is palatial... The business life seems to be flourishing though, no doubt with Israelis buying cheap junk, and everywhere there are the pestering little boys. An Israeli or other foreigner can be spotted immediately, if not by his way of dressing then by the cut and quality of his or her clothes. I shall spend only a couple of hours or so here and then return to Tel Aviv.

I had wanted to post the letter from Gaza, but was unsuccessful in my search for a post office. I wandered for a while through innumerable streets, many of which reeked of urine, before finally giving up.

At the beginning of October I went back up to Jerusalem and spent a couple of days with Colin S. staying at the British School of Archaeology. It was an old fashioned place that had until the war been quietly operating in

---

out however (after Sylvia had rung it) that the number was no longer in operation: a recorded message referred to another number for those seeking legal advice. Disappointed but undeterred, I put the matter in the hands of Irene's niece Beverly in Los Angeles. A couple of weeks later I came home late after a performance in *Cabaret* (see chapter 10) and, in the process of winding down, I was looking at my new e-mails in the early hours of the morning. There, amazingly, were a message from Beverly, who had just put the phone down to Diana, and one from Diana herself, containing the memorable opening lines:
I am in shock! I have goose-bumps. I just spoke to your niece Beverly... I am delighted to be reconnecting with you. I am totally amazed that you have been able to find me...

Jordanian Jerusalem. Colin was engaged in what archaeologists call "pot sticking", the sorting of hundreds of broken bits of ancient pottery so that they could as far as possible be stuck together in their original shape, and he let me help him.

G'vat volunteers, Jerusalem, September 1967

There was one final meeting I had fixed. Chaim Hertzog, later to become Israel's 6th President, was a retired Major-General of the Israeli Army. He was born in Belfast but grew up in Dublin where his father was the Chief Rabbi of Ireland (and of course spoke English with an Irish accent) and went to live in Palestine in the 1930s (serving in the British army during WW2). He was highly respected in Israel during the Six Day War for his daily broadcasts to the nation as official commentator on the state of the war. I had actually met him in London at Dad and Suzanne's house, as he worked for a time for Isaac Wolfson's organisation Great Universal Stores, as of course, indirectly, did Dad. Irene and I had been invited to his house in Tel Aviv for lunch earlier and now I wanted to ask him about the prospects of qualifying as a lawyer in Israel. His advice was, having got as far as I had in qualifying at the English Bar, to complete the necessary stages needed for call to the Bar and then set about qualifying in Israel. Needless to say, other events took over, and in fact I never did.

Irene had meanwhile returned from America, and for the early part of October we were effectively out of communication (our last letters to each other were dated 2nd and 3rd October respectively). It was thus a shock that the first news I had when I got back to London was that she was in University College Hospital Maternity Wing. I went straight there to find her in bed looking pale, sad and strained. "It's all over" she said tearfully. She had miscarried earlier that day.

It was a bitter blow for us, but, as already recounted in chapter 5, in the longer run life was good to us. Rachel was born, healthy and delightful, some 14½ months later. Our connection with Israel was by no means severed; although we were never to live there again we subsequently went back several times for short stays (firstly in the summer of 1969 when Rachel was seven months old).

Soon after my return I started as a pupil in chambers at the Bar. There could hardly have been a greater contrast between the work of the last months in agricultural and livestock farming and that of a barrister in London. The companionship of our group of volunteers (at least the few in it with whom we had become good friends) and the easy-going ways of the Israelis gave way to what seemed at first to be the tight, formal English atmosphere of the Bar and the courts. The transition came as a severe and even somewhat unpleasant shock. As a pupil to Sam Stammler my days began to be filled with the attempted study of thick bundles of papers tied with red tape that constituted his "briefs to counsel" (much of the content of which I was ill-equipped to understand, let alone master), conferences with clients and observing in court a man who was one of the leading commercial barristers of his day.

Much of the time I seemed to be way out of my depth.

Chapter 7

Malawi 1973 – 6

The Idea	224
Preparing for life in Malawi	227
The social and political background	230
Home life	235
Travel in Malawi and beyond	242
The practice of the law	247
Bell-bottom trousers	249
Jehovah's Witnesses	251
Traditional courts	252
The Roads Project	254
Ornithology, acting and other leisure pursuits	254
Leaving Malawi	258

The Idea

Actually it was Irene who suggested it, in effect a sort of working holiday abroad, early in 1972.

Most of the countries of the former British Empire had been granted independence in the decade 1957 to 1967. Immediately this happened parliamentary elections took place and local politicians (including a handful of Europeans who had become citizens) filled the legislatures. And since almost all adopted the Westminster system of government under which the executive is drawn from the majority party in Parliament, all the executive posts from Presidents or Prime Ministers downwards were likewise localised. Those taking the highest posts had naturally tended to have been leaders in colonial times of political parties that had, with varying degrees of insistence, urged or demanded independence.

There nevertheless remained (and would continue for some time to remain) large areas of work where there were insufficient numbers of local people with the necessary training or expertise to adequately administer the countries concerned. For example, though top civil service posts tended to be localised quite quickly, especially if purely administrative (e.g. District Commissioners and their staffs), there was still a shortage of capable and experienced professional local people to assign to public service posts at various levels. If there were not to be a collapse of public administration, experienced expatriates were thus needed to carry on in, or be recruited to, these posts[1]. In fact most, if not all, expatriate judges and at least some magistrates needed to be retained or recruited, as did professional staff at senior and middle levels in many areas of government: doctors, engineers, accountants, mining and agricultural experts (to mention a few) and of course lawyers.

There were thus a good number of openings, mainly on short (but usually extendable) 30 month contracts, within the Commonwealth for British professionals. These contracts were offered by the UK Government on request by Commonwealth countries and territories (both independent and dependent) as a form of indirect aid. Recruitment was undertaken mainly by the Crown Agents, and the scheme[2] provided for the contracted person to work for the government of the relevant Commonwealth jurisdiction as though recruited locally by it, but the UK government would top up his or her salary to that of an equivalent post at home. There were also important extra benefits attached to this kind of post such as free education for children of expatriate families.

In fact I had once previously been asked in the late 1960s by someone who had done so why I didn't consider working on such a contract myself. But I had not at that time been that long at the Bar in London and I was concentrating on gaining experience and making some headway in the profession. Nevertheless Irene's suggestion, though unexpected, wasn't, given the situation just described, entirely a bolt out of the blue.

It was a typical grey, depressing early winter's day, and she was feeling listless and frustrated. We had moved into 44 Temple Fortune Lane some 18 months earlier, Rachel was 3, and we wanted to have another child but seemingly couldn't. Irene was glancing through the newspaper and happened to see a Crown Agents' recruiting advertisement for Crown Counsel in Hong Kong. "What about applying?" she said. I didn't need much encouragement. We thought about it and starting making enquiries.

In the way that fate tends to operate, shortly afterwards Irene became pregnant, and so the proposal was put to one side for a while; she certainly wanted to undergo her pregnancy and have the baby in London, and indeed

---

[1] Although actually in Malawi this process took longer than in many other newly independent countries. For an explanation of "expatriates" see below p. 230.
[2] It was known as the Overseas Service Aid Scheme (OSAS). It operated for the benefit of Commonwealth (and some other) countries, and was administered through the UK Foreign and Commonwealth Office.

Jessie was duly born in November 1972, just over a month before Rachel's 4th birthday.

In the course of the next few months our enquiries resumed. It seemed that on appointment to Hong Kong shortage of housing (in practice flats) there meant that the family would have to spend up to six months in a hotel; this did not seem a very attractive idea for the two of us and two very young children. But further advertisements appeared from time to time, and one in particular seemed interesting: the Malawi Buying and Trade Agents (by-passing the Crown Agents) in London were recruiting a state advocate[3] for that country. I applied and was in due course accepted, and through the summer of 1973 we began planning for 30 months away from London and my career at the Bar on the lines previously mentioned. It wasn't an ideal time. Jessie had been a difficult baby at times, seemingly always crying (belying her soon-to-develop sunny personality – she probably picked up the tension from anxiety in Irene and me concerning the move).

However, on acceptance of the post we were recommended to attend, at the Government's expense, a few days' residential course at Farnham Castle, an institution specialising in acclimatisation courses for those going to work abroad. The course programme was formulated to enable us to learn something of the geography, ethnography and recent history of (in our case) Malawi, to learn tips on day to day living (in particular how to deal with insect pests) and to meet one or two native Malawians, and also British expatriates on leave or recently returned from that country. The experience was interesting and thoroughly worthwhile, although amongst many other things we learned was that just about every known serious tropical disease was endemic in Malawi!

It was also suggested that, as a lawyer, I ought to go and see Sir Bryan Roberts, up to about a year previously the Attorney-General and Secretary to the President and Cabinet in Malawi. Roberts had decided to retire from Malawi before his post was Africanised ("and while I'm still young enough to do other work") and at the time I met him was working in the Lord Chancellor's Department in London. He subsequently became a stipendiary magistrate, and I found it difficult to understand how a man who had had such an important and influential post could settle down to (in comparative terms) such a lowly job. During our discussion he left me in no doubt that I was going to work for a dictator ("if that bothers you, you obviously won't

---

[3] Lawyers working for Commonwealth governments were (depending on whether or not the Queen remained Head of State) usually styled crown or state *counsel*, but Malawi had adopted the latter designation for senior barristers, as an equivalent to Queen's Counsel in the UK and other Commonwealth countries; hence "state advocate".

go"). At that stage of things I was not to be put off, although, as I was soon to find out, working in a dictatorship would seem at times to nullify most of what I had previously learned about the function and practice of the law.

We decided that I would travel ahead (a common practice for those with young families) in order to settle into the job, hopefully also into a house, and get to some extent acclimatised to life in a tropical country, before sending for Irene and the girls. It was thus that I boarded a British Airways VC10 in mid-October 1973 bound for Blantyre.

Preparing for life in Malawi

I was enthralled to be back in the tropics. The intensity of the light, the smells of Africa, the fauna and flora, and indeed just about everything else, fascinated me. The romantic side of my nature was conscious of continuing, albeit somewhat late in the day, the tradition of helping to bring development and order to the "outposts of the Empire" (a phrase my father liked to use, slightly tongue in cheek). These were countries whose stamps I had eagerly collected as a child, and I often indulged in the daydream of how I would have liked to have been born a generation or two earlier and been involved in the high noon of colonial administration. Though the books had not yet been published at that time, I subsequently read, and have reread a number of times, Charles Allen's collections of reminiscences of those who lived and worked for large parts of their lives in the Empire starting with "Plain Tales from the Raj", and continuing with "Tales from the Dark Continent" and "Tales from the South China Seas". They were originally produced as sound recordings for BBC Radio 4.

For some reason I had thought I would be posted to Blantyre, but James Kalaile, the self-effacing young Malawian Government senior state advocate who was at the airport to meet me, told me it was to be to the Ministry of Justice headquarters in Zomba, where the Government of Malawi Ministries were still mainly situated.[4] This turned out to be lucky, for Zomba, a beautiful little town which lies at the foot of a small mountain range, seemed to me to be almost exactly what I had imagined a typical African colonial-style town would be, and was conducive to my daydreaming. As I arrived, the blossoms were out on the jacaranda and flamboyant trees that lined the streets. Its churches and market, and its offices and houses (at least those occupied by the more senior civil servants) with their typically wide wooden verandas often wrapped round entire

---

[4] In fact the move of the Government offices from Zomba to Lilongwe, in central Malawi, had been planned for some time and the first Ministries had already moved in 1973, before my arrival.

buildings, mostly built in the period between the nineteen-twenties to the nineteen-fifties, were delightful. One of these buildings, a small Government owned hotel known as the Government Hostel, was where I spent the first two weeks waiting for the allocation of a house.

Being still the formal seat of government, Zomba remained for the time being at least the country's capital, although it also housed one of the campuses of the University of Malawi. It was nowhere near the size of Blantyre[5]. Zomba's population thus consisted mainly of government, and to a lesser extent university, employees.

After a couple of weeks I was allocated a house on Mulunguzi Road, named after the small river which flowed through the town from the mountain behind. This road ran along the foot of the mountains and parallel with the newly tarmacked main road from Zomba to Lilongwe and onwards to the north of the country. Built in the late 1950s, the 3 bedroom house was simple but adequate, and had from its veranda, or *khonde* (the local Chichewa word that was universally used in Malawi), a sensational view southwards towards Malawi's highest mountains, the Mulanje Massif which rises to approximately 10,000 feet from a level of about 3,000 feet above sea level. The mountains ran close to the border with Mozambique, in those days still one of Portugal's African colonies. Our view of Mulanje changed according to the weather and the time of day, and though often I envied those who lived in the older houses situated higher up the hillside, our location certainly had, if only for this view, much in its favour.

Apart from work, my first tasks were to employ house servants, to buy a car, and to get the house ready and reasonably comfortable for Irene and the children. We had been briefed about the practice of employing servants (something that had been common in middle class families in Britain up to the Second World War, but had almost completely disappeared afterwards) at our introductory acclimatisation course at Farnham Castle. Quite simply it was the norm in a country where there was much unemployment and domestic service was considered good and honourable employment for those fortunate enough to get it. There was a tendency at that time, amongst those of about my age recruited in similar circumstances, to profess to disdain the idea of employing servants, and indeed views of this nature had been expressed at Farnham Castle before we left the UK. In fact even the word "servant" had seemed to be something those concerned found embarrassed to use. This was of course to be in ignorance of the social

---

[5] Actually Blantyre-Limbe, the twin towns situated about 45 km to the south west that jointly constituted by far the largest urban area in, and the commercial centre of, the country.

structure already referred to and assume it was the same as that in 1970s UK.

Rachel & Jessica with Zakariah & Yusuf, Zomba, Malawi, October 1973

Though employing living in servants was of course a new experience for us, I for one did not have a problem with it; indeed it obviously gave employment to someone who might not otherwise have had a job at all. And, for those new to it, the relationship did tend to give rise to unforeseen things; typically servants' personal problems being laid at one's feet and for which one naturally assumed a degree of concern, if not responsibility. It certainly wasn't the foundation for the kind of idle, exploitive "colonial" life that many people in the UK seemed to imagine it was.

It was conventional to employ two: a cook/house-servant for inside work and a garden "boy" for outside, although if there were small children often also a female ayah or nanny. The system for putting it about that one was in the market for employing servants was simply to inform acquaintances or work colleagues. They would inform their staff, and in no time at all applicants would begin to arrive at the house.

With the first of these I had beginner's luck. I had been told that those of the Yao tribe tended to be the best, and one such, Yusuf Amusa Chimombo (members of the Yao tribe were Muslims) presented himself on the first day. He looked neat and tidy, and had what seemed to be impeccable references from past employers. I had no difficulty in choosing him over the other candidates. In selecting a gardener, however, I had less luck, employing as I did someone who turned out to be an amusing and likeable but fairly useless individual named Zakariah. In practice, if the senior servant did not approve of the junior one he was sure to let the fact be known, and this process indeed led eventually to Zakariah being replaced after a few months by Lawrence, a man who, though not of the same tribe as himself, was recommended as reliable by Yusuf.

The process of buying a car was in practice simple. The price of new cars was prohibitively high and in practice one scanned the newspaper for used cars for sale, watched club notice-boards or put it about on the grapevine that one was in the market. Again, I was lucky; a white Datsun (made by Nissan) estate car became available and I bought it with the aid partly of an advance of salary that the OSAS scheme made possible for the purpose.

The social and political background

As a contracted British officer and family in Malawi, we were "expatriates". This contrasted with the permanent residents of the country, the vast majority of whom were of course Africans (the term "natives", which was thought to have a slightly colonial flavour, was no longer much used). The population was also made up of "Coloureds" (those of mixed African/European or African/Asian parentage); "Asians" or "Indians" (usually people of Indian descent, Hindus, Muslims and a few, mainly Goan, Christians), whose parents or grandparents had arrived in the country during the early part of the 20th century and were mainly traders and professionals; and finally "settlers".

This latter term, a common one in colonial times, was usually used to refer to Europeans who had bought land (mainly for farming) and made their permanent home in the country, some of whom became citizens of the country at independence. However, in contrast to countries such as Kenya and Rhodesia (as the country that subsequently became Zimbabwe was still called), not to speak of South Africa[6], where there were large numbers of such people, their number in Malawi was very small (probably not more than 500 or so).

The word "expatriate" was often shortened to "expat" and as such was in the eyes of local people in practice synonymous with "expert"; indeed, as

---

[6] In fact white South Africans, many of whom could trace their ancestry in that country back for hundreds of years, did not regard themselves as settlers at all, but as a particular kind of native Africans.

pronounced by Africans, the two words sounded virtually the same. We were employed to fill in where there was seen to be a shortage of local skills, and were often regarded by local people with a mixture of grudging respect and envy. We were generally much better educated and trained than local people, and with our Malawi Government salaries topped up by OSAS to the level an equivalent officer in the UK would earn, we earned much more than local people we were working alongside in the public sector.

In the eyes of most of us expatriates the level at which many things were done in Malawi verged on, if it didn't actually rate as, incompetence.

Although in our professional lives we expatriates obviously mixed freely with local people, that mixing did not often translate into personal friendships of the kind that involved off-duty association. For a start, African men tended to leave their wives at home if invited out socially and they tended not to be interested in the kinds of things that Europeans liked doing. So activities like playing golf or bridge, or sitting over drinks or snacks at the club, not to speak of more culturally specific social activities like amateur theatre, tended to be undertaken amongst expatriates alone, and indeed our circle of close friends and associates was, most of the time, composed entirely of those like ourselves.

Malawi at that time was a country in which the rule of law did not exist[7] and where there was no effective way of challenging the absolute power of the Government or, what for most purposes amounted to the same thing, of the only permitted political party, the Malawi Congress Party. For most purposes both meant in reality the Dictator (or "President for Life" as he was officially known), Dr Hastings Kamuzu Banda[8]. This had resulted in a police state in which the Government was able to suppress the slightest hint of any expression of unease with, or dislike of, its policies, or any aspect of public administration or individual in power, let alone opposition to any of them. This it did by locking up in prison in indefinite detention[9] any person

---

[7] By rule of law, I mean a framework of constitutional and other law under which basic freedoms (e.g. of speech, assembly) are in place and where the Government and its agencies (especially the police) are accountable to its people for its actions, which are subject to scrutiny by the courts.

[8] In fact he was always referred to officially and in the news media as "His Excellency the Life President, Ngwazi [*the unequalled one*] Dr H. Kamuzu Banda", sometimes shortened to "the Ngwazi". The "Hastings" part of his name was always reduced to an initial.

[9] In practice people were locked up for periods from a few months to many years, never knowing how long their incarceration would last. There was a further measure open to the Government: that of confiscation of property under the Forfeiture Act. Under it a person could be deprived of virtually everything he owned, which was declared forfeited to the Government.

who might have dared to state any such thing, at whatever level, or indeed anyone it saw, for any reason at all, as a threat.

Nor did such expression have to be in public; there were (as there always will be in such situations) people who, in order to ingratiate themselves with the authorities, would report to the latter things that individuals might say in private, and it was widely suspected, for example, that some house and club servants came into this category.

All this created a climate of fear, and a person was ill-advised to speak about the Government, or public affairs generally, unless with someone he or she knew could be trusted. In the case of Africans, this in practice meant talking in the most guarded way with those one worked alongside (most of whom in fact *were* indeed to be trusted) but it was not conducive to forming out of office hours friendships. Indeed, for the first and only time in our lives we developed the habit of looking warily around us before saying anything that could even possibly be construed as controversial, especially in a shop or other public place, in a club, or even in people's houses where the hosts were unsure of their servants.

Though expatriates were indeed sometimes subjected to detention, the more usual procedure in their case was for the President to sign an order under the Immigration Act declaring the person concerned to be a "prohibited immigrant". That meant the person together with any members of his or her family, had to leave the country, usually within 48 hours, and hope that friends would be able to sell their property and wind up their affairs locally as best they could. The person on whom such an order was served was referred to as having been "P.I.-ed". This did not occur often, as expatriates knew not to take risks, but certainly it happened in a handful of cases to people we knew of.

As part of the general paranoia about security in the country, the police and authorities generally had, as they seem to have in Africa generally, a deep suspicion of cameras, and they tended to assume that anybody who had one must by that very fact be a spy. This, while quite amusing as a general concept, was less so when one was caught up in it.

When first in Malawi I had in all innocence watched Dr Banda arriving to open Parliament (in a rather pale shadow of the Queen's annual ceremony in London) in Zomba. There I had without incident captured some of the scene on my cine camera. Some weeks later, I decided it would be good to have some photographs of the weekly Changing of the Guard at State House (in colonial times the Governor's, now the President's, residence) and went there at the appointed time. I had not been there for more than a minute or so and, with a new 35mm film in my camera, was lining up a picture on the gate through which the Guard would shortly march. Suddenly the police guard at the gate shouted at me in a peremptory tone "You! Come here!" Slightly anxiously, I did so.

"Why are you taking pictures of State House?"
"Actually I haven't taken a picture; I was just lining up and focussing my camera. As you can see, the film counter is still on zero."
"You were taking pictures of State House. I saw you."
"I've just explained. Anyway you can't see State House from where I was standing or even from here". (This was true; the building was surrounded by a high wall).
"Why were you taking pictures?"
"I wasn't; and anyway what law am I supposed to have I broken?"
"You wait here! And you give me your camera."

He made a telephone call, and shortly a police Land Rover arrived into which I was bundled and driven round to the police post at the rear of State House. There an interrogation began. It followed more or less the same format as with the guard at the gate, with me attempting to explain that I had done nothing wrong, and that, if I had the camera (which had meanwhile disappeared) I could anyway prove that I hadn't taken a picture. The interrogator, who wasn't interested in anything I had to say that wasn't a confession of being a Communist spy[10], decided that I needed to be passed on to the Post Commander, and I was duly taken before him in close arrest. The camera reappeared, held gingerly by its strap at the end of his finger by a police sergeant as though it were some sort of limpet mine.

Once again exactly the same monotonous questions were asked, and the same answers given by me. It was an unnerving experience: it dawned on me that I was not in rule-of-law Britain, but somewhere where in the final analysis the law meant very little, leaving me effectively totally without rights or recourse. My attempts to explain the workings of my camera were about as effective as if I had been trying to explain a computer to a deaf mute with zero interest in the subject matter.

Suddenly there dawned on me what would probably have come immediately to the mind of anyone, especially if not a lawyer, with more common sense

---

[10] Malawi was at that time in the right-wing camp of dictatorships, and Dr Banda was violently anti-communist. Malawi was, for example, one of the few countries in the world that not only had no diplomatic relations with Communist China, but actually had a Taiwanese "Chinese" embassy.

than I seemed to have at the time: the way out of this was not to try to prove my innocence (for anyway my guilt was, at least up to that point, taken for granted) but to drop names as hard and effectively as I possibly could. I said suddenly "I work as a state advocate in the Ministry of Justice. Ring Mr Richard Banda[11] the Attorney General and ask him to confirm who I am!"

Why I didn't think of this line before is still a mystery to me. At once the interrogation began to stall. The Post Commander left the room and a whispered conversation began in the corridor. I was left to stew for a while. After half an hour or so I was ordered downstairs again to the waiting Land Rover. As I got in, my camera was returned to me with the worst possible grace and with the snapped caution: "Don't ever take pictures of State House again". I was driven back to the gate where first arrested and ordered to get out and go on my way.

I discovered later the same day that the police had apparently taken my word for it that I worked for the Attorney-General, for when I told Richard Banda about the incident he confirmed that they had not in fact contacted him about me[12]. This fact actually sheds more light on the general situation.

Firstly, Europeans were generally supposed by the police and official authorities to be well-connected to those in power. In fact only a few were, though most of us could be, through our Embassies and High Commissions, potentially the cause of minor problems for the authorities in Malawi and adverse publicity abroad. We were thus to be treated with some care, for fear that there might be "consequences" if, for example, we were wrongly accused of an offence or (what was worse in their eyes) a political misdemeanour of some kind. I realised soon afterwards that this is probably why I was comparatively speedily released: the fear of what might happen to them if they got things wrong (questions, disciplinary proceedings, even demotion or dismissal, all conducted in the same non-rule of law context) probably outweighed any vague suspicions of me they might have entertained.

Yet, curiously, for most of us expatriates this kind of incident did not really undermine the experience of being in Malawi. There was so much to attract: the climate (only rarely oppressively hot) which encouraged an outdoor social life, the exotic fauna and flora (I began, under the mentorship of John Alder, of whom more later, to develop a largely latent life-long interest in

---

[11] Banda is a common name in Malawi. He was not related to the President.
[12] He also asked me, somewhat bizarrely in the circumstances, if I in fact still wanted to take the pictures I had planned to take, for if so he could arrange it. I declined his well-meant offer.

birds especially, and Irene started collecting butterflies), the beauty of the environment, especially in our six months in Zomba, the exotic places to visit, sport (I started playing golf and squash again after more than ten years), and the fact that in one's job one was able to make some sort of contribution at a fairly senior level. Actually, during my time in Malawi (and later in Kenya too) I had a recurring dream in which I found myself somehow back in the UK; and each time I woke with a huge sense of relief that I was still in Africa.

What the political climate did do was to bind us expatriates closer together and by that fact in a sense push us further away from the Africans. This was not because the latter were seen as "the enemy" in this situation; far from it, as they stood to lose much more than we did (and many did so). But it helped to foster a "them and us" situation: a division between the Africans all around us (whose representatives were in political control) and the Europeans, and to some extent also other minorities, Indians and Coloureds. We saw ourselves as largely helpless minority groups in a situation of usually mild but occasionally ugly oppression, and as competent professionals or business people in a sea of incompetence.

Home life

The first thing we needed to adapt to was living in the very small town that Zomba was in those days. Most Africans bought their food and necessities from the market in the centre of town, as to an extent did we. There was one supermarket, "Kandodo", one Bata shoe shop and one or two small all-purpose shops run by Indians. Irene recalls seeing a woman emerge from the Bata shop tottering on a pair of high heel shoes she had obviously just bought. She soon gave up the struggle of trying to manage them on the uneven ground in the street, took the shoes off, put them on her head and walked comfortably away.

Fish from Lake Malawi, mainly tilapia (known locally as *chambo*) was, at least at that time, in plentiful supply. Meat in the form of beef, mutton or pork, was on the other hand in short supply and tended to be tough, and if you wanted chicken the chances were that you had to buy a live one in the market, and kill and pluck it yourself (or, more usually, get your servant to do it). The availability of things that in Europe we tend to take for granted was not an established fact; basic necessities tended to run out without warning, and one was well advised to buy things like flour, salt and sugar when it was in stock[13].

---

[13] This applied later in Kenya too. It took Irene a while after returning to England to get used to not over-buying this sort of commodity "just in case".

In fact, if anything more than basic requirements were needed, it was in practice necessary to travel the 45 miles south west to Blantyre. It was a journey we quite often made, not only for shopping, but also to collect visitors from Blantyre Airport at the nearby township of Chileka.

Some basic knowledge about produce in the market was acquired only by experience. One day Irene saw some cucumber-shaped items between the size of a cucumber and a small marrow. On enquiring if they were good to eat, she was assured that they were and so she bought some (very cheaply – that should have been a clue). On getting home, she asked Yusuf about preparing them. He smiled politely and said "Madam, these are for the bath!" She had bought loofahs! Actually I believe the flesh of these things is edible when they are young, but all that remained in the instant case was the spongy but firm fibrous interior that is revealed when the outer skin is removed.

The proliferation of insects in the tropics is something that anyone living there has quickly to get used to. Mosquitoes were constant pests, mainly, but not exclusively, after dark and this meant that at night we had always to sleep under insect nets. And ants were everywhere. It became second nature to ensure that no food, particularly if sweet, was left uncovered, especially if out of the fridge. If not, there would within a very short space of time be a moving black trail leading to it from some access point in the floor or wall. Cockroaches too were very difficult to eradicate, as they were adept at concealing their flat bodies in tiny spaces. Suddenly switching on the light in the kitchen in the middle of the night would reveal just how many of these unwanted guests we entertained.

And this is not even to mention the huge variety of flies, bees, wasps and other insects that were everywhere. At one time, when the fireflies swarmed, our bedroom was almost lit up by them, and one or two of them had even managed to get underneath the sheet between the mattresses.

A particular wonder for the uninitiated was the swarming of large termites that emerged from their nests as the rains were about to begin. I remember attending a lecture at the university during which the room filled with these things with their approximately 5 inch (12.5 cm) wingspan. Nobody seemed to take much notice. Eventually they landed, their wings fell off, and the sexes would pair up and move off in line to try to start a new colony. Of course only the tiniest fraction succeeded in doing so. Some Africans used to stand under the street lamps during these swarms and catch the termites that were attracted by the light, remove their wings and eat them live.

Many of the routine jobs in the house were of course done by the house servant, and this included basic cooking, although in our case by no means all of it, and waiting at table. In fact the chief luxury that stays in my memory was that of being able to get up from the table at the end of a meal and just walk away from it. But Irene cooked too, especially if we were entertaining guests (which we did often).

On occasions the results of having someone share your kitchen could be bizarre. Both in Zomba and later after we had moved to Lilongwe, we had a garden in which we grew or attempted to grow various things – a pawpaw tree and a passion-fruit vine gave us good fruit in season, and Irene attempted, with our gardener's help, to grow tomatoes. When these were ripe for the first time, she decided to make the whole crop (which was actually quite small) into puree. Having successfully done this she considered that the puree would be enhanced by the addition of a little wine that was left over in a small bottle in the fridge and she duly poured the contents over it. Curiously, the liquid remained floating on the top of the puree and gave off a pungent smell. In a flash she realised that what she had poured was not wine at all, but paraffin: Yusuf had been using the fridge to store some of his personal effects. In one second our whole precious crop was ruined.

At the time of our arrival in Malawi, plans for the movement of the seat of Government from Zomba to Lilongwe were already well under way. Dr Banda had decided to shift the centre of gravity of the country from the south to the middle of the country, and as Malawi was at that time the only African country to have diplomatic relations with South Africa (apart from those countries immediately adjoining it), he had persuaded the South Africans to lend Malawi the money to build a new Capital City in Lilongwe. Some Ministries had already moved and plans were in place for the rest to do so shortly. Thus we knew from the outset that our time as residents of Zomba would be no more than about six months.

In fact it was almost exactly that. We were not looking forward to the move, having been a little spoiled by the experience of living in Zomba. We were loath to leave the general quiet beauty of the place, the views from our *khonde*, the easy proximity of the beautiful Ku Chawe hotel and restaurant up at the top, and on the edge of, the plateau of Zomba Mountain with its stupendous view of the countryside around, and the friends that we had quickly made. I also loved the old colonial type offices that had housed the Ministry of Justice. And the large variety of birds to be found on the large area of unused land adjoining our house had served as a perfect inducement to taking up what had up to then been only a latent interest: ornithology.

But on the appointed day a lorry arrived to load up all our household furniture and goods along with a crew of prisoners and their guards from Zomba gaol to do the manhandling. In positioning the vehicle, the driver backed it into and over the beautiful little gardenia bush in our garden that we had until then been intending to dig up and transport with us. Irene was so upset she lost her temper and raged at him, while he, the prisoners and the prison guards looked on in bewilderment. How could anyone (except a European, apparently) get so upset at damage to something useful only for firewood?

The distance by road to Lilongwe was roughly 180 miles and the journey took about 3½ hours. I had been there on at least one occasion before our move for a business meeting, and so knew the rough layout of the road. It was a journey we were to make many times subsequently. As it approached Dedza (about ⅔ of the way to Lilongwe) it ran for a while along the very border with Mozambique, and one could without any immigration formalities pull into the little Mozambique border town of the same name to a very acceptable Portuguese restaurant that accepted Malawi money[14].

Lilongwe had of course already existed as the main town in the Central Region of Malawi and with a population roughly equal to that of Zomba (somewhere around 25,000 at that time) was second equal in size, but the new Capital City, including Government offices, housing for staff, shops and a hotel, as well as plans for the Legislature and the High Court (presently in Zomba and Blantyre respectively), was in the course of being built on a virgin site about 3 miles to the east.

In fact the housing areas for higher grade Government officers had not been given names (even in Malawi at that time, not every street, square, bridge, park or location could be named after Dr Banda as "Kamuzu" Street, etc.) and the housing areas for middle to higher grade Government officers were known simply as Areas 10, 11 and 12. The third of these was for middle ranking officers like myself and our families.

The first house we were allocated had just been built in a new part of Area 12; it had no garden, but merely stretches of brown earth with tufts of planted grass that would eventually (actually in the tropics very quickly) become

---

[14] The kwacha (of which at independence there had been two to the pound sterling) divided into 100 tambala. Kwacha is a word from Chichewa (the dominant African language in Malawi) meaning "dawn".

lawns. Most of the houses nearby were still unoccupied, and the children especially felt isolated. At night we could hear the eerie whooping cries of hyenas; it was a depressing contrast to where we had come from. Never one to take a situation lying down, Irene went to work on the Capital City Development Corporation to get us another house. By virtue of her persistence and charm we were, within a month or so, allocated an alternative house: number 12, Area 12, located in part of the estate that had been in occupation for more than a year.

A small explanation is needed about addresses. In most of Africa, as indeed in most parts of the world, there was (and is) no postal delivery service directly to addressees, and the universal system was to rent a lockable pigeon-hole (known as a post-office, or PO, box) or, depending on the amount of mail expected, a private mail bag, at the local post office. Into these your letters and packages were put by the postal authorities and collected, daily or as often as necessary, by you, an employee or someone else you trusted with your box or bag key. In practice, unless there was some special reason to rent your own personal box, etc. it was normal to make use of that of your employer for receipt of personal mail. Thus, when we spoke of our "address", we normally gave the relevant PO Box or Bag number rather than (as in for example Western Europe, the USA, etc.) the house or flat and street where we resided. The most usual exception was when we needed to give directions as to how to get to the house; and for this purpose we referred to the house as "12/12".

The countryside around Lilongwe is comparatively flat, but 12/12 was at one edge of the estate in a row of houses on a small ridge at the highest point. This meant that from it there was, even though it was a single storey house (as all were at that time), an impressive view of the land around and an especially grand view of the sweep of the sky at night. This was all the more so as there was no light pollution of the kind that is normal in a large town or city, and it became a challenge for me to try to identify the southern hemisphere constellations, not only the obvious ones like the Southern Cross, which cannot be seen from the UK, but all of the prominent ones.

Our family with two small girls made it easy quickly to make friends. From early on in Zomba Irene made contact with Katrine Alder, the mother of two small girls of similar ages to our own and someone with whom she struck an immediate affinity. Whether Katrine's German, distantly Jewish[15],

---

[15] In fact her father's family, though originally Jewish, had converted to Christianity. But of course this, in Nazi Germany, counted for nothing and he and Katrine's mother (who was not Jewish) had to flee. They ended up working for the Anglican Church in Uganda, where Katrine and her brother were born and grew up.

family background made for a more than usual affinity is an open question, but she and her husband John, with whom I had much in common[16] became and remain, long after our mutual Malawi experience, close friends. John quickly became my mentor in all things to do with the natural world, particularly ornithology. Katrine was and is a very talented musician, as well as having many culinary and other skills, and John's wide-ranging, intelligent mind, as well as his very practical approach to things mechanical made, and continues to make, their friendship and company of great value to us.

We did have visitors from abroad while in Malawi. My father came through Blantyre on his way back home from a business trip to South Africa; he had refused point blank to stay with us in our house in Zomba, probably thinking we were living in a mud hut, and ensconced himself in the Mount Soche Hotel in Blantyre, from where we had to chauffeur him to and fro. Irene's father too came on at least one occasion and was able to wonder at so many things that were entirely new to him.

At a wedding, Lilongwe, Malawi, September 1975

For a longer visit, Irene's sister and brother-in-law Monica and Gunter, and their daughters Beverly and Miriam came to stay with us after visiting Gunter's sister and brother-in-law in Johannesburg. It was actually a memorable trip for Gunter especially, as he had spent the years of the Second World War as a refugee in Swaziland and there was much in Malawi

---

[16] Also much not in common, for he was from a Cotswold farming family.

that reminded him of those years. We were able to arrange for the family to stay for the fortnight or so they were to be in Malawi at the house of acquaintances, Arthur and Gwen Paine[17], who were on leave at the material time, and so they were able to have a taste of the full African expatriate experience, complete with the Paines' house servants to look after them.

However, the first shock for the family had been at the airport on arrival, when the book Monica had been reading: *Fear of Flying* by Erica Jong, was seized by the Customs as being one of the hundreds of books on the list of those officially banned in Malawi[18]. Irene had taken instruction meanwhile on the very difficult-to-master art of boning a chicken (removing the bones but putting the carcass back together again more or less as it would look with the bones still inside). Thoroughly pleased with her achievement, she proudly served it to the family for the first celebratory dinner at home, only to have Gunter ask, failing entirely to notice the context of his question as he ate it, if there were any decent restaurants in the town. We took them around to various spots in central Malawi that we thought might interest them, and at one point allowed Beverly, who had recently passed her driving test back home to drive our car. There was a learning experience in that too, for as she drove away the gear-lever came away in her hand.

Gunter actually needed to leave earlier than the rest of the family and fly from Lilongwe back to Blantyre and then back to the US via Johannesburg. We took him to Lilongwe airport at the appointed time only to find that the Malawi Airways plane that was due to take him to Blantyre had been commandeered by the Minister of Transport (probably for his own personal use). Gunter, at a loss to know what precisely to do, announced in raised tones that he was an American citizen and demanded to be flown to Blantyre (we quietly pointed out that this would not of itself particularly impress the natives). But he need not have worried, for the airline chartered a small 6-seater plane flown by a rather wild Australian pilot of our acquaintance, "Tas" Beatty, to take him and the two nuns who were his co-passengers down to get his connecting flight.

---

[17] Arthur was the Accountant-General for Malawi and, by this time nearing retirement, had spent almost forty years as a career colonial and then Commonwealth civil servant. Typical of many such people, he and his wife did not want to contemplate living in a northern European climate on their retirement and had a home in Cyprus to which they eventually intended to settle.

[18] The list, which was added to by notices in the official Gazette nearly every week, contained any book that espoused any kind of political philosophy of which Dr Banda disapproved, and any book that was considered to have content of a sexual nature. Some of the exclusions were fatuous: *The Green Revolution* was about agriculture, but had been reputedly banned for its supposed political content!

Travel in Malawi and beyond

Apart from a few South Africans, there were at that time almost no tourists in Malawi. It was comparatively inaccessible from Europe and those tourists who did visit Africa almost always went to the more spectacular game reserves and ocean beaches of South Africa, Kenya and Tanzania. There thus were many exotic and "unspoiled" places to visit in our spare time, the most obvious being Lake Malawi (always known as "The Lake"), a huge inland sea covering about 11,400 square miles. Apart from the lake steamers that plied between ports and the two Lake islands, Likoma and Chisumula[19] and were rarely seen from the shore, virtually the only means of transport on the lake were dugout canoes made from hollowed out tree trunks. In fact the steamers were used more than the roads to transport people and goods to the farther points on the Lake, for there was hardly any railway and the principal roads, except for the tarmac stretch between Blantyre and Lilongwe and most roads within towns, were laterite clay. On these in the dry season a vehicle going at more than minimal speed would send up a huge cloud of choking red dust (you automatically wound up all the windows when passing or being passed), and in the rainy season could be rutted by run-off rainwater and treacherously skid-inducing.

Air Malawi ran, besides a handful of international routes, an internal service from Blantyre to Lilongwe and then further north to Mzuzu and Karonga (at almost the northernmost point on the Lake). To get to Lilongwe by air from abroad one had to change planes at Blantyre[20], and occasionally I had reason in the course of work to take these latter flights. The volume of traffic was not large and I recall flying to Karonga in a ten-seater plane. For this not only the luggage, but the passengers too, had to be weighed, and on one flight a fierce argument broke out when a late-joining passenger was told that either he or his luggage, but not both, could go on the plane. The pilots were at that time always Europeans (if not literally, then South Africans, Rhodesians, Australasians or Americans), and on one occasion when the small plane was full I was directed by the pilot to the co-pilot's seat, not from any supposed flying expertise on my part, but more likely as being the only European passenger on board and less likely to panic if things got rough (he could not know that in rough weather in a small plane that was exactly what I was likely to do.)

We were introduced quite early on by the Alders to Palm Beach near the end of the south eastern fork of the Lake. It had until recently been a hotel, but

---

[19] These are Malawi territories, although situated within the area of the lake that belongs by international agreement to Mozambique.
[20] This was of course before the international airport was built at Lilongwe. Plans for this had already been drawn up by the time we were in Malawi.

had seen better days, particularly with the rise in the level of the lake in recent years, and the chalets that had been part of the hotel had been sold off and rented out, one of them to friends of the Alders[21]. Though rather basic in terms of facilities, it was an exquisite place. Overhanging part of the corrugated iron roof was a "Sausage Tree", whose large heavy "fruit" (seed pods) gave it its name. In season these would fall on the corrugated steel roof with a heavy and initially frightening thump. There was little to do at Palm Beach but swim, read and relax, and from time to time watch the wild monkeys and baboons (we had to be on our guard that they did not come into the chalet and steal food) and the occasional dugout canoe paddling by. The Lake had been described, with some justification, as being how the Mediterranean must have been before the advent of mass tourism; just so.

Except for Nyika Plateau in the north, Malawi has not the open savannah of large parts Kenya and Tanzania, and its wild country tends at lower levels to be scrubby brachystegia woodland (more commonly known as "bush"). While this does in fact support a wide variety of larger wildlife, the latter is often not easily seen and attempts at game viewing, even in wildlife parks or reserves, are likely to be frustrating. We did in fact visit the Nyika on one occasion and saw on its rolling hills the herds (sometimes large) of zebra, eland and roan antelope. They, or at least the young ones, are preyed on mainly by leopard, but this symbol of Malawi is an elusive night-time animal and not often seen. There are of course crocodiles and hippopotamus in the Lake, but these tended to avoid humans and were not often seen either.

We went to the Nyika with the Alders, and while staying at the Lodge there the children were jumping on their beds, when Rachel fell backwards, hit the back of her head on the bedstead and cut it very badly. What were we to do, miles from anywhere, let alone a doctor? There followed a typical African solution: the Nyika Warden was a European whose wife had some nursing skills. She didn't have the wherewithal to stitch the deep cut, but she applied some butterfly plasters and wound a bandage around Rachel's head. It did the trick. Jessie and the Alder children, Karen and Susan, were quite jealous of her get-up, and so Irene had the idea of including them by winding lavatory paper round their heads so that they could all look the same.

In the wake of David Livingstone, Malawi (then British Central Africa) attracted missionaries from the Scottish Presbyterian Church, and, though the Anglican and Roman Catholic Churches were well represented, the dominant church in the country was the Church of Central Africa Presbyterian (always known as the CCAP). The earliest mission was that

---

[21] Francis and Annabel Shaxson, with whom we later ourselves became friendly in Lilongwe, and quite often saw in later years at the Alders' house in Wiltshire or their own in Dorset.

established in 1876 at the eponymous Livingstonia and situated just to the east of the Nyika Plateau in a beautiful setting high on an escarpment overlooking the Lake. To get from there to the Lake you had to undergo a special experience in motoring by taking the dirt road down the escarpment that doubled back on itself in a series of about 15 hairpin bends. Though just about negotiable in a car without having to back in the process, this certainly was not the case for a bus or lorry.

The town that was farthest distance of all from the main centres of population was Karonga, a tiny trading centre at the north end of the Lake with a population of perhaps 5000 at that time. I needed to go there occasionally in order to prosecute the odd outstanding case of more than average severity in the tiny little rondavel that was the magistrate's court there. During these visits I discovered a tiny World War I military cemetery, an unexpected relic of the East African Campaign, during which British Empire forces fought running battles throughout the war with, but failed to tie down or defeat, the German colonial forces under General von Lettow Vorbeck. It is an Anglo-German cemetery, and besides the graves of individual European officers and NCOs from both sides there is a memorial to the African soldiers from both sides who died in this little out of the way and almost forgotten early skirmish (presumably their bodies were taken to tribal areas for burial). It reads:

Frieden   Peace

In memory of the African ranks
who died fighting at Karonga
14. 9. 1914

Unvergessen
[*unforgotten*]

To me there was an even more poignant sadness to this little out of the way cemetery than to the huge Commonwealth War Graves cemeteries in northern Europe. Who, I wondered, ever visited the grave of, among others, Gordon Merriman, who "died fighting at Karonga, Nyasaland, for his country, 9 September 1914 aged 29 years".

While in Karonga I remember dining at the home of one of the Indian traders there. I don't remember how the invitation arose but I do recall that the food was served by the man's wife, and that not only did she not eat with us, she retired to some back room while we ate, as one might have expected a servant to do. Most of the goods that reached Karonga did so by Lake

Steamer, but Indian traders would also travel the 14 hours or so each way by road to Blantyre to purchase the goods they needed for their little shops, an example of the hard work and enterprise that would not have begun to occur to most Africans as a necessary element in the running of a small business.

There were other places of interest too. At Ntchisi, northeast of Lilongwe on the way to Nkhotakota there was a Forestry Department bungalow, in a clearing at the edge of the fast disappearing rain forest, that one could rent. When we rented it for the second time, someone told us just before we left home that it was supposed to be haunted. Whether or not this was true we did not discover, but it did not induce peaceful nights of sleep. Another place we enjoyed visiting while living in Zomba was Milange in Mozambique, just over the border from Mulanje (the little town at the foot of the mountains of the same name) in Malawi. The wide dual carriageway main street in Milange seemed to go from nowhere to nowhere, but a Portuguese restaurant there served giant prawns piri-piri of the highest quality. The Portuguese soldiers stationed in Milange at that time also frequented the restaurant and would give impromptu renderings of *fado* (fate), unaccompanied sad songs that we had never heard anywhere else, before or since.

Malawi itself did not provide the only opportunities for travel in Central Africa. We had planned and booked a trip to the Luangwa Valley in Zambia in late 1974, one of whose attractions was game trekking (game viewing on foot), but shortly before we were due to go the Malawi Government made a rule that public officers (as I was) could not travel outside the country on leave unless they had requested and been granted permission to do so at least four weeks beforehand. This rule was effectively and unjustly made retrospective so that it covered not only journeys planned from then on, but also those already planned at the date the rule came into force[22], including of course ours. So we had to cancel.

We did however, in the following year, get to Rhodesia and spend a couple of days at the Victoria Falls, the fabulous *Mosi-oa-Tunya* (the Smoke that Thunders), located on the Zambezi River dividing modern Zimbabwe and Zambia. We had the good fortune to stay at the Victoria Falls Hotel, one of the oldest hotels in the town of Victoria Falls, a grand building with its

---

[22] Drafters of legislation are taught to use this device very sparingly indeed, as it can work injustice, but this was Malawi where such considerations were of low priority, if indeed they existed at all.

revolving ceiling fans that must rate with the dozen or so top traditional hotels in the world.[23]

It was dry season in Rhodesia at the time and so the falls were comparatively low (at their height, in spate, the spray is so thick that it is difficult to see the falls from many vantage points), yet the experience was unforgettable and one of those must-see-if-you-possibly-can sights of the world.

But vying with the falls as my main memory of that trip is that of a case of Scotch whisky.

Rhodesia was at that time the subject of international economic and trade sanctions. One of the obvious consequences of this was that imported commodities were in very short supply there, and some, like whisky, in high demand. We had been told by Rhodesians working in Malawi that the thing to do was to buy a case of whisky at Blantyre airport, declare it at the Rhodesian customs, pay whatever duty was due, and then sell it on at a considerable profit to a contact (we had been given the contact details of just such a person who owned or managed a hotel in Salisbury, as at that time the capital was called).

The first part of the scheme went entirely to plan. We arrived at Salisbury airport, paid the requisite import duty to a harassed woman customs officer, met the contact the following morning with our whisky and duly received payment which showed us a handsome profit. This was I believe my first and only attempt at playing the spiv. But as a novice spiv I learned the very important lesson that, if you are in this business you need to have an eye to every eventuality, especially disposal of the money.

I had received more money for the whisky than we could spend in a long weekend. It was illegal to export Rhodesian currency and, we were officially warned, one might be subjected to body search by the Rhodesian Customs on leaving the country to check that we were complying. We were due to fly back to Malawi about midday on the Monday morning and I still had Rhodesian Dollars to about the value of US$450. What were we to do? The only feasible thing seemed to be to hurriedly open a deposit account in a bank in Salisbury and send for the money later.

---

[23] Others we have visited include the Mount Nelson in Cape Town, the Peninsula in Hong Kong, and (myself only) Raffles in Singapore. When I was there in 1990 with Irene and nine-year old Jonno it had been demolished except for some outer walls, but was in the process of being rebuilt exactly to the original plans. But there are many famous hotels that we have not visited, including the famous Shepheard's Hotel in Cairo, the original of which was destroyed by fire during anti-British riots in 1952.

And indeed this is what I later set about doing once back in Malawi. But first I needed to answer questions in writing to the Bank's satisfaction. Where did I get this money? I replied that I had sold whisky on which the full import duty had been paid. Other questions followed, including to whom did I sell it? It began to dawn on me that I was potentially going to dig myself, and more particularly my contact, into a hole. Fearing that it might have required a licence to sell or buy, I decided that, although now I personally was beyond the jurisdiction of the Rhodesian authorities (and we were hardly in the area of extraditable offences) I had better rely on my right to silence. I told the bank that I was not willing to supply further information. Alright, they said, but until you can explain fully the circumstance in which you acquired it, the money stays here in Rhodesia, and in an account on which no interest is payable. And so it did!

Actually I was finally able to get the capital sum back once Rhodesia had become independent Zimbabwe and Mugabe's regime had taken over some five years later, in the early days when everything was still sweetness and light and the new government was still anxious to give a good impression to the world at large. I must be one of the comparatively few Europeans who can thank Robert Mugabe for doing me a small favour. There thus drew to a close my brush with the criminal law. What I had learned was that I actually needed to have had a further contact in Rhodesia who in turn had a relative or contact in Malawi (there were in fact quite a few such people) so that I could have given the first person the Rhodesian dollars and been repaid inside Malawi in Malawi currency. While this was no doubt strictly speaking illegal it was the kind of measure practised all over the world to get round the nuisance of exchange control.

The practice of the law

But of course the reason I was in Malawi at all was to help to create some stiffening in the administration in the practice of government law. The Ministry of Justice headquarters[24] to which I was assigned was a small, rather top-heavy, office consisting of an Attorney-General – after the departure of Sir Bryan Roberts (see above) this post had been Africanised and was now held by Richard Banda (of whom more later) – a Solicitor-General (an expatriate New Zealander, David Barwick), a First Parliamentary Counsel (an Irish expatriate, Nick Barron), a Malawian Director of Public Prosecutions (Friday Makuta), a head of the Civil Section

---

[24] There was also a Ministry of Justice office in Blantyre, consisting of four state advocates who were mainly concerned with appearing in cases before the High Court there; and a small office in Lilongwe with one more.

(James Villiera) and four others (one senior state advocate and three state advocates, including myself). Those of us in this last group (the "Indians", as opposed to the "chiefs") were expected to turn our hand to any kind of legal work.

In practice, the bulk of office work tended to be giving advice to the Police on the sufficiency or otherwise of evidence in serious criminal cases, especially if they were to be tried before the High Court (murder and, I think, armed robbery). The case files consisted mainly of witness statements, badly typed and translated into generally rather poor, sometimes unintentionally funny, English, and taken from people with some of the (to us) funniest names.

It was popular at that time to call male children something with a suffix "son", with sometimes slightly odd results (Lackson, Handison). Also popular were colours, especially Brown, Gold and Green (or Gleen – Africans had difficulty in distinguishing phonetically between R and L[25], as they did between B and W) and days of the week (as with the Director of Public Prosecutions himself, Friday Makuta) and months of the year. Sometimes spelling showed cute transliteration (Aubrey sometimes became Oberry), but the oddest names were selected at random: Flymo, Limited, Maglassi (glasses or spectacles), Mattress, Teapot, and sometimes combined with bizarre results: Gold Mattress, Brown Teapot and, best of all, Limited Willy![26]

Actually the range of work tended to be rather humdrum and there was often not enough to do. At one stage I asked if I could be employed part time as a magistrate, but that would have been complicated to arrange administratively even if there had been much enthusiasm for the idea. The one area that was completely new to me was the drafting of legislation. True, I had, in the stylised language which was used at the time, drafted pleadings in England, and had even advised on the drafting of some private legal documents, but Bills for Acts of Parliament, and the various kinds of subsidiary legislation (regulations, orders, etc.) made under them constituted an entirely new field. And anyway this area of work, especially the more difficult tasks, was Nick Barron's province. Unfolding events were about to throw me in at the deep end however.

---

[25] This led to an interesting rendering of my own name. Bearing in mind that for some reason Africans usually transformed to it to Rogers, it was sometimes spelled exactly as pronounced – LOJAS, or because words in African languages tend not to end with a consonant, Lojasi.

[26] I amused myself by postulating a situation where such a person might plead his name as a defence to a charge of rape!

Bell-bottom trousers

There were already enshrined in the law certain of Dr Banda dislikes. The Decency in Dress Act forbade a woman to wear a "mini-skirt", defined as one that did not cover her knees when standing upright. In fact prudishness ruled, for even pictures (usually in advertisements) in newspapers or magazines of women in underwear, or even bathing costumes, were blacked out by censors. And kissing scenes in films were cut, so that often a man and woman would seem to bend towards each other and then suddenly fly apart. Actually the ban on mini-skirts was a popular measure and reflected the views of many people, both men and women, at the time.

But things moved on from women's modesty to the Dictator's personal dislikes: women wearing trousers, and men with long hair, neither of which could have been rationally argued to be matters of decency. The Decency in Dress Act was amended to prohibit the former[27], while a ban on long hair was achieved by (an actually rather complicated) amendment to the section in the Penal Code dealing with "idle and disorderly persons", putting offenders into exactly the same category as beggars, prostitutes and those involved in unlawful gaming!

For some time it had been known that Dr Banda also strongly disapproved of flared trousers. This was a fashion that had established itself almost worldwide in the late 1960s, but because Dr Banda's whims were regarded as the law, the relevant trousers were effectively banned without recourse to any formal provision in statute. There must nevertheless have been some difficulties engendered by this situation. If police or (more likely) Malawi Congress Party warnings and threats failed, or if the police failed or refused to use strong-arm tactics against a perceived offender, on what charge could he be prosecuted? Eventually the Attorney-General was prevailed upon to prepare an amendment to the law. Nick Barron must have been either on leave or otherwise unable to undertake the task; and so Richard instructed me to do it.

Preparation of a Bill to amend the Decency in Dress Act to ban flared trousers (usually referred to as "bell bottoms") was, to say the least, an unusual subject for anyone beginning to turn their hand to parliamentary drafting.

---

[27] Though some exceptions had to be made, e.g. for Asian women who normally wore this kind of dress and, as a concession to tourism, when at a recognised resort on the Lake.

Even if, in the days long before the internet, there had been facilities for research into the law of other countries, I would not have found any precedent for a law that was remotely like what was now required of me; and no help whatever was forthcoming from any Government Ministry responsible for this bizarre area of human affairs. How, then, was the matter to be approached? How was I to define the offending garments? Presumably "bell bottoms" meant widening of trouser legs towards the bottom, as of course with sailors' trousers from which the expression originated. Did the term include shorts? (Probably not, I thought.) And, apart from the most obvious cases, how was the flaring to be recognised in practice, and the law enforced? Was any degree of flaring at all to be banned? If so most of my own personal pairs of trousers, as with those of many men living in Malawi, would have to be thrown away. It felt as though I had been given instructions by the Red Queen in "Alice through the Looking Glass".

I discussed the matter with the Attorney-General and he agreed that a reasonably small degree of flaring could not be seriously said, by any ordinary use of the words, to turn trousers into bell bottoms. Indeed the very use of this term seemed to indicate that objection was to the more extreme form of design that tends to surface in any innovative fashion. Some degree of flaring, we thought, had to be allowed if the law were not to seem altogether ridiculous, as well as being extremely difficult to enforce in practice. The question was what degree? Clearly a line had to be drawn somewhere.

The drawing of arbitrary lines is a necessary element in the making of rules. Clearly a person is for practical purposes no less capable on the day before his or her 18th birthday than on the day itself, yet the law makes a whole series of assumptions as to maturity and capacity on that day. Such lines have likewise to be drawn in setting things as different as speed limits, fishing quotas and guest capacity for the purpose of defining what constitutes a hotel; in practice a view has to be taken as to where a sensible line should be drawn in the relevant context. Thus by analogy and in a rather less than sensible context I was required, so to speak, to draw a line for flared trousers.

Common sense indicated that, for the purposes of the present rule, flaring had to mean a ratio between trouser bottoms and the narrowest part of the leg. The answer seemed to require some sort of survey of trousers in working use. Where better to start than on those in my own wardrobe? From these I formed the idea that a ratio of six to five[28] (i.e. widest to narrowest) would best define the maximum permissible flaring. This formula was not arrived at by the application of any scientific principles, nor after advice from an organisation that represented tailoring or pattern-cutting, but quite simply (in a novel and unconventional occupation for a legislative drafter) after I had measured all the trousers I could lay my hands on. As no-one could think of a better formula or way out of the dilemma, in the formula went to the draft Bill.

There was of course still the worry that bizarre enforcement problems would follow. Were the police going to have to be issued with tape measures, or pocket calculators? Would there need to be spot checks of trouser dimensions in shops or markets, schools or offices? Were suspects to be required to stand on a platform of sorts, or were the police going to have, literally, to stoop to measure at ground level? Would the offending trousers be subject to forfeiture by the convicting court? But there were, as there nearly always are, time pressures and the drafting had to stop somewhere. It is a sad but common state of affairs that, in the absence of drastic problems with enforcement, the drafter rarely gets feedback on how a law is operating once it is in force. There were probably very few prosecutions and there couldn't have been many enforcement problems, as I never did get answers to those questions.[29]

Jehovah's Witnesses
One of the things we state advocates were quite often called on to do was review case files relating to people who had been charged with belonging to an illegal organisation. The law stated that such people could be prosecuted only with the express sanction of the Director of Public Prosecutions (in whose name we were of course working). Almost always the people concerned were Jehovah's Witnesses.

This sect had been banned by Dr Banda's government. It is one of the tenets of the Witnesses' faith that they recognise only or mainly the Kingdom of God, rather than any earthly one, and this had called into question their loyalty to the Government, especially as some of them had, in the early days

---

[28] This became widely known in Malawi as the "six-fifths rule". The actual text, shorn of the embarrassing "legalese" in which I actually drafted it (not knowing any better at the time) read:
> *"'bell-bottom trousers' means trousers so made that the circumference of each leg measured along the bottom edge is greater than six-fifths of the circumference of the leg at its narrowest point."*

[29] The Decency in Dress Act was repealed after Malawi emerged, in the early 1990s, from Dr Banda's dictatorship.

of independence, foolishly and probably seditiously, called on their people not to recognise the new country.

In my mind, as in the minds of most of us lawyers in the Attorney-General's Chambers, sedition was one thing, but being criminalised simply for one's religious beliefs quite another. Those charged always admitted, indeed were proud of, their membership of the sect, and their rather pathetic statements to the police usually contained expressions of the fact that they would continue to believe in their articles of faith no matter what the Government did to them. Most had done nothing criminal except belong to the sect. But the evidence on the files clearly showed this and in the circumstances we had the very unpleasant duty to apply this unjust law and sanction prosecution. We hated doing so.

Traditional courts

The other thing we had qualms about was sanctioning prosecutions for murder. This was not because of any pity for the accused persons, but because of the circumstances under which they were to be tried. It needs to be explained by way of background that as a general rule the gathering of evidence in criminal cases in Malawi was poor, and the police tended to take the least line of resistance and proceed by way of a confession statement of the accused person if they possibly could. Once the prosecution authorities have this, there is usually no need to produce other evidence of guilt. Often, we suspected but could never know for sure, such statements were obtained by beatings or even torture applied to the unfortunate accused person.

In the late 1960s there had been a nasty series of ritual murders in Blantyre. Two men suspected to have been responsible were tracked down and brought to trial. Perhaps for reasons referred to above, the evidence against the accused men was thin. The judge of the High Court before whom they were tried found that, at the end of the prosecution case, the *only* evidence against one of them was the written confession statement by his co-accused implicating him. Now under English law (and probably other legal systems too), which applied in Malawi, this is not admissible evidence against the person so implicated unless admitted by him (which in the instant case it had not been). This is because there is every inducement for an accused person to want to blame, or share the blame with, someone else, particularly a co-accused. There being no other relevant or admissible evidence in that case against the accused man so implicated, the judge had no option but to acquit him.

When Dr Banda heard about this he went, as we would say colloquially today, ballistic. For a start he disliked the legal profession – often referring to them as "tricky lawyers". He went on the radio to state that Malawi was not going to continue to tolerate "foreign systems of justice" under which people could be acquitted "when everyone knows they are guilty". Accused persons would, he said, in future be tried "under an African system of justice" and he had directed that the necessary measures be taken.

There was already in existence a series of what were called Traditional Courts, which tried cases involving local law and custom. These were not as tightly bound by rules of evidence as the courts set up under the English law system. The plan was to create a new "super" (or Regional) Traditional Court to try homicide cases. It was to be composed of five judges, only one of whom was to be legally qualified (and in practice was usually a magistrate). No "tricky lawyers" (or indeed any at all) would be permitted to appear before it as advocates.

This system began operating quickly. As a concession, Dr Banda (who at the time besides being President-for-Life was also Minister for Justice) agreed that the new Traditional Court procedure would apply only to *Africans* charged with murder i.e. not to Europeans, Indians or those of mixed race. The reality, after all this, was that those who were appointed to sit on the court understood that it was their job to convict. Quite apart from flouting rights under the Constitution (which the Government in practice anyway ignored) this set the criminal law on its head, for a person was in practice deemed to be guilty unless and until he could prove otherwise[30].

It was one of the many things that sometimes made me wonder why I was doing what I was doing. I remember once saying to Nick Barron "we lawyers are just ciphers here"; he agreed. I had of course the option to resign, but I didn't. This was partly because, for all its shortcomings, and the fear under which people lived, Malawi was at the time a country where corruption was minimal and where good order and a kind of peace prevailed.

---

[30] Much of my information about the Regional Traditional Courts came from Leonard Unyolo, a Malawian colleague I liked and respected. He had originally been a court interpreter but had persuaded the Government to send him to study to get a law degree. He duly qualified and was working as a state advocate alongside me when I was first in Malawi. He subsequently became a magistrate and was one of those sitting fairly often in those Traditional Courts. His apotheosis came in 2002 when he was appointed Chief Justice of Malawi; a truly remarkable end to a career that had started very humbly.

The Roads Project

Another file that landed on my desk was a big one. It concerned Malawi's efforts to enforce a performance bond against the South African company that had been responsible for building the tarmac road between Zomba and Lilongwe. I can't remember the exact details of the claim (it must have concerned alleged poor workmanship or late completion of work) but South African lawyers acting for the company maintained they were not liable on the bond as it had not been executed properly by the Malawi Government and was therefore not binding on them. In the first part of their assertion they were, to my consternation, correct, although how far this would have nullified it was a thorny legal question. They hinted, however, that a settlement might be possible if a representative of the Malawi Government were to travel to Johannesburg to negotiate. That representative was to be me.

I arrived in South Africa and checked in at the Holiday Inn, Johannesburg, neutral ground where the negotiations were to take place. Feeling somewhat out of my depth I did my best (I remember smoking ten or so cigarettes from a flat South African pack of 30 and for the first time in my life actually feeling ill from smoking) and at the end we reached a tentative agreement that we would submit to our clients (in my case, the Ministry of Finance, through the Solicitor General)[31]. Though David Barwick, the incumbent in that post, agreed that I had done as well as could be expected in the circumstances, I later learned that it had been suggested (though not directly to me) by a Ministry of Finance official that I should have been personally surcharged for not having achieved a settlement to the total amount of the claim. Governments in Africa do not lose court cases brought in courts in their own jurisdictions.

Ornithology, acting and other leisure pursuits

Probably my personal top priority in Malawi outside work was to get to know the endemic birds. There was in those days no bird book specifically for the country and one needed to make use either of the rather cumbersome two-volume *Birds of the Southern Third of Africa* by Mackworth-Praed and Grant, or (as most of us did) the more compact single volume *Birds of South Africa* by Austin Roberts (which covered birds up to the Zambezi and hence contained most, but not quite all, of Malawi's birds). As my knowledge gradually increased I moved from the beginner's frantic riffling through the

---

[31] I checked out of my hotel leaving my dressing gown, I afterwards recalled, behind the bathroom door. Later, at my request, the manager posted it back to me in Malawi and I reimbursed him (this is relevant to what happened a year or so later).

pages of Roberts before the bird I was trying to identify disappeared (often before I'd even got the book open), to a more considered assessment of the relevant species.

I had never thought that bird-watching could be hazardous, and normally it isn't, but one day in a little patch of woodland near the centre of the new Lilongwe Capital City, wandering on my own with my head turned upward and my binoculars poised I heard a rustling noise behind me. I didn't always pay much attention to such diversions, but this time it was lucky I did, for turning I saw, about 10 yards away from me, a cobra rearing with its hood spread. I immediately backed away from it with measured steps, for instinctively I knew not to make a sudden movement. After what seemed a long time, but was probably a matter of seconds, the snake subsided. I was told afterwards that I had probably been unwise not to turn my back on it, for it was most likely a spitting cobra. These snakes were reputed to be able to aim their venom at the eyes of their prey, or any living thing they felt to be threatening them, with unerring accuracy. Although the result of this was not itself fatal to humans, it could cause temporary blindness and was not an experience to be recommended.

Irene too found interest in the huge butterfly species count. With John's encouragement, she began collecting specimens and learned something of the skills needed in setting them.

The amateur theatre became very much part of both our lives in Lilongwe. I had done a little acting in form and school plays at my Belmont prep school, although after the earliest years not in leading parts. As already recounted, only once did I audition for a part in a Mill Hill School play (Twelfth Night), but I read the lines so badly that I didn't get the part. Nevertheless my interest remained latent. About a year after arriving in Malawi I heard that the director of a play being put on by the Lilongwe Dramatic Society (LDS, an association consisting entirely of expatriates) was looking to audition for some unfilled parts in his current play. I rang him, and to my surprise he offered me the part over the telephone (only later did I realise that he was at the time desperate to fill the last few roles).

The play was actually an adaptation by the director, John Dench (a distant relative, he said, of the well-known actress Judi), of a novel entitled "Flight into Danger", and both the script and the set were to a high standard (the latter reproducing as it did the interior and cockpit of a passenger aircraft). It was however quickly apparent that by no means all those involved were particularly talented actors and I realised during the production that I had talents that were worth developing. Irene too was persuaded to audition for, and got, the lead part in the next production: an Agatha Christie whodunit "The Unexpected Guest".

The LDS was very lucky in having permanent access to the stage in the Lilongwe Scout Hall in the old town, something that is rare in London, where premises for putting on shows has in the cases of most amateur groups to be hired for the week of the performance only. We were also lucky in that we had, at least among the expatriate community, a more or less guaranteed audience, for apart from the one drive-in cinema, there was virtually no other public entertainment available. There was no television in Malawi in those days and for practical purposes most of our contact with the outside world was through the BBC World Service, reception of which tended to be patchy at its crackly best.

The lack of entertainment meant that, rather as people did up to the 1930s in Europe, we needed to provide our own. Thus, for any social gathering of the LDS, members would volunteer a cabaret: songs, sketches or instrumental pieces. One of the things that struck us on return to the UK was that at so-called parties people just seemed to sit or stand around and talk; our enthusiasm for these gatherings soon simmered down.

A fact of life in Malawi at the time was that any play to be performed in public had to be censored. An appointment had to be made for the censors (in practice often officials of the Malawi Congress Party) to attend, usually at one of the dress rehearsals but in any event before the first public performance. They would pick on language, or elements of costume, of which they disapproved, and require us to conform accordingly. The day of Irene's play censorship was a day in which she got an uncontrollable fit of giggles at the start when some white glue got accidentally squirted into someone's face. The censors must have wondered at Agatha Christie being played for laughs.

Things moved on. Although Irene decided that one lead performance was enough to constitute a career in drama, I continued acting and was in a number of productions, including "Birds on the Wing" in which I played a confidence trickster using a number of accents. In one performance ("the Gazebo") I had to overcome a situation in which the lead actress playing opposite me did not make her appearance on stage on the appropriate cue. There followed a short impromptu interchange between those of us left high and dry on stage of the "I wonder where she can be" type until, running out of off-the-cuff dialogue, I decided I had to manufacture some excuse to go to the door of the set and find out. There she was on the other side calmly chatting to a stage hand. The door opened downstage and I frantically waved her on; but this sharp confrontation with the effects of her absent-mindedness induced panic in her and on entering she promptly forgot her lines. It was not one of our most polished performances.

All this brought me to the point where I considered I was ready to direct a play (Alan Ayckbourne's "Relatively Speaking") shortly before leaving Malawi. The ground was laid for a pastime that continued to occupy me on and off afterwards in Kenya and London.

One of the attractive spin-offs of an expatriate existence was that one came into close contact with a very wide range of people with a wide range of skills: accountants, agronomists, engineers of various kinds (including one who specialised in building railways), lawyers, scientists of various kinds, and teachers, to name the most easily recallable. We even got to know in passing the expatriate who was the country's Commissioner of Prisons, an obese Geordie with the most enormous capacity for beer I have ever seen.

Besides the Alders, Alasdair MacLeod was another with whom we formed a life-long friendship. He was at that time an accountant working as a project finance officer with the Ministry of Works. During the time we were in Lilongwe his marriage broke down, his wife having left him taking their youngest son and leaving him with their two older ones, Colin and Douglas, one a year or so older and the other the same amount younger than Jessie. Alasdair had directed the first play in which I had a substantial part. We shared a school run with the children, as indeed we did indeed the voyage home on the S.A. Vaal at the end of our contract periods (although he was merely on leave and going back to Malawi to a different post). About 3 years later he married again, this time to Theresa (Terry) Braybrook, one of Rachel's teachers at Bishop Mackenzie School in Lilongwe and also a member of the GST whom we knew well. We have all maintained a long friendship.

We were not seeking it, but there was virtually no Jewish life in Malawi. Such as there was centred around a small Israeli community, most of whom were engaged in development training of one sort or another[32]. While in Lilongwe we were on the invitation list of the Israeli embassy (Malawi was one of the few African countries to have maintained diplomatic relations with Israel after the Yom Kippur War in October 1973) though we found

---

[32] We did become very friendly with one Israeli couple, Moshe and Leah Hagigi, (whose little son, Tal, was similar in age to Jessie). Moshe was an economist working in Malawi for the Ministry of Finance and they later migrated to Boston, Massachusetts, where he obtained a teaching post at one of the universities there. We kept in spasmodic touch with them, and actually went to visit them while Jessie was working a year in New York in 1995-6.

the ambassador, Shamai Laor, to be a difficult man who seemed to enjoy arguing, often, and usually in public, with his wife.

The other major pastime for me was a return to golf. I had ceased playing shortly after leaving the army. Living in Africa provided the only time in my life when I had a sustained period at the game. Though the course in Lilongwe was of standard design, in Zomba the nine-hole course had sand "browns" instead of greens, and a golfer needed to equip him- or herself with a scraper to smooth a path from the ball to the hole. Such few golf trophies as I have all come from this period.

Leaving Malawi

Promotion from the ranks of the public service to that of a politician, though in some ways vastly increasing a person's power, can be a dangerous proposition. Shortly before we left Malawi, Richard Banda, who had been promoted from Attorney-General to Minister of Justice during 1975, had apparently attracted the envy and dislike of the nasty people in politics who can flourish in a totalitarian regime. By maintaining the good will of the Dictator these people, usually a layer or two beneath him in the hierarchy, can do virtually anything in his name and in the vague name of state security. And because power tends to corrupt, the settling of scores is the kind of thing is almost certain to happen in such situations; and it certainly happened in Malawi.

A number of charges were manufactured against Richard. He did tell me what they were, but I have forgotten the details, save that they seemed so preposterous that it was obvious at once what was happening. Very quickly Dr Banda was persuaded that Richard was a subversive person and should be dismissed from the Malawi Congress Party. As the MCP was the sole political party, this meant automatic dismissal from his post as Minister and as an MP. He became overnight a "non-person". If that had been all, it would have been bad enough, but there now began a cat and mouse game in which there was a very real likelihood that he would end up in prison in indefinite detention.

As it happened Richard lived with his family only a short distance from where we did. Besides being professional colleagues we were to some extent personal friends, especially as Rachel was at school with, and very friendly with, his daughter Susan. It seemed natural to go round to the house to offer our moral support. Richard was, however, forthright in warning us, and I remember the gist of his words: "I'm touched by your support, but please do not come here again. This is not the UK. You are putting yourselves in potential danger if you are seen to be associating with me. As a friend I am asking you please not to do so."

This would not be the first time that we would see a Minister responsible for legal affairs dismissed and humiliated.

In fact Richard managed to avoid gaol, but he was put under house arrest in his house in Nkhata Bay for about three years. The story did have a happy ending however, for during his restriction the instigator of his downfall (and that of many others), Muwalo Nqamayo, the Minister of State in the President's Office, was finally brought to book[33]. He was eventually tried, together with his accomplice the Head of Special Branch (a man named Focus Gwedi), found guilty of, I think, treason and hanged. Richard was rehabilitated, appointed a magistrate and quite quickly rose through the ranks of the judiciary to become Chief Justice of Malawi[34].

There remained only our departure. There was little prospect of promotion for me even had Irene been keen on the idea of staying on for a further contract, and it seemed as though the African experience had run its course. I had known, after only a month or two in Malawi, that it would be difficult for me to go back to the Bar in London, or indeed to the UK at all, but there seemed little practical alternative.

Meanwhile the difficulty could be postponed for a few weeks. We sold off things that we did not want to take home, including a beige corduroy suit I had had made by a local tailor. I had always fancied one, even though it would be a little heavy for the tropics, and Irene when on leave had bought and brought back the requisite material. Unfortunately the African tailor had no previous experience of corduroy and did not realise that it has a pile, and that it is imperative that it be cut all the same way. The resulting suit was not so cut; it looked a bit like a Harlequin costume and was unwearable. We sold it for the cost of the material to our African neighbour, an eager buyer even when the "Harlequin effect" was pointed out to him.

---

[33] The story, which may have been true or partly true, was that at some point Muwalo had been in the process of targeting the Commissioner of Police himself. The latter, so the story goes, managed to arrange an audience with the President before his arrest, and told Dr Banda that he understood that he was to be next in line for disgrace, humiliation and detention. "It will be a privilege" the Commissioner is reported to have said to the President "to be in prison in detention with all those innocent people." Muwalo's demise is said to have started from this point.

[34] His second wife, Joyce, was sworn in as acting President of Malawi on the death of the previous incumbent, Bingu wa Mutharika (born in 1934 Brightson Webster Ryson Thom!), in April 2012.

We packed and arranged to send off what we were taking back with us, found jobs for our servants[35], surrendered our house and spent the last two or three days in the Lilongwe Hotel in the old town. We had arranged to travel home not by air, but by the longer journey by sea from Cape Town, South Africa (it was still possible to travel officially this way).

For practical purposes our journey required flying firstly to Johannesburg. It was theoretically possible to travel to South Africa overland through what was still then Rhodesia (now Zimbabwe), but that involved either a very long journey through Zambia first, or a slightly shorter one through part of Mozambique by way of Tete. But the latter country was in the middle of an insurrection against Portuguese rule that made its roads unsafe to travel on unless in armed convoy. With two little girls, both options were clearly impractical.

Our plan was thus to hire a car in Johannesburg and take a couple of weeks to drive to Cape Town. Arrival at the Holiday Inn in Johannesburg[36] was something of a revelation, especially for the children, after two and a half years in Malawi. When we came down to breakfast there was a bewildering array of different kinds of food, and Rachel and Jessie loaded their trays in the self-service breakfast room with all kinds of things (including little individual packets of cereal), far more than they could eat. Although the hotel did not operate a colour bar (this fact was unusual at the time), we were conscious of being in an apartheid situation, and in South Africa we sometimes wondered if we were in the correct part of a park or (later) beach. Signs stating *"net blankes"* (whites only) were to be seen on things like post office counters, public loos and park benches. It was at the time (1976) when the anti-apartheid movement was beginning to gain momentum, although as tourists we ourselves were not conscious of any incipient violence.

We got to the famous Kruger National Park. It had proved to be impossible to book at short notice, but we were helped by the German hotel manager who had seemingly been impressed by my having repaid the cost of returning my dressing gown the year previously. He managed through a contact, presumably at the German Embassy (I remember his opening words: *Ich habe hier einen guten Gast* – I have a good guest here), to get us booked into a part of one of the Park lodges normally reserved for diplomatic personnel.

---

[35] Yusuf went to work for Sandy and Cornell Dudley, American friends of the Alders and ourselves, with whom we remained in touch. Sadly, Yusuf died prematurely of an infected leg ulcer about 10 years later.
[36] The hotel I had stayed in while on Government business the year before.

The journey through South Africa was pleasant though uneventful. As it was May, and out of season for tourism, we found beaches largely deserted and had no trouble finding hotel accommodation. It was a pleasure to be able to use a camera, even at places like the docks in Cape Town, without fear of arrest. We visited, in East London and Cape Town, parents of South African friends living in England, and finally towards the end of May 1976 boarded the S A Vaal, one of the last two ships still sailing on a regular service between South Africa and England[37].

The journey on board contained the usual things. Jessie, together with Lisa and Tina the two little girls of our travelling companions from Malawi, John and Lorna Coote (from Belfast), won a prize in the fancy dress completion for their Three Blind Mice, and John, Alasdair MacLeod and I won the "Brain of the Vaal" quiz completion. I found my sea legs and recall in a rough patch of the ocean shortly after leaving Palma, Grand Canaria, lying in a bath whose water swished from side to side with the movement of the ship. Someone come into the loo next door and was violently sick and I thought to myself somewhat smugly how grand it was to be acclimatised to the sea.

We docked in Southampton on a misty, sunny morning in early June. In fact most of that summer remained sunny, as though to tease us with what English weather does not usually offer; it was the year when many of the country's reservoirs ran dry. But I was listless; I missed Africa.

---

[37] The other was the Union Castle Line *Windsor Castle*. Both ships were taken out of scheduled service just over a year later, when the competition from air freight and air passenger travel made them no longer a paying proposition.

Chapter 8

Kenya 1977 – 84

The Start	262
The Political Background	266
The House	269
Servants	273
Social Life	279
The Law	285
Crime	293
Sporting and Cultural Life	295
Wildlife	297
Safaris	299
Diani	299
The Aberdares	301
Mount Kenya	305
Suswa	306
Lake Turkana and Shaba	306
The journey back from Shaba	310
Leaving Kenya	314
Conclusion	319

The Start

Looking back on my life in Kenya some 30 years later it still seems as though the experience of the seven years there was a highlight that has never been repeated, at least not to the same intensity and certainly not for such a sustained period. Malawi had indeed paved the way and served as an introduction, but the full intensity of the African experience was still to come. I had known before leaving Malawi that in spite of the minor irritations of living in Africa (the most common of which formulated itself into the frustrated question "why, just for once, can't things be done with reasonable competence?") life in England would seem dull and flat by comparison.

Firstly there was my professional life. I had returned to my chambers at the Bar after Malawi and attempted to pick up where I had left off nearly three years before, but looking at it in retrospect it was almost as though I had outgrown that part of it. I began to be a little tired of the same pattern of most of the criminal cases that came my way: the same old lies; the same wonder that juries could be so stupid as to acquit on occasions against all common sense (even where the verdict was in my client's favour); the same pattern of procedure in court with what one police officer had succinctly described to me as "playing this elaborate game of cricket". And civil cases too seemed more and more like highly sophisticated but essentially silly games of posturing and trying to get one up on one's legal opponents.

Although I have never been particularly interested in politics, the political situation in the UK, which was gloomy in the extreme, seemed at that time to dominate everything. The country, far from being the world power that it had formerly professed to be, at least up to the Suez debacle in 1956, had now become something of an international laughing stock.

In particular, a succession of weak governments of both main parties had shown an inability or unwillingness to stand up to organised labour, and this had encouraged the ratcheting up of more and more demands for increased pay and softer working conditions. Strikes, always referred to in the news media euphemistically as "industrial action", seemed incessant (many of these were "unofficial" in that they were not called by the relevant trade unions themselves but were a result of action taken locally at the behest of shop stewards in individual factories)[1]. Added to that, the UK's economic situation was so parlous that for the first time in our history we suffered the indignity of having to negotiate a loan, in the autumn of 1976, from the International Monetary Fund.

It was an unhappy time, especially for one such as myself who would have much preferred to be in Africa. What was to be done?

Having before we went to Malawi been on and enjoyed an induction course at Farnham Castle in Surrey, we went back there to share our experiences with others who were going to Africa. One young man I came across while doing this was Nick Harwood, a barrister, who was about to go out to Kenya as state counsel. Envious of his luck, I asked him if he would, when he got there, let me know if there were any other vacancies. In due course he wrote to tell me that there was indeed a vacancy in the legislative drafting section of the Attorney-General's Chambers, although the applicant would need to be experienced in the skill. Even though I was not experienced (the highlight of my drafting career so far having been the drafting of the amending Bill in Malawi to make illegal the wearing of flared trousers) I decided that I would

---

[1] In fact strikes had become known abroad as "the British disease". It was not until Margaret Thatcher's government (elected in 1979) decided that the time had come to take a stand against this state of affairs that it began to improve.

apply. And somewhat to my surprise I was accepted, even apparently welcomed, by the interview board.

Once more, Irene, though reluctant, had agreed that we could go. Always one to see the advantages rather than the disadvantages offered by life, she recognised that, apart from probable job satisfaction for me, there were many things about life in Africa that would benefit us as a family, and the children in particular. There was also a down side, and one that had not fully come into my consciousness until we had grandchildren of our own: we would be taking our children away again from their grandparents. For Irene's parents in particular this was a big wrench and the separation not lightly borne.

But I was full of eager anticipation. Kenya had been a place I had wanted to get to during National Service and had heard many positive stories about the country from expatriates who had lived there. I knew that it was bigger in many senses than Malawi, with not only a much larger land area, but containing very diverse habitats (sea, lakes, rivers, mountains, plains, bush, forests and desert) and very diverse peoples. These were not only those of the Bantu stock (e.g. the Kikuyu, Kamba, Luhya and Meru tribes) which were dominant in East and Central Africa and made up over 50% of the population of Kenya, but also many from entirely different ethnic groups as well: nilotic people such as the Luo and Kalenjin; nilo-hamitic people (Maasai, Samburu, Turkana); significant numbers of Somalis and some Ethiopians; as well as minority European, Asian (mostly Indian) and mixed race people.

I also knew something of the history of British involvement in Kenya: the opening up of the country after the building of the Uganda Railway (from Mombasa through to Kampala) in the 1890s; the pioneer European farmers with their incredible tenacity; the ugly killings during the Mau Mau rising in the 1950s; the post-independence rivalry between the Kikuyu leader Jomo Kenyatta and the Luo leader Oginga Odinga.

Arrival in Nairobi in May 1977 was a rather different experience from that in Blantyre nearly four years before. To my surprise I was met at the airport by a European, a rather dour Scot, Norman Montgomery, who was near retirement but was at that time the Office Manager for the Attorney-General's Chambers. He was not in a true sense an expatriate as he had taken Kenya citizenship at or soon after independence. He surprised me by telling me on the journey from the airport that he was a keen amateur actor who had noticed from my CV that I was too. I don't know if that helped our relationship but, as far as anyone was able to do, I got on well with him thereafter.

I stayed for the first couple of nights in an unimposing hotel known as Brunner's. It was not comfortable and seemed to serve partly (from the noises coming from the rooms at night) as a place where rooms could be hired by the hour. It was actually demolished within a year and at that time its management was clearly not concerned about its standard or reputation. Unimpressed with it, to say the least, I moved to the 680 Hotel across the road, but this was an international standard hotel and expensive (I forget how much subsistence I was allowed per day, but this cost considerably more). Eventually someone told me about the Fairview Hotel, in Bishop's Road slightly out of the centre of town. Reasonably priced and set in attractive grounds, it was a family business owned and run by Charles Szlapak, soon to become a very good friend, and served very well indeed until such time as I could be allocated a house.

The man I was to work for, Charles Njonjo, though actually the Attorney-General, was in effect the Minister for Justice. More than that, he was the man working behind the scenes in the latter days of Jomo Kenyatta's presidency (which were clearly not going to last much longer, as the old man was getting frail both physically and mentally) to ensure that the then Vice-President, Daniel Arap Moi, would, against the wishes of most MPs, become the next President. Charles was a Kikuyu (his father was a Chief) but his wife Margaret was a European lady who had been born in Kenya. Thus with a mixed marriage it was unlikely that he would effectively be in the running for President himself, even if Margaret had wanted it (which she most certainly did not). Even so, it was not an exaggeration to say that at that time Charles was virtually running Kenya.

My first meeting with him was in the company of Ray Fleeton, an English solicitor who was for the time being First Parliamentary Counsel (and thus my direct boss), but due to retire within a few months. Charles, clearly the most generous of men (as in my experience prominent Africans tend to be) offered me the loan of his wife's car (a Mini estate, which she was not in fact using at the time) until I could fix myself up with one of my own. The prospect of working for such a powerful man was exhilarating.

The Political Background

Indeed, it was an interesting time to be in Kenya. Jomo Kenyatta[2] had been in power since self-government and then independence in 1963, although as already noted the country was now increasingly being run by those closest to him.

Though in theory anyone could form a political party, there was in practice only one permitted: the Kenya African National Union founded by Kenyatta and others in the 1940s[3]. Even so, the political atmosphere was much freer than had been the case in Malawi. Political detention existed as a last recourse, but unlike in Malawi it was not often applied, and though outspoken critics of the regime or those in power were likely to find life uncomfortable, e.g. by criminal prosecution on possibly dubious evidence, or by being undermined in other subtle ways, only a few were actually locked up in detention.

One such had been Oginga Odinga, the recognised leader of the Luo people from the area in the west of the country around Lake Victoria. Odinga, who had been Vice-President of Kenya at and after independence had, after disagreements with Kenyatta, resigned from this post in 1966 and formed the (mainly Luo) Kenya Peoples' Union. Relations with Kenyatta's government steadily worsened until, after there had been politically motivated riots in Kisumu (the Luo capital in western Kenya on Lake Victoria) in 1969, Odinga was arrested and put in detention for 2 years and the KPU effectively banned.

Only the single political party had existed since that time. The device for controlling the formation of political parties was the Societies Act, which required formal associations of persons to be registered with the Registrar-General (a post in the Office of the Attorney-General). Quite simply anything that looked like it might be a political party was refused registration (and hence, if it purported to function, was liable to prosecution as an illegal society). However, during my time as First Parliamentary Counsel (see below) I was instructed by Charles Njonjo, by then Minister for Constitutional Affairs, to draft an amendment to the Kenya Constitution

---

[2] Born Kamau wa Ngengi, he later, on baptism, become known as Johnstone Kamau. He took the name by which he was subsequently known when living in England in the late 1930s. "Kenyatta" is said to be a Maasai name for the beaded belt he habitually wore.

[3] Originally the Kenya African Union, it merged with other pre-independence parties and changed its name in 1960.

making KANU the sole permitted political party, so that what had been a *de facto* situation now became *de jure*[4].

Kenyatta in fact died in August 1978, just over a year after my arrival in the country. By chance the death occurred during a visit to Kenya by my sister Sarah and her husband Terry. During that time my office had seemed to be particularly quiet and I decided one day, most unusually for me, that after about an hour in the office I would take the rest of the morning off and accompany Sarah and Terry to the Nairobi Game Park (I had even told my secretary the lie that I was going to a meeting the Ministry of Health!).

In the way things you do can sometimes jump up and bite you, I returned to the office after lunch on that day to the news that Charles Njonjo had been frantically trying to find me most of the morning (asking everyone including the Ministry of Health, who of course had no idea where I was!) to discuss the situation. I actually had no inkling of what had happened until, summoned immediately on my return to go to Charles' office, when his secretary, Penny Hill[5], told me of the death announcement. Charles' anger at not being able to find me earlier was tempered by relief that he had after all got hold of me and fortunately he did not cross-examine me on where I had been.

I later learned that the announcement of the death had actually been delayed for some hours so that steps could be taken to have the Vice-President, Daniel arap Moi, quickly sworn in as acting President. This in turn was so that alternative plans by MPs to have their own nominee so sworn in could be forestalled. As this delay was assumed to have been orchestrated by Charles, it was carried forward as one of the resentments that MPs harboured against him and helped them later to plot his downfall. It was not the only resentment: Charles had a somewhat patrician manner (he always wore a three-piece pin-striped suit with a rose in his buttonhole, and was often ironically nicknamed "Sir Charles"), he did not suffer fools and often made scathing comments in public about Kenya's politicians (and others). Those

---

[4] It was with wry amusement that I later learned that when Kenya and other African countries had been forced in the late 1980s by aid donor countries (mainly in Europe and North America) to amend their constitutions to prevent one-party states and presidents-for-life, this offending Kenya constitutional amendment, from which politicians were now anxious to distance themselves, was referred to as the "Roger Rose amendment"!

[5] A young English woman with an interesting name. She was a distant relative (great, great granddaughter or thereabouts) of Rowland Hill, the man who introduced the penny post in Britain along with its first adhesive postage stamps, the penny black and twopence blue. Penny's previous job in the UK had been as secretary to the society of those who had been awarded the Victoria Cross.

who had been upset by him (and there were many) remembered; and bided their time.

But things quickly settled down, at least on the surface. Moi was sworn in and, though technically acting in the post, in the one-party system operating at the time everyone knew that, barring assassination or some kind of *coup d'état*, he would soon be confirmed in the post and remain President for as long as he wanted to. In fact, as will be seen, there was indeed to be an attempt to remove him before very long.

In the prevailing system, government was generally a *laissez faire* business, in which (there being no challenge to power from alternative parties or policy-making bodies offering voters different programmes) there were very few innovations; policies and legislation were formed or drafted mainly in response to obvious needs. Government Ministers, and indeed politicians generally, were assumed (probably correctly) to be corrupt; indeed one Minister was widely known as "Mr Five-percent", his usual rake-off for awarding Government contracts.

As is to be expected in a system where the Government is not really accountable before independent courts, the police tended to throw their weight around with impunity. For example, criminals, especially if armed, were if apprehended often shot dead at the scene of crime (to the relief of many people it has to be said). At a much lower level of crime, one day I returned to where I had parked my car in the centre of the city to find two men, the first holding the second in an arm-lock. The former explained that he was a plain-clothes police officer and had caught the other one in my car. Had I given him permission to enter it? I of course said I hadn't, whereupon a quite open punching up of the lying suspect began. There were actually two suspects, both of whom were getting a good clobbering from the police (to get them to confess) as I left the scene.

But there was generally nothing like the fear of the Government and the ruling party that had been so prevalent in Malawi.

Internationally Kenya, along with most other "Third World" countries, relied heavily on aid from national and international donors. Relations with South Africa were of course, at least on the surface, non-existent, as the Nationalist government in power there continued its separate development policy, then and since known universally by its Afrikaans name "Apartheid" (pronounced *apart-ate*, not, as so often incorrectly in the news media and elsewhere, *apart-ide*). International condemnation of this had become organised since about the mid-1970s and South Africa was becoming a pariah state.

However, the South African Government were putting out feelers. In the hope (not entirely without justification) that Charles Njonjo, who had been to Fort Hare University, a university for non-whites in South Africa, might be sympathetic to possible limited bilateral trade and overfly rights with Kenya, they sent a non-official citizen to Nairobi, actually a tall Jewish businessman and lay magistrate, Hymie Shippel, to discuss things with Charles. Behind the scenes arrangements were made to allow him to land in Nairobi with a South African passport.

One day I received a call in my office to the effect that "Mr Shipper" was downstairs waiting to see me. I had not up to then any notion of what was going on, but it quickly became apparent that I was to be the person through whom he was to be introduced to Charles; I suppose it was easier this way, rather than having to go straight to him. Hymie explained to me quite openly that he was there to explain to Charles South Africa's interest in buying certain raw materials (I think it was soda) from Kenya. His unofficial diplomatic mission was an obvious low key way to make overtures for, as he rather crudely put it, "if there is nothing on, then it's only Hymie Shippel that gets kicked in the teeth, not the South African Government". In fact nothing came of the overtures for, as Charles later told me, this was a good step further than he could go politically.

In fact this was not the only time that I, or we as a family, were to be used as a conduit for important meetings. But this is to get ahead of myself, and indeed full awareness of much of the above came gradually and later. For the moment I had more mundane things to attend to.

The House

As things turned out I had greater luck, at least in some respects, with the allocation of a house than I had had initially in Malawi. One of the most senior magistrates, by the name of Robert McCready, was about to retire and it was decided that I would take over the house that he had occupied for some years. It was a sprawling building, built at a guess originally in the 1920s but with an extension made probably in the 1950s. I was told that it had been the Attorney-General's house in colonial times and was frankly pleased and surprised to have been allocated it.

Set in just under an acre of ground located at the end of Chyulu Road opposite the rear entrance to the Nairobi Club and built without much architectural style, it had seen better days but was not quite in a state of disrepair. With its thick walls, it had 5 bedrooms, 2 bathrooms (the 1950s extension itself contained 2 bedrooms including what was to be ours plus a bathroom and lavatory), a large lounge with an extension area, a dining room and a breakfast room, plus a kitchen set slightly away from the main part of the house, accessed by a short corridor open on one side with a wire mesh screen. The original part of the house was constructed on slightly sloping ground, with low stone arches of tapering size underneath that gave a person just enough room to crawl under at the highest part. All the rooms in this part had high ceilings.

But before taking possession there were some administrative arrangements to attend to. McCready was a man of about 60 with a shock of white hair, and though rather dour-faced was reputed to be capable of turning on the charm, especially with women. Magistrates are never popular figures, but he was particularly disliked by those who had to come before him. In fact he was known generally to Africans as "Bwana Maximum" from his propensity to punish convicted criminals with the maximum sentence allowed by law.

Just before he and his wife moved out, they invited me to stay overnight at the house. As I might have guessed, there was an ulterior motive to this. Apparently they were going on termination of service leave to Europe for "eight weeks" and then retiring to a house they owned up-country near Naro Moro at the foot of Mount Kenya[6]. In the meantime, he informed me, I could of course use his furniture but he would deem it a favour if I would allow his three motor vehicles to remain on the property and look after his two dogs. I was pleased to be getting the house and so at that stage did not mind that it was obviously going also to serve the previous occupant for a while as a free warehouse, garage and kennel.[7]

Though some were functional, the pieces of furniture in the house were mostly ugly, flimsy and dreadful; but until I could get a basic Government furniture issue (which in the event would anyway not be nearly sufficient for such a large house) they at least served a purpose. As we acquired the Government issue and gradually added to it pieces of our own (purchased from expatriates who were leaving, either directly or from the auction house in town), one of the bedrooms and one of the servants' rooms were gradually

---

[6] While talking to him at the house, he mused that he thought he had "given good value" in his post. "I was" he told me "tough when I needed to be". Eventually some person or persons, possibly from among those who thought they had reason to hate him, took their revenge, for two or three years later McCready was found murdered at his home.

[7] As will be seen, the "while" turned out to be rather longer than expected.

filled, floor to ceiling, with stacked and unwanted McCready items. The vehicles (a Land Rover and two saloon cars) were parked out of the way and, though unsightly, were not sufficiently conspicuous to give the appearance of a second-hand vehicle lot and did not inconvenience us. The dogs were another matter.

They were neither of them dogs we would have chosen as pets or guard dogs, but the McCready bull terriers, a white female (Millie) and a piebald male (Mogsie), became by default our companions for the next months. Millie was docile and, I seem to remember, partially blind; Mogsie was muscular, highly strung, extremely lively and potentially vicious, and would bark hysterically at other dogs and passing humans. Although confined to the garden of our house, on one occasion he somehow got into the garden of the house next door occupied at that time by European expatriates like ourselves. They owned two red setters, one of which Mogsie savaged so badly that I think it had to be put down. We were mortified and offered to pay compensation, but it was graciously declined.

We didn't want the dogs to be inside the house (in fact, bearing in mind the climate, the space underneath it served as a good "home" for them), but they must have been previously allowed inside, at least at times, by their owners, for soon we began to suffer from itchy bites. It quickly became apparent that the lounge area was infested with fleas, something we at first suspected but fairly quickly confirmed when we began to notice them actually jumping from the floor on to us. A pest control firm had to be called in to fumigate the house.

That wasn't the end of pests. At various times we could hear animals of some sort scurrying around in the roof; they were probably squirrels or rats, but they did not appear inside the house and didn't trouble us or cause a problem. However, shortly after getting rid of the fleas a small swarm of African honey bees settled in one of the air-brick vents of the house. We could not ignore them, for the corridor in which the air-brick was situated was alive with bees, and they are known to be potentially much more aggressive than their European counterparts. At first our house servants (more of whom later) decided that getting rid of the swarm was a job they could handle. Their method was simply to spray insecticide all over the place; this of course merely caused the bees that were not killed (most) to get angry. In the end we had to call the pest control firm once again.

Actually some time later we had another, and much larger, swarm settle in a tree in the garden. Although it probably would not have caused a problem, we were less sanguine than we might have been after our first experience and quickly decided that this was a job for expert removal of the swarm as an entity. After Irene had finally got the relevant department of one of the Government Ministries to understand what she was talking about ("Yes, yes, bees. BEES – buzz, buzz") they came and effected a fairly expert removal job.

Returning to the house itself, it was about 5 months before we were finally able to get shot of the McCready dogs and effects. Encouraged by Sir James Wicks, the then Chief Justice, who heartily disliked McCready and was amused by the thought that he might be discomfited by me, I eventually threatened (by registered letter) that if his furniture were not cleared within a stated period, I would stack it in the garden. He duly came with three vans he had scrounged from the Ministry of Works, muttering that I had broken the agreement he had struck with me, and implying that I was guilty of ungentlemanly conduct. That was fortunately the last we ever saw of him.

It took months of frustration attempting to get necessary repairs and redecoration done to the house, and anyway we had to wait for the rains to come before we could see where the roof leaked, for it was a question of putting out buckets, or the children's paddling pool, in the relevant positions. In a rare fit of efficiency, the Ministry of Works inspector decided that the house needed rewiring. This job took about three months of on and off visits from "electricians", who would clamber about the house (including the area underneath already described) banging and shouting to each other and tramping about with gravel on their boots over the polished wooden floors. It all drove Irene up the wall to the extent that they decided it was better to wait until she had gone out before resuming work (no hardship, that) rather than face her anger.

In the meantime, the repainting of the house took place not once but twice. This was a not untypical kind of event, for the authorities, usually slow to do what was really required, would make a great show of doing what wasn't. I wouldn't have minded so much, but each time the painters left quantities of paint on the window panes (of which there were many) as well as the frames and I had to go round scraping the excess off with a razor blade.

We also decided that the "outdoor kitchen" was too far away to be of any use to Irene and persuaded the Ministry of Works to let us construct a kitchen in the breakfast room (they put in a sink, we had to supply a cooker, fridge and furniture). True to form, the work took place spasmodically and the Ministry workmen laid the floor with two different shades and sizes of tiles. When the job was about two-thirds complete there was another pause in the work, and when it finally resumed they found they had run out of stock of both these tile varieties and needed to complete the job with yet a third, giving the interior designer's equivalent of a patchwork quilt. But in the end I, even if Irene didn't, came to love the house.

The grounds contained, just to the rear of the kitchen four small rooms constructed as servants' quarters and also two garages. All were of corrugated steel construction (as was, in traditional style, the roof of the main house). Living in one of the green-painted garages was Mohammed, a Somali. He had been employed by McCready as a watchman in return for living rent-free in the garage, and the former had urged me to keep him on in this capacity ("the other Africans are terrified of Somalis" he had confided to me). So here was another accessory to the house. Soon afterwards Irene found an old flattened-out cardboard box outside the garage. She picked it up and was about to dispose of it when she was informed that it was Mohammed's prayer mat.

The garden of the house consisted in a large part of a thin layer of soil on a rock base; there was thus hardly any water-retaining capacity and consequently in the dry season everything turned quickly to dust. It is an enduring memory that when the rains finally came at the end of the main hot dry season (January to March) the children, and sometimes we ourselves, would go outside and stand in the downpour, rejoicing in the fact and smelling the fresh smell as the dust was being laid. Where the soil was of reasonable depth, however, it did support a variety of plants, especially trees and shrubs: jacaranda, bauhinia, mulberry, false pepper and two enormous Australian eucalyptus trees, as well as oleander, hibiscus and bougainvillea shrubs and, just by the front door, a bed of blue agapanthus lilies.

Servants

While I was staying at the Fairview Hotel prior to taking over the house, Charles Szlapak asked me if I was looking for a house servant; if so, he said, he knew a man who was seeking employment. The latter had worked for many years for a friend of his, a Dr Barton, who had retired and gone back to the UK. Charles described the potential servant as an older man but was convinced that he was honest and reliable. I was of course interested, and as far as I was concerned his age was an advantage (mature servants tended to be more reliable than young ones).

It was thus that Joseph Wanjau Manjari came into our lives. It was often difficult to judge the age of Africans, but Joseph was at that time probably in his fifties. He was a fairly tall, quite portly man with a kind round face who wore glasses. He spoke good English, though as with most Kenyans this was his third language, for he spoke firstly his native Kikuyu and secondly Swahili[8]. I had decided that I was going to learn basic Swahili, but Irene needed to communicate in English.

With his references I had no difficulty in deciding to engage Joseph from the time I first moved into the house. He turned out to be not a bad cook, although his idea of cleaning and keeping the house did not exactly coincide with ours. Like many Africans he had no appreciation of things that were probably of no consequence to his own life: thus he was simply unable to see that, for example, in changing bedclothes there was any point in matching pillows and duvet covers; or that after dusting pictures on the wall it was desirable to leave them with their tops and bottoms parallel to the ceiling.

My abiding memory of Joseph is of him dressed in a short sleeved safari suit and wearing an oilcloth apron that Irene had given him which advertised Marmite. But a typical picture is one of the last photographs we have of him, together with the nearly four-year-old Jonno, as we were in the process of vacating the house in Chyulu Road in late April 1984.

There was no doubt as to his loyalty, and the fact that he had our interests, and those of the children in particular, very much at heart. He had a great sense of humour and was particularly fond of Jonno, to whom he used to refer as "my friend". Though not an educated man by modern standards, he did have some basic reading and writing ability, although in common with most Africans the letters L and R tended for him to be interchangeable. At one stage we had our deep-freeze unit in the dining room and we had put magnetic letters on it for Jessie's sake. Joseph could not resist making use of these and one morning we came into breakfast to find spelled out on the deep-freezer door:

LECHER
JESCA

It took a few moments to work out that these were the girls' names. A tactful suggestion that Rachel's name in fact began with an R produced an amended version:

RECHER

---

[8] The *lingua franca* of East Africa generally that was, apart from comparatively small groups of people at the coast, virtually no-one's first language in Kenya; but it was in Tanzania, especially Zanzibar.

We had not the heart to take it further.

Joseph with Jonno, while preparing to leave Kenya, May 1984

One further example of Joseph's spelling that took my fancy was in a shopping list he prepared for me one day when Irene was away (in London having an amniocentesis test for her pregnancy at age 40 with Jonno):

                Shap
    Chees
    Piample
    Ovener creaner   not sply lup

This last phrase meant that he didn't want the spray-on oven cleaner but the rub-on type.

But hard or efficient work was not his strong suit, more especially if there was more than usual to do. On numerous occasions, if we were having a dinner party or other gathering at the house, he would complain of some ailment or other and report sick. He had, too, the supposed old soldier's ability to look as though he was busy when he wasn't. If, for example, we had been out during the day, we would often come back to find him just a little bit too busy in the lounge with a duster, almost certain that he had grabbed it as he heard our car coming into the drive. In fact a duster was sometimes to be found on the top of our tall Makonde[9] carving even when there was no housework to be done (he had forgotten to remove it), and were almost sure that this was the strategic position for his shows of industry with it.

On one occasion we had an unannounced visit from an escapee from the mental hospital. The man in question had removed his trousers before coming into our garden and climbed onto a low tree. Joseph seemed to feel personally responsible for this behaviour, and was mortified by the indignity of it. He rushed into his room to fetch a pair of his own trousers which he then persuaded the man to wear after he had coaxed him down from the tree, and then escorted him off the premises.

Our gardener was a simpler man altogether. We had for a very short time employed a man who knew very little about gardening, the height of whose work had been to arrange bits of leaves taken from other plants in the bed nearest to the front door to make letters that read:

FLOURS

I can't remember the details of his leaving us (it was probably at Joseph's prompting), but we were soon joined by John, who remained with us for some years as a gardener and general help around the house. John was from the Kamba tribe[10], but Joseph seemed to accept him, although every now and then he would mutter about John's inefficiency or mendacity, managing to imply that if we wanted to employ an incompetent and unreliable half-wit then that was our affair. John spoke hardly any English and this at least forced me along my path of learning to speak sufficient Swahili to be able to make myself understood. He also had a strong sense (as indeed do most African house-servants) of what is deemed to be "women's work" that would be quite impossible for him to undertake: for example washing clothes (though ironing was apparently in order, unless of women's underwear) or anything to do with child-minding (babysitting excepted).

One day John came into the house looking very down in the mouth, his arm in a home-made sling. He said he had been robbed at the bus stop the previous evening during which the thieves had used an iron bar; he did have a nasty graze on his left arm. But Joseph didn't believe his story and was convinced it was a lie to cover up to his wife the fact that he drank away the

---

[9] This still-prized possession, carved from ebony, is of the "bodies on bodies" style that was actually strongly influenced in the 1930s by missionaries and others to the Makonde people of what is today northern Mozambique and southern Tanzania.
[10] The Kamba are, as already noted, of Bantu stock, along with the Kikuyu and others.

money he said was taken from him. Finally John decided to leave us (we suspected that he had been worn down by Joseph) and we replaced him with Isaac, a Kikuyu recommended by Joseph, who must have fitted in harmoniously for no strong memory of him remains.

The Somali watchman bequeathed to us by McCready soon left. A while later we decided to employ another, although we quickly suspected that he was sleeping on the job. Indeed, on coming home one night we found him fast asleep on his back with his boots sticking out from under one of the garden shrubs; the entry of our car into the gravel drive of the house hadn't even woken him. After that we decided that there really wasn't much point.

After Jonno was born we employed ayahs[11], firstly Catherine and then Anna, to look after him. As most African women tend to be, both were good and very patient with him and he liked Anna especially. However, the story that stays most strongly in mind about Anna concerned something that came as a bolt out of the blue. It was 26 November 1983; Irene and the children had by this time to all intents and purposes left Kenya, having gone back to London the previous August to get our London house going again (after it had been rented out to a succession of tenants) and get the children established in schools. They would come out for the Christmas and Easter school holidays before we finally all left the following May. Meanwhile I was living in the house alone with the servants.

In the early hours of one morning Isaac knocked on my bedroom window saying that Anna needed urgently to get to hospital. I dressed quickly only to be informed that she was in labour (I hadn't even known that she was pregnant). She was accompanied by an older woman who was looking concerned. Having quickly recovered from the shock, I got both women into our little yellow Renault 5 car and thinking there would be no problem, as the Kenyatta Hospital was a mere 250 yards or so from the house, drove off in that direction. However, as we set off the women informed me that Anna had to be taken not to Kenyatta at all, but to Pumwani Maternity Centre on the far side of the city. I had never been there, had only the vaguest idea of where it was and my passengers seemed incapable of directing me. Even before we started off Anna had been groaning and crying, but some five minutes into the journey she began screaming with birth contraction pains. I was praying that she would not have the baby in the car.

In this state of mind I got lost in the maze of streets with which I was unfamiliar, and needed to find someone to ask directions, quickly. But it was

---

[11] The Swahili word for a nanny (as it is also in many Indian languages, I believe), derived from the Portuguese word *aia* (nurse).

about 3.00 am and there seemed to be no-one about. Finally I found a watchman dozing in a doorway; I got out of the car and prodded him. Rousing himself slightly, he gave me sleepy and rather vague directions and I drove on. Suddenly even louder and more anguished screams came from the back of the car, and I was struck in the back of the head by Anna's right foot which then lodged itself on the back of my seat. At the same time, while the car was going at some speed as I was frantically trying to get to the hospital, the older woman, a rather large person, was attempting to get from the front seat to the back (there was not much room for this type of manoeuvre in a Renault 5 at the best of times). It was then that I heard a baby's cry!

There was nothing for it but to stop the car so that the informal midwife could help with the final stages of birth. I got out, flagged down a taxi that was passing the other way and explained the predicament and he agreed to lead me to the maternity centre, actually not very far away. Meanwhile the baby had stopped crying (Oh God! I thought, the baby's dead). Once there, I left the women (and baby, very much alive) in the car and tore down a long entranceway. The person at reception seemed indifferent to my frantic tale of birth in my car (perhaps it was not an uncommon occurrence); and no, a doctor could not attend the car. Neither was there any kind of transport in the form of a trolley or even a wheelchair for the mother. In that depressingly often used phrase to indicate that nothing much would happen soon, it was suggested that I "take a seat".

The hospital was a dirty, dilapidated place with cockroaches crawling about everywhere; in fact it presented a typically urban African scene. After what seemed an age, a nurse was detailed to accompany me back to the car; she had instruments, so presumably she cut the umbilical cord (I did not pay close attention to that part of the proceedings) and she then carried the baby into the hospital. Poor Anna had to follow her on foot, dripping blood everywhere, down the long entranceway to be admitted. I hovered around in reception for a short while but realised there was nothing much more I could do, so feeling anxious but surplus to requirements I returned to the car. The older woman who had accompanied us had just finished mopping up the mess in the back with a *kanga* (the cloth African women drape around themselves like a skirt). Feeling not exactly as though a good night's work had been accomplished, I drove home and got back to bed at around 4.30 am.

In fact the baby boy, whom Anna named David, thrived. She had no husband or partner that we knew of. Anna got employment with another family and we kept in touch for some twenty years afterwards and periodically arranged for money to be got to her for the boy's education.

Social Life

From a social point of view Nairobi was quite unlike the places in Malawi in which we had lived. It had very much larger European and Asian populations and in particular a large diplomatic corps, as most countries had missions there covering east and central Africa, and there was also a large representation of international bodies of one sort or another, including the headquarters of the United Nations Environment Programme. This meant that it took rather longer to establish a circle of friends than it had done in Malawi. However we had, in David and Shirley Marks, friends from (in my case) the 1950s, when David and I had played rugby together for the Old Millhillians. They had by then been living Nairobi for a few years and they were very hospitable to us, in the early period especially.

Nevertheless we did quickly develop a social life. Very soon after I had moved in Harold and Lori Platt and their 6 year old daughter Gabriella came over from the house across the road at the side of our house to introduce themselves. Harold was a judge of the High Court and the family became close friends, especially as Gabriella, their only child, was close in age to Jessie. And, as in Malawi, we got to know people from varied walks of life that we would have been much less likely to meet in London. Acquaintance- and friendships came through our work, through sport, through friends of our children, and in Irene's case especially, through initial casual meetings.

Typical of this last was her striking up a friendship, shortly after her arrival, with Rosemary Kempsell at the Nairobi Club swimming pool. Rosemary had two little girls of approximately Jessie's age, and her husband John worked as Finance Director for Brooke Bond. Through Rosemary she decided to join, of all things, a bible study group run by a friend of Rosemary's, Francie Bowman, an American whose husband Bob was flying aeroplanes for a Norwegian missionary organisation[12].

---

[12] Francie and Bob returned to Boone, North Carolina, in the early 80s, but divorced not long afterwards. She later remarried Ralph Hall and we kept in touch over the years, visiting them, and they us, from time to time. Rosemary and John returned to England, soon after we did, to Sanderstead, Surrey, and it was of course much easier to remain in touch with them. Rosemary went on eventually to become a two-term World-wide President of the Mothers' Union (the principal women's organisation within the Anglican Church) and was eventually honoured with a CBE.

The girls of course made friends at school. Though they needed to work hard they had, largely due to the climate, a free and open life. Sometimes the unexpected happened, as when the children at Rachel's school (the Banda School[13]) were unable to get off the school bus one morning as there was a lion roaming around on the premises. Later, when the by then 14 year old Rachel was attending Henrietta Barnet School back in Hampstead Garden Suburb she took a while to adjust, not so much to the fact of an all-girls school, but to the almost entirely female staff and the fact that she could not see out of the high classroom windows.

To an extent social life was centred on the clubs, of which we belonged to two. The Nairobi Club was just across the road from our house, and as it had tennis and squash courts and most importantly a swimming pool (virtually at the bottom of our garden) we clearly had to join. It was still very old-fashioned, with a back bar to which only male members were allowed access, and a dining room to which we went occasionally to dine in an atmosphere that was reminiscent of England about thirty years before. The main lounge had leather armchairs and newspapers from England, albeit at least a day or two late, and some magazines, and there was also a reasonable lending library. In fact it was for me a fuddy-duddy old place (with some fuddy-duddy old European committee members) where time had stood still. I was always conscious of this and I loved it.

The club also had the inestimably valuable facility of its own borehole, which meant that there was always water for showers, something of which we were able to take advantage during periods when the mains water supply to our house was minimal or non-existent (quite often in the dry season). In fact we installed a hand pump adjacent to the entrance drive to our house to try to get water from the mains into our tank when pressure ran low, and the steady working of the pump handle to and fro was one of the jobs our gardener of the time seemed quite happy to undertake, with his mind in neutral gear, for periods of half an hour or so at a time.

In order to play golf it was necessary to join another club, and this we did at Karen. The club was located in that comparatively far-flung suburb west of Nairobi named after the Danish countess, Karen Blixen, who had lived there, grandly but not always happily from 1914 to 1930, when her lover Denys Finch-Hatton was killed in an air crash and her coffee farm (which had never been very successful) had burned down. Karen Club too had, besides a golf course, all the sports facilities of Nairobi Club, with the added advantage for

---

[13] No connection with the President of Malawi! The word *banda* in Swahili actually means a small house or hut.

me personally that there was a very good variety of birds to be seen in its grounds.

At Shirley's suggestion Irene took a course on guiding and then volunteered as a museum guide. She became quite knowledgeable about the exhibits, particularly those in sections of the museum that interested her. She was however stumped when one day a man came in asking about cuckoos; some that he owned apparently had a disease and he needed information. A visit to the bird gallery did not help to identify which species he was concerned about, until finally someone explained to her that the man was talking about his *kukus*, the Swahili word for chickens.

There was a small Jewish community in Nairobi, with a nucleus of twenty or so settler families. But the majority were Israelis, most of whom were working in the construction industry, particularly for the large company Solel Boneh that specialised in the building of roads.

From a position of extreme doubt I was increasingly coming to the realisation that I was an atheist and hence that religious life, necessarily predicated on there being a God, was without much meaning. But Jewish life tended anyway to be based on social contacts and gatherings rather than religious ones and we were good friends by this time with a number of the Jewish families, particularly our doctor, Vera Somen and her husband Michael, and the chairman of the Nairobi Hebrew Congregation, Charles Szlapak, and his wife Marian. I did even participate minimally in Jewish religious life in Nairobi. I was happy to support Charles and so, in spite of my non-belief I allowed my name to be put on the rota of those needed in order to get a *minyan*, a minimum of 10 adult males needed before services in a synagogue can be held. In the circumstances it seemed almost to be making a statement of rejection not to do so. This did not require attendance every week and though I regarded it as a bit of a chore, I didn't mind too much doing it.

We quite often found ourselves invited for Friday evening dinners at the Szlapaks, or at the flat of Charles' mother Rachel. These dinners were sometimes quite large affairs, with guests from out of town (who were not always Jewish) regularly invited. The Szlapak family were always generous hosts.

We also developed friendships with one or two more unlikely people. One such couple was an Israeli, Harry Barak, and his wife Leah. Whether or not that was Harry's original surname we never discovered; it probably wasn't, as he had emigrated to Israel as a young man from Australia, and Israelis were encouraged, if not required, to take Hebrew-derived names especially if they worked for the Israeli Government abroad. Harry gave out that he had an import/export business; however, it soon became clear from inference rather than information that he was primarily involved with "security" amongst the Israeli community.

Kenya had no formal diplomatic relations with Israel at the time (most African countries had broken off relations with Israel after the 1973 Yom Kippur War) so there was no Israeli Ambassador. But there was instead an informal Israeli Government representative in the person of Arye Oded, styled Israel's "Head of Trade Mission", with whom (together with his wife Esther) we also became friendly. Harry was obviously close to Arye, and both had a very cordial relationship with Charles Njonjo, by that time my direct boss.

Some time in, I think, early 1978 Harry invited us to his house to view a film of a momentous occasion for Israel: President Anwar Sadat's official visit the previous year to that country. Sadat had taken the bold decision in the context of the Muslim, let alone Arab, world that it was in Egypt's interest to end the "no peace, no war" stalemate and begin negotiations that would end with the signing of a peace treaty and the return to Egypt of all the Sinai peninsula captured by Israel in 1967. At the gathering at the Baraks' were, besides us, also the Odeds, Charles and Margaret Njonjo (at whose suggestion I think we had been invited), Charles Szlapak and, knocking back beer after beer to the point of becoming almost legless, the then Kenya Commissioner of Police, Ben Gethi.

We gradually realised that Harry was almost certainly the local representative of Mossad, Israel's renowned secret service. Whenever he came to our house he would discreetly take his hand gun from wherever he concealed it on his person and place it into one of the drawers of our chest in the hall.

A while later we arranged to have a dinner party at home to which we invited Charles and Margaret Njonjo. We also invited Harry and Leah, together with our neighbours Harold and Lori Platt. On hearing that the Njonjos had accepted, the servants, especially Joseph, worked themselves up to a fever pitch of excitement, and a huge effort was made (for once!) to have the house (and even its windows) thoroughly cleaned.

We had assured Charles and Margaret that it would be a "non-political" evening with just friends, all of whom were known to them. Charles was not thought from many points of view to be an ideal guest, as he had no small talk and on occasion was known to sit yawning until the earliest moment he and Margaret could decently leave. As an alcoholic beverage he drank only beer, but disliked the Kenya-brewed Tusker brands which were all most of us could get hold of, and was known to bring along his own evening supply – two bottles of imported German Löwenbräu, which indeed his police driver discreetly handed to me on their arrival.

A day or two before the dinner Harry had rung Irene and asked if he and Leah could bring along a guest. Irene was a bit put out and explained how we had assured the Njonjos that they would know everyone at the dinner; but Harry was persistent:

"Irene, trust me."
"Harry, this is a special evening for us, and we don't want to risk upsetting Charles."
"That certainly won't happen."
"Harry, I'm uneasy about it. Who is this person?"
"I can't tell you right now, but all I can say is that you have no need to worry, and furthermore you would be doing Israel a great favour."

After a certain amount of further dithering, Irene somewhat reluctantly agreed.

On the evening in question the Baraks arrived with their guest. He turned out to be David Kimche, a man of about fifty who, though Israeli, spoke English like the English public school boy he had originally been[14]. He was introduced that evening as a journalist and diplomat (a wonderful example of the truth, but not the whole truth – by a long shot!) but it was clear that he wanted to get the chance to talk for a while confidentially to Charles, which he did immediately after dinner. The others present, including ourselves, sensing the importance of the occasion kept a discreet distance. It was only some time afterwards that we learned that he was actually at the time the deputy head of Mossad.[15]

One of the particularly nice things about living in what to others seems an exotic place is that you get plenty of visitors, mainly family and friends, but

---

[14] Actually from a Swiss Jewish family, his name was already familiar to us as we had had for some time in our bookshelf in London a copy of the book he wrote together with his brother Jon about the Israel/Arab War of 1948-9 entitled "Both Sides of the Hill". We also knew that he and his brother had been born in London.

[15] He left this organisation in 1980, after almost 30-years, due to a quarrel with the then Mossad Chief, Yitzhak Hofi. Shortly after this the Israeli Foreign Minister at the time, Yitzhak Shamir, appointed him as the Ministry's Director-General. He died at the age of 82 in March 2010, when the Israeli newspaper Ha'aretz described him as "Israel's spymaster".

sometimes people you have never met before who are friends of friends. In the very early days we had a visit from Irene's niece Miriam who witnessed at first hand some of our initial trials and tribulations, particularly with the bull terriers. Joseph, who called her "Milly", had to make it clear he was not referring to the eponymous dog. In fact she and her sister Beverly were to visit us on another occasion. Those visits enabled us to see our life through the eyes of others.

One such visitor was Eva Sussman, a friend from New York, whom we took with us on a visit to Amboseli (actually the only time we stayed at that amazing place with its backdrop of Mt Kilimanjaro). On the way back to Nairobi in our Range Rover (that we had bought from our American friends, Francie and Bob Bowman, when they left a few months before) we noticed a group of people gathered around a vehicle that had stopped by the side of the road. We were flagged down by the European driver and discovered that the vehicle had knocked over (but not killed) a child and that the crowd surrounding it was rather hostile.

The occupants turned out to be the Briffit family, one of whose three children was in Jessie's class at school. The parents had perforce to sit it out and wait for the police to arrive (something that could take hours) but they begged us to take their three children, who were somewhat distressed, back home to Nairobi with us. There were already six of us in the car, but this was clearly important and somehow we fitted the three extra children in and made our way back home.

As all nine of us pulled up outside our house we saw another car parked outside; Alasdair and Terry MacLeod and their two boys, who were on their way to or from Malawi, had arrived, as we suddenly recalled they had said they would. We were now, so to speak out of the blue, thirteen people: five adults and eight children. Showing a special kind of ability to rise to the occasion, Irene organised somehow to feed the children and then the adults, after which I delivered the Briffit children back to their home (by which time fortunately their parents had returned). Eva Sussman told us a number of times afterwards how she had observed the whole sequence of events with wonder and respect.

But it was a natural thing for people to help each other out in bad situations in Africa, certainly more so than they would have done in Europe. Death was much closer to everyday life there. We were to experience that kind of help ourselves later on when we desperately needed it.

My most direct experience of death while in Nairobi was that of my secretary, Grace, some 18 months into my time there. She had gone into hospital to have a baby, and I had heard from Margaret Mulumba, her friend and my temporary replacement secretary, that she was not doing too well. I didn't think too much about it, births were after all sometimes difficult and I was particularly busy at work, until one day Margaret came into my office in floods of tears and told me Grace had died (Africans always seem to say "passed away") the previous day. I later learned that she had had high blood pressure and soon after giving birth had gone into a coma from which she never recovered.

Grace's body had been taken to the City Mortuary. A day or so afterwards I received a deputation of three from the office telling me they were going to view the body (a typical custom in Africa to show respect) and asking if I would join them. I have to admit that my first reaction was to want to chicken out, but I told myself that this was being silly and offered to take them in my car.

I had never been to a mortuary before. We arranged with one of the attendants to take us to view, and he opened what seemed like a huge fridge door to reveal three or four layers of stretchers end-on. My first impression was the bare soles of a pair of feet at eye level. Bodies were wrapped in blankets and some were doubled up on the stretchers. All we could see of Grace's body on the top row was her head. The four of us stood there a little sheepishly while the bored mortuary attendant leant against the doorpost and picked his teeth with a match. As we turned to leave, he slammed the door shut and shuffled off.

The Law

Of course the reason I had been able to get to Kenya at all was the fact that I was adjudged to be qualified to draft legislation, in spite of the fact that my experience of it in Malawi had been limited, albeit somewhat intense.[16] I was in effect to be the Second Parliamentary Counsel, the First being Ray Fleeton.

Ray, at that time in his late 50s, was a solicitor from Felpham in Sussex who had worked on one or two previous assignments for the Commonwealth Secretariat in the Pacific, and he was now working in Kenya under their auspices on a two-year contract.[17] He was ordinarily a mild enough person,

---

[16] See the section on the practice of the law in the chapter on Malawi.
[17] By an odd co-incidence, Ray's predecessor in office in Nairobi had been Giles Harwood (no relation to Nick Harwood who had helped me to get my present job). Giles, after a spell

but seemed often unable, or unwilling, to "ride" the many difficulties that were put in his way professionally by incompetence and lack of consideration in others, particularly the time pressures under which our drafting section was sometimes placed. All too often these time pressures turned out to be unjustified, and having been required to complete work by a (sometimes unrealistic) deadline, we would find that the "extremely urgent" matter then went to sleep for months (sometimes for good). We also, as is so often the case with parliamentary counsel in "developing" countries, suffered constantly from lack of proper instructions for drafting.

All of this made him irascible at times and some people he had to work with found him difficult. In fact he found life in Kenya sufficient of a trial for him and his wife Mary (they had no children) not to want to consider renewing his contract, which expired nine months after my arrival. Thus, unexpectedly, I found myself in line for his job. I had, I think, sufficiently impressed Charles Njonjo that I could do it and after a month or two acting in the post I was confirmed in it.

Drafting legislation is undertaken on the basis that Government departments make policies which, assuming they need the backing of law, are then put (or "translated") into legislative form by those of us who are called legislative, or parliamentary, counsel (though in Kenya, as in most Commonwealth countries, such officers actually work for the Government and not for Parliament). In everyday parlance they are known simply as "draftsmen" or, more usually in a modern gender-neutral world, "drafters".

In an ideal world, the relevant policies would be worked out in appropriate detail by the Government Department responsible for the matter in question and then given in the form of instructions to draft to the Attorney-General, which of course meant in practice the parliamentary counsel. But the world is usually a less than an ideal place, and such instructions as we received often tended to be ill-thought out or deficient. Two admittedly rather extreme examples can serve to illustrate what I mean.

There had been a spate of robberies in Nairobi undertaken by criminals dressed as police officers. Some bright spark in the Ministry responsible for crime had the idea that the answer to this problem was to ban the sale of any item of police uniform to the general public. I was called to a meeting to get instructions to draft the necessary legislation to do so. Now at that time a male police constable's uniform consisted of a black beret, a khaki tunic

---

in the Caribbean when his marriage had broken up, was afterwards appointed Chief Parliamentary Counsel in Malawi. I met him and discussed many things of mutual interest during visits we made there from Kenya.

shirt, khaki trousers and black boots. The accompanying cap badge, lanyard and belt were of course distinctive.

What, I asked politely, would banning the sale of such items achieve except for chaos in the clothing industry? How could any of the main items of uniform be legally distinguished from ordinary items of clothing of the same kind readily to be found on sale in shops and markets (and widely worn); were we, for example, seriously to consider banning the sale of black boots? The real problem was of course not that the relevant clothing was generally available, but that the criminals were impersonating police officers (something that, naturally, was already an offence under the Police Act). This deception could be achieved whether or not the clothing consisted of genuine items of police uniform. After the use of considerable tact I persuaded the Ministry officials that banning the sale of these items of clothing was not the way "to be seen to be doing something about the problem".

A rather bigger problem came up in the guise of what were known as "land cases". There had been for some time dissatisfaction on the part of civil litigants appearing before magistrates with the way in which their land dispute cases were handled. All too often the cases were the subject of delays, and partly for this reason the legal costs were high (and anyway it was alleged that lawyers were overcharging their clients and sometimes deliberately dragging the process out). But even worse, litigants often considered that the district magistrates hearing the cases had insufficiently understood or applied the facts. This led to appeals to the resident magistrates' courts and yet more expense. These appeals were sometimes launched on what the resident magistrates found to be insufficiently complete records of cases, which then had to be referred back to the original court.

The situation was clearly unacceptable and the President and Ministers had received many complaints about it. But instead of getting the courts to deal with the matters properly, or at least to make suggestions as to how things might be improved, President Moi's patience suddenly snapped and he went on the radio to explain that these problems had never existed when he was a young man: land cases had always been heard by the tribal elders then and resolved to the satisfaction of the parties to the disputes. He had therefore directed that there would be a return to that happy state of affairs and he had directed the Attorney-General accordingly.

I didn't hear the radio broadcast, which would anyway have been in Swahili, but the following morning the recently appointed Attorney-General (a lawyer by the name of Julius Kamere who was from the start clearly completely out of his depth in the post[18]) called me to his office to tell me about it. I said something to the effect that we would no doubt be getting instructions on the matter shortly. He replied that I had misunderstood; what the President had said (which boiled down to "land cases will be heard by elders") *were* the instructions, and the only ones we were going to get. The only clarifications were that no lawyers were to be allowed to appear in cases before the elders and that there was to be no appeal from their decisions.

I have often used this as a case study in how not to brief parliamentary counsel. In legislation everything relevant must be stated so that there can be no doubt as to exactly who or what is affected and how. But in this case every word in the "policy" quoted above needed detailed clarification. I presumed we were dealing with agricultural land, but at what point did a garden in which a person grew crops – as most people did – become dignified with this title? Could land within city limits or in a township constitute agricultural land? I had only the roughest of idea of what kinds of cases we were to provide for (rights to ownership or occupation; rights of way; rights to hunt or take crops, etc.) And who were the elders exactly? This was an easy enough question to answer in traditional societies, but things had moved on from the situation that had existed 30 to 40 years previously; there was much inter-tribal marriage, and anyway not all traditional societies had the same concept of elders. And what if one of the parties to a case were from a different tribe, or a European or Asian, or a company or corporation, or even the Government itself?

There were actually many other policy decisions that needed to be made (was some sort of land tribunal to be set up, and if so how exactly was it to be composed, and what was to be its procedure, and its power to enforce its decisions?) on which I had no help at all. I discussed the whole matter with one of the European resident magistrates who had had some experience of the cases concerned, and with his help I cobbled together something in the form of a Bill that I knew would be bound to be problematical, and probably beg as many questions as it purported to answer. I was right, but as I was to leave Kenya within a year or so of the enactment of the Bill I didn't actually have to deal with the fall-out.

---

[18] His sole qualification for it seemed to have been that he had undertaken conveyancing work for the President. He was appointed after Charles' immediate successor, James Karugu, the former Director of Public Prosecutions, had resigned after only a year in office, apparently over differences of opinion with Charles (see below p. 292). He too lasted only a year in office but for different reasons: he had become such an embarrassment to the Government that he had to be replaced. *His* successor was nearly as bad.

Sometimes the drafting of amendments to Bills that were going through the National Assembly needed to be done in a great hurry. I remember thinking that trying to do so in a corridor of the building, or even in the car park (when for some reason no rooms were available), as occasionally we needed to do, with Ministers and senior civil servants literally breathing down our necks, constituted less than ideal circumstances for producing our best work.

Though as a drafter one was not supposed to question policy (except to clarify it, or in the kind of circumstances mentioned above when its absurdity need to be tactfully pointed out) there were one or two instances where I was suspicious that there was a hidden agenda behind it. For instance towards the end of my time in Kenya I received instructions to draft a Bill to licence video rental shops (at that time video tapes were in the form of cassettes measuring 7½" x 4", or about 19 x 10 cm).

No real reason was given as to why this measure was thought to be in the public interest and I knew that firstly the people to be licensed were in practice virtually all Asians and secondly that the man behind the proposed licensing scheme was the former Commissioner for Customs and Excise who had been removed from his post for corruption and "shunted sideways" into the instructing Ministry. I thought there was a real likelihood that the legislation, if passed, would be used as a vehicle for corruption; indeed I thought it likely that only those who were prepared to pay bribes (as most Asians were) would get a licence. I asked for more details as to the policy. I didn't receive them; but then neither did I have the unpleasant task of drafting the Bill.

But the boot could be on the other foot, as I recalled in one letter:

> I was really angry the other day when I found a letter on the file from Elijah Mwangale [then Minister for Tourism and Wildlife] to the Attorney-General in September accusing me of putting up objections to some of his Ministry's (more fatuous) proposals "for reasons which we can only consider to be very dubious". So now, with an intimation that I have acted corruptly, I think I have, as they say, seen everything. The trouble is that [the current Attorney-General, Matthew Muli] will not lift a finger to back me up. Ah me!

I don't recall exactly what the complaint was about (I don't think it concerned the video shops, as that matter would not have come under the Ministry of Tourism) and presume that nothing came of it, as I do not seem to have referred to it further. Although the letter was signed by the Minister it was almost certainly composed by the official who felt aggrieved by my actions or omissions.

Sometimes corruption shocked me, not so much for its existence (everyone knew that) but in the way and by whom it was applied. One day I entered a senior official's office on a work matter. He was on the phone as I went in, saying something to the effect "You'll rig the ballot, won't you?" It may of course be that the matter was something trivial, and I certainly didn't know the context, but the fact that this was said, quite openly in my hearing, by a person of such seniority and standing was disquieting. I remember recalling the quote attributed to Stalin (though it could equally have been Robert Mugabe of Zimbabwe, or indeed any dictator) "It doesn't matter who votes; it's who counts the votes that matters".

However, the first Attorney-General under whom I had worked, Charles Njonjo, was fundamentally a very able, decent and generous man, who had trusted me from the outset to do my job to the best of my ability and backed me up if I needed it. I was very grateful for that; it was not always to be so with those that succeeded him. Charles was also a very religious man; indeed his Christian faith was to stand him in good stead through the events that came to pass later on.

Socially, life in the office was congenial. Charles tended to distrust the ability and competence of Africans (one of the things that was to count against him later), and all but one of the sections within his Ministry, which consisted of the Registrar-General's Department, and the Attorney-General's Chambers, were headed by expatriates[19]. Roger Tomkins was in charge of the commercial section, responsible for the legal aspects of Government borrowing, Government contracts and the granting of statutory licenses. I can still hear him, in his New Zealand accent, urging me to continue a career in drafting: "Stay with it, Rog! Parliamentary counsel are as rare as hens' teeth." In charge of the civil litigation section was Frank Shields who, perhaps not untypically for an Irishman, when off duty delighted in talking and drinking in equal measure.

Those expatriates who were closest to the centre of both my professional and our social life were Chris Edmonds, another New Zealander who worked with Roger for a time, Brian Suttill, who took over from Roger, and Peter Gray, who had started as a magistrate, but with my help managed to persuade the authorities to transfer him to my drafting section[20]. Professional

---

[19] The one exception was the prosecution section headed by the Director of Public Prosecutions.
[20] Chris afterwards joined a law firm in Perth, Western Australia, Brian went to Hong Kong for 12 years or so and became Registrar of the High Court there, and Peter joined Linklaters and Paines, one of the biggest firms of solicitors in London, soon becoming a partner and, through hard work and skill, earning a fortune.

and social life combined in our morning coffee breaks taken at one of the cafés in the centre of town. These were a mere five minutes' walk away from the office, across the flag-stoned grand open space surrounding Jomo Kenyatta's statue which was gradually turning green as the neglected grass growing between the stone slabs began to overwhelm them.

Charles Njonjo himself, to everyone's surprise, suddenly in late 1979 resigned his office as Attorney-General in order to "stand for Parliament". This action, in the *de facto* one-party state, did not of course mean what it is presumed to mean in a multi-party one, and he was duly returned, unopposed, as the MP for the Kikuyu constituency[21]. My own belief is that he had always felt slightly insecure in the constitutional but unelected post of Attorney-General, and wanted to consolidate his position by becoming Minister for Justice, a post that had ceased to exist since the early days of independence, but otherwise carry on as before. But he could not constitutionally be appointed to this office unless he became an "elected" MP[22].

Making a humorous point. Charles Njonjo centre, Sir James Wicks right. Nairobi, January 1980

---

[21] This is a reference to the town of that name, not the tribe.
[22] Kenya had, as most Commonwealth countries do, the Westminster style of government structure under which Government Ministers are appointed by the President from amongst MPs. As Attorney-General he did constitutionally have a seat in Parliament, but this was technically as the chief legal adviser to the Government rather than as a member of the Executive.

In the meantime, James Karugu, Director of Public Prosecutions under Charles, was appointed Attorney-General. A power dispute now arose, for James considered he should have all the powers that his predecessor had had, whereas Charles doubtless wanted him in a subordinate role. A sort of compromise was reached, under which Charles was appointed Minister for Constitutional Affairs, but the relationship between the two men soured and after a year in the post James resigned.

Now the heat gradually turned up on Charles himself, and things came to a head when he was out of the country in mid-1983. The political pressure from anti-Njonjo politicians became intense and President Moi finally made a speech stating, without mentioning a name, that "there is a traitor in our midst"; but everyone knew he was referring to Njonjo. I remember having to go to Charles' office for a meeting on a business matter at about that time. He came into the anti-room of the office where I was waiting and stated simply "I think I've had it, Roger."

I was actually as shocked as I was profoundly disappointed; I must have assumed that he would be able to ride the situation, or even turn the tables on his accusers. But this time they had nailed him. He was forced to resign and a Commission of Inquiry was appointed to look into allegations that he had abused his office. The Commission was to be chaired by an Appeal Court Judge, Cecil "Dusty" Miller. This was a truly bizarre state of affairs, for this man was in my opinion after having been at fairly close contact with him over a period of time, certifiably mad.

Miller was a black West-Indian (from Guyana) by birth, and had served in the RAF during the Second World War, something he seemed constantly to like to remind people. He later married a Kenyan lady and took Kenya citizenship. He was quite useless as a judge and had been appointed as Chairman of the Kenya Law Reform Commission on its formation in 1983 to get him out of harm's way, but did virtually nothing in that post. I had the misfortune to be appointed as the KLRC Secretary and it was in this situation that I witnessed his histrionics at one particular Commission meeting when he stood up, raised a bible he had brought for the purpose and started tearfully and incoherently babbling to the effect that anyone who thought he was not doing a good job as Chairman would feel the wrath of God. None of the rest of us present knew quite where to put ourselves. Miller was some time later (after the Njonjo Enquiry it has to be said) found wandering in the High Court building without his trousers.

The enquiry was not a trial, and so there was no question of a penalty in the form of imprisonment and/or fine being imposed but it did, as it was expected to, duly find Charles guilty of abuse of office and effectively put an end to his political career. The only slight saving grace so far as I was concerned was that I was not present in Kenya to witness all of this, as I had, with a heavy heart, left the country in May 1984[23].

Crime

Petty (and for that matter more serious) crime was never far away in Nairobi. We came to realise this very quickly after the spare wheel of the yellow Renault 5 we had imported from London was stolen within days of the car's arrival. One quickly learned that all car wheels had to be fitted with security nuts and the spare wheel had to be chained down, or else the car would likely be found resting on bricks with all its wheels missing. When I mentioned to Joe Lobo, the Goan clerk in our office, that it seemed that local people habitually stole wheels off cars he commented wryly "What *don't* they steal, Mr Rose? That is the question."

Burglaries too were rife, and expatriates used to regale each other with stories of them, sometimes quite nasty ones. We indeed suffered our own burglary quite early on, and quickly realised how inept we had been over matters of security. We were woken one night by the sound of the dogs barking, and when I went to investigate found that the door between the part of the house where our and Jessie's bedrooms were situated and that where Rachel's bedroom was, was locked (we had stupidly left the key in it). Frightened for Rachel's safety, and realising that even Irene could not squeeze through the windowpane-size metal grills in the bedroom windows, we shouted for the servants.

They came quickly enough, but in the meantime the burglars must have run away, for we later found some of our property, including our typewriter and the speakers for the stereo system, abandoned in the front garden. We deduced that they must have put a child through windows in the living room (they were too small for an adult to climb through) and the child had then unlocked the front door (again, with our key helpfully in the lock). We lost most of our sound equipment, a slide projector and portable radio plus a few other items including Rachel's prized "tackies" (trainers). Jessie, surprised

---

[23] We did continue to keep contact with Charles and his family, at one point visiting him and Margaret at their house in Kensington, London. He also briefed me to draft some legislation to set up a Lands Tribunal for Kenya in an attempt (somewhat ironic in view of what had happened to him) to assist President Moi to get re-elected in I think late 2002 (in the event the latter didn't get re-elected). Charles and Margaret also came to Jessie's wedding in 2006, but could not be persuaded to stay for the dinner afterwards.

that hers were not taken too, offered the explanation that the thief must have tried them on and decided they didn't suit him.

One Saturday morning I was in my office when I got a phone call from reception to say that "a certain European is downstairs waiting to see you". I was in the middle of doing something and told them to send him (I presumed it was a man) up to me on the first floor. Nothing happened and the phone went again to tell me the European was still waiting. Somewhat irritated I went the short distance downstairs, found no-one at all there and returned to my office. In doing so I bumped into a man in the corridor just outside it. Going back in I suddenly twigged that what had happened was a conspiracy to get me out of the office so that my wallet could be stolen and I had just seen the thief. However, in the time it took for me to put two and two together and check my jacket on the back of my chair he had got away.

I ran downstairs calling for the reception messengers to lock the front door and questioned them, but nobody admitted to having seen anyone or anything suspicious, and I had not recognised the voice of the person who had called me (but I would not have recognised that of any of the messengers, who often changed). I did not believe them, but there was not much I could actually do without extensive interrogation of those concerned, something I was not equipped to do. There had not been much money in my wallet, about the equivalent of £7.50, and no credit cards – we did not use them much in Nairobi. As usual in these cases the most annoying thing was the loss of the wallet itself and various membership cards in it. However, thankfully what the thief did *not* take was an envelope in another pocket of my jacket that *did* contain a considerable quantity of cash I had just changed with a friend who wanted to remit sterling to the UK. So I just counted my blessings.

When things went wrong, or were carried out with customary incompetence, we expatriates often used to raise our eyebrows and refer to "the K (Kenya) Factor". For once the K Factor had worked for rather than against me.

There were also the hard luck story merchants, who preyed mainly on tourists. Typically one would accost you and ask you jovially how you were and how you liked Nairobi and Kenya. A story would then emerge about how the individual concerned had a problem: he desperately needed to get to his home up country somewhere where his father/mother/ brother/sister/son/daughter was very sick but he didn't have enough for the bus fare as his money had been robbed/burgled/pick-pocketed. Could the person help him out with maybe something towards it; or maybe even ("because I can see that you are a generous and compassionate person") with all of it?

Another confidence trick preyed on the fact that Europeans tended not to recognise Africans they did not know well. A visitor would be approached in the street with great friendliness asked how he was and (with a slightly quizzical look) where he was staying. On being given the name of the hotel the trickster would then state something to the effect "Yes, I thought I recognised you. Surely you remember me – I'm James, from reception?" The non-committal reply would not deter him and he would then continue on the following lines: "Mr [*some random African name*] the under manager sent me down to town to pick up an order from [*a stated place*], but I only realised when I got here that he had forgotten to give me the money to pay for it. Would you be so kind as to lend me 500 shillings [*or whatever*] until I get back? I will get the money from the manager straight away and put it in an envelope in your pigeon-hole."

I have to admit falling for this myself on a return visit to Kenya in the 1990s. Although you might think in the cold light of analysis that you would not be fooled by such a story, the trickster catches you off guard (in my case I was deep in thought about something) and the bonhomie is extremely plausible. The very second I handed over the money (and the man disappeared) I realised I had been tricked.

A variation on this story in the case of residents would be for the trickster to assert that he was a ranger in the Game Park who "recognised" his victim.

As previously indicated[24], there was a robust approach to the law, which people tended to take into their own hands, as the following extract from a letter I wrote in October 1983 illustrates:

> There was a very nasty robbery at [Joseph's] *shamba* [i.e. plot of land] during the time I was in England, when I gather that one of his grandchildren was killed. Apparently the same gang tried to strike twice, the second time last weekend. This time Joseph's family with the help of neighbours managed to scare off two of the gang (one having received a broken arm) and caught the third who was then beaten to death by the householders.

Sporting and Cultural Life

A decade or more after independence, most of the sporting and cultural life in Nairobi was still essentially European. Africans played and enjoyed

---

[24] Page 268.

watching soccer, but other sports such as golf, rugby, cricket, hockey, tennis and squash, were played mainly by Europeans, although with increasing Asian participation especially in cricket and hockey. Africans too, if they attended the university, were gradually being drawn into rugby and cricket, and the mainly African university rugby side, calling itself the Mean Machine, played to a good standard. Attendance at the Nairobi Race Course too was mainly by Europeans.

Cultural life, in the sense of theatre, music and art was also almost entirely European (and in the theatre almost exclusively English). Nairobi had its own National Theatre, situated opposite the famous Norfolk Hotel. It had excellent facilities but like everything else in Nairobi that was not on the top of the politicians' list of things that needed attention, was starting to crumble for lack of money for maintenance. This was not altogether surprising, as it was seen as being there primarily for the benefit the European population. Nairobi had in addition its own purpose-built professional theatre, named after its founder, the Donovan Maule.

At least three amateur companies regularly put on performances: the Nairobi City Players, the Theatre Group and the Lavington Players (the last of which had their own scout-hall premises). Memberships of these were of course almost entirely European and the shows put on obviously reflected this, although occasionally Africans and Asians did take part. The larger shows and plays (the City Players specialised mainly in musicals) went on at the National Theatre or at other premises such as the French Cultural Centre, which had a suitable stage. Indeed, my first role in Nairobi was at the latter place in Peter Schaffer's *The Public Eye* which the Theatre Group put on there, together with Tom Stoppard's *The Real Inspector Hound*.

James Falkland had been a professional actor in the UK and was at that time the leading light in the Nairobi theatre scene. In 1978 he decided under the auspices of the Theatre Group to put on a production of Robert Bolt's *Vivat! Vivat Regina!* at the National Theatre. I was fortunate to be cast in one of the leading roles: that of the Queen's Secretary, Lord Cecil, in a production that was in a different dimension from anything else I had acted in, before or since. The play concerns the relationship between Queen Elizabeth I and Mary Queen of Scots, has a cast of over 20 and of course requires lavish late sixteenth century costumes. James managed to get British Airways to sponsor the play by flying out at no cost the costumes for the production which were hired from Bermans and Nathans, the main professional theatrical costumiers in London (BA possibly paid for the hiring charges as well). I learned a lot about acting and directing from James.

In about 1980 the professional Donovan Maule theatre began to run into trouble financially and, presumably because it could not afford to hire so many professionals, changed its programme to allow amateurs to appear. At this time I was cast as Mr Manningham in the Victorian melodrama *Gaslight* staged there (with the luxury of a professional set). But financial problems continued and Annabel Maule, daughter of the founder, soon found that she had to sell the theatre, to an Asian businessman. For a while plays continued there, but the new owner was not really interested in continuing what was essentially a European place of entertainment and eventually knocked it down in order to build an office block. The company running plays was taken over by James Falkland and others, renamed the Phoenix Theatre, and run from the basement of the Professional Centre next door, which was effectively converted into a small, intimate theatre.

The cultural gulf between the races can be demonstrated by small examples. One evening during a dress rehearsal at the National Theatre, an African security guard, either looking for the loo or just doing his rounds, and obviously completely unaware of what was going on, casually wandered across the front of the stage. Another time a stray dog, that had obviously gained access through a door that should have been kept shut by the security guards, did the same, but during a live performance.

There was however one area in which there was considerably more integration between the races: singing. Africans tend to love it and be very good at it. Our servant Joseph sang regularly as a bass in his church choir (we went once to hear his choir rehearsing and were impressed by their standard). We ourselves sang on two occasions in a 60 strong mixed race choir under the auspices of the Nairobi Music Society that performed Handel's *Messiah* at the Anglican Cathedral.

Wildlife

One of the principal joys of living in Nairobi, though the city itself was getting dirtier and uglier as each year passed, was its proximity to so many places that were desirable to visit. The Nairobi Game Park, which had a wide variety of game (or "games" as the African rangers tended to say) and for which we had an annual season ticket at minimal cost, was a mere ten minutes' drive from our house. In fact I soon became quite blasé about the animals there (giraffe, buffalo, various kinds of antelope, and ostrich were common, and lion and rhino fairly often to be seen) and became more preoccupied with looking for birds. And just beyond Langata to the west of Nairobi was a remnant of rain forest in which uncommon forest birds could occasionally be seen.

One did not even need to go to a game park to see large animals; there were often zebra and gazelle grazing in the rift valley as we approached Naivasha. Adjoining that little town is the lake that carries its name, and as it was only about an hour's drive from Nairobi this made possible delightful picnics there, often arranged at short notice at weekends, amid a huge variety of bird life. Many wild animals were commonly to be seen there, including hippo and waterbuck. Nakuru, with its soda lake and world famous flocks of flamingos (one of the true world natural history "experiences") was no more than an hour beyond Naivasha. Further than that, one could get to Lake Bogoria (like Lake Nakuru, a soda lake with usually a sizeable population of flamingos) and Lake Baringo, where hippo would come and graze at night in the grounds of the Lodge and where bird-watching was a special experience owing to the fact that it was an ecological niche between the desert and the fertile land further south.

Birding had of course been one of my main hobbies in Kenya, and during the seven years we spent there I managed to accrue a respectable list of just over 400 different species seen and identified, including nearly 60 in our own garden.

But for the real East Africa wildlife experience one needed to go further afield, to the Maasai Mara (actually the northern extension of the Serengetti Plains in Tanzania), to Amboseli or to Tsavo. These places, which are still comparatively free from human encroachment, consist mainly of grass savannah and support a greater density of large mammalian wildlife than anywhere else on earth. The huge numbers of wildebeest in migration in the Maasai Mara, and the large herds of elephants in Amboseli, with its sensational backdrop of Mount Kilimanjaro, are obvious examples. I went on one walking safari in Tsavo that gave a rare opportunity to see animals in an undisturbed environment; it was one of the few places where hippo could be seen out of the water during the day (they tend to emerge only under cover of darkness).

Inevitably some of the wildlife came into the category of pests. We were fortunate to live too close to the centre of the city to be visited by baboons, but those living further out often suffered from their raids and depredations. The pests we encountered (apart from fleas and bees) were no more than speckled mousebirds. These birds go about in small flocks and had a particular liking for the flowers on our bauhinia trees which, given the chance, they would do their best to strip. They annoyed me so much that I would shoot with an air rifle any that I could (those I did manage to down were immediately eaten – except for their long tail feathers – by the dogs).

Our encounters with bees had been comparatively mild affairs. An Israeli whom we first encountered in the intensive care ward of Nairobi Hospital in circumstances to be related had been attacked by a swarm of bees and was now fighting for his life. At the time his wife was about to give birth; the doctor in charge of him said that the birth would probably make or break him. To the immense joy of everybody, and slightly against the odds, he began to revive and his return to health was then quite quick. Soon afterwards he and his wife invited us to a party to celebrate the birth of their daughter "and other blessings".

Safaris

Safari has changed its meaning over the course of the last century. In fact it is simply a Swahili word meaning "a journey"; but in recent times (as in the expressions "on safari" or "wildlife safari", widely used in the tourist industry) it has come to mean the experience of being driven around a game park or reserve in a vehicle to look at the larger wild animals. I prefer to use the word in its original sense.

Diani

We spent many a holiday down at the Kenya coast, especially at Diani Beach, about 20 miles south of Mombasa. As getting there involved a 5 hour road journey from Nairobi to Mombasa and then a further hour or so getting the Kilindini ferry[25] and driving on to Diani, this could reasonably count as a safari. Sometimes we broke our journey on the way back by staying with Nick Harwood, the young man who had been partly instrumental in getting me to Kenya and who had been appointed State Counsel in Mombasa.

At Diani, our time was almost always spent at the Beachalets (a rather contrived name that was widely misquoted – though just as appropriately it has to be said – as *Beachlets*), a complex of about 10 chalets owned and run by a European couple, Harold and Jean Barker, who had retired there from Uganda. These were self-catering and fairly basic, although it was normal to employ a cook/house servant who was attached to the premises for the duration of the stay (in our case usually a pleasant man named Shadrack); and most had a view of the sea. There, the beach at low tide consisted of twenty yards or so of sand that gave way to smooth rock pools for about another thirty yards. About 100 yards beyond this was the coral reef, around

---

[25] Mombasa is situated on an island, linked at that time to the mainland by a man-made causeway to the east, a bridge to the north and the ferry to the south.

which we would snorkel, in wonder at the variety of fish to be seen (though all the large shells had generally been plundered for sale).

Jessie & Rachel wearing *kikois*, Diani, Kenya coast, April 1980

Standard dress for men and women consisted of a *kikoi*, a length of light cloth that could be tucked around the body somewhat like a sari for women, or round the waist for men. One could readily buy recently caught fish, including octopus and crayfish, from itinerant sellers who sold from boxes attached to their bicycles. In those days there were few of the itinerant sellers of tourist tat that became so irritating a feature of the coast generally in later years. For us it had all the charm of a comparatively wild coast.

On one occasion early in our time in Kenya we (that is Irene, a young American we had met at the coast, Marc Kupper, and myself - we had left the girls to play with friends) decided to hire a local boat to take a ride out to the far side of the reef and do some snorkelling from it. This was a typical fisherman's boat, basically a dugout canoe fitted with outriggers, a wooden mast and a sail made of thick polythene.

Our choice was unfortunate, for on the way out to the reef there was a sudden grating crack: to our consternation we saw that the mast had snapped in two near its base. The plastic sail suddenly enveloped everybody on board. Some frantic scrambling involving all four of us ensued until the sail could be wrapped around the broken mast and the whole assembly placed on top of one of the outriggers as close as possible to the hull. We began to proceed back to the shore with paddles, but the very considerable weight of the mast and sail placed in this way now severely unbalanced the boat. Shortly afterwards we stared with horror as the opposite outrigger began to rise gradually skywards as the boat slowly and sedately turned turtle, tipping us all into the sea.

Irene, not always noted for her agility in the sea, climbed on to the upturned hull in a flash; her instinct for self-preservation was impressive. Marc swam about with a concerned look, while I found myself treading water and, perhaps because of the anti-climax, simply unable to stop laughing. There was in fact no great danger, the shore was not too far and anyway there was "wreckage" to cling to. I don't remember the exact sequence of events afterwards; we were all eventually picked up by another boat and taken back to the shore, and presumably "our" boat was rescued together with its mast, before the latter sank to the bottom. For some reason none of us including myself could understand, when we reached the shore I decided to pay the boatman his hire fee nonetheless – he had after all nearly suffered the loss of his boat which was anyway going to need significant repair; and (after the initial scare) it had been a hilarious adventure.

Wildlife could intrude in unexpected ways. One evening a bush baby got into our chalet. Clearly frightened by both people and the light, it dashed into a bedroom and hid under a bed against the wall. The only way I could get it out was to fish around with a broom-handle until, in the odd kangaroo hopping gait they have, it finally made a dash for the open door.

But visits to places at the coast were not really "safaris" in the eyes of Kenya residents; for a safari one needed to travel not necessarily further but to more remote parts. In fact our first taste of a truly out of the way place was a camp named Bushwhackers off the Mombasa Road, that had originally been constructed to house a film crew (not incidentally "Out of Africa", which was filmed much later in 1985). We soon got used to the fact that some animal life (squirrels in particular) regarded it as their right to share our accommodation.

The Aberdares

This mountain range was so named in 1884 by the explorer Joseph Thompson after the Liberal peer/politician Lord Aberdare, at that time President of the Royal Geographical Society. Our first safari there was unplanned. Martin and Pat Thomas, with whom we became friendly through the children (their two girls were at school with Jessie), were with the British High Commission and a weekend at the Ark had been arranged for its staff in circumstances that either there were vacancies, or they were allowed to bring a limited number of friends. In any event, we as a family joined them and other High Commission staff. The Ark was one of the two best known hotels set in the middle of wildlife reserves (the other, Tree-tops, was even better known for its association with the then Princess Elizabeth who was staying there in February 1952 when the news came through that her father had died and that she had consequently become Queen). Set in front of a water hole habitually visited by a wide variety of animals and birds (including that rare and shy forest antelope, the bongo) both were ideal places from which to watch animals in comfort.

The weekend passed pleasantly and without much incident, and having the whole of Sunday at our disposal we decided to travel back to Nairobi by a roundabout route that would take us over the Aberdares. It was of course only a dirt road that crossed the mountains passing through the Aberdares Game Reserve, and we had at that time a normal two-wheel drive saloon car (a yellow Datsun). The ranger at the reserve entrance was non-committal about the state of the road, but told us that another two-wheel drive car had preceded us some time earlier that day. There looked to be fair weather around and I decided it would be worth chancing it. After all it would not be often that we had the opportunity to travel the road concerned.

To begin with all went well. Up on the top the countryside is open moorland with some wooded clumps; the only animals around seemed to be bushbuck, which have a bark not unlike a dog, and these we could hear rather than see. We stopped the car and walked around, though not far from the car as we noted what appeared to be the pug-marks of lion on the road. Suddenly, and seemingly out of nowhere, the sky blackened and it began to rain heavily; in a short space of time the dirt road became a sea of mud. Along this we slithered for a time before finally drifting sideways into the bank at the side of the road and getting stuck. Any attempt to move further simply involved the car wheels spinning to no effect. *Now* what?

I estimated that we were at a point just over half way between the gate we had passed though and the one on the other side, although I obviously couldn't be sure. It had at least after a comparatively short time stopped raining. There were two alternatives: either we should wait in the hope that a vehicle capable of helping us would arrive at some point; or else one of us (clearly me) would have to try to find a park ranger to help tow us out.

When in a situation of difficulty, I have always preferred to do something active if I can, rather than to wait passively for things to happen. It was thus that I began to walk towards what was hopefully the nearer of the reserve entrances, leaving Irene and the girls, who needed to sit it out with food rations consisting of a single packet of crisps. Although there were reputed to be leopard around, and we had already seen evidence that there were lion, I was in retrospect surprisingly little stressed by the thought of these animals, and in fact the only sounds I recall were from the continued occasional barking of bushbuck. Actually, what seemed of far more concern to me at the time was how long it would take to reach the reserve entrance.

I was spurred on by necessity and the thought of my abandoned family, although I knew they could retreat into the car if dangerous animals appeared[26]. After an hour or so of walking I finally caught sight of the rangers' hut by the entrance gate. Soon, over a proffered cup of African tea (tea, water, milk and sugar all boiled up together), a drink even the thought of which would normally have made me want to retch, but which now seemed like nectar itself, I was explaining our predicament.

The two rangers were helpful. They didn't have a vehicle, but their colleagues at the other gate (the one from which we had entered the park) had a Wildlife Department Land Rover, and they radioed for it to proceed to the spot where our car was stranded. Meanwhile I began the return journey on foot back to the car with one of the rangers, a small wiry man who proceeded to fix a panga[27] to his belt ("there are dangerous animals about!") and set off at such a fast pace I had a job to keep up.

To the relief of Irene and the girls, we reached them at more or less the same time as the Land Rover arrived from the other direction. The procedure was fairly routine: they fixed a towing rope to our car and off we went in tandem back to the gate from which I had just returned. As we were being towed our car seemed to waltz from side to side of the road as the fancy took it, for the traction of our tyres was minimal. This didn't matter too much until suddenly the road went downhill to a small and very narrow bridge over a stream. I was terrified that too much of a sideways slip just before the bridge could have had us missing the bridge altogether and in the stream. I had very little control of our car (I was to have an all too similar experience later in the day) and shut my eyes hoping that we would be roughly in line with the towing vehicle when we reached the bridge.

But our luck was in, and we made it unscathed to the gate. On the other side, leading away from the reserve down the mountainside, was (blessed relief)

---

[26] The only animals that would in practice be capable of taking on a motor vehicle were angry elephants. But there were no elephants around, and anyway nothing that should have upset them.
[27] The African term for a machete.

a tarmac road. In spite of the fact that it was by now dark, we felt relieved and even relaxed, having survived a minor adventure unscathed. On the way down the mountain a medium sized animal of the cat family jumped across the road in front of us; it seemed about the size of a leopard or a bit smaller, but without spots. Later inquiries confirmed that it was probably a Golden Cat, a species known to inhabit the Aberdares but nocturnal in its habits and rarely seen.

At the bottom the tarmac road ended. The state of the earth road we now entered, already churned into a morass, was similar to that of the track we had experienced at the top only considerably worse. After 20 minutes or so of trying to drive along it, with the car swerving about almost uncontrollably at times, I was beginning to feel desperately tired, but clung to the idea that we simply had to be back in Nairobi for the following day. Suddenly the car swerved about 130 degrees to the right and, as we came to a stop pointing in almost the opposite direction from that intended, our headlights were shining on a sign that read "Kinangop Mission Hospital 1 km".

Irene said steadily "We're going there to ask if we can stay for the night"; it was not a suggestion but an order. Protesting feebly, I manoeuvred the car on to the track. On arrival it soon became clear that we could be offered accommodation for the night; I felt myself involuntarily bursting into tears.

I say "soon" rather than "immediately", not because there was any lack of willingness to offer hospitality on the part of the nuns who operated the mission hospital, but rather that there was a language problem: they were Italian and seemed to speak only that and the local vernacular Kikuyu, rather than Swahili (in which I could at least have made myself understood – such little Italian as I know was acquired after that time). Eventually however one of the nuns was found who spoke English. She stated that we could not possibly attempt to get back to Nairobi that night. The priest who lived with them was away on leave in Italy and we could stay in his house for the night and attempt the journey back the following day, when at least we would have daylight to assist us.

The details remain hazy, but we were offered supper with the nuns, consisting of bread, butter and hard-boiled eggs (Jessie's muttered protest that she didn't like eggs was quickly sat on by Irene). I think the two little girls shared a room, separate from the one we were offered, and Jessie fell in love with the various little religious pictures and figures on surfaces and walls in the rooms of the priest's house.

In those days telephone communication was less efficient than later. The following morning, being unable to reach the Attorney General, I left a message for him telling him of our plight although, this being Africa, I later discovered that it had never reached him. We thanked the nuns profusely, left them a donation for the hospital, and arrived back in Nairobi after a difficult first part of the journey by about midday.

Mount Kenya

A favourite place of ours was the Naro Moro River Lodge, a small hotel at the foot of the west side of the mountain with a series of log cabins alongside the river of that name flowing down from the mountain. Here it tended to get quite cold at night and we became expert at laying and lighting log fires. It was situated about 12 miles south of the equator, itself just to the south of the little Kikuyu town of Nanyuki that would feature in a later safari.

Climbing the mountain itself was of course out of the question unless one made a specific expedition to do so. Mt Kenya is an extinct volcano and inside its crater is a plug of volcanic rock whose twin peaks, Batian and Nelion, rise to just over 17,000 feet. If one aims to ascend those peaks then true mountain climbing is involved, with all the necessary experience and climbing gear, but one can get to Point Lenana (c. 16,350 feet) merely by walking or scrambling.

Towards the end of 1979 with Chris Edmonds from the A-G's Chambers I did make such an expedition over a weekend. This involved climbing up to the Teleki Valley (around 14,000 feet) through a large area of waterlogged ground known as the vertical bog before nightfall on the Saturday, staying overnight in the wooden hut there (there are a number of these on various parts of the mountain) and attempting to get to Point Lenana on the Sunday morning.

The extreme cold at this altitude was novel and it was difficult to sleep (there were tame rats of some sort sharing our accommodation too), especially as we needed to get going at 4 am in order to make the best of the weather and give ourselves time to get to the top and back down again. I found the going at that height very difficult because of the lack of oxygen and needed to force myself repeatedly to climb 30 paces before stopping to rest. We reached what is called the Top Hut (around 15,750 feet I believe and the launching point for the top) by 7.15 am but by this time the main peaks were in cloud, which seemed to be getting lower by the minute. After some discussion Chris decided he would see how far he could get, although I did not want to risk it, especially as I was now very tired. Also I thought further deterioration in the weather might jeopardise our descent. Indeed, after a short while he returned, having come to the same conclusion. We made our way down uneventfully amid the amazing mountain scenery that surrounded us.

Suswa

Suswa is another extinct volcano situated in Kenya's Rift valley. It is a geological feature known as a shield volcano, a type of volcano named for the large area it covers and its low profile resembling a warrior's shield (when active they erupt highly fluid lava which travels farther than that erupted from more explosive volcanoes). The main attraction for speleologists, as those who study caves are called, is the spaces between passages of lava (tunnels that are in effect caves) that are formed from the lava flow. These can be extensive and in layers of up to three on top of each other, although often the "roof" of these collapses blocking the tunnels, sometimes completely.

Access to it was by very rough tracks that needed four-wheel drive vehicles, and Rachel and I went in our Land Rover after she and I had returned after leave in 1980 (while Irene stayed on In London for a few weeks with the younger ones). We were in a group of 16, some of whom were experienced cavers, and explored various caves, one of which was the roost of thousands of bats, most of which took off if someone made a sound. The smell in such a place of bat excrement is strong.

We all slept in a cave that was free of bats and, unlike on the mountains, pleasantly cool. The only other animals commonly found in the area are rock hyraxes, animals that are common in Africa and resemble large rabbits but without the long ears[28], and baboons. The experience of caving made me realise how free one needs to be of feelings of claustrophobia, for some of the passages we had to squeeze through, typically flat on our belly, can be very low and very narrow.

Lake Turkana and Shaba

A journey to the far north of Kenya was inevitably something of an adventure. The area is semi-desert, the climate accordingly hot and inhospitable and the roads few and of unreliable quality. It was a trip that I had wanted to make for some time, but knowing that Irene and the children

---

[28] They are not in fact closely related to rabbits, or any other living mammals, but to primitive hoofed mammals.

would probably not enjoy it I decided to wait until their absence on one of their annual visits back to England. Bryan Hudson had earlier written that he would like to come with me and flew out for the purpose. His visit was to be a longer one than he had intended.

Our vehicle was the Range Rover that Irene and I had bought from the Bowmans a year or so before. Without attempting to force the pace, it took about 3 days to get to Lake Turkana. There were few people around and we laid our camp beds on the ground at suitable stopping places for the night. However, at one point a young Samburu warrior, complete with spear, wandered into our camp-site. Having gone for a while, probably to watch birds, I returned and found him standing next to, and staring at, a concerned-looking Bryan, who had up to this point been attempting to write up his journal[29]. Asking myself what the explorers of this part of the world in the previous century like Joseph Thompson might have done[30], and anxious to establish good relations with the natives, I found to my relief that I could communicate with him in Swahili and offered him a cup of tea. This seemed to be acceptable to him, as he drank it and after a while wandered off into the bush.

I had volunteered to do most of the cooking and had also spent time looking for and trying to identify birds along the way. As always, the frustration in such situations is not often being able to get a good enough sighting of a bird to be confident of its particular features, especially where there is more than one possible candidate for identification in a given family of birds. But the journey had its many compensations. Quoting Bryan on the subject of a typical evening:

> We sat round the fire talking, just every so often leaning forward to put some dry sticks on the fire. It is the best part of the day. The meal is over, the washing up is done, our bed-rolls are out and we have the time to talk. We listen to the BBC overseas news at 8 pm which in a way distances [me] even further from Britain. Our problems are much simpler: will the vehicle start in the morning? We have used up our reserves of petrol (3 cans); where will we find [more]? Will the fire keep going overnight to enable us to restart it from the embers?

---

[29] Quite by chance, Bryan had contacted us after we had notified him and Sonja about our change of e-mail address offering to lend the journal itself, written up in a hard-cover "Kasuku" exercise book. His timing could not have been better, as I had reached the point of writing this particular section.

[30] Famously, when in a tight situation at one point in his travels, Thompson had made a great play of removing his false teeth from his mouth. This sufficiently impressed the natives that he possessed significant powers to work magic, and thus that any ideas of summarily killing him and his entourage had better be revised.

The terrain was increasingly volcanic as we got nearer to the lake, and this helped to increase the sense in us of having nearly accomplished a long, difficult and tiring journey. It was therefore a bit of a shock to see, as we passed the airstrip near the little town of Loyengalani, near the southern end of the lake, a group of tourists boarding a bus. They had clearly just been flown in, probably for an hour or two and, with all the modern conveniences supplied to them, looked as fresh as they might have done in Nairobi. We, by contrast, did not. We made our way to a little area near the town that served as a campsite overlooking the lake, where the Indian man in charge was happy to help us slake our by now enormous thirsts with bottles of beer at twice the normal price.

One of the peculiarities of that region is that, at any rate the time of year we were there, a strong dry wind gets up in the early morning and blows for most of the day. I think we stayed two nights and then decided that, having at least reached our goal, there was no point in staying any longer in that inhospitable climate. Apart from the view we had of the lake itself, there was nothing particularly attractive about the scenery, and the heat was oppressive. We did not even entertain any idea of swimming in the lake as there were crocodiles.

We decided that we would return via Shaba Game Reserve, adjoining the better known Samburu Reserve, north of Isiolo. Shaba was where Joy Adamson, the Austrian-born naturalist and (at least in Kenya) well-known tropical plant illustrator had lived. She had become world famous during her (third) marriage to George Adamson for having raised, and written a best-selling book about, a lioness cub, Elsa, and especially so after the book was made into a popular film. It was thus that the world had been shocked by the fact that in 1980 she was inexplicably murdered at her home.

One of the boundaries of Shaba, as with Samburu, is the Uaso Nyiro River[31]. Of some size there, it flows more or less due eastwards and eventually disappears into the desert in Somalia without ever reaching the sea. It was at a rough and ready campsite on the banks of this river that we decided to stay for the night. After a leisurely supper we prepared to sleep in the open,

---

[31] The first word is pronounced Wasso. And, as with all African words beginning with N followed by a Y or a consonant, "Nyiro" is not pronounced (as Europeans without experience of Africa sometimes think) *ner-yiro*, but as though the first letter were preceded by a barely sounded I or U. Thus, for example, Kilimanjaro is not *Kiliman jaro*, but *Kilima* (the mountain) *njaro* (that is great).

We had visited Samburu Reserve as a family a year or so previously, and had been struck by the number of elephants to be found there, especially around the river. Our car was even charged by a trumpeting baby elephant, which fortunately stopped some 20 metres from us. Even small elephants can give one a considerable fright.

as we had done for most of the journey. Taking up from Bryan's journal again:

> Our meal was chicken and noodle soup followed by tinned plums. At 9 pm we still felt hungry so we consumed a tin of pineapple. We talked until about ten, being interrupted by hippos calling each other in the river. We went down but I could see only big black shapes. The water is only 2-3 feet deep and the hippo come out at night for vegetation. The baboons had been making a row. I was somewhat concerned about sleeping as there was a lot of elephant dung around and I did not want to wake up in the night surrounded; God knows what I would do. Both of us agreed that it would be sensible to keep the fire going all night, so we pulled a dead tree trunk down and fed it on to the fire and placed our sleeping bags about 5 yards away.

It is a glorious thing for an urbanised individual like myself to lie, as we did for most of the journey, watching the stars and listening to the sounds of the night. But on that night I found it difficult to get to sleep as Bryan had started snoring, and I soon moved my bed a short distance from his, the other side of the fire, taking the opportunity to stoke it up a bit as I did so. I soon fell asleep.

At some time in the middle of the night something woke me; it must have been a kind of sixth sense, as there had been no discernible noise. As I lay in my sleeping bag I looked from side to side in the moonlight. There, standing about 15 yards away to my right were two lions.

I heard myself making the slightly noisy intake of breath that one sometimes effects to indicate shock or extreme surprise; only this time it was a quite involuntary gasp. The lions seemed slightly startled by this and jumped backwards a fraction just as domestic cats might do. My senses were fully alive as only they can be in mercifully rare situations of acute potential danger, and over thirty years later I can still picture the scene with perfect clarity. I could make out in the moonlight that they were probably young males. I immediately sensed that they did not seem to be threatening – in fact I remember thinking that if they had wanted to kill me they could easily have done so by now. Nevertheless, I thought, I can't just stay here helpless on the ground and I raised myself to a sitting position. This necessitated a sudden movement that again made the pair of lions jump backwards slightly. Having wriggled out of my sleeping bag, I moved slowly and deliberately away from them until I reached the Range Rover and climbed in.

My mind was racing as I watched the animals. There was an approximately twenty yard sided triangle joining where I now was in the Range Rover, where I had been sleeping, and where Bryan was still sleeping. What if they were to attack him? I had half-thought out ideas that in such an event I would dash to the fire and grab a by now barely alight piece of wood from it, although quite what I would do with it I was not sure.

While in this state of tense confusion I saw the two lions move slowly forward to where I had been sleeping. They sniffed my sleeping bag from one end to the other. Then perhaps thinking that my scent did not seem attractive as food, or perhaps simply that they weren't hungry, they seemed to lose interest, turned round and strolled off into the night.

Now what? Should I wake Bryan; but if so for what, as the danger had now passed? The only effect of such an action could be to scare him unnecessarily. There wasn't room for both of us to sleep in the vehicle, and I could hardly stay there myself and leave him outside. Nor did the situation seem to warrant both of us sitting the night out in the vehicle. I decided to get the fire going again, make sure that a panga was at hand and go back to where he was and try to go back to sleep. The snoring started again. I went back to near where I had been before the lions arrived and slept, this time fitfully.

Bryan's reaction on waking in the morning was to wonder what on earth had happened to me. I was not where I had been when he went to sleep (and, lying down, he could not see me in my new sleeping place). Furthermore, there was a panga next to him that had not been there the evening before. I couldn't resist giggling at his apparent state of anxiety before I revealed where I was. And then I began the explanation of the previous night's activities with "You won't believe this but..." Fortunately the lions' pug marks were clearly to be seen on the ground!

> I could find no lion pug marks nearer to me than 11 yards, where they had been sniffing Roger's bed. Breakfast this morning will be an anti-climax. Thank God Roger has cool nerves and didn't make any sudden movements.

The journey back from Shaba

Our journey back to Nairobi began normally enough. We packed up leisurely after *my* adventurous night and drove back through Isiolo where we stopped to fill up with petrol. Everything seemed to be proceeding normally, and then the Somali pump attendant said laconically as he was filling the tank:

"No more President. Army in control now."

As we drove off I said to Bryan that I was concerned, for this was not the sort of thing that people would say as a joke. But everything seemed to be normal and quiet and in due course we stopped for lunch at a trout farm run by Europeans near Timau on the northern slopes of Mount Kenya. It was there that we heard on the radio that the Kenya Air Force had risen against the Government, together with minor units of the army, but that the President had matters in hand. Hoping that everything would be calming down, we set off again.

Just before we entered Nanyuki we could see a line of cars that had stopped by the side of the road. We joined them and learned that there had been fighting in the town, which was the main Kenya Air Force base; no-one was sure how safe it was to proceed. We conferred, and the other drivers (all Africans) suggested that it would be best to proceed cautiously in a convoy headed by us ("they will be less likely to shoot Europeans"). We saw the logic of the suggestion and proceeded accordingly.

We got as far as the police station in Nanyuki where there was a road block and we were ordered to stop on some waste ground. I take up the story from Bryan's journal:

> We climbed out and watched (along with a motley gathering of armed police) two [army] land-rovers and two 3 tonners laden with troops edge forward 200 yards ahead. They dismounted and disappeared into some greenery on our left, but remounted in 10 minutes. As they started off one soldier dropped the magazine of his rifle and bullets fell out – the [army] convoy stopped. Again it edged forward, guns sticking out the side until it came to a cross-roads where all the men dismounted. I thought it wasn't the way I'd have done it; I'd have had them dismounted from where we were watching and we'd have moved down the road staggered ready for action left or right.

In fact none of what we had seen inspired much confidence! However, shortly afterwards an armed policeman came over to us and said it was safe to move through. Apparently the cross-roads had been held by a few air-force men:

> We saw them being disarmed and pushed into a vehicle. I watched one being marched in still carrying his .303 [rifle] – ridiculous, he ought to have been disarmed before.

Our journey back to Nairobi then proceeded in slow stages; there were a number of roadblocks, some manned by troops who were polite and efficient, others by those who, to say the least, were not either. If ordered out of the vehicle, we instinctively moved as in the presence of dangerous wild animals: not too quickly (that might literally trigger a response!) and not too slowly, but deliberately with apparent calm. We were lucky in that being Europeans we were in the eyes of the army unlikely to have had anything to do with the attempted coup, but Africans were sometimes harshly treated. A *matatu* (communal taxi/small bus) had been stopped:

> [it] was being pushed away by soldiers, its contents lying on the road. You feel somewhat sorry, but having done the same thing so many times myself I know you cannot afford the luxury of compassion. A bus load of people were in a ditch with their hands up and down on their knees. The bus was being given a thorough going over.

At one roadblock just before a roundabout as we approached Nairobi we were asked at gunpoint to produce identification. Bryan had his passport; I had only my Kenya driving licence (which had my photograph in it). A short interrogation followed:

"What are you doing?"
"I'm going home."
"Where's that?"
"Nairobi. I work there."
"Are you a Kenyan citizen?"
"No"
"You're a tourist then."

This last was not so much a question as a statement, but the lawyer in me baulked at giving false or misleading information. I was after all a non-citizen resident: I held a Kenya driving licence, something most unlikely in the case of a tourist, and I had already stated that I worked in Nairobi. I started to explain, but was cut short in a peremptory manner:

"If you're not a citizen, you must be a tourist."

Still thinking I need to clarify the position I opened my mouth again. Bryan snarled *sotto voce* at me "Just shut up!" He had seen what any non-lawyer would see, namely that this was a time for agreeing with those in (armed) authority over us and doing what we were told, not for "cavilling on the ninth part of a hair". I, at last, could now see it too.

"Yes, that's right"

As I had now clearly given the correct answer in the circumstances, we were allowed to proceed. You had, as Bryan said as we moved off, to understand their thinking: there had been some shooting, and their enemy could be anyone; that is not a situation for legal niceties. Bryan's journal continues:

> We drove carefully around the roundabout. A car that had probably failed to stop was nose up in the bushes of the roundabout, its back window shot out. On the right

there was a 20 yard mass of shoes and boots (army) lying around plus papers. Another vehicle had four shots through the windscreen. We drove carefully on. It was 5.45 pm and both of us knew we had somehow to get in before dark ... I saw two men running across the road carrying bolts of material, obviously looters. They disappeared into a block of flats...

[At the Museum Hill roundabout] a strange spectacle greeted us: the roundabout was jammed with abandoned vehicles for 60-80 yards on all roads leading into it. Buses and cars had been just left with doors open; one bus even had its headlights fully on.

We discussed what to do. We knew some fierce fighting had taken place in the centre and no-one was allowed there, but we had to take this road in order to get home. I gingerly [walked] down to the roundabout and could see it was feasible to get a vehicle around and then bump over the central tree boulevard on to the right route. Roger didn't think it a risk worth taking as nothing anyway was moving ... [he] decided to try to loop around; if the worst came to the worst we could call in and stop at friends. Neither of us felt that it was wise to be on the road at night.

We ran into 3 [army] land-rovers. Roger stopped. A soldier told us to wait ... I said to Roger "I'm going to ask to join the convoy". I climbed out and went to see the major in charge. I explained we were trying to get to Chyulu Road, we were unarmed, and we needed his protection – could we join the convoy? He smiled and so did all the soldiers in the back. Roger said it must be that I knew how to talk their language. I think on reflection it was the only course that offered us safety and secondly all troops like to feel wanted.

So we set off two land-rovers in front and a radio control one behind. They were returning to their barracks. We passed Jessica's school, the President's residence – highly guarded ...

We saw scenes of looting: windows smashed, furniture, bottles, clothing scattered everywhere. It's amazing how quickly others feather their nests during any trouble. The soldiers turned off into their barracks and with big smiles they gave a thumbs-up. We now had only 300 yards to go. Sporadic firing continued as we turned into the gates of home at 6.30 pm.

Joseph and John were overjoyed to see us return safely home; they had naturally been very worried. They told us that the coup had started at 3 am when the rebels, including armed students, had stormed the Voice of Kenya broadcasting station[32] and announced the overthrow of the government in the name of democracy. At about 8 am our next-door neighbour, a senior African civil servant, had been arrested and taken from his home. However, the army had remained loyal and seized back the radio station from the rebels who had been occupying it. The President had then broadcast to the

---

[32] We later deduced that this was why we had seen all the abandoned vehicles at the Museum Hill roundabout; the surrounding area had probably been swept by gunfire from the VOK building.

nation and appealed for calm and for everyone to attend work as usual the following day (Monday).

In fact the next few days were anything but normal. Contact with various people confirmed that it was pointless to try to get to the office or the centre of town the following day. We tried to contact Irene in London and Sonja in Packington without success, and stayed at home, hearing bursts of gunfire from time to time (probably, we thought, a nervous soldier or two firing at nothing and others joining in). The 6 pm to 6 am curfew that had been imposed meant that there was no possibility of going out visiting or to a restaurant in the evenings. Bryan had actually been due to fly back on Air Sudan shortly after our return, but obviously flights in and out of Nairobi had been suspended.

Little by little life returned to normal. We eventually got through on the telephone to the UK. There had been a good deal of looting during the period immediately after the failed coup, mainly from Asian owned shops in Westlands (a suburb that had suffered badly from looting, television pictures of which had been beamed round the world as typical). Bryan's journal continues for the Friday following the Sunday coup:

> We went into town and had a coffee at the Red Cow [*he means the Red Bull!*]. Still the city is getting back to normal. Bread has appeared, but many shops are having glass and protective grilles replaced. Many had been ripped out by the rebels and looters tying ropes to them and hauling them away by vehicle power. One of Roger's African colleagues has had his only two suits stolen from the dry cleaners when that was ransacked.

Finally, just over a week after our return, and after much uncertainty as to flights, Bryan got away to a rough journey back to London via Juba in Sudan. In doing so he experienced all of the frustrations of the incompetence of African officialdom, and in the intense heat of Juba.

Leaving Kenya

Leaving Kenya had almost been a much earlier event than planned. In the summer of 1978 Irene had gone back to London with the girls while I stayed in Nairobi. I received a phone call from her one day to say that she did not want to come back. The only way she would contemplate doing so would be if I came to London to persuade her to do so. Somewhat rattled, I told Charles Njonjo that I would have to make an emergency trip to London because of domestic problems. He immediately got on the telephone to Norman Montgomery and said he was "sending Rose to London with immediate effect" and to please arrange the ticket. Norman muttered to me later "He can't do this!" But he did. If you are big enough in Africa you can do almost anything. Happily, Irene was persuaded that life in Kenya should continue, at least for a while.

The "while" was of course a matter for negotiation. The plan had always been that we would consider leaving after my second 30 month contract expired (in March 1983), but I got an extension for a year to March 1984. I had hoped that I might be able to extend that to a full thirty month contract that would take us to September 1985 or even March 1986, but apart from the fact that Irene was not prepared to consider this, events conspired against it anyway.

The first was the death of Irene's father, at the age of 84, on 8th July 1982. As usual in the European summer, Irene had arranged to take the children back while I stayed in Nairobi (intending to take the trip to Lake Turkana with Bryan Hudson). Her plan had been to leave on Tuesday 6th, but both girls had open days at their respective schools that week, and Rachel was in a play (A Midsummer Night's Dream) and so the trip was postponed until the following Sunday. Late at night on Thursday 8th we got a telephone call from Beverly Saffrin to say that he had suffered a heart attack and died while playing bridge at the home of friends of his.

It was a cruel trick of fate for Irene, especially as the family decided to have the funeral on the very day she was travelling back.

While the death was not in itself a reason to leave, it was one of those events that accumulated in Irene's mind. The attempted coup had been another. We attended a small party on New Year's Eve 1982 at Nairobi Club and dolefully said to each other when toasting in the year 1983 that we did not think it was going to be a very good one. That was an understatement. In March, Irene's sister Monica came to stay for a while, depressed that her marriage had recently broken up. In the middle of that month Irene suffered from a bout of amoebic dysentery which was so bad that she had to be admitted for a short while to hospital and was incapacitated for a fortnight. She lost about 6 kilos in weight. However, the next major event in our lives was to set the seal on things.

In the period 1982-3 the Nairobi City Council had virtually ceased to function owing to a combination of corruption and incompetence. Its powers had been taken over, in a kind of "direct rule" situation by the Ministry for Local Government and the President had ordered that a "task force" be set up to make recommendations as to what should happen. Much against my will I had been co-opted as a member of this force. Its meetings were long and rambling and sometimes went on until late at night. In fact its last meeting to finalise the interim report finished at 2.45 am. I was both tired and fed up, as this work had to be done on top of my ordinary work. I was thus extremely glad to be able to persuade the Attorney-General to allow me to get away in late March for 11 days on one of our regular visits to Diani.

All began as normal; the journey to the village of Mtito Andei, approximately half way from Nairobi to Mombasa and where we always stopped for breakfast, was uneventful. Jessie always said how she felt excitement once we continued on the road past Nairobi airport as that meant we were going on holiday. We set off again after breakfast. Near Voi, roughly three quarters of the way, I suddenly felt our Range Rover go out of control: the back of the vehicle seemed to "fishtail", sliding from side to side. As I fought with the steering wheel and Irene involuntarily leaned across to help steady it, I felt the whole car begin to rock from side to side as well. Within seconds I was horribly aware that it was turning over sideways. In fact it performed a somersault, landing the right way up, but with the roof caved in. It had never left the tarmac and there was no other vehicle in sight.

There were known to be freak whirlwinds in that area of the road, partly, it was said, because of the cutting down of trees in the area. I afterwards worked out that what almost certainly had happened is that we had blown a rear tyre (causing the "fishtailing") and the combination of this and the wind acting on its comparatively high centre of gravity had caused the vehicle to turn a sideways somersault. At the time I was not of course aware of this, and was only dimly aware of what had happened to the others and to the car. Some of what follows has therefore of necessity been supplemented by Irene's recollections.

The somersault had caused the buckled metal of the roof to cut my head badly. I remember staggering out of the vehicle feeling very weak and dazed, doubtless suffering from concussion. Jessie and Jonno had been thrown from the vehicle as it somersaulted; Irene and Rachel were very shaken but comparatively unharmed. Jessie, it soon afterwards transpired, had been badly injured; Jonno, though he had many splinters of shattered window glass embedded in his arm, less so.

A European couple from Nairobi (their surname was Stuart-Smith) had been following not far behind us. They immediately stopped their car and insisted on driving us all (except for Rachel who stayed initially with the vehicle) to the hospital at Voi, mercifully only a short distance away. There it was quickly decided that I needed emergency attention to sew up the wound to my scalp. Someone was removed, very graciously, from a bed in favour of Jessie. My own memories are of being laid on a simple operating table with a bank of household-type light bulbs above it, of being asked how I felt and, dreading the thought of being operated on there, of beating my chest and saying that I felt fine!

The next thing I was aware of was the sensation of a very loud noise and a dim sight of what looked like wires in front of me. I actually remember thinking that perhaps I was dead, and that this was a sort of state of limbo. I put my hand in front of me to see if the wires were real.

A lot had happened in the meantime. Irene (again showing her ability to rise to the occasion) had been terrific. She telephoned friends in Nairobi: Charles Szlapak, Charles Njonjo, Vera Somen, Harold Platt and Rosemary Kempsell among others. Rosemary told her not to worry, she would organise something to help, although as she later admitted she had at that moment no idea how. But somehow, after co-operation between various people, the Flying Doctor Service was organised to fly to Voi and airlift us all back to Nairobi. Charles ordered the police to guard our car.

It was now that the real Africa began to bear on the situation: we could not be taken to Voi airstrip by ambulance as the hospital had no petrol for it! With the intervention of someone (probably Charles Njonjo) somehow petrol was obtained, I think from the police, and we were taken to the airstrip. While boarding the small plane Rachel inadvertently stepped on an acacia thorn that pierced her flip-flop and went into her foot. That was all Irene needed!

It was during the airlift back to Nairobi that I had come round. Jessie and I were laid out on stretcher-beds in the plane and the "wires" were tube drip-feeds to us both. Apparently I caused concern, in my attempt to verify whether I was alive, that I would detach the tubes. When we landed at Wilson Airport (the one used by smaller aircraft) all I could remember was vomiting (I had been given an anaesthetic soon after eating breakfast). Jessie and I were taken straight to the intensive care unit of Nairobi Hospital where Jessie was operated on immediately for a depressed fracture to her skull above the left eye.

I recovered very quickly, although my head need to be re-stitched (with I think about 40 stitches) in a further operation. Jessie was much more seriously injured: she was kept in the intensive care ward for 10 days, but shortly after her discharge from there she drifted into a coma. Against a background of intense worry for everyone, medical staff included, she regained consciousness after about 36 hours. Her injuries meant that for a while she was paralyzed down her right side, but with physiotherapy and great perseverance she proceeded to virtually teach herself to walk again, being finally released from hospital after about 5 weeks. Jessie initially had to write and paint with her left hand, but gradually near normal use returned to her right hand side. She was left with a slight wasting of her right arm and leg that resulted in about a 5% residual disability.

It was thus that plans to leave Kenya crystallised. Irene and the children would leave after the end of the next school term (actually the school year ran from January to December) and I would stay to wind things up until the end of the contract in March. It would take a month or so to completely sell up and settle our affairs, and so they would all come out to Nairobi in the December school holidays and possibly also at Easter.

And so, in July and August 1983 we departed from Nairobi at different times. Rachel was suddenly torn from her life in Nairobi, flying back to London on the evening of her last day at school in July to go to a Sport and Music Camp in England that both girls had attended the previous year. In view of Jessie's injuries (by now very much on the mend) we had decided that she should not go, and so Irene left with her and Jonno at the beginning of August, and I followed a fortnight later. I would return at the beginning of October; the others would begin life in London.

Paradoxically it was during this winding up period that in September 1983 I went with Irene to Hong Kong to attend the Commonwealth Law Conference that year as a representative of the Kenya Government. What we found was Hong Kong seemingly at the height of its glory, a little while before Margaret Thatcher's government decided to begin to negotiate its return to China. The 99 year lease of the "New Territories" (the bulk of the Colony's mainland area) was to terminate in 1997, China wanted the whole Colony returned to it then, and the originally ceded islands and tip of the mainland would not, it was obvious, be viable in the face of Chinese hostility.

After years in East and Central Africa, the opulence and availability of every material thing you could think of in Hong Kong and at comparatively little cost, were truly amazing. Various lawyer friends were working there or visiting at that time and we had the opportunity of dining one night at the Peninsula, one of the handful of truly great Commonwealth hotels.[33]

---

[33] See footnote 23 to chapter 7. Hong Kong's English language newspaper, the South China Morning Post, was also to me highly evocative of expatriate life.

Back in London, the girls were accepted into Henrietta Barnet School (Rachel) and, after a year at Child's Way School, the Mount (Jessie), while Jonno went to the kindergarten at Alyth Synagogue that both girls had attended at some point (Rachel before Malawi, and Jessie in the year between Malawi and Kenya). I soon learned from Irene that it was in fact 3½ year-old Jonno who seemed to miss life in Nairobi most. I recalled in a letter in November 1983 to Nanny that:

> He probably misses Kenya more than the rest of them, and has been really unhappy at being away from Anna, his ayah, from his garden, 'his' dogs, the servants, the sunshine and his friends. Whenever I have rung and spoken to him he has insisted on speaking to Anna too, and the poor little fellow has been very frustrated (as have we) by the fact that the line is at times very bad indeed. I feel really bad about him and asked Irene to send him back to me as I feel sure I could look after him. But Irene feels, I suppose correctly, that such a move would cause even more disruption, and the girls, especially Rachel, were very much against the idea of losing him, even temporarily.
>
> He is of course too young to fully appreciate what is going on. I remember how infinitely sad I felt when he asked me wistfully one day when we were all together in London "Daddy, are we going to stay here all the days?" Irene has written some little letters from him at his dictation. The last of these went (in part) "Say to Daddy leave the spade [his pride and joy] and then come back to me and bring me back to Kenya and then I'll see the spade – is that alright? I want to see Shimba and Chyulu [the dogs]... and Joseph and Anna and Platt [Harold Platt, our friend and neighbour]."

Irene had much to contend with in London, not least the medical attention of different kinds that Jessie needed. It was a huge relief that physiotherapy was bringing about sufficient improvement to the extent that a further operation could be thought on medical advice to be unnecessary, and the fear of epilepsy was retreating.

Conclusion

Although the disengagement period lasted just over a year, the acute pain of it struck me most forcibly just as soon as Irene and the children left for the UK at the beginning of August 1983. My letter dated 2nd August says it all:

> Dear Irene
> So you have really gone.
>
> I sit here feeling miserable to put down some thoughts on paper even before you have taken off from Nairobi, scarcely able to hold back the tears as I contemplate Jonno's "office" by my side[34], the scissors still where he threw them down barely three hours ago.

---

[34] This was a little blue table in the living-room extension where he had his things.

When I returned I could not resist visiting the vacated rooms and contemplating their awful bareness. Rachel's room has of course been empty for 2½ weeks, Jessie's, as one would expect, scrupulously tidy but so bare, Jonno's with the bed still as he left it just a short while ago when I lifted him out for the journey to the airport, and ours with your side of the bed likewise still rumpled from this afternoon's rest.

Yes, you will come back, but it won't be quite the same. Still there will be, for three or four weeks at Christmas, a brief return to the life we have had for the past six years. In spite of all the ups and downs, and the downs have been worse than anywhere else, I have never really felt so much sadness at the thought of leaving a place before, save perhaps the house in which I grew up in Edgware[35]. But that was in rather "watered down" circumstances as I was away at boarding school when the family moved to that house in the Bishops' Avenue which carries no fond memories at all.

At least I will have a few months to ease myself out of here, get completely used to the idea of leaving. Who knows? By the time next March arrives things may have got difficult enough for me actually to be quite glad to leave. Anyway, my father was right when he said that the fact of your all going will ensure my return.

Anyway, as Jessie would say, there is little point in going on with this maudlin letter. It has served to work out of me some of the excesses of sadness, and I can contemplate Jessie's farewell card and Jonno's drawings with happiness.

I enclose Lori Platt's address which you forgot to take.

Lots and lots of love and kisses to you all.
Roger

Almost thirty years would pass before I could bring myself to reread it.

---

[35] I am surprised that I made this comparison at the time. In retrospect the wrench referred to was nothing like so bad.

Chapter 9

Lawyer

The Start	321
1 Garden Court	328
The Kray trial	332
The dock brief	334
The Nigerian professor	336
Other cases	338
A very uncomfortable interlude 1984-5	341
Jersey 1985-6	344
The Crown Prosecution Service 1987	347
The Commonwealth Legal Advisory Service 1987-94	349
Legal consultant	351

The Start

The factors leading up to my becoming a barrister have already been considered[1], and I have given short glimpses into my subsequent life as a lawyer in Malawi and in Kenya. But for a fuller picture I need to go back to the beginning.

Firstly, an outline explanation of the way the legal profession worked at the time might be helpful. It was, as it still is, split between barristers (usually referred to collectively as the Bar[2]) on the one hand, and solicitors on the other. The two sub-professions were (as they still are) each governed by their own regulatory body: the General Council of the Bar (usually known as the Bar Council) on the one hand, and the Law Society on the other. In the 1960s there were in England and Wales[3] around 2000 barristers and probably twenty times that number of solicitors.

---

[1] See chapter 5.
[2] The name derives from the physical barrier that divided (and still often does) the area in a court in which the public are admitted from the area where judges, magistrates, juries and lawyers, and of course litigants in person, take their places. Hence a newly qualified barrister is "called to the Bar" and given the right to address the court from inside that area.
[3] Scotland and Northern Ireland constitute different legal jurisdictions, the former at least with its own law that had different origins from the English common law. Call to the Bar of England and Wales did and does not automatically entitle the barrister to practice in the other British jurisdictions. This is why it is incorrect to speak of "British law", as there is

There were and are two broad categories of legal work: criminal (both in prosecution and defence) and what is known as "civil" (basically anything other than criminal work). A person who wished for any reason to consult a lawyer would need to go to a solicitor; this could be for representation in a criminal case; for non-contentious civil business such as buying or selling property ("conveyancing"), getting a will or lease drawn up or drafting a contract; or for contentious civil business where there was a dispute that failing resolution between lawyers might end up in court. As a general rule most of this work was handled by solicitors alone. Much of the criminal work and some of the civil work was paid for under the state-assisted legal aid scheme.

With one minor exception in criminal cases[4], a barrister could be briefed only by a solicitor and not directly by a member of the public. In practice this briefing was done in two types of cases. Firstly those where court appearance was involved, in either civil or criminal cases. Solicitors did at that time have "right of audience" (i.e. to appear and plead on behalf of clients) in the lower levels of courts[5], but they normally preferred to leave that kind of work to barristers (usually known as "counsel") who specialised in court work, particularly as this often involved a considerable amount of waiting around for cases to be called; solicitors could use their time more efficiently and profitably in their offices. And of course solicitors had no choice where appearance in the Crown Court (in judge and jury criminal cases), the High Court or the Courts of Appeal were concerned. Secondly, briefs tended to be sent to counsel where complex or obscure points of law or evidence were involved that were likely to need research, particularly if litigation might result. While solicitors were perfectly capable of undertaking this kind of work, it tended to be more efficient for them to "seek counsel's opinion", particularly if consideration of the matter was going to be time-consuming. There was also the anomaly in the law that a barrister could not be sued for giving a negligent opinion.

For criminal cases there was at the time no official prosecuting service (such as the Attorney-General's Chambers in most Commonwealth countries, or the District Attorneys' Offices in the United States) and prosecutions were undertaken in the lower courts often by the police themselves or in the

---

technically no such thing (although statute law – i.e. Acts of Parliament and statutory instruments – does often apply to all British jurisdictions). Rather one speaks of "the law of England and Wales" or "the common law", and this latter is in fact the basis of the law of most of the countries in the Commonwealth, and of course the United States.

[4] See below p.338.

[5] Solicitors today have much wider rights of audience.

higher courts or more complex lower court cases by solicitors acting on behalf of the police. These solicitors would of course brief barristers in the circumstances already described, and so one could as a barrister alternate between prosecuting and defending (although in practice many tended to specialise in one or the other). After the establishment of the Crown Prosecution Service in the late 1980s the prosecution work formerly done by solicitors was taken over by that organisation, and its professional staff (many of whom had qualified as barristers) gradually attained wider rights of appearing in courts.

There was at that time a rigid division between the two professions, and any but formal professional contact between the two was forbidden. As a barrister one could not, for example, invite a solicitor, unless already a personal friend (and then only outside a professional environment), to a meal or even for a drink, except during the course of a case in which one was appearing. Certainly a solicitor could not be invited to dine at one of the Inns of Court. The idea behind this was as far as possible to prevent barristers from touting for business. Though there was some movement of individual lawyers between the professions this was discouraged and difficult and involved a period when the person concerned had to be neither one nor the other. Most Commonwealth countries and the United States had found this structure too complicated and unnecessary, and had fused the professions, sometimes long before.

The idea of joining the Bar, a respected profession, was attractive not only to me but as previously noted also to my father. From many points of view the choice seemed a good one: I was articulate, but did not waffle; I was good at getting to the heart of a problem; and the intellectual challenge of the law did not seem beyond me. And though I was less aware of it at the time than I became later, I had a well-developed sense of what is required in order to effectively present information (of whatever kind), i.e. that there is a need at some level to put on a performance to one's audience. Also, I fancied myself at what I saw as the sharp end of the legal profession, and considered that if I was not exactly God's gift to the courtrooms, I could be more effective and enjoy myself more in that environment than as a "backroom boy" in a legal office. In view of the turn my legal career later took this was supremely ironic.

I had discussed these things with Edward Griew, the son of former neighbours and friends of my parents in Dorset Drive, Edgware, who had for a time practised at the Bar but (largely for health reasons) had since taken up an academic post at Leicester University. He encouraged me to take up the profession, although he emphasised that for a successful career one needed to be "in the right set of chambers". However, failing family or other fairly intimate connections with those already at the Bar (and I had neither), and not knowing if or how I wanted to specialise, I did not see how I could know what the "right chambers" would be until I had actual experience of them.

My studies and my discussions with those I met along the way did not enlighten me very much about this. It was true that I met all sorts of people while, as a law student, eating the required three dinners in (in my case) the Middle Temple Hall each law term, but the majority of them were Commonwealth lawyers who would be returning to their own countries after call, or those in, or aiming for, odd specialist areas like church law or taxation law. The meals themselves were pleasant enough (we sat at long tables and ate in "messes" of four; wine was always included in the cost of the dinner) but it was difficult to see how the requirement to eat them contributed anything much of direct value to us as would-be lawyers. It seemed to be merely a tradition that had continued, much for its own sake, from the time when Bar students were required to be resident in the Inns of Court during their studies.

I would clearly have to learn where I should ideally end up by a process of trial and error.

My initiation into the profession involved one or two minor shocks. When I first went to see my pupil-master-to-be, Sam Stammler, on my return from Israel in the early autumn of 1967 I naturally went to shake his hand. "You won't do that when you come to the Bar" he said, gently but firmly. I withdrew my hand as though from a flame. There were traditions at the Bar on which I clearly needed instruction and this was the first. For no discernible reason, barristers never shook hands with each other, and this custom often led to a slight awkwardness when one was introduced, for example, to a new pupil or member of chambers, or indeed to any other barrister. Both parties were expected to nod to each other, often in practice awkwardly, rather than greet in the socially conventional way. Though I quickly got used to the custom, it didn't get to feel any more natural; it was as though we were frightened of passing on a contagious disease to each other and at times the required "stand-off" felt downright silly.

Another custom was that (unless closely acquainted, when of course first name terms were expected) barristers always called each other by their surnames alone, i.e. never prefaced with a "Mr" (I don't think the equivalent rule applied to women, of whom there were comparatively few at the Bar at that time, and I seem to remember the convention was to refer to them by both first and surnames). The "Mr" (or "Mrs" or "Miss") form of address needed to be used by barristers' clerks and chambers staff, and of course by clients.

Barristers invariably called their clerks (there would, depending on the size of the chambers, usually be a senior and one or more junior clerks) and other chambers staff by their first names, but in return the staff would always refer to a barrister as "Mr X", or face to face as "Sir". As in a similar situation in Officer Cadet School in the army, that formal form of address was sometimes delivered to pupils or novice barristers in a very mildly sarcastic tone. Once outside the Temple area, however, these formalities could and often did break down, and at an informal social function at which all were present the clerks could and would call barristers in their chambers, particularly the younger ones, by their first names.

Barristers' clerks were in fact quite powerful people (they were overwhelmingly men, but women were just beginning to encroach into the occupation). They were "self-made" in that they had no qualifications except their experience and were usually from lower middle class backgrounds. However, in spite of this class distinction the clerks were in a position to make or break the careers of novice barristers, for failing family or other connections in the solicitors' profession (i.e. contacts who would be prepared to brief young barristers on the basis of acquaintance alone), it was the clerks, and in practice only they, who could persuade instructing solicitors to allow "promising" young barristers in their chambers to be sent briefs. The clerk negotiated the fee on any brief with the instructing solicitors (barristers did not dirty their hands with haggling over money!) and took a percentage of each fee for doing so. In successful chambers they could and did become rich men.

There was another tradition at the Bar that was just beginning to break down: the dress code. Quite apart from formal court dress, most barristers still wore in chambers the formal black jacket and waistcoat and striped trousers of the kind that up to the Second World War civil servants, and those in the legal and other professions, had customarily worn. It was also, curiously, the dress usually adopted by cinema managers at the time, and it was not a get-up I had in mind for myself. I was not the only one of my generation to consider this type of dress to be outmoded by the late 1960s and promised myself I would never wear it.

It was, however, a requirement at the Bar that you wore a three-piece suit (i.e. with a waistcoat) when appearing in court, and it was necessary to buy your suits accordingly. The other more pragmatic element of a barrister's dress was the wearing of detached-collar shirts. This was not a requirement, but as court dress (in any but the magistrates' courts) required, besides the wig and gown, the wearing of a detachable wing collar and "bands" (the two white cotton strips worn at the neck in an inverted V that represented the tablets of the law given to Moses and which were inherited from clerical dress), it made sense merely to have to change only your collar rather than your whole shirt when dressing for court. This process of dressing was known as "robing".

An informal practice at the Bar which seemed just a little strange at first was the "proprietary reference". If for example you were briefed on behalf of a factory owner in a building dispute, you would always refer generally (though not formally when in court) to *"our* factory". This would apply whatever the subject matter of a civil dispute, so that when barristers were discussing their cases, either in conference or informally amongst themselves, you constantly heard references to such things as *"our* policy of insurance", *"our* vehicle" and even, to non-initiated ears, the rather odd-sounding *"our* wife" (or husband, or children). You yourself slipped into this habit almost without noticing it.

The arrangement in chambers (at 1 Essex Court in the Middle Temple area[6]) was that I would be Sam Stammler's pupil for six months. Sam was at the time one of the senior "juniors" at the Bar (this designation simply applied to any barrister, of however long standing, who had not "taken silk" and become a Queen's Counsel – as indeed Sam was to do a year or two later)[7]. He was a very public spirited man and already had two pupils, but it didn't take me long to realise that, even if I had had the required level of ability and interest (and I didn't think I had either), this was not the set of chambers for me. The work, which mainly involved company and commercial law disputes (and incidentally reputed to be "where the money is") was not what I wanted to do.

Socially, apart from Sam, whom I liked but who at the age of 42 or 43 seemed from my viewpoint at age 28 to be very much older than I was (and of course almost on another planet professionally), there was only one other member of chambers to whom I could relate easily: a Jewish South African lawyer in his mid-thirties, W. S. Getz. He was known at the Bar by his first

---

[6] The location of a set of chambers did not need to bear any relation to the Inns of Court to which its various members belonged.
[7] As a pupil you needed to pay a fee to your master for his trouble. I cannot remember what this was, but the amount was not really recompense him for the time and trouble taken, and many barristers refused to take pupils. By tradition, once a barrister had "taken silk" he or she could no longer take pupils anyway.

name, Wilfred, but his wife and close friends called him by his second, Sholom or Shol. He and his family had emigrated from South Africa two or three years previously. He had made a name for himself there by co-editing a text book on South African insurance law that doubtless helped him in his search for chambers in London. We became good friends and Irene and I maintained social contact throughout my time at the Bar and after our return from Africa. Sadly he died when only in his 50s of a brain tumour and we lost contact with his widow, Jill, afterwards.

I was acutely conscious of my lack of depth in legal education, especially as most of the barristers in Essex Court had law degrees. I was going to have to pick things up as I went along. In fact, although I was now "in" the profession and would in some months be formally called to the Bar, I found it difficult to think of myself as a lawyer (if someone asked me at a social gathering what I did for a living my explanation sounded to myself as though I were talking about somebody else). The exposure to courts that I had as Sam's pupil was exclusively the High Court or the Court of Appeal and did little to help understand the way things worked at the lower levels: the magistrates' courts (which heard mainly the more minor criminal cases and some matrimonial cases) and the county courts (which heard civil cases up to a certain value of claim). It was in these courts that I presumed that inevitably my career would start. As a matter of fact I was wrong.

As a pupil, you were entitled to take a brief after six months of pupillage. In fact I had been given one of a sort when in Sam Stammler's chambers. Not only was it the first time I appeared in court in my own right, but I needed to be "robed" for the occasion. The case involved a dispute before the Official Referee, a judicial officer of senior rank, but less than a High Court Judge. The Official Referee's court typically heard cases such as building disputes in which many documents needed to be referred to (and which were usually itemised in schedules)[8]. The case in question was one in which Sam had been briefed for the defendant in just such a building dispute, and the reason I was given the task was that though the plaintiff had sued our client, the claim was in reality against the company to whom the work had been subcontracted, and Sam had joined the subcontractor to the action as a "third party". I was thus sitting both literally and metaphorically in the middle of a lengthy dispute in which I, in theory at least, had nothing to do. If the plaintiff lost the action, then the company concerned would be ordered to pay the costs of both the defendant and the third party. If the plaintiff won,

---

[8] In fact about three quarters of Official Referee cases originated (as they still do) in the construction industry and typically concerned architects, engineers, surveyors, contractors, sub-contractors, house-builders, developers, property owners, building societies and other financial institutions, and local authorities.

then our client could and would recoup the amount of the judgement and costs from the third party (the company concerned was not legally represented in that case but appeared, as of course it was entitled to do, in the person of one of its directors).

It was not a conventional beginning to a career at the Bar, and I was kept alert through the enormous amount of detail (the case lasted about 2 weeks) by the fact that I might be called on to address the court. In fact I was, but I seem to remember only when counsels' closing speeches were made. I did not attend the judgement, which was reserved and given a week or two later, but I seem to remember that the plaintiff won.

But that kind of thing apart, if one did receive a brief oneself as a pupil in the second six months of pupillage it tended to be for the kinds of case no-one else wanted. These included *"pro bono"* briefs, i.e. at no fee at all; or so-called "watching briefs", that involved simply reporting what had happened in a case, as with my own first magistrates' court case (these cases tended to be briefed by solicitors acting for insurance companies); or other briefs almost certainly in the magistrates' courts at the minimum fee, which at the time was three guineas[9].

1 Garden Court

It was easy enough to get a pupillage at the Bar at the time, but what a qualified barrister needed to be able to do was to become a permanent member of chambers, as a so-called tenant[10]. Naturally it helped if you could be taken on as a pupil in chambers where that might be a possibility. Finding a set of chambers prepared to take you was not easy, but it was obviously easier if you were, as I was, already a pupil and the word could be put around by barristers and barristers' clerks. It turned out that I was lucky.

---

[9] £3.15 in today's money. Fees in a number of professions were traditionally (if somewhat illogically) set in this denomination of money that took its name from the regions in Africa where gold had been mined in the 17th and 18th centuries, including of course the Gold Coast – the former name for Ghana. The guinea coin's value was officially set in the early nineteenth century at 21 shillings, or one pound and one shilling (£1.05 in today's money). It was also used in betting (two of the English classic flat horseraces are still called the One Thousand and Two Thousand Guineas respectively – the amount of prize money originally paid to the winner) and in the giving of gifts of money. Such gifts to me at my Bar-mitzvah were almost exclusively in cheques drawn in these amounts, the "going rate" at the time being between two and five guineas depending on the generosity of the donor.

[10] His or her name could then be painted on the board at the entrance to the chambers announcing that he or she was (in theory at least) an established junior barrister.

By the spring of 1968 a set of chambers nearby, at 1 Garden Court, was looking for pupils. It had as its joint heads of chambers Charles Lawson QC and Lewis Hawser QC, and it undertook a wide variety of what was termed "common law" work (basically both criminal and civil non-specialist cases). There was a further connection in that Charles was a member of Coombe Hill Golf Club and knew Dad quite well. I was accepted to undertake a further pupillage with Brian Clapham, one of the senior "juniors" in those chambers. Though I was certainly not promised what was called "a seat" there at the end of the pupillage, it was hinted that it might happen if I gave a good enough account of myself.

Newly called to the Bar, 1968

Brian was as almost as complete a contrast to Sam as it was possible to get. Probably in his mid-fifties at the time, he was a man who specialised in run-of-the-mill court work. Though he loved his work and was competent at it he had nothing like the level of ability or practice that I had seen in Essex Court. He also seemed to me to be, both in conferences in chambers and in conducting cases in court, totally insensitive to the feelings of clients and witnesses, and he was often curt with them, sometimes to the point of rudeness. The idea that a client needed to feel he or she was being looked after, let alone valued, was something that never seemed to cross his mind. To him the challenge and fascination were in the cut and thrust of litigation and the minor ways in which he could use tactics to trump opposing lawyers in his cases; in these processes the client could be almost irrelevant. On several occasions I needed to smooth ruffled feathers by trying to imply, as I accompanied clients out of Brian's room, that *I* was sympathetic to their cases, even if he wasn't.

Still, though I certainly did not learn anything from Brian about human relations, I could at least understand and work on the briefs and it was something of a refreshing change to be involved with more everyday problems than those thrown up in disputes between large companies.

At about the same time as Brian took me on, he also took on a pupil from Hong Kong, Hon Tam-Chan[11]. Hon was about my age and had also come to the Bar late, having been an inspector in some area of Government work beforehand. He had a wife and young daughter at home, but his studies for the Bar meant that he had had to be away from home for a considerable period (it seems difficult to believe but I think it was as long as six years) with, due to the cost involved, no more than one or two visits home during the period. I'm not sure if the Hong Kong Government contributed towards his legal education[12], they probably did, but even so the process showed a kind of dedication that was remarkable. Hon later became Chairman of the Hong Kong Small Claims Court. He was on leave the first time I went to Hong Kong in 1983 and had retired by the time I next went there in 2009, so (not having the time or energy to make extensive enquiries as to his whereabouts) I never managed to meet him again.

By the end of 1968, after some six months as Brian's pupil, I was indeed offered a tenancy (or "seat") in chambers. Contrary to what I had experienced in Essex Court, the work was much more the kind I wanted to do, and the younger members of chambers were congenial and easy to get on with. For the time being at least, everything looked rosy.

The set of chambers at Garden Court comprised the ground floor and basement of what was probably a late 18th century building. The first and second floors were occupied by another set of chambers, and the top floor,

---

[11] The Chinese way of writing names is to state the surname first, and it was by his surname that Hon liked to be known. When a few months later we were both called to the Bar at the Middle Temple, the person calling out his name for formal admission mistakenly called him forward as "the Honourable Tam-Chan".

[12] At that time of course the territory was still a British dependency and would remain so for another 30 years.

as with so many buildings in the Temple, contained residential flats. The building faced the Middle Temple garden and Hall, although most of us who were more junior members of chambers had or shared rooms in the basement with no view but the legs of people passing by.

As a new member of chambers life was not that busy, but bit by bit small cases were channelled my way. They tended to be run of the mill cases, particularly careless driving cases in the magistrates' courts and landlord & tenant eviction cases in the County Courts. The driving cases were usually lost (the accused driver would usually, hardly surprisingly, want to contest the case however strong the evidence); and there was no option but for a landlord to bring a case to the County Court when a tenant was in breach of the terms of his or her lease (usually for non-payment of rent due) as domestic premises could not be repossessed without a court order. These latter cases tended to drag on, with adjournments being granted e.g. to allow time for a tenant to find money owing for rent, as the courts wanted to be seen to be lenient to litigants they saw as the weaker parties.
They were not necessarily always so as many landlords I came across were retired people renting out flats in their own homes to supplement meagre pensions.

In fact there was a set of chambers nearby with a youngish female head clerk named Celia with whom Arthur Dorset, our head clerk, sometimes exchanged briefs of the more general nature (i.e. not those marked for specific barristers) when we or they were particularly busy. She was on a visit to our chambers one day, and as I approached the clerks' room I overheard her telling Arthur to give a brief she was delivering to "the one I like". I entered and he immediately handed it to me. As I looked at her gratefully she was smiling cheekily. "She's a vamp, Sir!" came Arthur's mock warning.

Briefs to appear in what soon after my call to the Bar became known as the Crown Courts tended to start with cases where the accused person intended to plead guilty; these were heard by a judge alone. It was only slowly that one progressed to trials (i.e. where not guilty pleas had been or were to be entered) which were heard before a judge and jury.

If you were lucky, you could be briefed as a junior to a Queen's Counsel[13]. The rule was that QCs could not appear in court unless accompanied by a

---

[13] Senior barristers, who applied for this status once they were sufficiently confident that they had the experience and reputation sufficient to undertake the weightiest or most complex cases. They needed to be able to justify the higher fees their status commanded, including the briefing of a junior barrister to appear in court with them.

junior barrister. In civil cases this served some purpose, for in any but the most complex cases the junior would advise on the merits, and assuming it were to go forward to litigation he or she would draft the pleadings (the documents, known as the "statement of claim" and, if the case were to be contested, the "defence", setting out and possibly narrowing down the issues between litigants), and take care of what were called interlocutory proceedings (usually incidental issues that needed to be decided before a case came for full trial[14]). Assuming the case were considered important enough to brief a QC[15], the latter would usually come into the case at a late stage and lead the presentation of it in court.

But in criminal cases, where the stages before trial were almost always much simpler, there was little merit in the "two counsel" rule, as the junior, at any rate in run of the mill cases where there were not many legal issues, often had little to do. I was, however, briefly a beneficiary of this rule and became involved on the fringes of one of the largest and most infamous criminal trials of the 1960s.

The Kray trial

In the 1950s and 1960s the London criminal underworld was dominated by two rival gangs, known after those that ran them as the Richardsons and the Krays. The former, headed by Charlie and Eddie Richardson and operating in South London, specialised in large scale frauds and extortion rackets. They were particularly notorious for torturing victims and gang members whom they regarded as "transgressors". They were eventually arrested, tried, convicted and given long prison sentences in 1967, although they continued in crime after their respective releases.

The Kray twins, Ronnie and Reggie, were owners of night-clubs, mostly bought from the proceeds of violent crime, and operated various "protection rackets" in East and North-east London, mainly amongst owners of pubs and other night-clubs. The victims were required to pay "protection money" to the Kray gang; if they failed to do so their premises would be raided by the gang and "done over", often with consequential injury to personnel and considerable damage to property. The fear they engendered was usually

---

[14] Typically these were so called "Order XIV proceedings" (after the relevant provision in the High Court's rules of procedure) under which a plaintiff swore an affidavit to the effect that he or she truly believed that there was no defence to the action.

[15] In practice this normally meant that the case would be heard in the High Court, the Court of Appeal or what would now be the Supreme Court (at that time the Judicial Committee of the House of Lords).

enough to ensure their victims paid up, and it was also enough to ensure that for a long time nobody dared to give evidence against them.

However, by 1968 the police had finally managed to amass enough evidence to arrest the Krays and their gang on charges of murder and accessories to murder. Once it was seen that they were in custody, other witnesses could be persuaded to give evidence against them and consequently strengthen the case.

Ivor Richard QC was a senior member of our Garden Court chambers who had recently taken silk (he was incidentally also a Labour MP). He was briefed to appear for Freddie Foreman, a career criminal and one of the co-accused who had been involved in the disposal of the body of one of the victims whose deaths were the subject of the trial (in fact those who had been murdered were actually both themselves criminals loosely associated with the Kray gang). However, as Foreman was a comparatively minor figure in this particular trial, there was not all that much for Ivor to do; for his junior there was practically nothing.

Following the rules of the Bar, a junior was required to be in court with Ivor and was entitled to receive a fee for doing so. This largesse was shared between those of us young barristers in the chambers on a sort of rota basis if we were not otherwise occupied. Though not large, the relevant fees, which in effect were paid to us for doing virtually nothing except attend, were accepted gratefully if, in my case at least, with a touch of uneasy conscience. The experience obviously allowed those of us in this fortunate position to watch the various men concerned at close quarters. At one point I saw Reggie Kray, possibly to demonstrate that he was a man of finer feeling, get up in the dock to read a poem he had written about the young child ("little Connie") of one of his co-accused. The effect was bizarre and slightly embarrassing.

The trial ended in early 1969 with all but one of the accused being convicted. I was present when the presiding judge, Mr Justice Melford Stevenson, famously stated when sentencing the Kray twins "in my view society has earned a rest from your activities" and passed life sentences on them that did not allow for parole to be even considered for 30 years, and in effect meant that they would most likely spend the rest of their lives in prison. This must have been to the intense relief of many people. The judge is reported as having remarked some while afterwards that the Krays had told the truth only twice during the trial: when Reggie referred to a particular barrister as "a fat slob", and when Ronnie accused the judge of being biased.[16] In fact Ronnie died in Broadmoor (having in the meantime been certified insane) in 1995 aged 61, and Reggie was released on compassionate grounds after being diagnosed with inoperable bladder cancer in August 2000. He died some five weeks later shortly before his 67th birthday.

But most of the criminal cases in which I was involved were much, much lower down the scale of things.

In the early days I quite often attended what were then the Inner London Quarter Sessions (later to become Borough Crown Court) in Borough High Street with a brief (or more than one if I was lucky) on a plea of guilty. In these cases, if one were appearing for the defence, one made a so-called plea in mitigation. These were usually a bit of a farce: in the majority of cases the client would have a string of previous convictions on his record (something like ninety percent of my criminal clients were men), and there was little to say on his behalf, little at any rate that would affect the sentence the court would be bound to pass.

The dock brief

One day while waiting in court for such a case to be called a court police officer entered the witness box and announced that there was an application for a dock brief. I had not seen this procedure before: it was actually an uncommon event, as most persons charged with criminal offences of more than a trivial nature were able to get legal aid for their defence. At once most of the barristers attending the court made a rush for the door; only a few of us remained, almost certainly those who were either desperate for any work they could get or, like me, only vaguely aware of what was happening. An applicant of this kind was entitled to choose any barrister present to represent him[17], and needed to pay for the service only the basic fee of three guineas. As ill-luck would have it, he chose me.

I made my plea in mitigation in the case for which I was actually attending court and then went to see my new client. He was accused of theft by shoplifting. His case, which was an absolutely standard one of its type, took only a couple of minutes to read up. There was the usual statement from the store detective of the shop concerned to the effect that (as almost always happened

---

[16] This was not apparent from the record, and anyway the decision to convict was not of course his but the jury's. The Krays' appeals against conviction and sentence were later dismissed by the Court of Appeal.

[17] This was actually the only situation in which a barrister could appear in a case without having been briefed by a solicitor.

in such cases) he had been seen furtively looking around him before taking some things from shelves or counters in the shop (I can't remember what – I think some items from a supermarket), putting them into his own bag and then leaving the shop without paying. Again as was usual he was stopped outside the shop, taken back to the manager's office, the police called and the unpaid for items taken from him for use in evidence. There are probably dozens of such cases daily in London alone; the evidence is usually (as it was here) solid, and the accused person usually pleads guilty. From time to time a not-guilty plea is entered and a defence run, usually along the lines of lack of intention to steal e.g. in a fit of absentmindedness. Such defences are usually unconvincing and the court duly convicts and (unless the thief is then found to have a long list of previous similar convictions) passes a sentence of a fine or some form of community work.

My client's defence was not along these lines; it was simply that he did not do it.

In vain did I go through the prosecution witness statements with him to try to find out whether there was disagreement with any part of them or the construction put on what he was seen to have done. I was met with the same bland assertion that he did not do what he was accused of doing. At this stage of my career I had had some thin cases, but this was non-existent. The case was eventually called, he duly pleaded not guilty, a jury was sworn in and the trial went ahead. The evidence was indeed solid; I had no ammunition on which to cross examine prosecution witnesses, and indeed such questions as I did put to them probably served if anything only to make the case against my client stronger. At the end of the prosecution case I asked the judge if I could have a short adjournment to consult with my client. This, as the judge well knew, was code for "I'll do my best to get him to change his plea to guilty"; he of course granted the adjournment with the words: "Yes, Mr Rose, you give your client such advice as you think is appropriate".

Needless to say my attempt to get him to change his plea failed and I was met with the same stonewall assertion. The trial continued and my client gave evidence. When cross-examined he was unable to offer any explanation as to why the store detective (a woman) should have given evidence against him unless the events she described were true. The judge, as he was bound to, gave a short summing-up to the jury and at the end of it he asked them if they thought they needed to retire to consider their verdict. They muttered amongst themselves, indicated that they didn't, and convicted in about two minutes. This was in fact my record fastest time for losing a case in front of a jury. I forget what sentence my client was given;

it was probably a fine. He paid me my three guineas fee, stating rather unconvincingly that he *thought* he'd had his money's worth from the experience, and we both went on our way.

Actually he probably had some recognisable mental condition (though he was perfectly coherent) and had also probably earlier been refused legal aid on the basis that he had no apparent defence. I now understood why the barristers in court had made a general rush out when the application for the dock brief had first been announced.

The Nigerian professor

Occasionally a case could have quite unexpected repercussions. In September 1970 I needed to travel all the way to Chester-Le-Street in county Durham to appear on behalf of a Nigerian professor (from a university in Nigeria) who was opposing an application by his estranged wife (a white English woman) in the magistrates' court for custody of their son and payment of arrears of maintenance in the sum of over £400 (a considerable sum then). My brief contained all sorts of allegations against this woman, with whom the boy was living.

In magistrates' court proceedings at that time there was no way of getting systematically to what the issues between the parties were. In the higher civil courts there was a pre-trial exchange of documents between the parties known as "pleadings"[18] in which the basic facts of the case were recited and from which it was determined which matters in the case were agreed between them and which in issue. This was obviously an important process in saving time and money by not having to bring unnecessary witnesses and evidence to court. But in this case there were all sorts of allegations made by both sides and there was no way of knowing what issues were agreed except by discussion with the solicitor acting for the wife. I soon found that this was anyway a case in which my client was going to give no quarter.

At some point during the trial he produced an air-mail letter from his brother (who was in Nigeria) and demanded that it be put in evidence. I told him I could not do this: broadly speaking, documentary evidence is not admissible in court unless the person who wrote or made it is called before the court as a witness (this is under what is known to lawyers as the rule against hearsay [evidence]); clearly the brother could not be called as a witness in the present case. My client became very angry and continued to demand that I produce the letter to the court. I asked the court for a short adjournment so that I

---

[18] See above p. 332.

could try further to explain the law to him. During the adjournment he became almost hysterical, and waving the letter in question over his head as though it contained some kind of magic formula for winning his case which I was deliberately refusing to apply, he roundly denounced "British justice" and accused me of conspiring with the solicitor acting for his wife to make him lose the case.

I was taken aback: my first reaction was of disbelief and concern that I had not heard him correctly. It gradually dawned on me however that the man was, apart from anything else, paranoid. I told him that, if he believed what he had said, I had no alternative but to withdraw from the case immediately. He then seemed to calm down a little and said he did not want that. The accusation was anyway so fatuous that I could not accept that he had really believed it. The trial continued, and it became apparent that his estranged wife was a decent woman who was doing a good job in bringing up the child and who thoroughly deserved to have custody awarded her; further, that there was no good reason for the non-payment by my client of the arrears of maintenance. We duly and deservedly lost the case and the court made the orders sought by the wife. By this time my client seemed to accept the inevitable and we parted on what I thought were reasonably cordial terms.

But appearances were deceptive. To my consternation, about a month later I received from my instructing solicitors a copy of a long and rambling letter the professor had sent to them making numerous complaints and allegations about the handling of his case by them, by their agents (solicitors in Chester-Le-Street) and by me. He had copied it to the Legal Aid authorities (and hence effectively to the Law Society) and to the Bar Council. Much of it barely made sense. After a further few weeks I received another copy of the same letter from the Secretary to the Professional Conduct Committee of the Bar Council. It asked me to comment on only two of the allegations in the letter, one of which was that I did not have a proper conference with the client, and the other (turning the truth on its head) that I had continued to act after the client had terminated my retainer. Both were nonsense; I wrote explaining what had actually happened.

That was the last I heard of the matter. Though it was obvious the Bar Council were not going to take the matter any further, the process of having been reported to them on charges of professional incompetence and even misconduct was at the time both worrying and unpleasant. Doubtless the same applied to both firms of solicitors. Indeed in retrospect I could see that the client was an unpleasant and thoroughly devious man who was prepared to say anything at all (true or not) to serve his purpose. And the fact that he turned up at the court having driven all the way from where he was living in

Bromley, Kent, in his Mercedes car had caused some raised eyebrows and mutterings as to how it was that he had been granted legal aid.

Other cases

Between these extremes there were of course the vast majority of cases, most of which were unmemorable. I was, however, involved in one or two other murder cases, the most unusual of which involved a man who had lunged with a ceremonial sword that he kept over his lounge mantelpiece through his bathroom window at a burglar attempting to gain entry. The would-be burglar had made his escape but then keeled over and died some way down the street. The accused was a man with no previous convictions of any sort and although he was charged with murder this was clearly one of those cases that was going to end up with, at its highest, a conviction for manslaughter, with a high chance of an acquittal. Sadly the brief went somewhere else after he was granted bail (on strict terms) at the magistrates' court and I never found out what happened to him.

Occasionally situations resulting from a case could be bizarre. I had represented an Israeli man charged with, I think, a drugs offence. I was comparatively inexperienced at the time and "got involved" emotionally to the degree that I believed in his innocence, and was personally upset when he was convicted and given a short prison sentence (I think six months). Such a state of involvement is of course professionally to be avoided as, quite apart from unnecessary emotional wear and tear on the advocate, it may well do a disservice to the client in that it can remove the ability to make a rational assessment of the case.

Some six months later I was sitting with Irene in a coffee bar in Wigmore Street in London's West End after a visit to the theatre when someone I didn't immediately recognise approached me affably. It was the Israeli client, apparently none the worse for wear from the four months' imprisonment he had probably actually served. Bearing in mind the history of the case I found myself embarrassed and at a complete loss for words (I could hardly, I thought, ask him how he had found his time inside, at least not in public) and far less at ease that the former client, who did not seem to have any hard feelings about the case. It was part of my maturing process.

In fact, being briefed for the defence in drugs cases was a common experience in my early days at the Bar. It was not an area of practice that most of us barristers were too keen to be involved with, for some of the solicitors who seemed to specialise in this kind of work were thought of (especially by the police) as identifying too closely with their clients and even being suspect in their honesty. While engaged in these sorts of cases we needed to be very careful not to be "tarred with the same brush". That too was part of the maturing process.

Sometimes there was an unusual pleasure in winning a case. One of my clients, a small rather rotund Turkish man, had been charged with indecent assault. He was, I think, accused of "groping" a woman on the London Underground. The evidence against him was not that convincing and I was rather proud of my submission to the jury on the concept of personal space being different in different communities. They duly acquitted and my client was released from the dock. As he was sitting on a seat in front of it waiting to undergo his release formalities, the jury filed past him on their way out of court. He burst into tears of gratitude as they did so, thanking them profusely, and then did so again as he thanked me.

My father was interested from a distance in my career at the Bar and on a couple of occasions he came with Irene to listen to criminal cases in which I was appearing for the defence. The first of these happened to be a shop-lifting one that, while not quite on the level of the surreal irrationality of my earlier dock brief case, was nevertheless one that I was almost bound to lose. I don't remember the facts of this one but what I do recall was, as I was making what was clearly an ineffectual address to the jury, his remark to Irene (clearly audible to me, and possibly to the judge and jury): "they're not listening to him!" On the second occasion (I have forgotten what the case was about) I could clearly hear his not particularly *sotto voce* considered opinion on one of the female witnesses in the case: "she looks like a bit of a tart". Given my sensitive inexperience at the time, both were embarrassing.

It was recognised that bored and irritated judges who could not professionally speaking take out their frustration on accused persons, litigants or witnesses could and would do so on lawyers appearing before them, especially if obviously junior in rank. On one occasion I was sitting in court while a young, inexperienced and frankly not very capable young female barrister was attempting to make a plea in mitigation on behalf of her client at what were then called Middlesex Quarter Sessions[19] before Ewan Montague, a judge known for his irascibility. As she sat down he stared at her, paused and said sarcastically "You can't be serious!" If it hadn't been a courtroom I'm fairly sure she would have burst into tears.

---

[19] In fact in the very building in Parliament Square that now houses the Supreme Court of Appeal (formerly the Judicial Committee of the House of Lords) and the Judicial Committee of the Privy Council.

Although I did not ever have my competence challenged in this way, I did have an experience of being openly undermined by a judge in court. I was appearing in a case at the Old Bailey on behalf of a young man accused of some crime the details of which I have forgotten. From the start the judge seemed to take exception to my client, and seemingly also to me; perhaps he disapproved of the way in which I was conducting the case. He refused to grant my client bail over the weekend (the case had begun on a Friday) and remanded him in custody, a decidedly unusual (though strictly speaking permissible) step in a comparatively minor kind of case involving a young man, who had at that time of course not been convicted.

On the Monday the case concluded. Though I was unaware of the fact, as I was addressing the jury at the end of the evidence I must at some point have had my thumbs resting at the tips of my trouser pockets. As I was in full flow the judge pointedly interrupted me. "Mr Rose, I think it would show more respect to the jury" he said "if you were to take your hands out of your pockets". This blatant attempt to undermine me clearly embarrassed the jury and frankly angered me. Without thinking, I made an exaggeratedly humble and pretty obviously insincere apology to the jury, which of course embarrassed them even further. I cannot pretend that the intervention had affected the outcome of the case, but it certainly put me out of sorts and to some extent inevitably affected the rest of my address to the jury. My client was duly convicted, but perhaps because the judge had by then had his share of malign pleasure he did not sentence the young man to immediate imprisonment.

Sometimes cases would take a wholly unexpected turn. I was appearing for one of the accused in a case where four or five men were charged with affray: they had allegedly gone into a pub and "done it over" causing considerable damage to the premises. I forget what the motive was, or indeed the details of my client's defence (I think it was that he had done his best to prevent the outcome) and was rather proud of the fact that I had managed in cross-examination to "sap the strength" somewhat of the evidence against him, and was reasonably confident of an acquittal. To my surprise my client decided at the end of the prosecution case that he wanted to change his plea from not guilty to guilty. I found myself in the highly usual position of telling a client that, though the matter of the plea was of course a matter for him, and though the outcome of the case could not of course be certainly predicted, it was in my opinion likely to be in his favour. But he persisted and just said, without any further explanation, that he wanted to plead guilty (something an accused person may do at any stage of a trial). Perhaps he was just tired of lying (though I did not of course know this) and wanted to "come clean", if only to himself. I don't remember the outcome, but I think he received no more than a suspended prison sentence.

As a barrister, one's stock-in-trade in criminal cases was supposed to be representing clients who had pleaded not guilty, but occasionally an appearance on a plea of guilty could be important and might involve a considerable amount of work. A farmer had been driving his Landrover along a street when the trailer it was towing had become detached and careered into a motor car coming in the opposite direction causing fairly serious injury to at least one of its occupants. I was briefed to appear for the farmer in the magistrates' court on the road traffic charges arising.

The details after all this time are somewhat hazy, but the client was concerned among other things that that under his policy of insurance liability might be denied by his insurers on the ground that he had been negligent in allowing the accident to happen. So concerned was he that I was briefed to attend a conference with him so that the mechanical failure could be examined in detail. I needed to master the technicalities of the coupling device and the two theories there were about how it had managed to come loose. He duly pleaded guilty in court to the charges against him (I think this turned on a bent linking pin) and I needed to question the police officer in charge of the case closely to establish that my client's submissions as to the causes of the mechanical failure (which were barely foreseeable) were justified. In practice after a plea of guilty the police tend to be, as they were in this case, quite helpful on the technical details and our submissions were accepted by the court. My instructing solicitor told me afterwards that during the process the client (referring to my grasp of the technicalities of the case,) had at one point whispered "He's got it!" perhaps not having believed that I could or would.

Traffic cases where an accused person pleads guilty are expected to last only a matter of minutes, but this one lasted for something like an hour and a half and ended with (bearing in mind the gravity of the case) only a moderate fine. I must have appeared to do my work well, for a member of the public in the court came up to me afterwards, told me he had never heard a plea in mitigation like it and asked me for my details in case he ever needed to be represented in court. It was needless to say gratifying to have this unsolicited praise.

A very uncomfortable interlude 1984-5

That period of my career lasted for about seven years (including a period of almost a year after returning from Malawi in 1976). For a while after returning from Kenya I was unable to decide whether or not to go back to the Bar. Things were somewhat against me. The profession was going through one of its periods of self-regulating reduction as there were more barristers that there was comfortably enough work for. Against this background I needed to be able to persuade a set of chambers to take me on as a tenant (and this would be by no means a certainty, as my former chambers at 1 Garden Court had by then split three ways). I did not get much encouragement from Arthur Dorset, my former clerk: as so often happened with those of us who had spent time abroad, that time was not only of no interest at all to anyone who had not had a similar experience, but more importantly it was of negative value regarding getting employment back in London. It was as though one had gone backwards in time.

There was also the thought, still at the back of my mind, that I was after all not ideally suited to life at the Bar. I was irritated by the pretentious airs of many of my fellow barristers, who though by and large able, tended to be loud-mouthed and full of themselves, pompous in a word, far more so it seemed to me than those in the acting profession, of whom one might at least in theory expect such behaviour. But much more importantly there was the fact that I am not by nature a disputatious person and do not as a rule relish controversy or arguments (I never, for example, watch or listen to television or radio debates or discussions on "current issues"). This characteristic, combined with a nervousness as to the inevitably unpredictable nature of litigation (in my seven odd years at the Bar I never got over a tendency to worry about cases), made me tend to prefer to settle civil cases if I thought I could, rather than to battle them out in court. I thought that these were characteristics that would not in the long run serve me or my clients particularly well.

In view of my recent legal experience I had obviously made enquiries with the Parliamentary Counsel Office in London to see if I could get a job drafting legislation, but they told me that they did not (at that time) recruit new lawyers over the age of 30. I was 45. Suggestions were made by lawyer friends that a practicable plan would be to aim for chairmanship of a tribunal.[20] But that course of action would mean as a first step finding a set of chambers that specialised in the particular type of work concerned, persuading them (bearing in mind the professional climate of the time) to accept me, and undertaking that kind of work as a practitioner for a period of a few years. Only then could I practically speaking apply for this kind of minor judicial post. Quite simply it sounded to me like time-serving in order to achieve something that I wasn't at all sure I wanted anyway, and I rejected

---

[20] There were and are a number of these set up to hear cases in specialist areas of the law (asylum & immigration, employment, mental health, social security, etc.)

the idea. After the senior position I had held in Kenya, I really didn't fancy starting virtually at the bottom all over again; unless, that is, I was forced to. As fate would have it, and for a short while later on, that is in fact almost exactly what happened.

But for now the months were passing; I was getting desperate and depressed. It was the only time in my life when I have felt without hope; despair was feeding on itself, and at times I was convincing myself I would not find employment anywhere. Should I give up the law altogether and go and do something completely different? What a waste, I thought, of all that training and experience. There was a proposal that I might join Great Universal Stores, the company that had owned Beautility and for whom my father had gone to work after the sale of that company. On the strength of my being his son I was granted an interview with its managing director, Lord Wolfson, a personal friend of Dad's whom I had met on various social occasions. So searching was the interview that I compared the experience at the time with being interviewed by a cobra. But even if I had been prepared to leave the law for industry (something I had previously done in reverse) I did not like the idea of being given a job under these circumstances, especially as it seemed to me that Leonard Wolfson wanted to recruit someone to be what amounted to his personal spy within the organisation. It was nevertheless good of him to have considered me, something which I knew was mainly predicated on his liking and respect for Dad[21].

I did in fact discuss quite seriously with John Alder that we might together start a bird-watching safari business, and I made some enquiries along these lines, but it seemed that anyone involved would need to be first and foremost a kind of travel agent and only secondly a birding tour leader. In the former area I had no experience at all, and there was both figuratively and literally speaking serious competition already in the field. Mention of the plan to Dad elicited the terse response: "You'll lose every penny you put into it!"

It was while considering these plans that I saw an advertisement for a parliamentary draftsman in Jersey, Channel Islands. With Irene's blessing I answered it. This was something that I knew how to do. I flew over to St Helier for the interview and was offered the job. Someone actually wanted to employ me! I made my apologies to John, but he understood the "bird in the hand" situation I was in.

---

[21] I was actually passed on for another interview with a senior manager in the company, but he knew as well as I did that we were was just going the motions for the sake of form.

Jersey 1985-6

The Channel Islands are Crown Dependencies[22]. They are not part of the United Kingdom (but part of the wider but not much used term "the British Islands") and are self-governing but subject to the UK Government in matters of defence and foreign affairs. They were originally part of the Duchy of Normandy and became part of the lands of the monarchs of England with the accession of William the Conqueror in 1066, remaining so even after King Henry III formally renounced claims to mainland Normandy in 1259. Some half-hearted attempts have been made in history by France to seize them back, last in 1781, but these all ultimately failed. Famously, during World War II they were occupied by Germany (the only parts of the British Islands to be so), having been reluctantly abandoned by Britain as being for practical purposes militarily indefensible after the fall of France in 1940[23].

There were practical problems to the job. Whilst I could for a while work on the basis of commuting weekly (flying out early on Monday mornings and home on Friday afternoons) this could not be done indefinitely. Sooner or later the family would have to move to Jersey and all the necessary administrative consequences faced: the search for a house, and for schools, if not for Rachel (by this time aged 16 and a boarder at Mill Hill) then for Jessie and Jonno. But firstly I needed to test the water, to see how everything might work out.

Jersey is in general a pretty little island of approximately 45 square miles (very roughly about 9 miles east to west and 5 miles north to south). From a north to south elevation it is shaped like a wedge, with a comparatively steep northern side, tapering down to sea level. Geographically it is part of France, sitting, as do all the Channel Islands, in the shallow Bay of St Malo. The island is only about 12 miles south west of Cartaret on the Cherbourg Peninsula in Lower Normandy and about 35 miles north of the port of St Malo in Brittany. The shallow sea means that on its southern side when the tide is out huge stretches of shore are revealed (at La Roque at the south eastern point of the island a spring tide can cause the water to retreat nearly 2 miles, giving rise to a danger of being cut off by the incoming tide, which you can actually see advancing up the shore).

---

[22] As also is the Isle of Man, and further-flung territories such as Gibraltar, the Falkland Islands, St Helena and a number of small jurisdictions in the Caribbean, the best-known of which is the Cayman Islands. The Channel Islands consist of two "Bailiwicks": Jersey and Guernsey, of which the latter includes also the islands of Alderney and Sark and a couple of smaller ones.

[23] There is a lively collectors market in the Channel Islands in German Occupation artefacts and documents.

In a way everything is, by mainland standards, in miniature. England's smallest county, Rutland, is 152 square miles, or nearly three and a half times larger, and the whole of Jersey is very slightly larger in area than the city of Bristol.[24] At the time in question it had a population of about 80,000[25] of whom about a third lived in St Helier, in effect the only town. Though it was originally French-speaking, and with a particular dialect of Norman French[26], since World War II the English language has become totally dominant; indeed, by 1985 those residents who were not born in the island (and came mainly from the UK) easily outnumbered those who were. Even the Jersey English accent, which sounds rather like that of English-speaking South Africans, was and is less and less heard. And if one hears a language other than English spoken it will most likely be Portuguese, by the migrant mainly agricultural workers from Madeira, or standard French, by tourists from the mainland.

It was into this small world that I arrived in September 1985. As a drafter of legislation (by then all new legislation was entirely in English, and only some of the pre-World War II statutes were still in French) I was employed in the States Greffe, in effect the secretariat for the States (the slightly odd name by which Jersey's legislature is known), although we draftsmen had quite a close connection with lawyers working in the Attorney-General's office across the corridor. We were all accommodated in the building in Royal Square that housed both the States and the Royal Court. Bordered as it was by the St Helier Parish Church and the main pedestrianized shopping streets, King Street and Queen Street, and with the central market only a stone's throw away, the Square was the central point of St Helier and of Jersey life in general. I was staying at the pleasant enough though rather old-fashioned Royal Hotel in David Place that was about ten minutes' walk away from the Royal Square[27], a walk that was accompanied by the incessant cawing of the herring gulls that are to be found in any UK coastal town. In fact nowhere on the island is more than about 2½ miles from the sea.

---

[24] In terms of Commonwealth jurisdictions it is however many times larger in area than the smallest, Gibraltar (2.3 square miles), and about the same size as Montserrat and Grand Cayman in the Caribbean (both with much smaller populations).

[25] In recent years this has risen to around 100,000.

[26] As an example of Jersey French (or *Jèrriais*), the standard French language words of welcome for Jersey, which would be *Soyez le bienvenue à Jersey* become *Seyiz les bienv'nus à Jèrri.*

[27] As can be seen, the Channel Islands are very much attached to the monarchy! The loyal toast is to "The Queen, our Duke".

Actually it seemed to be quite a sleepy little world. Work was generally speaking not done under pressure and no-one seemed to expect a large output of Bills (there known by the French term *projets de loi*). As I anticipated would happen, I was allocated work that had lain around for a while unattended to (what we expatriates in Kenya used to call "the too-hard-to-do tray") including a large *projet* to redraft Jersey's Companies Law. I did not mind; I was glad to be back at work and happy that I could once again do something useful. And it was all quite matey: other lawyers would drift into my office for a chat and maybe a cup of coffee, and I into theirs. Nowadays one might almost compare it to working in an internet café, although of course at that time there was no internet, and it was a few years before the era when computers were the standard machines for work, legislative drafting included. At these times I was quickly exposed to local professional gossip, inevitably revealing the likes and dislikes of individuals: this one was lazy, that one incompetent, etc.

But though my work colleagues were pleasant and friendly enough, that was where it seemed to end. I was not invited for a drink during out-of-office hours, let alone for a meal. And I found it difficult to get to know anyone outside the office. For example, soon after arriving I got in touch with the birding people (the local branch of the Royal Society for the Protection of Birds) and offered to give them a talk on the birds of East Africa. I think I'd have jumped at the chance if I'd been them; but they merely thanked me and said that their programme for 1985-6 was already fixed and full – perhaps next year? I did go to some of their meetings, but was clearly going to have to work hard over a period before I could be accepted as anything but an outsider. There seemed to be a kind of insularity everywhere that was in such marked contrast to the atmosphere of the expatriate life we had known in Africa. But, as I constantly needed to remind myself, Jersey residents were not expatriates. This was their settled society; why should they be interested in, let alone put themselves out for, a newcomer? Getting together some sort of social life from scratch was clearly going to take a long time, I thought, even given Irene's propensity for making friends.

The work I was doing, while reasonably satisfying, seemed to offer little prospect of advancement. And though I truly relished the opportunity to walk Jersey's coast paths and the former railway track from La Corbière at the south-western point of the island to St Aubin after work on spring and summer evenings and to study the birds and wild flowers, all that was only one element in Jersey life even for me. In short, I soon began to realise that I would not in all honesty be able to ask Irene and the children to uproot themselves again for an existence with so many imponderables to it. My constant coming and going was meanwhile putting a strain on the marriage;

by the time I had fitted back into life with Irene and the children at the weekend, it was time to leave again.

In the late spring of 1986 I therefore gave my notice to the States Greffe and left the island in July. The dispiriting search for work would have to resume in London[28]. It was somewhat ironic that a new Attorney-General for Jersey, Philip Bailhache, had been appointed during my time there, but that I did not actually meet him until a couple of years or so later, at a conference of small Commonwealth jurisdictions in Bermuda, since which time he and his wife Linda became very good friends. We visited and stayed with them many times after that and through them saw aspects of life in the island that would have taken us years, if ever, to find for ourselves.[29]

The Crown Prosecution Service 1987

The CPS had been established only in 1986 following a Royal Commission report. I had been advised by Richard Williamson, by then a senior officer in the organisation whom I had first met in Kenya, to apply for a post while there was still significant recruiting taking place. Still feeling the desperation of the months before Jersey, I did so. When, early in 1987, I turned up to a building in Whitehall for the interview, because of my age (forty-seven) the staff there at first assumed I was a member of the interview panel.

I was accepted and posted to the London Branch of the Service that dealt with cases principally at Camberwell Green Magistrates' Court. At the time it was housed in temporary accommodation in a building adjoining Southwark Bridge. Our job was to advise on the sufficiency or otherwise of the evidence on police files and to take cases that were to be prosecuted (most) to court. But everything seemed to be in a half-baked state. The office where we lawyers sat had an air of makeshift about it, and the administrative office, in which the occupants had Radio London playing quite loudly all the time (mostly pop music), was untidy, undermanned and inefficient.

Typically I would be given "the remand list" for a morning at court, consisting mostly of cases where there was to be an application for bail or

---

[28] I was actually soon afterwards offered a job with Garth Thornton, author of the leading textbook on legislative drafting and then Chief Parliamentary Counsel for Western Australia. But the prospect of moving to Perth was beyond anything Irene (and, by that time, Rachel too) would seriously contemplate.

[29] Philip was appointed Bailiff of Jersey from 1995 to 2009 and received the knighthood that customarily goes with the post. He was subsequently the first retired Bailiff to seek and win election to the States, where he became in effect Minister responsible for foreign affairs.

for one reason or another an adjournment was being sought, either by the prosecution or defence. Occasionally there was a plea of guilty to be dealt with. Typically there would be between twelve and fourteen cases in the court morning list, and equally typically two or more of the prosecution files would be missing from my bundle for that morning due to inefficiency in the administration. In these cases the court eventually and rightly lost patience and dismissed them for want of prosecution. The situation of being on the receiving end of the court's displeasure for this sort of inefficiency that was not my personal fault never ceased to rankle; at times, both in court and in the office, I felt like screaming.

Occasionally I prosecuted at a trial (i.e. where the accused person pleaded not guilty), but most of these were driving cases. It was all a bit like being back at the Bar when I had first started, only under considerably worse circumstances. In those former days I would probably have had one case in a court's list and it would have been properly prepared. In the office things were mostly routine and dull. Our guidelines stipulated that a prosecution should not be sanctioned where in our opinion there was a less than 50% chance of a conviction, as quite clearly it was wrong that the courts should be burdened with cases that would probably, due to lack of sufficient, or sufficiently credible, evidence, end in an acquittal. A minority of cases was rejected for these reasons.

One day I got a call from a police officer in charge of one such case in which I personally had advised rejection; he was beside himself with anger:

> "We are here at the sharp end of things with the task of catching criminals, and when we do, you bloody people just sit there in your offices saying that prosecutions cannot go ahead, and at the same time pulling the rug from under our feet. You know what these criminals are doing? They're laughing at us? And all because of you."
>
> "I am truly sorry that you feel like that. We have guidelines under which we have to operate, but I assure you that it is not our intention to undermine the police. Very far from it."
>
> "Go to hell!"

The phone was slammed down on me.

One had to hope and believe that many of the frustrations associated with the job would lessen as the Service became fully manned and hopefully more efficient. But the situation in which I found myself was not at all to my liking; apart from anything else I thought that my general legal experience was being wasted. I resolved to get out of it just as soon as anything better turned up.

As luck would have it something did, and after a period of only a few months.

The Commonwealth Legal Advisory Service 1987-94

What presented itself was, if not exactly the perfect job, a complete contrast. An institution known as the British Institute of International and Comparative Law (BIICL) had been formed in about 1960, with Lord Denning, probably the most brilliant and well-known English judge of the twentieth century, as one of its founders and its first Chairman. It was essentially an academic institution that, as its name implied, undertook research and study into international law and the ways in which different legal systems operated. Neither were actually subjects of much interest to me, but set up under the auspices of this institute was a tiny organisation known as the Commonwealth Legal Advisory Service (CLAS) and a professional colleague in the Commonwealth Secretariat tipped me off that a new director was being sought for it. The reason why soon became clear.

BIICL occupied part of the building that housed the Institute of Advanced Legal Studies, at the Russell Square end of a long five-story high concrete edifice erected in the 1970s that runs the length of the western side of Bedford Way and must rank in my opinion as one of the ugliest office buildings in London. By the early 1980s BIICL was moribund, but it had been turned around by its current energetic director, Lady Hazel Fox. The wife of Lord Justice Michael Fox and step-daughter of Lord Denning (her mother was his second wife) Hazel generally speaking ran it effectively. She was an academic lawyer of some note and edited its professional journal, the International and Comparative Law Quarterly. But personal relations were not her strong suit and she tended to upset people working under her and ride roughshod over anyone who could not stand up to her. The previous director of CLAS (who came into this category) was a retired senior civil servant, and had lasted only a year before asking himself if he really needed the job in these circumstances. The expression "getting a hand-bagging" at that time applied in particular to those who had been browbeaten by the Prime Minister, Margaret Thatcher, but it could equally have applied to Hazel's manner of operation.

For me, however, almost anything was better than the CPS. And here at least I thought I could not only use such skills as I had to better advantage but also to get to travel a bit. CLAS had been set up in 1962 to offer a service to Commonwealth Attorneys-General, mainly in the form of comparative legislative precedents from other Commonwealth countries, and to encourage the exchange of ideas between Commonwealth governments. The idea of being part of this process very much appealed to me.

I had always been keen on the Commonwealth as an institution. My childhood had been during what were effectively the last days of the British Empire, and children of my generation were imbued with the idea that its rule had, at least in later times, been beneficial and its legacies worthwhile. Though the Commonwealth was (and is) often sneered at as a largely impotent and pointless relic of that Empire (itself in modern times an object of almost obligatory retrospective hate), it seemed to me that it embodied what had been the most enduring beneficial legacies of British rule: the political and administrative systems it had bequeathed, English law and of course the English language. I really believed (and still believe) in the benefits of these things and did not need to be convinced that the assistance that I might be able to give would be valuable. I went for an interview with the directors of BIICL at the House of Lords (Lord Robert Goff, the then Chairman, was a Law Lord) and after a very matey interview was given the job. It had the added attraction that the appointment was for three days a week, which left me free to develop skills in other directions if the opportunity arose. As will be seen, in fact they soon did.

It quickly became apparent that Hazel Fox was working her way out of BIICL and that a new director for the organisation was being sought. A very bright solicitor with experience in private practice and in working at the secretariat of the European Court of Human Rights in Strasbourg, and some fifteen years younger than I, was duly appointed. Actually the first I heard of this was from Hazel: "He'll be above you", she told me laconically, with her customary tact.

Actually for me things started well, and in the total of just over seven years that I spent in the post, I too turned a moribund organisation around. When I started CLAS was dealing with only a handful of cases annually. I took several trips to countries in different regions of the Commonwealth to promote the organisation and by the time I left in 1994 we were dealing with around 50 requests for assistance annually.[30]

---

[30] These included such varied topics as the law on court bailiffs, leadership codes, the current status of the death penalty, the control of prospecting for fossils, constitutional limits on the right to free speech, the right to bail pending appeal, armed force in aid of the civil power, and codes of conduct for Ministers, MPs and senior government officials.

But all the same, as time went on it became apparent that two things were working against me. The first was an identity problem for my organisation. In 1965, only three years after CLAS had come into being, the Commonwealth Secretariat was set up in London[31], and a Legal Division created within it in 1969. From then on, once that Division began to establish itself, there was a continuing problem. Even though initially quite small it still had more staff and considerably greater funding than CLAS (I had a single researcher for just a small proportion of the time I worked as director, otherwise I was on my own), and as its operations spread it inevitably began to cover partly the same ground. Because of its inevitably higher profile it was soon better-known than CLAS and there began to be an assumption that both were part of the same organisation. This made the payment of annual contributions to it on the part of Commonwealth jurisdictions more and more difficult to collect: they did not see why they had to pay these to two organisations that were operating in much the same areas of work.

The second problem was the relationship with the director of the parent organisation BIICL. I found him difficult to work with; as with his predecessor in office, he did not in my opinion manage people well or get the best from them. He seemed to demand ever more of those of us working within BIICL for no increase in pay or conditions: for example when my researcher left and I tentatively made arrangements for her replacement, he told me that I had no business doing so and quite simply vetoed the employment of another. The combination of these things began to rankle, and for the first time in my life I found myself increasingly unhappy about working alongside a person (as opposed to for an organisation) with whom I was not in phase. I was not the only one; individual lawyers began to leave. Finally, in spite of my enjoyment of working within the Commonwealth and the success I was having with CLAS, I decided that I too had had enough, and in June 1994 I gave notice that I would leave by the end of that year.

Legal consultant

Two things had anyway meanwhile been working for me in the background, and these helped me decide on a further change of direction and made it unlikely that I would find myself at the advanced age of fifty-five once more on the job market. Both involved new or resumed acquaintances.

The first was the result of my having previously attended a Commonwealth Law Conference in Ocho Rios, Jamaica, in 1986, shortly after leaving

---

[31] Its home was Marlborough House, set between The Mall and Pall Mall, that had previously be the residence of King George V's widow, Queen Mary, and then of her son's widow, Queen Elizabeth, the Queen Mother.

Jersey[32]. There I had run into someone who was to feature in a significant way for some time in my life subsequently: Keith Patchett, then Professor of Law at the University of South Wales in Cardiff. I had first met Keith in 1980 when he and his wife Audrey had come to a Commonwealth-sponsored law meeting held in Nairobi that he and another law professor from England were leading. We had entertained them all while they were there, and I had corresponded with Keith on professional matters afterwards, as I was attempting to get implemented in Kenya legislation that he had drafted[33]. Although not a legislative draftsman, he had a brilliant legal mind and could turn his hand apparently effortlessly to most legal professional things. In fact he had recently been commissioned to take over the legislative drafting course run at the Royal Institute of Public Administration (RIPA) in Regent's College, London,[34] and, knowing my background, asked me if I would be interested in giving an annual morning's lecture session on the course.

I had gone to the Ocho Rios conference to put out feelers about possible consultancy work in legislative drafting. Sitting one morning at the hotel having breakfast on my own I saw a couple of tables away, also by himself, Sir Clifford Hammett, then I think Chief Justice of Fiji. Here was an important person to talk to about possible avenues for work. However, my nature is to be cautious in such situations, and so instead of just walking over to him, I sat at my table, a glass of orange juice in my hand, deliberating on how I would open my intended conversation with him. Suddenly I felt liquid falling on to me and, startled, jumped up. So intently had I been concentrating on the proposed conversation that I had not noticed that my glass of orange juice was some way from my mouth as I tipped it towards me in order to drink. Most of the contents of the glass had poured straight into my lap.

In fact, although unintended in this way, it was rather a good opening gambit, for he couldn't help but notice my discomfort and laughed as I mopped myself dry with a serviette. We did get to talk, although in fact nothing came of our conversation.

---

[32] These conferences, run every three years or so, are meetings of judges and lawyers from all over the Commonwealth that take place in a different Commonwealth jurisdiction each time.

[33] A model Act on reciprocal enforcement of judgements.

[34] In 1992 RIPA sold off its International Division (under which the drafting course was run) to Capita plc in order to try to stay afloat. This was the era in which the Conservative Government in the UK had stated that it would not continue to use public money to prop up failing institutions. In fact the sale did not help to keep the RIPA parent company in being, and it was anyway wound up a short time later.

The second acquaintance was Sir William Dale, an ex-Commonwealth Relations Office Legal Adviser of some stature in the legal world whom I quickly got to know quite well[35]. He occupied an office on the ground floor of the Institute of Advanced Legal Studies ("IALS" in whose building on the first floor BIICL and CLAS were situated). He was of course very much interested in the Commonwealth, and hence as to the person who was given the task of running CLAS. It was thus natural that I was sent to speak to him very soon after having been appointed its director.

Bill Dale had for some years, from even before his retirement from the civil service in 1966, run under the auspices of the IALS a comprehensive Government Legal Advisers Course that lasted for about three months (a length of training that was extremely long by later standards). It contained in it a module of about month or so on legislative drafting, and, discovering that I was an ex-parliamentary counsel, he was glad at that stage to have me as possible lecturer in reserve, especially after my early discussions with him convinced him that I favoured the same plain language approach to drafting as he did. In fact he had written a book on the subject, in which he had compared (unfavourably) the current British style of drafting to those of France, Germany and Sweden[36].

In fact the lecturing didn't happen until 1990, when the IALS secured a big British Government contract to teach legislative drafting to Nigerians and Bill found he couldn't manage on his own (he was eighty-three by this time)[37]. From that time on he brought me in to the Legal Advisers Course as well, and thus it was that, for ten years, I became in effect his assistant and began to take over responsibility for the largest share of the teaching on it. As with seemingly everything in or related to the academic world, the work was poorly paid, but I enjoyed it and soon realised that teaching was a skill for which I had a natural talent.

It was actually not my first experience of teaching law. I had started in Nairobi, when the then Director of the Kenya School of Law, Tudor

---

[35] He later gave me a signed copy of his autobiography *Time Past Time Present* that chronicles a full and interesting life.
[36] *Legislative Drafting: A New Approach.* I was not able to impress him with the fact that I had read it, because I hadn't, although I had certainly heard of it. But he considered, as I did too, that legislation should be as far as possible comprehensible directly by those to be affected by it (and not have to be "interpreted" for them by lawyers), and that the old-fashioned forms of expression (dubbed mockingly by some as "legalese") should be replaced by modern formal English and the resulting rules structured so as to assist the reader as far as possible.
[37] Nigeria was at the time just returning to a constitutional and elected system of government after years of military rule.

Jackson, had asked me to lecture to students who were studying for the Kenya Bar professional exams, on the subject of civil procedure (i.e. the required legal procedures in all matters relating to civil litigation). This had been something of a struggle at first, especially as Kenya didn't operate the English civil procedure system, with which I was fairly familiar, but the Indian. However, I soon got the hang of it, both from the point of view of the teaching and also, surprisingly, the need occasionally to keep students in check. For example, one of the students once asked me cheekily: "Why do you look like Bob Astles?" (Astles was at the time the European Chief of Staff to Idi Amin, the gruesome dictator in Uganda[38]).

Soon after my involvement with Bill Dale's courses, Keith Patchett found himself wanting to disengage to an extent from the (for him) onerous directorship of the RIPA course. He lived in Cardiff and the weekly commuting for what was then a ten-week course was becoming more of a strain. In early 1992 he was also involved with a drafting course for Nigerians at Regent's College, and invited me to share the lecturing on it. We worked together well and the experience led to an invitation to join him as joint-Director of Studies at RIPA on their annual course. Five years later he dropped out of the course altogether and left it to me to run on my own.

With Keith Patchett, Cardiff 2001

---

[38] Amin was notorious for having, amongst many other unpleasant things, expelled at very short notice all those of Asian origin from the country in the early 1970s. Something of the bizarre and at times terrifying nature of his regime can be gathered from the film *The Last King of Scotland* (the title referring to Amin's liking for appearing in Scottish-style military uniforms).

These consultancy jobs with IALS and RIPA gave me a platform from which to develop a career in teaching. In 1993 I was invited by the Commonwealth Secretariat to run a two-week course in Malaysia, and this was repeated the following year. By 1994 I had decided that I had enough potential to earn a living as a consultant without needing to hold on to my post at CLAS and, as has already been seen, I was not by then sorry to cut my link to it or its parent organisation BIICL. Thus began a career as a teacher of legislative drafting. Besides the courses in London, it would involve travel to a large number of overseas countries during the following twenty-five years to run short courses.[39]

The work was varied, as were the conditions under which I needed to undertake it. These ranged from at one extreme countries like Gibraltar and Malaysia where they knew exactly what they wanted and organised things well, to Ethiopia, Liberia and Nigeria where neither attribute applied. I was, at the end these latter assignments, thoroughly glad to get out of the country concerned, not because I felt myself to be in any personal danger, but because I was fed up with the general incompetence surrounding whatever I had tried to do. Indeed, getting out of Monrovia, Liberia, in December 2009 after my flight back to London via Accra, Ghana, was cancelled (due, I subsequently discovered to the runway having been blocked by airport staff protesting that they had not been paid) was an adventure of such proportions that I wrote it up in some detail.[40]

A typically African experience is summed up in my letter to Irene from Nairobi in January 1997. I had undertaken an evaluation exercise on the state of legislative drafting capacity there for the British High Commission the previous year and this had led to them agreeing to fund a 12 week legislative drafting course to be run by me. It was good to be back amongst so much that was familiar and the course actually turned out to be a success, but on the very first day things did not get off to a good start:

> The inevitable happened this morning. I arrived at the Law School, where the course is being held, to find –
> (a) the Principal, Mr Njagi, had not been officially informed that the course was to run there and so had nothing prepared;
> (b) only 4 of the 12 lawyers who are to be on the course were actually there (2 more turned up after an hour);
> (c) others, including James Hamilton[41] and the Principal himself were there, having been informed on Friday afternoon (incorrectly) that there was to be

---

[39] At the time of writing these have been in Brunei, Ethiopia, Ghana, Gibraltar, Kenya, Liberia, Malaysia, the Maldives, Nigeria, Pakistan and South Africa (some several times).
[40] It would unbalance the story here. See Appendix II.
[41] A friend and former principal partner in Hamilton, Harrison & Matthews, one of the leading law firms in Kenya. By this time he had retired from private practice and was the

an official opening of the course by the Attorney-General and the British High Commissioner (this is supposed to be on <u>Wednesday</u> morning).

After a largely wasted morning I got angry. I said I would not proceed with running the course until –
(a) the filthy classroom was cleaned and the floor polished;
(b) the screen for the overhead projector (both supplied by the British High Commission) was replaced by one which worked; and
(c) <u>all</u> the participants were assembled.

I rather laid into the BHC people, said that the whole show was a shambles which was wasting my time and their money, and requested (or rather demanded) that if things had not been righted by tomorrow we go and see the Attorney-General.

Well, I think that enough people are now sufficiently embarrassed (I said that, amongst other things, the shambles was a discourtesy to me personally) to get things put right. We shall see. It's the Africa we know and love (!)

The matters were attended to and the number of students originally detailed to attend (some of whom were apparently on leave) made up by a sort of Press Gang operation in which three or four lawyers from the A-G's Chambers were on the Tuesday morning to their surprise summarily ordered out of their offices to attend the course in order fill the quota. It was not the best way of ensuring dedication to it.

Bill Dale died in 2000 at the age of ninety-three. I was out of the country at the time, but on my return I was offered the chance to in effect take his place with the directorship of what was about to become the Sir William Dale Centre for Legislative Studies in the IALS. But I had no difficulty in turning the job down. The then director of IALS, Barry Rider, wanted me to undertake the work on a full-time basis: "the trouble is" he whined "we have very little money". When he threw in the comment that they would like me to make the course "a little more academic" (whatever that was supposed to mean) I knew I had no need to give the offer serious consideration. I did not even discuss the doubtless measly salary they were prepared to pay, while at the same time denying me the opportunity to earn outside money as a consultant. There was a repercussion to this temerity: except for minor involvement in one of their courses in 2002, I was never again invited to lecture on courses run at the IALS.

Although training constituted the bulk of my work from 1995 on, I always strongly resisted the idea that my courses are in any way academic; one of my fears was that they would become of less practical value and that I would

---

energetic Chairman of the Kenya Law Reform Commission (the body that had been set up while I was in Nairobi and had got off to a particularly bad start – see above chapter 8, p 292).

end up as my idea of a university don, a man somewhat divorced from the real world. The fact that one of the lawyers I most respected, Keith Patchett[42], was an academic lawyer didn't seem to reduce this irrational fear. But my teaching was anyway of practical skills for lawyers who mostly needed to go back to their offices and exercise them immediately. Besides, I did also undertake legislative drafting assignments from time to time, and in 2011 was first commissioned to draft model legislation for the Commonwealth Secretariat[43].

Teaching a class in Brunei. October 2013

Teaching is about involvement, both from the point of view of the teacher and the students. Legislative drafting tends to be thought of as a dull subject: if I'm asked at a cocktail party type gathering what I do, the questioner's eyes usually glaze over at my response, and sometimes he or she finds a pressing need to go and speak to someone over at the other side of the room. But actually there are no dull subjects; only dull people. I'm sure that over the years drafting has not seemed so to the vast majority of my students. Often they have really enjoyed it. One afternoon in the autumn of 2015 during what was to be the last legislative drafting course I ran at RIPA (its

---

[42] Keith suffered bad health for a number of years once he had reached his mid-seventies, and died in early 2014 at the age of 82.
[43] These have resulted in model Integrity in Public Life and Judicial Service Commission Acts.

parent company, Capita, decided to close it down in March 2016) my students had an almost riotously funny time, and the continuing laughter engendered could easily be heard outside the classroom. "What on earth was going on in your class?" I was asked by one of the other directors of studies during the subsequent tea-break. "Oh, we were just considering the efforts of some of the class to draft effective rules" I said.

Hilarity doesn't fit in with most people's conception of what is involved in the drafting of legislation.

Chapter 10
Gathering the Threads

Introduction	359
Politics	362
Religion	364
"More to Life"	368
The Arts	
Music	372
Theatre	375
Poetry, literature & language	380
Painting and architecture	382
Natural History	385
Collecting	388
Miscellaneous other interests	
Carpentry	395
Cooking	396
Travel	396
Sport	397
Dress	398
Family	399
Irene	399
Rachel	401
Jessica	402
Jonathan	403

Introduction

For most people the first half of their lives, or at least their lives up to about their mid-40s, are the most varied. A host of new experiences comes to us during that period, after which things tend to settle into a pattern of family, job and the continuance of outside interests that have been cultivated in the first period. My own life has followed this pattern, and although in this "second half" I have had many interesting experiences and had the opportunity to travel widely, especially in the course of my work, there have been few fundamental changes to, or strong influences on, my life. Notice however that I use the word "few" rather than "no".

Another factor relevant to my story is the way that memory works. Old people constantly remark on two things: firstly the apparent paradox that it is easier to remember things from fifty years ago than it is from a day ago.

Secondly that time seems to play tricks on us, so that an event that we think happened five years ago, we find when we have records that enable us to check on it, to have actually taken place ten years ago. I have not made a study of these phenomena, and actually scientists may come up with qualifying or contradictory evidence, but actually I think there are simple explanations for them.

As to the first of these, as one gets older life experiences constantly increase and the brain becomes to an extent saturated with them, so that ability to distinguish between them inevitably decreases. As a simple example, I can quite well remember exactly the times I went to the cinema or theatre as a young child, and the first few times I went abroad, but as an old person there are so many experiences of this type that there is inevitably difficulty in recalling them individually unless they have made an outstanding impression. And it is anyway not all events from our early days that come easily and sharply into focus; much of the detail is, in the absence of documentary evidence or the chance recollection of a close relative or friend, simply lost.

The second and interrelated matter is connected I think to proportions of one's life. Five years in the life of a child constitutes an enormous proportion of it; but for a septuagenarian that proportion is quite small. Hence, I believe, the apparent distortion in the different concepts of periods of time that have passed.

It is these things that explain why this story, and I think it is not untypical of its kind, concentrates far more on the period of my life to 1984, when I became 45, than it does on the period subsequently, and why it is that this chapter concentrates on individual facets of my life and family and pays little attention to chronology. In fact I always think of the year 1984, when the period in Africa came to an end, as a watershed year: life before it and life after it were in some ways quite different[1]. The former had been a series of expeditions into the unknown, while the latter mostly involved adapting to the known. This is not to suggest that life before was better or happier than life subsequently (in many ways I am happier in my seventies than I was as a young man), but in retrospect the latter has probably been more predictable and less exciting.

---

[1] To be more precise the watershed was the 26th May of that year, when I finally returned from Africa. As has been noted (chapter 8), for Irene and the children that disengagement had for practical purposes come nearly ten months earlier, in August 1983.

I have already looked at my working career[2]. What I want to do in this final chapter is to examine some of the things that have been important for me outside my work. They are so different that trying to place them in some sort of meaningful order is pointless, but I will start with the wider life issues that have affected me (though, as will be seen, not necessarily deeply) and then move on to the more personal ones.

Probably in common with a good few of my generation I find that many things that fill the newspapers are trite and uninteresting. I think the cult of celebrities, though probably inevitable, is shallow and silly and I am annoyed by television reporting of issues in the news that tries to involve its audience by concentrating on *victims*: wherever possible a camera is stuck in the face of someone weeping, or failing that people are encouraged to whinge about something they don't like. But then I tell myself that the news media have to write or present *something*, and there usually isn't that much happening that is really of interest. I read the Times not for its news (the standard of which I consider to have dropped to that of the Daily Express or the Daily Mail twenty or thirty years ago) but for the occasional interesting leading or columnist's article, for its columns on nature and the weather, and not least for its Sudoku and crossword puzzles.

Apart from family and relationships, the widest issues in most of our lives are probably religion and politics, both subjects on which my father used to say (doubtless following received wisdom) that one should refrain from discussing in company as it was impossible to make any headway. Religion involves a series of beliefs in the supernatural that are incapable of proof or disproof (superstitions in a word), and politics involves differences of opinion on the best form of governance (from national down to local or even workplace level) that are likewise usually incapable of proof except after a period of trial. The relevant beliefs and opinions are nevertheless usually strongly and rigidly held and discussion is unlikely to change them, so in a sense my father was right.

While reading a historical novel recently I came across the following telling passage that very effectively sums up the way mankind has thought throughout the ages, and in many respects still does:

> How men fear the chaos of the world, I thought, and the yawning eternity thereafter. So we build patterns to explain its terrible mysteries and reassure ourselves that we are safe in this world and beyond.[3]

---

[2] In chapters 3 and 9 particularly.
[3] The words of Matthew Shardlake, the hunchbacked hero in *Dissolution*, the first of C. J. Sansom's series of 6 novels set in the latter part of the reign of King Henry VIII.

He is actually speaking about both religion and politics.

Family, August 1989

Politics

In my teenage years I was told by my history teacher that it was to be expected that, given circumstances of reasonable economic stability, the young would want society to be reformed and the old would prefer the *status quo*. The latter, in the words of the old platitude, tend to be more conservative because they usually have more to conserve. In terms of UK politics that proposition translates (albeit only very roughly indeed) into the young voting Labour and the old Conservative. It is of course only a trend; many if not most people vote for one or the other party, or a different party, as a matter of personal or family habit[4]. However, the above pattern ascribed to the young and the old has by and large applied to me.

---

[4] In fact the notion that had always hitherto existed: that there are only two main political parties in the UK, has since 2010 seemed to be no longer necessarily valid, as evidenced by the political coalition necessarily formed that year between the Conservatives and Liberal Democrats, and the leap into the political unknown brought about by the (to me unexpected and unwanted) decision for the UK to leave the European Union following the referendum on the matter conducted in June 2016.

I used to think as a young man that I was interested in politics, but the truth is that have not usually followed peacetime current political affairs closely. I have never had the urge to be a social crusader (though I can respect those who are) and I dislike and distrust the politics of extremism. Though I first voted Conservative, as my parents did, I changed to Labour as I began to think as young people tend to do about (in my case rather vague) concepts of social justice. However my support for the centre left had definite boundaries. For example in my youth there was vociferous support mainly from the more extreme political left for the Campaign for Nuclear Disarmament, some of its adherents even going so far as to advocate that the UK should disarm unilaterally. I have never had any sympathy with such ideas, and when in the 1960s I voted Labour it was on the understanding that the party did not support it. But actually political debates, as with most arguments over the things that do not really matter that much (and I think there are very few that really do), usually bore me.

In did in fact vote for New Labour in the early years of this century. I thought it was a reasonable alternative to a Conservative Party that was by the end of the 1990s riven by dissent, and I had a good deal of respect for Tony Blair, one of New Labour's architects. I retain this, in spite of the popular opinion in the years since he left office in 2007, based on hindsight, that lambasts him for his having taken the country into the Iraq War (my own view is that on balance it was the right decision at the time). But actually I am, and think that certainly since my thirties have been, a natural adherent to the centre right. My thinking tends towards respect and admiration for those that try to do things for themselves, rather than sympathy for those that expect things to come to them or be done for them: what I sometimes think of as the "whinge culture" that seems constantly to be encouraged by the left-leaning BBC.

This does not mean that I think that State benefits should not apply to those that genuinely need help, and I am hugely grateful for the enormous benefit of the National Health Service. Centre politics are anyway largely a question of where the emphasis is put. My good friend from my days at the Bar, Shol Getz, who had a politically left outlook, used to say that he started off from the premise that strikes in industry were right. I have usually started from the opposite viewpoint.

A centre right political viewpoint is in the early part of the twenty-first century to an extent unfashionable in the middle class circles in which Irene and I have moved, and in which "Champagne Socialism" has for many decades been the vogue. Leftist politics are at any rate what many people of our acquaintance say they believe in.

Religion

I have previously explained my lack of religious belief.[5] Had I lived in past times I think I might possibly have been able to believe in God; there were many things that were unexplained, natural phenomena in particular including the origins of human life, that were once mysterious but which we now know about in detail. In the days before science was able to explain so much of what goes on around us it might just have made sense, for example, to believe in the story of God's creation of the world in Genesis.

But it can never have made sense to believe in Adam and Eve as the first humans created by God. Just to take the simplest of examples, where did their son Cain's wife come from? Or the wife of Seth, Adam's third son who replaced the murdered Abel and who we are told was born to Adam and Eve when they were aged a hundred and thirty? And, we are further told, at the time of the birth of Cain's son Enoch, Cain was building a city that he called after the child. Who was to populate this city? And could anyone seriously have believed that Methuselah was nine hundred and sixty-nine when he died? And moving on into the bible a bit can a rational person believe, for example, in the feeding of the five thousand with two loaves and five fishes, the converting of water into wine, or some of the other miracles ascribed to Jesus?

Theists today protest that this sort of story is today mostly accepted as just symbolism or allegory and that we have no need to take all parts of the bible literally. But, to quote Richard Dawkins:

> We pick and choose which bits of scripture to believe, which bits to write off as symbols or allegories. Such picking and choosing is a matter of personal decision, just as much, or as little, as the atheist's decision to follow this moral precept or that was a personal decision, without an absolute foundation. If one of these is "morality flying by the seat of its pants" so is the other.[6]

And throughout the ages people have read into the bible, or the Koran, justifications for just about anything, murder of course included.

I had occasion after a visit to Israel (a country I hugely admire) in early 2016 to return home on an El Al flight whose passengers consisted mainly of ultra-orthodox Jews (with British passports). I was one of the few "normal" people in my part of the plane. Doubtless it can be said that these people

---

[5] See chapter 1, p. 44 and following.
[6] *The God Delusion.* Bantam Press 2006, p.238.

show the same range of human attributes as any other social grouping of people, but I find them physically unattractive and baffling. What is it that induces men to wear a uniform of strange black outfits with wide-brimmed hats, white shirts and bits of string dangling from their trousers, not to speak of the ugly ringlets of hair dangling from the temples of many of them? And if this is strange it is nothing compared to the bizarre outfits some of them wear on the Sabbath. And why do their women have to wear wigs if they are married (actually I probably wouldn't be aware of this unless I knew that this is what they are required to do)? To answer my own question, it is of course the power of sections of human society over the individuals in it that forces such egregious behaviour. I understand this intellectually, but I have never been able to fully grasp how people can readily be induced to go completely against the grain of modern living. But I suppose they do not consider that they are doing so, and that everybody else is out of step.

On a number of occasions, someone has said to me (usually about an aspect of Christianity) "We believe that…" My question arising from this has been "But what do *you* believe?" to which the answer is usually "Well, *that* I suppose." I have been tempted to say, but of course don't, "You *suppose*?" It is simply evidence that what is called belief is really only a subscription to a particular culture that holds to a set of superstitions.

Indeed, the power of superstition (and into this category come all religious faiths that I know of) can be overwhelming. Think of the astronomer Galileo: in 1616, an Inquisitorial Commission declared that his stated opinion (following the findings of Copernicus) that the earth revolved around the sun rather than the other way round was "foolish and absurd in philosophy, and formally heretical since it explicitly contradicts … the sense of Holy Scripture." He was ordered to abandon that opinion on pain of conviction for heresy. Later, in 1632, he was in fact condemned for heresy anyway and sentenced by the Inquisition to imprisonment, though the sentence was commuted to house arrest (which continued for the remaining ten years of his life), and publication of any of his works was forbidden.

This is the kind of thing that can happen when people imagine that theirs is the only true religion, and are powerful, or desperate, enough to try to ensure that anything that is considered by them as threatening this appalling belief must be stamped out. In today's world this kind of thinking is mostly confined to Muslims of the more extreme kind, particularly those savagely barbaric adherents of the so-called Islamic State.

But I need to clarify that I am not at all arguing that religious faith itself is undesirable; indeed it undoubtedly has usually been, and remains, a strong force for good in the world, and I am mindful that, for example, a whole body of morals and ethics has been built up over the centuries in the Jewish religion alone. The kind of bigotry described above that has existed in former times (particularly in times before science began to explain the world in terms that were incontrovertible to thinking people) is fortunately in modern times comparatively rare in the western world. And although the kind of behaviour it can lead to, particularly in Muslims, can be gruesome, this is because of the crude and vicious nature of some of the people professing it, rather than the religion itself. In spite of my own lack of belief in God, I continue to be interested in what religions have to contribute to the world, and some people I can think of in whose company I am most happy to be are churchmen and rabbis[7]. I do nevertheless think that religious belief is becoming more and more difficult to sustain amongst thinking people in the modern world.

And there the matter might rest, except for the question whether my lack of belief nevertheless leaves me Jewish, and thus raises the never totally satisfactorily answered question: who or what is a Jew?[8]

One probably needs to believe in God to call oneself a Christian; so does one also have to so believe to call oneself a Jew? In other words, though there is probably no such thing as a secular Christian (and I say only "probably", as many people, though atheists or agnostics, might still happily regard themselves as belonging to a Christian culture) can there be a secular Jew? At base I think it has to do with adherence (however loosely) to a culture that is different from that of the mainstream, in my case of course that of Christian England and the UK[9].

In fact in past times, when religion really mattered (in the sense that adherence to religions other than the recognised one could lead to limitations being imposed on such things as ownership of real estate, membership of certain professions, and formal status in society) and it was easier to believe in God, I might, assuming I had a free choice in the matter, have thought it

---

[7] In particular Reform Rabbis David Woznica, Charles Emmanuel and Colin Eimer.

[8] The two terms here used remind me of Jonathan Miller's retort in the satirical comedy show *Beyond the Fringe* in the early 1960s to the statement by one of the others that he was a Jew. "I'm not a Jew," he replied, "I'm Jew*ish*. I don't go the whole hog".

[9] This is not of course to lose sight of the enormous disparities in belief and ceremonial between different sects of Christianity itself as practised in the UK, with Roman Catholicism at one end of the spectrum and Quakerism at the other. Indeed, when one adds to these the many other sects of Christianity both orthodox (e.g. Russian, Greek, Syrian, Coptic and Ethiopian) and "low church" non-conformist, it can be seen that it is probably misleading, except in the widest sense of belief in Jesus being the redeeming son of God, to speak of a Christian culture.

was a good idea to convert to Christianity. In the nineteenth and early twentieth century many Jews in Germany and other western European countries including Britain did that (I imagine even if they did not firmly believe in the Christian idea of God) as it was clearly easier to swim with the tide of the predominant culture (and not of course foreseeing the rise of National Socialism in Germany)[10]. I myself had a mainly Christian education and, as previously noted in chapter 1, doubtless because of this I have always felt more at home with Christian religious services than Jewish ones. But today I can intellectually no more believe in the Christian God, and the necessary attendant beliefs in the Immaculate Conception and the Resurrection, than the Jewish one.

To some extent the discussion is artificial, for decisions on culture and religion tend in practice to be made not so much by individuals alone as in the context of a family, or of a marriage or partnership. To take my own case, the loss of a Jewish identity is and has always been for Irene something not for a moment to be contemplated. I have recognised this, it to an extent sets the tone of our marriage and I am comfortable with it.

So how can I define myself? Short of conversion to another religion do I remain Jewish? Even if I were to convert, would I be regarded by those who had known me before as "the converted Jew"? I believe I probably would. Those of us born into a Jewish culture are a bit different from the mainstream, just as are those who are born in Britain into e.g. a Greek, Spanish or Polish culture (though these latter are of course still Christian), not to speak of those from the Middle East and beyond whose cultures and religions are in general very different indeed[11]. Though I am probably not taken for Jewish by those who do not know me, once I declare that fact I am probably seen, whether I like it or not, as necessarily being part of that different culture, and even though I lack the belief in God that underpins the culture must therefore be considered (and consider myself) a secular Jew.

While that is so for me in my lifetime, it need not apply necessarily down the generations. If my children, grandchildren or beyond, or some of them, choose not to associate themselves with Jewish culture and marry or partner those that are from outside it, the Jewish part of their heritage will probably gradually fade and eventually disappear altogether.

---

[10] In Britain the most famous examples were of course the Disraeli family.
[11] Not of course exclusively so. A number of well-educated friends and acquaintances from Muslim, Hindu and Parsee cultures think like me and lead lives that are very similar to mine.

"More to Life"

If religion has not had much direct effect on my life then something that in a sense came out of it has indeed done so.

As has been seen, except for my work in Jersey, in the two-year period from leaving Nairobi up to mid-1986, things had not gone well for me. In July of that year my work in the island finished and I was once again unemployed. In the meantime, in June, Irene had attended a weekend self-development course in London that she thought had been very helpful to her. It was apparent from hints rather than direct proposals that she wanted me to take it too. I was to say the least unenthusiastic; in those days the kinds of course that I understood it to be were less well-known than they became later, and I was anyway of the opinion that in adversity one should do ones best to sort out personal problems oneself. It was, so I had it in my mind, only self-indulgent people, or people I held as being in some way strange, who, unless their problems were manifestly chronic, went in for psycho-therapy or even counselling[12]. I did not see myself as a person of either kind, and did not consider the problems I had were of that magnitude.

Irene was nevertheless persistent. In the end I thought I had better take a look. Things were not at that time smooth in our marriage and I thought I had better be seen to be trying my best to keep things together. If we were to break up I could not then be accused of having failed to "leave no stone unturned" in my own search for a solution to our problems. I went to an introductory evening at a London hotel with Irene in August. I don't remember much about it save for talking at some length to a youngish man, introduced as David Templer, who seemed "normal" and sensible. He explained the course to me in terms that seemed to make sense, and I agreed to give it a go.

The programme to which I was introduced, originally known as the Life Training (later as More to Life), was created by two American former ministers of the Episcopalian Church, Brad Brown and Roy Whitten, in the early 1980s in San José, California, although the programme and basic weekend course they devised was not a religious one and was offered as being equally effective whatever a person's belief or non-belief. Brad and Roy soon enrolled others (who became known as trainers) to assist them in presenting the programme. In 1984 someone from London who had taken the basic course in California and was impressed with its effectiveness arranged for it to be brought to London. There it soon began running every

---

[12] I also had it (on no particular evidence) that Americans readily went in for this type of thing.

two months or so, led by one or sometimes two of these trainers who were flown over from the USA for the purpose. By the time I became involved it was run over a very full weekend, starting on a Friday evening until midnight and then on Saturday and Sunday until the same time. About 80 people had signed up for the course with me.

With Brad Brown, co-founder of More to Life, September 2003

At first I thought I had joined a bunch that contained some of the strange people I had feared might be attracted to this kind of thing. There was a large volunteer administrative "team" helping to run the weekend that contained people who introduced themselves at the beginning. Hardly any of them seemed to belong to the same world as I did. For instance, a number of men and women described themselves as "re-birthers" (it was explained to me at the time what this was, but I have long since forgotten). "What" I asked myself "have I got myself into here?" But I am not a quitter, and having signed up for something I usually see it through.

People were invited at various points during the weekend to "share" relevant experiences (the American usage of this word was new to me then in this context; I would have said "describe" or "tell about"). Some of these "shares" I regarded as rather pathetic: "How can that possibly be a problem" I would say to myself about a typically snivelling young woman with the microphone whom I found not only undeserving of my sympathy but positively irritating; or "Why doesn't the trainer just tell her to get a grip of herself?" Nevertheless slowly but surely some people's stories (particularly, but by no means only, from men) did resonate with me as touching on problems with which I could identify.

We were invited to undergo a series of exercises, known as processes, designed to get us not only to recall difficult times in, or aspects of, our lives, and to examine them in depth, but in particular to feel the feelings associated with them. From the outset I found this difficult. For example, on one occasion when I had volunteered to take the microphone and was relating the difficulty I had had in returning to London from Africa two years before, the trainer, Sue Oldham, asked me at some point how I felt. Having at her invitation already gone on for a little while about the story (too long, I thought), I said "I feel that I am boring the pants off everybody". "That's a thought, not a feeling" she said (she also verified that I was not in fact boring people). It was my first introduction not only to this common inexactitude of language, but to the fact that emotions are always accompanied by feelings somewhere in the body. In my experience women are much better at identifying these feelings than men, and I am probably worse at doing so than most men. It was nevertheless an important lesson.

At some point on the Sunday morning I suddenly "got it", and began to see myself, and those around me, in a new light. From being someone who had been for some while depressed, turned inward and held back, I became connected to those around me, both fellow students and administrative team. It had come about especially after a cathartic exercise called at that time a "No Process" during which I had with help managed to feel and to shed two years of resentment at having been (as I previously saw it) "forced" to leave Kenya against my will.[13] I was shown that I had in fact made my own choice to come back. I could have made the choice to stay; there would have been consequences arising from such a decision, but the important thing to see was that there was, as there always is, a choice to be made. Even doing nothing involves, consciously or unconsciously, a choice.

Obviously the weekend experience did not change me in the sense of making me a different person, but what it did do was to make me much more aware of myself and what was going on around me than I had been hitherto[14]; and it gave me a series of exercises I could use to help to get me out of difficult times. Actually I do not use them very often, but I am conscious that I can and that sometimes I am making a choice not to do so. The understanding

---

[13] This process (pronounced by Americans with a short "o" as in "cross") was later changed slightly and renamed. John Alder, who took the course when it still had its original name, used to call it a "Nose press".

[14] One of the watchwords of the course was "notice". A big sign was displayed in the training room with just that one word on it.

that we all have the power to free ourselves from depression and general "negativity" was and is supremely empowering.

Involvement with More to Life could have ended there, but other courses were additionally offered, on such things as personal relationships, relationships with money, the dramas that people present, etc., and there was also the opportunity to become a mentor within the programme and teach courses to others on self-esteem and on purposefulness. Irene chose to do so and ran such courses for many years, besides working part-time for the organisation at its London headquarters in Belsize Park.

Quite apart from the benefit to both of us of those separate weekend courses we first took, and subsequently various others, we became in effect part of a community of people who, because they have been through the same self-examination processes, we found very congenial. They are largely down-to-earth and easy-to-be-with men and women from all walks of life who are not afraid to openly and frankly tell the truth about themselves and their lives. David Templer, the man I had first been introduced to, in fact became the first British trainer, and he and his partner Maggie Spooner, and many others over the years, have become good friends.

Irene gets her BSc, April 1993

The Arts

Music

Unlike most people I know, music has been important to me all my life. I have never learned to play a musical instrument or to sight-read music (though obviously I can see where notes are higher or lower, longer or shorter) and my knowledge of musical structure and harmony is rudimentary. But music "speaks" to me and I can, if in the right mood, get carried quite away by it, even to the point of tears. This does not have to be in a formal concert environment, and can be even when hearing music casually on the radio.

But I need to clarify that when I speak of music I do not include "pop" music[15]. I think I remember correctly the famous violinist Yehudi Menuhin being reported as having politely turned down a request that he should perform together with the Beatles, and when pressed for a reason he said that there was in the pop genre "very little musical content". While in the case of the Beatles themselves that would be an unfair comment on some of their later work, and I do in fact like the occasional song in this genre, in general this comment holds true for me, and I am actually repelled by the sight of scruffily or ridiculously dressed musicians and singers leaping about on stage with or without electric guitars and screaming into microphones.

But my tastes are by no means restricted to what is generally called classical music (probably "serious music" would be a better label) and I very much like singers and bands/orchestras of what these days come under the general and also misleading label "easy listening"[16]. I also like much film music, some jazz, most swing music of the 1930s and 40s, "folk" music and a wide variety of ethnic music (Greek and Israeli popular music in particular), including Indian classical music, although the music of China and Japan is generally a little too far from the normal range of other music to interest me.

But top of my list are the pieces of music that so much draw me into them that they usually induce me to drop whatever I am doing and listen entranced whenever I hear them on the radio or elsewhere. To name but a few and in no particular order: Beethoven's 9th Symphony (the Choral, especially the

---

[15] I am conscious that within this term are various sub-genres of music, e.g. rock, heavy metal, the kind of spoken "rap" music, etc. but with few exceptions I have no liking for any of them.
[16] Light music might be a better term, although that tends to be reserved for lighter serious music of composers such as Eric Coates, Haydon Wood, Robert Farnon or Ronald Binge. The last of these, whose works *Elizabethan Serenade* and *Sailing By* are consistently played on the radio (and both have reached Classic FM's top 300) was the father of our friend Maggie Spooner mentioned above.

final movement) or his *Moonlight* sonata; Mozart's trio *Soave sia il Vento* (may the wind be fair) from *Cosi Fan Tutte*, the *Lacrimosa* (tears) from his Requiem Mass, or *Ave Verum Corpus* (behold the true body); Bach's chorus *Wir setzen uns mit Tränen nieder* (we sit down in tears) from the St Matthew Passion, or the chorale *Wachet auf ruft uns die Stimme* (Sleepers wake!) from his cantata no. 140; Gregorio Allegri's *Miserere*; Thomas Tallis' *Spem in Alium* (I never had hope in anything but God); Vaughan Williams' *Fantasia on a Theme of Thomas Tallis* or *The Lark Ascending*; G F Handel's *He shall feed his flock* or *I know that my redeemer liveth* from the Messiah or the fanfare-like *La Réjouissance* (the rejoicing) from the Music for the Royal Fireworks; Antonio Vivaldi's *Nulla in Mundo Pax sincera* (no true peace in this world); Samuel Barber's *Adagio*... There are at least as many again.

Nor does the "drop everything" factor apply to classical music alone. There are many songs that stop me in my tracks too: Stephen Sondheim's *Send in the Clowns* is probably my all-time favourite, but others (again in no particular order) are close behind: Cole Porter's *Begin the Beguine* and *I've got you under my Skin*; Charles Trenet's *La Mer* (the sea); the Carpenters' *We've only just begun* and *Yesterday once more*; Consuela Velasquez' *Besame Mucho* (kiss me passionately), Frank Sinatra singing *Goodbye* and *Willow weep for me*; Paul Simon's *Bridge over Troubled Water* and *Graceland* (the whole albums); Abba's *Voulez Vous* and *The Day Before you Came*; Don McLean's *Vincent* (see also below under painting); and many more...

I was captivated in the 1960s by the singing of Joan Baez (though I found her too-often-heard facile leftist political statements irritating) and later in a similar style by Irish singers and songwriters Lorina McKennit and Enya. And I love Greek popular singing too, especially by Georgos Dlaras and Dimitris Mitropanos. There is an enormous amount for me also in the music of the English composer John Barry[17], John Williams (the composer), John Williams (the classical guitarist), Ludovico Einaudi and Phillip Glass; and this is not even to speak of Latin American music, especially tango, or the wonderful pan-pipe music from the Andes. And I love to listen, particularly late at night, to Gregorian chant. There is a great wealth of marvellous music, and it is so easily available to us. Our ancestors had to create their own; we are so very lucky.

---

[17] In particular his wonderfully evocative theme music for "Out of Africa", a film that struck personal chords sufficiently to reduce me to tears when I first saw it, and some of his lesser known but equally great non-film pieces, of which the best for me are "The Beyondness of Things" and "Give me a Smile" (the latter I used as theme music when directing "Separate Tables" – see below).

In fact so much music is constantly available on radio programmes such as Classic FM (*"Tha warld's greatest music"*) that I have needed to limit my access to it for fear of tiring of good music from overexposure, or having it as just mindless background noise. In the case of Classic FM this abstention is not difficult owing not only to the fact that it is a commercial station with constant irritating advertisement breaks, but also the tendency of its presenters to use irritating clichés: I get a little tired of being told to "sit back, relax and unwind" (a similar cliché to that used by airline pilots at the beginning of a flight), or that I am "in for a treat" with the next piece of music. And I can't abide the sickly-sweet tones of some of its presenters, especially some of the women, whose programmes I make a point of not listening to.

But so much for the "passive" or purely listening aspect of music. Given the fact that I have never learned to play an instrument[18] the only musical sound I could actively make was, as I once heard a lecturer on African music say, "with my face". Part of me had believed since school days that I could not really sing (the experience of being shifted to different sides of the piano in music lessons at Belmont has been described in chapter 1). True, I knew I could sing effectively in unison, as I had done for years singing hymns and psalms in the school chapel, for a short while singing other music too in the Choral Society at Mill Hill, and occasionally in a chorus in stage musicals. And so long as I had a leader for more difficult bits I could sing in harmony in a choir (on more than one occasion in Handel's *Messiah*).

Nevertheless, in later life I was still a bit unsure of my ability. In fact of course singing is largely a matter of confidence; most people can actually sing, even though they think or persuade themselves they can't. Abstaining from singing is usually a matter of choice (i.e. from timidity) rather than because of any real lack of ability. I discovered this for myself when I joined a group called "Singing for Pleasure" in 2012. The teacher for this little group of some 15 amateur singers, Helen Swift, was determined to do what she could to allow us in her class to reach our potential, and we were all required to sing solo at different times during each two-hour session. More than that, we were encouraged to insert variations into the notes of a song, particularly at the end of it.

Singing solo is of course a quite different proposition from singing in unison, and when I'm "out on a limb" in this way there is usually a little internal voice in my head constantly saying to me "You're going to get the

---

[18] And don't want to, as I fear the standard I could reach, particularly in this late stage in my life, would be bound to be low.

wrong note!" The object is to train oneself to ignore or drive through this "mind-talk" and simply go for the song. Many of the songs I have chosen to sing solo were from my favourites stated above. The pleasure for me in achieving something in this way has been enormous, and it encouraged me to audition for and take a singing part in more than one musical show.

And then of course there is dancing. I have been lucky to have in Irene a dancing partner who is very good. There is still a (fading) hope that we might get our Latin American dancing to a better standard, especially the tango. To me this is the dance that represents the summit of the art; its rhythms seem to grab me somewhere between the shoulder blades, and to dance it well one needs to be able to move like a panther.

Theatre

For most people, involvement with the theatre is as audience. Though I have of course seen my fair share of theatrical productions, this kind of entertainment is one in which as a general rule I prefer to participate rather than to watch. Whereas singing is an art I have needed to work at, acting is one that has always come fairly naturally to me, both in the sense of being able to realistically represent another character and of the equally important awareness of the positioning of myself and others on stage. I once answered an advertisement in the Times calling for participants to appear on a television show about Amateur Dramatics. Someone on the production team telephoned me and asked me why it was I liked dressing up in other peoples' clothes. It was a silly question: the reason I like acting is that I like telling a story. I did participate but my contribution was edited out of the screened show![19]

Something of my potential must have been apparent to my teachers early on, for at Belmont I had some small leading roles at an early age, but there was no particular encouragement for me to continue acting afterwards either there or at Mill Hill, and, not at that time being aware that I had an above average ability, I did not push myself to do so. Any willingness to go further lay dormant until suddenly an opportunity arose to take it up again in Malawi. Experiences in the theatre in Malawi and Kenya have been related in the relevant chapters.

---

[19] It was one of a series presented by Esther Ranson in the 1990s. In fact, as I should have known, she and the producer were not really interested in why people acted, or on exploring anything but the highly unusual or sensational, e.g. where someone had had a heart attack on stage, or where a woman had had a baby in the wings.

In London I had originally joined what became the Garden Suburb Theatre in the short period back in London between Malawi and Kenya, when I was given a tiny part in the pantomime *Alice in Wonderland* in early 1976 (that of the lion in the lion and unicorn duo) wearing for the purpose a ridiculous outfit and undertaking in the role an equally ridiculous "fight" choreographed by Terry Rogers, more of whom below. But pantomime is supposed to be ridiculous, and as already described in chapter 1 it is a form of entertainment that as a child I found incomprehensible and which I have grown neither to appreciate nor enjoy.

My main involvement in acting with the GST started after my return from Kenya in 1984 and throughout the years since then I was involved in numerous productions. A few of these were memorable for me: playing Colonel Pickering in Bernard Shaw's *Pygmalion* (1986), Sir Robert Morton in Terrence Rattigan's *The Winslow Boy* (1991), various roles and Ralph Nickleby respectively in adaptations of *The Canterbury Tales* (1990) and *Nicolas Nickleby* (1998), Uncle Ben in Arthur Miller's *Death of a Salesman* (2001, which we also took to the Isle of Man the following year for their Festival of Plays), Stanton Case in Miller's *Broken Glass* (2003) and Herr Schultz in the musical *Cabaret* (2016).

On one night during the production of *Pygmalion* something happened that still makes me smile whenever I think of it. At one point in a scene involving me as Pickering, Professor Higgins (played by Bill Critchley) and others, Higgins needed to sink into a chaise longue. Unfortunately the stage crew had forgotten to put chocks under the casters of the chaise and as he threw himself a little too violently into it, it careered backwards and collided with the bottom of one of the scenery "flats" with sufficient force to dislodge the braces and weights behind it holding it in place. The 8ft x 4ft flat seemed to lurch forward in slow motion and topple on to Bill who, acting instinctively, was by that time positioned beneath it with his arms outstretched above his heading. Imagine the scene: the principal actor, with his back to the audience, literally propping up the scenery. It seemed to me to epitomise "coarse acting" and to my shame, instead of immediately going to help him (actually the flats, though large, are canvas stretched on frames and not all that heavy), all I did in the first instance was to go up to him and tell him I'd never seen anything so funny in my life. Not surprisingly in retrospect, he was furious. All of this was of course in full view of the audience. As I began to gather my wits and help him, we were rescued by the curtain (these were still the days, unusual later on, when use was made of the main theatre curtains, or "tabs" as they are known in the profession) and, after the stage crew had reset the scenery, needed to begin that scene again.

In *Nicolas Nickleby* I was required in the role of the miserly uncle, Ralph Nickleby, to commit suicide by hanging myself on stage towards the end of the play. To do so I needed to wear a harness under my costume with a hook attached that I was required subtly to attach to the upper part of the noose before jumping off a ledge and letting myself swing in the air "dead". Before I knew anything about the apparatus I had expressed my nervousness about the safety of the process to the director, Richard Kinder. "Don't worry" he replied "I need you for more than one performance!" In fact the resulting "suicide" was sufficiently realistic to cause occasional gasps from members of the audience.

The sad fact about acting is, however, that there are increasingly few decent roles for older people, and from having been involved with acting in at least one production a year, my involvement since the turn of the present century has been considerably less. Interestingly, the only two productions since 2003 I have been in were productions that required me both to act and to sing solo: Alan Ayckbourn's comedy *A Chorus of Disapproval* in 2014 and the well-known musical *Cabaret* in early 2016 (the stage sore and script for this show is different and I think has considerably more depth than the film version).

In both I was lucky in that the directors, Francis Beckett and Nick Hastings respectively, knew me well and what I could do, and were prepared to offer me good parts in spite of my age. Actually both shows were very well received, and in general I was pleased that I was able to contribute some depth to that latter dark musical. With the considerable amount of singing and dancing required, it was a big stretch for the director and all of us involved.

I myself had directed plays in Malawi and Kenya, but my first attempt at doing so for a full production in London (as opposed to a rehearsed play-reading) for the GST was in 2003 with Terence Rattigan's *Separate Tables*. This, which we put on at what later became the Henrietta Barnet School auditorium was a great success and we won the prize for the best overall play in the Barnet Festival of plays for that year.

My next attempt at directing, could, however, hardly have been more of a contrast or turned out worse. It was Michael Frayne's *Benefactors* in 2007, and in that production everything that could go wrong did. I had difficulty with casting: it had a cast of only four, but so few auditioned that I was forced to accept those who did (although by and large they were in fairness actors I was happy to have), and then in getting sufficient rehearsal time (one member of the cast needed to take time out on holiday). Cuts to the text that I had wanted to make were not accepted by the copyright holders and I had to reinsert them at the last minute, wrong-footing the cast. I had not had been able to get a set designer or stage manager and needed to rely on a fairly bare set. The result of all this was that the opening performance at the Gatehouse in Highgate was like a rather bad dress rehearsal. This time we came last in the entries for the Barnet Festival, the adjudicator giving the opinion that the production was in effect rather like a rehearsed play-reading[20]. She was right. I was so upset by the whole thing that I vowed to myself that I would not attempt to direct again. Memory of the experience caused me to shudder inwardly for years afterwards.

Nevertheless, after the debacle with *Benefactors* I was persuaded by Terry Rogers, the choreographer of my lion fight back in 1976 and by 2010 the chairman of the GST, to direct a rehearsed play-reading. "Come on; we all have failures!" he said, urging me to get out of my negative mood and just do something again. The result was my direction in that year of a rehearsed play-reading of *The God of Carnage* by the French playwright Yasmina Reza. This time I promised myself that instead of a full production that seemed like a rehearsed play-reading, this would be the other way around: a rehearsed play-reading that looked like a full production. And I was lucky to have both a talented cast and a first-class venue.[21] I was really pleased with the result.

I have admired Reza's work since seeing a production of that play on the London Stage[22]. In fact she made her name earlier with *Art*, a three-hander which ran in London for eight years from 1996. I decided I would like to direct it. Alas, one of the difficulties for amateur groups, especially in London, is getting acting rights. *Art*, we were told by Samuel French the copyright holders, was simply not available for us. Oh well, I thought, why not do a full production of *The God of Carnage*? But that was not available either. However her play *Life x 3* was; even though it was my third choice, I decided to give it a go. It is an interesting play in which essentially the

---

[20] A production in which the cast read from their scripts but otherwise act as though in a full production. In practice the set is usually quite crude as there is neither time nor money to build anything much. The process also places limitations on what actors can do, as they have only one hand free for props and activities.

[21] It went on at the Finchley Youth Theatre, a venue not normally available to us for full productions. The cast of Stiofan Lanigan-O'Keefe, Emma Pleas, Toby Moore and Miriam Clarke could hardly have been bettered.

[22] Reza is the daughter of an Iranian father and a Hungarian violinist mother (both Jewish) and grew up in Paris. *The God of Carnage* was later made into a film entitled simply *Carnage*, directed by Roman Polanski and featuring Kate Winslet and Jodie Foster as the two women in the cast of four.

same scene is played three times, but with a subtly different interplay between the four characters each time.

The venue this time was the Bull Theatre in Barnet. Originally a pub, the conversion was made around 1990 and the premises are now used mainly as the Susie Earnshaw Theatre School. The theatre has a good-size auditorium for us (seating 150) and good theatre facilities, although the stage is rather wide and without much depth and has (unless there is a rear curtain) a stage exit on only one side. The main drama however came to be over the stage management for the production.

Bernard Smith had been my stage manager for *Separate Tables* ten years before. A management consultant of rather dour aspect, he was a good organiser and had contributed a good deal to the success of that show. When some time later I was complaining to him about what had happened in *Benefactors* he told me that I should have asked him to stage manage it. Yes, I thought, he's right. So it was that he was the person I naturally turned to for *Life x 3*. And this time (May 2013) I had a really good cast.[23]

I hardly saw Bernard before the last couple of rehearsals, but things did not look good when we were getting into the theatre on the Sunday before the show (we were to open on the Wednesday). As we were moving in the stage set and furniture he seemed to be constantly simmering with anger and snapping at people. What is more he developed a proprietary attitude to the task and seemed to assume that nothing could be done in the theatre by anybody (including me as director) without his permission. He even purported to refuse to allow any changes to be made to the set once we had erected it. By the first dress rehearsal his attitude was affecting the cast.

It was enough. During a sleepless Monday night (we had one further dress rehearsal to go before opening) I decided that Bernard was acting not *with* me and the cast but against us, and he had to go; if not, it was a virtual certainty that the show would not reach its potential. And we were after all in a competition. It was a bold decision to have to make so late in the day and I did not know how we would manage. I did not even know if he would purport to override my authority and claim that *he* could sack *me*. I rang him the following morning and told him that though I respected his ability, I simply could not work with him any longer. He rang me back subsequently to say that he and his partner, Pauline, who was in charge of props, would come round to our house later that morning. I had half feared that they wanted to offer some sort of compromise (which I told myself I was not

---

[23] Stiofan Lanigan-O'Keefe, Emma Pleas, Nick Hastings and Emma Sullivan.

going to accept); but they didn't, they just came to deliver keys and props in their possession and wash their hands of the show. As I had expected would be the case, Pauline said she also could not continue, and no, she was not prepared to instruct anybody as to what needed doing as regards props.

It was a turning point. Veronica Woolf, who had been my production assistant, stated when I rang her to give her the news that she thought she could do what was necessary to stage manage the show. I was almost in tears with relief. The cast too heaved a collective sigh of relief, and between all of us we worked out solutions for the problems raised by the events described.

It would be nice to be able to report a fairy-tale finish, but in fact we came only third in the Barnet Festival competition for that year. For what it's worth, I thought our production deserved better and was in fact among the best things of its kind the Garden Suburb Theatre had done in recent years[24].

Poetry, literature & language

None of these subjects was one that particularly struck a chord with me in my school days. They have grown on me since, although poetry that has no recognisable structure remains almost as much a mystery to me as abstract art. In fact the beauty of the flow of language is something that has gradually crept up on me, and the reading and reciting of poetry (in a rather conservative way – as with novels, see below) is something that has become in the late stages of my life genuinely enjoyable.

Shakespeare is always held up as the greatest poet and playwright that ever lived (at least by English speakers), but my exposure to his works at school seemed to do little to convince me of this. It is true that I enjoyed Henry IV Part 1, which had a series of plots and sub-plots, but the language itself (once I had understood it) did not strike me with its beauty. And as I got older it was more apparent to me that many of the plots of his plays were not very believable, and by modern standards at least even a bit silly (Comedy of Errors, Much Ado about Nothing) or, for me personally, unduly gruesome (Richard III, Julius Caesar, Othello).

---

[24] Two of the cast (Stiofan and Emma P) did at least get nominations for best actor and actress; but the other two could in my opinion equally well have done so. It was our bad luck that in that year the standard was, in the words of the Festival Chairman, particularly high. We were up against two productions in particular that must have been exceptional and had really impressed the adjudicator. To be fair to Bernard, it transpired not long afterwards that Pauline had cancer (in fact she died in 2015), and although we had no inkling of that at the time, assuming it was known to both of them it would undoubtedly have affected their attitude towards all sorts of things.

Nonetheless, there are undoubtedly many passages of very fine writing and I have enjoyed reciting on a few occasions extracts from a presentation entitled "Shakespeare in Medicine" put together by a friend and former senior pathologist, Howard Jacobs. Further, I have sufficiently loved two pieces in particular (the Prologue to Henry V, and the "To be or not to be" speech from Hamlet) to incorporate them into my repertoire of pieces I can recite by heart and occasionally share with various groups of people who seem happy enough to come along and listen.

In fact for these recitals comic verse has been much more popular than serious poetry (of which most people seem to be wary, probably fearing that it might be beyond their comprehension). In an age when entertainment is available all the time on television or through the medium of computers, reading or reciting poetry (let alone doing so from memory), and reading prose, aloud seem to have become almost obsolete as forms of entertainment. Many of the comic pieces were made popular by Stanley Holloway in the days when "knives and forks" entertainment in restaurants and night clubs while guests ate or drank was common[25]. Other exponents were Noel Coward and the Grenada-born singer Leslie Hutchinson ("Hutch"), and recordings of all three were widely played on old-fashioned gramophone records in my childhood.

I have never consciously read "literature" (in the sense of classic novels) for its own sake, and for example the works of well-known writers of the nineteenth century (Dickens, Eliot, Thackeray, Trollope, etc.) do not really interest me. But good fictional writing set in, or partly in, my own lifetime is something that in a conservative way I am very much attracted to, none more so than in series of novels that are set particularly well in a time and background that interests me. For a detailed description of the final days of British rule in India, Paul Scott's "Raj Quartet" of novels (together with its wonderfully humorous sequel "Staying On") is to my mind a masterpiece, as is the "Strangers and Brothers" series of eleven novels by C P Snow that chronicle upper middle class English life in the period from about 1920 to 1970, and I have read and enjoyed nearly all of the novels by Graham Greene. To a lesser extent I have enjoyed also the twelve novels of Anthony Powell's "Dance to the Music of Time" series, set in much the same period

---

[25] In particular the verses by Marriot Edgar (a half-brother of the novelist Edgar Wallace) in the "Albert and the Lion" vein and Weston and Lee's bitter-sweet cockney rhyme "Brahn Boots". But this form of entertainment is not in fact dead: Peter Christie (a friend and almost exactly contemporary pupil at Mill Hill School) and his group "Instant Sunshine" are a wonderful example of the continuation of this genre.

as those of Snow, and Lawrence Durrell's "Alexandria Quartet" set in Egypt in the 1930s.

In a lighter vein, I have been since childhood an enthusiastic reader and re-reader of Sherlock Holmes short stories and novels, and have read with interest and pleasure, as well as huge respect for the research involved, the historical novels of Mary Renault set in ancient Greece (previously recalled in chapter 6), and those of C J Sansom set in England in the Tudor period. I have of course enjoyed many other individual novels over the years, although unlike in the case of my mother reading of these has never occupied a large proportion of my reading time.

It will be apparent that language and its spoken and written use are of interest, and indeed important, to me. I am disconcerted at what I see as the dumbing down of language, particularly in television and radio, and by the fact that so many who appear there seem to need to go to great lengths to persuade us that they are not "posh". This silliness leads to a coarsening of spoken language itself, for example by the use of a glottal stop in place of a final "t" in a word and constant use of cliché expressions with virtually no meaning that are favoured by people who are not used to thinking before (or even while) they speak: "at the end of the day", "that's what it's all about (in' it?), and "know what I mean?" Sometimes, in a meaningless flood of words, all three are rolled together.

Worst of all, following the example of younger Americans, is the beginning of spoken sentences, and the punctuation of every three or four words thereafter, with the contextually meaningless word "like". When this nonsense finally passes, as it surely must, future generations will wonder how, for example, "I'm/was like…" (or even "Like, I'm/was like…") came to mean "I said" or "I thought"; how "I was like yeah/no" meant "I agreed/disagreed"; or how "I was like oh my God" came to mean "I was surprised/upset". I believe this brand of diseased language started in America in the early 1960s among the "hippy generation" before spreading to English speakers under about age 50 everywhere, including those whose first language is not English.

Painting and architecture

It is in these areas of the arts that I have always considered myself to be the least educated. This is not to say that I have no appreciation at all for either, but I have always thought that it is somewhat rudimentary. In my late teens I made an effort to look at the pictures of some of artists of the so-called modern school of painting (in fact a general name for painting that did not represent, at least not directly, the subject-matter of the picture, or which did not even purport to represent anything concrete). Though today we take for granted the works that in my childhood and adolescence were still novel (and when first shown quite shocking to the unsuspecting public, for example these of the early cubists), they really no more "speak to me" now than they did then. I remember, for example, being intrigued when at school by a painting by the Swiss artist Paul Klee entitled *Spectacles in a Tantrum* (a name to remember, it has to be admitted) and others by the same artist consisting largely of coloured squares; but intrigued in the sense that I simply could not make them out or get any idea as to what attracted people to them. I experienced the same blank emotion many decades later when looking at the much loved and prized collection of mainly abstract paintings of friends, Alan and Cherry Figgis.

Neither have I ever been in the least attracted by eighteenth century baroque painting. But I do really enjoy looking at some paintings: the 17th century Dutch School for example, or the landscapes of John Constable. But though I like the French Impressionists (and in similar vein those of J W M Turner, the English artist who was in some ways their forerunner), I have never been able to get particularly excited about the work of Paul Cezanne or Vincent Van Gogh (except indirectly through Don McLean's truly wonderful song *Vincent*, whose final poignant words could well apply to me [26]). And I never fail to be moved by the huge, dominating painting in the National Gallery in London, *The Execution of Lady Jane Grey* by the French painter Paul Delaroche. That is realism in its strongest form.

But, to repeat the old platitude, beauty is after all in the eye of the beholder, and I am content in having a true liking for certain types of paintings and prints. For example those by an old friend, Ilana Richardson, of striking Mediterranean scenes, almost always without people, many of which are on our walls; those of marine scenes by artists such as Montague Dawson or Geoff Hunt, or railway scenes by, among others, Terence Cuneo and David Shepherd, or wildlife scenes (the first "grown-up" book I ever bought, with money from my Bar-mitzvah, was *Wild Chorus*, a volume by, and illustrated with the bird paintings of, Peter Scott). And I never tire of the wonderful representations of middle-American life in the 1930s to 1950s by Norman Rockwell, who painted most of his pictures on contract to the Saturday Evening Post magazine to produce one each month.

---

[26] "…Now I think I know what you tried to say to me,
And how you suffered for your sanity,
And how you tried to set them free.
They would not listen, they're not listening still.
Perhaps they never will."

Another of the comparatively early books I bought was called simply *European Architecture in Colour*. This was in 1961 when the publishers Thames and Hudson were among the first to produce coloured books on various subjects in the arts. It is nice and heavy, and I spent much time looking at its illustrations. And although I cannot claim any special feeling for the art form, I never fail to be amazed when looking at pictures of buildings designed by the American architect Frank Lloyd Wright, especially bearing in mind that his earliest buildings date from the 1890s.

Some of the world's most famous buildings do of course induce in me, as with most people, a sense of wonder. Among those I have been lucky enough to see "in the flesh" I count Stonehenge, medieval gothic cathedrals such as Salisbury and Chartres, the magnificent Ottoman Blue Mosque in Istanbul, the amazing Taj Mahal mausoleum in Agra, and the equally amazing Opera House in Sydney. The same wonder exists for me too in some ruins, and I think (to mention just a few) the sheer scale of the remains of the ancient Egyptian temples at Karnak and Luxor cannot but impress, as does the crumbling Parthenon in Athens. And though I have not actually been to that particular site, the deliberate destruction of some of the Roman remains in Palmyra, Syria, by the unspeakably barbaric adherents to the so-called Islamic State in 2015, induced in me (as it did in almost everybody with knowledge of the remains) a feeling of horror.[27]

With Cliff & Sarah, January 1998

---

[27] Especially as they had reportedly used the site for some of the grizzly public beheadings with large knives of those of whom they disapproved (inevitably mainly other Muslims).

Natural History

It is a matter of mild regret that as a child there wasn't anyone I knew who could tell me about the natural world. After being shown a little book on birds by Keith MacDonald, a boy whose family lived down the road from us in Dorset Drive, Edgware, entitled *The Observer's Book of Birds*, I had requested a copy of it as a birthday or Christmas present[28]. Although hardback and cloth-bound, it was by modern standards badly illustrated and with only alternate double pages in colour.[29] I of course knew the common birds that came to our suburban gardens in Edgware and The Bishops' Avenue, but I would have loved to have been taken somewhere where there might have been a chance of having the less common ones pointed out to me.

I also later asked for and received as a present for my tenth birthday in 1949 from my grandmother Windy another book Keith had shown me entitled *Birds, Trees and Flowers*. I lost or gave away my original copy but bought a replacement some forty years later as a memento. Published by Odhams originally in 1947, it is also a product of its time, with mainly black and white photographs and a few not very good or particularly relevant coloured illustrations, and it contains a series of what are really essays on different aspects of each subject. It was not written for children and I didn't read much of it, but, indifferent as they were, the pictures helped familiarise me with the names and appearances of species.

In the absence of anyone to help me, I thus needed to instruct myself. I was full of good intentions but at first made little progress. I remember, for instance, telling Irene not long after I met her how much I wanted to get up very early at the appropriate time of year in order to listen to the dawn chorus of birdsong; but I don't recall actually doing it (except by chance in bed) until many years later. In fact it was not until I went to Malawi in the early 1970s, where I found a mentor in John Alder, that I was able really to begin to get gradually to know birds and their classifications, typical habitats and habits. My latent interest was at last able to be fed, and the appetite, as they say, grew with the feeding. Bearing in mind that there are just under ten thousand known bird species in the world, there is enough variation in birdwatching alone (let alone deeper study) for a lifetime's occupation.

---

[28] Keith was in fact at school with me at Belmont and Mill Hill, where he later became Ridgeway's Head of House, but he was three years older than me and our paths did not cross very much.

[29] Colour printing was at the time expensive. *Birds* was actually the first volume in what became a large series of books for spotters (it was succeeded by a book on wild flowers that I also had). First published in 1937, a first edition of *Birds* in a dust jacket can now fetch hundreds of pounds on the collectors' market.

The appreciation and study of birds inevitably leads to an interest in their habitats, and while only a percentage live mainly in trees, a working knowledge of the different species of tree helps enormously (if only to be able to say to one's birding partner(s) "Quick! In the lower left edge of that oak/poplar/ash"). In Africa this was more difficult, as most of the species are known only by their botanical Latin names, but in England where there are far fewer species, getting on top of the subject is comparatively easy. And although the one doesn't necessarily follow from the other, I found that an interest in trees led to cultivating an (again latent) interest in wild flowers. As a child I had read books about the countryside (by Beatrix Potter, Alison Uttley and others) that contained descriptions of wildflowers, many of which had the oddest of names and I wanted to be able to picture them in my mind. What exactly were Ivy-leaved toadflax, Jack-by-the-hedge, Dog's mercury, Charlock, Ragged Robin, Herb Robert, Rest-harrow, Enchanter's nightshade, Hemlock water dropwort, Sheep's-bit (or Devil's-bit) scabious and Good King Henry (to name but a handful)? I really wanted to know.[30] For me, the naming of species is important; the bird, tree or flower (or indeed other animal life) can then become part of my own life list. It is a kind of collecting.

Of course in Africa birding had at times been spectacular; who could forget the sight of the many hundreds of flamingos that were to be found at the soda-lakes in Kenya's Rift Valley, Lakes Nakuru and Bogoria? Or the wealth of general bird-life at Lakes Naivasha and Baringo? In fact for me the excitement of Africa was not only the sighting of large wild animals (spectacular though these could be), but the *sounds* of the wild, and these are above all of birds. One needs to be camping out to hear them properly; driving or being driven around is not conducive to listening unless you are prepared to stop and switch off the engine for minutes at a time. The opportunities for camping in the wild (which for me essentially had to be done when the family were away in England) though limited certainly existed. It is from these safaris in particular that I recall those sounds: the Cuc-*curr*-oo of the seemingly ubiquitous African ring-necked dove, the duetting of D'Arnaud's barbets, the extraordinary call of the aptly nicknamed "water-bottle bird" (the white-browed coucal), the cry of the equally aptly named "go-away bird" (the grey turaco), the exquisite bell-like duetting of tropical boubous, and many more... I miss them.

A superficial knowledge of aspects of natural history such as I have is at least a start in understanding how the world works, i.e. how species interact with their environments. In the richer countries of the world efforts are being

---

[30] My study of wildflowers really began during the nine months I spent in Jersey.

made, albeit late in the day, to conserving what is left (in the case of England not much), but in many parts of the world not even lip-service is paid, as tropical rain forests are relentlessly cut down square kilometre by square kilometre in "slash and burn" operations[31]. The usable wood is carted away, the rest burned and the laid-bare land used for agriculture (although areas that have contained forest are often not in fact much good for that purpose) or to plant in place of the native trees huge areas of non-indigenous commercial ones like rubber trees, or oil palms, that constitute in effect deserts that are largely devoid of native flora and fauna[32].

But to dwell on things that one cannot individually affect is wretched, and I have wanted to enjoy what I can, in Africa and in Europe in particular, but in America and Asia too, while I can.

Walking is of course the best way to indulge a love of natural history, and in doing so I am never without binoculars. Living in the north-west quadrant of London we are never that far away from the Chiltern Hills, an area that, though not exactly wild, contains half a dozen or so of my favourite walks. And on two occasions over the years I have taken a few days off to walk firstly the north Norfolk coast path (from Hunstanton to Cromer) and secondly the Thames path from its source to Goring, near Reading[33]. It is good to be out, largely alone, with the sea (or the river) and time to notice things.

During my local walks I kept at one time an annual record of the bird species I saw on Hampstead Heath and its environment. My aim on a walk has always been the sighting of at least 15 different species, below which an hour or two's birding would count as poor. But it was sometimes possible to see (or in some cases at least to hear) as many as 30, and by my estimate the total count of bird species that one could reasonably expect to see over a period in this area (the count varies a little between winter and summer and of course includes water birds) is around 50. Naturally the time of year for this is crucial, as once the trees are substantially in foliage (from about early May), sighting of most bird species is considerably more difficult, and the period from about mid-July when most birds cease breeding (and hence singing) until about mid-November, by which time the leaves have

---

[31] This has happened to such an extent in Indonesia that the air for hundreds of miles has from time to time been polluted by the smoke from burning whatever cannot be economically extracted.

[32] As is, in of course a very much smaller way, the planting in England of exotic tree species such as Leyland Cypress.

[33] I had wanted to do the complete walk downstream to the Thames Barrier, but that needed another week that I did not have.

substantially fallen, is generally the least profitable time of all for seeing birds. Correspondingly, the best time is from mid-March until the end of April when birds are starting to breed, and are hence at their most active and can readily be seen and heard.

My interest in the subject has broadened slightly in my later years to horticulture. Not, I hasten to add, in the form of active creative gardening myself (my contributions to this take the form of the most basic of tasks, mainly grass-cutting and hedge-trimming), but rather in enjoyment of and wonder at the knowledge, imagination and ability shown by those who are passionately involved. This is so whether the gardens are local (where people, many of whom are friends and acquaintances, open their gardens for a day each year to the public) or on the grander national or even international scale. I always like to see the television presentations from the Royal Horticultural Society flower shows at Chelsea in May and Hampden Court in July each year, and Monty Don's "Gardener's World" is a television programme which, when each series is running, I try not to miss.

Collecting

I have always been a collector. Partly, as already been seen, this involves nothing more than the mere sighting of many different species of bird, animal or plant life; but I believe the passion for collecting proper always has its main focus on gathering together things that the collector finds for some reason attractive. Interestingly, I believe that around 90% of what I call true collectors are male.

Attendance at a collectors' fair will reveal stalls selling all sorts of things the collection of which most people would consider eccentric (lengths of barbed wire are the oddest "collectables" I personally have seen). I was some time ago given by an amused family member a little book entitled "Men and Collections" illustrated with photographs of proud collectors surrounded by the various things they have gathered together. Among these are traffic cones, blow-lamps, little individual packets of sugar, post-boxes (full-size outdoor ones), sand samples, and live tarantulas! The things that are prized do not of course need to have particular, or indeed any, intrinsic value (except perhaps in the sense of rarity value among collectors themselves).

My own taste has by comparison been very conventional, limited as it has been to stamps, cigarette (and similar) cards, postcards and books, although in the cases of the first three categories not at the same time. For me there is a satisfaction in bringing order out of chaos, in gathering, sorting and arranging items into sets or series and deriving a particular pleasure from knowing these to be complete. In some ways it is like assembling a jigsaw puzzle: the pieces need to be found one or two at a time and then fitted together to create the complete picture. The interesting thing is that when the puzzle has been completed it is usually a matter for admiration for only a short while before the assembler becomes bored with it and breaks it up. For the jigsaw puzzle assembler, as for the collector, the sport is in the chase rather than the final capture. In the words of Robert Louis Stevenson:

> To travel hopefully is a better thing than to arrive, and the true success is to labour.[34]

Sometimes particular collectables have such a following that items are collected solely or mainly as an investment. This has of course long been so in the case of paintings, but is also very much the case with coins (and increasingly banknotes too) and stamps. Investment for its own sake has, however, never been the reason for my own collecting, and I can never quite get used to the idea that something attractive (which is presumably why it is collectable) can be bought and simply placed in a bank vault or equivalent[35]. While it is true that a sensible collector needs to build a collection that is likely to increase in value, and this means collecting to a pattern or theme likely to be marketable in the event of sale, making money out of my collections has never been more than the smallest part of what has driven me.

As with many people, my collecting began when at school with stamps. Typically we schoolboy collectors would collect those of Britain and what was still called the British Empire, stamps that were attractive and the most readily available. In modern times, commemorative stamps, i.e. those marking a particular event or on a particular theme, are central to the hobby, but in those days they were rare and in the UK and elsewhere they were issued only for what were thought of as important events.[36] But even though in my early collecting days the stamps of the UK were mainly the regular or "definitive" sets of fairly ordinary stamps, countries in the Empire often had

---

[34] Though I would substitute "pleasure" for "success". As an eleven- or twelve-year-old I was required at school to write an essay on the first half of the quotation. As was the case with most of my English essays, the process of writing it was torture.

[35] For example, Stanley Gibbons offers various "capital protected" investment plans under which customers deposit £10,000 or more for between five and ten years, which buys them a portfolio of between five and seven rare stamps to be kept at home or stored and insured at Stanley Gibbons' office. The "protected" aspect of the plan means that return of at least the sum invested is guaranteed. Whatever that process is, it is not philately.

[36] The very first UK ones were issued to commemorate the British Empire Exhibition at Wembley in 1924 at face value of 1d and 1½d (i.e. old pennies – worth rather less than half of a modern one), but in 1963 the number of these issues began to increase until in modern times between 10 and 20 commemorative sets are issued annually.

pictorial definitive issues of attractively colourful stamps, none more so than tiny island dependencies such as the Cayman Islands, Turks and Caicos Islands, Falkland Islands and Pitcairn Islands, whose real postal needs were actually tiny[37].

In my adult years my own collection was of the stamps of British Africa and Middle East (Iraq, Transjordan and Palestine). It was a huge subject, although I limited myself to collecting only used (i.e. cancelled or franked) stamps, and to stamps issued up to the time of independence of the individual countries or 1962 (whichever was earlier). My particular favourites in the collection were some good examples of the well-known Cape of Good Hope unperforated triangular stamps; some of the early issues from Rhodesia (subsequently Zambia and Zimbabwe), particularly a large series depicting King George V and Queen Mary known as "double-heads"; and the early issues from what was originally known as the Oil Rivers Protectorate (the coastal strip that in 1894 became the Niger Coast Protectorate[38]). I sold the collection at auction in the 1980s (it had lain in a small trunk in the bank during our years in Africa) and the proceeds went largely to finance school education for the children that had been free while living abroad.

While working in Jersey in 1985-6 I came upon a shop in St Helier that sold all sorts of collectables, including interesting stocks of cigarette cards. These recalled the motley and quite small collection of cards that our grandmother had given to Cliff and me, as previously noted in chapter 1. I had maintained a latent interest in the cards, and so it was that, freed so to speak of my stamp collection, I began collecting cigarette cards.

I had always associated these with the issues of the 1930s, many of which had adhesive backs so that they could be stuck into purpose-made cardboard albums that sold for a penny. In fact, however, the issuing of cigarette cards had started in the USA in the 1880s and spread to the UK about a decade later. In those early years the American entrepreneur James Duke had caused the merger of most of the US tobacco companies under the name of the American Tobacco Company and by the turn of the century Duke made it known that his company wanted to take over British tobacco companies too.

---

[37] Indeed, some of these kinds of stamps, particularly those of high face value, are examples of what are today offered by dealers as investments. On the other hand, some jurisdictions (for example the Gulf States) issued at one time so many stamps that were obviously aimed at the philately trade and not needed for postal use that Stanley Gibbons refused to list them in their catalogues.

[38] In 1900 this became part of the Southern Nigeria Protectorate. It wasn't until 1914 that this was unified with Northern Nigeria to form a single colony.

This caused the leading ones among them to band together to form the Imperial Tobacco Company.[39]

Cigarette cards are generally collected in sets, and these ranged in numbers from 12 to 100 cards, although by the 1930s the commonest numbers were 25 and 50 cards per set. Typical of these were various series of motor cars, ships and railway engines, sports and theatrical personalities of the day, and various natural history subjects. Among the more unusual subjects in my collection were cards depicting fortune-telling, optical illusions, time & money in different countries (a framed set of which hangs on our wall still), the language of flowers, and (a timely issue at about the time of the Munich crisis in 1938) air-raid precautions.

Similar to cigarette cards is a category of what are termed "trade cards", those of similar size but issued by manufacturers of other things and similarly given away with their products, e.g. tea (Brooke Bond in particular), chocolate (Fry's being the most prominent), soap and many others. I collected some of the more attractive of these too, but there was one particular category of them that began to interest me in the 1990s to the exclusion of the others, those of the Liebig Extract of Meat Company[40]. Liebig cards, as they are generally called, were first produced in about 1872 and except for small breaks during the two world wars continued to be offered until 1976.[41] In ten years or so I built a collection of these that was almost complete from about 1896; but the difficulty (and hence of course the associated expense) is in finding those in the first 160 or so sets of cards issued up to about 1885.

By about the late 1990s I had, in the way of a jig-saw puzzle assembler, tired of the process of collecting cigarette and ordinary trade cards and I sold most of them at auction (as I had done with my stamps also), retaining just a few that were of special interest and the Liebig cards. It was time to take my first

---

[39] The principal companies were W D & H O Wills (easily the largest), John Player & Sons, Lambert & Butler, and later Ogden and Churchman. But a sort of merger of the US and UK giants was indeed formed for production of tobacco and tobacco products outside those countries, under the name of the British American Tobacco Company (BAT).
[40] They sold their products in Britain under the trade name Oxo.
[41] During this time some 1870 different sets were issued (the precise number depends on the catalogue used). A little larger than the largest size of cigarette cards but still considerably smaller than postcards, Liebig cards were usually published in sets of six and covered a huge range of different subjects. They were offered mainly in France, Germany, Belgium, Holland, Italy and Switzerland (with occasional sets in English distributed in the UK and the USA) and often published simultaneously in different languages, although from about 1940 onwards (with a gap only between the years 1943 and 1947) they were issued for use only in Belgium and Italy.

tentative steps into postcards. There are millions of these to choose from, and unlike the previous things I had collected, there are few authoritative listings of any of them and no catalogues in the sense of comprehensive dealers' lists of prices.

In the UK, postcards were originally plain cards with the stamp printed on them that could be bought only at the Post Office; the address was to be written on the side with the printed stamp, and the message on the other (these cards could still be bought during my childhood). The idea of *picture* postcards was not taken up officially in the UK until 1894, when the Post Office authorised the sending of privately printed cards with a picture on part of one side and the address on the other. These originally conformed to the size of the official cards (somewhat smaller and squarer than they later became), but by the early 1900s what became known as "divided-back" postcards were being produced in the format still followed today, allowing one complete side to consist of a picture and the reverse divided between space for the message and that for the address.

The hey-day of postcards was in fact the period from the turn of the twentieth century until the First World War. In those days before the telephone (how often in my reveries have I thought what bliss that must have been!), at least for any but commercial use and in the houses of the richest people, the postcard was a cheap and efficient way of communicating: the cards were sold at a penny (plain, i.e. black and white or sepia) and two-pence (coloured), the inland postage rate was one halfpenny and the rate for sending abroad one penny (there was of course no air mail). Added to that there was a comprehensive postal service that offered two collections and as many as three deliveries a day; within many localities if one posted a letter or card before 9.00 am delivery could be expected to be made later the same day.

As with most beginners I started collecting historical views of where I live, what in the hobby is called "topography". Hampstead Garden Suburb is a sought-after, limited and not particularly interesting topographical subject, but there were many postcards of Hampstead and Hampstead Heath, both of which were popular with both locals and tourists at the turn of the twentieth century, and these were mostly easy to find. In fact, being keen to see how places that I know well have changed over the decades, I built up a small collection of postcards of north-west London suburbs.

I soon noticed that the most striking and well-produced Hampstead cards were from one publisher whose logo "LL" and a number appeared with the caption on the picture side of each card. This was in fact the logo of Levy

Fils et Cie, a firm of what had originally been Jewish photographers based in Paris, and from the numbers one could get some idea of the total number of the cards produced in a series. I decided that I would switch to collecting only or mainly LL cards, and theirs from other locations in England too (they were issued only for towns and places of tourist interest south of a line from the Severn to the Wash), and not long after that LLs from other countries as well (mainly France, French North Africa and Egypt). I was not alone in my preference and in 2003 joined a circle of LL collectors that meets twice a year in Reading.

What I particularly like about these postcards is their contribution to social history, and central to my collection has been the beach and street scenes of the early twentieth century, the latter often crowded with horse buses, carriages and cabs and, slightly later, single- and double-decker trams and motor buses. But of course also shown are people coming and going, and a card can often be dated, at least approximately, from the vehicles depicted and the styles of dress. Because the publishers were French, in cases where there were English captions (i.e. on the cards of England, the Channel Islands and Egypt) the misprints and translations were occasionally funny. An Egyptian card of a riverside scene is captioned "The smelling of the Nile". While this might be unintentionally accurate, what was intended was "the *swelling* of the Nile". Another is captioned "Walk upon Ass" (in later printings, more felicitously, "Donkey riding"!) And a First World War card states curiously that it depicts "English soldiers laring cower" (taking cover!)

In general I do not buy a book unless I can get something from it. This doesn't necessarily mean that I intend to read it from cover to cover: some books are of course purely for reference and others are for reading only in part. Nor do I necessarily have to read a book when first bought, and some have remained on my shelves for many years until I get round to reading them (and sometimes this never actually happens). But I have nonetheless collected some books that I cannot pretend I need except for the pleasure of dipping into them from time to time. Into this category come most of the many books I have on natural history and in particular a collectable series published by Collins known as the "New Naturalist Series".

I well remember these books from my childhood.[42] They were highly thought of and each had a remarkably distinctive dust jacket designed by

---

[42] The first in the series, *Butterflies* (of Britain), together with the third on *London's Natural History* were published in November 1945 soon after the end of the Second World War (they were not initially published in the order of the numbers in the series assigned to them) at a

Clifford and Rosemary Ellis, whose work continued for most of the first seventy books of the series up to the death of Clifford in 1985. I recall the tables in W H Smiths bookshop in Edgware on which they were displayed as they were published, and from time to time noticed one or two of them in peoples' bookshelves. In 1988 I managed to buy a set of them that was nearly complete up to number 67, and in the years that followed I gradually obtained the missing volumes, or better copies of the ones I had (the condition of a book is of paramount importance to collectors). From then on (the series had by that time reached 74 volumes) I began to buy them as they were published[43].

Collectors want these in hardback editions. Collins, the publishers, had decided however that by 1983 there were too many unsold remainders from their print runs and that they would continue to publish books in the series mainly in paperback format, with only a very limited number of hardback editions, mainly for libraries. In consequence the print runs of the next two in the series were cut to 725 hardback copies, but this caused such an outcry among collectors that Collins thereafter reversed their decision and increased their print runs to double that amount. In the inevitable way that collecting affects the market, since that time the demand for those two particular issues has been such that they now fetch over £2,000 each for copies in fine condition.[44]

There are two other series that I have collected. The one published by A & C Black in the early years of the twentieth century that became known as "Black's Colour Books",[45] were the first to be produced at what were considered to be reasonable prices for books with large numbers of illustrations printed wholly in colour. Beautifully produced and with attractive cloth covers, they are mainly on individual countries. The second series are British topographical books published by Batsford, from the early 1930s through to the mid-1950s. They are copiously illustrated with contemporary photographs, but the distinguishing features common to them all are their dust jackets on which appear the highly individual designs of

---

price of 16 shillings (£0.80), and a further seven were published in remaining years of the 1940s. By the end of that decade the price had risen to 21 shillings (£1.05).

[43] At the time of writing there are 133 in the series and the price has risen to £60 for the latest ones.

[44] These are nos. 70 *The Natural History of Orkney*, and 71 *British Warblers*, both published in 1985, shortly before I had started taking an interest in the books. I bought both in 1988-9 at book fairs and at what seemed then to be the very high prices of £90 and £100 respectively.

[45] There were two main series of these: the so-called "20/- [i.e. £1.00] Series" and the smaller "7/6 [£0.37.5] Series". Each had an illustrator whose water-colour paintings were sometimes produced specifically for the series.

Brian Cooke. These too are books I remember being on sale during my childhood.

These series apart, I have always liked to have books on my shelves that reflect my various interests; it is the collecting habit that induces me to want to own these books, rather than, say, borrowing them from a library (in modern times a fast disappearing institution) or, in the cases of recently published books, reading from an electronic reading machine such as Kindle, a device that has never held any interest for me.

I like reading popular history from all periods, and in this regard I find outstanding Simon Shama's 3-volume work "A History of Britain" and Norman Davies single volume "The Isles"[46]. But the period that most interests me it is that covering the years from about 1880 to 1980 (anything more recent than that is really too near in time to be looked at objectively). And books that chronicle the British Empire tend to be particular favourites, with first among these the 3-volume "Pax Britannica" series by James Morris (who was later to change gender into Jan Morris) which I bought when they were published in the 1970s. The Empire's apogee and virtual demise coincide with the above period.[47]

Miscellaneous other interests

Carpentry

I have always liked making things, and in this I include not only construction but also the process of painting and decorating; there is great satisfaction in standing back (literally) from something I have created. In my childhood this fondness found its outlet in constructing Meccano models, but later, especially after my time in the furniture business where I saw daily how furniture was constructed, it turned to carpentry.

Never having practised this skill with any degree of regularity, it has been largely a matter of re-instructing myself each time I undertake a particular

---

[46] In fact I have heard the slightly abridged audio version of Shama's work brilliantly read by Timothy West right through at least three times. The same apples to the Davies book, the audio version of which is read by Andrew Sachs.

[47] Although there are still a small number of British overseas dependencies, mostly in the Caribbean: Anguilla, Bermuda, British Virgin Islands, Cayman Islands, Falkland Islands, Gibraltar, Montserrat, St Helena, Turks & Caicos Islands and a handful of other tiny ones with minimal populations. And other countries in the Commonwealth that long ago became independent still retain Queen Elizabeth as their Head of State: Australia – though there is constant debate on its becoming a republic – Canada, New Zealand, Jamaica, Papua New Guinea and several others in the Caribbean and the Pacific.

project; but these have come up from time to time, mostly in the form of installing fitted wardrobes, cupboards and shelves, especially on first moving into our house in Temple Fortune Lane, and as Rachel and Jessica and their families have moved, or re-moved. At these times, quite apart from the work itself, I have enjoyed the process of selecting the necessary materials[48] at DIY warehouses, getting 8ft x 4ft boards cut to size and the feeling while mingling with others doing so of leading a separate life as an artisan.

Generally things have gone well, although on one occasion when taking a load of about eight MDF panels for wardrobe ends and doors to Rachel's house I had insufficiently secured it with ropes to the roof-rack of the car. As I braked at a red light on a downhill junction in Maida Vale, the load shot forward free of the restraining ropes and the boards cascaded along the bonnet of the car into the road in front of me. Fortunately there was no other car there at the time, and as I had anyway braked slowly and all but stopped there was no real momentum to the slide. But it was to say the least embarrassing to have to pick up the panels one by one (with the help of a sympathetic passer-by) and reload and re-secure them properly.

Cooking

Here, my interest has rested on good intentions rather more than results, but I have nevertheless from time to time tried to produce meals that are tasty, even if the results are not always up to the standard I would like. I have great admiration for those cooks who can think up interesting dishes and pass on recipes that need comparatively little in the way of preparation time. And I admire Irene's ability to rustle up dishes apparently from nowhere, especially from left-over food. Baking too is something that interests me, although at the time of writing I have tried only to produce bread.

Both skills are ones that ideally require either a period of apprenticeship or else years of practice in order to produce food to a high standard. Whilst I don't expect ever to be able to do that, I do at least hope that practice will lead me to be able to achieve greater things.

Travel

I have previously described how the urge to travel had obsessed me in my young adulthood. The experiences I had been lucky enough to have for the

---

[48] These days mostly MDF (medium density fibreboard) for panels, softwood of various dimensions for anchoring and bracing strips and bearers, and the necessary metal hinges, handles and other fittings.

23 years from 1961 through to 1984 had gone a good way to satisfying this obsession, and the opportunities afforded me by my work after returning from living in Africa enabled visits to a wide range of mainly Commonwealth countries, especially in Africa, south-east Asia, Australasia and the Caribbean.

In some ways it was enough, for with one exception I find I no longer want to visit countries or places unless there is a particular reason for doing so (work or to see and/or stay with family or friends). Indeed, there are now parts of the world that, in the absence of these factors, barely interest me at all (Eastern Europe, Russia and the former Asian satellite countries of the USSR) or to which I would need an amount of persuasion to visit as a tourist (South America, China, Japan). There is, by contrast, one area of the world that I would go to again and again if free to do so: the Indian sub-continent (including Burma), and particularly India itself. In these countries there are many beautiful old places that have been restored and converted to hotels (particularly Maharajahs' guest houses and even former palaces) which I particularly love. Travel has for me much to do with a love of history, particularly British history in its widest sense, and the areas mentioned as being of little interest do not of course have any such connection.

Sport

I have already recounted how in my school days sport was a predominant interest; with comparatively minor exceptions it has not, however, been so since. I follow international rugby and to some extent international cricket, if they involve England, but my interest in both games is not particularly partisan and though I like to see my country win I actually prefer to see a good game, even though they lose. Thanks to television, I can sometimes get pleasure too from watching golf or athletics, but I do not make a special effort to do this. I am however disgusted at the tribalism that is demonstrated around sport, particularly soccer, and how international tournaments for this game regularly induce packs of young men from one nation to violently attack those of another (English "fans" are particularly notorious for this barbaric ugliness). In former times they might have found outlets for their pent-up violence in the armed forces.

My own participation in sports after school was limited for a short while to rugby (see chapter 5), golf and squash, but except for occasional visits to golf ranges, and an even more occasional game, I effectively ceased to play golf about a year after returning from Africa. My golf clubs, originally bought second-hand while in Malawi, have become almost museum pieces: the "woods" actually have wooden heads and all have leather grips. My squash continued for about ten years afterwards, but as one gets older it becomes an increasingly bad idea to continue with a game that can put enormous strains on the body unless one is able to play consistently, and this I was unable to do when I needed to make frequent visits abroad. So "sports" participation in my later years has been confined to the gym, where I can watch my gradually diminishing performance. When as a nine-year-old my father took my brother Cliff and me to the Opening Ceremony of the 1948 London Olympic Games on a boiling hot August day, there gradually appeared on a big board at one end of Wembley Stadium laboriously put up, letter by letter and by hand, the statement "The important thing in the Olympic Games is not winning but taking part". In modern times such a statement would be regarded as cant; nevertheless, in my visits to the gym I like to bear it in mind. In the words of a friend "At least you go!"

Dress

Surprisingly to some, I do take an interest in clothes, although, as with those of comparatively advanced age, in a rather mild and conservative way. Social conventions as to dress are of course very strong, and it is usually important to people of all ages to be seen in what are thought of to be correct clothes. "Correct" in this context does not necessarily have any connection with smartness or even style, but in the main involves following the herd (we are after all social animals). We are careful when inserting individualities into our dress not to go too far in pushing the boundaries of acceptability; those who do so are seen as wanting to make a statement of some sort, and we tend to refer to them as either eccentric or exhibitionist or both. This applies to any group in society; just as much for example to students as it does to those in e.g. business, religious or gay circles. It has always been so.

Something else that has always existed is the (usually mild) dislike of the old for the tastes and styles of the young, or at least those younger than themselves. In my own case this takes the form of dislike of particular items of clothing: of baseball type caps (and irritation at the silliness of a fashion that requires them as often as not to be worn back to front or sideways); of trainers and collarless tee-shirts (except for the purposes for which they were originally intended – gym or sports, or additionally in the case of the latter, pyjamas); of "draw-string" trousers (which to me look slovenly); and of jeans with store-bought deliberate defects, or splits in the legs so that the wearers' knees show. However, my greatest dislike is for what I consider to be affectations among those of my own generation when they attempt to imitate, in my view inappropriately, the styles of the young. In my parents' generation such people were referred to as "mutton dressed as lamb".

Though I do not like what I think of as excessive formality in any area of life, I decry the modern fashion for dressing down, especially among men, and I find it offensive that people can see fit to attend what I think of as public "occasions" (opera, theatres, concerts, etc.) dressed inappropriately. "Casual" is the word that tends to apply to dress that is not formal, largely I suppose because it is thought to indicate a relaxed attitude to life on the part of the wearer. Of course in truth it does nothing of the sort (a relaxed attitude is mainly an inner quality), and if worn inappropriately simply marks the wearer as someone who cannot be bothered to take trouble over his appearance (I use the masculine pronoun advisedly, as this phenomenon is much more usually seen in men). It is I think the same syndrome that induces people to put their feet up on chairs in public places and on seats on public transport: it marks them out for me not as "relaxed" but simply as bad-mannered.

Though I personally prefer not to have to wear a tie unless fairly strict convention requires it (usually work-related situations or visiting fuddy-duddy places like London clubs), I tend to wear a jacket for what I think of as "an occasion", and this includes a private lunch or dinner party or visit to a smart restaurant just as much as to a theatre or concert. If someone can go to the trouble to prepare a meal for me and others then the least I can do is make a little effort to dress accordingly. However the "smart casual" absence of a tie does not in my mind excuse a resulting untidy collapsed shirt front; the tie-less appearance requires a shirt whose collar "stands up".

Family

My family of origin I described in chapter 1, but I want finally to say something about my own nuclear family. I have left this dominatingly important aspect of my life until last because this account has been primarily about the things that have happened to me and the background to them; it is an account *for* my wife, children and grandchildren (and also of course anyone else who is interested) not *about* them. But their importance to my life cannot be underestimated.

Irene

I have described in chapter 5 something of Irene's background and the circumstances that got us together. It has been a partnership that in spite of difficulties between us at times has worked well. She has qualities that I lack: she is often patient where I am impatient, often understanding of people where I am dismissive of them, often generous where I might be inclined to be mean, often bold in facing a situation where I might be inclined to try to avoid it. But above all she is often tenacious where I am inclined to give in. When we first got together all those years ago I was in a seemingly unresolvable quandary about what I could do in the way of changing my career. Her reaction was along the lines of "Well, what would you ideally like to do about it?" and she proceeded to suggest practical lines of approach and how I needed to get going and do something positive rather than simply bemoan my lot. She has said to me on quite a few occasions (in relation to that and other things both large and small) "You give up too easily".

Left to right: Miriam Zacuto and Beverley Woznica (Irene's nieces), Monica Samuels (Irene's sister), Irene, Debbi Grant (Irene's cousin). Los Angeles, November 2011

But her overwhelmingly obvious quality is her ability to establish friendships and get on well with people; the people she doesn't like are very few and far between. When I first knew her she seemed to be constantly meeting people she knew in the street (this was even a bit irritating at times). I recall that when speaking to her father and asking for his blessing to marry her I mentioned this quality: "Yes" he said with admirable conciseness "she is very popular." This aspect of her character was summed up by the middle-aged Irish teller in what used to be our local bank branch (who liked talking to her customers – all very fine if there wasn't a queue, but there usually was). She volunteered to me one day when I had finally got to the front of the queue and was asking her about a matter Irene had been dealing with "Your wife is such a lovely person!"

One of the chief benefits of this has been a social life, both in London and abroad, that has been full and wide, and our house has often been a place for friends from out of town to stay, the latter especially since our children have left. I am delighted that this has been so.

Rachel

Being the first-born, Rachel's arrival on 26th December 1968 was something of a wonder to me, and I described the experience in chapter 5. Our little girl grew up to be, outwardly at least, the most like me of my three children: she doesn't like wasting words and is very focussed; she is quick-witted and somewhat intolerant of those she sees as not reaching the standards she expects from them; like me she is untidy in the short term, but has nevertheless an ordered mind; and (here the characteristics start to diverge a little) she is undoubtedly an especially good organiser of people. I suspect that, also like me, she prefers an approach to tasks that is not necessarily the obvious one, and an originality of thought is almost certainly an attribute that has enabled her to win a number of trophies in competitions (run by the personnel management trade journal) for her training programmes. Head of Talent Management for Europe with Fujitsu is not only her official job title at the time of writing, it is about as good a description of what she does best as it is possible to get.

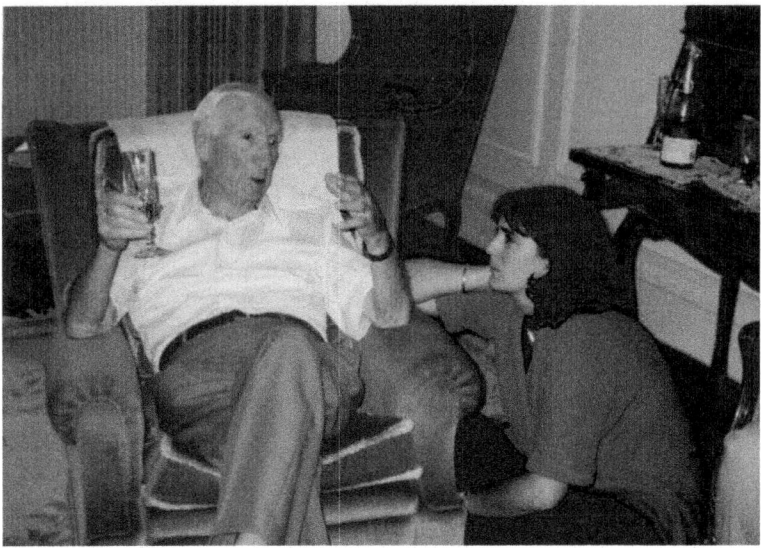

Dad aged 88 with Rachel September 1998. He died almost exactly 6 years later.

From a very early age she liked order, and I recall her (fruitless) attempts at the age of about 20 months to try to get a litter of kittens to stay in the same place at the same time. As she grew, it was clear that she had well-above average ability at school, and this led me to intervene on her behalf in Nairobi when on first arrival at the Banda School she was placed in a class that she considered too low for her. The headmaster, Douglas Dalrymple, impressed that she should think so, told me that usually requests to him were the other way round (i.e. to move a child *down* a class or year). He put her up a year in consequence and she flourished. Rachel also showed her ability to cope with life generally at the age of 14 when the road accident in Kenya in March 1983 had Jessie and me in hospital. She assisted Irene in running day to day affairs in a way that impressed.

Generosity is one of the characteristics that comes strongly to mind in relation to her, and the giving of presents takes on, especially at Christmas, the quality of an art form.

In our house in Nairobi Rachel and Jessica shared a bedroom after the birth of Jonno. The difference of approach to tidiness (in Rachel's case lack if it) led to Irene having to place a physical dividing line down the centre of the room.

Jessica

In contrast to her sister, Jessie is outwardly very much like her mother. She has a similarly wide circle of friends, and the same "un-academic" outlook on life in that she has never felt inclined to absorb knowledge that was not of direct relevance to her day to day affairs; yet she has a fundamental common sense that has enabled her to organise her own fairly complex family life especially well.

Also like her mother, she has a particularly positive sense of what life has to offer. She has, for example, never let the minor residual disabilities from the road accident in Kenya described in chapter 8 bother her; indeed her expressed attitude at the time was that (in spite of having been in a dangerous coma at one point and having been temporarily partially paralysed down one side of her body) it was a lucky thing that the accident had happened when it did, as the previous year Nairobi hospital did not have a children's ward. And when Irene refused on religious grounds to celebrate Christmas in Africa (a decision she reversed when back in London), Jessie took it on herself to festively decorate a small shrub in our Nairobi garden.

Jessie, born on 13th November 1972, not only showed considerable artistic talent early on (we have a still-life on the wall painted by her at the age of 16 which is remarkably mature) but was prepared to work at it, and spent one school holiday making little pieces of ornamental jewellery out of Fimo[49] so that she could (and did) sell them at the market at Camden Lock. Though she did not go to art school, her university course involved the study of clothing and textiles, and with this background, and considering her particular liking for the whole concept of shops and shopping, her job at the time of writing as a buyer for T K Maxx could not be better suited to her abilities. So much so that the days when she is required to "comp-shop" (tour shops noting what is being offered by her company's competitors) are days that she considers she is not working at all.

She has an infectious laugh and an unusually strong ability to engage with people that has served her well in her business as well as her private life, so that she is often able to negotiate good business terms; her suppliers like her. She has an attention to detail (and a focus of mind on what she wants done that is like my own) and a feeling for shape, design and beauty that causes her own family home to be kept as she kept her own room (or part of it) as a little girl: tidy, well-ordered and with a well-developed sense of positioning and colour.

Jonathan

In some circles it was at one time considered politically incorrect to attempt to compare children to their parents: each was supposed to be seen as being simply a person in his or her own right. Devoid of the word "simply" the latter observation is of course incontrovertible, but I have never had a problem with stating what is obvious to me, namely that the process of the passing of genes in the ratio of 50% from each parent is bound to produce likenesses, some of which will be more apparent than others. So if Rachel is essentially her father's daughter, and Jessica her mother's, what of Jonno?

By the time of his birth in Kenya on 18th May 1980 I was used to having daughters and was quite prepared for a third. It was therefore almost a surprise when our friend and obstetrician Max Bennun delivered him in Nairobi Hospital with the cheerful announcement "Here's your little boy" (unlike with the girls, and even though the birth needed to be assisted with suction, this time I was present).

---

[49] A modelling clay that sets hard when baked in the oven.

In over-simplified summary (because I am neither a paediatrician nor a child psychologist) my own view is that he has quite simply a "down the middle" mixture of the characteristics of both his parents and so comparisons are difficult and anyway to an extent pointless. He is sharp-witted, yet highly empathetic; practical-minded, adaptable, and (I understand often *not* the case with the youngest child in a family) highly responsible. At university he was stated to be capable of obtaining a first-class degree (his subject was politics), but knew that in order to do so he would have to severely cut down on sports and social activities in his final year. He was not prepared to do this, rightly in my opinion, and was content with a "2:1".

From the outset he was a very physical and well-co-ordinated child, so it was not a surprise that he should later turn out to be good at all sports. In these things he seems to have inherited those talents of my own father to a greater degree than I did. Not only that, but a combination of ability and responsibility meant that he was appointed Captain of Rugby at UCS School and elected Rugby Club Captain at Nottingham University (corresponding to President of Rugby in some universities). Additionally at school he was in the first XI soccer side in his penultimate year and agreed in his final year to be appointed captain of the second XI; and he was for three years the school first XI cricket side's opening bowler and middle order batsman. It is the kind of ability that I aspired to at a similar time in my life but simply did not have.

At school there had been something of a "drug problem" amongst a few of the boys; Jonno, by nature a peacemaker, took a lead in helping to deal socially with the fall-out from this so that there did not need to be any expulsions. His chosen career in management consultancy is thus, in spite of many difficulties, one to which he is well suited both figuratively and literally: he has always had a strong sense of dress style, and impeccably dressed in a business suit, and wearing shirts that are made to measure, he looks ready for anything. In fact I must be one of the few fathers who has inherited clothes (though not suits and shirts) from his son.

Indeed the taking of responsibility is something that all three of our children readily do, sometimes too much so, so that undue worry is taken on for things that are really down to others.

Irene and I consider that we can congratulate ourselves on them and the way in which they have made the best use of their talents. This is not of course to ignore their partners, about whom I am less qualified to write meaningfully, and at the time of writing the three grandchildren they have between them produced are truly a delight for us. It is too early in their lives to attempt meaningfully to assess these children's abilities, but some emerging characteristics do nevertheless stand out: Charlie's unusual creativity, Ollie's sturdy curiosity and powers of observation, and Rosie's powers of observation and outstanding potential in dance and sport. These attributes will give each of them very good chances of making their mark in their lives.

Family, September 2016
Back row: Charlie, Rosie. Ollie, Nick (Rachel's husband)
Front row: Rachel, Jonno, Roger, Irene, Jessie, John (Jessie's husband)

Epilogue

The foregoing chapters contain the essence of my story. I hope that by relating both the main events and some of the minor ones that have taken place in my life, and some of the background to them, I have been able to bring into reasonably sharp focus what has made me the person I am.

Whilst many people might say that attempting to rate one's life is an unnecessary "add-on" to an autobiography, for me it is important to try to do so. The interesting question is as to what measure I should use to rate it. Can I, for instance, look back on it and consider that it has been "successful"? If so, what is success? Do I have to have got somewhere near what is considered generally to be the top of my profession to have achieved it? If so, then mine has been very modest indeed; perhaps it doesn't rate as success at all. Yet, in the narrow field of the law in which I have worked for some forty years I am one of the best. Is that success? Of a sort, clearly. But am I asking the right question? Is this concept of success valid?

It is an interesting question that was brought into focus recently by a friend, Phiroze Neemuchwala, who had written a paper on success and asked Irene and me for our comments on it. He is a psycho-therapist, and in the course of his work had asked fifty or so people from different walks of life what they thought success was. After eliciting the expected responses about having money or status (preferably both) he conducted a small survey among a dozen professional people or people with inherited wealth, each of whom was rated as "successful" by his or her peers, asking them to rate their own success in life on a scale of one to ten. Somewhat to his surprise he found that few of them scored over six.

Phiroze then put the same questions to a carpenter friend of his. When the man rated his success with a score of nine, my friend's interest was sufficiently aroused by the fact to want to ask the man to tell him more detail about his day to day life. After needing to verify that he was actually serious in his request, the carpenter told him about the way he spent a typical week. As a result, among the words that came to my friend's mind were "varied", "balanced", "interesting" and "relaxed". It was also apparent that the man had a very good relationship with his wife. Phiroze was struck by how many different things were going on in the man's life – and about how not a single one of them depended on being an "important" person, or being affluent.

By contrast, Phiroze thought of his "successful" friends and realised that their lives were often monothematic, stressed, repetitive and hurried. What kind of success was this and was it worth having if, as was usually the case with those questioned, they didn't have time to do the things they really liked doing? Money or status could not replace these things.

So perhaps success should be given a wider meaning, more in line with what we think if as happiness? In fact I find it difficult to disentangle the two attributes.

There is an adage that happiness is like a butterfly: if you actively pursue it, it will probably elude you; but if you cease to think about it, it may well come and land on your shoulder. I think success, in its wider and to my mind truer sense, is much the same. The nearest I can get to a definition of it is:

> The ability to feel good about myself and what I have achieved, or am achieving, that is worthwhile in my life.

Clearly, by this definition, my rating of the success of my life will depend to some extent on my state of mind when I stop to consider it. Nevertheless I do really think that within its terms my life has had the necessary ingredients for success: my work in the law has been varied and interesting, I have always had a wide variety of interests outside it, and there has been a good balance between them. And in spite of differences and strains at times I have had a very good relationship with Irene and with my children and grandchildren.

Success is clearly by the above measure a subjective not an objective attribute, for I am very much aware that the events in my life that I have described and challenges that I have overcome may often be of little interest to others. I illustrate what I mean (with some exaggeration for effect!) with a notional dinner party conversation where one of the guests states that he has recently crossed Antarctica:

Guest 2: "Really? How interesting. Was it cold?"

Antarctic traveller: "Yes, minus 50 some of the time."

Guest 2: "Really? That's even colder than last weekend. Do you know when I came out of T K Maxx on Saturday it had started to snow, and the wind was so strong I had to put up the hood of the padded jacket I was wearing. Actually I had bought that there too, last September for £25! You know they have some really good bargains. In fact on Saturday I didn't find much that I wanted, but I bought some socks and, you'll never believe this, a Samsonite suitcase for £35! It'll be perfect for when we go on our cruise next summer to the Mediterranean. Did you see on television that Marvel

Tours are offering special discounts if you book before the end of March? We are so glad we did. Mind you, we hope we don't get stuck with the kind of people who were sharing our table last year, they were awful!"

Guest 3: "I bet they weren't as bad as the couple we met in Marbella last summer…"

Probably the most important thing I have learned in life, and this was one of the central messages from More to Life, is to esteem myself. This emphatically does not mean having an inflated view of my worth; rather it means quite simply being glad to be me. True self-esteem means not being unduly concerned about what others might think of us, or about the lack of impact on others of what we have done; it is the value to ourselves of who we are and what we have achieved that counts. This state of mind is not necessarily easy to achieve: many people probably never really do so, others do so only occasionally and fleetingly; and for some it can mean undergoing psychological counselling at some level. Certainly I have not always been able to esteem myself in this way.

Notice however that I state above that we should not be "unduly concerned" about what others think of us. I am not advocating that other people's feelings and opinions should be ignored, even less that we should consider ourselves at liberty deliberately to upset other people by what we say or do (unless of course in situations, usually work related, where we might have no choice but to take harsh or unpalatable decisions regarding others).

In simple terms, our goal in life as I see it is to be truly aware of, and content with, our capabilities and the contributions we can make in any area of it. This doesn't mean a "God-willing" attitude to life (passing the responsibility to a deity for what is or is not accomplished – more likely the latter), nor should it be taken to be an excuse for not attempting to stretch ourselves at times. Rather, I think, it involves recognising our abilities (and, even better, our passions) and following and applying them where we can, whether in work, social intercourse, or sport or other recreation.

If we can be so aware of these abilities and passions, and can feed them with varied and interesting ingredients of life experience, then, as with Phiroze's friend, I think success as I defined it above is and will continue to be achieved.

I do not think I could pass on more valuable advice.

APPENDIX I

Selected correspondence sent from abroad[1]

Liberia, December 2009[2]

Dear All

The phenomenon that some of you received my last e-mail but not all is apparently typical of what happens from here. Some messages simply disappear, so be aware that some from your end may not get through to me. And even logging on to Hotmail is by no means a certainty. Even so, what I have is more than I expected. I will shorten the odds by including you all.

There was really heavy rain Sunday night, such as one experiences only in the tropics. The hotel has a whole series of corrugated steel rooves, so you can imagine the decibel level!

A telling, though rather charming scene unfolded before me yesterday morning as I sat on the hotel terrace having breakfast. The terrace overlooks the ocean, as the hotel name implies, but there is no beach (only a rocky shore) and there is a potholed road between. Chugging up the road came a water bowser, which stopped just below me, the driver placing a large stone behind one of the back wheels to supplement the brakes, and began to deliver fresh water to the hotel (I have since learned that there is no piped water in Monrovia, let alone Liberia, except to a few standpipes). Shortly afterwards, a number of people, mainly brightly clothed young women and girls, arrived with a variety of brightly coloured plastic bowls of various sizes. I soon realised why. As the bowser started pumping water and the pump pressure rose, it became apparent that the transmission hose was full of leaks. The people had come to fill their bowls and obtain their daily water supply from these leaks. Precious commodities like this must not be wasted!

We drove to our first appointment yesterday along the potholed roads of Monrovia (I remember V S Naipaul in "A Bend in the River" describing vehicles in what is now the Congo proceeding on such roads as though they were stately galleons riding the waves). At one point my driver started muttering about the slow speed at which the car in front was being driven. With his left hand on the steering wheel and his right simultaneously clutching his mobile phone and sounding the horn, he overtook the car, dodging pedestrians in the middle of the road and cursing its driver roundly

---

[1] What follows is a small, but representative, fraction of correspondence that has survived in e-mail form.

[2] The correspondence that follows arose out of a two-week consultancy to teach a course in legislative drafting I had undertaken in Monrovia under the auspices of the United Nations Mission in Liberia.

and loudly as he did so. He then slowed down to the speed we were going at previously.

I was involved in a series of meetings, including with the (lady) Minister of Justice that were jolly enough, but seemed to serve little real purpose. They had been set up by Gillian Dare, the UK Political Counsellor & Resident Representative (the only UK "official" here). She is an energetic lady in her 50s, who works incredibly hard (though, as she says, there is really nothing else to do in Monrovia) and is well-versed in the country and its history, some of which she related to me over drinks and a plate of humus here at the hotel at the end of the afternoon.

The timetable of this morning's events is revealing. For my own amusement I made a note of the times.

The plan was that I would be collected from the hotel at 8.20 am so as to be able to set things up for the course before the official opening at 9.00 am (actually the collection time was not suggested by me but by Charles Gibson). So, naturally, just before that time I was waiting in the hotel reception.

At 8.40 I received a phone call from Charles to tell me that he was on his way. No reason was offered for the delay. I didn't ask for one and was actually pretty relaxed about the whole thing, as they could hardly start without me. After further phone calls both ways (I am becoming a dab hand at using a mobile; you would think I had been doing it all my life) the car finally came for me at 9.20, exactly an hour after the appointed time.

I arrived at the Liberian Institute of Public Administration (LIPA) where the course is being held at 9.25, finding 10 or so people there (out of at least 30 expected). People wandered in after that until, at 9.50, there was a sort of mutual decision to make a start. This turned out to be a false start, as just then some more important people were found to be arriving. Things finally got going, still without the Speaker of the House of Representatives, one of the key Liberians, at 10.00 am, exactly an hour late.

During the formal speeches (mercifully short) that followed people still kept arriving, accompanied each time by the loud squeaking of the un-oiled hinges of the door. At 10.25, just as the opening ceremony was concluding...

[I break off here as it is dark and all the electricity in the hotel has just gone off – but in the event only for a minute or so]

...with some administrative announcements, the Speaker arrived, full of bonhomie and waving cheery apologies to all. The proceedings had then to be reopened for him to say his piece.

I finally got going with the course at around 11.35. Needless to say, no arrangements had been made for me to be able to use the computer (LCD?) projector, as I had requested in advance. That might happen tomorrow, if I am very lucky. But the sessions went very well and I think most of the participants (some of whom seem to change from one hour to the next) enjoyed themselves. During lunch (taken in the training room) a group of the men started arguing about a point raised during the previous session. The pitch of voices got so loud that I thought it might end in violence. But it didn't.

Lots of love to all

R

Dear All

I will answer individual messages individually, but this method of bringing you observations saves constant cutting and pasting.

I have had little opportunity of seeing Monrovia, not that there is really much to see. It's probably superficially a bit like Nairobi might have been in about 1920, though not as well planned, and I'm sure dirtier. There is pretty dire poverty everywhere (though the people are certainly not in rags). Rubbish litters the streets, although not as badly as might be the case, and most bits of exposed grass seem to be covered most of the time with washing laid out to dry in the sun. Sad little stalls selling things to eat, usually staffed by young girls fanning the flies away, appear at intervals

I get very little exercise. The somewhat battered and faded sign outside the Oceanview Hotel advertises what it offers (not much), including "exercise facilities". When I asked about these, I was told that they had tried to install them but "the materials didn't work". Your guess as to what that means is as good as mine. You remember the philosophical comment of the typical African servant who has just smashed a favourite crystal jug: "Its time had come"? Well, the statement above seems to me equivalent to the opposite: "Its time has not yet come". True, there is a swimming pool, but this is tiny and not very inviting.

So in the mornings I walk to LIPA (it's rather as an East African might pronounce RIPA!) where the course is held. This takes about 12 minutes, about the time from home to the station at home, but the route lies partly up a fairly steep hill. So, in spite of the fact that the sun, at around 8.45 am, is not yet really punishing (temperature a mere 30° or so) I arrive somewhat damp.

The classes are chaotic. After some days I have made it understood that I prefer them not to use mobile phones while I'm teaching. I don't even mean that the phones should be switched off (there isn't the slightest chance of that happening) but I do object to trying to talk over one (or more) of my course participants holding animated conversations on them in classroom sessions. I have at least made that point, and so now the person receiving a call makes a bolt for the door, usually sweeping papers off desks as he or she does so.

Most of them are bored by the details of legislative drafting (and it is no problem openly falling asleep – or as one participant offered "you listen better with your eyes closed"!) and so I try to keep the details to a minimum and encourage them to wander off the point (not at all difficult). I think Andrew and Augustus from my London course, both alternating in the training room as "observers", are a bit embarrassed by their countrymen. But I just go with the flow. As I found in Nigeria, this discipline thing is (at least in Africa) bigger than I am.

Two of the participants are extremely large ladies (you should see what they eat in the lunch and tea breaks!). One is called Macdilla, which I think is a good name, rather appropriately in this case, for a giant hamburger. The other is Ophelia, who elects to be called Fifi, except that she spells it (with some logic, it must be said) Phe-Phe. We also have a normal sized young woman whose name is Cecelia and who, like Sophie's little one, is called Sisi (she spells it, again with logic, Ce-Ce).

More to follow when I have a bit more energy

Love R

Dear All

I haven't really described my room in the Krystal Oceanview Hotel, Monrovia. I am privileged in that it is in the "main" part of the hotel, up 2 small flights of unsteady-feeling wooden stairs. This is not a good route to have to take if you are a bit decrepit or unsteady, for the banister is so loose it might very well come away in your hand, and its use as a steadying or guide rail is not advised.

At the top of the stairs you reach a landing with four bedrooms, eccentrically numbered: the two that face you have 12 and 20 respectively on the doors, while those at each end (one of which is mine) have no numbers at all. My room key however is for room 31. This is actually the Ghassan A. H. Basma Suite, but I didn't notice this for several days, as the wooden notice advertising it is in shadow high up on the wall where (if you were looking for it) you would not expect to find it. I idly amuse myself by trying to guess the number of the room at the other end (is there a sequence that runs: x, 12, 20, 31? Rachel this is more your line).

As I mentioned before, the room is certainly large and 40 years ago or so might have been well-appointed. There is a sort of dressing room off it and a bathroom off that. In the dressing room there was once a built-in wardrobe, but it has long since lost its sliding doors (probably for firewood!) and looks forlorn with its collection of assorted mangy wire coat hangers and an empty neon strip-light holder. But, as has doubtless long been realised, it is surplus to requirements anyway, for there is a perfectly good wardrobe in the bedroom itself. The bathroom has formica facings coming away in places. These are good hiding-places for cockroaches, and switching on the light at night I see them scuttling for cover. But they are quite small and I've seen only two or three so far.

The sheets on the double bed at the moment are unusual. The bottom sheet has M. Gerrard in huge manuscript type letters flourished over it. Jessie will know if M. Gerrard is a famous designer of bed linen, but I rather suspect the sheets may have been created from linen used for something else, an exhibition stand say. The top sheet has a "divided down the middle" black and white pattern with "Stress and Relax" in large letters (twice). I sleep on the "Stress" side.

My dinner tonight was not untypical. The food actually isn't bad, but it takes forever to arrive. I ordered a seafood pizza. After 20 minutes the waiter came to tell me that they were out of shrimps, should they still go ahead? I said yes. As I read chapters (note the plural) of my book I was more and more aware of a man at the next table sitting with a lap-top in front of him and talking loudly into his mobile phone. This is of course commonplace, but right in one's ear it is a bit enervating after a while. Unusually for here the conversation was in an African language (the *lingua franca* is pidgin English, which is actually almost as incomprehensible) heavily punctuated by the universal African *Eeh*! In the end I moved to another table some way away off.

Finally my pizza arrived, complete with "shrimps" (actually prawns) after all. I couldn't eat it all and, as has happened before, the left-over segments were gratefully received by one of the waitresses to take home for her child.

Tomorrow it's back to the bear garden of a classroom!

Love R

Dear All
So glad others too have enjoyed my "postcards from Monrovia". To continue:

The first thing I do every afternoon on returning to the hotel after classes is have a pee. This is because the superbly misdescribed "rest room" at LIPA is best avoided. There is one lavatory bowl in a large not over-clean room, which serves for everyone on the course but, this being Monrovia, has no running water with which to flush it. So flushing has to be done periodically by hand with a bucket, although I admit I haven't enquired as to the details of how often this needs to be done in practice. And I do not like even to think about the possibility of diarrhoea.

Some of the characters in my class deserve a mention. The Assistant Minister of Justice is an able young woman, in her mid-thirties I would guess, who did a post-graduate degree in the US. She normally dresses well and soberly, but on Saturday (clearly a "dressing down" day in government circles here) she appeared in a brilliant yellow tee shirt and shorts with "Support Maryland" on the front and a hideous peaked cap to match (there may have been the name of a football or baseball team as well; I was so blinded by the outfit I can't remember). The only things missing from this bizarre get-up were a set of cheer-leader's pom-poms.

One of the more vocal members of the class is the aptly named Chattah. He is the comedian of the group, always nattily dressed in a shiny suit with an immaculately tied and tie-pinned bright green, yellow or purple tie, and always with a breast pocket handkerchief to match. He periodically has others in stitches. I can't understand what he says (though I'm assured it's in English) but enjoy the rowdiness it produces.

Then there is a man who always appears in a large Stetson hat (he removes it for classes and places its delicately upturned brim on his desk). I don't know what his real name is, but he is the Chief Clerk to one of the Houses of Parliament and elects to be called Esquire. It's apparently his idea of how a senior professional man should be addressed (and prompted others to ask me about the use of this "title" in the UK). The equivalent might be for me to put it out that I'd like to be known as "Your Honour" or possibly even "My Lord".

One or two of the other names are interesting. One very charming and polite young man is called Handison (a good blend of Henderson and Anderson, with overtones of being useful about the house). Another (a young man, over six feet tall and one of the most gifted at shouting down those who have the temerity to argue with him) is named Dubuisi. I made a strong effort early on to remember this accurately by thinking, just before I said his name, of Debussy. But otherwise any attempt at a comparison between his personality and the gentle music of that impressionist composer gives about as extreme a mismatch as you could imagine.

More later if I have time (events begin to crowd in on one towards the end of a course).

Love R

Dear Irene

Yes, there are indeed many horrible stories if one wants to dredge them up (even Augustus had to flee for his life from Liberia and live in a refugee camp with thousands of others across the border in Ivory Coast).

Harold Platt always used to say that Africans, and he was talking of East Africans who are by and large considerably milder, were full of every kind of human emotion (from generosity through to cruelty) at double the intensity of us Europeans. I reckon that in West Africa you can probably multiply this by three.

But all those horrible things happened (and for sure will happen again somewhere, sometime, as the world gets increasingly overpopulated) and, unless it is one's job to do so, I don't think it is profitable for anybody to dwell on them. For this same reason I usually tend to avoid yet more morbid exposure to the European holocaust of the 1940s. One has to accentuate the positive; and find humour where one can. As I hope I have conveyed, it is not difficult to find it here.

Love
Roger

Dear All

My note to Miry and Irene yesterday stated how I had not been paid my daily allowance money and might have to creep out of the hotel at the dead of night. Today I was informed that (by some miracle) my cheque from UNDP was ready, but that I must collect it from them before 12 noon. I later learned that this was because those who had actually turned up for work there today (a small minority) were leaving at that time, doubtless to join all those who had taken the day off, for a UN Christmas party!

That was the easy part. They couldn't pay me cash (apparently that is against the rules) and so I was given a cheque that I needed to go to a commercial bank to cash. My heart sank, recalling that in Nairobi if you got in and out of a bank in under an hour you were doing exceptionally well. And this is Monrovia.

I was driven through the streets of the city, seething with people and with vehicles proceeding round the crowds and in and out of the potholes at a snail's pace, and after the half hour it took thus to cover the necessary mile or so we arrived at the bank. Inside people were queuing and milling about everywhere; if I'd been an ordinary customer I'd have been there for the rest of the day. But I was (at least for today) a "UN customer". After various enquiries by my minder we walked up some narrow, dirty stairs to where the "UN Department" of the bank was situated.

This was a tiny, grubby, partitioned-off little office with a woman with an American accent (such people are known as American Liberians and form an aristocracy here) sitting behind an office desk. To my astonishment she proceeded to cash the cheque without fuss, but (and here's the catch) the amount was just over $1600 and she had notes only for $10 and under. So I had to be paid in two "bricks" of money. You have also to remember that US dollars are legal tender here, so the money I received has mostly been in circulation in Liberia for some time and most of the notes (as with most African money most of the time) are too filthy and disgusting for words.

I will need only $300 or so to pay my food bill at the hotel. The remaining repulsive little bundles will need to be taken home and deposited in a bank in London. But I have as yet to obtain a copy voucher to prove where the money comes from (I was in such a rush at UNDP that I forgot to ask for one) and unless I have this my London bank will suspect that I am trying to launder the street proceeds of selling crack cocaine, and probably be under a duty to inform the police accordingly.

I'm actually looking forward to getting back to normality.

Love to all
Roger

PS. I just had to tell you that at the closing ceremony this evening (more later) I was asked to make sure that I personally send the greetings of the people of Liberia to Her Majesty the Queen, and to Gordon Brown[3], and to pass on the invitation for them to come to Liberia.

Dear Irene

The main news is that <u>I think</u> I'm on tonight's BA flight from Accra. It is supposed to leave just before midnight GMT (also the time here in Accra). This should get into LHR at around 6.35 am tomorrow. However, there have been so many slips along the way that I won't actually believe it until the plane is in the air. I can't use the mobile here (I've tried), and frankly it's not worth getting another Sim Card for one call, so I have logged on to the Internet at the Golden Tulip Hotel here in Accra, at which I have stayed overnight and am still today, at vast expense ($200 per night B & B). Electing to pay cash, I had to hand this over in advance. The room is good. I had a nice shower last night, but it was so late that I didn't sleep much.

I've had so many adventures on this journey home that, having nothing else to do today but wait for this evening's plane, I decided to write it all up. Though I say it myself, it is quite a story. Some of the details you know already, and it will suffice at this stage to say that a replacement Kenya Airways flight came into Monrovia at about 11 pm last night (I had been at the airport since 6 pm) and took off with all of us on the cancelled flight to Accra at about 1 am this morning, arriving at 2.30 am. I was given an economy boarding card in error, but I was past caring, just glad to get out of Monrovia.

My problems began all over again at Accra with having to get a transit visa (needed to leave the airport). The officials here were without exception curt, rude and arrogant (perhaps partly in response to being kept up so long for a late flight). In the end they seized my passport (giving me a receipt) to ensure that I pay the relevant transit visa which, if I get away within 48 hours of landing will be $20 instead of the $100 they were going to charge me. Having deliberately left consideration of my case until last (I actually didn't care; it was so late anyway) I finally got away from the airport at 4.15 am, fortunately with a young American who had arranged to stay at this hotel and had also arranged for the hotel courtesy bus to collect us. If I hadn't run into him at the visa counter I would not have had any idea where to go to spend the night. The porters at the airport are aggressive, rather unpleasant licensed beggars, who snatch your bags and demand money for doing nothing that one couldn't do equally well oneself.

---

[3] At that time Britain's Prime Minister.

I got a hotel taxi to take me to British Airways office this morning, where I could speak only on the phone to someone from the reception desk. She said she had put me on tonight's flight (business class). She said she'd have to charge me $70 for the administration. Another argument about it being "circumstances beyond my control". She said she'd put a note to that effect on the booking. But I don't trust anyone here any more. I'll be so glad to get out of West Africa.

I'll try to keep you posted if there are any more changes.

Lots of love, and hopes of an early return.

Roger

For the full written-up account of leaving Liberia after this assignment had been completed, see Appendix II

New Zealand, December 2011[4]

Here I am on the coast at Coromandel, amid the delightful scenery that this part of the country is known for. Going through my head incessantly have been the lines of Edward Lear I once learned as a child:

On the coast of Coromandel,
Where the early pumpkins grow,
In the middle of the woods
Lived the Yonghy-Bonghy-Bo.
Two old chairs and half a candle,
One old jug without a handle
These were all his worldly goods:
In the middle of the woods,
These were all the worldly goods
Of the Yonghy-Bonghy-Bo...

It goes on at some length about his doomed courtship with Lady Jingly who has milk-white Dorking hens (I refreshed my memory by looking it up on the internet).

But, disappointment, disappointment! I've discovered that the Yonghy-Bonghy-Bo didn't live here in New Zealand after all. The name is simply taken from the British Navy ship, *HMS Coromandel*, which bought (or took) local timber for masts for sailing ships in the 1820s. The name actually comes from the Coromandel Coast in

---

[4] The reason for this journey was a conference for the Pacific Region of the Commonwealth called to debate and discuss a model Integrity in Public Life Act that I had drafted for the Commonwealth Secretariat.

India, i.e. the south eastern coastal strip of what is today Tamil Nadu, roughly from Madras southwards (the name is a corruption of *Cholamandalam*, the Tamil name for "land of the Tamils"). *That's* where Edward Lear had in mind!

The Internet can make us all instant pundits.

The last evening in Hamilton I went to a "Blue Grass" concert with Susan, her partner Tom, and Felicity (whose husband Roger did not want to come). The main part of the concert was given by a visiting American quartet called "X Train" whose virtuosity with banjo, mandolin and guitar quite "blew me away" (as it did the others I was with). I have never heard anything quite so good, especially in a type of music with which I am only vaguely familiar. In fact it so happened that they were performing last night once again very near to where I was staying (Thames, at the foot of the Coromandel peninsula) and I did something I have never done before: I went to a concert by the same musicians on successive nights! I enjoyed it as much the second time.

I got to the Jacaranda Lodge (there is actually only one rather feeble looking Jacaranda tree in the grounds) on the recommendation of the Mana retreat, an establishment quite near here that had in turn been recommended to me by some of the MTL people in Hamilton (Brad and Ann Brown had stayed there when in NZ). I tried ringing them several times but never got anything but a recorded message. I went there. It is very "spiritual" (only vegetarian food, etc. etc.) indeed so spiritual that there was not a single corporeal being in sight anywhere, even though the whole establishment was wide open to the world. I wandered through the place at leisure and then sat down in their spiritual library to read a book. After about ¾ hour I heard a car and found someone connected with the place.

Actually, somewhat to my relief by this time, they had no vacancy for accommodation as they were starting a men's "retreat weekend" later that day and all the staff had buggered off in the meantime.

"But you could join the retreat weekend!"

I muttered a feeble excuse and asked if they could recommend anywhere else; hence the Jacaranda, where I am staying for 2 nights

It is an absolutely delightful bed and breakfast just outside the town of Coromandel, run by Robin (an energetic woman in her sixties). Soon after I arrived I heard her speaking to a young woman friend of hers in, of all things, Hebrew (the friend is an Israeli married to a Kiwi), albeit in Robin's case with a New Zealand accent! It turns out that Robin is Jewish, studied Hebrew at university in Auckland and lived for some 6 years in Israel. Her surname is Münch – that of the husband from whom she has been, she tells me, divorced for over 30 years.

On her suggestion I discovered something else: an amazing little railway at Driving Creek, just outside *our* Coromandel. It was built by an extraordinary man, Barry Brickell, now 76, who has two main interests in life: designing and building railways and making pottery. The one was originally built to gather clay for the other, but soon took on a life of its own. You can take an hour's round trip on the railway that climbs a steep hillside, by an intricate series of spirals and reversing points, and now ends in a rotunda-like structure, with an impressive view over the coastline far below, that he has called the "Eyefull Tower"(!)

The trip before mine was full of simpering Indians and Japanese, who got off the train and posed toothily by and up against it for so long for endless permutations of photographs that *our* departure had to be delayed slightly.

Later I went for a walk near to Colville that Robin encouraged me to go on. It turned out not to be for the faint hearted: a solid climb of about an hour and a quarter, occasionally very steep, of the kind that has you thinking that the summit must surely be round the next bend (but never is). That wouldn't have been so bad if it hadn't been for the fact that most of the walk was in a howling gale; and there was the hazard of cattle that refused to budge. But there were stupendous views from the top.

She had the grace to offer me a Radox bath on my return.

The weather here seems to follow a pattern at the moment: the mornings are mostly cloudy, the sky clearing by about early afternoon. But the wind has been almost non-stop since I arrived in the country.

The other guests at the Jacaranda last night were a couple from England who never stopped talking, to each other and anybody else present, usually at the same time. It was an interesting breakfast. Fortunately they left immediately afterwards.

New Zealand went to the polls today for a general election. Robin is glued to the gradually emerging results on television, which seem to indicate a centre-right National party victory.

Yesterday I had what I think would have been an amazing experience even for those not particularly interested in bird-watching. There is a place called Muriwai Beach on the coast due west of Auckland that is well known here for its enormous sweep of surfing beach but, more to the present point, its cliffs and an off-shore rocky island house in the breeding season (September – January) a colony of *many hundreds* of gannets, and to a lesser extent white-fronted terns. What is more, it is possible to see the gannets in particular from viewing points close by. I have *never* been so near to such large wild birds (just a little smaller than Canada geese, though of course a slightly different shape); not only were the nearest ones to us only about 6 feet away on the other side of an open-structured fence, but the wind was such that some of them hovered in the air near to us almost within touching distance. The birds nest on the ground in huge tightly compacted groups, but just out of pecking distance from each other, and we could see clearly many downy chicks and all the social interaction between the adult birds.

This country is full of amazing places. Kay had rung the Waitakere (pronounced Wye-*tak*-ery) Estate Hotel near Auckland to say that she had "a VIP guest from England" that she would like to show round the place. By the time we got there the receptionist seemed to think that I was visiting with a view to setting up an international conference, and, not daring to catch Kay or Richard's eye, I felt duly obliged to play the part (and in due course came away with a full "conference pack" of materials). The hotel, originally a private dwelling, dates in its present form from about the 1970s and is set in a valley surrounded by a huge tract of native rain forest (they seem to call it "bush" here) with stupendous views all around.

Today we walked around North Head, a vantage point for the various parts of Auckland that had housed a gun battery from the late nineteenth century up to and including the Second World War. I think I explained previously that Richard has had more than one career, but for the past decade or so has been a Master captaining various ferries running between the city and its offshore islands, and so is familiar with absolutely everything that takes place in the local waters.

I'll try and write more later. It's actually quite difficult to find the time while staying with friends.

Love
R

Bandar Seri Begawan, Brunei, October 2013

Dear Irene
…The course went well on the first day, I think. Yesterday morning (Monday) there was what was billed as a "share and discuss session", but the sharing was 95% by me and there was not much discussion. But there were about 30 people present, including a princess, one of the Sultan's daughters, who sat in a special rather throne-like chair in front of everybody else, so the atmosphere was rather formal.

It was my "honour" to sit next to her during the tea-break which, true to Malay style (most of the population are Malays) was more of a full-size meal. I don't know where they put it all (well, some are a bit fat). The princess, who apparently is about 40 but looks much younger, didn't have much to say (one addresses her as "Your Highness" or "Princess"). I felt rather sorry for her. There must be hardly anyone outside her family she can talk to normally person to person….

All love
Roger

Dear Irene

Yesterday, as I told you, it was a particular pleasure to have been sought out by Salman Nabi who was one of the participants on the course in Islamabad in I think 1995 that I ran with Keith (that was the time we - Audrey included - visited Arshi's parents)[5]. Salman is now working here as a consultant to the Government, having retired as head of the legal division of Pakistan's Income Tax Department. He told me he had learned that I was here from the articles I told you about in the Brunei Times (I'll bring a copy of the relevant paper home with me). We are to meet up for lunch on Friday. The comparatively young women in the drafting section here were fascinated that two acquaintances from 20 odd years ago should suddenly meet up so to speak in their office. I recall with particular pleasure that Salman took me on a trip up to the hill station at Murree, quite near to Islamabad and Rawalpindi, on the free last day I was there. With its Anglican church, it was almost a little piece of British India…

All love
Roger

Gibraltar, February 2014[6]

Dear Irene
Everything seems suddenly familiar again - Gibraltar with its narrow little streets and down-market pubs and tourists (even at this time of the year). It's all so reminiscent of St Helier in Jersey. The Rock Hotel is exactly the same in the way it manages maintain its standards at good second-rate.

Feeling rumpled and tired after my arrival at the hotel last night in what seemed almost like a hurricane, and having been simultaneously blasted and soaked in my efforts to get a taxi at Gibraltar Airport after the long tedious journey by coach from Malaga (to where the plane had, as previously reported, been diverted) I had trouble finding my room (no. 210). Rather like that hotel I stayed at in Monrovia, Liberia, the numbering of rooms here is eccentric: a sign at the top of the stairs points to rooms 201 -212, yet for some reason there is no 202, 209 or 211. I thought it was my state of shell-shock that had me wandering up and down the corridor silently cursing, but no, I confirmed the missing numbers in the cool light of today. Having finally found it, the room is actually large and rather nice in its old-fashioned way – for instance you have to lock and unlock the door with a conventional key that has

---

[5] I was running the course with my colleague and mentor Keith Patchett, and his wife Audrey had accompanied him for the duration. Arshi Haque is a friend from London whom we first got to know as the mother of a friend of Jonno's at primary school in London. Her father was a retired group captain from the Pakistan Air Force

[6] This was actually the second year in succession that I had visited Gibraltar to run a drafting course there. The first year Irene had joined me for part of the time, hence the occasional references to things remembered.

to be jiggled a bit in the lock – although the fitted carpets are a bit rucked up. The bed could reasonably comfortably sleep three.

There are the same old (literally) waiters in the dining room who appear mostly to be doing their work in their sleep, except that mine had to wake up for a moment as he brought my main course tonight: "Very 'ot" he muttered as he almost threw the plate down in front of me shaking his hands as he walked off. And indeed it was; the heat radiating from the plate as I leant over it to take a forkful of food gave the sensation of having a face massage. The food here usually manages to taste as though it had been cooked by me on an off night (good intentions, bad execution). Tonight was no exception, and the piping-hot chicken breast was over-cooked (probably at least in part by the plate).

Today the weather has been fine but very windy, and hence not so warm (I was glad I had my overcoat). The wind dropped a bit this evening and I sat for a while on the room balcony, but wherever in this small space I positioned myself I seemed to get drops of water falling on me (it wasn't raining so they must have been from overflow pipes from the rooms above). Perhaps it's not such a bad thing that the Rock could book me in only until Wednesday, when I will have to move to Eliott's Hotel…

Love and hugs
Roger

Dear Irene
I checked in to Eliott's Hotel after work this afternoon. I walked here from the office, checked in and took a taxi on a round trip to pick up my case that I had left at the Rock. The hotel is part of a small Irish group (its other hotels are 4 in Dublin and one in Annapolis, USA). They advertise themselves as "Distinctive Hotels Distinguished by Excellence". What bollocks!

Apart from anything else, the management is illiterate. There is a printed note in the bathroom stating:

> "Gibraltar is an isthmus enjoying a privileged climate comprising pleasant temperatures and radiant sunshine".

Gibraltar, as even Ollie and Charlie would probably know, isn't an isthmus; it's a peninsula. As for the advert-speak, I've not heard of a "privileged" climate before (did it go to a fee-paying school, I wonder?), and how, I ask myself, can "radiant" sunshine be different from the ordinary variety?

The dining room serves the same sort of food as the Rock (to be fair, marginally better). I had the "special" tonight: the badly photocopied sheet on which it was announced reminded me suddenly of Joseph's writing on the freezer in Nairobi:

Fillet Code
Served with Cream
spinach sauce, much
Potatoes and veg's

It took me a short while to decipher the Fillet Code; I just had to have it (together with its much potatoes and veg's). Waiters rush in and out of the kitchen door (it has kick marks at the bottom and greasy hand marks at shoulder level) but in spite of all the flying about the service is at slow motion tempo. It didn't matter; I wasn't in a hurry (it doesn't do to be in a hurry here).

Love R

Dear Irene

…Hotel dinners continue to amuse (so long as one's expectations continue to be low). There is one table I always choose for this meal as it is the only one with sufficient light for comfortable reading. There was only one waiter in the dining room tonight, rushing around as usual to little effect; all the others had been grabbed for what must have been a Valentine's Day dinner in the conference room. From the kitchen you could hear the staff shouting at each other in Spanish; nearly all the lower levels of staff in all hotels and restaurants in Gibraltar are Spanish people who live across the border in La Linea, and they all seem to shout at each other.

Periodic crashes also could be heard coming from the kitchen (one so loud it sounded like a door being kicked in, causing all five of us in the dining room to start in alarm), and then in the dining room itself the flying waiter accidentally dropped what sounded like a glass stopper as it hit the tiled floor and rolled round a bit. He mopped up what had spilt and then crashed around at the sideboard as he removed quantities of crockery or cutlery from it, or stowed others back into it. The first morning at breakfast I inadvertently sat at the dining table next to this sideboard and was nearly deafened by the racket, but as I am now getting to be an old hand around here I'm beginning to know what and where to avoid.

In fact only three tables were occupied tonight (the others by two British couples who didn't seem to speak at all – perhaps they were in shock from all the noise), but it still took about 20 minutes to get my first course (crispy duck spring roll – in reality rubber duck spring roll). Dreadful music played in the background. And then my steak arrived only 10 minutes after the rubber duck and caught me quite off guard. Not expecting the waiter for another 20 minutes or so, I jumped in surprise when he suddenly appeared at my shoulder, nearly knocking the plate out of his hand.

I have to report that the steak was actually good, though more than I could eat.

As I moved out of the dining room, everywhere seemed suddenly tranquil. I called and got into the empty lift and, facing the doors, pushed the button for my floor. The doors closed, but the lift did not move. As I turned round I found a youngish man standing behind me smiling vacantly. It was one of those short interludes in which you begin to doubt your sanity. The man had definitely not been there when I got into the lift; what's more he could not have followed me in, as I was facing the doors all the time. I suffered a momentary panic.

It suddenly dawned on me that at this level the lift has a back set of doors as well, and that these open directly into the kitchen; they were now closing. In a flash all was revealed. I apologised to the man on the way down for my idiotic misunderstanding of the situation. He continued to smile vacantly, signalling to me vaguely that he did not understand a word of English.

All love
Roger

Dear Irene

...Today I walked in the other direction up past the Moorish Castle (an ugly bunker of a place, you may remember) to the viewing point overlooking the isthmus where the airport is and La Linea (we were up there last year with Gail). That's worth doing, but as I walked around I thought what a capacity the people here have for making the worst of a potentially beautiful place. Some of the old Mediterranean style houses are nice, and in the centre of town some of these have been kept in good repair, but most of the buildings in the town (and elsewhere) are superbly ugly. And outside the centre of town (where presumably some effort is made to tidy up) there is litter all over the place, including seemingly dumped piles of plastic bags of refuse, usually being picked over by gulls and pigeons (and doubtless monkeys too – I saw a few of those yesterday and today, though not at the rubbish).

One of the waiters in the dining room has befriended me. He poured me an unsolicited (and unwanted) extra glass of wine this evening. Rachel writes that the hotel sounds like Fawlty Towers; though I have seen only clips from that series, I imagine she's right. I seem to be the only man at dinner time who wears a jacket. Though the women diners sometimes make a bit of an effort, most of the men (particularly the younger ones) seem to be in a competition as to who can look the scruffiest. I feel old; not in the sense of decrepit, weary or overcome by life, far from it, but simply in the sense of having a set of values that obviously belongs to a time that has passed (not only as regards dress; also language, communication generally, sport, education, the former Empire, etc.)

All love
Roger

Dear Irene

It was raining this evening when I went in to dinner (actually it had been a pleasant spring day earlier – I had lunch with Paul and it was warm enough to sit outside). An English couple preceding me into the dining-room were telling the waiter at the reception desk in that curious language affecting a slight foreign accent that English people often seem to use when addressing a foreigner, and spoken slowly in a loud voice as though he or she were a half-wit:

> "We come from Cuba. It raining there too." [*Translation* – We were in Cuba recently; it was raining there as well]

I'm not sure what kind of reaction was expected to this fascinating information (which was presented in mock indignation – implying that it's not supposed to rain anywhere outside England). The waiter merely smiled weakly and showed them to a table.

My table, the only one not in semi-darkness, nowadays has a reserved sign on it (for me!) The waiter merely tells me what the special dish is (no more photocopied details, unfortunately) and asks me what colour my glass of wine is to be (only one brand is offered in single-glass-sized small bottles). But preferential treatment doesn't extend to fast service: I don't have a starter, but my dish still takes 30 – 40 minutes to arrive.

Tomorrow I'm meeting Gail after work – we'll have tea and a chat in the Veranda Bar (it is at street level and has no veranda). She has a house in Spain, and Paul tells me she had a slight run-in with the Spanish authorities a few months ago following which her car (that she used to leave on the Spanish side of the border) was torched! Maybe I'll find out more.

Dear Irene

…I was entertained this evening by Paul and five others from the office, all of whom were on my course either this year (three of the young men) or last (two of the women – Yvette and Claire – both of whom of course remember you). We went to a restaurant in Irish Town (actually the name of a road in the old part of town) that was excellent.

It was a nice change from the hotel, where I seem to have established routines. For example I always have the same things for breakfast (which frankly isn't much cop) and usually smile and nod there to an older woman (she's probably younger than I am) who seems to be on her own and whom I had placed as "county" English (she wears pearls and a cardigan round her shoulders). She's a change from the run of guests here, I can tell you.

As we were both by the lift the other morning she suddenly said "You are vurking here?" in a German accent. It didn't fit in at all with my preconception; almost as bizarre as if little Rosie had suddenly spoken to me in Spanish (which you will remember, according to her, she can speak). Anyway, having got over the surprise at my complete misreading of the lady, my immediate expectation was that she was going to make some kind of complaint to me (maybe I hadn't bowed to her as appropriate). But far from it: she told me how nice it was to see a person (me) "reading a book zees days, razer than vun of zose machines". I muttered something suitably appreciative in agreement. We old people of class have to stick together.

All love
Roger

Accra, Ghana, June 2014[7]

I though you would like some snapshots from the Golden Tulip Hotel, Accra:
1. Although I had to pay the total bill for the room (inc. breakfast) on arrival @ over £200 per day, each day my key fails to open the door when I come back in the afternoon and I have to get it re-activated. I complain but get blank looks.
2. There is no plug for the bath (in fact I use the shower anyway).
3. The television doesn't work properly (the picture keeps going into a distorted "letterbox" mode). Although I have taught myself how to get it as it should be, it slips back every 10 minutes or so.
4. The air-conditioner in the bedroom doesn't work properly and showered me with spray when I tried to turn it on. Fortunately I don't need or want it as there is one in the lounge/ante room.
5 The only decoration consists of 2 pictures approx 25" x 30" next to each other on the wall in the lounge/ante-room. They are identical photographs of the *Arc de Triomphe* in Paris!

Love Roger

---

[7] A visit on behalf of the Commonwealth Secretariat to evaluate the effects of their support for legislative drafting in Africa. There was a sequel to the story. I had inadvertently been booked in, and paid, for four nights at the Golden Tulip instead of three. I was told when checking out that all I needed to do was to reclaim the amount overpaid when I got home. I tried to do so over the following months but nothing happened and the hotel seemed to be what my grandmother used to call "cocking a deaf 'un". I feared I was going to have to forget about it. However, later that year on my RIPA course in London I had some Ghanaians, including an MP who I discovered was not only an influential man but also a director of the Golden Tulip. At my request he called the hotel from London and explained the problem I was having. The overpaid money was credited to me next day! It's not what you know…

Nairobi, Kenya, June 2014[8]

Dear Charles

Thank you again for your hospitality and company during last week (in particular it was a great convenience to be able to sort myself out at your house yesterday afternoon). I'm sorry that I had to dash off rather precipitately last night and that I didn't have the opportunity to say goodbye properly to you, but the gridlocked roads resulting from the President's visits yesterday constituted extenuating circumstances! In the event it took about 25 minutes for my taxi to get down the main road from Nairobi Club to the Highway roundabout, and another 25 from there to the airport. So we timed it just about right. The flight was on time (after **three** security checks of our hand baggage plus one of our hold baggage - all other airports that I know of manage with one) and though almost full went without a hitch, and I finally got home at about 8.15 am London time (10.15 Kenya time).

It was good in some ways to be back in Nairobi after such a long time and I had some interesting meetings - some of those in top legal positions had been my students when I used to give occasional lectures at the Kenya School of Law under Tudor Jackson. The centre of the city hasn't changed that much, but all buildings except the newish ones look rather down-at-heel, both outside and inside. The concept of maintenance and renewal that has been a cornerstone of Fairview policy seems hardly to exist anywhere else (I understand the family's reasons for selling the hotel, but it may be a pity for travellers). However, the abiding memory is of stationary lines of vehicles on both sides of the Highway and the approaches to it. The new Nairobi by-pass I saw under construction in the Karen area will probably be too little (and in a sense too late). It's the story of modern Africa.

Best regards
Roger

Nairobi, February 2015[9]

Dear Irene
Here I am in the dining room at the Fairview at 10.15 am (7.15 am your time and probably about the time Jessie will be arriving from Australia). I am waiting for my room to be got ready, but I have no complaint about that as check-out is later.

The journey was LONG; not so much the flight, which went more or less according to schedule, but it took over an hour to get through immigration and pay for the

---

[8] A visit on the same consultancy as that to Accra above. The note is to Charles Szlapak, a good friend from our time in Kenya and former owner of the Fairview Hotel, where I had been staying.

[9] The occasion of this visit was to assess the needs of Kenya with regard to training in legislative drafting.

necessary visa (£30 in sterling). The KQ flight was actually the first of at least two, and there was a huge queue behind me as I went through to collect my case and arrange a taxi to the hotel. It then took *an hour and forty minutes* to get from the airport to Bishops Road (solid traffic almost all of the way) and then we were stopped by the GSU[10] for a security check just before reaching the hotel. The taxi driver reckons that with the GSU presence (obviously more because of the Israeli Embassy across the road than the Fairview) this is the safest place in Nairobi.

The flight was pretty full, though the middle seat next to me in the central three was vacant. Kenya Airways are OK, but as so often in African contexts their cabin staff seem to be going through the motions of their job rather than "living it". They give me the impression that they are saying to themselves "we're not really sure why we're supposed to do this, but that's what we've been told to do so we'd better do it." For example, the steward who offered me dinner did so from behind me (where I couldn't see him) and in my ear, so that I started in surprise. By his lights his job is to hand out dinners; I don't think the idea that the work involves performing a service impinges on his consciousness, and even if it does the concept is probably without much meaning.

I have a meeting with the Law School this afternoon. They are coming to collect me after lunch and take me to Karen. It's warm (quite pleasant actually, I expected it to be hotter) and partly cloudy today.

All love
Roger

Dear Irene

I have just come back from having dinner with Vera & Michael[11]; we went to an Italian restaurant in Westlands. I took a taxi back and forth as they don't like driving any distance from home at night. Though, as you know, they remarried about a year ago (it would have been sooner when their sons were all here, but they couldn't track down their divorce papers) they do not live together, except when in London, where they have been often for medical treatment for Mike. He was in Vera's words "at Death's door" about a year ago with some kind of skin cancer, but has responded well to some new treatment given in London and is now doing well. The three of us had a very good and jolly evening.

This afternoon for an hour or so I took a trip down Memory Lane, visiting the Nairobi Club and Chyulu Road. What a contrast! The former seems (rather comfortingly to me) to be exactly the same as it was 30 years ago (the lounge where you can read newspapers hasn't changed one jot). One comparatively small difference is that the rear entrance to the swimming pool that used to be opposite

---

[10] The General Service Unit, a militarised gendarmerie set up in the early days of Kenya's independence.
[11] Vera Somen had been our GP when we lived in Kenya. In fact Michael died in early 2016.

our house is now closed off (the car park is still there but the access to it is from the road at the back). So, being unable to exit at that point I had to retrace my steps back around the cricket field and through the clubhouse.

It was easy to see why. The only thing the same as it was on "our side" of Chyulu Road is the ugly dilapidated house at the beginning, although that is now part of an ugly little conglomeration of kiosks and small downmarket shops. Our house, along with every other one in the block that included the road were the Suttills used to live has disappeared without trace, and mostly high-rise office and apartment blocks have gone up in their places. Our site now contains an ugly 8-story glass office block called KMA House fronting on to the road that used to be to the side of us. Next to it, on the plot where 3-year-old Jonno used to call through the fence to the "boys", is an apartment block containing at a guess about 120 flats. The Platts' house, across what is now a main road, is still there but almost certainly not for much longer.

I hope this message is not too full of mistakes: I discovered when I got home that I had left my glasses behind at the restaurant. This was my second pair! The first one went missing on my way from the airport yesterday morning, so I am doing my best to write without, using large letters on the computer.

All love
R

Putrajaya, Malaysia, November 2015[12]

Dear All
Irene I got your various messages and am glad that everything seems to be going well.

As a matter of fact I went out this afternoon after work to the local shopping mall to get myself some coffee and biscuits to bring back to the hotel. This is because the hotel coffee is disgusting (even Nescafé tastes better) and I have remembered some of my food and drink rules for Malaysia: never drink coffee, unless in a very high class hotel, and never eat beef, which is always tough, stringy and tasteless.

Shopping malls are depressingly the same everywhere, and I actually thought as I walked around that, but for the little Malay women all imprisoned in their headscarves, I could easily have been walking around the mall at Thousand Oaks, or one of the newer ones in London for that matter. Many of the shops are actually the same, and with the same centre rows of little kiosks selling things you can do without, the same escalators, the same mindless wandering around…Anyway I got what I was looking for, at Cold Storage (very big supermarket chain) and left as

---

[12] This visit was to run a two-week drafting course for lawyers who had recently joined the Attorney-General's Chambers as drafters, and some others.

quickly as possible, getting back to the hotel as thunder and lightning round about, and that pre-rain wind, threatened a tropical storm.

I had complained about various things here at the Everly Hotel. The next day a skinny young Chinese man of about 18 (well, give or take) wearing a crumpled white shirt and no tie came up to me in the dining room as I was having dinner and announced himself as Loo, the hotel manager. Loo has in fact risen above his name and seen to it that I get what I want in the dining room. My requests are modest: merely that I don't have to have the set meal each evening, the main course of which is always loaded with rice. I can now have anything I like to a ceiling of 80 ringgit (about £14, which goes further here).

Putrajaya is not a place that tourists come to (at least not if they have any sense) and the hotel seems to be full of Malay families, which makes breakfast (average to below average standard) a bit of a scrum. Loo told me I could have a table set apart (at least I think he did, accents here make spoken English often difficult to understand, he might have been advising me to make an early start) but actually I anyway prefer to go early before the dining room is full of people milling around. I still haven't quite overcome the jetlag and find myself waking very early in the morning. The view from my room is pleasant, overlooking as it does a large (probably artificial) lake.

I'm collected each day by an official driver at 8.45 am and driven the eight minutes or so to a complex of offices where the course is being held on the first floor. It's actually going very well. The course participants range from keen but not too bright, to really rather stupid, in other words much as usual, but they seem to be enjoying the experience. I am being well looked after by those on the course who seem to have been appointed class monitors. We finish at 4.00 pm. I have told them they can call me Roger, rather than Sir. Some now call me Sir Roger.

I have invited Koid and Yoong over for lunch on Saturday.

Lots of love
Roger

Dear All

The course ... was a great success today. I think I have enrolled most of the nineteen participants into the subject and they seem to be enjoying themselves (I got them working on things almost from the beginning). The main trouble is that I sometimes have difficulty in understanding what they say, especially if they don't speak up.

I went for a little walk at lunchtime – not much to see and not very interesting, as Putrajaya is a modern concrete jungle. Aspects of the hotel continue to be mildly irritating. At dinner tonight (it is now 9.50 pm) no-one seemed to know what I was to be charged (the AG's Office are anyway paying for my B & B and dinner) and hence what I needed to sign. After a huddle that took five minutes (the junior person at the desk had to call his senior, and that person had to call someone else) I was presented with a bill for 0.00 ringgit. What, I asked, was the point of signing for a zero debit? This caused more confusion. I asked for the manager; "unfortunately" he (or she) was not available. I rolled my eyes, not for the first time here; it's not the fault of the staff, who are doing their incompetent best, but lack of proper management. I'll try to sort it out tomorrow...

Dear All

I've just come back to my room on the tenth floor of the Everly Hotel, Putrajaya, in the lift that annoyingly announces each one as it stops there (for the blind presumably) and, in some language presumably meant to be English, it informs us that we have arrived at what sounds like "the hair floor". Once unlocked with the touch-card, my bedroom door needs a hefty shoulder charge to it to get it open, though I don't actually have to take a run at it.

Inside, I mostly do not have the air-conditioning on, as if I do it is extremely uncomfortable sitting at the "desk" with my lap-top as the blast of cold air is then directed straight at me (there is no way of adjusting the vents, believe me I've tried). I think it's a cunning plan to save electricity. Oh, and this morning I had to complain at the reception as the wi-fi kept going off. Though I didn't see Loo (he must normally hide in his office – notice that I have stopped myself from making the obvious silly remark – or else possibly the young man I spoke to last week was an impostor, for I have never seen him since) things definitely then took a turn for the better.

Enough of this nonsense. There's nothing much to report. I had a really good day with Koid and Yoong yesterday, the gist of which I copied to Irene. For much of the time, though, we were stuck in heavy traffic. Those of us from London and Los Angeles would have, as I did in this respect, felt very much at home. It didn't matter; there was no rush to get anywhere and they are good company. My ears take a little while to re-attune to the Malaysian accent in general and for the first half hour or so I just trust that I am nodding and smiling in the right places and hope they are not asking me a question. Koid is a walking encyclopaedia of alternative medicine recipes, some of which she has sent through. She and Miriam Shepherd[13] would have a lot to say to one another. Having retired from the Central Bank she is now a member of a disciplinary tribunal that deals with various kinds of financial operators.

One thing from yesterday sticks in my mind. As we were going back to the car from the flea market, there was a rather plump woman (Indian I think, but she could have been a Malay without a headscarf) sitting on the kerb with, when I actually looked at her, a smiley face. I hadn't taken much notice and presumed she was begging, but Yoong stopped, spoke to her and found that she was selling little homemade

---

[13] The mother of our son-in-law Nick.

cakes on behalf of a charity that tries to help unmarried mothers (I'm sure Islam highly disapproves of them). Obviously she could not afford a "pitch" in the market. He put some money into the cardboard box with a slot in the top that she proffered (I'm sure it was more than the value of the cakes he bought from her) and we went on our way. I thought that was a nice gesture and said so.

There is a path most of the way round the artificial lake on which the Everly Hotel stands (seriously, I think they got the idea from Canberra, Australia, where a similar feature, Lake Burley Griffin, is named after the American architect who designed the city). The lake here is quite extensive and I have walked only a small part of it, mostly this morning before it got too hot. Lots of herons, storks and water birds generally.

…Thanks for all the pictures of Ollie's party, Jessie. One notices how the children are already beginning to pass out of the "cute" to the "fun" stage.

The course starts again tomorrow. I'm sure this week will go quickly.

Love to all
Roger

Appendix II

Exodus from LIBERIA

Chapter 1
When things go wrong

Actually, air travel within Africa most of the time is generally not too bad; but if anything should go wrong with your travel arrangements, as recently happened to me, then heaven help you!

My story concerns the ramifications of a connecting flight being cancelled (as the first leg of my recent homeward journey Monrovia/Accra/London was). I would guess that within Africa such an occurrence is not infrequent. I certainly remember incidences of it happening while we lived there, so much so that in Malawi (where the Minister of Transport or other senior personage would occasionally commandeer an Air Malawi plane for his own personal use) there was an established stand-by routine involving transferring passengers to small private aircraft chartered on an *ad hoc* basis for those occasions.

However, cancellations and their ramifications appear somewhat outside the administrative capacity of airline and airport officials in West Africa today. Indeed, as I will tell, many of these people seem at times actually to take a sadistic delight in making life for those of us unfortunate enough to be affected as difficult and miserable as possible. But let us get this in perspective. Though cancellation is probably common enough, it still affects only a fairly small percentage of flights. I need to start by describing the *normal situation* for an air traveller embarking at Monrovia, Liberia, in the latter part of 2009.

To put this into its context, I also need to explain some background. The American airline, Delta, had been planning to run flights into and out of Monrovia (presumably via Accra, Ghana) for some time. But they postponed the plan earlier that year as they apparently considered, after inspection, that the airport security there was insufficient for their purposes. I believe much of what follows may be a direct result of this decision.

Chapter 2
Roberts International Airport, Monrovia. A little queuing and some shocks

Bear in mind that I had to endure the procedure outlined below on successive days: Saturday 12th and Sunday 13th December 2009. The variations may be of some interest and are noted. This is what normally happens:

Firstly, if more than one flight is leaving, there is a queue of 50 yards or so long in the open air waiting simply to get inside the terminal building. Imagine the 30° or so heat and 90% humidity, the crowds, and the fact that there are no airport trolleys and seemingly no help whatsoever in manoeuvring your heavy cases, which you must somehow do yourself for the first half hour or so of the procedure together with your hand baggage.

When you eventually reach the terminal door you find an airport official conducting a ticket and passport check. Having passed this, you are now funnelled into a narrow corridor about 15 yards long, at the end of which there is another check of exactly the same documents. As with many of the procedures that follow, it is difficult to understand the reason for it, as there is no way an interloper could join the queue at this stage. But that is to be logical, and thus of course completely to miss the point, which is that "security", whether to any effect or not, must not only be in place, but (to borrow a lawyer's principle about justice) must manifestly be seen to be in place.

Still with all your heavy luggage, you must then again queue for your name to be manually checked against the passenger list (or "manifest" as I believe it is called in the trade: a long roll of continuous computer print-out). After your name is found (this takes a minute or two of searching) and ticked off, your ticket and passport are then checked again (3 times already now). Half an hour or so of solid queuing has passed (remember the heat!) and you haven't even reached the check-in desk.

It's now that the real fun starts. There is of course what passes in Africa for a queue at each of the three Kenya Airways (KQ) check-in desks (the procedure is just the same for any other airlines operating out of Monrovia, as I was able to witness on the Sunday). People are milling about, dumping cases, pushing and shoving, shouting and gesticulating, and quite shamelessly queue-barging, in the general direction equally of both the Economy and Business Class desks (the signs above them are ignored in practice and business travellers get no privileges whatever). You are certainly sweating and probably fanning yourself with anything to hand, for there is no air-conditioning (well, there is, but it's not working).

The mostly female check-in clerks tap-tap on their keyboards and stare for what seems like aeons of time frowning at their screens without even looking up; they frankly give a discouraging impression of not really knowing what they are doing or why. The "queues" move forward at about two feet every 10 minutes. When, after exercising exemplary patience over a long period of time, you have finally been checked in and your case has disappeared (always a bad moment, that), don't make the mistake of thinking that the process is finished. You must continue to wait at the desk (causing even more of a logjam of people), because the single ticketing machine is overloaded and takes another while (5 or 6 minutes in my case) to print your boarding card.

You need to be reminded at this point that I had to go through this whole procedure twice. Shortly after getting my boarding card on the second occasion I discovered that in spite of my business class ticket Monrovia/Accra I had been allocated an economy class seat by the check-in clerk. But by then I was so relieved to have one at all that I didn't even care.

> *With a palpable sense of achievement and relief, you now begin to queue all over again, this time for immigration (passport) control. Before you get there – you've guessed – there is another check: this time of your boarding card and passport.*

For me, the first time at passport control, though seeming to take ages, was uneventful. The second time, the woman in the booth riffled roughly through my passport, as though counting banknotes (the document is beginning to look a little dog-eared).

"Where's the entry stamp!" she snapped, grumpily and accusingly, almost flinging the passport back to me.

I found it and showed her, as I handed the passport back. She riffled further.

"Where's the exit stamp!" [i.e. the one inserted the day before], once again shoving the document back to me.

Well, the entry and exit stamps *were* on different pages of my passport, *and* different ones again from the Liberian visa itself. This was clearly too much for her to handle. Again I needed patiently to show her where it was [*I promise you I'm not making this up*].

> *So, Immigration have checked your passport and boarding card yet again (this makes 5 times; there will be a sixth before boarding the plane), and now comes the* piece de resistance*. It is time to queue yet again, in order to experience the security searches.*

> *"Stand and wait behind the red line!" barks a security guard as you approach the area. When your turn eventually comes, you are ordered to march smartly forward to the checking tables.*

> *The first point to make is that, as you can easily see, <u>the security X-ray machine is not working</u>: no-one is "manning it" and its screen is blank. Nevertheless, its conveyor belt is running and through it everything has to go, including shoes, jackets, lap-tops and everything metal. Shoeless, beltless, with trousers slipping a little, we pass through the archway detector (on the second day, this was not working either). But, so far, apart from the non-functioning machinery, the procedure is normal.*

> There then follows for <u>everyone</u> a physical search of everything in their cabin baggage.

I should explain that I had put in my small rucksack two envelopes containing most of the $1300 subsistence I had been paid at the last minute by the UN in filthy $10 notes (see my previous letter), as the bundles were far too bulky to put in my pocket, let alone my wallet. And the rucksack in turn was in the cabin case.

On Saturday's search the two envelopes containing the money were fished out of the rucksack by the security guard.

> "What's in these?" he asked, waving them in front of my face. I gulped.
> "Cash that I've just been paid by the UN" I replied truthfully, in what sounded to myself almost like a falsetto voice.

I tried to lay emphasis on the provenance of the money (it <u>might</u> just make him pause, but I wasn't hopeful). Even were I inclined to do so, there was no point in trying to bluff: he had the envelopes in his hand.

> "How much?"
> "$1300" I stuttered.

My heart now felt like it was in my mouth and racing madly, knowing as I did that he now had me potentially over a barrel. Having some experience of Africa, particularly West Africa, my mind started to run riot. I was convinced that he would now sternly tell me something to the effect that "it is a very serious offence (in Liberia they would say "a felony") to try to smuggle so much cash out of the country". I was imagining that there would in all likelihood follow an unpleasant interlude involving calling an armed accomplice and arrest would be threatened if not actually effected. I would then be "softened up" by being put in a corner of the room to sweat (in more senses than one) while the perilous situation I was in was given time to sink in, and while panic started to take hold of me as I watched all the other passengers pass through to the departure lounge. When the time was finally judged to be right and I was thought to be sufficiently malleable, I would be offered a way of "getting round" this little problem. It would probably involve parting with anything up to 50% of the cash.

But to my indescribable joy and amazement my vivid nightmare evaporated. The guard simply put the envelopes back in the rucksack and waved me through. My legs were shaking and I felt limp, yet at the same time I almost wanted to hug him with relief. Sweat was now running so freely that it had thoroughly soaked my shirt, my underpants and the top half of my trousers as I walked, slightly unsteadily and uncomfortably, into the departure lounge...

For Sunday's search the sweat was again running profusely. I had toyed with the idea of putting the cash into my heavy suitcase, but I thought that this could well go astray during the broken journey to come, and the events of the previous day had by now emboldened me a little. I had thus taken the only flimsy precaution I could and put the cash into the front compartment of the rucksack, which has a hidden zip.

But this time the event turned out to be something of an anti-climax. To my intense relief the (different) guard ignored my rucksack altogether. But he seized, of all things, the dispenser containing my favourite "Polo" shower gel (which I had almost forgotten at the hotel and thrown in to my cabin case at the last minute). Unfortunately, it had "200 ml" on the container.

> "You're not allowed to have more than 100 ml of liquid" he said sternly, pointing to a grubby notice on the wall.
> "But it's not liquid" I replied, as I demonstrated the fact by squeezing a little on to my hand, "and it's only half full anyway".

Don't try to be logical in situations like this; it seldom works. He merely repeated his statement, snatched the container out of my hand and flung it into a corner of the room, where it spattered a little of the shower gel on to the wall. Doubtless then considering he had done his "duty" at my expense, he waved me through. Once more, I was soaked in the sweat of tension and relief.

> "Whatever you say" I said, cravenly.

> *At last! You have jumped through all the hoops and are finally in the departure lounge. This has been fairly recently built and at first glance actually seems like paradise after the purgatory you have come through. Until, that is, you realise that the metal seats are hard. That there are around you merely three small shops with absolutely nothing worth buying in them and a rather unattractive and crowded bar that seems to have been there longer than the rest of the departure area; and that there is still a long wait ahead.*

And the feeling of well-being evaporated altogether when we were informed, after three hours or so of waiting and being told that our plane was delayed, that the flight had now been cancelled, "for operational reasons".

Chapter 3
Cancellation of a flight

I assumed at first that the reason for the cancellation was that the plane had been diverted to another route. I know from Nairobi days, when we had a friend working for BA, that the African airlines sometimes do this so that they don't have to cancel flights on European or American routes. If they do that too often, it could lead to losing landing rights, whereas that's much less likely to happen on an African route.

But no, the reason as later rumoured turned out to be much more bizarre. The story was that work was being carried out on the runway at Monrovia Airport. The KQ flight was, so I was told, informed *after take-off from Accra* (an hour and a half's flying time away) that it could not land in Monrovia for the time being and should divert to Freetown, Sierra Leone (an hour's flight beyond Monrovia) and wait for the go-ahead to be given to land. According to this version of events, work on the runway ceased, unfinished, at about 9 pm, and thus the authorities couldn't let the flight land. It therefore had to go all the way back to Accra. Poor passengers! Some 5 hours of flying, plus several hours on the ground at Freetown, had served only to land them back exactly where they had started. And poor us!

I must admit that, even for Africa, aspects this story sounded a bit far-fetched. After I got home I heard of another, and probably more likely, version of the events. This was that the official responsible for signing the cheques for the November salaries for the airport staff had left for Christmas leave without doing so. There had not in fact been work in progress on the runway at all, but the staff had been protesting at non-payment of their salaries by deliberately parking trucks on it. According to my informant this rings true; it seems that the police and the army had not been paid last month either.

Whatever the cause, the effect on passengers, both on the unfortunate plane and waiting to board it, was the same. After half an hour or so of shouting and waving of arms by us, the dispossessed, the senior KQ official told us we should take back our checked-in luggage from the arrivals hall, and go to their office in town on the following morning (Sunday) to have our tickets reissued.

Chapter 4
Consequences of a cancellation

You have to bear in mind that Monrovia Airport is nearly an hour and a half's drive from the centre of town, there is no hotel nearby, and no arrangements whatever had been made for passengers to get back into town. You can imagine our states of mind as we were once more left to haul our heavy luggage without the help of a trolley. There was some talk of KQ getting hold of a bus, but I decided that, even if it materialised (and I had severe doubts) its journey would probably take forever, as people would need to be dropped off at all sorts of places or else the bus would drop everyone at a central point in town some way from my hotel. So I decided to take a taxi back to town. I had been warned that they were expensive, as taxis in Africa almost always are, but there seemed no practicable alternative.

Agreeing prices with taxi drivers is something I really loathe doing. I had been told that the fare ought to be around US$25, a price I eventually seemed to settle on, after extensive haggling with the group of "taxi-men" that had suddenly appeared around me from nowhere. One of them then loaded my luggage into the boot of his car, but he then started complaining that $25 was not enough, and just stood waiting outside the car. It was then that all the frustrations of the evening began to boil over and I lost patience. I got out, opened the boot, dragged my cases (large and small) out and said that he obviously wasn't interested and that I would get "the Kenya Airways bus".

"No, no! I'll take you" he said, with what appeared to be sincerity.
"Well, let's get going then!" I replied grumpily.

The luggage went back into the boot. But still clearly hoping for another person who could be induced to share the ride with me and whom he could fleece for another $25, he started the car, crawled for a few yards and stopped again. Once again I decided to confront the situation head on. For a second time I got out and pulled the cases out (in retrospect I was quite proud of my strength, bearing in mind the heat and all I'd been through that evening), and began marching off with all my luggage. Quite where I was proposing to go at that point hadn't for the moment occurred to me.

"No, no! I will take you". This time said with apparent urgency.

After a short stand-off period, during which I realised that actually I had little option but to go with him, the cases went back in (for the third time now) and the driver started off in the general direction of Monrovia.

"But you must give me a little tip of $5 or so" he whined as we drove away.
"We agreed a price" I snapped back. And then, after more muttering from him, I heard myself almost shout "Just shut up and drive to town!"

It was to some extent a war of nerves: he could very well stop the car in the middle of nowhere and refuse to proceed further, thus effectively blackmailing me for the extra money. But my "masterful" act seemed to work. The journey wasn't exactly full of matey exchanges between us, but after just over an hour I was back at my hotel. I gave him an extra $3.

My return to the hotel was not at all to the surprise of the reception clerk, who had obviously seen this sort of thing before.

Chapter 5
A new flight is arranged

We had been told to be at the KQ office in town in the morning "between 8 and 12 noon" on Sunday. I will spare you the details and merely say that for once Africa worked in my favour. My Liberian UN organiser/driver was *two hours late* in picking me up. I'm not exaggerating; he was using his own car had had to find someone on a Sunday to get a puncture mended. Arriving at the KQ office just before noon, I found dozens of people sitting around, with clerks tapping at keyboards, staring intently at computer screens and doing nothing much else. Mercifully, shortly after my arrival, the top KQ man announced that another plane would be coming in that evening at 9 pm and that everyone should just turn up at 6 pm at the airport with his or her Saturday's ticket and these would be somehow there transmogrified into Sunday's. I had, by pure good luck, coolly missed a couple of hours of useless frustration.

There are some high points in the story. Back at the hotel the previous evening I had contacted the British Resident Representative (there is no longer a British Embassy and so Gillian Dare is now the UK's sole official presence in Liberia) and she invited me to a lunch she was hosting at her flat on Sunday. No-one there was especially surprised by my plight, and one of the guests offered to drive me to the airport (which was lucky as my UN organiser rang me just before the time to leave for the airport to tell me he couldn't get hold of an official car). Dropping me at the airport, my acquaintance further told me to ring him if there were any further problems over getting away. I was almost weeping with gratitude.

I have already described the second round of procedure at the airport on Sunday evening. Suffice it to say that I had arrived at 6 pm; the promised plane did indeed eventually arrive, though not until 11.30 pm, and took off with us on board at about 1.00 am, arriving in Accra without further adventure at 2.30 am on Monday morning.

Chapter 6
Fun and games in Accra Part I. "Go to the back of the queue!"

There now began the next round, in its own way as full of the unpleasantly unexpected as the first. The first thing was that Ghanaian officials I happened to come across on my arrival seemed without exception curt, rude and arrogant. But doubtless some allowance should be made for the fact that it was now well into the early hours of the morning, and they had probably been required to stay at their posts just for our benefit (though that is far from the most appropriate word here).

My first problem was at the immigration booth. The official tossed my passport back to me almost contemptuously.

"You've got to have an immigration visa. Go and get it over there." he said tersely, waving vaguely in the direction from which I'd just come.

I went back to the visa booth (which I hadn't even noticed before – there is nothing and no-one to tell you what you need to do or where you have to go) and eventually tried to explain my predicament, namely that it had been intended that I should get a connecting flight from Accra on Saturday night, which I had missed because the first flight was cancelled.

"When are you leaving Ghana?"
"I don't know yet, as I haven't been able to contact British Airways."
"You have to have a visa to get out of the airport."
"How much does that cost?"
"US$100."
Staggering slightly I exclaimed "But I'm only in transit, and that against my will!"
"Where's your ticket?"
"Here. But it's now out of date."

This was my first mistake. I learned later that I should simply and boldly have told them that I was booked on the BA flight leaving that night. The bluff might well have worked (as indeed it did for 2 savvy Americans who were travelling with me and due out on Delta). But at that stage, an innocent abroad, I was not even sure that there *was* a BA flight, and I certainly wasn't booked on it. I also later learned that BA anyway have no office at the airport, even during normal business hours.

> "How do I know you are going to leave within 48 hours?"
> "I can't prove that until I can book the flight. I can't do that until tomorrow." I said, digging myself deeper into my self-made pit.
> "You have to pay $100."

Subsequently I thought ruefully how telling the truth often serves in Africa merely to get one into trouble; perhaps this in turn makes lying something that is so readily resorted to. At this stage I discovered that a "transit visa" costs only $20. But the immigration official continued to refuse to issue me one, as I couldn't "prove" my entitlement to it. What should I do? Just grit my teeth and pay the $100 for the privilege of being in the country against my will and hopefully for less than 24 hours? I sought advice from one of the Americans, Frank, with whom I'd got matey during the long waits in Monrovia:

> "You're on expense account aren't you? Claim it." He said, as though the problem was a "no-brainer".

Well, no, actually I wasn't. And an unhappy mixture of tight-fistedness and rebelliousness in my character made me persist. It fleetingly passed through my mind to spend the night in the airport and I actually mentioned this to the official; but my heavy case was still in the arrival hall, to which I couldn't yet get access, and I probably wouldn't be able to contact BA from "flight-side" anyway. However, possibly in view of my patently hollow threat, the immigration official grudgingly decided to call his boss. This of course meant waiting further and going to the back of the queue again, but it was anyway so late (around 3.30 am by now) that I was really past caring about time.

Eventually a compromise was reached with the boss. Immigration would hold on to my passport. If I could prove to them that I was leaving within 48 hours they would release it on payment of $20. Otherwise I would have to pay $100. I was given an official receipt for my passport and told I could go. It was now 4.15 am. It crossed my mind to wonder how I was ever going to able to get back through immigration to retrieve the passport, but I mentally shelved the problem for the moment. Tomorrow (or rather later today) could take care of itself.

Fortunately the other American, George, who had been at the visa desk with me, was still in the arrival hall when I reached it, waiting for the courtesy bus to the Golden Tulip Hotel. I joined him (up till then I hadn't the faintest clue where I would spend the night). On the way to the bus we were harassed by a gang of airport porters who seized our trolleys and aggressively demanded money for wheeling them to the minibus about 30 yards away. A group of them followed in our wake. It was made clear to us in a darkly threatening manner that suitable tips (I had nothing less than $1 notes) had to go to the men who wheeled the trolleys there, and (doubtless because $1 was considered insufficient) another $1 each to yet other men who were assigned to wheel them back! In case I might think of objecting, my way to the bus was physically blocked by the gang until I paid both sums. It was my first experience of a Ghanaian protection racket. George, for whom the scene was clearly not new, took it all philosophically.

At the hotel I registered, and paid the requisite $200 B & B! As I elected to offload some of my dirtiest $10 notes by paying cash, this has to be done in advance (the notes had then to be verified as genuine under a machine at reception; almost to my surprise they passed the check). At 4.40 am I finally got to my room.

Chapter 7
Fun and Games in Accra Part II. "Unfortunately we can't check you in without your Passport"

The following morning, after about 2 hours sleep, there was another minor highlight. A smooth and comparatively cheap and pleasant hotel taxi ride got me to the BA office and back. It was luckily a simple matter to arrange my flight for that night, but BA would have to charge me $70 for the administration. Again I had to argue "circumstances beyond my control". The booking clerk seemed to be sympathetic.

After kicking my heels at the Golden Tulip for most of the rest of the day (and starting to record this story) I got the courtesy bus to the airport deliberately early, and was first in the queue when BA opened their check-in facilities (half an hour later than the advertised time – about normal for West Africa). I knew exactly what would happen: BA would tell me that, unfortunately, they wouldn't be able to check me in without a passport. But on the other hand the immigration department wouldn't release my passport until I could prove that I was flying that night (effectively by showing them a boarding card). There was a potential stalemate. I was going to need to mount a charm offensive of the highest order.

Those who know me well will also know that this is not the sort of thing that I am usually noted for. But, having got a booking on BA, I was determined to get out of Accra that night or bust.

I started with the first BA official and got the expected answer. I explained the stalemate situation.

> "Look, I really need your help. Do you think I could speak to the manager?" [*This is an approach I learned many years ago from my late mother-in-law, Rose Lyons*].

A little huddle of BA staff developed, and eventually I was approached by someone who appeared to be in charge. I patiently explained my dilemma again, waving my official immigration receipt and adding something like:

> "British Airways have a reputation for getting their passengers out of trouble".
> [*OK... I know, I know*]

A further little huddle developed.

> "OK. Go and check in over there" said the manager, pointing to a particular desk.

Pleased with myself and ecstatically grateful to him, I approached the woman checking in, who seemed pleasant and ready to help. My spirits began to soar. Then she said:

> "Look, I really want to help you, but, unfortunately, though you are booked on tonight's flight, you have not been ticketed."
> "What does that mean? What do I have to do?"
> "You need to go and see them at the desk over there."

I joined a small queue "over there". It turned out to be the wrong one. I was directed to a window marked "tickets" in front of which was another small queue. I got to the front; the woman at the hatch seemed pleasant:

> "How are you this evening?" I said "I have this little problem which I'm told that only you can solve for me." (I explained again).

Willingly enough, she tap-tapped on the keyboard.

> "Unfortunately (that word again!) we can't ticket you because your ticket is basically a Kenya Airways one, and the system won't let me in. You'll have to go to them".

Tears of frustration began to well up in me; but, focussed grimly on my purpose, I gained control of myself.

> "I really appreciate your help; I know I couldn't manage without you. But could you possibly spare one of your staff to show me where to go?"

James, a young member of the BA staff in uniform, was standing nearby picking his nose. He was detailed to guide me. The KQ office is a long way off in another part of the airport buildings, but after a certain amount of trial and error rushing around in the clammy heat we found the correct office. A large woman was sitting at a desk, concentrating on eating something out of a plastic bag with a fork. Once again:

> "How are you? What a nice office you have here! [*OK...but put yourself in my shoes!*]. Look, I have a problem that I think that only you might be able to solve. James can explain."

James explained. At least here was someone from KQ who knew about the cancelled flight. Without pausing from her eating, she made some calls on a phone whose handset cable was so twisted she could barely lift it above the machine (this was actually convenient as she had to bend low over it and thus had less of a distance to convey her food to her mouth). At the third attempt some sort of number was dictated to her and written down. The magic number! James took the paper and I literally nearly fell over myself with thanks, tripping over the waste-paper bin on the way out. On the way back, elated, I promised James a tip.

We had to go back to two separate BA offices again, but this time James simply barged to the front of the queues. Finally a "ticket" (a print-out on a boarding card) emerged. I gave James $10 and practically blew kisses to the ticketing woman. *And there was no $70 administration charge to pay.*

I ran back to the original BA check-in desk, which was somehow miraculously free, and handed the ticket to the woman there as though it was a diploma certificate I'd just been awarded. She checked me in as I supplied details of my passport (expiry date, etc.)

> "Tell your boss I said you should be promoted!" I told her as I took my precious boarding card.

Now for stage 2: the retrieval of my passport. More laying it on with a trowel, this time at the information desk. Finally Hannah was deputed to take me through the labyrinths of the airport, through security points (more flattery required), and right to the visa office at the beginning of the arrival hall. Both men from early that morning were there; they waved to me cheerily! They smiled and nodded when I showed them the boarding card, then (after I paid $20 and got the relevant stamp) they gave me back my passport as though awarding me the Duke of Edinburgh's Award for Initiative. I deserved it!

Chapter 8
In Paradiso

Once more back in the departure hall I gave Hannah $10. I then went uneventfully through passport control, wishing everyone in sight a Happy Christmas, and collapsed into the Club Lounge. There I spent an hour simply gazing into space, regaining my equilibrium, congratulating myself for what I had managed to accomplish and nervously fingering my passport and boarding card to remind myself that I wasn't dreaming.

When finally on board the aircraft and talking casually to the male cabin staff, I felt overwhelmingly (and possibly disproportionately) glad to be back among "my people" who spoke "my language" (I don't mean English); people who just knew what they were doing and why, and quietly got on with it.

I have <u>never</u> enjoyed a flight so much.

Lightning Source UK Ltd.
Milton Keynes UK
UKOW01f2257210717
305814UK00003B/23/P